Eric Ambler

A COFFIN FOR DIMITRIOS

JUDGMENT ON DELTCHEV

PASSAGE OF ARMS

Eric Ambler

A COFFIN FOR DIMITRIOS

JUDGMENT ON DELTCHEV

PASSAGE OF ARMS

*Three Complete Novels
in One Volume*

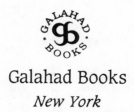

Galahad Books
New York

Published in 1992 by
Galahad Books
A division of LDAP, Inc.
386 Park Avenue South
New York, New York 10016

Galahad Books is a registered trademark of LDAP, Inc.
Published by arrangement with Alfred A. Knopf, Inc.

Library of Congress Catalog Card Number: 92-72501

ISBN: 0-88365-805-4
Designed by Hannah Lerner.

Printed in the United States of America.

Contents

A COFFIN
FOR
DIMITRIOS

One

〰〰〰〰〰〰〰〰〰

ORIGINS OF AN OBSESSION

A FRENCHMAN NAMED Chamfort, who should have known better, once said that chance was a nickname for Providence.

It is one of those convenient, question-begging aphorisms coined to discredit the unpleasant truth that chance plays an important, if not predominant, part in human affairs. Yet it was not entirely inexcusable. Inevitably, chance does occasionally operate with a sort of fumbling coherence readily mistakable for the workings of a selfconscious Providence.

The story of Dimitrios Makropoulos is an example of this.

The fact that a man like Latimer should so much as learn of the existence of a man like Dimitrios is alone grotesque. That he should actually see the dead body of Dimitrios, that he should spend weeks that he could ill afford probing into the man's shadowy history, and that he should ultimately find himself in the position of owing his life to a criminal's odd taste in interior decoration are breath-taking in their absurdity.

Yet, when these facts are seen side by side with the other facts in the case, it is difficult not to become lost in superstitious awe. Their very absurdity seems to prohibit the use of the words "chance" and "coincidence." For the sceptic there remains only one consolation: if there should be such a thing as a superhuman Law, it is administered with sub-human inefficiency. The choice of Latimer as its instrument could have been made only by an idiot.

During the first fifteen years of his adult life, Charles Latimer became a lecturer in political economy at a minor English university. By the time he was thirty-five he had, in addition, written three books. The first was a study of the influence of Proudhon on nineteenth-century Italian political thought. The second was entitled: *The Gotha Programme of 1875*. The third was an assessment of the economic implications of Rosenberg's *Der Mythus des zwanzigsten Jahrhunderts*.

It was soon after he had finished correcting the bulky proofs of the last work, and in the hope of dispelling the black depression which was the aftermath of his temporary association with the philosophy of National Socialism and its prophet, Dr. Rosenberg, that he wrote his first detective story.

A Bloody Shovel was an immediate success. It was followed by *"I," said the Fly* and *Murder's Arms*. From the great army of university professors who write detective stories in their spare time, Latimer soon emerged as one of the shamefaced few who could make money at the sport. It was, perhaps, inevitable that, sooner or later, he would become a professional writer in name as well as in fact. Three things hastened the transition. The first was a disagreement with the university authorities over what he held to be a matter of principle. The second was an illness. The third was the fact that he happened to be unmarried. Not long after the publication of *No Doornail This* and following the illness, which had made inroads on his constitutional reserves, he wrote, with only mild reluctance, a letter of resignation and went abroad to complete his fifth detective story in the sun.

It was the week after he had finished that book's successor that he went to Turkey. He had spent a year in and near Athens and was longing for a change of scene. His health was much improved but the prospect of an English autumn was uninviting. At the suggestion of a Greek friend he took the steamer from the Piræus to Istanbul.

It was in Istanbul and from Colonel Haki that he first heard of Dimitrios.

A letter of introduction is an uneasy document. More often than not, the bearer of it is only casually acquainted with the giver who, in turn, may know the person to whom it is addressed even less well. The chances of its presentation having a satisfactory outcome for all three are slender.

Among the letters of introduction which Latimer carried with him to Istanbul was one to a Madame Chávez, who lived, he had been told, in a villa on the Bosphorus. Three days after he arrived, he wrote to her and received in reply an invitation to join a four-day party at the villa. A trifle apprehensively, he accepted.

For Madame Chávez, the road from Buenos Ayres had been as liberally paved with gold as the road to it. A very handsome Turkish woman, she had successfully married and divorced a wealthy Argentine meat broker and, with a fraction of her gains from these transactions, had purchased a small palace which had once housed a minor Turkish royalty. It stood, remote and inconvenient of access, overlooking a bay of fantastic beauty and, apart from the fact that the supplies of fresh water were insufficient to serve even one of its nine bathrooms, was exquisitely appointed. But for the other guests and his hostess's Turkish habit of striking her servants violently in the face when they displeased her (which was often), Latimer, for whom such grandiose discomfort was a novelty, would have enjoyed himself.

The other guests were a very noisy pair of Marseillais, three Italians, two young Turkish naval officers and their "fiancées" of the moment and an assortment of Istanbul business men with their wives. The greater part of the time they spent in drinking Madame Chávez's seemingly inexhaustible supplies of Dutch gin and dancing to a gramophone attended by a servant who went on steadily playing records whether the guests happened to be dancing at the moment or not. On the pretext of ill-health, Latimer excused himself from much of the drinking and most of the dancing. He was generally ignored.

It was in the late afternoon of his last day there and he was sitting at the end of the vine-covered terrace out of earshot of the gramophone, when he saw a large chauffeur-driven touring car lurching up the long, dusty road to the villa. As it roared into the courtyard below, the occupant of the rear seat flung the door open and vaulted out before the car came to a standstill.

He was a tall man with lean, muscular cheeks whose pale tan contrasted well with a head of grey hair cropped Prussian fashion. A narrow frontal bone, a long beak of a nose and thin lips gave him a somewhat predatory air. He could not be less than fifty, Latimer thought, and studied the waist below the beautifully cut officer's uniform in the hope of detecting the corsets.

He watched the tall officer whip a silk handkerchief from his sleeve, flick some invisible dust from his immaculate patent-leather riding boots, tilt his cap raffishly and stride out of sight. Somewhere in the villa, a bell pealed.

Colonel Haki, for this was the officer's name, was an immediate success with the party. A quarter of an hour after his arrival, Madame Chávez, with an air of shy confusion clearly intended to inform her guests that she regarded herself as hopelessly compromised by the Colonel's unexpected appearance, led him on to the terrace and introduced him. All smiles and gallantry, he clicked heels, kissed hands, bowed, acknowledged the salutes of the naval officers and ogled the business men's wives. The performance so fascinated Latimer that, when his turn came to be introduced, the sound of his own name made him jump. The Colonel pump-handled his arm warmly.

"Damned pleased indeed to meet you, old boy," he said.

"Monsieur le Colonel parle bien anglais," explained Madame Chávez.

"Quelques mots," said Colonel Haki.

Latimer looked amiably into a pair of pale grey eyes. "How do you do?"

"Cheerio—all—the—best," replied the Colonel with grave courtesy, and passed on to kiss the hand of, and to run an appraising eye over, a stout girl in a bathing costume.

It was not until late in the evening that Latimer spoke to the Colonel again. The Colonel had injected a good deal of boisterous vitality into the party; cracking jokes, laughing loudly, making humorously brazen advances to the wives and rather more surreptitious ones to the unmarried women. From time to time his eye caught Latimer's and he grinned deprecatingly. "I've got to play the fool like this—it's expected of me," said the grin; "but don't think I like it." Then, long after dinner, when the guests had begun to take less interest in the dancing and more in the progress of a game of mixed strip poker, the Colonel took him by the arm and walked him on to the terrace.

"You must excuse me, Mr. Latimer," he said in French, "but I should very much like to talk with you. Those women—phew!" He slid a cigarette case under Latimer's nose. "A cigarette?"

"Thank you."

Colonel Haki glanced over his shoulder. "The other end of the terrace is more secluded," he said; and then, as they began to walk: "you know, I came up here to-day specially to see you. Madame told me you were here and really I could not resist the temptation of talking with the writer whose works I so much admire."

Latimer murmured a non-committal appreciation of the compliment. He was in a difficulty, for he had no means of knowing whether the Colonel was thinking in terms of political economy or detection. He had once startled and irritated a kindly old don who had professed interest in his "last book," by asking the old man whether he preferred his corpses shot or bludgeoned. It sounded affected to ask which set of books was under discussion.

Colonel Haki, however, did not wait to be questioned. "I get all the latest *romans policiers* sent to me from Paris," he went on. "I read nothing but *roman policiers*. I would like you to see my collection. Especially I like the English and American ones. All the best of them are translated into French. French writers themselves, I do not find sympathetic. French culture is not such as can produce a *roman policier* of the first order. I have just added your *Une Pelle Ensanglantée* to my library. Formidable! But I cannot quite understand the significance of the title."

Latimer spent some time trying to explain in French the meaning of "to call a spade a bloody shovel" and to translate the play on words which had given (to those readers with suitable minds) the essential clue to the murderer's identity in the very title.

Colonel Haki listened intently, nodding his head and saying: "Yes, I see, I see it clearly now," before Latimer had reached the point of explanation.

"Monsieur," he said when Latimer had given up in despair, "I wonder whether you would do me the honour of lunching with me one day this week. I think," he added mysteriously, "that I may be able to help you."

Latimer did not see in what way he could be helped by Colonel Haki but said that he would be glad to lunch with him. They arranged to meet at the Pera Palace Hotel three days later.

It was not until the evening before it that Latimer thought very much more about the luncheon appointment. He was sitting in the lounge of his hotel with the manager of his bankers' Istanbul branch.

Collinson, he thought, was a pleasant fellow but a monotonous companion. His conversation consisted almost entirely of gossip about the doings of the English and American colonies in Istanbul. "Do you know the Fitzwilliams," he would say. "No? A pity, you'd like them. Well, the other day . . ." As a source of information about Kemal Ataturk's economic reforms he had proved a failure.

"By the way," said Latimer after listening to an account of the goings-on of the Turkish-born wife of an American car salesman, "do you know of a man named Colonel Haki?"

"Haki? What made you think of him?"

"I'm lunching with him to-morrow."

Collinson's eyebrows went up. "*Are* you, by Jove!" He scratched his chin. "Well, I know *of* him." He hesitated. "Haki's one of those people you hear a lot about in this place but never seem to get a line on. One of the people behind the scenes, if you get me. He's got more influence than a good many of the men who are supposed to be at the top at Ankara. He was one of the Gazi's own particular men in Anatolia in nineteen-nineteen, a deputy in the Provisional Government. I've heard stories about him then. Bloodthirsty devil by all accounts. There was something about torturing prisoners. But then both sides did that and I dare say it was the Sultan's boys that started it. I heard, too, that he can drink a couple of bottles of Scotch at a sitting and stay stone cold sober. Don't believe that though. How did you get on to him?"

Latimer explained. "What does he do for a living?" he added. "I don't understand these uniforms."

Collinson shrugged. "Well, I've *heard* on good authority that he's the head of the secret police, but that's probably just another story. That's the worst of this place. Can't believe a word they say in the Club. Why, only the other day . . ."

It was with rather more enthusiasm than before that Latimer went to his luncheon appointment the following day. He had judged Colonel Haki to be something of a ruffian and Collinson's vague information had tended to confirm that view.

The Colonel arrived, bursting with apologies, twenty minutes late, and hurried his guest straight into the restaurant. "We must have a whisky-soda immediately," he said and called loudly for a bottle of "Johnnie."

During most of the meal he talked about the detective stories he had read, his reactions to them, his opinions of the characters and his preference for murderers who shot their victims. At last, with an almost empty bottle of whisky at his elbow and a strawberry ice in front of him, he leaned forward across the table.

"I think, Mr. Latimer," he said again, "that I can help you."

For one wild moment Latimer wondered if he were going to be offered a job in the Turkish secret service; but he said: "That's very kind of you."

"It was my ambition," continued Colonel Haki, "to write a good *roman policier* of my own. I have often thought that I could do so if I had the time. That is the trouble—the time. I have found that out. But . . ." He paused impressively.

Latimer waited. He was always meeting people who felt that they could write detective stories if they had the time.

"But," repeated the Colonel, "I have the plot prepared; I would like to make you a present of it."

Latimer said that it was very good indeed of him.

The Colonel waved away his thanks. "Your books have given me so much pleasure, Mr. Latimer. I am glad to make you a present of an idea for a new one. I have not the time to use it myself, and, in any case," he added magnanimously, "you would make better use of it than I should."

Latimer mumbled incoherently.

"The scene of the story," pursued his host, his grey eyes fixed on Latimer's, "is an English country house belonging to the rich Lord Robinson. There is a party for the English week-end. In the middle of the party, Lord Robinson is discovered in the library sitting at his desk—shot through the temple. The wound is singed. A pool of blood has formed on the desk and it has soaked into a paper. The paper is a new Will which the Lord was about to sign. The old Will divided his money equally between six persons, his relations, who are at the party. The new Will, which he has been prevented from signing by the murderer's bullet, leaves all to one of those relations. Therefore"—he pointed his ice cream spoon accusingly—"one of the five other relations is the guilty one. That is logical, is it not?"

Latimer opened his mouth, then shut it again and nodded.

Colonel Haki grinned triumphantly. "That is the trick."

"The trick?"

"The Lord was murdered by none of the suspects, but by the butler, whose wife had been seduced by this Lord! What do you think of that, eh?"

"Very ingenious."

His host leaned back contentedly and smoothed out his tunic. "It is only a trick, but I am glad you like it. Of course, I have the whole plot worked out in detail. The *flic* is a High Commissioner of Scotland Yard. He seduces one of the suspects, a very pretty woman, and it is for her sake that he solves the mystery. It is quite artistic. But, as I say, I have the whole thing written out."

"I should be very interested," said Latimer with sincerity, "to read your notes."

"That is what I hoped you would say. Are you pressed for time?"

"Not a bit."

"Then let us go back to my office and I will show you what I have done. It is written in French."

Latimer hesitated only momentarily. He had nothing better to do, and it might be interesting to see Colonel Haki's office.

"I should like to go back with you," he said.

The Colonel's office was situated at the top of what might once have been a cheap hotel, but which, from the inside, was unmistakably a government building, in Galata. It was a large room at the end of a corridor. When they went in a uniformed clerk was bending over the desk. He straightened his back, clicked his heels and said something in Turkish. The Colonel answered him and nodded a dismissal.

The Colonel waved Latimer to a chair, gave him a cigarette and began rummaging in a drawer. At last he drew out a sheet or two of typewritten paper and held it out.

"There you are, Mr. Latimer. The *Clue of the Bloodstained Will*, I have called it, but I am not convinced that that is the best title. All the best titles have been used, I find. But I will think of some alternatives. Read it, and do not be afraid to say frankly what you think of it. If there are any details which you think should be altered, I will alter them."

Latimer took the sheets and read while the Colonel sat on the corner of his desk and swung a long, gleaming leg.

Latimer read through the sheets twice and then put them down. He was feeling ashamed of himself because he had wanted several times to laugh. He should not have come. Now that he *had* come, the best thing he could do was to leave as quickly as possible.

"I cannot suggest any improvements at the moment," he said slowly; "of course, it all wants thinking over; it is so easy to make mistakes with problems of this sort. There is so much to be thought of. Questions of British legal procedure, for instance . . ."

"Yes, yes, of course." Colonel Haki slid off the desk and sat down in his chair. "But you think you can use it, eh?"

"I am very grateful indeed for your generosity," said Latimer evasively.

"It is nothing. You shall send me a free copy of the book when it appears." He swung round in his chair and picked up the telephone. "I will have a copy made for you to take away."

Latimer sat back. Well, that was that! It could not take long to make a copy. He listened to the Colonel talking to someone over the telephone and saw him frown. The Colonel put the telephone down and turned to him.

"You will excuse me if I deal with a small matter?"

"Of course."

The Colonel drew a bulky manila file towards him and began to go through the papers inside it. Then he selected one and glanced down it. There was silence in the room.

Latimer, affecting preoccupation with his cigarette, glanced across the desk. Colonel Haki was slowly turning the pages inside the folder, and on his face was a look that Latimer had not seen there before. It was the look of the expert attending to the business he understood perfectly. There was a sort of watchful repose in his face that reminded Latimer of a very old and experienced cat contemplating a very young and inexperienced mouse. In that moment he revised his ideas about Colonel Haki. He had been feeling a little sorry for him as one feels sorry for anyone who has unconsciously made a fool of himself. He saw now that the Colonel stood in need of no such consideration. As his long, yellowish fingers turned the pages of the folder, Latimer remembered a sentence of Collinson's: "There was something about torturing prisoners." He knew suddenly that he was seeing the real Colonel Haki for the first time. Then the Colonel looked up and his pale eyes rested thoughtfully on Latimer's tie.

For a moment Latimer had an uncomfortable suspicion that although the man across the desk appeared to be looking at his tie, he was actually looking into his mind. Then the Colonel's eyes moved upwards and he grinned slightly in a way that made Latimer feel as if he had been caught stealing something.

He said: "I wonder if you are interested in *real* murderers, Mr. Latimer."

Two

THE DOSSIER OF DIMITRIOS

LATIMER FELT HIMSELF redden. From the condescending professional he had been changed suddenly into the ridiculous amateur. It was a little disconcerting.

"Well, yes," he said slowly. "I suppose I am."

Colonel Haki pursed his lips. "You know, Mr. Latimer," he said, "I find the murderer in a *roman policier* much more sympathetic than a real murderer. In a *roman policier* there is a corpse, a number of suspects, a detective and a gallows. That is artistic. The real murderer is not artistic. I, who am a sort of policeman, tell you that squarely." He tapped the folder on his desk. "Here is a real murderer. We have known of his existence for nearly twenty years. This is his dossier. We know of one murder he may have committed. There are doubtless others of which we, at any rate, know nothing. This man is typical. A dirty type, common, cowardly, scum. Murder, espionage, drugs— that is the history. There were also two affairs of assassination."

"Assassination! that argues a certain courage, surely?"

The Colonel laughed unpleasantly. "My dear friend, Dimitrios would have nothing to do with the actual shooting. No! His kind never risk their skins like that. They stay on the fringe of the plot. They are the professionals, the *entrepreneurs*, the links between the business men, the politicians who desire the end but are afraid of the means, and the fanatics, the idealists who are prepared to die for their convictions. The important thing to know about an assassination or an attempted assassination is not who fired the shot, but who paid for the bullet. It is the rats like Dimitrios who can best tell you that. They are always ready to talk to save themselves the inconvenience of a prison cell. Dimitrios would have been the same as any other. Courage!" He laughed again. "Dimitrios was a little cleverer than some of them. I'll grant you that. As far as I know, no government has ever caught him and there is no photograph in his dossier. But we knew him all right and so did

11

Sofia and Belgrade and Paris and Athens. He was a great traveller, was Dimitrios."

"That sounds as though he's dead."

"Yes, he is dead." Colonel Haki turned the corners of his thin mouth down contemptuously. "A fisherman pulled his body out of the Bosphorus last night. It is believed that he had been knifed and thrown overboard from a ship. Like the scum he was, he was floating."

"At least," said Latimer, "he died by violence. That is something very like justice."

"Ah!" The Colonel leaned forward. "There is the writer speaking. Everything must be tidy, artistic, like a *roman policier*. Very well!" He pulled the dossier towards him and opened it. "Just listen, Mr. Latimer, to this. Then you shall tell me if it is artistic."

He began to read.

"Dimitrios Makropoulos." He stopped and looked up. "We have never been able to find out whether that was the surname of the family that adopted him or an alias. He was known usually as Dimitrios." He turned to the dossier again. "Dimitrios Makropoulos. Born eighteen eighty-nine in Larissa, Greece. Found abandoned. Parents unknown. Mother believed Roumanian. Registered as Greek subject and adopted by Greek family. Criminal record with Greek authorities. Details unobtainable." He looked up at Latimer. "That was before he came to our notice. We first heard of him at Izmir [1] in nineteen twenty-two, a few days after our troops occupied the town. A *Deunme* [2] named Sholem was found in his room with his throat cut. He was a moneylender and kept his money under the floorboards. These were ripped up and the money had been taken. There was much violence in Izmir at that time and little notice would have been taken by the military authorities. The thing might have been done by one of our soldiers. Then, another Jew, a relation of Sholem's, drew the attention of the military to a negro named Dhris Mohammed, who had been spending money in the cafés and boasting that a Jew had lent him the money without interest. Inquiries were made and Dhris was arrested. His replies to the court-martial were unsatisfactory and he was condemned to death. Then he made a confession. He was a fig-packer and he said that one of his fellow workmen, whom he called Dimitrios, had told him of Sholem's wealth hidden under the floorboards of his room. They had planned the robbery together and had entered Sholem's room by night. It had been Dimitrios, he said, who had killed the Jew. He thought that Dimitrios, being registered as a Greek, had escaped and bought a passage on one of the refugee ships that waited at secret places along the coast."

[1] *Smyrna.*
[2] *Jew turned Moslem.*

He shrugged. "The authorities did not believe his story. We were at war with Greece, and it was the sort of story a guilty man might invent to save his neck. They found that there had been a fig-packer named Dimitrios, that his fellow workmen had disliked him and that he had disappeared." He grinned. "Quite a lot of Greeks named Dimitrios disappeared at that time. You could see their bodies in the streets and floating in the harbour. This negro's story was unprovable. He was hanged."

He paused. During this recital he had not once referred to the dossier.

"You have a very good memory for facts," commented Latimer.

The Colonel grinned again. "I was the President of the court-martial. It was through that that I was able to mark down Dimitrios later on. I was transferred a year later to the secret police. In nineteen twenty-four a plot to assassinate the Gazi was discovered. It was the year he abolished the Caliphate and the plot was outwardly the work of a group of religious fanatics. Actually the men behind it were agents of some people in the good graces of a neighbouring friendly government. They had good reasons for wishing the Gazi out of the way. The plot was discovered. The details are unimportant. But one of the agents who escaped was a man known as Dimitrios." He pushed the cigarettes towards Latimer. "Please smoke."

Latimer shook his head. "Was it the same Dimitrios?"

"It was. Now, tell me frankly, Mr. Latimer. Do you find anything artistic there? Could you make a good *roman policier* out of that? Is there anything there that could be of the slightest interest to a writer?"

"Police work interests me a great deal—naturally. But what happened to Dimitrios? How did the story end?"

Colonel Haki snapped his fingers. "Ah! I was waiting for you to ask that. I knew you would ask it. And my answer is this: it *didn't* end!"

"Then what happened?"

"I will tell you. The first problem was to identify Dimitrios of Izmir with Dimitrios of Edirné.[3] Accordingly we revived the affair of Sholem, issued a warrant for the arrest of a Greek fig-packer named Dimitrios on a charge of murder and, with that excuse, asked foreign police authorities for assistance. We did not learn much, but what we did learn was sufficient. Dimitrios had been concerned with the attempted assassination of Stambulisky in Bulgaria which had preceded the Macedonian officers' *putsch* in nineteen twenty-three. The Sofia police knew very little but that he was known there to be a Greek from Izmir. A woman with whom he had associated in Sofia was questioned. She stated that she had had a letter from him a short time before. He had

---

[3]*Adrianople.*

given no address, but as she had had very urgent reasons for wishing to get in touch with him she had looked at the postmark. It was from Edirné. The Sofia police obtained a rough description of him that agreed with that given by the negro in Izmir. The Greek police stated that he had had a criminal record prior to nineteen twenty-two and gave those particulars of his origin. The warrant is probably still in existence; but we did not find Dimitrios with it.

"It was not until two years later that we heard of him again. We received an inquiry from the Yugoslav Government concerning a Turkish subject named Dimitrios Talat. He was wanted, they said, for robbery; but an agent of ours in Belgrade reported that the robbery was the theft of some secret naval documents and that the charge the Yugoslavs hoped to bring against him was one of espionage on behalf of France. By the first name and the description issued by the Belgrade police we guessed that Talat was probably Dimitrios of Izmir. About the same time our Consul in Switzerland renewed the passport, issued apparently at Ankara, of a man named Talat. It is a common Turkish name; but when it came to entering the record of the renewal it was found from the number that no such passport had been issued. The passport had been forged." He spread out his hands. "You see, Mr. Latimer? There is your story. Incomplete. Inartistic. No detection, no suspects, no hidden motives, merely sordid."

"But interesting, nevertheless," objected Latimer. "What happened over the Talat business?"

"Still looking for the end of your story, Mr. Latimer? All right, then. Nothing happened about Talat. It is just a name. We never heard it again. If he used the passport we don't know. It does not matter. We have Dimitrios. A corpse, it is true, but we have him. We shall probably never know who killed him. The ordinary police will doubtless make their inquiries and report to us that they have no hope of discovering the murderer. This dossier will go into the archives. It is just one of many similar cases."

"You said something about drugs."

Colonel Haki began to look bored. "Oh, yes. Dimitrios made a lot of money once I should think. Another unfinished story. About three years after the Belgrade affair we heard of him again. Nothing to do with us but the available information was added to the dossier as a routine matter." He referred to the dossier. "In nineteen twenty-nine, the League of Nations Advisory Committee on the illicit drug traffic received a report from the French Government concerning the seizure of a large quantity of heroin at the Swiss frontier. It was concealed in a mattress in a sleeping car coming from Sofia. One of the car attendants was found to be responsible for the smuggling but all he could or would tell the police was that the drug was to have been collected in Paris by a man who worked at the rail terminus. He did not know the man's name and had never spoken to him; but he described him. The man in question was later arrested. Questioned, he admitted the charge but claimed that he knew nothing of the destination of the drug. He received one consignment a month which was collected by a third man. The police set a trap for this third man and caught him only to find that there was a fourth intermediary. They arrested six men in all in connection with that affair and only obtained one real clue. It was that the man at the head of this peddling organisation was a man known as Dimitrios. Through the medium of the Committee, the Bulgarian Government then revealed that they had found a clandestine heroin laboratory at Radomir and had seized two hundred and thirty kilos of heroin ready for delivery. The consignee's name was Dimitrios. During the next year the French succeeded in discovering one or two other large heroin consignments bound for Dimitrios. But they did not get very much nearer to Dimitrios himself. There were difficulties. The stuff never seemed to come in the same way twice and by the end of that year, nineteen thirty, all they had to show in the way of arrests were a number of smugglers and some insignificant peddlars. Judging by the amounts of heroin they did find, Dimitrios must have been making huge sums for himself. Then, quite suddenly, about a year after that, Dimitrios went out of the drug business. The first news the police had of this was an anonymous letter which gave the names of all the principal members of the gang, their life histories and details of how evidence against every one of them might be obtained. The French police had a theory at the time. They said that Dimitrios himself had become a heroin addict. Whether that is true or not, the fact is that by December, the gang was rounded up. One of them, a woman, was already wanted for fraud. Some of them threatened to kill Dimitrios when they were released from prison but the most any of them could tell the police about him was that his surname was Makropoulos and that he had a flat in the seventeenth *arrondissement*. They never found the flat and they never found Dimitrios."

The clerk had come in and was standing by the desk.

"Ah," said the Colonel, "here is your copy."

Latimer took it and thanked him rather absently.

"And that was the last you heard of Dimitrios?" he added.

"Oh, no. The last we heard of him was about a year later. A Croat attempted to assassinate a Yugoslav politician in Zagreb. In the confession he made to the police, he said that friends had obtained the pistol he used from a man named Dimitrios in Rome. If it was Dimitrios of Izmir he must have returned to his old profession. A dirty type. There are a few more like him who should float in the Bosphorus."

"You say you never had a photograph of him. How did you identify him?"

"There was a French *carte d'identité* sewn inside the lining of his coat. It was issued about a year ago at Lyons to Dimitrios Makropoulos. It is a visitor's *carte* and he is described as being without occupation. That might mean anything. There was, of course, a photograph in it. We've turned it over to the French. They say that it is quite genuine." He pushed the dossier aside and stood up. "There's an inquest to-morrow. I have to go and have a look at the body in the police mortuary. That is a thing you do not have to contend with in books, Mr. Latimer—a list of regulations. A man is found floating in the Bosphorus. A police matter, clearly. But because this man happens to be on my files, my organisation has to deal with it also. I have my car waiting. Can I take you anywhere?"

"If my hotel isn't too much out of your way, I should like to be taken there."

"Of course. You have the plot of your new book safely? Good. Then we are ready."

In the car, the Colonel elaborated on the virtues of *The Clue of the Blood-stained Will*. Latimer promised to keep in touch with him and let him know how the book progressed. The car pulled up outside his hotel. They had exchanged farewells and Latimer was about to get out when he hesitated and then dropped back into his seat.

"Look here, Colonel," he said, "I want to make what will seem to you a rather strange request."

The Colonel gestured expansively. "Anything."

"I have a fancy to see the body of this man Dimitrios. I wonder if it would be impossible for you to take me with you."

The Colonel frowned and then shrugged. "If you wish to come, by all means do so. But I do not see . . ."

"I have never," lied Latimer quickly, "seen either a dead man or a mortuary. I think that every detective story writer should see those things."

The Colonel's face cleared. "My dear fellow, of course he should. One cannot write about that which one has never seen." He signalled the chauffeur on. "Perhaps," he added as they drove off again, "we can incorporate a scene in a mortuary in your new book. I will think about it."

The mortuary was a small corrugated iron building in the precincts of a police station near the mosque of Nouri Osmanieh. A police official, collected *en route* by the Colonel, led them across the yard which separated it from the main building. The afternoon heat had set the air above the concrete quivering and Latimer began to wish that he had not come. It was not the weather for visiting corrugated iron mortuaries.

The official unlocked the door and opened it. A blast of hot, carbolic-laden air came out, as if from an oven, to meet them. Latimer took off his hat and followed the Colonel in.

There were no windows and light was supplied by a single high-powered electric lamp in an enamel reflector. On each side of a gangway which ran down the centre, there were four high, wooden trestle tables. All but three were bare. The three were draped with stiff, heavy tarpaulins which bulged slightly above the level of the other trestles. The heat was overpowering and Latimer felt the sweat begin to soak into his shirt and trickle down his legs.

"It's very hot," he said.

The Colonel shrugged and nodded towards the trestles. "They don't complain."

The official went to the nearest of the three trestles, leaned over it and dragged the tarpaulin back. The Colonel walked over and looked down. Latimer forced himself to follow.

The body lying on the trestle was that of a short, broad-shouldered man of about fifty. From where he stood near the foot of the table, Latimer could see very little of the face, only a section of putty-coloured flesh and a fringe of tousled grey hair. The body was wrapped in a mackintosh sheet. By the feet was a neat pile of crumpled clothing: some underwear, a shirt, socks, a flowered tie and a blue serge suit stained nearly grey by sea water. Beside this pile was a pair of narrow, pointed shoes, the soles of which had warped as they had dried.

Latimer took a step nearer so that he could see the face.

No one had troubled to close the eyes and the whites of them stared upwards at the light. The lower jaw had dropped slightly. It was not quite the face that Latimer had pictured; rather rounder and with thick lips instead of thin, a face that would work and quiver under the stress of emotion. The cheeks were loose and deeply lined. But it was too late now to form any judgment of the mind that had once been behind the face. The mind had gone.

The official had been speaking to the Colonel. Now he stopped.

"Killed by a knife wound in the stomach, according to the doctor," translated the Colonel. "Already dead when he got into the water."

"Where did the clothes come from?"

"Lyons, all except the suit and shoes which are Greek. Poor stuff."

He renewed his conversation with the official.

Latimer stared at the corpse. So this was Dimitrios. This was the man who had, perhaps, slit the throat of Sholem, the Jew turned Moslem. This was the man who had connived at assassinations, who had spied for France. This was the man who had trafficked in drugs, who had given a gun to a Croat terrorist and who, in the end, had himself died by violence. This putty-coloured bulk was the end of an Odyssey. Dimitrios had returned at last to the country whence he had set out so many years before.

So many years. Europe in labour had through its pain seen for an instant a new glory, and then had collapsed to welter again in the agonies of war and fear. Governments had risen and fallen; men and women had worked, had starved, had made speeches, had fought, had been tortured, had died. Hope had come and gone, a fugitive in the scented bosom of illusion. Men had learned to sniff the heady dreamstuff of the soul and wait impassively while the lathes turned the guns for their destruction. And through those years, Dimitrios had lived and breathed and come to terms with his strange gods. He had been a dangerous man. Now, in the loneliness of death, beside the squalid pile of clothes that was his estate, he was pitiable.

Latimer watched the two men as they discussed the filling-in of a printed form the official had produced. They turned to the clothes and began making an inventory of them.

Yet at some time Dimitrios had made money, much money. What had happened to it? Had he spent it or lost it? "Easy come, easy go," they said. But had Dimitrios been the sort of man to let money go easily, howsoever he had acquired it? They knew so little about him! A few odd facts about a few odd incidents in his life, that was all the dossier amounted to! No more. And for every one of the crimes recorded in the dossier there must have been others, perhaps even more serious. What had happened in those two- and three-year intervals which the dossier bridged so casually? And what had happened since he had been in Lyons a year ago? By what route had he travelled to keep his appointment with Nemesis?

They were not questions that Colonel Haki would bother even to ask, much less to answer. He was the professional, concerned only with the unfanciful business of disposing of a decomposing body. But there must be people who knew and knew of Dimitrios, his friends (if he had had any), and his enemies, people in Smyrna, people in Sofia, people in Belgrade, in Adrianople, in Paris, in Lyons, people all over Europe, who *could* answer them. If you could find those people and get the answers you would have the material for what would surely be the strangest of biographies.

Latimer's heart missed a beat. It would be an absurd thing to attempt, of course. Unthinkably foolish. If one did it one would begin with, say, Smyrna and try to follow one's man step by step from there, using the dossier as a rough guide. It would be an experiment in detection really. One would, no doubt, fail to discover anything new; but there would be valuable data to be gained even from failure. All the routine inquiries over which one skated so easily in one's novels one would have to make oneself. Not that any man in his senses would dream of going on such a wild goose chase—heavens no! But it was amusing to play with the idea and if one were a little tired of Istanbul . . .

He looked up and caught the Colonel's eye.

The Colonel grimaced a reference to the heat of the place. He had finished his business with the official. "Have you seen all you wanted to see?"

Latimer nodded.

Colonel Haki turned and looked at the body as if it were a piece of his own handiwork of which he was taking leave. For a moment or two he remained motionless. Then his right arm went out, and, grasping the dead man's hair, he lifted the head so that the sightless eyes stared into his.

"Ugly devil, isn't he?" he said. "Life is very strange. I've known about him for nearly twenty years and this is the first time I've met him face to face. Those eyes have seen some things I should like to see. It is a pity that the mouth can never speak about them."

He let the head go and it dropped back with a thud on to the table. Then, he drew out his silk handkerchief and wiped his fingers carefully. "The sooner he's in a coffin the better," he added as they walked away.

Three

≈≈≈≈≈≈≈≈≈≈≈≈≈≈≈

NINETEEN
TWENTY-TWO

IN THE EARLY hours of an August morning in nineteen twenty-two, the Turkish Nationalist Army under the command of Mustafa Kemal Pasha attacked the centre of the Greek army at Dumlu Punar on the plateau two hundred miles west of Smyrna. By the following morning, the Greek army had broken and was in headlong retreat towards Smyrna and the sea. In the days that followed, the retreat became a rout. Unable to destroy the Turkish army, the Greeks turned with frantic savagery to the business of destroying the Turkish population in the path of their flight. From Alashehr to Smyrna they burnt and slaughtered. Not a village was left standing. Amid the smouldering ruins the pursuing Turks found the bodies of the villagers. Assisted by the few half-crazed Anatolian peasants who had survived, they took their revenge on the Greeks they were able to overtake. To the bodies of the Turkish women and children were added the mutilated carcasses of Greek stragglers. But the main Greek army had escaped by sea. Their lust for infidel blood still unsatisfied, the Turks swept on. On the ninth of September, they occupied Smyrna.

For a fortnight, refugees from the oncoming Turks had been pouring into the city to swell the already large Greek and Armenian populations. They had thought that the Greek army would turn and defend Smyrna. But the Greek army had fled. Now they were caught in a trap. The holocaust began.

The register of the Armenian Asia Minor Defence League had been seized by the occupying troops, and, on the night of the tenth, a party of regulars entered the Armenian quarters to find and kill those whose names appeared on the register. The Armenians resisted and the Turks ran amok. The massacre that followed acted like a signal. Encouraged by their officers, the Turkish troops descended next day upon the non-Turkish quarters of the city and began systematically to kill. Dragged from their houses and hiding places, men, women and children were butchered in the streets which soon became littered with mutilated bodies. The wooden walls of the churches, packed with refugees, were drenched with benzine and fired. The occupants who were not burnt alive were bayoneted as they tried to escape. In many parts looted houses had also been set on fire and now the flames began to spread.

At first, attempts were made to isolate the blaze. Then, the wind changed, blowing the fire away from the Turkish quarter, and further outbreaks were started by the troops. Soon, the whole city, with the exception of the Turkish quarter and a few houses near the Kassamba railway station, was burning fiercely. The massacre continued with unabated ferocity. A cordon of troops was drawn round the city to keep the refugees within the burning area. The streams of panic-stricken fugitives were shot down pitilessly or driven back into the inferno. The narrow, gutted streets became so choked with corpses that, even had the would-be rescue parties been able to endure the sickening stench that arose, they could not have passed along them. Smyrna was changed from a city into a charnel-house. Many refugees had tried to reach ships in the inner harbour. Shot, drowned, mangled by propellers, their bodies floated hideously in the blood-tinged water. But the quayside was still crowded with those trying frantically to escape from the blazing waterfront buildings toppling above them a few yards behind. It was said that the screams of these people were heard a mile out at sea. *Giaur Izmir*—infidel Smyrna—had atoned for its sins.

By the time that dawn broke on the fifteenth of September, over one hundred and twenty thousand persons had perished; but somewhere amidst that horror had been Dimitrios, alive.

As, sixteen years later, his train drew into Smyrna, Latimer came to the conclusion that he was being a fool. It was not a conclusion that he had reached hastily or without weighing carefully all the available evidence. It was a conclusion that he disliked exceedingly. Yet there were two hard facts that were inescapable. In the first place, he might have asked Colonel Haki for assistance in gaining access to the records of the court-martial and confession of Dhris Mohammed but had not been able to think of a reasonable excuse for doing so. In the second place, he knew so little Turkish that, even assuming that he could gain access to the records without Colonel Haki's help, he would be unable to read them. To have set out at all on this fantastic and slightly undignified wild goose chase was bad enough. To have set out without, so to speak, a gun and ammunition with which to make the killing was crass idiocy. Had he not been installed within an hour of his arrival in an excellent hotel, had his room not possessed a very comfortable bed and a view across the gulf to the sun-drenched, khaki hills that lay beyond it and, above all, had he not been offered a dry Martini by the French proprietor who greeted him, he would have abandoned his experiment in detection and returned forthwith to Istanbul. As it was . . . Dimitrios or no Dimitrios, he might as well see something of Smyrna now that he was in the place. He partly unpacked his suitcases.

On his second morning in Smyrna, he went to the proprietor of his hotel and asked to be put in touch with a good interpreter.

Fedor Muishkin was a self-important little Russian of about sixty with a thick, pendulous underlip which flapped and quivered as he talked. He had an office on the waterfront and earned his living by translating business documents and interpreting for the masters and pursers of foreign cargo vessels using the port. He had been a Menshevik and had fled from Odessa in nineteen-nineteen; but although, as the hotel proprietor pointed out sardonically, he now declared himself in sympathy with the Soviets, he had preferred not to return to Russia. A humbug, mind you; but at the same time a good interpreter. If you wanted an interpreter, Muishkin was the man.

Muishkin himself also said that he was the man. He had a high-pitched, husky voice and scratched himself a great deal. His English was accurate but larded with slang phrases that never seemed quite to fit their contexts. He said: "If there is anything I can do for you just give me the wire. I'm dirt cheap."

"I want," Latimer explained, "to trace the record of a Greek who left here in September, nineteen twenty-two."

The other's eyebrows went up. "Nineteen twenty-two, eh? A Greek who left here?" He chuckled breathlessly. "A good many of them left here then." He spat on one forefinger and drew it across his throat. "Like that! It was damnawful the way those Turks treated those Greeks. Bloody!"

"This man got away on a refugee ship. His name was Dimitrios. He was believed to have conspired with a negro named Dhris Mohammed to murder a moneylender named Sholem. The negro was tried by a military court and hanged. Dimitrios got away. I want to inspect, if I can, the records of the evidence taken at the trial, the confession of the negro and the inquiries concerning Dimitrios."

Muishkin stared. "Dimitrios?"

"Yes."

"Nineteen twenty-two?"

"Yes." Latimer's heart jumped. "Why? Did you happen to know him?"

The Russian appeared to be about to say something and then to change his mind. He shook his head. "No. I was thinking that it was a very common name. Have you permission to examine the police archives?"

"No. I was hoping that you might be able to advise me as to the best way of getting permission. I realise, of course, that your business is only concerned with making translations, but if you could help me in this matter I should be very grateful."

Muishkin pinched his lower lip thoughtfully. "Perhaps if you were to approach the British Vice-Consul and request him to secure permission. . . ?" He broke off. "But excuse me," he said; "why do you want these records? I ask, not because I cannot mind my own damn business, but that question may be asked by the police. Now," he went on slowly, "if it were a *legal* matter and quite above board and Bristol fashion, I have a friend with influence who might arrange the matter quite cheap."

Latimer felt himself redden. "As it happens," he said as casually as he could, "it *is* a legal matter. I could, of course, go to the Consul, but if you care to arrange this business for me then I shall be saved the trouble."

"A pleasure. I shall speak to my friend to-day. The police, you understand, are damnawful and if I go to them myself it will cost plenty. I like to protect my clients."

"That's very good of you."

"Don't mention it." A faraway look came into his eyes. "I like you British, you know. You understand how to do business. You do not haggle like those damn Greeks. When a man says cash with order you pay cash with order. A deposit? O.K. The British play fair. There is a mutual confidence between all parties. A chap can do his best work under such circumstances. He feels . . ."

"How much?" interrupted Latimer.

"Five hundred piastres?" He said it hesitantly. His eyes were mournful. Here was an artist who had no confidence in himself, a child in business matters, happy only in his work.

Latimer thought for a moment. Five hundred piastres was less than a pound. Cheap enough. Then he detected a gleam in the mournful eyes.

"Two hundred and fifty," he said firmly.

Muishkin threw up his hands in despair. He had to live. There was his friend, too. He had great influence.

Soon after, having paid over one hundred and fifty piastres on account of a finally agreed price of three hundred (including fifty piastres for the influential friend), Latimer left. He walked back along the quayside not unpleased with his morning's work. He would have preferred, it was true, to have examined the records himself and to have seen the translation done. He would have felt more like an investigator and less like an inquisitive tourist; but there it was. There was always the chance, of course, that Muishkin might have in mind the pocketing of an easy one hundred and fifty piastres; but somehow he did not think so. He was susceptible to impressions and the Russian had impressed him as being fundamentally, if not superficially, honest. And there could be no question of his being deceived by manufactured documents. Colonel Haki had told him enough about the Dhris Mohammed court-martial to enable him to detect that sort of fraud. The only thing that could go wrong was that the friend would prove unworthy of his fifty piastres.

The following day, Muishkin arrived, sweating profusely, very shortly before the time of the evening meal, and Latimer was drinking an apéritif. Muishkin came towards him waving his arms and rolling his eyes despairingly and, throwing himself into an armchair, emitted a loud gasp of exhaustion.

"What a day! Such heat!" he said.

"Have you got the translation?"

Muishkin nodded wearily, put his hand in his inside pocket and drew out a bundle of papers.

"Will you have a drink?" said Latimer.

The Russian's eyes flickered open and he looked round like a man regaining consciousness. He said: "If you like. I will have an absinthe, please. *Avec de la glace.*"

The waiter took the order and Latimer sat back to inspect his purchase.

The translation was handwritten and covered twelve large sheets of paper. Latimer glanced through the first two or three pages. There was no doubt that it was all genuine. He began to read it carefully.

NATIONAL GOVERNMENT OF TURKEY
.. TRIBUNAL OF INDEPENDENCE

By order of the officer commanding the garrison of Izmir, acting under the Decree Law promulgated at Ankara on the eighteenth day of the sixth month of nineteen twenty-two in the new calendar.

Summary of evidence taken before the Deputy-President of the Tribunal, Major-of-Brigade Zia Haki, on the sixth day of the tenth month of nineteen twenty-two in the new calendar.

"The Jew, Zakari, complains that the murder of his cousin, Sholem, was the work of Dhris Mohammed, a negro fig-packer of Buja.

"Last week, a patrol belonging to the sixtieth regiment discovered the body of Sholem, a Deunme moneylender, in his room in an unnamed street near the Old Mosque. His throat had been cut. Although this man was neither the son of True Believers nor of good reputation, our vigilant police instituted inquiries and discovered that his money had been taken.

"Several days later, the complainant, Zakari, informed the Commandant of Police that he had been in a café and seen the man Dhris showing handfuls of Greek money. He knew Dhris for a poor man and was surprised. Later, when Dhris had become drunk, he heard him boast that the Jew Sholem had lent him money without interest. At that time he knew nothing of the death of Sholem but when his relations told him of it he remembered what he had seen and heard.

"Evidence was heard from Abdul Hakk, the owner of the Bar Cristal, who said that Dhris had shown this Greek money, a matter of several hundreds of drachmas, and had boasted that he had had it from the Jew Sholem without interest. He had thought this strange for Sholem was a hard man.

"A dock-worker named Ismail also deposed that he had heard this from the prisoner.

"Asked to explain how he came into possession of the money, the murderer at first denied that he had had the money or that he had ever seen Sholem and said that as a True Believer, he was hated by the Jew Zakari. He said that Abdul Hakk and Ismail had also lied.

"Questioned sternly by the Deputy-President of the Tribunal, he then admitted that he had had the money and that it had been given to him by Sholem for a service he had done. But he could not explain what this service had been and his manner became strange and agitated. He denied killing Sholem and in a blasphemous way called upon the True God to witness his innocence.

"The Deputy-President then ordered that the prisoner be hanged, the other members of the Tribunal agreeing that this was right and just."

Latimer had come to the end of a page. He looked at Muishkin. The Russian had swallowed the absinthe and was examining the glass. He caught Latimer's eye. "Absinthe," he said, "is very good indeed. So cooling."

"Will you have another?"

"If you like." He smiled and indicated the papers in Latimer's hand. "That's all right, eh?"

"Oh yes, it looks all right. But they are a little vague about their dates, aren't they? There is no doctor's report either, and no attempt to fix the time of the murder. As for the evidence, it seems fantastically feeble to me. Nothing was proved."

Muishkin looked surprised. "But why bother to prove? This negro was obviously guilty. Best to hang him."

"I see. Well, if you don't mind, I'll go on glancing through it."

Muishkin shrugged, stretched himself luxuriously and signalled to the waiter. Latimer turned a page and went on reading.

STATEMENT MADE BY THE MURDERER, DHRIS MOHAMMED, IN THE PRESENCE OF THE GUARD-COMMANDANT OF THE BARRACKS IN IZMIR AND OTHER TRUE WITNESSES

"It is said in the book that he shall not prosper who makes lies and I say these things in order to prove my innocence and to save myself from the gallows. I have lied but now I will tell the truth. I am a True Believer. There is no god but God.

"I did not kill Sholem. I tell you I did not kill him. Why should I lie now? Yes, I will explain. It was not I but Dimitrios who killed Sholem.

"I will tell you about Dimitrios and you will believe me. Dimitrios is a Greek. To Greeks he is a Greek but to True Believers he says that he is also a Believer and that it is only with the authorities that he is a Greek because of some papers signed by his foster-parents.

"Dimitrios worked with others of us in the packing sheds and he was hated by many for his violence and for his bitter tongue. But I am a man who loves other men as brothers and I would speak with Dimitrios sometimes as he worked and tell him of the religion of God. And he would listen.

"Then, when the Greeks were fleeing before the victorious army of the True God, Dimitrios came to my house and asked me to hide him from the terror of the Greeks. He said that he was a True Believer. So I hid him. Then, our glorious army came to our aid. But Dimitrios did not go because he was, by reason of this paper signed by his foster-parents, a Greek and in fear of his life. So he stayed in my house and when he went out dressed like a Turk. Then, one day, he said certain things to me. There was the Jew Sholem, he said, who had much money, Greek pieces and some gold, hidden below the floor of his room. It was the time, he said, to take our revenge upon those who had insulted the True God and His Prophet. It was wrong, he said, that a pig of a Jew should have the money rightfully belonging to True Believers. He proposed that we should go secretly to Sholem, bind him and take his money.

"At first I was afraid, but he put heart into me, reminding me of the book which says that whosoever fights for the religion of God, whether he be slain or victorious, will surely find a great reward. This is now my reward: to be hanged like a dog.

"Yes, I will go on. That night after the curfew we went to the place where Sholem lived and crept up the stairs to his room. The door was bolted. Then Dimitrios knocked and called out that it was a patrol to search the house and Sholem opened the door. He had been in bed and he was grumbling at being woken from his sleep. When he saw us he called upon God and tried to close the door. But Dimitrios seized him and held him while I went in as we had arranged and searched for the loose board which concealed the money. Dimitrios dragged the old man across the bed and kept him down with his knee.

"I soon found the loose board and turned round full of joy to tell Dimitrios. He had his back turned towards me and was pressing down on Sholem with the blanket to stifle his cries. He had said that he himself would bind Sholem with rope which we had brought. I saw him now draw out his knife. I thought that he was meaning to cut the rope for some purpose and I said nothing. Then, before I could speak, he drove the knife into the old Jew's neck and pulled it across his throat.

"I saw the blood bubble and spurt out as if from a fountain and Sholem rolled over. Dimitrios stood away and watched him for a moment then he looked at me. I asked him what he had done and he answered that it was necessary to kill Sholem for fear that he should point us out to the police. Sholem was still moving on the bed and the blood was still bubbling, but Dimitrios said that he was certainly dead. After that, we took the money.

"Then, Dimitrios said that it was better that we should not go together but that each should take his share and go separately. That was agreed. I was afraid then, for Dimitrios had a knife and I had none and I thought he meant to kill me. I wondered why he had told me of the money. He had said that he needed a companion to search for the money while he held Sholem. But I could see that he had meant from the first to kill Sholem. Why then had he brought me? He could have found the money for himself after he had killed the Jew. But we divided the money equally and he smiled and did not try to kill me. We left the place separately. He had told me the day before that there were Greek ships lying off the coast near Smyrna and that he had overheard a man saying that the captains of these ships were taking refugees who could pay. I think that he escaped on one of those ships.

"I see now that I was a fool of fools and that he was right to smile at me. He knew that when my purse becomes full my head becomes empty. He knew, God's curses fall upon him, that when I sin by becoming drunk I cannot stop my tongue from wagging. I did not kill Sholem. It was Dimitrios the Greek who killed him. Dimitrios . . ." (*here followed a stream of unprintable obscenities*). "There is no doubt in what I say. As God is God and as Mohammed is His Prophet, I swear that I have said the truth. For the love of God, have mercy."

A note was appended to this, saying that the confession had been signed with a thumb print and witnessed. The record went on:

"The murderer was asked for a description of this Dimitrios and said:

"'He has the look of a Greek but I do not think he is one because he hates his own countrymen. He is shorter than I am and his hair is long and straight. His face is very still and he speaks very little. His eyes are brown and tired-looking. Many men are afraid of him but I do not understand this as he is not strong and I could break him with my two hands.'

"N.B. The height of this man is 185 centimetres.

"Inquiries have been made concerning the man Dimitrios at the packing sheds. He is known and disliked. Nothing has been heard of him for several weeks and he is presumed to have died in the fire. This seems likely.

"The murderer was executed on the ninth day of the tenth month of nineteen twenty-two in the new calendar."

Latimer returned to the confession and examined it thoughtfully. It rang true; there was no doubt about that. There was a circumstantial feeling about it. The negro, Dhris, had obviously been a very stupid man. Could he have invented those details about the scene in Sholem's room? A guilty man inventing a tale would surely have embroidered it differently. And there was his fear that Dimitrios might have been going to kill him. If he himself had been responsible for the killing he would not have thought of that. Colonel Haki had said that it was the sort of story that a man might invent to save his neck. Fear did stimulate even the most sluggish imaginations; but did it stimulate them in quite that sort of way? The authorities obviously had not cared very much whether the story was or was not true. Their inquiries had been pitiably halfhearted; yet even so they had tended to confirm the negro's story. Dimitrios had been presumed to have died in the fire. There was no evidence offered to support the presumption. It had, no doubt, been easier to hang Dhris Mohammed than to conduct, amidst all the terrible confusion of those October days, a search for a hypothetical Greek named Dimitrios. Dimitrios had, of course, counted on that fact. But for the accident of the Colonel's transfer to the secret police, he would never have been connected with the affair.

Latimer had once seen a zoophysicist friend of his build up the complete skeleton of a prehistoric animal from a fragment of fossilised bone. It had taken the zoophysicist nearly two years and Latimer, the economist, had marvelled at the man's inexhaustible enthusiasm for the task. Now, for the first time, he understood that enthusiasm. He had unearthed a single twisted fragment of the mind of Dimitrios and now he wanted to complete the structure. The fragment was small enough but it was substantial. The wretched Dhris had never had a chance. Dimitrios had used the negro's dull wits, had played upon his religious fanaticism, his simplicity, his cupidity with a skill that was terrifying. "We divided the money equally and he smiled and did not try to kill me." Dimitrios had smiled. And the negro had been too preoccupied with his fear of the man whom he could have broken with his two hands to wonder about that smile until it was too late. The brown, tired-looking eyes had watched Dhris Mohammed and understood him perfectly.

Latimer folded up the papers, put them in his pocket and turned to Muishkin.

"One hundred and fifty piastres, I owe you."

"Right," said Muishkin into his glass. He had ordered and was now finishing his third absinthe. He set down his glass and took the money from Latimer. "I like you," he said seriously; "you have no *snobisme*. Now you will have a drink with me, eh?"

Latimer glanced at his watch. "Why not have some dinner with me first?"

"Good!" Muishkin clambered laboriously to his feet. "Good," he repeated and Latimer saw that his eyes were unnaturally bright.

At the Russian's suggestion they went out to a restaurant, a place of subdued lights and red plush and gilt and stained mirrors, where French food was served. It was crowded and the atmosphere was thick with cigarette smoke. They sat down in upholstered chairs which exuded wafts of stale scent.

"*Ton*," said Muishkin looking round. He seized the menu and after some deliberation chose the most expensive dish on it. With their food they drank a syrupy, resinous Smyrna wine. Muishkin began to talk about his life. Odessa, nineteen eighteen. Stambul, nineteen nineteen. Smyrna, nineteen twenty-one. Bolsheviks. Wrangel's army. Kiev. A woman they called The Butcher. They used the abattoir as a prison because the prison had become an abattoir. Terrible, damnawful atrocities. Allied army of occupation. The English sporting. American relief. Bed bugs. Typhus. Vickers guns. The Greeks—God, those Greeks! Fortunes waiting to be picked up. Kemalists. His voice droned on while outside, through the cigarette smoke, beyond the red plush and the gilt and the white tablecloths, the amethyst twilight had deepened into night.

Another bottle of syrupy wine arrived. Latimer began to feel sleepy.

"And after so much madness, where are we now?" demanded Muishkin. His English had been steadily deteriorating. Now, his lower lip wet and quivering with emotion, he fixed Latimer with the unwavering stare of the drunk about to become philosophical. "Where now?" he repeated and thumped the table.

"In Smyrna," said Latimer and realised suddenly that he had drunk too much of the wine.

Muishkin shook his head irritably. "We grade rapidly to damnawful hell," he declared. "Are you a Marxist?"

"No."

Muishkin leaned forward confidentially. "Neither me." He plucked at Latimer's sleeve. His lip trembled violently. "I'm a swindler."

"Are you?"

"Yes." Tears began to form in his eyes. "I damn well swindled you."

"Did you?"

"Yes." He fumbled in his pocket. "You are no snob. You must take back fifty piastres."

"What for?"

"Take them back." The tears began to course down his cheeks and mingle with the sweat collecting on the point of his chin. "I swindled you, Mister. There was no damn friend to pay, no permission, nothing."

"Do you mean that you made up those records yourself?"

Muishkin sat up sharply. *"Je ne suis pas un faussaire,"* he asserted. He wagged a finger in Latimer's face. "This type came to me three months ago. By paying large bribes"—the finger stabbed emphatically—"large bribes, he had obtained the permissions to examine the archives for the dossier on the murder of Sholem. The dossier was in the old Arabic script and he brought photographs of the pages to me to translate. He took the photographs back, but I kept the translation on file. You see? I swindled you. You paid fifty piastres too much. Faugh!" He snapped his fingers. "I could have swindled five hundred piastres, and you would have paid. I am too soft."

"What did he want with this information?"

Muishkin looked sulky. "I can mind my own damn nose in the business."

"What did he look like?"

"He looked like a Frenchman."

"What sort of a Frenchman?"

But Muishkin's head had sagged forward on to his chest and he did not answer. Then, after a moment or two, he raised his head and stared blankly at Latimer. His face was livid and Latimer guessed that he would very shortly be sick. His lips moved.

"Je ne suis pas un faussaire," he muttered; "three hundred piastres, dirt cheap!" He stood up suddenly, murmured, *"Excusez-moi,"* and walked rapidly in the direction of the toilet.

Latimer waited for a time then paid the bill and went to investigate. There was another entrance to the toilet and Muishkin had gone. Latimer walked back to his hotel.

From the balcony outside the window of his room, he could see over the bay to the hills beyond. A moon had risen and its reflection gleamed through the tangle of crane jibs along the quay where the steamers berthed. The searchlights of a Turkish cruiser anchored in the roadstead outside the inner port swung round like long white fingers, brushed the summits of the hills and were extinguished. Out in the harbour and on the slopes above the town pinpoints of light twinkled. A slight warm breeze off the sea had begun to stir the leaves of a rubber tree in the garden below him. In another room of the hotel a woman laughed. Somewhere in the distance a gramophone was playing a tango. The turntable was revolving too quickly and the sound was shrill and congested.

Latimer lit a final cigarette and wondered for the hundredth time what the man who looked like a Frenchman had wanted with the dossier of the Sholem murder. At last he pitched his cigarette away and shrugged. One thing was certain: he could not possibly have been interested in Dimitrios.

Four

≋≋≋≋≋≋≋≋≋

MR. PETERS

Two DAYS LATER, Latimer left Smyrna. He did not see Muishkin again.

The situation in which a person, imagining fondly that he is in charge of his own destiny, is, in fact, the sport of circumstances beyond his control, is always fascinating. It is the essential element in most good theatre from the *Œdipus* of Sophocles to *East Lynne*. When, however, that person is one-self and one is examining the situation in retrospect, the fascination becomes a trifle morbid. Thus, when Latimer used afterwards to look back upon those two days in Smyrna, it was not so much his ignorance of the part he was play-ing but the bliss which accompanied the ignorance that so appalled him. He had gone into the business believing his eyes to be wide open, whereas, actually, they had been tightly shut. That, no doubt, could not have been helped. The galling part was that he had failed for so long to perceive the fact. Of course, he did himself less than justice; but his self-esteem had been punc-tured; he had been transferred without his knowledge from the role of sophisticated, impersonal weigher of facts to that of active participator in a melodrama.

Of the imminence of that humiliation, however, he had no inkling when, on the morning after his dinner with Muishkin, he sat down with a pencil and a notebook to arrange the material for his experiment in detection.

Some time early in October nineteen twenty-two, Dimitrios had left Smyrna. He had had money and had probably purchased a passage on a Greek steamer. The next time Colonel Haki had heard of him he had been in Adrianople two years later. In that interim, however, the Bulgarian police had had trouble with him in Sofia in connection with the attempted assassination of Stambulisky. Latimer was a little hazy as to the precise date of that attempt but he began to jot down a rough chronological table.

TIME	PLACE	REMARKS	SOURCE OF INFORMATION
1922 (October)	—Smyrna	Sholem	Police Archives
1923 (early part)	—Sofia	Stambulisky	Colonel Haki
1924 — —	—Adrianople	Kemal attempt	Colonel Haki
1926 — —	—Belgrade	Espionage for France	Colonel Haki
1926 — —	—Switzerland	Talat passport	Colonel Haki
1929-31 (?) —	—Paris	Drugs	Colonel Haki
1932 — —	—Zagreb	Croat assassin	Colonel Haki
1937 — —	—Lyons	*Carte d'identité*	Colonel Haki
1938 — —	—Istanbul	Murdered	Colonel Haki

The immediate problem, then, was quite clear-cut. In the six months following the murder of Sholem, Dimitrios had escaped from Smyrna, made his way to Sofia and become involved in a plot to assassinate the Bulgarian Prime Minister. Latimer found it a trifle difficult to form any estimate of the time required to become involved in a plot to kill a Prime Minister; but it was fairly certain that Dimitrios must have arrived in Sofia soon after his departure from Smyrna. If he had indeed escaped by Greek steamer he must have gone first to the Piræus and Athens. From Athens he could have reached Sofia overland, via Salonika, or by sea, via the Dardanelles and the Golden Horn to Bourgaz or Varna, Bulgaria's Black Sea port. Istanbul at that time was in Allied hands. He would have had nothing to fear from the Allies. The question was: what had induced him to go to Sofia?

However, the logical course now was to go to Athens and tackle the job of picking up the trail there. It would not be easy. Even if attempts had been made to record the presence of every refugee among the tens of thousands who had arrived, it was more than probable that what records still existed, if any, were incomplete. There was no point, however, in anticipating failure. He had several valuable friends in Athens and if there was a record in existence it was fairly certain that he would be able to get access to it. He shut up his notebook.

When the weekly boat to the Piræus left Smyrna the following day, Latimer was among the passengers.

During the months following the Turkish occupation of Smyrna, more than eight hundred thousand Greeks returned to their country. They came, boatload after boatload of them, packed on the decks and in the holds. Many of them were naked and starving. Some still carried in their arms the dead children they had had no time to bury. With them came the germs of typhus and smallpox.

War-weary and ruined, gripped by a food shortage and starved of medical supplies, their motherland received them. In the hastily improvised refugee camps they died like flies. Outside Athens, on the Piræus, in Salonika, masses of humanity lay rotting in the cold of a Greek winter. Then, the Fourth Assembly of the League of Nations, in session in Geneva, voted one hundred thousand gold francs to the Nansen relief organisation for immediate use in Greece. The work of salvage began. Huge refugee settlements were organised. Food was brought and clothing and medical supplies. The epidemics were stopped. The survivors began to sort themselves into new communities. For the first time in history, large scale disaster had been halted by goodwill and reason. It seemed as if the human animal were at last discovering a conscience, as if it were at last becoming aware of its humanity.

All this and more, Latimer heard from a friend, one Siantos, in Athens. When, however, he came to the point of his inquiries, Siantos pursed his lips.

"A complete register of those who arrived from Smyrna? That is a tall order. If you had seen them come . . . So many and in such a state . . ." And then followed the inevitable question. "Why are you interested?"

It had occurred to Latimer that this question was going to crop up again and again. He had accordingly prepared his explanation. To have told the truth, to have explained that he was trying, for purely academic reasons, to trace the history of a dead criminal named Dimitrios would have been a long and uneasy business. He was, in any case, not anxious to have a second opinion on his prospects of success. His own was depressing enough. What had seemed a fascinating idea in a Turkish mortuary might well, in the bright, warm light of a Greek autumn, appear merely absurd. Much simpler to avoid the issue altogether.

He answered: "It is in connection with a new book I am writing. A matter of detail that must be checked. I want to see if it is possible to trace an individual refugee after so long."

Siantos said that he understood and Latimer grinned ashamedly to himself. The fact that one was a writer could be relied upon to explain away the most curious extravagances.

He had gone to Siantos because he knew that the man had a Government post of some importance in Athens; but now his first disappointment was in store for him. A week went by and, at the end of it, Siantos was able to tell him only that a register was in existence, that it was in the custody of the municipal authorities and that it was not open to inspection by unauthorised persons. Permission would have to be obtained. It took another week, a week of waiting, of sitting in *kafenios*, of being introduced to thirsty gentlemen with connections in the municipal offices. At last, however, the permission was forthcoming and the following day Latimer presented himself at the bureau in which the records were housed.

The inquiry office was a bare tiled room with a counter at one end. Behind the counter sat the official in charge. He shrugged over the information Latimer had to give him. A fig-packer named Dimitrios? October nineteen twenty-two? It was impossible. The register had been compiled alphabetically by surname.

Latimer's heart sank. All his trouble, then, was to go for nothing. He had thanked the man and was turning away when he had an idea. There was just a remote chance . . .

He turned back to the official. "The surname," he said, "may have been Makropoulos."

He was dimly aware, as he said it, that behind him a man had entered the inquiry office through the door leading to the street. The sun was streaming obliquely into the room and for an instant a long, distorted shadow twisted across the tiles as the new-comer passed the window.

"Dimitrios Makropoulos?" repeated the official. "That is better. If there was a person of that name on the register we will find him. It is a question of patience and organisation. Please come this way."

He raised the flap of the counter for Latimer to go through. As he did so he glanced over Latimer's shoulder.

"Gone!" he exclaimed. "I have no assistance in my work of organisation here. The whole burden falls upon my shoulders. Yet people have no patience. I am engaged for a moment. They cannot wait." He shrugged. "That is their affair. I do my duty. If you will follow me, please."

Latimer followed him down a flight of stone stairs into an extensive basement occupied by row upon row of steel cabinets.

"Organisation," commented the official; "that is the secret of modern state-craft. Organisation will make a greater Greece. A new empire. But patience is necessary." He led the way to a series of small cabinets in one corner of the basement, pulled open one of the drawers and began with his fingernail to flick over a series of cards. At last he stopped at a card and examined it carefully before closing the drawer. "Makropoulos. If there is a record of this man we shall find it in drawer number sixteen. That is organisation."

In drawer number sixteen, however, they drew a blank. The official threw up his hands in despair and searched again without success. Then inspiration came to Latimer.

"Try under the name of Talat," he said desperately.

"But that is a Turkish name."

"I know it. But try it."

The official shrugged. There was another reference to the main index. "Drawer twenty-seven," announced the official a little impatiently; "are you sure that this man came to Athens? Many went to Salonika. Why not this fig-packer?"

This was precisely the question that Latimer had been asking himself. He said nothing and watched the official's fingernail flicking over another series of cards. Suddenly it stopped.

"Have you found it?" said Latimer quickly.

The official pulled out a card. "Here is one," he said. "The man was a fig-packer, but the name is Dimitrios Tala*dis*."

"Let me see." Latimer took the card. Dimitrios Taladis! There it was in black and white. He had found out something that Colonel Haki did not know. Dimitrios had used the name Talat before nineteen twenty-six. There could be no doubt that it *was* Dimitrios. He had merely tacked a Greek suffix on to the name. He stared at the card. And there were here some other things that Colonel Haki did not know.

He looked up at the beaming official. "Can I copy this?"

"Of course. Patience and organisation, you see. My organisation is for use. But I must not let the record out of my sight. That is the regulation."

Under the now somewhat mystified eyes of the apostle of organisation and patience Latimer began to copy the wording on the card into his notebook, translating it as he did so into English. He wrote:

NUMBER T.53462

NATIONAL RELIEF ORGANISATION

Refugee Section: ATHINAI

Sex: Male. *Name*: Dimitrios Taladis. *Born*: Salonika, 1889. *Occupation*: Fig-packer. *Parents*: Believed dead. *Identity Papers or Passport*: Identity card lost. Said to have been issued at Smyrna. *Nationality*: Greek. *Arrived*: October 1, 1922. *Coming from*: Smyrna. *On examination*: Able-bodied. No disease. Without money. Assigned to camp at Tabouria. Temporary identity paper issued. *Note*: Left Tabouria on own initiative, November 29th, 1922. Warrant for arrest, on charge of robbery and attempted murder, issued in Athinai, November 30, 1922. Believed to have escaped by sea.

Yes, that was Dimitrios all right. The date of his birth agreed with that supplied by the Greek police (and based on information gained prior to nineteen twenty-two) to Colonel Haki. The place of birth, however, was different. According to the Turkish dossier it had been Larissa. Why had Dimitrios bothered to change it? If he were giving a false name, he must have seen that the chances of its falsity being discovered by reference to the registration records were as great for Salonika as for Larissa.

Salonika, eighteen eighty-nine! Why Salonika? Then Latimer remembered. Of course! It was quite simple. In eighteen eighty-nine Salonika had been in Turkish territory, a part of the Ottoman Empire. The registration records of that period would, in all probability, not be available to the Greek authorities. Dimitrios had certainly been no fool. But why had he picked on the name Taladis? Why had he not chosen a typical Greek name? The Turkish "Talat" must have had some special association for him. As for his identity card issued in Smyrna, that would naturally be "lost" since, presumably, it had been issued to him in the name of Makropoulos by which he was already known to the Greek police.

The date of his arrival fitted in with the vague allusions to time made in the court-martial. Unlike the majority of his fellow refugees, he had been able-bodied and free from disease when he had arrived. Naturally. Thanks to Sholem's Greek money, he had been able to buy a passage to the Piræus and travel in comparative comfort instead of being loaded on to a refugee ship with thousands of others. Dimitrios had known how to look after himself. The fig-packer had packed enough figs. Dimitrios the Man had been emerging from his chrysalis. No doubt he had had a substantial amount of Sholem's money left when he had arrived. Yet to the relief authorities he had been "without money." That had been sensible of him. He might otherwise have been forced to buy food and clothing for stupid fools who had failed to provide, as he had provided, for the future. His expenses had been heavy enough as it was; so heavy that another Sholem had been needed. No doubt he had regretted Dhris Mohammed's half share.

"Believed to have escaped by sea." With the proceeds of the second robbery added to the balance from the first, he had no doubt been able to pay for his passage to Bourgaz. It would obviously have been too risky for him to have gone overland. He had only temporary identity papers and might have been stopped at the frontier, whereas in Bourgaz, the same papers issued by an international relief commission with considerable prestige would have enabled him to get through.

The official's much-advertised patience was showing signs of wearing thin. Latimer handed over the card, expressed his thanks in a suitable manner and returned thoughtfully to his hotel.

He was feeling pleased with himself. He had discovered some new information about Dimitrios and he had discovered it through his own efforts. It had been, it was true, an obvious piece of routine inquiry; but, in the best Scotland Yard tradition, it had called for patience and persistence. Besides, if he had not thought of trying the Talat name . . . He wished that he could have sent a report of his investigations to Colonel Haki, but that was out of the question. The Colonel would probably fail to understand the spirit in which the experiment in detection was being made. In any case, Dimitrios himself would by this time be mouldering below ground, his dossier sealed and forgotten in the archives of the Turkish secret police. The main thing was now to tackle the Sofia affair.

He tried to remember what he knew about post-war Bulgarian politics and speedily came to the conclusion that it was very little. In nineteen twenty-three Stambulisky had, he knew, been head of a government of liberal tendencies; but of just how liberal those tendencies had been he had no idea. There had been an attempted assassination and later a military *coup d'état* carried out at the instigation, if not under the leadership of the I.M.R.O., the International Macedonian Revolutionary Organisation. Stambulisky had fled from Sofia, tried to organise a counter-revolution and been killed. That was the gist of the affair, he thought. But of the rights and wrongs of it (if any such distinction were possible), of the nature of the political forces involved, he was quite ignorant. That state of affairs would have to be remedied; and the place in which to remedy it would be Sofia.

That evening he asked Siantos to dinner. Latimer knew him for a vain, generous soul who liked discussing his friends' problems and was flattered when, by making judicious use of his official position, he could help them. After giving thanks for the assistance in the matter of the municipal register, Latimer broached the subject of Sofia.

"I am going to trespass on your kindness still further, my dear Siantos."

"So much the better."

"Do you know anyone in Sofia? I want a letter of introduction to an intelligent newspaperman there who could give me some inside information about Bulgarian politics in nineteen twenty-three."

Siantos smoothed his gleaming white hair and grinned admiringly. "You writers have bizarre tastes. Something might be done. Do you want a Greek or a Bulgar?"

"Greek for preference. I don't speak Bulgarian."

Siantos was thoughtful for a moment. "There is a man in Sofia named Marukakis," he said at last. "He is the Sofia correspondent of a French news agency. I do not know him myself, but I might be able to get a letter to him from a friend of mine." They were sitting in a restaurant, and now Siantos glanced round furtively and lowered his voice. "There is only one trouble about him from your point of view. I happen to know that he has . . ." The voice sunk still lower in tone, Latimer was prepared for nothing less horrible than leprosy. ". . . Communist tendencies," concluded Siantos in a whisper.

Latimer raised his eyebrows. "I don't regard that as a drawback. All the Communists I have ever met have been highly intelligent."

Siantos looked shocked. "How can that be? It is dangerous to say such things, my friend. Marxist thought is forbidden in Greece."

"When can I have that letter?"

Siantos sighed. "Bizarre!" he remarked. "I will get it for you to-morrow. You writers. . . !"

Within a week the letter of introduction had been obtained, and Latimer, having secured Greek exit and Bulgarian ingress visas, boarded a night train for Sofia.

The train was not crowded and he had hoped to have a sleeping car compartment to himself; but five minutes before the train was due to start, luggage was carried in and deposited above the empty berth. The owner of the luggage followed very soon after it.

"I must apologise for intruding on your privacy," he said to Latimer in English.

He was a fat, unhealthy-looking man of about fifty-five. He had turned to tip the porter before he spoke, and the first thing about him that impressed Latimer was that the seat of his trousers sagged absurdly, making his walk reminiscent of that of the hind legs of an elephant. Then Latimer saw his face and forgot about the trousers. There was the sort of sallow shapelessness about it that derives from simultaneous over-eating and under-sleeping. From above two heavy satchels of flesh peered a pair of pale-blue, bloodshot eyes that seemed to be permanently weeping. The nose was rubbery and indeterminate. It was the mouth that gave the face expression. The lips were pallid and un-defined, seeming thicker than they really were. Pressed together over unnaturally white and regular false teeth, they were set permanently in a saccharine smile. In conjunction with the weeping eyes above it, it created an impression of sweet patience in adversity, quite startling in its intensity. Here, it said, was a man who had suffered, who had been buffeted by fiendishly vindictive Fates as no other man had been buffeted, yet who had retained his humble faith in the essential goodness of Man: here, it said, was a martyr who smiled through the flames,—smiled yet who could not but weep for the misery of others as he did so. He reminded Latimer of a high church priest he had known in England who had been unfrocked for embezzling the altar fund.

"The berth was unoccupied," Latimer pointed out; "there is no question of your intruding." He noted with an inward sigh that the man breathed very heavily and noisily through congested nostrils. He would probably snore.

The new-comer sat down on his berth and shook his head slowly. "How good of you to put it that way! How little kindness there is in the world these days! How little thought for others!" The bloodshot eyes met Latimer's. "May I ask how far you are going?"

"Sofia."

"Sofia. So? A beautiful city, beautiful. I am continuing to Bucuresti. I do hope that we shall have a pleasant journey together."

Latimer said that he hoped so too. The fat man's English was very accurate, but he spoke it with an atrocious accent which Latimer could not place. It was thick and slightly guttural, as though he were speaking with his mouth full of cake. Occasionally, too, the accurate English would give out in the middle of a difficult sentence, which would be completed in very fluent French or German. Latimer gained the impression that the man had learned his English from books.

The fat man turned and began to unpack a small attaché-case containing a pair of woollen pyjamas, some bed socks and a dog-eared paper-backed book. Latimer managed to see the title of the book. It was called *Pearls of Everyday Wisdom* and was in French. The fat man arranged these things carefully on the shelf and then produced a packet of thin Greek cheroots.

"Will you allow me to smoke, please?" he said, extending the packet.

"Please do. But I won't smoke just now myself, thank you."

The train had begun to gather speed and the attendant came in to make up their beds. When he had gone, Latimer partially undressed and lay down on his bed.

The fat man picked up the book and then put it down again.

"You know," he said, "the moment the attendant told me that there was an Englishman on the train, I knew that I should have a pleasant journey." The smile came into play, sweet and compassionate, a spiritual pat on the head.

"It's very good of you to say so."

"Oh, no, that is how I feel."

"You speak very good English."

"English is the most beautiful language, I think. Shakespeare, H. G. Wells —you have some great English writers. But I cannot yet express all my ideas in English. I am, as you will have noticed, more at ease with French."

"But your own language . . . ?"

The fat man spread out large, soft hands on one of which twinkled a rather grubby diamond ring. "I am a citizen of the world," he said. "To me, all countries, all languages are beautiful. If only men could live as brothers, without hatred, seeing only the beautiful things. But no! There are always Communists etcetera."

Latimer said: "I think I'll go to sleep now."

"Sleep!" apostrophized his companion raptly; "the great mercy vouchsafed to us poor humans. My name," he added inconsequentially, "is Mister Peters."

"It has been very pleasant to have met you, Mr. Peters," returned Latimer firmly. "We get into Sofia so early that I shan't trouble to undress."

He switched off the main light in the compartment leaving only the dark blue emergency light glowing and the small reading lights over the berths. Then he stripped a blanket off his bed and wrapped it round him.

Mr. Peters had watched these preparations in wistful silence. Now, he began to undress, balancing himself dexterously against the lurching of the train as he put on his pyjamas. At last he clambered into his bed and lay still for a moment, the breath whistling through his nostrils. Then he turned over on his side, groped for his book and began to read. Latimer switched off his own reading lamp. A few moments later he was asleep.

The train reached the frontier in the early hours of the morning and he was awakened by the attendant for his papers. Mr. Peters was still reading. His papers had already been examined by the Greek and Bulgarian officials in the corridor outside and Latimer did not have an opportunity of ascertaining the nationality of the citizen of the world. A Bulgarian customs official put his head in the compartment, frowned at their suitcases and then withdrew. Soon the train moved on over the frontier. Dozing fitfully, Latimer saw the thin strip of sky between the blinds turn blue-black and then grey. The train was due in Sofia at seven. When, at last, he rose to dress and collect his belongings, he saw that Mr. Peters had switched off his reading lamp and had his eyes closed. As the train began to rattle over the network of points outside Sofia, he gently slid the compartment door open.

Mr. Peters stirred and opened his eyes.

"I'm sorry," said Latimer, "I tried not to waken you."

In the semi-darkness of the compartment, the fat man's smile looked like a clown's grimace. "Please don't trouble yourself about me," he said. "I was not asleep. I meant to tell you that the best hotel for you to stay at would be the Slavianska Besseda."

"That's very kind of you; but I wired a reservation from Athens to the Grand Palace. It was recommended to me. Do you know it?"

"Yes. I think it is quite good." The train began to slow down. "Good-bye, Mr. Latimer."

"Good-bye."

In his eagerness to get to a bath and some breakfast it did not occur to Latimer to wonder how Mr. Peters had discovered his name.

Five

≋≋≋≋≋≋≋≋≋≋≋≋≋≋≋≋

NINETEEN
TWENTY-THREE

Latimer had thought carefully about the problem which awaited him in Sofia.

In Smyrna and Athens it had been simply a matter of gaining access to written records. Any competent private inquiry agents could have found out as much. Now, however, things were different. Dimitrios had, to be sure, a police record in Sofia; but, according to Colonel Haki, the Bulgarian police had known very little about him. That they had, indeed, thought him of very little importance was shown by the fact that it was not until they had received the Colonel's inquiry that they had troubled to get a description of him from the woman with whom he was known to have associated. Obviously it was what the police had *not* got in their records, rather than what they had got, which would be interesting. As the Colonel had pointed out, the important thing to know about an assassination was not who had fired the shot but who had paid for the bullet. What information the ordinary police had would no doubt be helpful; but their business would have been with shot-firing rather than bullet-buying. The first thing he had to find out was who had or might have stood to gain by the death of Stambulisky. Until he had that basic information it was idle to speculate as to the part Dimitrios had played. That the information, even if he did obtain it, might turn out to be quite useless as a basis for anything but a Communist pamphlet, was a contingency that he was not for the moment prepared to consider. He was beginning to like his experiment and was unwilling to abandon it easily. If it were to die, he would see that it died hard.

On the afternoon of his arrival he sought out Marukakis at the office of the French news agency and presented his letter of introduction.

The Greek was a dark, lean man of middle age with intelligent, rather bulbous eyes and a way of bringing his lips together at the end of a sentence as though amazed at his own lack of discretion. He greeted Latimer with the watchful courtesy of a negotiator in an armed truce. He spoke in French.

"What information is it that you need, Monsieur?"

"As much as you can give me about the Stambulisky affair of nineteen twenty-three."

Marukakis raised his eyebrows. "So long ago? I shall have to refresh my memory. No, it is no trouble, I will gladly help you. Give me an hour."

"If you could have dinner with me at my hotel this evening, I should be delighted."

"Where are you staying?"

"The Grand Palace."

"We can get a better dinner than that at a fraction of the cost. If you like, I will call for you at eight o'clock and take you to the place. Agreed?"

"Certainly."

"Good. At eight o'clock then. *Au'voir*."

He arrived punctually at eight o'clock and led the way in silence across the Boulevard Maria-Louise and up the Rue Alabinska to a small side-street. Half way along it there was a grocer's shop. Marukakis stopped. He looked suddenly self-conscious. "It does not look very much," he said doubtfully; "but the food is sometimes very good. Would you rather go to a better place?"

"Oh no, I'll leave it to you."

Marukakis looked relieved. "I thought that I had better ask you," he said and pushed open the door of the shop.

Two of the tables were occupied by a group of men and women noisily eating soup. They sat down at a third. A moustachioed man in shirt sleeves and a green baize apron lounged over and addressed them in voluble Bulgarian.

"I think you had better order," said Latimer.

Marukakis said something to the waiter who twirled his moustache and lounged away shouting at a dark opening in the wall that looked like the entrance to the cellar. A voice could be heard faintly acknowledging the order. The man returned with a bottle and three glasses.

"I have ordered vodka," said Marukakis. "I hope you like it."

"Very much."

"Good."

The waiter filled the three glasses, took one for himself, nodded to Latimer and, throwing back his head, poured the vodka down his throat. Then he walked away.

"*A votre santé*," said Marukakis politely. "Now," he went on as they set their glasses down, "that we have drunk together and that we are comrades, I will make a bargain with you. I will give you the information and then you shall tell me why you want it. Does that go?"

"It goes."

"Very well then."

Soup was put before them. It was thick and highly spiced and mixed with sour cream. As they ate it Marukakis began to talk.

In a dying civilisation, political prestige is the reward not of the shrewdest diagnostician but of the man with the best bedside manner. It is the decoration conferred on mediocrity by ignorance. Yet there remains one sort of political prestige that may still be worn with a certain pathetic dignity; it is that given to the liberal-minded leader of a party of conflicting doctrinaire extremists. His dignity is that of all doomed men: for, whether the two extremes proceed to mutual destruction or whether one of them prevails, doomed he is, either to suffer the hatred of the people or to die a martyr.

Thus it was with Monsieur Stambulisky, leader of the Bulgarian Peasant Agrarian Party, Prime Minister and Minister for Foreign Affairs. The Agrarian Party, faced by organised reaction, was immobilised, rendered powerless by its own internal conflicts. It died without firing a shot in its own defence.

The end began soon after Stambulisky returned to Sofia early in January nineteen twenty-three, from the Lausanne Conference.

On January the twenty-third, the Yugoslav (then Serbian) Government lodged an official protest in Sofia against a series of armed raids carried out by Bulgarian *comitadji* over the Yugoslav frontier. A few days later, on February the fifth, during a performance celebrating the foundation of the National Theatre in Sofia at which the King and Princesses were present, a bomb was thrown into a box in which sat several government ministers. The bomb exploded. Several persons were injured.

Both the authors and objects of these outrages were readily apparent.

From the start, Stambulisky's policy towards the Yugoslav Government had been one of appeasement and conciliation. Relations between the two countries had been improving rapidly. But an objection to this improvement came from the Macedonian Autonomists, represented by the notorious Macedonian Revolutionary Committee, which operated in both Yugoslavia and in Bulgaria. Fearing that friendly relations between the two countries might lead to joint action against them, the Macedonians set to work systematically to poison those relations and to destroy their enemy Stambulisky. The attacks of the *comitadji* and the theatre incident inaugurated a period of organised terrorism.

On March the eighth, Stambulisky played his trump card by announcing that the Narodno Sobranie would be dissolved on the thirteenth and that new elections would be held in April.

This was disaster for the reactionary parties. Bulgaria was prospering under the Agrarian Government. The peasants were solidly behind Stambulisky.

An election would have established him even more securely. The funds of the Macedonian Revolutionary Committee increased suddenly.

Almost immediately an attempt was made to assassinate Stambulisky and his Minister of Railways, Atanassoff, at Haskovo on the Thracian frontier. It was frustrated only at the last moment. Several police officials responsible for suppressing the activities of the *comitadji*, including the Prefect of Petrich, were threatened with death. In the face of these menaces, the elections were postponed.

Then, on June the fourth, the Sofia police discovered a plot to assassinate not only Stambulisky but also Muravieff, the War Minister, and Stoyanoff, the Minister of the Interior. A young army officer, believed to have been given the job of killing Stoyanoff, was shot dead by the police in a gun fight. Other young officers, also under the orders of the terrorist Committee, were known to have arrived in Sofia, and a search for them was made. The police were beginning to lose control of the situation.

Now was the time for the Agrarian Party to have acted, to have armed their peasant supporters. But they did not do so. Instead, they played politics among themselves. For them, the enemy was the Macedonian Revolutionary Committee, a terrorist gang, a small organisation quite incapable of ousting a government entrenched behind hundreds of thousands of peasant votes. They failed to perceive that the activities of the Committee had been merely the smokescreen behind which the reactionary parties had been steadily making their preparations for an offensive. They very soon paid for this lack of perception.

At midnight on June the eighth all was calm. By four o'clock on the morning of the ninth, all the members of the Stambulisky Government, with the exception of Stambulisky himself, were in prison and martial law had been declared. The leaders of this *coup d'état* were the reactionaries Zankoff and Rouseff, neither of whom had ever been connected with the Macedonian Committee.

Too late, Stambulisky tried to rally his peasants to their own defence. Several weeks later he was surrounded with a few followers in a country house some hundreds of miles from Sofia and captured. Shortly afterwards and in circumstances which are still obscure, he was shot.

It was in this way that, as Marukakis talked, Latimer sorted out the facts in his own mind. The Greek was a fast talker but liable, if he saw the chance, to turn from fact to revolutionary theory. Latimer was drinking his third glass of tea when the recital ended.

For a moment or two he was silent. At last he said: "Do you know who put up the money for the Committee?"

Marukakis grinned. "Rumours began to circulate some time after. There were many explanations offered; but, in my opinion, the most reasonable and, incidentally, the only one I was able to find any evidence for, was that the money had been advanced by the bank which held the Committee's funds. It is called the Eurasian Credit Trust."

"You mean that this bank advanced the money on behalf of a third party?"

"No, I don't. The bank advanced the money on its own behalf. I happened to find out that it had been badly caught owing to the rise in the value of the *Lev* under the Stambulisky administration. In the early part of nineteen twenty-three, before the trouble started in earnest, the *Lev* doubled its value in two months. It was about eight hundred to the pound sterling and it rose to about four hundred. I could look up the actual figures if you are interested. Anyone who had been selling the *Lev* for delivery in three months or more, counting on a fall, would face huge losses. The Eurasian Credit Trust was not, nor is for that matter, the sort of bank to accept a loss like that."

"What sort of a bank is it?"

"It is registered in Monaco which means not only that it pays no taxes in the countries in which it operates but also that its balance sheet is not published and that it is impossible to find out anything about it. There are lots more like that in Europe. Its head office is in Paris but it operates in the Balkans. Amongst other things it finances the clandestine manufacture of heroin in Bulgaria for illicit export."

"Do you think that it financed the Zankoff *coup d'état*?"

"Possibly. At any rate it financed the conditions that made the *coup d'etat* possible. It was an open secret that the attempt on Stambulisky and Atanassoff at Haskovo was the work of foreign gunmen imported and paid by someone specially for the purpose. A lot of people said, too, that although there was a lot of talking and threatening, the trouble would have died down if it had not been for foreign *agents provocateurs*."

This was better than Latimer had hoped.

"Is there any way in which I can get details of the Haskovo affair?"

Marukakis shrugged. "It is over fifteen years old. The police might tell you something but I doubt it. If I knew what you wanted to know . . ."

Latimer made up his mind. "Very well, I said I would tell you why I wanted this information and I will." He went on hurriedly. "When I was in Stambul some weeks ago I had lunch with a man who happened to be the chief of the Turkish Secret Police. He was interested in detective stories and wanted me to use a plot he had thought of. We were discussing the respective merits of real and fictional murderers when, to illustrate his point, he read me the dossier of a man named Dimitrios Makropoulos or Dimitrios Talat. The man had been a scoundrel and a cut-throat of the worst sort. He had murdered a man in Smyrna and arranged to have another man hanged for it. He had been involved in three attempted assassinations including that of Stambulisky. He had been a French spy and he had organised a gang of drug pedlars in Paris. The day before I heard of him he had been found floating dead in the Bosphorus. He had been knifed in the stomach. For some reason or other I was curious to see him and persuaded this man to take me with him to the mortuary. Dimitrios was there on a table with his clothes piled up beside him.

"It may have been that I had had a good lunch and was feeling stupid but I suddenly had a curious desire to know more about Dimitrios. As you know, I write detective stories. I told myself that if, for once, I tried doing some detecting myself instead of merely writing about other people doing it, I might get some interesting results. My idea was to try to fill in some of the gaps in the dossier. But that was only an excuse. I did not care to admit to myself then that my interest was nothing to do with detection. It is difficult to explain but I see now that my curiosity about Dimitrios was that of the biographer rather than of the detective. There was an emotional element in it, too. I wanted to explain Dimitrios, to account for him, to understand his mind. Merely to label him with disapproval was not enough. I saw him not as a corpse in a mortuary but as a man, not as an isolate, a phenomenon, but as a unit in a disintegrating social system."

He paused. "Well, there you are, Marukakis! That is why I am in Sofia, why I am wasting your time with questions about things that happened fifteen years ago. I am gathering material for a biography that will never be written, when I ought to be producing a detective story. It sounds unlikely enough to me. To you it must sound fantastic. But it is my explanation."

He sat back feeling very foolish. It would have been better to have told a carefully thought out lie.

Marukakis had been staring at his tea. Now he looked up.

"What is your own private explanation of your interest in this Dimitrios?"

"I've just told you."

"No. I think not. You deceive yourself. You hope *au fond* that by rationalizing Dimitrios, by explaining him, you will also explain that disintegrating social system you spoke about."

"That is very ingenious; but, if you will forgive my saying so, a little oversimplified. I don't think that I can accept it."

Marukakis shrugged. "It is my opinion."

"It is very good of you to believe me."

"Why should I not believe you? It is too absurd for disbelief. What do you know of Dimitrios in Bulgaria?"

"Very little. He was, I am told, an intermediary in an attempt to assassinate Stambulisky. That is to say there is no evidence to show that he was going to do any shooting himself. He left Athens, wanted by the police for robbery and attempted murder, towards the end of November nineteen twenty-two. I found that out myself. I also believe that he came to Bulgaria by sea. He was known to the Sofia police. I know that because in nineteen twenty-four the Turkish secret police made inquiries about him in connection with another matter. The police here questioned a woman with whom he was known to have associated."

"If she were still here and alive it would be interesting to talk to her."

"It would. I've traced Dimitrios in Smyrna and in Athens where he called himself Taladis, but so far I have not talked to anyone who ever saw him alive. Unfortunately, I do not even know the woman's name."

"The police records would contain it. If you like I will make inquiries."

"I cannot ask you to take the trouble. If I like to waste my time reading police records there is nothing to prevent my doing so, but there is no reason why I should waste your time too."

"There is plenty to prevent your wasting your time reading police records. In the first place, you cannot read Bulgarian and in the second place, the police would make difficulties. I am, God help me, an accredited journalist working for a French news agency. I have certain privileges. Besides"—he grinned—"absurd as it is, your detecting intrigues me. The baroque in human affairs is always interesting, don't you think?" He looked round. The restaurant had emptied. The waiter was sitting asleep with his feet on one of the tables. Marukakis sighed. "We shall have to wake the poor devil to pay him."

On his third day in Sofia, Latimer received a letter from Marukakis.

My dear Mr. Latimer, (he wrote in French)

Here, as I promised, is a précis of all the information about Dimitrios Makropoulos which l have been able to obtain from the police. It is not, as you will see, complete. That is interesting, don't you think! Whether the woman can be found or not, I cannot say until I have made friends with a few more policemen. Perhaps we could meet to-morrow.

Assuring you of my most distinguished sentiments.

N. Marukakis

Attached to this letter was the précis:

POLICE ARCHIVES, SOFIA 1922–24

Dimitrios Makropoulos. *Citizenship*: Greek. *Place of birth*: Salonika. *Date*: 1889. *Trade*: Described as fig-packer. *Entry*: Varna, December 22nd 1922, off Italian steamer *Isola Bella*. *Passport or Identity Card*: Relief Commission Identity Card No. T.53462.

At police inspection of papers in Café Spetzi, Rue Perotska, Sofia, June 6th 1923, was in company of woman named Irana Preveza, Greek-born Bulgar. D. M. known associate of foreign criminals. Proscribed for deportation, June 7th 1923. Released at request and on assurances of A. Vazoff, June 7th 1923.

In September 1924 request received from Turkish Government for information relating to a fig-packer named "Dimitrios" wanted on a charge of murder. Above information supplied a month later. Irana Preveza when questioned reported receiving letter from Makropoulos at Adrianople. She gave following description:

Height: 182 centimetres. *Eyes*: brown. *Complexion*: dark, clean-shaven. *Hair*: dark and straight. *Distinguishing marks*: none.

At the foot of this précis, Marukakis had added a handwritten note.

N.B. This is an ordinary police dossier only. Reference is made to a second dossier on the secret file but it is forbidden to inspect this.

Latimer sighed. The second dossier contained, no doubt, the details of the part played by Dimitrios in the events of nineteen twenty-three. The Bulgarian authorities had evidently known more about Dimitrios than they had been prepared to confide to the Turkish police. To know that the information was in existence, yet to be unable to get at it was really most irritating.

However, there was much food for thought in what information was available. The most obvious tit-bit was that on board the Italian steamer *Isola Bella* in December 1922, between the Piræus and Varna in the Black Sea, the Relief Commission Identity Card number T.53462 had suffered an alteration. "Dimitrios Taladis" had become "Dimitrios Makropoulos." Either Dimitrios had discovered a talent for forgery or he had met and employed someone with such a talent.

Irana Preveza! A real clue that and one that would have to be followed up very carefully. If she were still alive there must surely be some way of finding her. For the moment, however, that task would have to be left to Marukakis. Incidentally, the fact that she was of Greek extraction was suggestive, Dimitrios would probably not have spoken Bulgar.

"Known associate of foreign criminals," was distinctly vague. What sort of criminals? Of what foreign nationality? And to what extent had he associated with them? And why had attempts been made to deport him just two days before the Zankoff *coup d'etat*? Had Dimitrios been one of the suspected assassins for whom the Sofia police had been searching during that critical week? Colonel Haki had pooh-poohed the idea of his being an assassin at all. "His kind never risk their skins like that." But Colonel Haki had not known everything about Dimitrios. And who on earth was the obliging A. Vazoff who had so promptly and effectively intervened on behalf of Dimitrios? The answers to those questions were, no doubt, in that secret second dossier. Most irritating!

He had sent a note to Marukakis, and on the following morning received a telephone call from him. They arranged to meet again for dinner that evening.

"Have you got any farther with the police?"

"Yes. I will tell you everything when we meet this evening. Good-bye."

By the time the evening came, Latimer was feeling very much as he had once used to feel while waiting for examination results: a little excited, a little apprehensive and very much irritated at the decorous delay in publishing information which had been in existence for several days. He smiled rather sourly at Marukakis.

"It is really very good of you to take so much trouble."

Marukakis flourished a hand. "Nonsense, my dear friend. I told you I was interested. Shall we go to the grocer's shop again? We can talk there quietly."

From then until the arrival of the tea he talked incessantly about the position of the Scandinavian countries in the event of a major European war. Latimer began to feel as baleful as one of his own murderers.

"And now," said the Greek at last, "as to this question of your Dimitrios, we are going on a little trip to-night."

"What do you mean?"

"I said that I would make friends with some policeman and I have done so. As a result I have found out where Irana Preveza is now. It was not very difficult. She turns out to be very well known—to the police."

Latimer felt his heart begin to beat a little faster. "Where is she?" he demanded.

"About five minutes' walk away from here. She is the proprietress of a *Nachtlokal* called *La Vierge St. Marie.*"

"*Nachtlokal?*"

He grinned. "Well, you could call it a night club."

"I see."

"She has not always had her own place. For many years she worked either on her own or for other houses. But she grew too old. She had money saved, and so she started her own place. About fifty years of age, but looks younger. The police have quite an affection for her. She does not get up until ten in the evening, so we must wait a little before we try our luck at talking to her. Did you read her description of Dimitrios? No distinguishing marks! That made me laugh."

"Did it occur to you to wonder how she knew that his height was exactly one hundred and eighty-two centimetres?"

Marukakis frowned. "Why should it?"

"Very few people know even their own heights exactly."

"What is your idea?"

"I think that that description came from the second dossier you mentioned, and not from the woman."

"And so?"

"Just a moment. Do you know who A. Vazoff is?"

"I meant to tell you. I asked the same question. He was a lawyer."

"Was?"

"He died three years ago. He left much money. It was claimed by a nephew living in Bucuresti. He had no relations living here." Marukakis paused and then, with an elaborate air of simplicity, added: "He used to be on the board of directors of the Eurasian Credit Trust. I was keeping that as a little surprise for you later, but you may have it now. I found out from the files. Eurasian Credit Trust was not registered in Monaco until nineteen twenty-six. The list of directors prior to that date is still in existence and open to inspection if you know where to find it."

"But," spluttered Latimer, "this is most important. Don't you see what . . ."

Marukakis interrupted him by calling for the bill. Then he glanced at Latimer slyly. "You know," he said, "you English are sublime. You are the only nation in the world that believes that it has a monopoly of ordinary common sense."

Six

~~~~~~~~~~~~~~~~~~~~~~~~~~~~~~~

CARTE POSTALE

LA VIERGE ST. MARIE was situated, with somewhat dingy logic, in a street of houses behind the church of *Sveta Nedelja*. The street was narrow, sloping and poorly lit. At first it seemed unnaturally silent. But behind the silence there were whispers of music and laughter—whispers that would start out suddenly as a door opened and then be smothered as it closed again. Two men came out of a doorway ahead of them, lit cigarettes and walked quickly away. The footsteps of another pedestrian approached and then stopped as their owner went into one of the houses.

"Not many people about now," commented Marukakis; "too early."

Most of the doors were panelled with translucent glass and had dim lights showing through them. On some of the panels the number of the house was painted; painted rather more elaborately than was necessary for ordinary purposes. Other doors bore names. There was *Wonderbar, O.K. Jymmies Bar, Stambul, Torquemada, Vitocha, Le Viol de Lucrece* and, higher up the hill, *La Vierge St. Marie.*

For a moment they stood outside it. The door looked less shabby than some of the others. Latimer felt to see if his wallet was safe in his pocket as Marukakis pushed open the door and led the way in.

They found themselves in a low-ceilinged room about thirty feet square. At regular intervals round the pale blue walls were placed oval mirrors supported by papier-mâché cherubim. The spaces between the mirrors were decorated haphazard with highly stylised pictures, painted on the walls, of monocled men with straw-coloured hair and nude torsos, and women in tailor-made costumes and check stockings. In one corner of the room was a minute bar; in the opposite corner the platform on which sat the band—four listless negroes in white "Argentine" blouses. Near them was a blue plush curtained doorway. The rest of the wall space was taken up by small cubicles which rose to the shoulder height of those sitting at the tables set inside them. A few more tables encroached on the dance-floor in the centre.

When they came in there were about a dozen persons seated in the cubicles. The band was still playing and two girls who looked as though they might presently form part of the cabaret were dancing solemnly together.

"Too early," repeated Marukakis disappointedly. "But it will be gayer soon."

A waiter swept them to one of the cubicles and hurried away, to reappear a moment or two later with a bottle of champagne.

"Have you got plenty of money with you?" murmured Marukakis; "we shall have to pay at least two hundred leva for this poison."

Latimer nodded. Two hundred leva was about ten shillings.

The band stopped. The two girls finished their dance, and one of them caught Latimer's eye. They walked over to the cubicle and stood smiling down. Marukakis said something. Still smiling, the two shrugged their shoulders and went away. Marukakis looked doubtfully at Latimer.

"I said that we had business to discuss, but that we would entertain them later. Of course, if you don't want to be bothered with them . . ."

"I don't," said Latimer firmly and then shuddered as he drank some of the champagne.

Marukakis sighed. "It seems a pity. We shall have to pay for the champagne. Someone may as well drink it."

"Where is La Preveza?"

"She will be down at any moment now, I should think. Of course," he added thoughtfully, "we could go up to her." He raised his eyes significantly towards the ceiling. "It is really quite refined, this place. Everything seems to be most discreet."

"If she will be down here soon there seems to be no point in our going up." He felt an austere prig and wished that the champagne had been drinkable.

"Just so," said Marukakis gloomily.

But an hour and a half passed by before the proprietress of *La Vierge St. Marie* put in an appearance. During that time things certainly did become gayer. More people arrived, mostly men, although among them were one or two peculiar-looking women. An obvious pimp, who looked very sober, brought in a couple of Germans who looked very drunk and might have been commercial travellers on the spree. A pair of rather sinister young men sat down and ordered Vichy water. There was a certain amount of coming and going through the plush-curtained door. The cubicles were all occupied and extra tables were set up on the dance-floor which soon became a congested mass of swaying, sweating couples. Presently, however, the floor was cleared

and a number of the girls who had disappeared some minutes before to replace their clothes with a bunch or two of artificial primroses and a great deal
of sun-tan powder, did a short dance. They were followed by a youth dressed
as a woman who sang songs in German; then they reappeared without their
primroses to do another dance. This concluded the cabaret and the audience
swarmed back on to the dance-floor. The atmosphere thickened, became hotter and hotter.

Through smarting eyes Latimer was idly watching one of the sinister young
men offering the other a pinch of what might have been snuff, but which was
not, and wondering whether he should make another attempt to slake his thirst
with the champagne, when suddenly Marukakis touched his arm.

"That will be her," he said.

Latimer looked across the room. For a moment a couple on the extreme
corner of the dance-floor obstructed the view; then the couple moved an inch
or two, and he saw her standing motionless by the curtained door by which
she had entered.

She possessed that odd blowzy quality that is independent of good clothes
and well-dressed hair and skillful maquillage. Her figure was full but good
and she held herself well; her dress was probably expensive, her thick, dark
hair looked as though it had spent the past two hours in the hands of a hair-
dresser. Yet she remained, unmistakably and irrevocably, a slattern. There
was something temporary, an air of suspended animation, about her. It seemed
as if at any moment the hair should begin to straggle, the dress slip down
negligently over one soft, creamy shoulder, the hand with the diamond
cluster ring which now hung loosely at her side reach up to pluck at pink
silk shoulder straps and pat abstractedly at the hair. You saw it in her dark
eyes. The mouth was firm and good-humoured in the loose, raddled flesh about
it; but the eyes were humid with sleep and the carelessness of sleep. Now
they were open and watchful, moving about while the mouth smiled a greeting here and there. Latimer watched her turn suddenly and go towards
the bar.

Marukakis beckoned to the waiter and said something to him. The man
hesitated and then nodded. Latimer saw him weave his way towards where
Madame Preveza was talking to a fat man with his arm round one of the cabaret
girls. The waiter whispered something. Madame Preveza stopped talking and
looked at him. He pointed towards Latimer and Marukakis, and for a moment her eyes rested dispassionately on them. Then she turned away, said a
word to the waiter and resumed her conversation.

"She'll come in a minute," said Marukakis.

Soon she left the fat man and went on making her tour of the room, nodding, smiling indulgently. At last she reached their table. Involuntarily, Latimer got to his feet. The eyes studied his face.

"You wished to speak with me, Messieurs?" Her voice was husky, a little harsh, and she spoke in strongly accented French.

"We should be honoured if you would sit at our table for a moment," said Marukakis.

"Of course." She sat down beside him. Immediately the waiter came up. She waved him away and looked at Latimer. "I have not seen you before, Monsieur. Your friend I have seen, but not in my place." She looked sideways at Marukakis. "Are you going to write about me in the Paris newspapers, Monsieur? If so, you must see the rest of my entertainment—you and your friend."

Marukakis smiled. "No, Madame. We are trespassing on your hospitality to ask for some information."

"Information?" A blank look had come into the dark eyes. "I know nothing of any interest to anybody."

"Your discretion is famous, Madame. This, however, concerns a man, now dead and buried, whom you knew over fifteen years ago."

She laughed shortly and Latimer saw that her teeth were bad. She laughed again, uproariously, so that her body shook. It was an ugly sound that tore away her slumberous dignity, leaving her old. She coughed a little as the laughter died away. "You pay the most delicate compliments, Monsieur," she gasped. "Fifteen years! You expect me to remember a man that long? Holy Mother of Christ, I think you shall buy me a drink after all."

Latimer beckoned to the waiter. "What will you drink, Madame?"

"Champagne. Not this filth. The waiter will know. Fifteen years!" She was still amused.

"We hardly dared to hope that you would remember," said Marukakis a trifle coldly. "But if a name means anything to you . . . it was Dimitrios—Dimitrios Makropoulos."

She had been lighting a cigarette. Now she stopped still with the burning match in her fingers. Her eyes were on the end of the cigarette. For several seconds the only movement that Latimer saw in her face was the corners of her mouth turning slowly downward. It seemed to him that the noise about them had receded suddenly, that there was cotton wool in his ears. Then she slowly turned the match between her fingers and dropped it on to the plate in front of her. The eyes did not move. Then, very softly, she said: "I don't like you here. Get out—both of you!"

"But . . ."

"Get out!" Still she did not raise her voice or move her head.

Marukakis looked across at Latimer, shrugged and stood up. Latimer followed suit. She glared up at them sullenly. "Sit down," she snapped; "do you think I want a scene here?"

They sat down. "If you will explain, Madame," said Marukakis acidly, "how we can get out without standing up we should be grateful."

The fingers of her right hand moved quickly and grasped the stem of a glass. For a moment Latimer thought that she was going to break it in the Greek's face. Then her fingers relaxed and she said something in Greek too rapid for Latimer to understand.

Marukakis shook his head. "No, he is nothing to do with the police," Latimer heard him reply. "He is a writer of books and he seeks information."

"Why?"

"He is curious. He saw the dead body of Dimitrios Makropoulos in Stambul a month or two ago, and he is curious about him."

She turned to Latimer and gripped his sleeve urgently. "He is dead? You are sure he is dead? You actually saw his body?"

He nodded. Her manner made him feel oddly like the doctor who descends the stairs to announce that all is over. "He had been stabbed and thrown into the sea," he added and cursed himself for putting it so clumsily. In her eyes was an emotion he could not quite identify. Perhaps, in her way, she had loved him. A slice of life! Tears should follow.

But there were no tears. She said:

"Had he any money on him?"

Slowly, uncomprehendingly, Latimer shook his head.

"*Merde!*" she said viciously; "the son of a diseased camel owed me a thousand French francs. Now I shall never see it back. *Salop!* Get out, both of you, before I have you thrown out!"

It was nearly half-past three before Latimer and Marukakis left *La Vierge St. Marie.*

The preceding two hours they had spent in Madame Preveza's private office, a beflowered room filled with furniture: a walnut grand piano draped in a white silk shawl with a fringe and pen-painted birds in the corners of it, small tables loaded with bric-a-brac, many chairs, a browning palm tree in a bamboo stand, a chaise-longue and a large roll-top desk in Spanish oak. They had reached it, under her guidance, via the curtained door, a flight of stairs and a dimly lit corridor with numbered doors on either side of it and a smell that had reminded Latimer of an expensive nursing home during visiting hours.

The invitation had been the very last thing that he had expected. It had come close on the heels of her final exhortation to them to "get out." She had become plaintive; apologised. A thousand francs was a thousand francs. Now she would never see it. Her eyes had filled with tears. To Latimer she had seemed fantastic. The money had been owing since nineteen twenty-three. She could not seriously have expected its return after fifteen years. Perhaps somewhere in her mind she had kept intact the romantic illusion that one day Dimitrios would walk in and scatter thousand franc notes like leaves about her. The fairy tale gesture! Latimer's news had shattered that illusion and when her first anger had gone she had felt herself in need of sympathy. Forgotten had been their request for information about Dimitrios. The bearers of the bad news must know how bad their news had been. She had been saying farewell to a legend. An audience had been necessary, an audience who would understand what a foolish, generous woman she was. Their drinks she had said, rubbing salt in the wound, were on the house.

They had seated themselves side by side on the chaise-longue while she had rummaged in the roll-top desk. From one of the innumerable pigeonholes she had produced a small dog-eared notebook. The pages of it had rustled through her fingers. Then:

"February the fifteenth, nineteen twenty-three," she had said suddenly. The notebook had shut with a snap and her eyes had moved upwards calling upon Heaven to testify to the accuracy of the date. "That was when the money became due to me. A thousand francs and he promised faithfully that he would pay me. It was due to me and he had received it. Sooner than make a big scene—for I detest big scenes—I said that he could borrow it. And he said that he would repay me, that in a matter of weeks he would be getting plenty of money. And he did get that money but he did not pay me my thousand francs. After all I had done for him, too!

"I picked that man up out of the gutter, Messieurs. That was in December. Dear Christ, it was cold. In the eastern provinces people were dying quicker than you could have machine-gunned them—and I have seen people machine-gunned. At that time I had no place like this, you understand. Of course, I was a girl then. Often I used to be asked to pose for photographs. There was one that was my favourite. I had on just a simple drape of white chiffon, caught in at the waist with a girdle, and a crown of small white flowers. In my right hand which rested—so—upon a pretty, white column, I held a single red rose. It was used for postcards, *pour les amoureux*, and the photographer coloured the rose and printed a very pretty poem at the bottom of the card." The dark, moist lids had drooped over her eyes and she had recited softly:

"Je veux que mon coeur vous serve d'oreiller,
"Et à votre bonheur je saurai veiller.

"Very pretty, don't you think?" The ghost of a smile had tightened her lips. "I burnt all my photographs several years ago. Sometimes I am sorry for that but I think that I was right. It is not good to be reminded always of the past. That is why, Messieurs, I was angry to-night when you spoke of Dimitrios; for he is of the past. One must think of the present and of the future.

"But Dimitrios was not a man that one forgets easily. I have known many men but I have been afraid of only two men in my life. One of them was the man I married and the other was Dimitrios. One deceives oneself, you know. One thinks that one wants to be understood when one wants only to be half-understood. If a person really understands you, you fear him. My husband understood me because he loved me and I feared him because of that. But when he grew tired of loving me I could laugh at him and no longer fear him. But Dimitrios was different. Dimitrios understood me better than I understood myself; but he did not love me. I do not think he could love anyone. I thought that one day I should be able to laugh at him too, but that day never came. You could not laugh at Dimitrios. I found that out. When he had gone I hated him and told myself that it was because of the thousand francs he owed to me. I wrote it down in my book as proof. But I was lying to myself. He owed me more than a thousand francs. He had always cheated me over the money. It was because I feared him and could not understand him as he understood me that I hated him.

"I was living in a hotel then. A filthy place, full of scum. The *patron* was a dirty bully, but friendly with the police; and while one paid for one's room one was safe, even if one's papers were not in order.

"One afternoon I was resting when I heard the *patron* shouting at someone in the next room. The walls were thin and I could hear everything. At first I paid no attention, for he was always shouting at someone, but after a while I began to listen because they were speaking in Greek and I understand Greek. The *patron* was threatening to call in the police if the room was not paid for. I could not hear what was said in reply for the other man spoke softly; but at last the *patron* went out and there was quiet. I was half-asleep when suddenly I heard the handle of my door being tried. The door was bolted. I watched the handle turn slowly as it was released again. Then there was a knock.

"I asked who was there but there was no answer. I thought that perhaps it was one of my friends and that he had not heard me so I went to the door and unbolted it. Outside was Dimitrios.

"He asked in Greek if he could come in. I asked him what he wanted and he said that he wanted to talk to me. I asked him how he knew that I spoke Greek but he did not answer. I knew now that he must be the man in the next room. I had passed him once or twice on the stairs and he had always seemed very polite and nervous as he stood aside for me. But now he was not nervous. I said that I was resting and that he could come to see me later if he wished. But he smiled and pushed the door open and came in and leaned against the wall.

"I told him to get out, that I would call the *patron*; but he only smiled and stayed where he was. He asked me then whether I had heard what the *patron* had said and I replied that I had not heard. I had a pistol in the drawer of my table and I went to it; but he seemed to guess what I was thinking for he moved across the room as if by accident and leaned against the table as if he owned the place. Then he asked me to lend him some money.

"I was never a fool. I had a thousand leva pinned high up in the curtain but only a few coins in my bag. I said that I had no money. He seemed not to take any notice of that and began to tell me that he had not eaten anything since the day before, that he had no money and that he felt ill. But all the time he talked his eyes were moving, looking at things in the room. I can see him now. His face was smooth and oval and pale and he had very brown, anxious eyes that made you think of a doctor's eyes when he is doing something to you that hurts. He frightened me. I told him again that I had no money but that I had some bread if he wanted it. He said: 'Give me the bread.'

"I got the bread from the drawer and gave it to him. He ate it slowly, still leaning against the table. When he had finished he asked for a cigarette. I gave him one. Then he said that I needed a protector. I knew then what he was after. I said that I could manage my own affairs. He said that I was a fool and that he could prove it. If I would do as he said he would get five thousand leva that day and give me half of it. I asked what he wanted me to do. He told me to write a note that he would dictate. It was addressed to a man whose name I had never heard and simply asked for five thousand leva. I thought he must be mad and to get rid of him I wrote the note and signed it 'Irana.' He said that he would meet me at a café that evening.

"I did not trouble to keep the appointment. The next morning he came again to my room. This time I would not let him in. He was very angry and said that he had two thousand five hundred leva for me. Of course, I did not believe him but he pushed a thousand leva note under the door and said that I should have the rest when I let him in. So I let him in. He gave me immediately another fifteen hundred leva. I asked him where he had got it and he said that he had delivered the note himself to the man who had given him the money immediately.

"I have always been discreet. I am not interested in the real names of my friends. Dimitrios had followed one of them to his home, had found out his real name and that he was an important man and then with my note in his hand had threatened to tell his wife and daughters of our friendship unless he paid.

"I was very angry. I said that for the sake of two thousand five hundred leva, I had lost one of my good friends. Dimitrios said that he could get me richer friends. He said, too, that he had given the money to me to show that he was serious and that he could have written the note himself and gone to my friend without telling me.

"I saw that this was true. I saw also that he might go to other friends unless I agreed with him. So Dimitrios became my protector and he *did* bring me richer friends. And he bought himself very smart clothes and sometimes went to the best cafés.

"But soon, someone I knew told me that he had become involved in politics and that he often went to certain cafés that the police watched. I told him that he was a fool, but he took no notice. He said that soon he would make a lot of money. Often he left Sofia for several days at a time. He did not tell me when he went and I did not ask. But I knew that he had made important friends, for, once, when the police were making difficulties about his papers, he laughed and told me not to worry about the police. They would not dare to touch him, he said.

"But one morning he came to me in great agitation. He looked as if he had been travelling all night and had not shaved for several days. I had never seen him so nervous. He took me by the wrists and said that if anyone asked me I must say that he had been with me for the last three days. I had not seen him for over a week but I had to agree and he went to sleep in my room.

"Nobody asked me about him; but later that day I read in the newspaper that an attempt had been made on Stambulisky at Haskovo and I guessed where Dimitrios had been. I was frightened. An old friend of mine, whom I had known before Dimitrios, wanted to give me an apartment of my own. When Dimitrios had had his sleep and gone, I went to my friend and said that I would take this apartment.

"I was afraid when I had done it, but that night I met Dimitrios and told him. I had expected him to be angry but he was quite calm and said that it would be best for me. Yet I could not tell what he was thinking because he always looked the same, like a doctor when he is doing something to you that hurts. I took courage and reminded him that we had some business to settle.

He agreed and said that he would meet me three days later to give me all the money that was due to me.

"Three days later I waited for him in the café and he did not come. Several weeks after that I saw him and he said that he had been away but that if I would meet him on the following day, he would pay me the money he owed. The meeting place was a café in the Rue Perotska, a low place that I did not like.

"This time he came as he had promised. He said that he was in difficulties about money, that he had a great sum coming to him and that he would pay me within a few weeks.

"I wondered why he had kept the appointment merely to tell me that; but later I understood why. He had come to ask me a favour. He had to have certain letters received by someone he could trust. They were not his letters but those of a friend of his, a Turk named Talat. If this friend could give the address of my apartment, Dimitrios himself would collect the letters when he paid me my money.

"I agreed. I could do nothing else. It meant that if Dimitrios had to collect these letters from me he would have to pay me the money. But I knew in my heart and he knew too that he could have collected the letters and not paid me a sou and I could have done nothing.

"We were sitting there drinking coffee—for Dimitrios was very mean in cafés—when the police came in to inspect papers. It was quite usual at that time but it was not good to be found in that café because of its reputation. Dimitrios had his papers in order but because he was a foreigner they took his name and mine because I was with him. When they had gone he was very angry; but I think he was angry not because of their taking his name but because they had taken my name as being with him. He was much put out and told me not to trouble about the letters as he would arrange for them with someone else. We left the café and that was the last time I saw him."

She had had a Mandarine-Curaçao in front of her and now she had drunk it down thirstily. Latimer had cleared his throat.

"And the last you heard of him?"

Suspicion had flickered for an instant in her eyes. Latimer had said: "Dimitrios is dead, Madame. Fifteen years have gone by. Times have changed in Sofia."

Her queer, taut smile had hovered on her lips.

"'Dimitrios is dead, Madame.' That sounds very curious to me. It is difficult to think of Dimitrios as dead. How did he look?"

"His hair was grey. He was wearing clothes bought in Greece and in France. Poor stuff." Unconsciously he had echoed Colonel Haki's phrase.

"Then he did not become rich?"

"He did once become rich, in Paris, but he lost his money."

She had laughed. "That must have hurt him." And then suspicion again: "You know a lot about Dimitrios, Monsieur. If he is dead . . . I don't understand."

"My friend is a writer," Marukakis had put in; "he is naturally interested in human nature."

"What do you write?"

"Detective stories."

She had shrugged. "You do not need to know human nature for that. It is for love stories and romances that one must know human nature. *Romans policiers* are ugly. *Folle Farine* I think is a lovely story. Do you like it?"

"Very much."

"I have read it seventeen times. It is the best of Ouida's books and I have read them all. One day I shall write my memoirs. I have seen a lot of human nature you know." The smile had become a trifle arch and she had sighed and fingered a diamond brooch.

"But you wish to know more of Dimitrios. Very well. I heard of Dimitrios again a year later. One day I received a letter from him, from Adrianople. He gave a poste restante address. The letter asked me if I had received any letters for this Talat. If I had I was to write saying so but to keep the letters. He said that I was to tell nobody that I had heard from him. He promised again to pay me the money he owed me. I had no letters addressed to Talat and wrote to tell him so. I also said that I needed the money because, now that he had gone away, I had lost all my friends. That was a lie but I thought that by flattering him I would perhaps get the money. I should have known Dimitrios better. He did not even reply.

"A few weeks after that a man came to see me. A type of *fonctionnaire* he was, very severe and businesslike. His clothes looked expensive. He said that the police would probably be coming to question me about Dimitrios.

"I was frightened at that but he said that I had nothing to fear. Only I must be careful what I said to them. He told me what to say: how I must describe Dimitrios so that the police would be satisfied. I showed him the letter from Adrianople and it seemed to amuse him. He said that I could tell the police about the letter coming from Adrianople but that I must say nothing about this name Talat. He said that the letter was a dangerous thing to keep and burnt it. That made me angry but he gave me a thousand-leva note and asked me if I liked Dimitrios, if I was a friend. I said that I hated him. Then he said that friendship was a great thing and that he would give me five thousand leva to say what he had told me to the police."

She had shrugged. "That is being serious, Messieurs. Five thousand leva!

When the police came I said what this man had asked me to say and the following day an envelope with five thousand leva in it arrived by post. There was nothing else in the envelope, no letter. That was all right. But listen! About two years later I saw this man in the street. I went up to him; but the *salop* pretended that he had not seen me before and called the police to me. Friendship is a great thing."

She had picked up the book and put it back in its pigeonhole.

"If you will excuse me, Messieurs, it is time I returned to my guests. I think I have talked too much. You see, I know nothing about Dimitrios that is of any interest."

"We have been most interested, Madame."

She had smiled. "If you are not in a hurry, Messieurs, I can show you more interesting things than Dimitrios. I have two most amusing girls who . . ."

"We are a little pressed for time, Madame. Another night we should be delighted. Perhaps you would allow us to pay for your drinks."

She had smiled. "As you wish, Messieurs, but it has been most agreeable talking to you. No, no, please! I have a superstition about money being shown in my own private room. Please arrange it with the waiter at your table. You will excuse me if I don't come down with you? I have a little business to attend to. *Au 'voir, Monsieur. Au 'voir, Monsieur. A bientôt.*"

The dark, humid eyes had rested on them affectionately. Latimer had found himself feeling absurdly distressed at the leave-taking.

It had been a *gérant* who had responded to their request for a bill. He had had a brisk, cheerful manner.

"Eleven hundred leva, Messieurs."

"What!"

"The price you arranged with Madame, Messieurs."

"You know," Marukaki remarked as they waited for their change, "I think one does wrong to disapprove altogether of Dimitrios. He had his points."

"Dimitrios was employed by Vazoff acting on behalf of the Eurasian Credit Trust to do work in connection with getting rid of Stambulisky. It would be interesting to know how they recruited him, but that is a thing we shall never know. However, they must have found him satisfactory because they employed him to do similar work in Adrianople. He probably used the name Talat there."

"The Turkish police did not know that. They heard of him simply as 'Dimitrios,'" put in Latimer. "What I cannot understand is why Vazoff— it obviously was Vazoff who visited La Preveza in nineteen twenty-four— allowed her to tell the police that she had had that letter from Adrianople."

"For only one reason, surely. Because Dimitrios was no longer in Adrianople." Marukakis stifled a yawn. "It's been a curious evening."

They were standing outside Latimer's hotel. The night air was cold. "I think I'll go in now," he said.

"You'll be leaving Sofia?"

"For Belgrade. Yes."

"Then you are still interested in Dimitrios?"

"Oh, yes." Latimer hesitated. "I can't tell you how grateful I am to you for your help. It has been a miserable waste of time for you."

Marukakis laughed and then grinned apologetically. He said: "I was laughing at myself for envying you your Dimitrios. If you find out any more about him in Belgrade I should like you to write to me. Would you do that?"

"Of course."

But Latimer was not to reach Belgrade.

He thanked Marukakis again and they shook hands; then he went into the hotel. His room was on the second floor. Key in hand, he climbed the stairs. Along the heavily carpeted corridors his footsteps made no sound. He put the key in the lock, turned it and opened the door.

He had been expecting darkness and the lights in the room were switched on. That startled him a little. The thought flashed through his mind that perhaps he had mistaken the room; but an instant later he saw something which disposed of that notion. That something was chaos.

Strewn about the floor in utter confusion were the contents of his suitcases. Draped carelessly over a chair were the bedclothes. On the mattress, stripped of their bindings, were the few English books he had brought with him from Athens. The room looked as if a cageful of chimpanzees had been turned loose in it.

Dazed, Latimer took two steps forward into the room. Then a slight sound to the right of him made him turn his head. The next moment his heart jolted sickeningly.

The door leading to the bathroom was open. Standing just inside it, a disembowelled tube of toothpaste in one hand, a massive Lüger pistol held loosely in the other and on his lips a sweet, sad smile, was Mr. Peters.

Seven

≋≋≋≋≋≋≋≋≋≋≋≋

HALF A MILLION FRANCS

M R. PETERS TOOK a firmer grasp of his pistol. "Would you be so good," he said gently, "as to shut the door behind you? I think that if you stretched out your right arm you could do it without moving your feet." The pistol was now levelled in an unmistakable fashion.

Latimer obeyed. Now, at last, he felt very frightened indeed. He was afraid that he was going to be hurt; he could already feel the doctor probing for the bullet. He would insist on an anæsthetic. He was afraid that Mr. Peters was not used to the pistol, that he might fire accidentally. He was afraid of moving his hand too quickly lest the sudden movement should be misinterpreted. The door closed. He began to shake from head to foot and could not decide whether it was anger, fear or shock that made him do so. Suddenly he made up his mind to say something.

"What the hell does this mean?" he demanded harshly and then swore. It was not what he had intended to say and he was a man who very rarely swore. He was sure now that it was anger that was making him tremble. He glowered into Mr. Peters' wet eyes.

The fat man lowered his pistol and sat down on the edge of the mattress. "This is most awkward," he said unhappily. "I did not expect you back so soon. Your *maison close* must have proved disappointing. The inevitable Armenian girls, of course. Appealing enough for a while and then merely dull. I often think that perhaps this great world of ours would be a better, finer place if . . ." He broke off. "But we can talk about that another time." Carefully he put the remains of the toothpaste tube on the bedside table. "I had hoped to get things tidied a little before I left," he added.

Latimer decided to play for time. "Including the books, Mr. Peters?"

"Ah, yes, the books!" He shook his head despondently. "An act of vandalism. A book is a lovely thing, a garden stocked with beautiful flowers, a magic carpet on which to fly away to unknown climes. I am sorry. But it was necessary."

"What was necessary? What are you talking about?"

Mr. Peters smiled a sad, long-suffering smile. "A little frankness, Mr. Latimer, *please*. There could be only one reason why your room should be searched and you know it as well as I do. I can see your difficulty, of course. You are wondering exactly where I stand. If it is any consolation to you, however, I may say that my difficulty is in wondering exactly where *you* stand."

This was fantastic. In his exasperation, Latimer forgot his fears. He took a deep breath.

"Now look here, Mr. Peters, or whatever your name is, I am very tired and I want to go to bed. If I remember correctly, I travelled with you in a train from Athens several days ago. You were, I believe, going to Bucharest. I, on the other hand, got off here in Sofia. I have been out with a friend. I return to my hotel to find my room in a disgusting mess, my books destroyed and you flourishing a pistol in my face. I conclude that you are either a sneak thief or a drunk. But for your pistol, of which I am, I confess, afraid, I should already have rung for assistance. But it seems to me on reflection that thieves do not ordinarily meet their victims in first-class sleeping cars, nor do they tear books to pieces. Again, you do not appear to be drunk. I begin, naturally, to wonder if, after all, you may not be mad. If you are, of course, I can do nothing but humour you and hope for the best. But if you are comparatively sane I must ask you once more for an explanation. I repeat, Mr. Peters; what the hell does this mean?"

Mr. Peters' tear-filled eyes were half-closed. "Perfect," he said raptly; "perfect! No, no, Mr. Latimer, keep away from the bell push, please. That is better. You know, for a moment I was almost convinced of your sincerity. Almost. But, of course, not quite. It really is not kind of you to try to deceive me. Not kind, not considerate and such a waste of time."

Latimer took a step forward. "Now listen to me . . ."

The Lüger jerked upwards. The smile left Mr. Peters' mouth and his flaccid lips parted slightly. He looked adenoidal and very dangerous. Latimer stepped back quickly. The smile slowly returned.

"Come now, Mr. Latimer. A little frankness, please. I have the best of intentions towards you. I did not seek this interview. But since you have returned so unexpectedly, since I could no longer meet you on a basis of, may I say, disinterested friendship, let us be frank with one another." He leaned forward a little. "Why are you so interested in Dimitrios?"

"Dimitrios!"

"Yes, dear Mr. Latimer, Dimitrios. You have come from the Levant. Dimitrios came from there. In Athens you were very energetically seeking his record in the relief commission archives. Here in Sofia you have employed an agent to trace his police record. Why? Wait before you answer. I have no animosity towards you. I bear you no ill-will. Let that be clear. But, as it happens, I too am interested in Dimitrios and because of that I am interested in you. Now, Mr. Latimer, tell me frankly where you stand. What—forgive the expression, please—is your game?"

Latimer was silent for a moment. He was trying to think quickly and not succeeding. He was confused. He had come to regard Dimitrios as his own property, a problem as academic as that of the authorship of an anonymous sixteenth-century lyric. And now, here was the odious Mr. Peters, with his shabby god and his smiles and his Lüger pistol, claiming acquaintance with the problem as though he, Latimer, were the interloper. There was, of course, no reason why he should be surprised. Dimitrios must have been known to many persons. Yet he had felt instinctively that they must all have died with Dimitrios. Absurd, no doubt, but . . .

"Well, Mr. Latimer." The fat man's smile had lost none of its sweetness, but there was an edge to his husky voice that made Latimer think of a small boy pulling the legs off flies.

"I think," he said slowly, "that if I am going to answer questions, I ought to be allowed to ask some. In other words, Mr. Peters, if you will tell me what *your* game is, I will tell you about mine. I have nothing at all to hide, but I have a curiosity to satisfy. Do you mind telling me what you hoped to find here—in the bindings of my books or in the tube of toothpaste?"

"I was looking for an answer to my question, Mr. Latimer. But all I found was this." He held up a sheet of paper. It was the chronological table which Latimer had jotted down in Smyrna. As far as he remembered, he had left it folded in a book he had been reading. "You see, Mr. Latimer, I felt that if you hid papers between the leaves of books, you might also hide more interesting papers in the bindings."

"It wasn't intended to be hidden."

But Mr. Peters took no notice. He held up the paper delicately between a finger and thumb—a schoolmaster about to consider a schoolboy essay. He shook his head.

"And is this all you know about Dimitrios, Mr. Latimer?"

"No."

"Ah!" He gazed pathetically at Latimer's tie. "Now who, I wonder, is this Colonel Haki, who seems so well informed and so indiscreet? The name is Turkish. And poor Dimitrios was taken from us at Istanbul, was he not? And you have come from Istanbul, haven't you?"

Involuntarily, Latimer nodded and then could have kicked himself, for Mr. Peters' smile broadened.

"Thank you, Mr. Latimer. I can see that you are prepared to be helpful. Now let us see. You were in Istanbul, and so was Dimitrios, and so was Colonel Haki. There is a note here about a passport in the name of Talat. Another Turkish name. And there is Adrianople and the phrase 'Kemal attempt.' 'Attempt'—ah, yes! Now, I wonder if you translated that word literally from the French '*attentat.*' You won't tell me? Well, well. I think that perhaps we may take that for granted. You know it almost looks as if you have been reading a Turkish police dossier. Now, doesn't it, eh?"

Latimer had begun to feel rather foolish. He said: "I don't think you're going to get very far that way. You're forgetting that for every question you ask you're going to have to answer one. For example, I should very much like to know whether you ever actually met Dimitrios."

Mr. Peters contemplated him for a moment without speaking. Then: "I don't think that you are very sure of yourself, Mr. Latimer," he said slowly. "I have the idea that I could tell you much more than you could tell me." He dropped the Lüger into his overcoat pocket and got to his feet. "I think I must be going," he added.

This was not at all what Latimer expected or wanted, but he said "Good night" calmly enough.

The fat man walked towards the door. But there he stopped. "Istanbul," Latimer heard him murmur thoughtfully. "Istanbul. Smyrna nineteen twenty-two, Athens the same year, Sofia nineteen twenty-three. Adrianople—no, because he comes from Turkey." He turned round quickly. "Now, I wonder . . ." He paused, and then seemed to make up his mind. "I wonder if it would be very stupid of me to imagine that you might be thinking of going to Belgrade in the near future. Would it, Mr. Latimer?"

Latimer was taken by surprise, and, even as he began to say very decidedly that it would be more than stupid of Mr. Peters to imagine any such thing, he knew by the other's triumphant smile that his surprise had been detected and interpreted.

"You will like Belgrade," Mr. Peters continued happily; "such a beautiful city. The views from the Terazija and the Kalemegdan! Magnificent!"

Latimer pulled the bedclothes off the chair and sat down facing him.

"Mr. Peters," he said, "in Smyrna I had occasion to examine certain fifteen-year-old police records. I afterwards found out that those same records had been examined three months previously by someone else. I wonder if you would like to tell me if that someone else was you."

But the fat man's watery eyes were staring into vacancy. A slight frown gathered on his forehead. He said, as though he were listening to Latimer's voice for mistakes in intonation: "Would you mind repeating that question?"

Latimer repeated the question.

There was another pause. Then Mr. Peters shook his head decidedly. "No, Mr. Latimer, it was not I."

"But you were yourself making inquiries about Dimitrios in Athens, weren't you, Mr. Peters? You were the person who came into the bureau while I was asking about Dimitrios, weren't you? You made a rather hurried exit, I seem to remember. Unfortunately I did not see it, but the official there commented on it. And it was design, not accident, that brought you to Sofia on the train by which I was travelling, wasn't it? You also took care to find out from me—very neatly, I admit—at which hotel I was staying, before I got off the train. That's right, isn't it?"

Mr. Peters was smiling sunnily again. He nodded. "Yes, Mr. Latimer, all quite right. I know everything that you have done since you left the record bureau in Athens. I have already told you that I am interested in anyone who is interested in Dimitrios. Of course, you found out all about this man who had been before you in Smyrna?"

The last sentence was put in a little too casually. Latimer said: "No, Mr. Peters, I did not."

"But surely you were interested?"

"Not very."

The fat man sighed. "I do not think that you are being frank with me. How much better if . . ."

"Listen!" Latimer interrupted rudely. "I'm going to be frank. You are doing your level best to pump me. I'm not going to be pumped. Let that be clear. I made you an offer. You answer my questions and I'll answer yours. The only questions you've answered so far have been questions to which I had already guessed the answers. I still want to know why you are interested in this dead man Dimitrios. You said that you could tell me more than I could tell you. That may be so. But *I* have an idea, Mr. Peters, that it is more important for you to have my answers than it is for me to have your answers. Breaking into hotel rooms and making this sort of mess isn't the sort of thing any man does in a spirit of idle inquiry. To be honest, I cannot for the life of me conceive of any reason for your interest in Dimitrios. It did not occur to me that perhaps Dimitrios had kept some of that money he earned in Paris. . . . You know about that, I expect?" And in response to a faint nod from Mr. Peters: "Yes, I thought you might. But, as I say, it did occur to me that Dimitrios might have hidden his treasure and that you were interested in finding out where. Unfortunately my own information disposes of that possibility. His belongings were on the mortuary table beside him, and there wasn't a penny piece there. Just a bundle of cheap clothes. And as for . . ."

But Mr. Peters had stepped forward and was staring down at him with a peculiar expression on his face. Latimer allowed the sentence he had begun to trail off lamely into silence. "What is the matter?" he added.

"Did I understand you to say," said the fat man slowly, "that you actually saw the body of Dimitrios in the mortuary?"

"Yes; what of it? Have I carelessly let slip another useful piece of information?"

But Mr. Peters did not answer. He had produced one of his thin cheroots and was lighting it carefully. Suddenly he blew out a jet of smoke and started to waddle slowly up and down the room, his eyes screwed up as if he were in great pain. He began to talk.

"Mr. Latimer, we must reach an understanding. We must stop this quarrelling." He halted in his tracks and looked down at Latimer again. "It is absolutely essential, Mr. Latimer," he said, "that I know what you are after. No, no, please! Don't interrupt me. I admit that I probably need your answers more than you need mine. But I cannot give you mine at present. Yes, yes, I heard what you said. But I am talking seriously. Listen, please.

"You are interested in the history of Dimitrios. You are thinking of going to Belgrade to find out more about him. You cannot deny that. Now, both of us know that Dimitrios was in Belgrade in nineteen twenty-six. Also, I can tell you that he was never there after nineteen twenty-six. Why are you interested? You will not tell me. Very well. I will tell you something more. If you go to Belgrade you will not discover a single trace of Dimitrios. Furthermore, you may find yourself in trouble with the authorities if you pursue the matter. There is only one man who could and would, under certain circumstances, tell you what you want to know. He is a Pole, and he lives near Geneva.

"Now then! I will give you his name and I will give you a letter to him. I will do that for you. But first I must know why you want this information. I thought at first that you might perhaps be connected with the Turkish police—there are so many Englishmen in the Near Eastern police departments these days—but that possibility I no longer consider. Your passport describes you as a writer, but that is a very elastic term. Who are you, Mr. Latimer, and what is your game?"

He paused expectantly. Latimer stared back at him with what he hoped was an inscrutable expression. Mr. Peters, unabashed, went on:

"Naturally, when I ask what your game is, I use the phrase in a specific sense. Your game is, of course, to get money. But that is not the answer I need. Are you a rich man, Mr. Latimer? No? Then what I have to say may be simplified. I am proposing an alliance, Mr. Latimer, a pooling of resources. I am aware of certain facts which I cannot tell you about at the moment. You, on the other hand, possess an important piece of information. You may not know that it is important, but nevertheless it *is*. Now, my facts alone are not worth a great deal. Your piece of information is quite valueless without my facts. The two together, however, are worth at the very least"—he stroked his chin—"at the very least five thousand English pounds, a million French francs." He smiled triumphantly. "What do you say to that?"

"You will forgive me," replied Latimer coldly, "if I say that I cannot understand what you're talking about, won't you? Not that it makes any difference whether you do or don't. I am *tired*, Mr. Peters, *very* tired. I want badly to go to bed." He got to his feet and, pulling the bedclothes on to the bed, began to remake it. "There is, I suppose, no reason why you should not know why I am interested in Dimitrios," he went on as he dragged a sheet into position. "The reason is certainly nothing to do with money. I write detective stories for a living. In Stambul I heard from a Colonel Haki, who is something to do with the police there, about a criminal named Dimitrios, who had been found dead in the Bosphorus. Partly for amusement—the sort of amusement that one derives from crossword puzzles—partly from a desire to try my hand at practical detection, I set out to trace the man's history. That is all. I don't expect you to understand it. You are probably wondering at the moment why I couldn't think of a more convincing story. I am sorry. If you don't like the truth, you can lump it."

Mr. Peters had listened in silence. Now he waddled to the window, pitched out his cheroot and faced Latimer across the bed.

"Detective stories! Now, that is most interesting to me, Mr. Latimer. I am so fond of them. I wonder if you would tell me the names of some of your books."

Latimer gave him several titles.

"And your publisher?"

"English, American, French, Swedish, Norwegian, Dutch or Hungarian?"

"Hungarian, please."

Latimer told him.

Mr. Peters nodded slowly. "A good firm, I believe." He seemed to reach a decision. "Have you a pen and paper, Mr. Latimer?"

Latimer nodded wearily towards the writing-table. The other went to it and sat down. As he finished making the bed and began to collect his belongings from the floor, Latimer heard the hotel pen scratching over a piece of the hotel paper. Mr. Peters was keeping his word.

At last he finished and the chair creaked as he got up. Latimer, who was replacing some shoe trees, straightened his back. Mr. Peters had recovered his smile. Goodwill oozed from him like sweat.

"Here, Mr. Latimer," he announced, "are three pieces of paper. On the first one is written the name of the man of whom I spoke to you. His name is Grodek—Wladyslaw Grodek. He lives just outside Geneva. The second is a letter to him. If you present that letter he will know that you are a friend of mine and that he can be frank with you. He is retired now, so I think I may safely tell you that he was at one time the most successful professional agent in Europe. More secret naval and military information has passed through his hands than through those of any other one man. It was always accurate, what is more. He dealt with quite a number of governments. His headquarters were in Brussels. To an author I should think he would be very interesting. You will like him, I think. He is a great lover of animals. A beautiful character *au fond*. Incidentally, it was he who employed Dimitrios in nineteen twenty-six."

"I see. Thank you very much. What about the third piece of paper?"

Mr. Peters hesitated. His smile became a little smug. "I think you said that you were not rich."

"No, I am not rich."

"Half a million francs, two thousand five hundred English pounds, would be useful to you?"

"Undoubtedly."

"Well, then, Mr. Latimer, when you have tired of Geneva I want you to—how do you say?—to kill two birds with one stone." He pulled Latimer's chronological table from his pocket. "On this list of yours you have other dates besides nineteen twenty-six still to be accounted for if you are to know what there is to know about Dimitrios. The place to account for them is Paris. That is the first thing. The second is that if you will come to Paris, if you will put yourself in touch with me there, if you will consider, then, the pooling of resources, the alliance that I have already proposed to you, I can definitely guarantee that in a very few days you will have at least two thousand five hundred English pounds to pay into your account—half a million French francs!"

"I do wish," retorted Latimer irritably, "that you would be a little more explicit. Half a million francs for doing what? Who is going to pay this money? You are far too mysterious, Mr. Peters—far too mysterious to be true."

Mr. Peters' smile tightened. Here was a Christian, reviled but unembittered, waiting steadfastly for the lions to be admitted into the arena.

"Mr. Latimer," he said gently, "I know that you do not trust me. That is the reason why I have given you Grodek's address and that letter to him. I want to give you concrete evidence of my goodwill towards you, to prove that my word is to be trusted. And I want to show that I trust you, that I believe what you have told me. At the moment I cannot say more. But if you will believe in and trust me, if you will come to Paris, then here, on this piece of paper, is an address. When you arrive send a *pneumatique* to me. Do not call, for it is the address of a friend. If you will simply send a *pneumatique* giving me your address, I will be able to explain everything. It is perfectly simple."

It was time, Latimer decided, to get rid of Mr. Peters.

"Well," he said, "this is all very confusing. You seem to me to have jumped to a lot of conclusions. I had not definitely arranged to go to Belgrade. It is not certain that I shall have time to go to Geneva. As for going on to Paris, that is a thing which I could not possibly consider at the moment. I have a great deal of work to do, of course, and . . ."

Mr. Peters buttoned up his overcoat. "Of course." And then, with a curious urgency in his tone: "But if you *should* find time to come to Paris, do please send me that *pneumatique*. I have put you to so much trouble, I should like to make restitution in a practical way. Half a million francs is worth considering, eh? And I would guarantee it. But we must trust one another. That is most important." He held out his hand. "Good night, Mr. Latimer. I won't say 'good-bye.' "

Latimer took the hand. It was dry and very soft.

"Good night."

At the door he half turned. "Half a million francs, Mr. Latimer, will buy a lot of good things. I do hope that we shall meet in Paris. Good night."

"I hope so, too. Good night."

The door closed and Mr. Peters was gone; but to Latimer's overwrought imagination it seemed as if his smile, like the Cheshire cat's, remained behind him, floating in the air. He leaned against the door and surveyed for an instant the upturned suitcases. Outside it was beginning to get light. He looked at his watch. Five o'clock. The business of clearing up the room could wait. He undressed and got into bed.

Eight

GRODEK

It WAS ELEVEN o'clock when Latimer, having been awake for about a quarter of an hour, finally opened his eyes. There, on the bedside table, were Mr. Peters' three pieces of paper. They were an unpleasant reminder that he had some thinking to do and some decisions to make. But for their presence and the fact that in the morning light his room looked like a rag-picker's workshop, he might have dismissed his recollections of the visitation as being no more than part of the bad dreams which had troubled his sleep. He would have liked so to dismiss them. But Mr. Peters, with his mystery, his absurd references to half millions of francs, his threats and his hintings, was not so easily disposed of. He . . .

Latimer sat up in bed and reached for the three pieces of paper.

The first, as Peters had said, contained the Geneva address:

> *Wladyslaw Grodek,*
> *Villa Acacias*
> *Chambésy.*
> *(At 7 km. from Geneva.)*

The writing was scratchy, florid and difficult to read. The figure seven was made with a stroke across the middle in the French way.

He turned hopefully to the letter. It consisted of only six lines and was written in a language and with an alphabet which he did not recognise, but which he concluded was probably Polish. It began, as far as he could see, without any preliminary "Dear Grodek," and ended with an indecipherable initial. In the middle of the second line he made out his own name spelt with what looked like a "Y" instead of an "I." He sighed. He could, of course, take the thing to a bureau and have it translated, but Mr. Peters would no doubt have thought of that, and it was unlikely that the result would supply any sort of answer to the questions that he, Latimer, badly wanted answered: the questions of who and what was Mr. Peters.

He turned to the second address:

> *Mr. Peters,*
> *aux soins de Caillé,*
> *3, Impasse des Huit Anges,*
> *Paris 7.*

And that brought his thoughts back to their starting point. Why, in the name of all that was reasonable, should Mr. Peters want him to go to Paris? What was this information that was worth so much money? Who was going to pay for it?

He tried to remember at exactly what point in their encounter Mr. Peters had changed his tactics so abruptly. He had an idea that it had been when he had said something about having seen Dimitrios in the mortuary. But there could surely be nothing in that. Could it have been his reference to the "treasure" of Dimitrios that had . . .

He snapped his fingers. Of course! What a fool not to think of it before! He had been ignoring an important fact. Dimitrios had not died a natural death. *Dimitrios had been murdered.*

Colonel Haki's doubts of the possibility of tracing the murderer and his own preoccupation with the past had caused him to lose sight of the fact or, at any rate, to see in it no more than a logical ending to an ugly story. He had failed to take into account the two consequent facts; that the murderer was still at large (and probably alive) and that there must have been a motive for the murder.

A murderer and a motive. The motive would be monetary gain. What money? Naturally, the money that had been made out of the drug-peddling business in Paris, the money that had so unaccountably disappeared. Mr. Peters' references to half millions of francs did not seem quite as fantastic when you looked at the problem from that point of view. As for the murderer—why not Peters?

But at that Latimer frowned. Dimitrios had been stabbed. He began to reconstruct the picture in his mind, to see Peters stabbing someone. Yet the picture seemed wrong. It was difficult to see Peters wielding a stabbing knife. The difficulty made him begin to think again. There really was no reason at all even to suspect Peters of the murder. And even if there had been a reason, the fact of Peters' murdering Dimitrios for his money still did not explain the connection (if a connection existed) between that money and the half millions of francs (if they existed). And, anyway, what was this mysterious piece of information he was supposed to possess? It was all very like being faced by an algebraic problem containing many unknown quantities and having only one biquadratic equation with which to solve it. If he *were* to solve it . . .

Now why should Peters be so anxious for him to go to Paris? Surely it would have been just as simple to have pooled their resources (whatever that might mean) in Sofia. Confound Mr. Peters! Latimer got out of bed and turned on his bath. Sitting in the hot, slightly rusty water he reduced his predicament to its essentials.

He had a choice of two courses of action.

He could go back to Athens, work on his new book and put Dimitrios and Marukakis and Mr. Peters and this Grodek out of his mind. Or, he could go to Geneva, see Grodek (if there were such a person) and postpone making any decision about Mr. Peters' proposals.

The first course was obviously the sensible one. After all, the justification of his researches into the past life of Dimitrios had been that he was making an impersonal experiment in detection. The experiment must not be allowed to become an obsession. He had found out some interesting things about the man. Honour should be satisfied. And it was high time he got on with the book. He had his living to earn and no amount of information about Dimitrios and Mr. Peters or anyone else would compensate for a lean bank balance six months hence. As for the half a million francs, that could not be taken seriously. Yes, he would return to Athens at once.

He got out of the bath and began to dry himself.

On the other hand there was the matter of Mr. Peters to be cleared up. He could not reasonably be expected to leave these things as they were and hurry off to write a detective story. It was too much to ask of any man. Besides, here was *real* murder: not neat, tidy book-murder with corpse and clues and suspects and hangman, but murder over which a chief of police shrugged his shoulders, wiped his hands and consigned the stinking victim to a coffin. Yes, that was it. It was real. Dimitrios was or had been real. Here were no strutting paper figures, but tangible evocative men and women, as real as Proudhon, Montesquieu and Rosa Luxemburg.

Aloud Latimer murmured: "Comfortable, very comfortable! You want to go to Geneva. You don't want to work. You're feeling lazy and your curiosity has been aroused."

He shaved, dressed, collected his belongings, packed and went downstairs to inquire about the trains to Athens. The reception clerk brought him a timetable and found the Athens page.

Latimer stared at it in silence for a moment. Then:

"Supposing," he said slowly, "that I wanted to go to Geneva from here."

On his second evening in Geneva, Latimer received a letter bearing the Chambésy postmark. It was from Wladyslaw Grodek and was in answer to a letter Latimer had sent enclosing Mr. Peters' note.

Herr Grodek wrote briefly and in French:

> *Villa Acacias, Chambésy*
> *Friday*
>
> *My dear Mr. Latimer,*
> *I should be pleased if you could come to the Villa Acacias for luncheon to-morrow. Unless I hear that you cannot come, my chauffeur will call at your hotel at eleven-thirty.*
> *Please accept the expression of my most distinguished sentiments.*
>
> *Grodek*

The chauffeur arrived punctually, saluted, ushered Latimer ceremoniously into a huge chocolate-coloured *coupé de ville*, and drove off through the rain as if he were escaping from the scene of a crime.

Idly, Latimer surveyed the interior of the car. Everything about it from the inlaid wood panelling and ivory fittings to the too-comfortable upholstery suggested money, a great deal of money. Money, he reflected, that, if Peters were to be believed, had been made out of espionage. Unreasonably he found it odd that there should be no evidence in the car of the sinister origin of its purchase price. He wondered what Herr Grodek would look like. He might possibly have a pointed white beard. Peters had said that he was a Polish national, a great lover of animals and a beautiful character *au fond.* Did that mean that superficially he was an ugly character? As for his alleged love of animals, that meant nothing. Great animal lovers were sometimes pathetic in their hatred of humanity. Would a professional spy, uninspired by any patriotic motives, hate the world he worked in? A stupid question.

For a time they travelled along the road which ran by the northerly shore of the lake; but at Pregny they turned to the left and began to climb a long hill. About a kilometre farther on, the car swung off into a narrow lane through a pine forest. They stopped before a pair of iron gates which the chauffeur got out to open. Then they drove on up a steep drive with a right-angle turn in the middle to stop at last before a large, ugly *chalet.*

The chauffeur opened the door and he got out and walked towards the door of the house. As he did so it was opened by a stout, cheerful-looking woman who looked as though she might be the housekeeper. He went in.

He found himself in a small lobby no more than six feet wide. On one wall was a row of clothes pegs draped carelessly with hats and coats, a woman's and a man's, a climbing rope and an odd ski-stick. Against the opposite wall were stacked three pairs of well-greased skis.

The housekeeper took his coat and hat and he walked through the lobby into a large room.

It was built rather like an inn with stairs leading to a gallery which ran along two sides of the room, and a vast cowled fireplace. A wood fire roared in the grate and the pinewood floor was covered with thick rugs. It was very warm and clean.

With a smiling assurance that Herr Grodek would be down immediately, the housekeeper withdrew. There were armchairs in front of the fire and Latimer walked towards them. As he did so there was a quick rustle and a Siamese cat leaped on to the back of the nearest chair and stared at him with hostile blue eyes. It was joined by another. Latimer moved towards them and they drew back arching their backs. Giving them a wide berth, Latimer made his way to the fire. The cats watched him narrowly. The logs shifted restlessly in the grate. There was a moment's silence; then Herr Grodek came down the stairs.

The first thing that drew Latimer's attention to the fact was that the cats lifted their heads suddenly, stared over his shoulder and then jumped lightly to the floor. He looked round. The man had reached the foot of the stairs. Now he turned and walked towards Latimer with his hand outstretched and words of apology on his lips.

He was a tall, broad-shouldered man of about sixty with thinning grey hair still tinged with the original straw colour which had matched the fair, clean-shaven cheeks and blue-grey eyes. His face was pear-shaped, tapering from a broad forehead, past a small tight mouth to a chin which receded almost into the neck. You might have put him down as an Englishman or Dane of more than average intelligence; a retired consulting engineer, perhaps. In his slippers and his thick baggy tweeds and with his vigorous, decisive movements he looked like a man enjoying the well-earned fruits of a blameless and worthy career.

He said: "Excuse me, please, Monsieur. I did not hear the car arrive."

His French, though curiously accented, was very ready and Latimer found the fact incongruous. The small mouth would have been more at home with English.

"It is very kind of you to receive me so hospitably, Monsieur Grodek. I don't know what Peters said in his letter, because . . ."

"Because," interrupted the tall man heartily, "you very wisely have never troubled to learn Polish. I can sympathise with you. It is a horrible tongue.

You have introduced yourself to Anton and Simone here." He indicated the cats. "I am convinced that they resent the fact that I do not speak Siamese. Do you like cats? Anton and Simone have critical intelligence, I am sure of it. They are not like ordinary cats, are you, *mes enfants*?" He seized one of them and held it up for Latimer's inspection. "*Ah, Simone cherie, comme tu es mignonne! Comme tu es bête!*" He released it so that it stood on the palms of his hands. "*Allez vite! Va promener avec ton vrai amant, ton cher Anton!*" The cat jumped to the floor and stalked indignantly away. Grodek dusted his hands lightly together. "Beautiful, aren't they! And so human. They become ill-tempered when the weather is bad. I wish so much that we could have had a fine day for your visit, Monsieur. When the sun is shining the view from here is very pretty."

Latimer said that he had guessed from what he had seen that it would be. He was puzzled. Both his host and his reception were totally unlike those he had expected. Grodek might look like a retired consulting engineer, but he had a quality which seemed to render the simile absurd. It was a quality that derived somehow from the contrast between his appearance and his quick, neat gestures, the urgency of his small lips. You could picture him without effort in the role of lover; which was a thing, Latimer reflected, that you could say of few men of sixty and few of under sixty. He wondered about the woman whose belongings he had seen in the entrance lobby. He added lamely: "It must be agreeable here in the summer."

Grodek nodded. He had opened a cupboard by the fireplace. "Agreeable enough. What will you drink? English whisky?"

"Thank you."

"Good. I, too, prefer it as an apéritif."

He began to splash whisky into two tumblers. "In the summer I work out-side. That is very good for me but not good for my work, I think. Do you find that you can work out of doors?"

"No, I don't. The flies. . . ."

"Exactly! the flies. I am writing a book, you know."

"Indeed. Your memoirs?"

Grodek looked up from the bottle of soda water he was opening and Latimer saw a glint of amusement in his eyes as he shook his head. "No, Monsieur. A Life of St. Francis. I confidently expect to be dead before it is finished."

"It must be a very exhaustive study."

"Oh yes." He handed Latimer a drink. "You see, the advantage of St. Francis from my point of view is that he has been written about so extensively that I need not go to sources for my material. There is no original research for me to do. The work therefore serves its purpose in permitting me to live here in almost absolute idleness with an easy conscience." He raised his glass. "*A votre santé.*"

"*A la vôtre.*" Latimer was beginning to wonder if his host were, after all, no more than an affected ass. He drank a little of his whisky. "I wonder," he said, "if Peters mentioned the purpose of my visit to you in the letter I brought with me from Sofia."

"No, Monsieur, he did not. But I received a letter from him yesterday which did mention it." He was putting down his glass and he gave Latimer a side-long look as he added: "It interested me very much." And then: "Have you known Peters long?"

There was an unmistakable hesitation at the name. Latimer guessed that the others' lips had been framing a word of a different shape.

"I have met him once or twice. Once in a train, once in my hotel. And you, Monsieur? You must know him very well."

Grodek raised his eyebrows. "And what makes you so sure of that, Monsieur?"

Latimer smiled easily because he felt uneasy. He had, he felt, committed some sort of indiscretion. "If he had not known you very well he would surely not have given me an introduction to you or asked you to give me informa-tion of so confidential a character." He felt pleased with that speech.

"Monsieur," said Herr Grodek; "I wonder what your attitude would be if I were to ask an impertinent question; if I were, for instance, to ask you to tell me seriously if a literary interest in human frailty were your only reason for approaching me."

Latimer felt himself redden. "I can assure you . . ." he began.

"I am quite certain that you can," Grodek interrupted smoothly. "But—forgive me—what are your assurances worth?"

"I can only give you my word, Monsieur, to treat any information you may give me as confidential," retorted Latimer stiffly.

The other sighed. "I don't think I have made myself quite clear," he said carefully. "The information itself is nothing. What happened in Belgrade in nineteen twenty-six is of little importance now. It is my own position of which I am thinking. To be frank, our friend Peters has been a little indiscreet in sending you to me. He admits it but craves my indulgence and asks me as a favour—he recalls that I am under a slight obligation to him—to give you the information you need about Dimitrios Talat. He explains that you are a writer and that your interest is merely that of a writer. Very well! There is one thing, however, which I find inexplicable." He paused, picked up his glass and drained it. "As a stu-dent of human behaviour, Monsieur," he went on, "you must have noticed that most persons have behind their actions one stimulus which tends to dominate all others. With some of us it is vanity, with others the gratification of the senses, with still others the desire for money, and so on. Er—Peters happens to be one of those with the money stimulus very highly developed. Without being unkind to him, I think I may tell you that he has the miser's love of money for its own sake. Do not misunderstand me, please. I do not say that he will act only under that money stimulus. What I mean is that I cannot from my knowledge of Peters imagine him going to the trouble of sending you here to me and writing to me in the way he has written, in the interests of the English detective story. You see my point? I am a little suspicious, Monsieur. I still have enemies in this world. Supposing, therefore, that you tell me just what your relations with our friend Peters are. Would you like to do that?"

"I should be delighted to do so. Unfortunately I cannot do so. And for a very simple reason. I don't know what those relations are myself."

Grodek's eyes hardened. "I was not joking, Monsieur."

"Nor was I. I have been investigating the history of this man Dimitrios. While doing so I have met Peters. For some reason that I do not know of, he, too, is interested in Dimitrios. He overheard me making inquiries in the relief commission archives in Athens. He then followed me to Sofia and approached me there—behind a pistol, I may add—for an explanation of my interest in this man, who, by the way, was murdered some weeks ago before I ever heard of him. He followed this up with an offer. He said that if I would meet him in Paris and collaborate with him in some scheme he had in mind we should each profit to the extent of half a million francs. He said that I possessed a piece of information which, though valueless by itself, would, when used in conjunction with information in his possession, be of great value. I did not believe him and refused to have anything to do with his scheme. Accordingly, as an inducement to me and as evidence of his goodwill, he gave me the note to you. I had told him, you see, that my interest was that of a writer and admitted that I was about to go to Belgrade to collect more information there if I could. He told me that you were the only person who could supply it."

Grodek's eyebrows went up. "I don't want to seem too inquisitive, Monsieur, but I should like to know how you knew that Dimitrios Talat was in Belgrade in nineteen twenty-six."

"I was told by a Turkish official with whom I became friendly in Istanbul. He described the man's history to me; his history, that is, as far as it was known in Istanbul."

"I see. And what, may I ask, is this so valuable piece of information in your possession?"

"I don't know."

Grodek frowned. "Come now, Monsieur. You ask me for my confidences. The least you can do is to give me yours."

"I am telling you the truth. I don't know. I talked fairly freely to Peters. Then, at one point in the conversation, he became excited."

"At what point?"

"I was explaining, I think, how I knew that Dimitrios had no money when he died. It was after that that he started talking about this million francs."

"And how *did* you know?"

"Because when I saw the body everything taken from it was on the mortuary table. Everything, that is, except his *carte d'identité* which had been removed from the lining of his coat and forwarded to the French authorities. There was no money. Not a penny."

For several seconds Grodek stared at him. Then he walked over to the cupboard where the drinks were kept. "Another drink, Monsieur?"

He poured the drinks out in silence, handed Latimer his and raised his glass solemnly. "A toast, Monsieur. To the English detective story!"

Amused, Latimer raised his glass to his lips. His host had done the same. Suddenly, however, he choked and, dragging a handkerchief from his pocket, set his glass down again. To his surprise, Latimer saw that the man was laughing.

"Forgive me, Monsieur," he gasped; "a thought crossed my mind that made me laugh. It was"—he hesitated a fraction of a second—"it was the thought of our friend Peters confronting you with a pistol. He is quite terrified of firearms."

"He seemed to keep his fears to himself quite successfully." Latimer spoke a trifle irritably. He had a suspicion that there was another joke somewhere, the point of which he had missed.

"A clever man, Peters." Grodek chuckled and patted Latimer on the shoulder. He seemed suddenly in excellent spirits. "My dear chap, please don't say that I have offended you. Look, we will have luncheon now. I hope you will like it. Are you hungry? Greta is really a splendid cook and there is nothing Swiss about my wines. Afterwards, I will tell you about Dimitrios and the trouble he caused me, and Belgrade and nineteen twenty-six. Does that please you?"

"It's very good of you to put yourself out like this."

He thought that Grodek was about to laugh again, but the Pole seemed to change his mind. He became instead very solemn. "It is a pleasure, Monsieur. Peters is a very good friend of mine. Besides, I like you personally, and we have so few visitors here." He hesitated. "May I be permitted as a friend to give you a word of advice, Monsieur?"

"Please do."

"Then, if I were in your place, Monsieur, I should be inclined to take our friend Peters at his word and go to Paris."

Latimer was perplexed. "I don't know . . ." he began slowly.

But the housekeeper, Greta, had come into the room.

"Luncheon!" exclaimed Grodek with satisfaction.

Later, when he had an opportunity of asking Grodek to explain his "word of advice," Latimer forgot to do so. By that time he had other things to think about.

Nine

~~~~~~~~~~~~~~~~~~~~~~~~~~~~~~~~~

BELGRADE, 1926

M EN HAVE LEARNED to distrust their imaginations. It is, therefore, strange to them when they chance to discover that a world conceived in the imagination, outside experience, does exist in fact. The afternoon which Latimer spent at the Villa Acacias, listening to Wladyslaw Grodek, he recalls as, in that sense, one of the strangest of his life. In a letter (written in French) to the Greek, Marukakis, which he began that evening, while the whole thing was still fresh in his mind, and finished on the following day, the Sunday, he placed it on record.

Geneva
Saturday

My dear Marukakis,

I remember that I promised to write to you to let you know if I discovered anything more about Dimitrios. I wonder if you will be as surprised as I am that I have actually done so. Discovered something, I mean; for I intended to write to you in any case to thank you again for the help you gave me in Sofia.

When I left you there, I was bound, you may remember, for Belgrade. Why, then, am I writing from Geneva?

I was afraid that you would ask that question.

My dear fellow, I wish that I knew the answer. I know part of it. The man, the professional spy, who employed Dimitrios in Belgrade in nineteen twenty-six, lives just outside Geneva. I saw him to-day and talked with him about Dimitrios. I can even explain how I got into touch with him. I was introduced. But just why I was introduced and just what the man who introduced us hopes to get out of it I cannot imagine. I shall, I hope, discover those things eventually. Meanwhile, let me say that if you find this mystery irritating, I find it no less so. Let me tell you about Dimitrios.

Did you ever believe in the existence of the "master" spy? Until to-day I most certainly did not. Now I do. The reason for this is that I have spent the

82

greater part of to-day talking to one. l cannot tell you his name, so I shall call him, in the best spy-story tradition, "G."

G. was a "master" spy (he has retired now) in the same sense that the printer my publisher uses is a "master" printer. He was an employer of spy labour. His work was mainly (though not entirely) administrative in character.

Now I know that a lot of nonsense is talked and written about spies and espionage, but let me try to put the question to you as G. put it to me.

He began by quoting Napoleon as saying that in war the basic element of all successful strategy was surprise.

G. is, I should say, a confirmed Napoleon-quoter. No doubt Napoleon did say that or something like it. I am quite sure he wasn't the first military leader to do so. Alexander, Cæsar, Genghis Khan and Frederick of Prussia all had the same idea. In nineteen eighteen Foch thought of it, too. But to return to G.

G. says that "the experiences of the 1914–18 conflict" showed that in a future war (that sounds so beautifully distant, doesn't it?) the mobility and striking power of modern armies and navies and the existence of air forces would render the element of surprise more important than ever; so important, in fact, that it was possible that the people who got in with a surprise attack first might win the war. It was more than ever necessary to guard against surprise, to guard against it, moreover, *before* the war had started.

Now, there are roughly twenty-seven independent states in Europe. Each has an army and an air force and most have some sort of navy as well. For its own security, each of those armies, air forces and navies must know what each corresponding force in each of the other twenty-six countries is doing— what its strength is, what its efficiency is, what secret preparations it is making. That means spies—armies of them.

In nineteen twenty-six G. was employed by Italy; and in the spring of that year he set up house in Belgrade.

Relations between Yugoslavia and Italy were strained at the time. The Italian seizure of Fiume was still as fresh in Yugoslav minds as the bombardment of Corfu; there were rumours, too (not unfounded as it was learned later in the year) that Mussolini contemplated occupying Albania.

Italy, on her side, was suspicious of Yugoslavia. Fiume was held under Yugoslav guns. A Yugoslav Albania alongside the Straits of Otranto was an unthinkable proposition. An independent Albania was tolerable only as long as it was under a predominantly Italian influence. It might be desirable to make certain of things. But the Yugoslavs might put up a fight. Reports from Italian agents in Belgrade indicated that in the event of war Yugoslavia intended to protect her seaboard by bottling herself up in the Adriatic with minefields laid just north of the Straits of Otranto.

I don't know much about these things, but apparently one does not have to lay a couple of hundred miles' worth of mines to make a two-hundred-mile wide corridor of sea impassable. One just lays one or two small fields without letting one's enemy know just where. It is necessary, then, for them to find out the positions of those minefields.

That, then, was G.'s job in Belgrade. Italian agents found out about the minefields. G., the expert spy, was commissioned to do the real work of discovering where they were to be laid, without—a most important point this—without letting the Yugoslavs find out that he had done so. If they did find out, of course, they would promptly change the positions.

In that last part of his task G. failed. The reason for his failure was Dimitrios.

It has always seemed to me that a spy's job must be an extraordinarily difficult one. What I mean is this. If I were sent to Belgrade by the British Government with orders to get hold of the details of a secret mine-laying project for the Straits of Otranto, I should not even know where to start. Supposing I knew, as G. knew, that the details were recorded by means of markings on a navigational chart of the Straits. Very well. How many copies of the chart are kept? I would not know. Where are they kept? I would not know. I might reasonably suppose that at least one copy would be kept somewhere in the Ministry of Marine; but the Ministry of Marine is a large place. Moreover, the chart will almost certainly be under lock and key. And even if, as seems unlikely, I were able to find in which room it is kept and how to get to it, how should I set about obtaining a copy of it without letting the Yugoslavs know that I had done so?

When I tell you that within a month of his arrival in Belgrade, G. had not only found out where a copy of the chart was kept, but had also made up his mind how he was going to copy that copy *without the Yugoslavs knowing*, you will see that he is entitled to describe himself as competent.

How did he do it? What ingenious manœuvre, what subtle trick made it possible? I shall try to break the news gently.

Posing as a German, the representative of an optical instrument-maker in Dresden, he struck up an acquaintance with a clerk in the Submarine Defence Department (which dealt with submarine nets, booms, mine-laying and mine-sweeping) of the Ministry of Marine!

Pitiful, wasn't it! The amazing thing is that he himself regards it as a very astute move. His sense of humour is quite paralysed. When I asked him if he ever read spy stories, he said that he did not, as they always seemed to him very naïve. But there is worse to come.

He struck up this acquaintance by going to the Ministry and asking the doorkeeper to direct him to the Department of Supply, a perfectly normal request

for an outsider to make. Having got past the door-keeper, he stopped someone in a corridor, said that he had been directed to the Submarine Defence
Department and had got lost and asked to be re-directed. Having got to the
S.D. Department, he marched in and asked if it was the Department of Supply. They said that it was not, and out he went. He was in there not more than
a minute, but in that time he had cast a quick eye over the personnel of the
department, or, at all events, those of them he could see. He marked down
three. That evening he waited outside the Ministry until the first of them came
out. This man he followed home. Having found out his name and as much as
he could about him, he repeated the process on succeeding evenings with the
other two. Then he made his choice. It fell on a man named Bulić.

Now, G.'s actual methods may have lacked subtlety; but there was considerable subtlety in the way he employed them. He himself is quite oblivious
of any distinction here. He is not the first successful man to misunderstand
the reasons for his own success.

G.'s first piece of subtlety lay in his choice of Bulić as a tool.

Bulić was a disagreeable, conceited man of between forty and fifty, older
than most of his fellow clerks and disliked by them. His wife was ten years
younger than he, dissatisfied and pretty. He suffered from catarrh. He was in
the habit of going to a café for a drink when he left the Ministry for the day,
and it was in this café that G. made his acquaintance by the simple process of
asking him for a match, offering him a cigar and, finally, buying him a drink.

You may imagine that a clerk in a government department dealing with
highly confidential matters would naturally tend to be suspicious of café acquaintances who tried to pump him about his work. G. was ready to deal with
those suspicions long before they had entered Bulić's head.

The acquaintance ripened. G. would be in the café every evening when Bulić
entered. They would carry on a desultory conversation. G., as a stranger to
Belgrade, would ask Bulić's advice about this and that. He would pay for Bulić's
drinks. He let Bulić condescend to him. Sometimes they would play a game of
chess. Bulić would win. At other times they would play four-pack *bezique* with
other frequenters of the café. Then, one evening, G. told Bulić a story.

He had been told by a mutual acquaintance, he said, that he, Bulić, held an
important post in the Ministry of Marine.

For Bulić the "mutual acquaintance" could have been one of several men
with whom they played cards and exchanged opinions and who were vaguely
aware that he worked in the Ministry. He frowned and opened his mouth. He
was probably about to enter a mock-modest qualification of the adjective "important." But G. swept on. As chief salesman for a highly respectable firm of
optical instrument-makers, he was deputed to obtain an order due to be placed

by the Ministry of Marine for binoculars. He had submitted his quotation and had hopes of securing the order but, as Bulić would know, there was nothing like a friend at court in these affairs. If, therefore, the good and influential Bulić would bring pressure to bear to see that the Dresden company secured the order, Bulić would be in pocket to the tune of twenty thousand dinar.[1]

Consider that proposition from Bulić's point of view. Here was he, an insignificant clerk, being flattered by the representative of a great German company and promised twenty thousand dinar, as much as he ordinarily earned in six months, for doing precisely nothing. If the quotation were already submitted, there was nothing to be done there. It would stand its chance with the other quotations. If the Dresden company secured the order he would be twenty thousand dinar in pocket without having compromised himself in any way. If they lost it *he* would lose nothing except the respect of this stupid and misinformed German.

G. admits that Bulić did make a half-hearted effort to be honest. He mumbled something about his not being sure that his influence could help. This, G. chose to treat as an attempt to increase the bribe. Bulić protested that no such thought had been in his mind. He was lost. Within five minutes he had agreed.

In the days that followed, Bulić and G. became close friends. G. ran no risk. Bulić could not know that no quotation had been submitted by the Dresden company as all quotations received by the Department of Supply were confidential until the order was placed. If he were inquisitive enough to make inquiries, he would find, as G. had found by previous reference to the *Official Gazette*, that quotations for binoculars had actually been asked for by the Department of Supply.

G. now got to work.

Bulić, remember, had to play the part assigned to him by G., the part of influential official. G., furthermore, began to make himself very amiable by entertaining Bulić and the pretty but stupid Madame Bulić at expensive restaurants and night clubs. The pair responded like thirsty plants to rain. Could Bulić be cautious when, having had the best part of a bottle of sweet champagne, he found himself involved in an argument about Italy's overwhelming naval strength and her threat to Yugoslavia's seaboard? It was unlikely. He was a little drunk. His wife was present. For the first time in his dreary life, his judgment was being treated with the deference due to it. Besides, he had his part to play. It would not do to seem to be ignorant of what was going on behind the scenes. He began to brag. He himself had seen the very plans

---

[1] *The Yugoslav* dinar *is worth a little less than the French franc.*

that in operation would immobilise Italy's fleet in the Adriatic. Naturally, he had to be discreet, but . . .

By the end of that evening G. knew that Bulić had access to a copy of the chart. He had also made up his mind that Bulić was going to get that copy for him.

He made his plans carefully. Then he looked round for a suitable man to carry them out. He needed a go-between. He found Dimitrios.

Just how G. came to hear of Dimitrios is not clear. I fancy that he was anxious not to compromise any of his old associates. One can conceive that his reticence might be understandable. Anyway, Dimitrios was recommended to him. I asked in what business the recommender was engaged. I hoped, I admit, to be able to find some link with the Eurasian Credit Trust episode. But G. became vague. It was so very long ago. But he remembered the verbal testimonial which accompanied the recommendation.

Dimitrios Talat was a Greek-speaking Turk with an "effective" passport and a reputation for being "useful" and at the same time discreet. He was also said to have had experience in "financial work of a confidential nature."

If one did not happen to know just what he was useful for and the nature of the financial work he had done, one might have supposed that the man under discussion was some sort of accountant. But there is, it seems, a jargon in these affairs. G. understood it and decided that Dimitrios was the man for the job in hand. He wrote to Dimitrios—he gave me the address as though it were a sort of American Express poste restante—care of the Eurasian Credit Trust in Bucharest!

Dimitrios arrived in Belgrade five days later and presented himself at G.'s house just off the Knez Miletina.

G. remembers the occasion very well. Dimitrios, he says, was a man of medium height who might have been almost any age between thirty-five and fifty—he was actually thirty-seven. He was smartly dressed and . . . But I had better quote G.'s own words:

"He was chic in an expensive way, and his hair was becoming grey at the sides of his head. He had a sleek, satisfied, confident air and something about the eyes that I recognised immediately. The man was a pimp. I can always recognise it. Do not ask me how. I have a woman's instinct for these things."

So there you have it. Dimitrios had prospered. Had there been any more Madame Prevezas? We shall never know. At all events, G. detected the pimp in Dimitrios and was not displeased. A pimp, he reasoned, could be relied upon not to fool about with women to the detriment of the business in hand. Also Dimitrios was of pleasing address. I think that I had better quote G. again:

"He could wear his clothes gracefully. Also he looked intelligent. I was pleased by this because I did not care to employ riff-raff from the gutters. Sometimes it was necessary but I never liked it. They did not always understand my curious temperament."

G., you see, was fussy.

Dimitrios had not wasted his time. He could now speak both German and French with reasonable accuracy. He said:

"I came as soon as I received your letter. I was busy in Bucharest but I was glad to get your letter as I had heard of you."

G. explained carefully and with circumspection (it did not do to give too much away to a prospective employee) what he wanted done. Dimitrios listened unemotionally. When G. had finished, he asked how much he was to be paid.

"Thirty thousand dinar," said G.

"Fifty thousand," said Dimitrios, "and I would prefer to have it in Swiss francs."

They compromised on forty thousand to be paid in Swiss francs. Dimitrios smiled and shrugged his agreement.

Meanwhile, Bulić was finding life more pleasant than it had ever been before. He was being entertained at rich places. His wife, warmed by unfamiliar luxury, no longer looked at him with contempt and distaste in her eyes. With the money they saved on the meals provided by the stupid German she could drink her favourite cognac; and when she drank she became friendly and agreeable. In a week's time, moreover, he might become the possessor of twenty thousand dinar. There was a chance. He felt very well, he said one night, and added that cheap food was bad for his catarrh. That was the nearest he came to forgetting to play his part.

The order for the binoculars was given to a Czech firm. *The Official Gazette*, in which the fact was announced, was published at noon. At one minute past noon, G. had a copy and was on his way to an engraver on whose bench lay a half-finished copper die. By six o'clock he was waiting opposite the entrance to the Ministry. Soon after six, Bulić appeared. He had seen the *Official Gazette*. A copy was under his arm. His dejection was visible from where G. stood. G. began to follow him.

Ordinarily, Bulić would have crossed the road before many minutes had passed, to get to his café. To-night he hesitated and then walked straight on. He was not anxious to meet the man from Dresden.

G. turned down a side street and hailed a taxi. Within two minutes his taxi had made a detour and was approaching Bulić. Suddenly, he signalled to the driver to stop, bounded out on to the pavement and embraced Bulić delightedly. Before the bewildered clerk could protest, he was bundled into the taxi and G. was pouring congratulations and thanks into his ear and pressing a cheque for twenty thousand dinar into his hand.

"But I thought you'd lost the order," mumbles Bulić at last.

G. laughs as if at a huge joke. "Lost it!" And then he "understands." "Of course! I forgot to tell you. The quotation was submitted through a Czech subsidiary of ours. Look, does this explain it?" He thrusts one of the newly printed cards into Bulic's hand. "I don't use this card often. Most people know that these Czechs are owned by our company in Dresden." He brushes the matter aside. "But we must have a drink immediately. Driver!"

That night they celebrated. His first bewilderment over, Bulić took full advantage of the situation. He became drunk. He began to brag of the potency of his influence in the Ministry until even G., who had every reason for satisfaction, was hard put to it to remain civil.

But towards the end of the evening, he drew Bulić aside. Estimates, he said, had been invited for rangefinders. Could he, Bulić, assist? Of course he could. And now Bulić became cunning. Now that the value of his co-operation had been established, he had a right to expect something on account.

G. had not anticipated this, but, secretly amused, he agreed at once. Bulić received another cheque; this time it was for ten thousand dinar. The understanding was that he should be paid a further ten thousand when the order was placed with G.'s "employers."

Bulić was now wealthier than ever before. He had thirty thousand dinar. Two evenings later, in the supper room of a fashionable hotel, G. introduced him to a Freiherr von Kiessling. The Freiherr von Kiessling's other name was, needless to say, Dimitrios.

"You would have thought," says G., "that he had been living in such places all his life. For all I know, he may have been doing so. His manner was perfect. When I introduced Bulić as an important official in the Ministry of Marine, he condescended magnificently. With Madame Bulić he was superb. He might have been greeting a princess. But I saw the way his fingers moved across the palm of her hand as he bent to kiss the back of it."

Dimitrios had displayed himself in the supper room before G. had affected to claim acquaintance with him in order to give G. time to prepare the ground. The "Freiherr," G. told the Bulićs after he had drawn their attention to Dimitrios, was a very important man. Something of a mystery, perhaps; but a very important factor in international big business. He was enormously rich and was believed to control as many as twenty-seven companies. He might be a useful man to know.

The Bulićs were enchanted to be presented to him. When the "Freiherr"

agreed to drink a glass of champagne at their table, they felt themselves
honoured indeed. In their halting German they strove to make themselves
agreeable. This, Bulić must have felt, was what he had been waiting for all
his life: at last he was in touch with the people who counted, the real people,
the people who made men and broke them, the people who might make him.
Perhaps he saw himself a director of one of the "Freiherr's" companies, with
a fine house and others dependent on him, loyal servants who would respect
him as a man as well as a master. When, the next morning, he went to his
stool in the Ministry, there must have been joy in his heart, joy made all the
sweeter by the faint misgivings, the slight pricklings of conscience which could
so easily be stilled. After all, G. had received his money's worth. He, Bulić,
had nothing to lose. Besides, you never knew what might come of it all. Men
had taken stranger paths to fortune.

The "Freiherr" had been good enough to say that he would have supper
with Herr G. and his two charming friends two evenings later.

I questioned G. about this. Would it not have been better to have struck
while the iron was hot? Two days gave the Bulićs time to think. "Precisely,"
was G.'s reply; "time to think of the good things to come, to prepare themselves for the feast, to dream." He became preternaturally solemn at the thought
and then, grinning, suddenly quoted Goethe at me. *Ach! warum, ihr Götter,
ist unendlich, alles, alles, endlich unser Glück nur?* G., you see, lays claim to
a sense of humour.

That supper was the critical moment for him. Dimitrios got to work on
Madame. It was such a pleasure to meet such pleasant people as Madame—
and, of course, her husband. She—and her husband, naturally—must certainly come and stay with him in Bavaria next month. He preferred it to his
Paris house and Cannes was sometimes chilly in the spring. Madame would
enjoy Bavaria; and so, no doubt, would her husband. That was, if he could
tear himself away from the Ministry.

Crude, simple stuff, no doubt; but the Bulićs were crude, simple people.
Madame lapped it up with her sweet champagne while Bulić became sulky.
Then the great moment arrived.

The flower girl stopped by the table with her tray of orchids. Dimitrios
turned round and, selecting the largest and most expensive bloom, handed it
with a little flourish to Madame Bulić with a request that she accept it as a
token of his esteem. Madame would accept it. Dimitrios drew out his wallet
to pay. The next moment a thick wad of thousand-dinar notes fell from his
breast pocket on to the table.

With a word of apology Dimitrios put the money back in his pocket. G.,
taking his cue, remarked that it was rather a lot of money to carry in one's

pocket and asked if the "Freiherr" always carried as much. No, he did not. He had won the money at Alessandro's earlier in the evening and had forgotten to leave it upstairs in his room. Did Madame know Alessandro's? She did not. Both the Bulićs were silent as the "Freiherr" talked on: they had never seen so much money before. In the "Freiherr's" opinion Alessandro's was the most reliable gambling place in Belgrade. It was your own luck not the croupier's skill that mattered at Alessandro's. Personally he was having a run of luck that evening—this with velvety eyes on Madame—and had won a little more than usual. He hesitated at that point. And then: "As you have never been in the place, I should be delighted if you would accompany me as my guests later."

Of course, they went; and, of course, they were expected and preparations had been made. Dimitrios had arranged everything. No roulette—it is difficult to cheat a man at roulette—but there was *trente et quarante*. The minimum stake was two hundred and fifty dinar.

They had drinks and watched the play for a time. Then G. decided that he would play a little. They watched him win twice. Then the "Freiherr" asked Madame if she would like to play. She looked at her husband. He said, apologetically, that he had very little money with him. But Dimitrios was ready for that. No trouble at all, Herr Bulić! He personally was well known to Alessandro. Any friend of his could be accommodated. If he should happen to lose a few dinar, Alessandro would take a cheque or a note.

The farce went on. Alessandro was summoned and introduced. The situation was explained to him. He raised protesting hands. Any friend of the "Freiherr" need not even ask such a thing. Besides, he had not yet played. Time to talk of such things if he had a little bad luck.

G. thinks that if Dimitrios had allowed the two to talk to one another for even a moment, they would not have played. Two hundred and fifty dinar was the minimum stake, and not even the possession of thirty thousand could overcome their consciousness of the value in terms of food and rent of two hundred and fifty. But Dimitrios did not give them a chance to exchange misgivings. Instead, as they were waiting at the table behind G.'s chair, he murmured to Bulić that if he, Bulić, had time, he, the "Freiherr," would like to talk business with him over luncheon one day that week.

It was beautifully timed. It could, I feel, have meant only one thing to Bulić: "My dear Bulić, there really is no need for you to concern yourself over a paltry few hundred dinar. I am interested in you, and that means that your fortune is made. Please do not disappoint me by showing yourself less important than you seem now."

Madame Bulić began to play.

Her first two hundred and fifty she lost on *couleur*. The second won on *inverse*. Then, Dimitrios, advising greater caution, suggested that she play *à cheval*. There was a *refait* and then a second *refait*. Ultimately she lost again.

At the end of an hour the five thousand dinar's worth of chips she had been given had gone. Dimitrios, sympathising with her for her "bad luck," pushed across some five hundred dinar chips from a pile in front of him and begged that she would play with them "for luck."

The tortured Bulić may have had the idea that these were a gift, for he made only the faintest sound of protest. That they had not been a gift he was presently to discover. Madame Bulić, thoroughly miserable now and becoming a little untidy, played on. She won a little; she lost more. At half-past two Bulić signed a promissory note to Alessandro for twelve thousand dinar. G. bought them a drink.

It is easy to picture the scene between the Bulićs when at last they were alone—the recriminations, the tears, the interminable arguments—only too easy. Yet, bad as things were, the gloom was not unrelieved; for Bulić was to lunch the following day with the "Freiherr." And they were to talk business.

They did talk business. Dimitrios had been told to be encouraging. No doubt he was. Hints of big deals afoot, of opportunities for making fabulous sums for those who were in the know, talk of castles in Bavaria—it would all be there. Bulić had only to listen and let his heart beat faster. What did twelve thousand dinar matter? You had to think in millions.

All the same, it was Dimitrios who raised the subject of his guest's debt to Alessandro. He supposed that Bulić would be going along that very night to settle it. He personally would be playing again. One could not, after all, win so much without giving Alessandro a chance to lose some more. Supposing that they went along together—just the two of them. Women were bad gamblers.

When they met that night Bulić had nearly thirty-five thousand dinar in his pocket. He must have added his savings to G.'s thirty thousand. When Dimitrios reported to G.—in the early hours of the following morning—he said that Bulić had, in spite of Alessandro's protests, insisted on redeeming his promissory note before he started to play. "I pay my debts," he told Dimitrios proudly. The balance of the money he spent, with a flourish, on five hundred dinar chips. To-night he was going to make a killing. He refused to drink. He meant to keep a cool head.

G. grinned at this and perhaps he was wise to do so. Pity is sometimes too uncomfortable; and I do find Bulić pitiable. You may say that he was a weak fool. So he was. But Providence is never quite as calculating as were G. and Dimitrios. It may bludgeon away at a man, but it never feels between his ribs with a knife. Bulić had no chance. They understood him and used their understanding with devilish skill. With the cards as neatly stacked against me as they were against him, I should perhaps be no less weak, no less foolish. It is a comfort to me to believe that the occasion is unlikely to arise.

Inevitably he lost. He began to play with just over forty chips. It took him two hours of winning and losing to get rid of them. Then, quite calmly, he took another twenty on credit. He said that his luck must change. The poor wretch did not even suspect that he might be being cheated. Why should he suspect? The "Freiherr" was losing even more than he was. He doubled his stakes and survived for forty minutes. He borrowed again and lost again. He had lost thirty-eight thousand dinar more than he had in the world when, white and sweating, he decided to stop.

After that it was plain sailing for Dimitrios. The following night Bulić returned. They let him win thirty thousand back. The third night he lost another fourteen thousand. On the fourth night, when he was about twenty-five thousand in debt, Alessandro asked for his money. Bulić promised to redeem his notes within a week. The first person to whom he went for help was G.

G. was sympathetic. Twenty-five thousand was a lot of money, wasn't it? Of course, any money he used in connection with orders received was his employers', and he was not empowered to do what he liked with it. But he himself could spare two hundred and fifty for a few days if it were any help. He would have liked to do more, but . . . Bulić took the two hundred and fifty.

With it G. gave him a word of advice. The "Freiherr" was the man to get him out of his difficulty. He never lent money—with him it was a question of principle, he believed—but he had a reputation for helping his friends by putting them in the way of earning quite substantial sums. Why not have a talk with him?

The "talk" between Bulić and Dimitrios took place after a dinner for which Bulić paid and in the "Freiherr's" hotel sitting-room. G. was out of sight in the adjoining bedroom.

When Bulić at last got to the point, he asked about Alessandro. Would he insist on his money? What would happen if he were not paid?

Dimitrios affected surprise. There was no question, he hoped, of Alessandro's not being paid. After all, it was on his personal recommendation that Alessandro had given credit in the first place. He would not like there to be any unpleasantness. What sort of unpleasantness? Well, Alessandro held the promissory notes and could take the matter to the police. He hoped sincerely that that would not happen.

Bulić was hoping so, too. Now, he had everything to lose, including his post at the Ministry. It might even come out that he had taken money from G. That might even mean prison. Would they believe that he had done nothing in return for those thirty thousand dinar? It was madness to expect them to do so. His only chance was to get the money from the "Freiherr"—somehow.

To his pleas for a loan Dimitrios shook his head. No. That would simply make matters worse, for then he would owe the money to a friend instead of to an enemy; besides, it was a matter of principle with him. At the same time, he wanted to help. There was just one way; but would Herr Bulić feel disposed to take it? That was the question. He scarcely liked to mention the matter; but, since Herr Bulić pressed him, he knew of certain persons who were interested in obtaining some information from the Ministry of Marine that could not be obtained through the usual channels. They could probably be persuaded to pay as much as fifty thousand dinar for this information if they could rely upon its being accurate.

G. said that he attributed quite a lot of the success of his plan (he deems it successful in the same way that a surgeon deems an operation successful when the patient leaves the operating theatre alive) to his careful use of figures. Every sum from the original twenty thousand dinar to the amounts of the successive debts to Alessandro (who was an Italian agent) and the final amount offered by Dimitrios was carefully calculated with an eye to its psychological value. That final fifty thousand, for example. Its appeal to Bulić was twofold. It would pay off his debt and still leave him with nearly as much as he had had before he met the "Freiherr." To the incentive of fear they added that of greed.

But Bulić did not give in immediately. When he heard exactly what the information was, he became frightened and angry. The anger was dealt with very efficiently by Dimitrios. If Bulić had begun to entertain doubts about the *bona fides* of the "Freiherr" those doubts were now made certainties; for when he shouted "dirty spy," the "Freiherr's" easy charm deserted him. Bulić was kicked in the abdomen and then, as he bent forward retching, in the face. Gasping, for breath and with pain and bleeding at the mouth, he was flung into a chair while Dimitrios explained coldly that the only risk he ran was in not doing as he was told.

His instructions were simple. Bulić was to get a copy of the chart and bring it to the hotel when he left the Ministry the following evening. An hour later the chart would be returned to him to replace in the morning. That was all. He would be paid when he brought the chart. He was warned of the consequences to himself if he should decide to go to the authorities with his story, reminded of the fifty thousand that awaited him and dismissed.

He duly returned the following night with the chart folded in four under his coat. Dimitrios took the chart in to G. and returned to keep watch on Bulić while it was photographed and the negative developed. Apparently Bulic had nothing to say. When G. had finished he took the money and the chart from Dimitrios and went without a word.

G. says that in the bedroom at that moment, when he heard the door close behind Bulić and as he held the negative up to the light, he was feeling very pleased with himself. Expenses had been low; there had been no wasted effort; there had been no tiresome delays; everybody, even Bulić, had done well out of the business. It only remained to hope that Bulić would restore the chart safely. There was really no reason why he should not do so. A very satisfactory affair from every point of view.

And then Dimitrios came into the room.

It was at that moment that G. realised that he had made one mistake.

"My wages," said Dimitrios, and held out his hand.

G. met his employee's eyes and nodded. He needed a gun and he had not got one. "We'll go to my house now," he said and started towards the door.

Dimitrios shook his head deliberately. "My wages are in your pocket."

"Not your wages. Only mine."

Dimitrios produced a revolver. A smile played about his lips. "What I want is in your pocket, *mein Herr*. Put your hands behind your head."

G. obeyed. Dimitrios walked towards him. G., looking steadily into those brown anxious eyes, saw that he was in danger. Two feet in front of him Dimitrios stopped. "Please be careful, *mein Herr*."

The smile disappeared. Dimitrios stepped forward suddenly and, jamming his revolver into G.'s stomach, snatched the negative from G.'s pocket with his free hand. Then, as suddenly, he stood back. "You may go," he said.

G. went. Dimitrios, in turn, had made *his* mistake.

All that night men, hastily recruited from the criminal cafés, scoured Belgrade for Dimitrios. But Dimitrios had disappeared. G. never saw him again.

What happened to the negative? Let me give you G.'s own words:

"When the morning came and my men had failed to find him, I knew what I must do. I felt very bitter. After all my careful work it was most disappointing. But there was nothing else for it. I had known for a week that Dimitrios had got into touch with a French agent. The negative would be in that agent's hands by now. I really had no choice. A friend of mine in the German Embassy was able to oblige me. The Germans were anxious to please Belgrade at the time. What more natural than that they should pass on an item of information interesting to the Yugoslav Government?"

"Do you mean," I said, "that you deliberately arranged for the Yugoslav authorities to be informed of the removal of the chart and of the fact that it had been photographed?"

"Unfortunately, it was the only thing I could do. You see, I had to render

the chart worthless. It was really very foolish of Dimitrios to let me go; but
he was inexperienced. He probably thought that I should blackmail Bulić into
bringing the chart out again. But I realised that I should not be paid much for
bringing in information already in the possession of the French. Besides, my
reputation would have suffered. I was very bitter about the whole affair. The
only amusing aspect of it was that the French had paid over to Dimitrios half
the agreed price for the chart before they discovered that the information on
it had been rendered obsolete by my little *démarche*."

"What about Bulić?"

G. pulled a face. "Yes, I was sorry about that. I always have felt a certain
responsibility towards those who work for me. He was arrested almost at once.
There was no doubt as to which of the Ministry copies had been used. They
were kept rolled in metal cylinders. Bulić had folded this one to bring it out
of the Ministry. It was the only one with creases in it. His fingerprints did the
rest. Very wisely he told the authorities all he knew about Dimitrios. As a
result they sent him to prison for life instead of shooting him. I quite expected
him to implicate me, but he did not. I was a little surprised. After all it was I
who introduced him to Dimitrios. I wondered at the time whether it was because he was unwilling to face an additional charge of accepting bribes or
because he felt grateful to me for lending him that two hundred and fifty dinar.
Probably he did not connect me with the business of the chart at all. In any
case, I was pleased. I still had work to do in Belgrade, and being wanted by
the police, even under another name, might have complicated my life. I have
never been able to bring myself to wear disguises."

I asked him one more question. Here is his answer:

"Oh, yes, I obtained the new charts as soon as they had been made. In quite
a different way, of course. With so much of my money invested in the enterprise I could not return empty handed. It is always the same: for one reason
or another there are always these delays, these wastages of effort and money.
You may say that I was careless in my handling of Dimitrios. That would be
unjust. It was a small error of judgment on my part, that is all. I counted on
his being like all the other fools in the world, on his being too greedy; I thought
he would wait until he had had from me the forty thousand dinar due to him
before he tried to take the photograph as well. He took me by surprise. That
error of judgment cost me a lot of money."

"It cost Bulić his liberty." I am afraid I said it a trifle vindictively, for he
frowned.

"My dear Monsieur Latimer," he retorted stiffly, "Bulić was a traitor and
he was rewarded according to his deserts. One cannot sentimentalise over him.
In war there are always casualties. Bulić was very lucky. I should certainly

have used him again, and he might ultimately have been shot. As it was, he went to prison. For all I know he is still in prison. I do not wish to seem callous, but I must say that he is better off there. His liberty? Rubbish! He had none to lose. As for his wife, I have no doubt that she has done better for herself. She always gave me the impression of wanting to do so. I do not blame her. He was an objectionable man. I seem to remember that he tended to dribble as he ate. What is more, he was a nuisance. You would have thought, would you not, that on leaving Dimitrios that evening he would have gone there and then to Alessandro to pay his debt? He did not do so. When he was arrested late the following day he still had the fifty thousand dinar in his pocket. More waste. It is at times like those, my friend, that one needs one's sense of humour."

Well, my dear Marukakis, that is all. It is, I think, more than enough. For me, wandering among the ghosts of old lies, there is comfort in the thought that you might write to me and tell me that all this was worth finding out. You might. For myself, I begin to wonder. It is such a poor story, isn't it? There is no hero, no heroine; there are only knaves and fools. Or do I mean only fools?

But it really is too early in the afternoon to pose such questions. Besides, I have packing to do. In a few days I shall send you a post card with my name and new address on it in the hope that you will have time to write. In any case, we shall, I hope, meet again very soon. *Croyez en mes meilleurs souvenirs.*

Charles Latimer

Ten

≈≈≈≈≈≈≈≈≈

THE EIGHT
ANGELS

IT WAS ON a slate-grey November day that Latimer arrived in Paris.

As his taxi crossed the bridge to the Ile de la Cité, he saw for a moment a panorama of low, black clouds moving quickly in the chill, dusty wind. The long façade of the houses on the Quai de Corse were still and secretive. It was as if each window concealed a watcher. There seemed to be few people about. Paris, in that late autumn afternoon, had the macabre formality of a steel engraving.

It depressed him, and as he climbed the stairs of his hotel in the Quai Voltaire he wished fervently that he had gone back to Athens.

His room was cold. It was too early for an apéritif. He had been able to eat enough of his meal on the train to render an early dinner unnecessary. He decided to inspect the outside of number three, Impasse des Huit Anges. With some difficulty he found the Impasse tucked away in a side street off the Rue de Rennes.

It was a wide, cobbled passage shaped like an L and flanked at the entrance by a pair of tall iron gates. They were fastened back, against the walls that supported them, with heavy staples, and had evidently not been shut for years. A row of spiked railings separated one side of the Impasse from the blank side-wall of the adjoining block of houses. Another blank cement wall, unguarded by railings but protected by the words "DEFENSE D'AFFICHER, LOI DU 10 AVRIL 1929" in weatherbeaten black paint, faced it.

There were only three houses in the Impasse. They were grouped out of sight of the road, in the foot of the L, and looked out through the narrow gap between the building on which bill-posting was forbidden and the back of a hotel over which drainpipes writhed like snakes, on to yet another sightless expanse of cement. Life in the Impasse des Huit Anges would, Latimer thought, be rather like a rehearsal for Eternity. That others before him had found it so was suggested by the fact that, of the three houses, two were shuttered and obviously quite empty, while the third, number three, was occupied on the fourth and top floors only.

Feeling as if he were trespassing, Latimer walked slowly across the irregular cobbles to the entrance of number three.

The door was open and he could see along a tiled corridor to a small, dank yard at the back. The concierge's room, to the right of the door, was empty and showed no signs of having been used recently. Beside it, on the wall, was nailed a dusty board with four brass name slots screwed to it. Three of the slots were empty. In the fourth was a grimy piece of paper with the name "CAILLÉ" clumsily printed on it in violet ink.

There was nothing to be learned from this but the fact, which Latimer had not doubted, that Mr. Peters' accommodation address existed. He turned and walked back to the street. In the Rue de Rennes he found a post office where he bought a *pneumatique* letter-card, wrote in it his name and that of his hotel, addressed it to Mr. Peters and dropped it down the chute. He also sent a post card to Marukakis. What happened now depended to a great extent on Mr. Peters. But there was something he could and should do: that was to find out what, if anything, the Paris newspapers had had to say about the breaking up in December nineteen thirty-one of a drug-peddling gang.

At nine o'clock the following morning, being without word from Peters, he decided to spend the morning with newspaper files.

The paper he finally selected for detailed reading had made a number of references to the case. The first was dated November 29, 1931. It was headed: "DRUG TRAFFICKERS ARRESTED," and went on:

"A man and a woman engaged in the distribution of drugs to addicts were arrested yesterday in the Alésia quarter. They are said to be members of a notorious foreign gang. The police expect to make further arrests within a few days."

That was all. It read curiously, Latimer thought. Those three bald sentences looked as if they had been lifted out of a longer report. The absence of names, too, was odd. Police censorship, perhaps.

The next reference appeared on December the fourth under the heading: "DRUG GANG, THREE MORE ARRESTS."

"Three members of a criminal drug distributing organisation were arrested late last night in a café near the Porte d'Orléans. *Agents* entering the café to make the arrests were compelled to fire on one of the men who was armed and who made a desperate attempt to escape. He was slightly wounded. The other two, one of whom was a foreigner, did not resist.

"This brings the number of drug gang arrests to five, for it is believed that the three men arrested last night belonged to the same gang as the man and woman arrested a week ago in the Alésia quarter.

"The police state that still more arrests are likely to be made, as the Bureau Général des Stupéfiants has in its possession evidence implicating the actual organisers of the gang.

"Monsieur Auguste Lafon, director of the Bureau, said: 'We have known of this gang for some time and have conducted painstaking investigations into their activities. We could have made arrests but we held our hands. It was the leaders, the big criminals whom we wanted. Without leaders, with their sources of supply cut off, the army of drug pedlars that infests Paris will be powerless to carry on their nefarious trade. We intend to smash this gang and others like it.' "

Then, on December the eleventh, the newspaper reported:

DRUG GANG SMASHED
NEW ARRESTS

"Now we have them all," says Lafon

THE COUNCIL OF SEVEN

"Six men and one woman are now under arrest as a result of the attack launched by Monsieur Lafon, director of the Bureau Général des Stupéfiants, on a notorious gang of foreign drug traffickers operating in Paris and Marseilles.

"The attack began with the arrest two weeks ago of a woman and her male accomplice in the Alésia quarter. It reached its climax yesterday with the arrest in Marseilles of two men believed to be the remaining members of the gang's 'Council of Seven,' which was responsible for the organisation of this criminal enterprise.

"At the request of the police we have hitherto remained silent as to the names of those arrested as it was desired not to put the others on their guard. Now that restriction has been lifted.

"The woman, Lydia Prokofievna, is a Russian who is believed to have come to France from Turkey with a Nansen passport in 1924. She is known in criminal circles as 'The Grand Duchess.' The man arrested with her was a Dutchman named Manus Visser who, through his association with Prokofievna, was sometimes referred to as 'Monsieur le Duc.'

"The names of the other five under arrest are; Luis Galindo, a naturalised Frenchman of Mexican origin, who now lies in hospital with a bullet wound in the thigh, Jean-Baptiste Lenôtre, a Frenchman from Bordeaux, and Jacob Werner, a Belgian, who were arrested with Galindo, Pierre Lamare or 'Jojo,' a Niçois, and Frederik Petersen, a Dane, who were arrested in Marseilles.

"In a statement to the press last night, Monsieur Lafon said: 'Now we have them all. The gang is smashed. We have cut off the head and with it the brains. The body will now die a speedy death. It is finished.'

"Lamare and Petersen are to be questioned by the examining magistrate to-day. It is expected that there will be a mass-trial of the prisoners."

In England, Latimer reflected, Monsieur Lafon would have found himself in serious trouble. It hardly seemed worthwhile trying the accused after he and the press between them had already pronounced the verdict. But then, the accused was always guilty in a French trial. To give him a trial at all was, practically speaking, merely to ask him whether he had anything to say before he was sentenced.

With the arrest of the "Council of Seven," interest in the case seemed to wane. The fact that "The Grand Duchess" had been transferred to Nice to stand trial there for a fraud committed three years previously may have been responsible for this. The trial of the men was dealt with briefly. All were sentenced: Galindo, Lenôtre and Werner to fines of five thousand francs and three months' imprisonment, Lamare, Petersen and Visser to fines of two thousand francs and one month's imprisonment.

Latimer was amazed by the lightness of the sentences. Lafon was outraged but not amazed. But for the existence of a set of obsolete and wholly ridiculous laws, he thundered, the whole six would have been imprisoned for life.

The newspaper did not mention the fact that the police had failed to find Dimitrios. That was not surprising. The police were not going to tell the press that the arrests were made possible only by a dossier obligingly supplied by some anonymous well-wisher whom they suspected of being the leader of the gang. All the same, it was irritating to Latimer to find that he knew more than the newspaper he had relied upon to clarify the affair for him.

He was about to shut the file in disgust when his attention was caught by an illustration. It was a smudgy reproduction of a photograph of three of the prisoners being led from the court by detectives to whom they were handcuffed. All three had turned their faces away from the camera but the fact of their being handcuffed had prevented them from concealing themselves effectively.

Latimer left the newspaper office in better spirits than those in which he had entered it.

At his hotel a message awaited him. Unless he sent a *pneumatique* making other arrangements, Mr. Peters would call upon him at six o'clock that evening.

Mr. Peters arrived soon after half-past five. He greeted Latimer effusively.

"My *dear* Mr. Latimer! I cannot tell you how pleased I am to see you. Our last meeting took place under such inauspicious circumstances that I hardly dare hope . . . But let us talk of pleasanter things. Welcome to Paris! Have

you had a good journey? You are looking well. Tell me, what did you think
of Grodek? He wrote telling me how charming and sympathetic you were. A
good fellow, isn't he? Those cats of his! He worships them."

"He was very helpful. Do, please, sit down."

"I knew he would be."

For Latimer, Mr. Peters' sweet smile was like the greeting of an old and
detested acquaintance. "He was also mysterious. He urged me to come to Paris
to see you."

"Did he?" Mr Peters did not seem pleased. His smile faded a little. "And
what else did he say, Mr. Latimer?"

"He said that you were a clever man. He seemed to find something I said
about you amusing."

Mr. Peters sat down carefully on the bed. His smile had quite gone. "And
what was it you said?"

"He insisted upon knowing what business I had with you. I told him all
I could. As I knew nothing," went on Latimer spitefully, "I felt that I could
safely confide in him. If you do not like that, I am sorry. You must remember that I am still in complete ignorance concerning this precious scheme of
yours."

"Grodek did not tell you?"

"No. Could he have done so?"

The smile once more tightened his soft lips. It was as if some obscene plant
had turned its face to the sun. "Yes, Mr. Latimer, he could have done so. What
you have told me explains the flippant tone of his letter to me. I am glad you
satisfied his curiosity. The rich are so often covetous of others' goods in this
world of ours. Grodek is a dear friend of mine but it is just as well that he
knows that we stand in no need of assistance. He might otherwise be tempted
by the prospect of gain."

Latimer regarded him thoughtfully for a moment. Then:

"Have you got your pistol with you, Mr. Peters?"

The fat man looked horrified. "Dear me no, Mr. Latimer. Why should I
bring such a thing on a friendly visit to you?"

"Good," said Latimer curtly. He backed towards the door and turned the
key in the lock. The key he put in his pocket. "Now then," he went on grimly,
"I don't want to seem a bad host but there are limits to my patience. I have
come a long way to see you and I still don't know why. I want to know why."

"And so you shall."

"I've heard that before," answered Latimer rudely. "Now before you start
beating about the bush again there are one or two things *you* should know. I
am not a violent man, Mr. Peters. To be honest with you, I dread violence.

But there are times when the most peace-loving among us must use it. This may be one of them. I am younger than you and, I should say, in better condition. If you persist in being mysterious I shall attack you. That is the first thing.

"The second is that I know who you are. Your name is not Peters but Petersen, Frederik Petersen. You are a member of the drug-peddling gang organised by Dimitrios and you were arrested in December nineteen thirty-one, fined two thousand francs and sentenced to one month's imprisonment."

Mr. Peters' smile was tortured. "Did Grodek tell you this?" He asked the question gently and sorrowfully. The word "Grodek" might have been another way of saying "Judas."

"No. I saw a picture of you this morning in a newspaper file."

"A newspaper. Ah, yes! I could not believe that my friend Grodek. . ."

"You don't deny it?"

"Oh, no. It is the truth."

"Well then, Mr. Petersen . . ."

"Peters, Mr. Latimer. I decided to change the name."

"All right then—Peters. We come to my third point. When I was in Istanbul I heard some interesting things about the end of that gang. It was said that Dimitrios betrayed the lot of you by sending to the police, anonymously, a dossier convicting the seven of you. Is that true?"

"Dimitrios behaved very badly to us all," said Mr. Peters huskily.

"It was also said that Dimitrios had become an addict himself. Is that true?"

"Unhappily, it is. Otherwise I do not think he would have betrayed us. We were making so much money for him."

"I was also told that there was talk of vengeance, that you all threatened to kill Dimitrios as soon as you were free."

"*I* did not threaten," Mr. Peters corrected him. "Some of the others did so. Galindo, for example, was always a hot-head."

"I see. You did not threaten; you preferred to act."

"I don't understand you, Mr. Latimer." And he looked as if he really did not understand.

"No? Let me put it to you this way. Dimitrios was murdered near Istanbul roughly two months ago. Very shortly after the time when the murder could have taken place, you were in Athens. That is not very far from Istanbul, is it? Dimitrios, it is said, died a poor man. Now is that likely? As you have just pointed out, his gang made a lot of money for him in nineteen thirty-one. From what I have heard of him, he was not the man to lose money he had made. Do you know what is in my mind, Mr. Peters? I am wondering whether it would not be reasonable to suppose that you killed Dimitrios for his money. What have you to say to that?"

Mr. Peters did not answer for a moment but contemplated Latimer unhappily in the manner of a good shepherd about to admonish an erring lamb.

Then he said: "Mr. Latimer, I think that you are very indiscreet."

"Do you?"

"And also very fortunate. Just suppose that I had, as you suggest, killed Dimitrios. Think what I should be forced to do. I should be forced to kill you also, now shouldn't I?" He put his hand in his breast pocket. It emerged holding the Lüger pistol. "You see, I lied to you just now. I admit it. I was so curious to know what you were going to do if you thought that I was unarmed. Besides, it seemed so impolite to come here carrying a pistol. The fact that I did not bring the pistol with me because of you would be a difficult one to prove. So I lied. Do you understand my feelings a little? I am so anxious to have your confidence."

"All of which is as skillful a reply to an accusation of murder as one could wish for."

Mr. Peters put away his pistol wearily. "Mr. Latimer, this is not a detective story. There is no *need* to be so stupid. Even if you cannot be discreet, at least use your imagination. Is it likely that Dimitrios would make a Will in my favour? No. Then how do you suppose that I could kill him for his money? People in these days do not keep their wealth in treasure chests. Come now, Mr. Latimer, let us please be sensible. Let us eat dinner together and then talk business. I suggest that after dinner we drink coffee in my apartment—it is a little more comfortable than this room—though if you would prefer to go to a café I shall understand. You probably disapprove of me. I really cannot blame you. But at least let us cultivate the illusion of friendship."

For a moment Latimer felt himself warming to Mr. Peters. True, the last part of his appeal had been accompanied by an almost visible accretion of self-pity; but he had not smiled. Besides, the man had already made him feel a fool: it would be too much if he made him feel a prig as well. At the same time . . .

"I am as hungry as you," he said; "and I can see no reason why I should prefer a café to your apartment. At the same time, Mr. Peters, anxious though I am to be friendly, I feel that I should warn you now that unless I have, this evening, a satisfactory explanation of your asking me to meet you here in Paris, I shall—half a million francs or no half a million francs—leave by the first available train. Is that clear?"

Mr. Peters' smile returned. "It could not be clearer, Mr. Latimer. And may I say how much I appreciate your frankness?"

"Where shall we dine? There is a Danish place near here, isn't there?"

Mr. Peters struggled into his overcoat. "No, Mr. Latimer, as you are doubtless well aware, there is not." He sighed unhappily. "It is unkind of you to make fun of me. And in any case I prefer French cooking."

Mr. Peters' capacity for making him feel a fool was, Latimer reflected as they descended the stairs, remarkable.

At Mr. Peters' suggestion and expense they ate in a cheap restaurant in the Rue Jacob. Afterwards they went to the Impasse des Huit Anges.

"What about Caillé?" said Latimer as they climbed the dusty stairs.

"He is away. At the moment I am in sole possession."

"I see."

Mr. Peters, who was breathing heavily by the time they had reached the second landing, paused for a moment. "You have concluded, I suppose, that I am Caillé."

"Yes."

Mr. Peters began to climb again. The stairs creaked under his weight. Latimer, following two or three stairs behind, was reminded of a circus elephant picking its way unwillingly up a pyramid of coloured blocks to perform a balancing trick. They reached the fourth floor. Mr. Peters stopped and, standing panting before a battered door, hauled out a bunch of keys. A moment later he pushed open the door, pressed a switch and waved Latimer in.

The room ran from front to back of the house and was divided into two by a curtain to the left of the door. The half beyond the curtain was of a different shape from that which contained the door as it included the space between the end of the landing, the rear wall and the next house. The space formed an alcove. At each end of the room was a tall French window.

But if it was, architecturally speaking, the sort of room that one would expect to find in a French house of that type and age, it was in every other respect fantastic.

The first thing that Latimer saw was the dividing curtain. It was of imitation cloth of gold. The walls and ceiling were distempered an angry blue and bespattered with gold five-pointed stars. Scattered all over the floor, so that not a square inch of it showed, were cheap Moroccan rugs. They overlapped a good deal so that in places there were humps of three and even four thicknesses of rug. There were three huge divans piled high with cushions, some tooled leather ottoman seats and a Moroccan table with a brass tray upon it. In one corner stood an enormous brass gong. The light came from fretted oak lanterns. In the centre of it all stood a small chromium-plated electric radiator. There was a choking smell of upholstery dust.

"Home!" said Mr. Peters. "Take your things off, Mr. Latimer; would you like to see the rest of the place?"

"Very much."

"Outwardly, just another uncomfortable French house," commented Mr. Peters as he toiled up the stairs again; "actually an oasis in a desert of discomfort. This is my bedroom."

Latimer had another glimpse of French Morocco. This time it was adorned by a pair of crumpled flannel pyjamas.

"And the toilet."

Latimer looked at the toilet and learned that his host had a spare set of false teeth.

"Now," said Mr. Peters, "I will show you something curious."

He led the way out on to the landing. Facing them was a large clothes cupboard. He opened the door and struck a match. Along the back of the cupboard was a row of metal clothes pegs. Grasping the centre one, he turned it like a latch and pulled. The back of the cupboard swung towards them and Latimer felt the night air on his face and heard the noises of the city.

"There is a narrow iron platform running along the outside wall to the next house," explained Mr. Peters. "There is another cupboard there like this one. You can see nothing because there are only blank walls facing us. Equally, no one could see us should we choose to leave that way. It was Dimitrios who had this done."

"Dimitrios!"

"Dimitrios owned all three of these houses. They were kept empty for reasons of privacy. Sometimes, they were used as stores. These two floors were used for meetings. Morally, no doubt, the houses still belong to Dimitrios. Fortunately for me, he took the precaution of buying them in my name. I also conducted the negotiations. The police never found out about them. I was able, therefore, to move in when I came out of prison. In case Dimitrios should ever wonder what had happened to his property, *I* took the precaution of buying them from myself in the name of Caillé. Do you like Algerian coffee?"

"Yes."

"It takes a little longer to prepare than French but I prefer it. Shall we go downstairs again?"

They went downstairs. Having seen Latimer uncomfortably ensconced amid a sea of cushions, Mr. Peters disappeared into the alcove.

Latimer got rid of some of the cushions and looked about him. It was odd to feel that the house had once belonged to Dimitrios. Yet the evidence around him of the tenancy of the preposterous Mr. Peters was a good deal odder. There was a small (fretted) shelf above his head. On it were paperbound books. There was *Pearls of Everyday Wisdom*. That was the one he had been reading in the train from Athens. There was, besides, Plato's Symposium, in French and uncut, an anthology called *Poèmes Erotiques*, which had no author's name on it and had been cut, Æsop's Fables in English, Mrs Humphry Ward's *Robert Elsmere* in French, a German Gazetteer, and several books by Dr. Frank Crane in a language which Latimer took to be Danish.

Mr. Peters came back carrying a Moroccan tray on which were a curious looking coffee percolator, a spirit lamp, two cups and a Moroccan cigarette box. The spirit lamp he lighted and put under the percolator. The cigarettes he placed beside Latimer on the divan. Then he reached up above Latimer's head, brought down one of the Danish books and flicked over one or two of the pages. A small photograph fluttered to the floor. He picked it up and handed it to Latimer.

"Do you recognise him, Mr. Latimer?"

It was a faded head and shoulders photograph of a middle-aged man with . . . Latimer looked up. "It's Dimitrios!" he exclaimed. "Where did you get it?"

Mr. Peters took the photograph from Latimer's fingers. "You recognise it? Good." He sat down on one of the ottoman seats and adjusted the spirit lamp. Then he looked up. If it had been possible for Mr. Peters' wet, lustreless eyes to gleam, Latimer would have said that they were gleaming with pleasure.

"Help yourself to cigarettes, Mr. Latimer," he said. "I am going to tell you a story."

Eleven

≈≈≈≈≈≈≈≈≈≈≈≈≈≈≈≈≈≈

PARIS, 1928–1931

"**Y**ES, MR. LATIMER, most of us go through life without knowing what we want of it. But Dimitrios, you know, was not like that. Dimitrios knew exactly what he wanted. He wanted money and he wanted power. Just those two things; as much of them as he could get. The curious thing is that I helped him to get them.

"It was in nineteen twenty-eight that I first set eyes on Dimitrios. It was here in Paris. I was, at the time, the part-owner, with a man named Giraud, of a *boîte* in the Rue Blanche. We called it *Le Kasbah Parisien* and it was a very gay and cosy place with divans and amber lights and rugs. I had met Giraud in Marrakesh and we decided that everything should be just like a place we knew there. Everything was Moroccan; everything, that is, except the band for dancing which was South American.

"We opened it in nineteen twenty-six which was a good year in Paris. The Americans and English, but especially the Americans, had money to spend on champagne and the French used to come, too. Most Frenchmen are senti-mental about Morocco unless they have done their military service there. And the *Kasbah was* Morocco. We had Arab and Senegalese waiters and the cham-pagne actually came from Meknes. It was a little sweet for the Americans but very nice all the same and quite cheap.

"For two years we made money and then, as is the way with such places, the clientèle began to change in character. We had more French and fewer Americans, more *maquereaux* and fewer gentlemen, more *poules* and fewer *chic* ladies. We still made a profit but it was not as great and we had to do more for it. I began to think that it was time to move on.

"It was Giraud who brought Dimitrios to *Le Kasbah.*

"I had met Giraud when I was in Marrakesh. He was a half-caste, his mother being an Arab and his father a French soldier. He was born in Algiers and had a French passport.

"I do not know exactly how he met Dimitrios. I think that it was at some *boîte* higher up the Rue Blanche; for we did not open until eleven o'clock and Giraud liked to dance at other places beforehand. But, one evening, he brought Dimitrios into *Le Kasbah* and then took me aside. He remarked that profits had been getting smaller and said that we could make some money for ourselves if we did business with this friend of his, Dimitrios Makropoulos.

"The first time I saw Dimitrios I was not impressed by him. He was, I thought, just such a type of *maquereau* as I had seen before. His clothes fitted tightly and he had greying hair and polished fingernails and he looked at women in a way that those who came to *Le Kasbah* would not like. But I went over to his table with Giraud and we shook hands. Then he pointed to the chair beside him and told me to sit down. One would have thought that I was a waiter instead of the *patron*."

He turned his watery eyes to Latimer. "You may think, Mr. Latimer, that, for one who was not impressed, I remember the occasion very clearly. That is true. I do remember it clearly. You understand, I did not then know Dimitrios as I came to know him later. He made his impression without seeming to do so. At the time he irritated me. Without sitting down, I asked him what he wanted.

"For a moment he looked at me. He had very soft, brown eyes, you know. Then he said: 'I want champagne, my friend. Have you any objection? I can pay for it, you know. Are you going to be polite to me or shall I take my business proposals to more intelligent people?'

"I am an even-tempered man. I do not like trouble. I often think how much pleasanter a place this world of ours would be if people were polite and softly spoken with one another. But there are times when it is difficult. I told Dimitrios that nothing would induce me to be polite to him and that he could go when he pleased.

"But for Giraud he would have gone and I should not be sitting here talking to you. Giraud sat down at the table with him, apologising for me. Dimitrios was watching me while Giraud was speaking, and I could see that he was wondering about me.

"I was now quite sure that I did not want to do business of any kind with this Dimitrios; but because of Giraud I agreed to listen, and we sat down together while Dimitrios told us what his proposal was. He talked very convincingly, and at last I agreed to do what he wanted. We had been in association with Dimitrios for several months, when one day . . ."

"Just a moment," interrupted Latimer; "what was this association? Was this the beginning of the drug peddling?"

Mr. Peters hesitated and frowned. "No, Mr. Latimer, it was not. Dimitrios was connected at the time with what I believe you call the white slave traffic.

It is such an interesting phrase to me. 'Traffic'—a word full of horrible significance. 'White slave'—consider the implications of the adjective. Does anyone talk nowadays about the coloured slave traffic? I think not. Yet the majority of the women involved are coloured. I fail to see why the consequences of the traffic should be any more disagreeable to a white girl from a Bucharest slum than to a negro girl from Dakar or a Chinese girl from Harbin. The League of Nations Committee is unprejudiced enough to appreciate that aspect of the question. They are intelligent enough, too, to mistrust the word 'slave.' They refer to the 'traffic in women.'

"I have never liked the business. It is impossible to treat human beings as one would treat ordinary inanimate merchandise. There is always trouble. There is always the possibility, too, that in an isolated case the adjective 'white' might have a religious instead of a merely racial application. From my experience, I should say that the possibility is remote; but there it is. I may be illogical and sentimental, but I should not care to be associated with anything like that. Besides, the overhead expenses of a trafficker in what is considered a fair way of business are enormous. There are always false birth, marriage and death certificates to be obtained and travelling expenses and bribes to pay quite apart from the cost of maintaining several identities. You have no idea of the cost of forged documents, Mr. Latimer. There used to be three recognised sources of supply: one in Zürich, one in Amsterdam and one in Brussels. All neutrals! Odd, isn't it? You used to be able to get a false-real Danish passport—that is, a real Danish passport treated chemically to remove the original entries and photograph and then filled in with new ones—for, let me see, about two thousand francs at the present rate of exchange. A real-false—manufactured from start to finish by the agent—would have cost you a little less, say fifteen hundred. Nowadays you would have to pay twice as much. Most of the business is done here in Paris now. It is the refugees, of course. The point is that a trafficker needs plenty of capital. If he is known there are always plenty of people willing to provide it, but they expect fantastic dividends. It is better to have one's own capital.

"Dimitrios had his own capital; but he also had access to capital which was not his own. He represented certain very rich men. He was never at a loss for money. When he came to Giraud and me he was in a different sort of difficulty. Owing to League of Nations activities the laws in quite a number of countries had been altered and tightened up in such a way that it was sometimes very difficult indeed to get women from one place to another. All very praiseworthy, but a great nuisance to men like Dimitrios. It was not that it made it impossible for them to do their business. It didn't. But it made things more complicated and expensive for them.

"Before Dimitrios came to us he had had a very simple technique. He knew people in Alexandria who would advise him about their requirements. Then he would go to, say, Poland, recruit the women, take them to France on their own passports and then ship them from Marseilles. That was all. It was enough to say that the girls were going to fulfil a theatrical engagement. When the regulations were tightened up, however, it was no longer as simple. The night he came to *Le Kasbah* he told us that he had just encountered his first trouble. He had recruited twelve women from a *Madame* in Vilna, but the Poles would not let him bring them out without guarantees as to their destination and the respectability of their future employment. Respectability! But that was the law.

"Naturally, Dimitrios had told the Polish authorities that he would provide the guarantees. It would have been fatal for him not to have done so, for then he would have been suspect. Somehow he had to obtain the guarantees. That was where Giraud and I came in. We were to say that we were employing the girls as cabaret dancers and deal with any inquiries that might be made by the Polish Consular authorities. As long as they stayed in Paris for a week or so, we were perfectly safe. If inquiries were made after that we knew nothing. They had completed their engagement and gone. Where they had gone to was no business of ours.

"That was the way Dimitrios put it to us. He said that for our part of the affair he would pay us five thousand francs. It was money easily earned, but I was doubtful; and it was Giraud who finally persuaded me to agree. But I told Dimitrios that my agreement only applied to this particular case and that I could not consider myself committed to helping him again. Giraud grumbled, but agreed to accept the condition.

"A month later Dimitrios came to see us again, paid us the balance of the five thousand francs and said that he had another job for us. I objected; but, as Giraud immediately pointed out, we had had no trouble on the first occasion and my objection was not very firm. The money was useful. It paid the South Americans for a week.

"I believe now that Dimitrios lied to us about that first five thousand francs. I do not think that we earned it. I think he gave it to us simply to gain our confidence. It was like him to do a thing like that. Another man might try to trick you into serving his ends; but Dimitrios bought you. Yet he bought you cheaply. He set one's common sense fighting against one's instinctive suspicions of him.

"I have said that we earned that first five thousand francs without trouble. The second caused us a lot of trouble. The Polish authorities made some *chi-chi* and we had the police visiting us and asking questions. Worse, we had to have these women in *Le Kasbah* to prove that we were employing them. They could not dance a step and were a great inconvenience to us, as we had to be amiable to them in case one should go to the police and tell the truth. They drank champagne all the time, and if Dimitrios had not agreed to pay for it we should have lost money.

"He was, of course, very apologetic and said that there had been a mistake. He paid us ten thousand francs for our trouble and promised that if we would continue to help him there would be no more Polish girls and no more *chi-chi*. After some argument we agreed, and for several months we were paid our ten thousand francs. We had during that time only occasional visits from the police, and there was no unpleasantness. But at last we had trouble again. This time it was because of the Italian authorities. Both Giraud and I were questioned by the examining magistrate for the district and kept for a day at the Commissariat. The day after that I quarrelled with Giraud.

"I say that I quarrelled. It would be more correct to say that our quarrel became open. He was crude and stupid and he sometimes tried to cheat me. He was suspicious, too; suspicious in a loud, stupid way like an animal; and he encouraged the wrong sort of clientèle. His friends were detestable; *maquereaux*, all of them. He used to call people '*mon gar.*' He would have been better as the *patron* of a *bistro*. For all I know he may be one now; but I think it more likely that he is in a prison. He often became violent when he was angry and sometimes injured people badly.

"That day after our unpleasantness with the police I said that we should have no more to do with this business of the women. That made him angry. He said that we should be fools to give up ten thousand francs a month because of a few police and that I was too nervous for his taste. I understood his point of view. He had had much to do with the police both in Marrakesh and Algiers, and he had a contempt for them. As long as he could keep out of prison and make money he was satisfied. I have never thought that way. I do not like the police to be interested in me, even though they cannot arrest me. Giraud was right. I was nervous. But although I understood his point of view I could not agree with it, and I said so. I also said that, if he wished, he could buy my share in *Le Kasbah Parisien* for the amount of money I had originally invested.

"It was a sacrifice on my part, you know, but I was tired of Giraud and wanted to be rid of him. I did get rid of him. He agreed immediately. That night we saw Dimitrios and explained the situation to him. Giraud was delighted with his bargain and enjoyed himself very much cracking clumsy jokes at my expense. Dimitrios smiled at these jokes; but when Giraud left us alone for a moment, he asked me to leave soon after he did and meet him at a café as he had something to say to me.

"I very nearly did not go. On the whole, I think that it was as well that I did go. I profited by my association with Dimitrios. There are, I think, very few associates of Dimitrios who could say as much; but I was lucky. Besides, I think that he had a respect for my intelligence. Generally he could bluff me, but not always.

"He was waiting in the café for me, and I sat down beside him and asked him what he wanted. I was never polite to him.

"He said: 'I think you are wise to leave Giraud. The business with the women has become too dangerous. It was always difficult. Now I have finished with it.'

"I asked him if he proposed to tell Giraud that and he smiled.

"'Not yet,' he said; 'not until you have your money from him.'

"I said suspiciously that he was very kind, but he shook his head impatiently. 'Giraud is a fool,' he said. 'If you had not been there with him, I should have made other arrangements about the women. Now, I am offering you a chance to work with me. I should be a fool if I made you angry with me to begin with by costing you your investment in *Le Kasbah*."

"Then he asked me if I knew anything about the heroin business. I did know a little about it. He then told me that he had sufficient capital to buy twenty kilogrammes a month and finance its distribution in Paris and asked me if I were interested in working for him.

"Now, twenty kilogrammes of heroin is a serious thing, Mr. Latimer. It is worth a lot of money. I asked him how he proposed to distribute so much. He said that, for the moment, that would be his affair. What he wanted me to do was to negotiate the purchases abroad and find ways of bringing it into the country. If I agreed to his proposal I was to begin by going to Bulgaria as his representative, dealing with suppliers there of whom he already knew and arranging for the transport of the stuff to Paris. He offered me ten per cent. of the value of every kilo I supplied him with.

"I said that I would think it over, but my mind was already made up. With the price of heroin as it was then, I knew that I would make nearly twenty thousand francs a month. I knew also that he was going to make a great deal more than that for himself. Even if, with my commission and expenses, he had to pay in effect fifteen thousand francs a kilo for the stuff, it would be good business for him. Selling heroin by the gramme in Paris, one can get nearly one hundred thousand francs a kilo for it. With the commissions to the actual pedlars and others, he would make not less than thirty thousand francs on each kilo. That meant over half a million francs a month for him. Capital is a wonderful thing if one knows just what to do with it and does not mind a little risk.

"In the September of nineteen twenty-eight I went to Bulgaria for Dimitrios with instructions from him to get the first twenty kilos to him by November. He had already begun to make arrangements with agents and pedlars. The sooner I could get the stuff the better.

"Dimitrios had given me the name of a man in Sofia who would put me in touch with the suppliers. This man did so. He also arranged for the credits with which I was to make the purchases. He . . ."

Latimer had an idea. He said suddenly: "What was this man's name?"

Mr. Peters frowned at the interruption. "I do not think that you ought to ask me that, Mr. Latimer."

"Was it Vazoff?"

Mr. Peters' eyes watered at him. "Yes, it was."

"And were the credits arranged through the Eurasian Credit Trust?"

"You evidently know a great deal more than I had thought." Mr. Peters was obviously not pleased by the fact. "May I ask . . . ?"

"I was guessing. But you need not have worried about compromising Vazoff. He died three years ago."

"I am aware of it. Did you guess that Vazoff was dead? And how much more guessing have you done, Mr. Latimer?"

"That is all. Please continue."

"Frankness . . ." began Mr. Peters and then stopped and drank his coffee. "We will return to the subject," he said at last. "Yes, Mr. Latimer, I admit that you are right. Through Vazoff, I purchased the supplies Dimitrios needed and paid for them with drafts on Eurasian Credit Trust of Sofia. There was no difficulty about that. My real task was to transport the stuff to France. I decided to send it by rail to Salonika and ship it from there to Marseilles."

"As heroin?"

"Obviously not. But I must confess it was difficult to know how to disguise it. The only goods which come into France from Bulgaria regularly, and which would not, therefore, be subject to special examination by the French Customs, were things like grain and tobacco and attar of roses. Dimitrios was pressing for delivery and I was at my wits' end." He paused dramatically.

"Well, how *did* you smuggle it?"

"In a coffin, Mr. Latimer. The French, I reflected, are a race with a great respect for the solemnity of death. Have you ever attended a French funeral? *Pompe funèbre*, you know. It is most impressive. No Customs official, I felt certain, would care to play the ghoul. I purchased the coffin in Sofia. It was a beautiful thing with very fine carving on it. I also purchased a suit of mourning clothes and accompanied the coffin myself. I am a man who responds very readily to emotion and really I was most moved by the marks of simple respect for my grief shown by the stevedores who handled the coffin at the dock. Not even my own personal luggage was examined at the Customs.

"I had warned Dimitrios, and a hearse was waiting for me and the coffin. I was pleased by my success, but Dimitrios, when I saw him, shrugged. I could not, he said very reasonably, arrive in France with a coffin every month. I think he thought the whole affair a little unbusinesslike. He was right, of course. He had, however, a suggestion. There was an Italian shipping line which ran one cargo steamer a month from Varna to Genoa. The stuff could be shipped to Genoa in small cases and manifested as special tobacco consigned to France. That would prevent the Italian Customs examining it. There was a man in Nice who could arrange for the transport of the stuff from Genoa by bribing the warehouse people to release it from bond and then smuggling it through by road. I wished to know how that would affect my financial interest in the supplies. He said that I should lose nothing as there was other work for me to do.

"It was curious how we all accepted his leadership almost without question. Yes, he had the money; but there was more than that to it. He dominated us because he knew precisely what he wanted and precisely how to get it with the least possible trouble and at the lowest possible cost. He knew how to find the people to work for him, too; and, when he had found them, he knew how to handle them.

"There were seven of us who took our instructions directly from Dimitrios and not one was the sort of person to take instructions easily. For instance, Visser, the Dutchman, had sold German machine guns to the Chinese, spied for the Japanese and served a term of imprisonment for killing a coolie in Batavia. He was not an easy man to handle. It was he who made the arrangements with the clubs and bars through which we reached the addicts.

"You see, the system of distribution was very carefully organised. Both Lenôtre and Galindo had for several years been peddling drugs which they bought from a man in the employ of a big French wholesale drug manufacturer. That sort of thing used to be quite easy before the nineteen thirty-one regulations. Both those men knew well those who needed the stuff and where to find them. Before Dimitrios came on the scene they had been dealing mostly in morphine and cocaine and always they had been handicapped by limited supplies. When Dimitrios offered them unlimited supplies of heroin they were quite ready to abandon the wholesale chemist and sell their clients heroin.

"But that was only one part of the business. Drug addicts, you know, are always very eager to get other people to take drugs too. Consequently, your circle of consumers is ever widening. It is most important, as you may imagine, to see that when you are approached by new customers they are not representatives of the *Brigade des Stupéfiants* or other similar undesirables. That was where Visser's work came in. The would-be buyer would come to, say, Lenôtre in the first place on the recommendation of a regular customer known to Lenôtre. But, on being asked for drugs, Lenôtre would pretend to be astonished. Drugs? He knew nothing of such things. Personally, he never used them. But, if one did use them, he had heard that the place to go to was the So-and-So Bar. At the So-and-So Bar, which would be on Visser's list, the prospective customer would receive much the same sort of answer. Drugs? No. Nothing of that kind at the So-and-So Bar but if it should be possible to call in again the following night, there might possibly be someone who could help. The following night, the Grand Duchess would be there.

"She was a curious woman. She had been brought into the business by Visser and was, I think, the only one of us Dimitrios had not found for himself. She was very clever. Her capacity for weighing up complete strangers was extraordinary. She could, I think, tell the most cleverly disguised detective just by looking at him across a room. It was her business to examine the person who wanted to buy and decide whether he or she should be supplied or not and how much was to be charged. She was very valuable to us.

"The other man was the Belgian, Werner. It was he who dealt with the small pedlars. He had been a chemist at one time and he used, I believe, to dilute the heroin with pigments under the pretext of testing its purity. Dimitrios never mentioned that part of the business.

"Some dilution very soon became necessary. Within six months of our beginning, I had had to increase the monthly heroin supply to fifty kilos. And I had other work to do. Lenôtre and Galindo had reported in the early stages that, if they were to get all the business they knew of, they would have to have morphine and cocaine to sell as well as heroin. Morphine addicts did not always like heroin and cocaine addicts would sometimes refuse it if they could get cocaine elsewhere. I had then to arrange for supplies of morphine and cocaine. The morphine problem was a simple one as it could be supplied at the same time and by the same people as the heroin; but the cocaine was a different matter. For that, it was necessary to go to Germany. I had plenty to do.

"We had our troubles, of course. They usually came to my part of the business. By the time we had been operating for a year, I had made several alternative arrangements for bringing in our supplies. In addition to the Genoa route for heroin and morphine which Lamare handled, I had come to terms with a sleeping-car attendant on the Orient Express. He used to take the stuff aboard at Sofia and deliver it when the train was shunted into the siding in Paris. It was not a very safe route and I had to take elaborate precautions to protect myself in case of trouble, but it was rapid. Cocaine used to come in in cases of machinery from Germany. We had also begun to receive consignments of heroin from an Istanbul factory. These were brought by a cargo boat which left them floating outside the port of Marseilles in anchored containers for Lamare to collect at night.

"There was one week of disaster. In the last week of the June of nineteen twenty-nine, fifteen kilos of heroin were seized on the Orient Express and the police arrested six of my men including the sleeping-car attendant. That would have been bad enough; but during the same week Lamare had to abandon a consignment of forty kilos of heroin and morphine near Sospel. He himself escaped but we were in a serious difficulty, for the loss of those fifty-five kilos meant that we were left with only eight kilos to meet commitments for over fifty. None was due on the Istanbul boat for several days. We were in despair. Lenôtre and Galindo and Werner had a terrible time. Two of Galindo's clientèle committed suicide and in one of the bars there was a *fracas* in which Werner had his head cut.

"I did the best I could. I went to Sofia myself and brought back ten kilos in a trunk; but that was not enough. Dimitrios did not, I must say, blame me. It would have been unfair to have done so. But he was angry. He decided that, in future, reserve stocks must be held. It was soon after that week that he bought these houses. Until then we had always met him in a room over a café near the Porte d'Orléans. Now he said that these houses should be our headquarters. We never knew where he lived and could never get in touch with him until he chose to telephone one or other of us. We were to discover later that this ignorance of his address put us at a disastrous disadvantage. But other things happened before we made that discovery.

"The task of creating stocks was left to me. It was by no means easy. If we were both to create stocks and to maintain existing supplies we had to increase the size of the consignments. That meant that there was a greater risk of seizure. It also meant that we had to find more new methods of bringing the stuff in. Things were complicated, too, by the Bulgarian Government's closing down the factory at Radomir from which we drew the bulk of our supplies. It soon opened again in a different part of the country; but inevitably there were delays. We were forced to rely more and more upon Istanbul.

"It was a trying time. In two months we lost by seizure no less than ninety kilos of heroin, twenty of morphine and five of cocaine. But, in spite of ups and downs, the stock increased steadily. By the end of nineteen thirty, we had, beneath the floorboards of those houses next door, two hundred and fifty kilos of heroin, two hundred odd kilos of morphine, ninety kilos of cocaine and a small quantity of prepared Turkish opium."

Mr. Peters poured out the remainder of the coffee and extinguished the spirit lamp. Then he took a cigarette, wetted the end of it with his tongue and lit it.

"Have you ever known a drug addict, Mr. Latimer?" he asked suddenly.

"I don't think so."

"Ah, you don't *think* so. You do not know for certain. Yes, it is possible for a drug-taker to conceal his little weakness for quite a time. But he—and especially *she*—cannot conceal it indefinitely, you know. The process is always roughly the same. It begins as an experiment. Half a gramme, perhaps, is taken through the nostrils. It may make you feel sick the first time; but you will try again and the next time it will be as it should be. A delicious sensation, warm, brilliant. Time stands still; but the mind moves at a tremendous pace and, it seems to you, with incredible efficiency. You were stupid; you become highly intelligent. You were unhappy; you become carefree. What you do not like you forget; and what you do like you experience with an intensity of pleasure undreamed of. Three hours of Paradise. And afterwards it is not too bad; not nearly as bad as it was when you had too much champagne. You want to be quiet; you feel a little ill at ease; that is all. Soon you are yourself again. Nothing has happened to you except that you have enjoyed yourself amazingly. If you do not wish to take the drug again, you tell yourself you need not do so. As an intelligent person you are superior to the stuff. Then, therefore, there is no logical reason why you should not enjoy yourself again, is there? Of course there isn't! And so you do. But this time it is a little disappointing. Your half a gramme was not quite enough. Disappointment must be dealt with. You must wander in Paradise just once more before you decide not to take the stuff again. A trifle more; nearly a gramme perhaps. Paradise again and still you don't feel any the worse for it. And since you don't feel any the worse for it, why not continue? Everybody knows that the stuff does ultimately have a bad effect on you; but the moment you detect any bad effects *you* will stop. Only fools become addicts. One and a half grammes. It really is something to look forward to in life. Only three months ago everything was so dreary; but now . . . Two grammes. Naturally, as you are taking a little more it is only reasonable to expect to feel a little ill and depressed afterwards. It's four months now. You must stop soon. Two and a half grammes. Your nose and throat get so dry these days. Other people seem to get on your nerves, too. Perhaps it is because you are sleeping so badly. They make too much noise. They talk so loudly. And what are they saying? Yes, *what*? Things about *you*, vicious lies. You can see it in their faces. Three grammes. And there are other things to be considered; other dangers. You have to be careful. Food tastes horrible. You cannot remember things that you have to do; important things. Even if you should happen to remember them, there are so many other things to worry you apart from this beastliness of having to live. For instance, your nose keeps running: that is, it is not really running but you think it must be, so you have to keep touching it to make sure. Another thing: there is always a fly annoying you. This terrible fly never *will* leave you alone and in peace. It is on your face, on your hand, on your neck. You must pull yourself together. Three and a half grammes. You see the idea, Mr. Latimer?"

"You don't seem to approve of drug-taking."

"Approve!" Mr. Peters stared, aghast. "It is terrible, *terrible*! Lives are ruined. They lose the power to work yet they must find money to pay for their special stuff. Under such circumstances people become desperate and may even do something criminal to get it. I see what is in your mind, Mr. Latimer. You feel that it is strange that I should have been connected with, that I should have made money out of, a thing of which I disapprove so sternly. But consider. If *I* had not made the money, someone else would have done so. Not one of those unfortunate creatures would have been any better off and I should have lost money."

"What about this ever-increasing clientèle of yours? You cannot pretend that all of those your organisation supplied were habitual drug-takers before you went to work."

"Of course they were not. But that side of the business was nothing to do with *me*. That was Lenôtre and Galindo. And I may tell you that Lenôtre and Galindo and Werner, too, were themselves addicts. They used cocaine. It is harder on the constitution but, whereas one can become a dangerous heroin addict in a few months, one can spend several years killing oneself with cocaine."

"What did Dimitrios take?"

"Heroin. It was a great surprise to us the first time we noticed it. We would meet him in this room as a rule at about six o'clock in the evening. It was on one of those evenings in the spring of nineteen thirty-one when we had our surprise.

"Dimitrios arrived late. That in itself was unusual; but we took little notice of it. As a rule, at these meetings, he would sit very quietly with his eyes half-closed, looking a little troubled as though he had a headache, so that even when one became used to him one constantly wished to ask if all was well with him. Watching him sometimes I used to be amazed at myself for allowing myself to be led by him. Then I would see his face change as he turned to meet some objection from Visser—it was always Visser who objected—and I would understand. Visser was a violent man and quick and cunning as well; but he seemed a child beside Dimitrios. Once when Dimitrios had been making a fool of him, Visser pulled out a pistol. He was white with rage. I could see his finger squeezing the trigger. If I had been Dimitrios, I should have prayed. But Dimitrios only smiled in the insolent way he had and, turning his back on Visser, began to talk to me about some business matter. Dimitrios was always quiet like that, even when he was angry.

"That was why we were so surprised that evening. He came in late and he stood inside the door looking at us for nearly a minute. Then he walked over to his place and sat down. Visser had been saying something about the *patron* of a café who had been making trouble and now he went on. There was nothing remarkable about what he was saying. I think he was telling Galindo that he must stop using the café as it was unsafe.

"Suddenly, Dimitrios leaned across the table, shouted '*Imbecile!*' and spat in Visser's face.

"Visser was as surprised as the rest of us. He opened his mouth to speak but Dimitrios did not give him time to say anything. Before we could grasp what was happening, he was accusing Visser of the most fantastic things. The words poured out and he spat again like a guttersnipe.

"Visser went white and got to his feet with his hand in the pocket where he kept his pistol; but Lenôtre, who was beside him, got up, too, and whispered something to him which made Visser take his hand from his pocket. Lenôtre was used to people who had been taking drugs and he and Galindo and Werner had recognised the signs as soon as Dimitrios had entered the room. But Dimitrios had seen Lenôtre whisper and turned to him. From Lenôtre he came to the rest of us. We were fools, he told us, if we thought that he did not know that we were plotting against him. He called us a lot of very unpleasant names in French and Greek. Then he began to boast that he was cleverer than the rest of us together, that but for him we should be starving, that he alone was responsible for our success (which was true though we did not like to be told it) and that he could do with us as he wished. He went on for half an hour, abusing us and boasting alternately. None of us said a word. Then, as suddenly as he had started, he stopped, stood up and walked out of the room.

"I suppose that we should have been prepared for treachery after that. Heroin addicts have a reputation for it. Yet we were not prepared. I think it may have been that we were so conscious of the amount of money he was making. I only know that, when he had gone, Lenôtre and Galindo laughed and asked Werner if the boss were paying for the stuff he used. Even Visser grinned. A joke was made of it, you see.

"Next time we saw Dimitrios he was quite normal and no reference was made to his outburst. But as the months went by, although we had no more outbursts, he became bad-tempered and little difficulties would make him angry. His appearance was changing, too. He looked thin and ill and his eyes were dull. He did not always come to the meetings.

"Then, we had our second warning.

"Early in September, he announced suddenly that he proposed to reduce the consignments for the next three months and use our stock. This startled us and there were many objections. I was one of the objectors. I had had a great deal of trouble building up the stock and did not want to see it distributed without reason. The others reminded him of the trouble they had had when supplies ran out before. But Dimitrios would not listen. He had been warned, he said, that there was to be a new drive by the police. Not only, he said, would so large a stock compromise us seriously if it were discovered; but its seizure would be a serious financial loss. He, too, was sorry to see it go but it was best to play for safety.

"I do not think that the notion that he might be liquidating his assets before he got out occurred to any of us; and you may say that for people of experience we were very trusting. You would be right to say that. With the exception of Visser we seemed always to be on the defensive in our dealings with Dimitrios. Even Lydia, who understood so much about people, was defeated by him. As for Visser, he was too paralysed by his own conceit to believe that anyone, even a drug addict, could betray him. Besides, why should we suspect him? We were making money, but he was making more, much more. What logical reason was there for suspecting him? Who could possibly have foreseen that he would behave like a madman?"

He shrugged. "You know the rest. He turned informer. We were all arrested. I was in Marseilles with Lamare when we were caught. The police were quite clever. They watched us for a week before they took us. They hoped, I think, to catch us with some of the stuff. Luckily, we noticed them the day before we were due to take delivery of a big consignment from Istanbul. Lenôtre and Galindo and Werner were not so lucky. They had some of the stuff in their pockets. The police tried, of course, to make me tell them about Dimitrios and showed me the dossier he had sent them. They might as well have asked me for the moon. Visser, I found out later, knew more than the rest of us, but he did not tell the police what it was. He had other ideas. He told the police that Dimitrios had had an apartment in the seventeenth arrondissement. That was a lie. Visser wanted to get a lighter sentence than the rest of us. He did not. He died not long ago, poor fellow." Mr. Peters heaved a sigh and produced one of his cheroots.

Latimer touched his second cup of coffee. It was quite cold. He took a cigarette and accepted a light from his host's match.

"Well?" he said when he saw that the cheroot was alight. "What then? I am still waiting to hear how I am to earn a half a million francs."

Mr. Peters smiled as if he were presiding at a Sunday School treat and Latimer had asked for a second currant bun. "That, Mr. Latimer, is part of another story."

"What story?"

"The story of what happened to Dimitrios after he disappeared from view."

"Well, what *did* happen to him?" Latimer demanded testily.

Without replying, Mr. Peters picked up the photograph that lay on the table and handed it to him again.

Latimer looked at it and frowned. "Yes, I've seen this. It's Dimitrios all right. What about it?"

Mr. Peters smiled very sweetly and gently. "That, Mr. Latimer, is a photograph of Manus Visser."

"What on earth do you mean?"

"I told you that Visser had other ideas about using the knowledge he had been clever enough to acquire about Dimitrios. What you saw on the mortuary table in Istanbul, Mr. Latimer, was Visser after he had tried to put those ideas into practice."

"But it was Dimitrios. I saw . . ."

"You saw the body of Visser, Mr. Latimer, after Dimitrios had killed him. Dimitrios himself, I am glad to say, is alive and in good health."

Twelve

MONSIEUR C.K.

LATIMER STARED. HIS jaw had dropped and he knew that he looked ridiculous and that there was nothing to be done about the fact. Dimitrios was alive. It did not even occur to him to question the statement seriously. He knew instinctively that it was true. It was as if a doctor had warned him that he was suffering from a dangerous disease of the symptoms of which he had been only vaguely aware. He was surprised beyond words, resentful, curious and a little frightened; while his mind began to work feverishly to meet and deal with a new and strange set of conditions. He shut his mouth, then opened it again to say, feebly: "I can't believe it."

Mr. Peters was clearly gratified by the effect of his announcement.

"I scarcely hoped," he said, "that you would have had no suspicions of the truth. Grodek, of course, understood. He had been puzzled by certain questions I asked him some time ago. When you came he was even more curious. That was why he wanted to know so much. But as soon as you told him that you had seen the body in Istanbul, he understood. He saw at once that the one thing that rendered you unique from my point of view was the fact of your having seen the face of the man buried as Dimitrios. It was obvious. Not to you, perhaps. I suppose that when one sees a perfect stranger on a mortuary slab and a policeman tells one that his name is Dimitrios Makropoulos, one assumes, if one has your respect for the police, that one has the truth of the matter. I *knew* that it was not Dimitrios you saw. But—I could not prove it. You, on the other hand, can. *You* can identify Manus Visser." He paused significantly and then, as Latimer made no comment, added: "How did they identify him as Dimitrios?"

"There was a French *carte d'identité*, issued in Lyons a year ago to Dimitrios Makropoulos, sewn inside the lining of his coat." Latimer spoke mechanically. He was thinking of Grodek's toast to the English detective story and of Grodek's inability to stop himself laughing at his own joke. Heavens! what a fool the man must have thought him!

"A French *carte d'identité*!" echoed Mr. Peters. "That I find amusing. Very amusing."

"It had been pronounced genuine by the French authorities and it had a photograph in it."

Mr. Peters smiled tolerantly. "I could get you a dozen genuine French *cartes d'identité*, Mr. Latimer, each in the name of Dimitrios Makropoulos and each with a different photograph. Look!" He drew a green *permis de séjour* from his pocket, opened it and, with his fingers over the space taken up by the identifying particulars, displayed the photograph in it. "Does that look very much like me, Mr. Latimer?"

Latimer shook his head.

"And yet," declared Mr. Peters, "it *is* a genuine photograph of me taken three years ago. I made no effort to deceive. It is simply that I am not *photogénique*, that is all. Very few men are. The camera is a consistent liar. Dimitrios could have used photographs of anyone with the same type of face as Visser. That photograph I showed you a few moments ago is of someone like Visser."

"If Dimitrios is still alive, where is he?"

"Here in Paris," Mr. Peters leaned forward and patted Latimer's knee. "You have been very reasonable, Mr. Latimer," he said kindly. "I shall tell you everything."

"It's very good of you," said Latimer bitterly.

"No, no! You have a *right* to know," said Mr. Peters warmly. He pursed his lips with the air of one who knows justice when he sees it. "I shall tell you everything," he said again and lit another cheroot.

"As you may imagine," he went on, "we were all very angry with Dimitrios. Some of us threatened revenge. But, Mr. Latimer, I have never been one to beat my head against a wall. Dimitrios had disappeared and there was no way of finding him. The indignities of prison life a memory, I purged my heart of malice and went abroad to regain my sense of proportion. I became a wanderer, Mr. Latimer. A little business here, a little business there, travel and meditation—that was my life. Two years ago I met Visser in Rome.

"I had not, of course, seen him for five years. Poor fellow! he had had a bad time. A few months after his release from prison he was pressed for money and forged a cheque. They sent him back to prison for three years and then, when he came out, deported him. He was almost penniless and he could not work in France where he knew useful people. I could not blame him for feeling bitter.

"He asked me to lend him money. We had met in a café and he told me that he had to go to Zürich to buy a new passport but that he had no money. His Dutch passport was useless because it was in his real name. I would have liked to have helped him; for, although I had never liked him very much, I felt sorry for him; but I decided to refuse.

"At my refusal he became angry and accused me of not trusting him to pay a debt of honour, which was a foolish way for him to talk. Then he pleaded with me. He could prove, he said, that he would be able to repay the money and began to tell me some interesting things.

"I have said that Visser had known a little more about Dimitrios than the rest of us. That was true. He had taken a lot of trouble finding it out. It was just after that evening when he had pulled out a pistol to threaten Dimitrios and Dimitrios had turned his back upon him. Nobody had treated him like that before and he wished to know more about the man who had humiliated him: that, at least, is what I believe. He himself said that he had suspected that Dimitrios would betray us; but that, I knew, was nonsense. Whatever his reason, however, he decided to follow Dimitrios when he left the Impasse.

"The first night that he tried he was unsuccessful. There was a large closed car waiting at the entrance to the Impasse and Dimitrios was driven off in it before Visser could find a taxi in which to follow. The second night he had a hired car ready. He did not come to the meeting but waited for Dimitrios in the Rue de Rennes. When the closed car appeared, Visser drove off after it. Dimitrios stopped outside a big apartment house in the Avenue de Wagram and went inside while the big car drove away. Visser noted the address and about a week later, at a time when he knew that Dimitrios would be here in this room, he called at the apartment house and asked for Monsieur Makropoulos. Naturally, the concierge knew of no one of that name but Visser gave him money and described Dimitrios and found that he had an apartment there in the name of Rougemont.

"Now Visser, for all his conceit, was no fool. He knew that Dimitrios would have foreseen that he might be followed and guessed that the Rougemont apartment was not his only place. Accordingly he set himself to watch Monsieur Rougemont's comings and goings. It was not long before he discovered that there was another way out of the apartment house at the rear and that Dimitrios used to leave that way.

"One night when Dimitrios left by the back entrance Visser followed him. He did not have far to go. He found that Dimitrios lived in a big house just off the Avenue Hoche. It belonged, he found, to a titled and very *chic* woman. I shall call her Madame la Comtesse. Later Visser saw Dimitrios leave with her for the opera. Dimitrios was *en grande tenue* and they had a large Hispano to take them there.

"At that point Visser lost interest. He knew where Dimitrios lived. No doubt he felt that he had in some way obtained his revenge by discovering that much.

He must, too, have been tired of waiting about in the streets. His curiosity was satisfied. What he had discovered was, after all, very much what he might have expected to discover. Dimitrios was a man with a large income. He was spending it in the same way as other men with large incomes.

"They told me that, when Visser was arrested in Paris, he said very little about Dimitrios. Yet he must have had ugly thoughts, for he was by nature a violent man and very conceited. It would have been useless, in any case, for him to have tried to have Dimitrios arrested, for he could only have sent them to the apartment in the Avenue de Wagram and the house of Madame la Comtesse off the Avenue Hoche and he knew that Dimitrios would have gone away. He had, as I said, other ideas about his knowledge.

"I think that, to begin with, he had intended to kill Dimitrios when he found him; but as he began to get short of money his hatred of Dimitrios became more reasonable. He probably remembered the Hispano and the luxury of the house of Madame la Comtesse. She would perhaps be worried to hear that her friend made his money by selling heroin and Dimitrios might be ready to pay good money to save her that worry. But it was easier to think about Dimitrios and his money than it was to find them. For several months after he was released from prison early in nineteen thirty-two, Visser looked for Dimitrios. The apartment in the Avenue de Wagram was no longer occupied. The house of Madame la Comtesse was shut up and the concierge said that she was in Biarritz. Visser went to Biarritz and found that she was staying with friends. Dimitrios was not with her. Visser returned to Paris. Then he had what I think was quite a good idea. He himself was pleased with it. Unfortunately for him, it came a little too late. He remembered one day that Dimitrios had been a drug addict, and it occurred to him that Dimitrios might have done what many other wealthy addicts do when their addiction reaches an advanced stage. He might have entered a clinic to be cured.

"There are five private clinics near Paris which specialise in such cures. On the pretext of making inquiries as to terms on behalf of an imaginary brother, Visser went to each one in turn, saying that he had been recommended by friends of Monsieur Rougemont. At the fourth his idea was proved to be good. The doctor in charge asked after the health of Monsieur Rougemont.

"I think that Visser derived a certain vulgar satisfaction from the thought of Dimitrios being cured of a heroin addiction. The cure is terrible, you know. The doctors go on giving the patient drugs, but gradually reduce the quantity. For him the torture is almost unbearable. He yawns and sweats and shivers for days, but he does not sleep and he cannot eat. He longs for death and babbles of suicide; but he has not the strength left to commit it. He shrieks and screams for his drug and it is withheld. He . . . But I must not bore you with horrors,

Mr. Latimer. The cure lasts three months and costs five thousand francs a week. When it is over the patient may forget the torture and start taking drugs again. Or he may be wiser and forget Paradise. Dimitrios, it seems, was wise.

"He had left the clinic four months before Visser visited it; and so Visser had to think of another good idea. He *did* think of it, but it involved going to Biarritz again and he had no money. He forged a cheque, cashed it and set off again. He reasoned that as Dimitrios and Madame la Comtesse had been friends, she would probably know his present whereabouts. But he could not simply go to her and ask for his address. Even if he could have invented a pretext for doing so, he did not know under what name Dimitrios was known to her. There were difficulties, you see. But he found a way to overcome them. For several days he watched the villa where she was staying. Then, when he had found out enough about it, he broke into her room one afternoon, when the house was empty except for two drowsy servants, and looked through her baggage. He was looking for letters.

"Dimitrios had never liked written records in our business, and he never corresponded with any of us. But Visser had remembered that on one occasion Dimitrios had scribbled an address for Werner on a piece of paper. I remembered the occasion myself. The writing had been curious: quite uneducated, with clumsy, badly formed letters and many flourishes. It was this writing that Visser was looking for. He found it. There were nine letters in the writing. All were from an expensive hotel in Rome. I beg your pardon, Mr. Latimer. You said something?"

"I can tell you what he was doing in Rome. He was organising the assassination of a Yugoslav politician."

Mr. Peters did not seem impressed. "Very likely," he said indifferently; "he would not be where he is to-day without that special organising ability of his. Where was I? Ah, yes! the letters.

"All were from Rome and all were signed with initials which I shall tell you were 'C. K.' The letters themselves were not what Visser had expected. They were very formal and stilted and brief. Most of them said no more than that the writer was in good health, that business was interesting and that he hoped to see his dear friend soon. No *tu-toi*, you know. But in one he said that he had met a relation by marriage of the Italian royal family and in another that he had been presented to a Rumanian diplomat with a title. He was very pleased with these encounters, it seems. It was all very *snob*, and Visser felt that Dimitrios would certainly wish to buy his friendship. He noted the name of the hotel and, leaving everything as he found it, went back to Paris *en route* for Rome. He arrived in Paris the following morning. The police were waiting for him. He was not, I should think, a very clever forger.

"But you may imagine the poor fellow's feelings. During the three interminable years that followed he thought of nothing but Dimitrios; of how near he had been to him and how far he was now. He seemed, for some strange reason, to regard Dimitrios as the one responsible for his being in prison again. The idea served to feed his hatred of him and strengthen his resolve to make him pay. He was, I think, a little mad. As soon as he was free he got a little money in Holland and went to Rome. He was over three years behind Dimitrios, but he was determined to catch up with him. He went to the hotel and, posing as a Dutch private detective, asked to be permitted to see the records of those who had stayed there three years before. The *affiches* had, of course, gone to the police, but they had the bills for the period in question and he had the initials. He was able to discover the name which Dimitrios had used. Dimitrios had also left a forwarding address. It was a poste restante in Paris.

"Visser was now in a new difficulty. He knew the name; but that was useless unless he could get into France to trace the owner of it. It was no use his writing his demands for money. Dimitrios would not go on calling for letters for three years. And yet he could not enter France without being turned at the frontier or risking another term of imprisonment. He had somehow to get a new name and a new passport, and he had no money with which to do so.

"I lent him three thousand francs; and I will confess to you, Mr. Latimer, that I felt myself to be truly stupid. Yet I was sorry for him. He was not the Visser I had known in Paris. Prison had broken him. Once his passions had been in his eyes, but now they were in his mouth and cheeks. One felt he was getting old. I gave him the money out of pity and to get rid of him. I did not believe his story. I never expected to hear from him again. You may, therefore, imagine my astonishment when, a year ago, I received here a letter from him enclosing a *mandat* for the three thousand francs.

"The letter was very short. It said: 'I have found him as I said I would. Here, with my profound thanks, is the money you lent me. It is worth three thousand francs to surprise you.' That was all. He did not sign it. He gave no address. The *mandat* had been bought in Nice and posted there.

"That letter made me think, Mr. Latimer. Visser had recovered his conceit. He could afford to indulge it to the extent of three thousand francs. That meant that he had a great deal more money. Conceited persons dream of such gestures, but they very rarely make them. Dimitrios must have paid; and since he was not a fool he must have had a very good reason for paying.

"I was idle at the time, Mr. Latimer; idle and a little restless. It might be interesting, I thought, to find Dimitrios for myself and share in Visser's good fortune. It was not greed that prompted me, Mr. Latimer; I should not like you to think that. I was *interested*. Besides, I felt that Dimitrios owed me something for the discomforts and indignities I had experienced because of him. For two days I played with the idea. Then, on the third day I made up my mind. I set out for Rome.

"As you may imagine, Mr. Latimer, I had a difficult time and many disappointments. I had the initials, which Visser, in his eagerness to convince me, had revealed, but the only thing I knew about the hotel was that it was expensive. There are, unfortunately, a great many expensive hotels in Rome. I began to investigate them one after the other; but when, at the fifth hotel, they refused, for some reason, to let me see the bills for nineteen thirty-two, I abandoned the attempt. Instead, I went to an Italian friend of mine in one of the Ministries. He was able to use his influence on my behalf and, after a lot of *chi-chi* and expense, I was permitted to inspect the Ministry of Interior archives for nineteen thirty-two. I found out the name Dimitrios was using, and I also found out what Visser had not found out—that Dimitrios had taken the course, which I myself took in nineteen thirty-two, of purchasing the citizenship of a certain South American republic which is sympathetic in such matters if one's pocket-book is fat enough. Dimitrios and I had become fellow citizens.

"I must confess, Mr. Latimer, that I went back to Paris with hope in my heart. I was to be bitterly disappointed. Our consul was not helpful. He said that he had never heard of Señor C. K. And yet another disappointment awaited me. The house of Madame la Comtesse off the Avenue Hoche had been empty for two years.

"You would think, would you not, that it would be easy to find out where a *chic* and wealthy woman was? It was most difficult. The *Bottin* gave nothing. Apparently she had no house in Paris. I was, I will confess, about to abandon the search when I found a way out of my difficulty. I reflected that a fashionable woman like Madame la Comtesse would be certain to have gone somewhere for the winter sports season that was just over. Accordingly, I commissioned Hachettes to purchase for me a copy of every French, Swiss, German and Italian winter sports and social magazine which had been published during the previous three months.

"It was a desperate idea, but it yielded results. You have no idea how many such magazines there are, Mr. Latimer. It took me a little over a week to go through them all carefully, and I can assure you that by the middle of that week I was very nearly a social-democrat. By the end of it, however, I had recovered my sense of humour. If repetition makes nonsense of words it makes even more fantastic nonsense of smiling faces, even if their owners are rich. Besides, I had found what I wanted. In one of the German magazines for February there was a small paragraph which said that Madame la Comtesse was at St. Anton for the winter sports. In a French magazine there was a *couturier's* picture of her in skating clothes. I went to St. Anton. There are not many hotels there, and I soon found that Monsieur C. K. had been in St. Anton at the same time. He had given an address in Cannes.

"At Cannes I found that Monsieur C. K. had a villa on the Estoril, but that he himself was abroad on business at the moment. I was not discontented. Dimitrios would return to his villa sooner or later. Meanwhile I set myself to discover something about Monsieur C. K.

"I have always said, Mr. Latimer, that the art of being successful in this life of ours is the art of knowing the people who will be useful to one. I have in my time met and done business with many important people—people, you know, who are informed of what goes on and why—and I have always taken care to be helpful to them. It has paid me.

"So, where Visser might have had to prowl about in the darkness in search of his information, I was able to get mine from a friend. It proved easier than I had expected to do so, for I found that, in certain circles, Dimitrios, with the name of Monsieur C. K., had become quite important. In fact, when I learned just how important he had become, I was pleasantly surprised. I began to realise that Visser must be living on the money he got from Dimitrios. Yet what did Visser know? Only that Dimitrios had dealt illegally in drugs; a fact that it would be difficult for him to prove. He knew nothing about the dealings in women. I did. There must, I reasoned, be other things, too, which Dimitrios would prefer not to be generally known. If, before I approached Dimitrios, I could find out some of those things, my financial position would be very strong indeed. I decided to see some more of my friends.

"Two of them were able to help me. Grodek was one. A Rumanian friend of mine was another. You know of Grodek's acquaintance with Dimitrios when he called himself Talat. The Rumanian friend told me that in nineteen twenty-five Dimitrios had had questionable financial dealings with Codreanu, the lamented leader of the Rumanian Iron Guard, and that he was known to, but not wanted by, the Bulgarian police.

"Now there was nothing criminal about any of those affairs. Indeed, Grodek's information depressed me somewhat. It was unlikely that the Yugoslav Government would apply for extradition after so many years; while, as for the French, they might hold that, as Dimitrios had rendered some sort of service to the Republic in nineteen twenty-six, he was entitled to a little tolerance in the matter of dealings in drugs and women. I decided to see what I could find out in Greece. A week after I arrived in Athens and while I was still trying unsuccessfully to trace in the official records a reference to my particular Dimitrios, I read in an Athens paper of the discovery, by the Istanbul police, of the body of a Greek from Smyrna with the name of Dimitrios Makropoulos."

He raised his eyes to Latimer's. "Do you begin to see, Mr. Latimer, why I found your interest in Dimitrios a little difficult to explain?" And then, as Latimer nodded: "I, too, of course, inspected the Relief Commission dossier; but I followed you to Sofia instead of going to Smyrna. I wonder if you would care to tell me now what you found out from the police records there?"

"Dimitrios was suspected of murdering a moneylender named Sholem in Smyrna in nineteen twenty-two. He escaped to Greece. Two years later, he was involved in an attempt to assassinate Kemal. He escaped again, but the Turks used the murder as a pretext for issuing a warrant for his arrest."

"A murder in Smyrna! That makes it even clearer." Mr. Peters smiled. "A wonderful man, Dimitrios, don't you think? So economical."

"What do you mean?"

"Let me finish my story and you will see. As soon as I read that newspaper paragraph, I sent a telegram to a friend in Paris asking him to let me know the whereabouts of Monsieur C. K. He replied two days later, saying that Monsieur C. K. had just returned to Cannes after an Ægean cruise with a party of friends in a Greek diesel yacht which he had chartered two months previously.

"Do you see now what had happened, Mr. Latimer? You tell me that the *carte d'identité* was a year old when they found it on the body. That means that it was obtained a few weeks before Visser sent me that three thousand francs. You see, from the moment Visser found Dimitrios, he was doomed. Dimitrios must have made up his mind at once to kill him. You can see why. Visser was dangerous. He was such a conceited fellow. He might have blurted out indiscretions at any time when he had been drinking and wanted to boast. He would have to be killed.

"Yet, see how clever Dimitrios was! He could have killed Visser at once, no doubt. But he did not do so. His economical mind had evolved a better plan. If it were necessary to kill Visser, could he not dispose of the body in some advantageous way? Why not use it to safeguard himself against the consequences of that old indiscretion in Smyrna? It was unlikely that there would be consequences, but here was his chance to make certain of the fact. The body of the villain, Dimitrios Makropoulos, would be delivered to the Turkish police. Dimitrios, the murderer, would be dead and Monsieur C. K. would be left alive to cultivate his garden. But he would require a certain amount of co-operation from Visser himself. The man would have to be lulled into feeling secure. So, Dimitrios smiled and paid up and set about getting the identity card which was to go with Visser's dead body. Nine months later, in June, he invited his good friend Visser to join him on a yachting trip."

"Yes, but how could he have committed the murder on the yachting trip? What about the crew? What about the other passengers?"

Mr. Peters looked knowing. "Let me tell you, Mr. Latimer, what I should have done if I had been Dimitrios. I should have begun by chartering a Greek yacht. There would be a reason for its being a Greek yacht: its home port would be the Piræus.

"I should have arranged for my friends, including Visser, to join the yacht at Naples. Then I should have taken them on their cruise and returned a month later to Naples, where I should have announced that the cruise would end. They would disembark; but I should stay on board saying that I was returning with the yacht to the Piræus. Then I should take Visser aside privately and tell him that I had some very secret business to transact in Istanbul, that I proposed to go there on the yacht and that I should be glad of his company. I should ask him not to tell the disembarking passengers who might be angry because I had not asked them and to return to the yacht when they had gone. To poor, conceited Visser, the invitation would be irresistible.

"To the captain I should say that Visser and I would leave the yacht at Istanbul and return overland, after we had transacted our business, to Paris. He would sail the yacht back to the Piræus. At Istanbul Visser and I would go ashore together. I should have left word with the crew that we would send for our baggage when we had decided where we should be staying for the night. Then, I should have taken him to a *boîte* I know of in a street off the Grande Rue de Pera; and later that night I should find myself poorer by ten thousand French francs, while Visser would be at the bottom of the Bosphorus at a place where the current would carry him, when he was rotten enough to float, out to Seraglio Point. Then I should take a room in a hotel in the name and with the passport of Visser, and send a porter to the yacht with a note authorising him to collect both Visser's luggage and mine. As Visser, I would leave the hotel in the morning for the station. His baggage, which I should have searched overnight to see that there was nothing in it to identify it as Visser's, I would deposit in the *consigne*. Then I would take the train for Paris. If inquiries about Visser are ever made in Istanbul, he left by train for Paris. But who is going to inquire? My friends believe he left the yacht at Naples. The captain and crew of the yacht are not interested. Visser has a false passport, he is a criminal: such a type has an obvious reason for disappearing of his own free will. Finish!"

Mr. Peters spread out his hands. "That is how it would occur to me to deal with such a situation. Perhaps Dimitrios managed it a little differently; but that is what might well have happened. There is one thing, however, that I am quite sure he did. You remember telling me that some months before you arrived in Smyrna, someone examined the same police records that you examined there? That must have been Dimitrios. He was always very cautious.

No doubt he was anxious to find out how much they knew about his appearance, before he left Visser for them to find."

"But that man I told you about looked like a Frenchman."

Mr. Peters smiled reproachfully. "Then you were *not* quite frank with me in Sofia, Mr. Latimer. You *did* inquire about this mysterious man." He shrugged. "Dimitrios does look like a Frenchman now. His clothes are French."

"You've seen him recently?"

"Yesterday. Though he did not see me."

"You know exactly where he is in Paris, then?"

"Exactly. As soon as I discovered his new business I knew where to find him here."

"And, now that you have found him, what next?"

Mr. Peters frowned. "Come now, Mr. Latimer. I am sure that you are not quite as obtuse as all that. You know and can prove that the man buried in Istanbul is not Dimitrios. If necessary you could identify Visser's photographs on the police files. I, on the other hand, know what Dimitrios is calling himself now and where to find him. Our joint silence would be worth a lot of money to Dimitrios. With Visser's fate in mind, we shall know, too, how to deal with the matter. We shall demand a million francs. Dimitrios will pay us, believing that we shall come back for more. We shall not be as foolish as to endanger our lives in that way. We shall rest content with half a million each—nearly three thousand pounds sterling, Mr. Latimer—and quietly disappear."

"I see. Blackmail on a cash basis. No credit. But why bring me into the business? The Turkish police could identify Visser without my help."

"How? They identified him as Dimitrios and buried him. They have seen perhaps a dozen or more dead bodies since then. Weeks have gone by. Are they going to remember Visser's face well enough to justify their beginning expensive extradition proceedings against a rich foreigner because of their fourteen years old suspicions about a sixteen years old murder? My dear Mr. Latimer! Dimitrios would laugh at me. He would do with me as he did with Visser: give me a few thousand francs here and there to keep me from making myself a nuisance with the French police and to keep me quiet until, for safety's sake, I could be killed. But you have seen Visser's body and identified it. You have seen the police records in Smyrna. He knows nothing about you. He will have to pay or run an unknown risk. He is too cautious for that. Listen. In the first place, it is essential that Dimitrios does not discover our identities. He will know me, of course, but he will not know my present name. In your case, we shall invent a name. Mr. Smith, perhaps, as you are English. I shall approach Dimitrios in the name of Petersen and we shall arrange to meet him outside Paris at a place of our own choosing to receive our million francs. That is the last that he will see of either of us."

Latimer laughed but not very heartily. "And do you really suppose that I shall agree to this plan of yours?"

"If, Mr. Latimer, your trained mind can evolve a more ingenious plan, I shall be only too happy to . . ."

"My trained mind, Mr. Peters, is concerned with wondering how best to convey this information which you have given me to the police."

Mr. Peters' smile became thin. "The police? What information, Mr. Latimer?" he inquired softly.

"Why, the information that . . ." Latimer began impatiently and then stopped, frowning.

"Quite so," nodded Mr. Peters approvingly. "You have no real information to convey. If you go to the Turkish police they will no doubt send to the French police for Visser's photographs and record your identification. What then? Dimitrios will be found to be alive. That is all. I have not, you may remember, told you the name that Dimitrios uses now or even his initials. It would be impossible for you to trace him from Rome as Visser and I traced him. Nor do you know the name of Madame la Comtesse. As for the French police, I do not think that they would be interested either in the fate of a deported Dutch criminal or excited by the knowledge that somewhere in France there is a Greek using a false name who killed a man in Smyrna in nineteen twenty-two. You see, Mr. Latimer, you cannot act without me. If, of course, Dimitrios should prove difficult, then it might be desirable to take the police into our confidence. But I do not think that Dimitrios will be difficult. He is very intelligent. In any case, Mr. Latimer, why throw away three thousand pounds?"

Latimer considered him for a moment. Then he said: "Has it occurred to you that I might not want that particular three thousand pounds? I think, my friend, that prolonged association with criminals has made it difficult for you to follow some trains of thought."

"This moral rectitude . . ." began Mr. Peters wearily. Then he seemed to change his mind. He cleared his throat. "If you wished," he said with the calculated bonhommie of one who reasons with a drunken friend, "we could inform the police *after* we had secured the money. Even if Dimitrios were able to prove that he had paid money to us, he could not, however unpleasant he wished to be, tell the police our names or how to find us. In fact, I think that that would be a very wise move on our part, Mr. Latimer. We should then be quite sure that Dimitrios was no longer dangerous. We could supply the police anonymously with a dossier as Dimitrios did in nineteen thirty-one. The retribution would be just." Then his face fell. "Ah, no. It is impossible. I am afraid that the suspicions of your Turkish friends might fall upon you, Mr. Latimer. We could not risk that, could we!"

But Latimer was scarcely listening. He knew that what he had made up his mind to say was foolish and he was trying to justify its folly. Peters was right. There was nothing he could do to bring Dimitrios to justice. He was left with a choice. Either he could go back to Athens and leave Peters to make the best deal he could with Dimitrios or he could stay in Paris to see the last act of the grotesque comedy in which he now found himself playing a part. The first alternative being unthinkable, he was committed to the second. He really had no choice. To gain time he had taken and lighted a cigarette. Now he looked up from it.

"All right," he said slowly; "I'll do what you want. But there are conditions."

"Conditions?" Mr. Peters' lips tightened. "I think that a half share is more than generous, Mr. Latimer. Why my trouble and expenses alone . . . !"

"Just a moment. I was saying, Mr. Peters, that there are conditions. The first should be very easy for you to fulfil. It is simply that you yourself retain all the money that you are able to squeeze from Dimitrios. The second . . ." he went on and then paused. He had the momentary pleasure of seeing Mr. Peters disconcerted. Then, he saw the watery eyes narrow quite appreciably. Mr. Peters' words as they issued from his mouth were charged with suspicion.

"I don't think I quite understand, Mr. Latimer. If this is a clumsy trick . . ."

"Oh no. There is no trick, clumsy or otherwise, Mr. Peters. 'Moral rectitude' was your phrase, wasn't it? It will do. I am prepared, you see, to assist in blackmailing a person when that person is Dimitrios; but I am not prepared to share in the profits. So much the better for you, of course."

Mr. Peters nodded thoughtfully. "Yes, I see that you might think like that. So much the better for me, as you say. But what is the other condition?"

"Equally inoffensive. You have referred mysteriously to Dimitrios's having become a person of importance. I make my helping you get your million francs conditional on your telling me exactly *what* he has become."

Mr. Peters thought for a moment, then shrugged. "Very well. I see no reason why I should not tell you. It so happens that the knowledge cannot possibly be of any help to you in discovering his present identity. The Eurasian Credit Trust is registered in Monaco and the details of its registration are not therefore open to inspection. Dimitrios is a member of the Board of Directors."

Thirteen

RENDEZVOUS

IT WAS TWO o'clock in the morning when Latimer left the Impasse des Huit Anges and began to walk slowly in the direction of the Quai Voltaire.

At the corner of the Boulevard St. Germain there was a café open. He went inside and was served with a glass of beer by the bored mute behind the zinc. He drank some of his beer and gazed vacantly about him like a person who has strayed into a museum for shelter from the rain. He wished that he had gone to bed after all. He paid for his beer and took a taxi back to his hotel. He was tired, of course: that was the trouble.

In his room, Latimer sat down by the window and gazed out across the black river to the lights which it reflected and the faint glow in the sky beyond the Louvre. His mind was haunted by the past, by the confession of Dhris, the negro, and by the memories of Irana Preveza, by the tragedy of Bulić and by a tale of white crystals travelling west to Paris, bringing money to the fig-packer of Izmir. Three human beings had died horribly and countless others had lived horribly that Dimitrios might take his ease. If there *were* such a thing as Evil, then this man. . . .

But it was useless to try to explain him in terms of Good and Evil. They were no more than baroque abstractions. Good Business and Bad Business were the elements of the new theology. Dimitrios was not evil. He was logical and consistent; as logical and consistent in the European jungle as the poison gas called Lewisite and the shattered bodies of children killed in the bombardment of an open town. The logic of Michael Angelo's *David*, Beethoven's quartets and Einstein's physics had been replaced by that of the *Stock Exchange Year Book* and Hitler's *Mein Kampf*.

Yet, Latimer reflected, although you could not stop people buying and selling Lewisite, although you could do no more than "deplore" a number of slaughtered children, there were in existence means of preventing one particular aspect of the principle of expediency from doing too much damage.

Most international criminals were beyond the reach of man-made laws; but Dimitrios happened to be within reach of one law. He had committed at least two murders and had therefore broken the law as surely as if he had been starving and had stolen a loaf of bread.

It was easy enough, however, to say that he was within reach of the Law: it was not as easy to see how the Law was to be informed of the fact. As Mr. Peters had so carefully pointed out, he, Latimer, had no information to give the police. But was that an altogether true picture of the situation? He *had* some information. He knew that Dimitrios was alive and that he was a director of the Eurasian Credit Trust, that he knew a French Countess who had had a house off the Avenue Hoche and that he or she had had an Hispana Suiza car, that both of them had been in St. Anton that year for the winter sports and that he had chartered a Greek yacht in June, that he had a villa on the Estoril and that he was now the citizen of a South American republic. Surely, then, it must be possible to find the person with those particular attributes. Even if the names of the directors of the Eurasian Credit Trust were unobtainable, it ought to be possible to get the names of the men who had chartered Greek yachts in June, of the wealthy South Americans with villas on the Estoril and of the South American visitors to St. Anton in February. If you could get those lists, all you would have to do would be to see which names (if there should be more than one) were common to the three.

But how did you get the lists? Besides, even if you could persuade the Turkish police to exhume Visser and then apply officially for all that information, what sort of proof would you have that the man you had concluded to be Dimitrios, was in fact, Dimitrios? And supposing that you could convince Colonel Haki of the truth, would he have enough evidence to justify the French extraditing a director of the powerful Eurasian Credit Trust? If it had taken twelve years to secure the acquittal of Dreyfus, it could take at least as many years to secure the conviction of Dimitrios.

He undressed wearily and got into bed.

It looked as if he were committed to Mr. Peters' blackmailing scheme. Lying in a comfortable bed with his eyes closed, he found the fact that in a few days' time he would be, technically speaking, one of the worst sorts of criminals no more than odd. Yet, at the back of his mind there was a certain discomfort. When the reason for it dawned on him, he was mildly shocked. The simple truth was that he was feeling afraid of Dimitrios. Dimitrios was a dangerous man; more dangerous by far than he had been in Smyrna and Athens and Sofia because he now had more to lose. Visser had blackmailed him and died. Now, he, Latimer, was going to blackmail him. Dimitrios had never hesitated to kill a man if he had deemed it necessary to do so; and, if he had deemed it necessary in the case of a man who threatened to expose him as a drug pedlar, would he hesitate in the case of two men who threatened to expose him as a murderer?

It was most important to see that, hesitation or no hesitation, he was not given the opportunity. Mr. Peters had proposed the taking of elaborate precautions.

The first contact with Dimitrios was to be established by letter. Latimer had seen a draft of the letter and had found it gratifyingly similar in tone to a letter he himself had written for a blackmailer in one of his books. It began with sinister cordiality, by trusting that, after all these years, Monsieur C. K. had not forgotten the writer and the pleasant and profitable times they had spent together, went on to say how pleasing it was to hear that he was so successful and hoped sincerely that he would be able to meet the writer who would be at the So-and-so Hotel at nine o'clock on the Thursday evening of that week. The writer concluded with an expression of his *"plus sincère amitié"* and a significant little postscript to the effect that he had chanced to meet someone who had known their mutual friend Visser quite well, that this person was most anxious to meet Monsieur K. and that it would be so unfortunate if Monsieur K. could not arrange to keep the appointment on Thursday evening.

Dimitrios would receive that letter on the Thursday morning. At half past eight on the Thursday evening, "Mr. Petersen" and "Mr. Smith" would arrive at the hotel chosen for the interview and "Mr. Petersen" would take a room. There they would await the arrival of Dimitrios. When the situation had been explained, Dimitrios would be informed that he would receive instructions as to the payment of the million francs on the following morning and told to go. "Mr. Petersen" and "Mr. Smith" would then leave.

Precautions would now have to be taken to see that they were not followed and identified. Mr. Peters had not specified what sort of precautions but had given assurances that there would be no difficulties.

That same evening, a second letter would be posted to Dimitrios telling him to send a messenger with the million francs, in *mille* notes to a specified point on the road outside the cemetery of Neuilly at eleven o'clock on the Friday night. There would be a hired car waiting for him there with two men in it. The two men would have been recruited for the purpose by Mr. Peters. Their business would be to pick up the messenger and drive along the Quai National in the direction of Suresnes until they were quite sure that they were not being followed and then to make for a point on the Avenue de la Reine near the Porte de St. Cloud where "Mr. Petersen" and "Mr. Smith" would be waiting to receive the money. The two men would then drive the messenger back to Neuilly. The letter would specify that the messenger must be a woman.

Latimer had been puzzled by this last provision. Mr. Peters had justified it by pointing out that if Dimitrios came himself there was just a chance that he might prove too clever for the men in the car and that "Mr. Petersen" and "Mr. Smith" would end up lying in the Avenue de la Reine with bullets in their backs. Descriptions were unreliable and the two men would have no certain means of knowing in the dark if a man presenting himself as the messenger were Dimitrios or not. They could make no such mistake about a woman.

Yes, Latimer reflected, it was absurd to imagine that there could be any danger from Dimitrios. The only thing he had to look forward to was the meeting with this curious man whose path he had stumbled across. It would be strange, after he had heard so much about him, to meet him face to face; strange to see the hand which had packed figs and driven the knife into Sholem's throat, the eyes which Irana Preveza and Wladyslaw Grodek and Mr. Peters had remembered so well. It would be as if a waxwork in a chamber of horrors had come to life.

For a time he stared at the narrow gap between the curtains. It was getting light. Very soon he fell asleep.

He was disturbed towards eleven by a telephone call from Mr. Peters, who said that the letter to Dimitrios had been posted and asked if they could have dinner together "to discuss our plans for to-morrow." Latimer was under the impression that their plans had already been discussed, but he agreed. The afternoon he spent alone at the Vincennes Zoo. The subsequent dinner was tedious. Little was said about their plans, and Latimer concluded that the invitation had been another of Mr. Peters' precautions. He was making sure that his collaborator, who now had no financial interest in the business, had not changed his mind about collaborating.

On the pretext of having a headache, Latimer escaped soon after ten o'clock and went to bed. When he awoke the following morning he actually had a headache and concluded that the carafe burgundy which his host had recommended so warmly at dinner had been even cheaper than it had tasted. As his mind crept slowly back to consciousness he had, too, a feeling that something unpleasant had happened. Then he remembered. Of course! Dimitrios had by now received the first letter.

He sat up in bed to think about it and, after a moment or two, came to the profound conclusion that if it were easy enough to hate and despise blackmailing when one wrote and read about it, the act of blackmailing itself called for rather more moral hardihood, more firmness of purpose, than he, at any rate, possessed. It made no difference to remind oneself that Dimitrios was a criminal. Blackmail was blackmail, just as murder was murder. Macbeth would probably have hesitated at the last minute to kill a criminal Duncan just as much as he hesitated to kill the Duncan whose virtues pleaded like angels. Fortunately, or unfortunately, he, Latimer, had a Lady Macbeth in the person of Mr. Peters. He decided to go out to breakfast.

The day seemed interminable. Mr. Peters had said that he had arrangements to make in connection with the car and the men to drive in it, and that he would meet Latimer at a quarter to eight, after dinner. Latimer spent the morning walking aimlessly in the Bois and, in the afternoon, went to a cinema.

It was toward six o'clock and after he had left the cinema that he began to notice a slight breathless feeling in the region of the solar plexus. It was as if someone had dealt him a light blow there. He concluded that it was Mr. Peters' corrosive burgundy fighting a rearguard action and stopped in one of the cafés on the Champs Elysées for an *infusion*. But the feeling persisted, and he found himself becoming more and more conscious of it. Then, as his gaze rested for a moment on a party of four men and women talking excitedly and laughing over some joke, he realised what was the matter with him. He did not want to meet Mr. Peters. He did not want to go on this blackmailing expedition. He did not want to face a man in whose mind the uppermost thought would be to kill him as quickly and quietly as possible. The trouble was not in his stomach. He had cold feet.

The realisation annoyed him. Why should he be afraid? There was nothing to be afraid of. This man Dimitrios was a clever and dangerous criminal, but he was far from being superhuman. If a man like Peters could . . . but then Peters was used to this sort of thing. He, Latimer, was not. He ought to have gone to the police as soon as he had discovered that Dimitrios was alive and risked being thought a troublesome crank. He should have realised before that, with Mr. Peters' revelations, the whole affair had taken on a completely different complexion, that it was no longer one in which an amateur criminologist (and a fiction writer at that) should meddle. You could not deal with real murderers in this irresponsible fashion. His bargain with Mr. Peters, for example: what would an English judge say to that? He could almost hear the words:

"As for the actions of this man Latimer, he has given an explanation of them which you may find difficult to believe. He is, we have been told, an intelligent man, a scholar who has held responsible posts in universities in this country and written works of scholarship. He is, moreover, a successful author of a type of fiction which, even if it is properly regarded by the average man as no more than the pabulum of adolescent minds, has, at least, the virtue of accepting the proposition that it is the business of right-thinking men and women to assist the police, should the opportunity present itself, in preventing crime and in capturing criminals. If you accept Latimer's explanation,

you must conclude that he deliberately conspired with Peters to defeat the ends of justice and to act as an accessory before the fact of the crime of blackmail for the sole purpose of pursuing researches which he states had no object other than the satisfaction of his curiosity. You may ask yourselves if that would not have been the conduct of a mentally unbalanced child rather than that of an intelligent man. You must also weigh carefully the suggestion of the prosecution that Latimer did in fact share in the proceeds of this blackmailing scheme and that his explanation is no more than an effort to minimise his part in the affair."

No doubt a French judge could make it sound even worse.

It was still too early for dinner. He left the café and walked in the direction of the Opera. In any case, he reflected, it was too late now to do anything. He was committed to helping Mr. Peters. But was it too late? If he went to the police now, this minute, something could surely be done.

He stopped. This minute! There had been an *agent* sauntering along the street through which he had just come. He retraced his steps. Yes, there was the man, leaning against the wall, swinging his baton and talking to someone inside a doorway. Latimer hesitated again, then crossed the road and asked to be directed to the police *Poste*. It was three streets away, he was told. He set off again.

The entrance to the *Poste* was narrow and almost entirely concealed by a group of three *agents* deep in a conversation which they did not interrupt as they made way for him. Inside was an enamelled plate indicating that inquiries should be made on the first floor and pointing to a flight of stairs with a thin iron banister rail on one side and a wall with a long, greasy stain on it on the other. The place smelt strongly of camphor and faintly of excrement. From a room adjacent to the entrance hall came a murmur of voices and the clacking of a typewriter.

His resolution ebbing with every step, he went up the stairs to a room divided into two by a high wooden counter, the outer edges of which had been worn smooth and shiny by the palms of innumerable hands. Behind the counter a man in uniform was peering with the aid of a hand-mirror into the inside of his mouth.

Latimer paused. He had yet to make up his mind how he was going to begin. If he said: "I was going to blackmail a murderer to-night, but I have decided to hand him over to you instead," there was more than a chance that they would think him mad or drunk. In spite of the urgent need for immediate action, he would have to make some show of beginning at the beginning. "I was in Istanbul some weeks ago and was told of a murder committed there in nineteen twenty-two. Quite by chance, I have found that the man who did it is here in Paris and is being blackmailed." Something like that. The uniformed man caught a glimpse of him in the mirror and turned sharply round.

"What do you want?"

"I should like to see Monsieur le Commissaire."

"What for?"

"I have some information to give him."

The man frowned impatiently. "What information? Please be precise."

"It concerns a case of blackmail."

"You are being blackmailed?"

"No. Someone else is. It is a very complicated and serious affair."

"Your *carte d'identité*, please."

"I have no *carte d'identité*. I am a temporary visitor. I entered France four days ago."

"Your passport, then."

"It is at my hotel."

The man stiffened. The frown of irritation left his face. Here was something that he understood and with which long experience had enabled him to deal. He spoke with easy assurance.

"That is very serious, Monsieur. You realise that? Are you English?"

"Yes."

He drew a deep breath. "You must understand, Monsieur, that your papers must always be in your pocket. It is the law. If you saw a street accident and were required as a witness, the *agent* would ask to see your papers before you were permitted to leave the scene of the accident. If you had not got them, he could, if he wished, arrest you. If you were in a *boîte de nuit* and the police entered to inspect papers, you would certainly be arrested if you carried none. It is the law, you understand? I shall have to take the necessary particulars. Give me your name and that of your hotel, please."

Latimer did so. The man noted them down, picked up a telephone and asked for "*Septième*." There was a pause, then he read out Latimer's name and address and asked for confirmation that they were genuine. There was another pause, of a minute or two this time, before he began to nod his head and say: "*Bien, bien.*" Then he listened for a moment, said: "*Oui, c'est ça,*" and put the telephone back on its hook. He returned to Latimer.

"It is in order," he said; "but you must present yourself with your passport at the Commissariat of the Seventh Arrondissement within twenty-four hours. As for this complaint of yours, you can make that at the same time. Please remember," he went on tapping his pencil on the counter for emphasis, "that your passport must always be carried. It is obligatory to do so. You are English, and so nothing more need be made of the affair; but you must report to the Commissariat in your arrondissement, and in future always remember to carry your passport. *Au 'voir, Monsieur.*" He nodded benevolently with an air of knowing his duty to be well done.

Latimer went out in a very bad temper. Officious ass! But the man was right, of course. It had been absurd of him to go into the place without his passport. Complaint, indeed! In a sense he had had a narrow escape. He might have had to tell his story to the man. He might well have been under arrest by now. As it was, he had not told his story and was still a potential blackmailer.

Yet the visit to the police *Poste* had eased his conscience considerably. He did not feel quite as irresponsible as he had felt before. He had made an effort to bring the police into the affair. It had been an abortive effort; but short of collecting his passport from the other side of Paris and starting all over again (and that, he decided comfortably, was out of the question) there was nothing more he could do. He was due to meet Mr. Peters at a quarter to eight in a café in the Boulevard Hausmann. But by the time he had finished a very light dinner the curious feeling had returned to his solar plexus and the two brandies which he had with his coffee were intended to do more than pass the time. It was a pity, he reflected as he went to keep his appointment, that he could not accept even a small share of the million francs. The cost of satisfying his curiosity was proving, in terms of frayed nerves and an uneasy conscience, practically prohibitive.

Mr. Peters arrived ten minutes late with a large, cheaplooking suitcase and the too matter-of-fact air of a surgeon about to perform a difficult operation. He said, "Ah, Mr. Latimer!" and sitting down at the table, ordered a raspberry liqueur.

"Is everything all right?" Latimer felt that the question was a little theatrical, but he really wanted to know the answer to it.

"So far, yes. Naturally, I have had no word from him because I gave no address. We shall see."

"What have you got in the suitcase?"

"Old newspapers. It is better to arrive at a hotel with a suitcase. I do not wish to have to fill up an *affiche* unless I am compelled to do so. I decided finally upon a hotel near to the Ledru-Rollin Metro. Very convenient."

"Why can't we go by taxi?"

"We shall go by taxi. But," added Mr. Peters significantly, "we shall return by the Metro. You will see." His liqueur arrived. He poured it down his throat, shuddered, licked his lips and said that it was time to go.

The hotel chosen by Mr. Peters for the meeting with Dimitrios was in a street just off the Avenue Ledru. It was small and dirty. A man in his shirtsleeves came out of a room marked "Bureau," chewing a mouthful of food.

"I telephoned for a room," said Mr. Peters.

"Monsieur Petersen?"

"Yes."

The man looked them both up and down. "It is a large room. Fifteen francs for one. Twenty francs for two. Service, twelve and a half per cent."

"This gentleman is not staying with me."

The man took a key from a rack just inside the Bureau and, taking Mr. Peters' suitcase, led the way upstairs to a room on the second floor. Mr. Peters looked inside it and nodded.

"Yes, this will do. A friend of mine will call for me here soon. Ask him to come up, please."

The man withdrew. Mr. Peters sat on the bed and looked round approvingly. "Quite nice," he said, "and very cheap."

"Yes, it is."

It was a long, narrow room with an old hair carpet, an iron bedstead, a wardrobe, two bent wood chairs, a small table, a screen and an enamelled iron *bidet*. The carpet was red; but by the washbasin was a threadbare patch, black and shiny with use. The wall-paper depicted a trellis supporting a creeping plant, a number of purple discs and some shapeless pink objects of a vaguely clinical character. The curtains were thick and blue and hung on brass rings.

Mr. Peters looked at his watch. "Twenty-five minutes before he is due. We had better make ourselves comfortable. Would you like the bed?"

"No, thank you. I suppose you will do the talking."

"I think it will be best." Mr. Peters drew his Lüger pistol from his breast pocket, examined it to see that it was loaded and then dropped it into the right-hand pocket of his overcoat.

Latimer watched these preparations in silence. He was now feeling quite sick. He said suddenly: "I don't like this."

"Nor do I," said Mr. Peters soothingly; "but we must take precautions. It is unlikely, I think, that they will be needed. You need have no fears."

Latimer remembered an American gangster picture that he had once seen. "What is to prevent him from walking in here and shooting us both?"

Mr. Peters smiled tolerantly. "Now, now! You must not let your imagination run away with you, Mr. Latimer. Dimitrios would not do that. It would be too noisy and dangerous for him. Remember, the man downstairs will have seen him. Besides, that would not be his way."

"What is his way?"

"Dimitrios is a very cautious man. He thinks very carefully before he acts."

"He has had all day to think carefully."

"Yes, but he does not yet know how much we know, and if anyone else knows what we know. He would have to discover those things. Leave everything to me, Mr. Latimer. I understand Dimitrios."

Latimer was about to point out that Visser had probably had the same idea, and then decided not to do so. He had another, more personal, misgiving to air.

"You said that when Dimitrios paid us the million francs that would be the last he heard of us. Has it occurred to you that he may not be content to let things rest in that way? When he finds that we don't come back for more money he may decide to come after us."

"After Mr. Smith and Mr. Petersen? We should be difficult to find under those names, my dear Mr. Latimer."

"But he knows your face already. He will see mine. He could recognise our faces, whatever we chose to call ourselves."

"But first he would have to find out where we were."

"My photograph has appeared once or twice in newspapers. It may do so again. Or supposing my publisher decided to spread my photograph over the wrapper of a book. Dimitrios might easily happen to see it. There have been stranger coincidences."

Mr. Peters pursed his lips. "I think you exaggerate, but"—he shrugged—"since you feel nervous perhaps you had better keep your face hidden. Do you wear spectacles?"

"For reading."

"Then put them on. Wear your hat, too, and turn up the collar of your coat. You might sit in the corner of the room where it is not so light. In front of the screen. It will blur the outlines of your face. There."

Latimer obeyed. When he was in position, with his collar buttoned across his chin and his hat tilted forward over his eyes, Mr. Peters surveyed him from the door and nodded.

"It will do. I still think it unnecessary; but it will do. After making all these preparations we shall feel very foolish if he does not come."

Latimer, who was feeling very foolish anyway, grunted. "Is there any likelihood of his not coming?"

"Who knows?" Mr. Peters sat on the bed again. "A dozen things might happen to prevent him. He might not, for some reason, have received my letter. He may have left Paris yesterday. But, if he has received the letter, I think that he will come." He looked at his watch again. "Eight forty-five. If he *is* coming, he will soon be here."

They fell silent. Mr. Peters began to trim his nails with a pair of pocket scissors.

Except for the clicking of the scissors and the sound of Mr. Peters' heavy breathing, the silence in the room was complete. To Latimer it seemed almost tangible; a dark grey fluid that oozed from the corners of the room. He began to hear the watch ticking on his wrist. He waited for what seemed an eternity before looking at it. When he did look it was ten minutes to nine. Another eternity. He tried to think of something to say to Mr. Peters to pass the time. He tried counting the complete parallelograms in the pattern of the wall-paper between the wardrobe and the window. Now he thought he could hear Mr. Peters' watch ticking. The muffled sound of someone moving a chair and walking about in the room overhead seemed to intensify the silence. Four minutes to nine.

Then, so suddenly that the sound seemed as loud as a pistol shot, one of the stairs outside the door creaked.

Mr. Peters stopped trimming his nails and, dropping the scissors on the bed, put his right hand in his overcoat pocket.

There was a pause. His heart beating painfully, Latimer gazed rigidly at the door. There was a soft knock.

Mr. Peters stood up and, with his hand still in his pocket, went to the door and opened it.

Latimer saw him stare for a moment into the semi-darkness of the landing and then stand back.

Dimitrios walked into the room.

Fourteen

~~~~~~~~~~~~~~~~~~~~~~~~~~~

THE MASK OF DIMITRIOS

A MAN'S FEATURES, the bone structure and the tissue which covers it, are the product of a biological process; but his face he creates for himself. It is a statement of his habitual emotional attitude; the attitude which his desires need for their fulfilment and which his fears demand for their protection from prying eyes. He wears it like a devil mask; a device to evoke in others the emotions complementary to his own. If he is afraid, then he must be feared; if he desires, then he must be desired. It is a screen to hide his mind's nakedness. Only a few men, painters, have been able to see the mind through the face. Other men in their judgments reach out for the evidence of word and deed that will explain the mask before their eyes. Yet, though they understand instinctively that the mask cannot be the man behind it, they are generally shocked by a demonstration of the fact. The duplicity of others must always be shocking when one is unconscious of one's own.

So, when at last Latimer saw Dimitrios and tried to read in the face of the man staring across the room at him the evil which he felt should be there, it was of that sense of shock which he was conscious. Hat in hand, in his dark, neat French clothes, with his slim, erect figure and sleek grey hair, Dimitrios was a picture of distinguished respectability.

His distinction was that of a relatively unimportant guest at a large diplomatic reception. He gave the impression of being slightly taller than the one hundred and eighty-two centimetres with which the Bulgarian police had credited him. His skin had the creamy pallor which succeeds in middle age a youthful sallowness. With his high cheekbones, thin nose and beak-like upper lip he might well have been the member of an Eastern European legation. It was only the expression of his eyes that fitted in with any of Latimer's preconceived ideas about his appearance.

They were very brown and seemed at first to be a little screwed up, as if he were short-sighted or worried. But there was no corresponding frown or contraction of the eyebrows; and Latimer saw that the expression of anxiety, height of the cheek-bones and the way the eyes were set in or short-sightedness was an optical illusion due to the head. Actually, the face was utterly expressionless, as impassive as that of a lizard.

For a moment the brown eyes rested on Latimer; then, as Mr. Peters closed the door behind him Dimitrios turned his head and said in strongly accented French: "Present me to your friend. I do not think that I have seen him before."

Latimer very nearly jumped. The face of Dimitrios might not be revealing, but the voice certainly was. It was very coarse and sharp, with an acrid quality that made nonsense of any grace implicit in the words it produced. He spoke very softly, and it occurred to Latimer that the man was aware of the ugliness of his voice and tried to conceal it. He failed. Its promise was as deadly as the rattle of a rattlesnake.

"This is Monsieur Smith," said Mr. Peters. "There is a chair behind you. You may sit down."

Dimitrios ignored the suggestion. "Monsieur Smith! An Englishman. It appears that you knew Monsieur Visser."

"I have *seen* Visser."

"That is what we wanted to talk to you about, Dimitrios," said Mr. Peters.

"Yes?" Dimitrios sat down on the spare chair. "Then talk and be quick. I have an appointment to keep. I cannot waste time in this way."

Mr. Peters shook his head sorrowfully. "You have not changed at all, Dimitrios. Always impetuous, always a little unkind. After all these years no word of greeting, no word of regret for all the unhappiness you caused me. You know, it was most unkind of you to hand us all over to the police like that. We were your friends. Why did you do it?"

"You still talk too much," said Dimitrios. "What is it you want?"

Mr. Peters sat down carefully on the edge of the bed. "Since you insist on making this a purely business meeting—we want money."

The brown eyes flickered towards him. "Naturally. What do you want to give me for it?"

"Our silence, Dimitrios. It is very valuable."

"Indeed? How valuable?"

"It is worth at the very least a million francs."

Dimitrios sat back in the chair and crossed his legs. "And who is going to pay you that for it?"

"You are, Dimitrios. And you are going to be glad to get it so cheaply."

Then Dimitrios smiled.

It was a slow tightening of the small, thin lips; nothing more. Yet there was something inexpressibly savage about it: something that made Latimer feel glad that it was Mr. Peters who had to face it. At that moment, he felt, Dimitrios was far more appropriate to a gathering of man-eating tigers than to a diplomatic reception, however large. The smile faded. "I think," he said, "that you shall tell me now precisely what you mean."

To Latimer, who would, he knew, have responded promptly to the menace in the man's voice, Mr. Peters' bland hesitation was maddeningly reckless. He appeared to be enjoying himself.

"It is so difficult to know where to begin."

There was no reply. Mr. Peters waited for a moment and then shrugged. "There are," he went on, "so many things that the police would be glad to know. For instance, I might tell them who it was who sent them that dossier in nineteen thirty-one. And it would be such a surprise for them to know that a respectable director of the Eurasian Credit Trust was really the Dimitrios Makropoulos who used to send women to Alexandria."

Latimer thought that he saw Dimitrios relax a little in his chair. "And you expect me to pay you a million francs for that? My good Petersen, you are childish."

Mr. Peters smiled. "Very likely, Dimitrios. You were always inclined to despise my simple approach to the problems of this life of ours. But our silence on those matters would be worth a great deal to you, would it not?"

Dimitrios considered him for a moment. Then: "Why don't you come to the point, Petersen? Or perhaps you are only preparing the way for your Englishman." He turned his head. "What have you to say, Monsieur Smith? Or is neither of you very sure of himself?"

"Petersen is speaking for me," mumbled Latimer. He wished fervently that Mr. Peters would get the business over.

"May I continue?" inquired Mr. Peters.

"Go on."

"The Yugoslav police, too, might be interested in you. If we were to tell them where Monsieur Talat . . ."

"*Par example!*" Dimitrios laughed malignantly. "So Grodek has been talking. Not a sou for that, my friend. Is there any more?"

"Athens, nineteen twenty-two. Does that mean anything to you, Dimitrios? The name was Taladis, if you remember. The charge was robbery and attempted murder. Is that so amusing?"

Into Mr. Peters' face had come the look of unsmiling, adenoidal viciousness that Latimer had seen for a moment or two in Sofia. Dimitrios stared at him unblinkingly. In an instant the atmosphere had become deadly with a naked hatred that to Latimer was quite horrible. He felt as he had once felt when, as a child, he had seen a street fight between two middle-aged men. He saw Mr. Peters draw the Lüger from his pocket and weigh it in his hands.

"You have nothing to say to that, Dimitrios? Then I shall go on. A little earlier that year you murdered a man in Smyrna, a moneylender. What was his name, Monsieur Smith "'

"Sholem."

"Sholem, of course. Monsieur Smith was clever enough to discover that, Dimitrios. A good piece of work, don't you think? Monsieur Smith, you know, is very friendly with the Turkish police; almost, one might say, in their confidence. Do you still think that a million francs is a lot to pay, Dimitrios?"

Dimitrios did not look at either of them. "The murderer of Sholem was hanged," he said slowly.

Mr. Peters raised his eyebrows. "Can that be true, Monsieur Smith?"

"A negro named Dhris Mohammed was hanged for the murder, but he made a confession implicating Monsieur Makropoulos. An order was issued for his arrest in nineteen twenty-four. The charge was murder; for the Turkish police were anxious to catch him for another reason. He had been concerned in an attempt to assassinate Kemal in Adrianople."

"You see, Dimitrios, we are very well informed. Shall we continue?" He paused. Dimitrios still stared straight in front of him. Not a muscle of his face moved. Mr. Peters looked across at Latimer. "Dimitrios is impressed, I think. I feel sure he would like us to continue." He went on.

"Monsieur Smith has told you that he saw Visser. It was in a mortuary in Istanbul that he saw him. As I told you, he is very friendly with the Turkish police, and they showed him the body. They told him that it was the body of a criminal named Dimitrios Makropoulos. It was foolish of them to be so easily deceived, was it not? But even Monsieur Smith was deceived for a while. Fortunately I was able to tell him that Dimitrios was still alive." He paused. "You do not wish to comment? Very well. Perhaps you would like to hear how I discovered where you were and who you were." Another silence. "No? Perhaps you would like to know how I knew that you were in Istanbul at the time poor, silly Visser was killed; or how easily Monsieur Smith was able to identify a photograph of Visser with the dead man he saw in the mortuary." Another silence. "No? Perhaps you would like to be told how easy it would be for us to arouse the interest of the Turkish police in the curious case of a dead murderer who is alive, or of the Greek police in the case of the refugee from Smyrna who left Tabouria so suddenly. I wonder if you are thinking that it would be difficult for us to prove that you *are* Dimitrios Makropoulos, or Taladis, or Talat, or Rougemont, after such a long time has elapsed. Are you thinking that, Dimitrios? You do not wish to answer? Then let me tell you that it would be quite easy for us to prove. I could identify you as Makropoulos, and so could Werner or Lenôtre or Galindo or the Grand Duchess. One of them is sure to be alive and within reach of the police. Any of them would be glad to help to hang you. Monsieur Smith can swear that the man buried in Istanbul is Visser. Then there is the crew of the yacht you chartered in June. They knew that Visser went with you to Istanbul. There is the concierge in the Avenue de Wagram. He knew you as Rougemont. Your present passport would not be a very good protection to a man with so many false names, would it? And even if you submitted to a little *chantage* from the French and Greek police, Monsieur Smith's Turkish friends would not be as accommodating. Do you think that a million francs is too much to pay for saving you from the hangman, Dimitrios?"

He stopped. For several long seconds Dimitrios continued to stare at the wall. Then at last he stirred and looked at his small gloved hands. His words, when they came, were like stones dropped one by one into a stagnant pool. "I am wondering," he said, "why you ask so little. Is this million all that you are asking?"

Mr. Peters sniggered. "You mean, are we going to the police when we have the million? Oh, no, Dimitrios. We shall be fair with you. This million is only a preliminary gesture of goodwill. There will be other opportunities for you. But you will not find us greedy."

"I am sure of that. You would not want me to become desperate, I think. Are you the only ones who have this curious delusion that I killed Visser?"

"There is no one else. I shall want the million in *mille* notes to-morrow."

"So soon?"

"You will receive instructions as to how you are to give them to us, by post, in the morning. If the instructions are not followed exactly you will not be given a second chance. The police will be approached immediately. Do you understand?"

"Perfectly."

As Dimitrios stood up an idea seemed to occur to him. He turned to Latimer. "You have been very silent, Monsieur. I wonder if you have been understanding that your life is in your friend Petersen's hands. If, for example, he decided to tell me your real name and where you might be found, I should very likely have you killed."

Mr. Peters showed his white false teeth. "Why should I deprive myself of Monsieur Smith's help? Monsieur Smith is invaluable. He can prove that Visser is dead. Without him you could breathe again."

Dimitrios took no notice of the interruption. "Well, Monsieur Smith?"

Latimer looked up into the brown anxious-seeming eyes and thought of

Madame Preveza's phrase. They were certainly the eyes of a man ready to do something that hurt, but they could have belonged to no doctor. There was murder in them.

"I can assure you," he said, "that Petersen has no inducement to kill me. You see . . ."

"You see," put in Mr. Peters quickly, "we are not fools, Dimitrios. You can go now."

"Of course." Dimitrios went towards the door, but at the threshold he paused.

"What is it?" said Mr. Peters.

"I should like to ask Monsieur Smith two questions."

"Well?"

"How was this man whom you took to be Visser dressed when he was found?"

"In a cheap blue serge suit. A French *carte d'identité*, issued at Lyons a year previously, was sewn into the lining. The suit was of Greek manufacture, but the shirt and underwear were French."

"And how was he killed?"

"He had been stabbed in the side and then thrown into the water."

Mr Peters smiled "Are you satisfied, Dimitrios?"

Dimitrios stared at him. "Visser," he said slowly, "was too greedy. You will not be too greedy, will you, Petersen?"

Mr. Peters gave him stare for stare. "I shall be very careful," he said. "You have no more questions to ask? Good. You will receive your instructions in the morning."

Dimitrios went without another word. Mr. Peters shut the door, waited a moment or two, then, very gently opened it again. Motioning to Latimer to remain where he was, he disappeared on to the landing. Latimer heard the stairs creak. A minute later he returned.

"He has gone," he announced. "In a few minutes we, too, shall go." He sat down again on the bed, lit one of his cheroots and blew the smoke out as luxuriously as if he had just been released from bondage. His sweet smile came out again like a rose after a storm. "Well," he said, "that was Dimitrios about whom you have heard such a great deal. What did you think of him?"

"I didn't know what to think. Perhaps, if I had not known so much about him, I should have disliked him less. I don't know. It is difficult to be reasonable about a man who is obviously wondering how quickly he can murder you." He hesitated. "I did not realise that you hated him so much."

Mr. Peters did not smile. "I assure you, Mr. Latimer, that it was a surprise to me to realise it. I did not like him. I did not trust him. After the way he betrayed us all, that was understandable. It was not until I saw him in this room just now that I realised that I hated him enough to kill him. If I were a superstitious man, I should wonder if perhaps the spirit of poor Visser had entered into me." He stopped, then added "*Salop!*" under his breath. He was silent for a moment. Then he looked up. "Mr. Latimer, I must make an admission. I must tell you that even if you had agreed to the offer I made you, you would not have received your half million. I should not have paid you." He shut his mouth tightly as if he were prepared to receive a blow.

"So I imagine," said Latimer dryly. "I very nearly accepted the offer just to see how you would cheat me. I take it that you would have made the real time for the delivery of the money an hour or so earlier than you would have told me, and that, by the time I arrived on the scene, you and the money would have gone. Was that it?"

Mr. Peters winced. "It was very wise of you not to trust me, but very unkind. But I suppose that I cannot blame you. But it was not to abase myself that I admitted to having tried to deceive you. It was to defend myself. I would like to ask you a question."

"Well?"

"Was it—forgive me—was it the thought that I might betray you to Dimitrios that made you refuse my offer to share the money with you?"

"It never occurred to me."

"I am glad," said Mr. Peters solemnly. "I should not like you to think that of me. You may dislike me, but I should not care to be thought cold-blooded. I may tell you that the thought did not occur to me either. There you see Dimitrios! We have discussed this matter, you and I. We have mistrusted one another and looked for betrayal. Yet it is Dimitrios who puts this thought in our heads. I have met many wicked and violent men, Mr. Latimer, but I tell you that Dimitrios is unique. Why do you think he suggested to you that I might betray you?"

"I imagine that he was acting on the principle that the best way to fight two allies is to get them to fight each other."

Mr. Peters smiled. "No, Mr. Latimer. That would have been too obvious a trick for Dimitrios. He was suggesting to you in a very delicate way that *I* was the unnecessary partner and that you could remove me very easily by telling him where I could be found."

"Do you mean that he was offering to kill you for me?"

"Exactly. He would have only you to deal with then. He does not know, of course," added Mr. Peters thoughtfully, "that you do not know his present name." He stood up and put on his hat. "No, Mr. Latimer, I do not like Dimitrios. Do not misunderstand me, please. I have no moral rectitude. But

Dimitrios is a savage beast. Even now, though I know that I have taken every precaution, I am afraid. I shall take his million and go. If I could allow you to hand him over to the police when I have done with him, I would do so. He would not hesitate if the situation were reversed. But it is impossible."

"Why?"

Mr. Peters looked at him curiously. "Dimitrios seems to have had a strange effect on you. No, to tell the police afterwards would be too dangerous. If we were asked to explain the million francs—and we could not expect Dimitrios to remain silent about them—we should be embarrassed. A pity. Shall we go now? I shall leave the money for the room on the table. They can take the suitcase for a *pourboire*."

They went downstairs in silence. As they deposited the key, the man in his shirt-sleeves appeared with an *affiche* for Mr. Peters to complete. Mr. Peters waved him away. He would, he said, fill it in when he returned.

In the street he halted and faced Latimer.

"Have you ever been followed?"

"Not to my knowledge."

"Then you will be followed now. I do not suppose that Dimitrios had any real hope of our leading him to our homes, but he was always thorough." He glanced over Latimer's shoulder. "Ah, yes. He was there when we arrived. Do not look round, Mr. Latimer. A man wearing a grey mackintosh and a dark soft hat. You will see him in a minute."

The hollow feeling which had disappeared with the departure of Dimitrios jolted back into its position in Latimer's stomach. "What are we to do?"

"Return by Metro, as I said before."

"What good will that do?"

"You will see in a minute."

The Ledru-Rollin Metro station was about a hundred yards away. As they walked toward it the muscles in Latimer's calves tightened and he had a ridiculous desire to run. He felt himself walking stiffly and self-consciously.

"Do not look round," said Mr. Peters again.

They walked down the steps to the Metro. "Keep close to me now," said Mr. Peters.

He bought two second-class tickets and they walked on down the tunnel in the direction of the trains.

It was a long tunnel. As they pushed their way through the spring barriers, Latimer felt that he could reasonably glance behind him. He did so, and caught a glimpse of a shabby young man in a grey raincoat about thirty feet behind them. Now the tunnel split into two. One way was labelled: "*Direction* Pte. de Charenton," the other: "*Direction* Balard." Mr. Peters stopped.

"It would be wise now," he said, "if we appeared to be about to take leave of one another." He glanced out of the corners of his eyes. "Yes, he has stopped. He is wondering what is going to happen. Talk, please, Mr. Latimer, but not too loudly. I want to listen."

"Listen to what?"

"The trains. I spent half an hour here listening to them this morning."

"What on earth for? I don't see . . ."

Mr. Peters gripped his arm and he stopped. In the distance he could hear the rumble of an approaching train.

"*Direction* Balard," muttered Mr. Peters suddenly. "Come along. Keep close to me and do not walk too quickly."

They went on down the right-hand tunnel. The rumble of the train grew louder. They rounded a bend in the tunnel. Ahead was the green automatic gate.

"*Vite!*" cried Mr. Peters.

The train was by now almost in the station. The automatic door began to swing slowly across the entrance to the platform. As Latimer reached it and passed through with about three inches to spare, he heard, above the hiss and screech of pneumatic brakes, the sound of running feet. He looked round. Although Mr. Peters' stomach had suffered some compression, he had squeezed himself through on to the platform. But the man in the grey raincoat had, in spite of his last-minute sprint, left it too late. He now stood, red in the face with anger, shaking his fists at them from the other side of the automatic gate.

They got into the train a trifle breathlessly.

"Excellent!" puffed Mr. Peters happily. "Now do you see what I meant, Mr. Latimer?"

"Very ingenious."

The noise of the train made further conversation impossible.

Mr. Peters touched his arm. They were at Chatelet. They got out and took the Porte d'Orléans *correspondance* to St. Placide. As they walked down the Rue de Rennes, Mr. Peters hummed softly. They passed a café.

Mr. Peters stopped humming. "Would you like some coffee, Mr. Latimer?"

"No, thanks. What about your letter to Dimitrios?"

Mr. Peters tapped his pocket. "It is already written. Eleven o'clock is the time. The junction of the Avenue de la Reine and the Boulevard Jean Jaurès is the place. Would you like to be there, or are you leaving Paris to-morrow?" And then, without giving Latimer a chance to reply: "I shall be sorry to say good-bye to you, Mr. Latimer. I find you so sympathetic. Our association has, on the whole, been most agreeable. It has also been profitable to me." He sighed. "I feel a little guilty, Mr. Latimer. You have been so patient and helpful and yet you go unrewarded. You would not," he inquired a trifle anxiously, "accept a thousand francs of the money? It would help to pay your expenses."

"No, thank you."

"No, of course not. Then, at least, Mr. Latimer, let me give you a glass of wine. That is it! A celebration! Come, Mr. Latimer. There is no taste in nothing. Let us collect the money together to-morrow night. You will have the satisfaction of seeing a little blood squeezed from this swine Dimitrios. Then we will celebrate with a glass of wine. What do you say to that?"

They had stopped at the corner of the street which contained the Impasse. Latimer looked into Mr. Peters' watery eyes. "I should say," he said deliberately, "that you are wondering if there is a chance that Dimitrios might decide to call your bluff and thinking that it might be a good idea to have me in Paris until you have the money actually in your pocket."

Mr. Peters' eyes slowly closed. "Mr. Latimer," he said bitterly, "I did not think . . . I would not have thought that you could have put such a construction on . . ."

"All right, I'll stay." Irritably, Latimer interrupted him. He had wasted so many days: another one would make no difference. "I'll come with you to-morrow, but only on these conditions. The wine must be champagne; it must come from France, not Meknes, and it must be a vintage *cuvée* of either nineteen nineteen, twenty or twenty-one. A bottle," he added vindictively, "will cost you at least one hundred francs."

Mr. Peters opened his eyes. He smiled bravely. "You shall have it, Mr. Latimer," he said.

Fifteen

~~~~~~~~~~~~~~~~~~~~~~~~~~~~~~~

THE STRANGE TOWN

M<small>R</small>. PETERS AND Latimer took up their positions at the corner of the Avenue de la Reine and the Boulevard Jean Jaurès at half-past ten, the hour at which the hired car was due to pick up the messenger from Dimitrios opposite the Neuilly cemetery.

It was a cold night, and as it began to rain soon after they arrived, they stood for shelter just inside the *porte cochère* of a building a few yards along the Avenue in the direction of the Pont St. Cloud.

"How long will they be getting here?" Latimer asked.

"I said that I would expect them by eleven. That gives them half an hour to drive from Neuilly. They could do it in less, but I told them to make quite certain that they were not followed. If they are in doubt they will return to Neuilly. They will take no chances. The car is a Renault *coupé-de-ville*. We must have patience."

They waited in silence. Now and again Mr. Peters would stir as a car that might have been the hired Renault approached from the direction of the river. The rain trickling down the slope formed by the subsidence of the cobbles formed puddles about their feet.

Suddenly Mr. Peters grunted: "*Attention!*"

"Are they coming?"

"Yes."

Latimer looked over Mr. Peters' shoulder. A large Renault was approaching from the left. As he looked it began to slow down as if the driver were uncertain of the way. It passed them, the rain glistening in the beams of the headlights, and stopped a few yards farther on. The outline of the driver's head and shoulders were just visible in the darkness, but blinds were pulled down over the rear windows. Mr. Peters put his hand in his overcoat pocket.

"Wait here, please," he said to Latimer, and walked towards the car.

"*Ça va?*" Latimer heard him say to the driver. There was an answering "*Oui*." Mr. Peters opened the rear door and leaned forward.

Almost immediately he withdrew a pace and closed the door. In his left hand was a package. "*Attendez,*" he said, and walked back to where Latimer was standing.

"All right?" said Latimer.

"I think so. Will you strike a match, please?"

Latimer did so. The package was the size of a large book, about two inches thick and was wrapped in blue paper and tied with string. Mr. Peters tore away the paper at one of the corners and exposed a solid wad of *mille* notes. He sighed. "Beautiful!"

"Aren't you going to count them?"

"That pleasure," said Mr. Peters seriously, "I shall reserve for the comfort of my home." He crammed the package into his overcoat pocket, stepped on to the pavement and raised his hand. The Renault started with a jerk, swung round in a wide circle and splashed away on its return journey. Mr. Peters watched it go with a smile.

"A very pretty woman," he said. "I wonder who she can be. But I prefer the million francs. Now, Mr. Latimer, a taxi and then your favourite champagne. We have earned it, I think."

They found a taxi near the Porte de St. Cloud. Mr. Peters enlarged on his success.

"With a type like Dimitrios it is necessary only to be firm and circumspect. We put the matter to him squarely; we let him see that he has no choice but to agree to our demands, and it is done. A million francs. Very nice! One almost wishes that one had demanded two million. But it would have been unwise to be too greedy. As it is, he believes that we shall make fresh demands and that he has time to deal with us as he dealt with Visser. He will find that he has deceived himself. This is very satisfactory to me, Mr. Latimer: as satisfying to my pride as it is to my pocket. I feel, too, that I have, in some measure, avenged poor Visser's death. I have suffered. Now I have my reward." He patted his pocket. "It would be amusing to see Dimitrios when at last he realises how he has been tricked. A pity that we shall not be there."

"Shall you leave Paris immediately?"

"I think so. I have a fancy to see something of South America. Not my own adopted fatherland, of course. It is one of the terms of my citizenship that I never enter the country. A hard condition, for I would like for sentimental reasons to see the country of my adoption. But it cannot be altered. I am a citizen of the world and must remain so. Perhaps I shall buy an estate somewhere, a place where I shall be able to pass my days in peace when I am old.

You are a young man, Mr. Latimer. When one is my age, the years seem shorter and one feels that one is soon to reach a destination. It is as if one were approaching a strange town late at night when one is sorry to be leaving the warm train for an unknown hotel and wishing that the journey would never end."

He glanced out of the window. "We are nearly home. I have your champagne. It was, as you warned me, very expensive. But I have no priggish objections to a little luxury. It is sometimes agreeable and, even when it is disagreeable, it serves to make us appreciate simplicity. Ah!" The taxi had stopped at the end of the Impasse. "I have no change, Mr. Latimer. That seems odd with a million francs in one's pocket, does it not? Will you pay, please?"

They walked down the Impasse.

"I think," said Mr. Peters, "that I shall sell these houses before I go to South America. One does not want property on one's hands that is not yielding a profit."

"Won't they be rather difficult to sell? The view from the windows is a little depressing, isn't it?"

"It is not necessary to be always looking out of the windows. They could be made into very nice houses."

They began the long climb up the stairs. On the second landing Mr. Peters paused for breath, took off his overcoat and got out his keys. They continued the climb to his door.

He opened it, switched on the light, and then, going straight to the largest divan, took the package from his overcoat pocket and undid the string. With loving care he extracted the notes from the wrappings and held them up. For once his smile was real.

"There, Mr. Latimer! A million francs! Have you ever seen so much money at once before? Nearly six thousand English pounds!" He stood up. "But we must have our little celebration. Take off your coat and I will get the champagne. I hope that you will like it. I have no ice, but I put it in a bowl of water. It will be quite cool."

He walked towards the curtained-off part of the room.

Latimer had turned away to take off his coat. Suddenly he became aware that Mr. Peters was still on the same side of the curtain and that he was standing motionless. He glanced round.

For a moment he thought that he was going to faint. The blood seemed to drain away suddenly from his head, leaving it hollow and light. A steel band seemed to tighten round his chest. He felt that he wanted to cry out, but all he could do was to stare.

Mr. Peters was standing with his back to him, and his hands were raised above his head. Facing him in the gap between the gold curtains was Dimitrios, with a revolver in his hand.

Dimitrios stepped forward and sideways so that Latimer was no longer partly covered by Mr. Peters. Latimer dropped his coat and put up his hands. Dimitrios raised his eyebrows.

"It is not flattering," he said, "for you to look so surprised to see me, Petersen. Or should I call you Caillé?"

Mr. Peters said nothing. Latimer could not see his face, but he saw his throat move as if he were swallowing.

The brown eyes flickered to Latimer. "I am glad that the Englishman is here, too, Petersen. I am saved the trouble of persuading you to give me his name and address. Monsieur Smith, who knows so many things and who was so anxious to keep his face hidden, is now shown to be as easy to deal with as you are, Petersen. You were always too ingenious, Petersen. I told you so once before. It was on the occasion when you brought a coffin from Salonika. You remember? Ingenuity is never a substitute for intelligence, you know. Did you really think that I should not see through you?" His lips twisted. "Poor Dimitrios! He is very simple. He will think that I, clever Petersen, will come back for more, like any other blackmailer. He will not guess that I may be bluffing him. But, just to make sure that he does not guess, I will do what no other blackmailer ever did. I will tell him that I *shall* come back for more. Poor Dimitrios is such a fool that he will believe me. Poor Dimitrios has no intelligence. Even if he finds out from the records that, within a month of my coming out of prison, I had succeeded in selling three unsaleable houses to someone named Caillé, he will not dream of suspecting that I, clever Petersen, am also Caillé. Did you not know, Petersen, that before I bought these houses in your name they had been empty for ten years? You are such a fool."

He paused. The anxious brown eyes narrowed. The mouth tightened. Latimer knew that Dimitrios was going to kill Mr. Peters and that there was nothing that he could do about it. The wild beating of his heart seemed to be suffocating him.

"Drop the money, Petersen."

The wad of notes hit the carpet and spread out like a fan.

Dimitrios raised the revolver.

Suddenly, Mr Peters seemed to realise what was about to happen. He cried out: "No! You must . . ."

Then Dimitrios fired. He fired twice and with the earsplitting noise of the explosions Latimer heard one of the bullets thud into Mr. Peters' body.

Mr. Peters emitted a long-drawn-out retching sound and sank forward on to his hands and knees with blood pouring from his neck.

Dimitrios stared at Latimer. "Now you," he said.

At that moment Latimer jumped.

Why he chose that particular moment to jump he never knew. He never even knew what prompted him to jump at all. He supposed that it was an instinctive attempt to save himself. Why, however, his instinct for self-preservation should have led him to jump in the direction of the revolver which Dimitrios was about to fire is inexplicable. But he did jump, and the jump did save his life; for, as his right foot left the floor, a fraction of a second before Dimitrios pressed the trigger, he stumbled over one of Mr. Peters' thick tufts of rug and the shot went over his head into the wall.

Half dazed and with his forehead scorched by the blast from the muzzle of the revolver, he hurled himself at Dimitrios. They went down together with their hands at each other's throats, but immediately Dimitrios brought his knee up into Latimer's stomach and rolled clear of him.

He had dropped his revolver, and now he went to pick it up. Gasping for breath, Latimer scrambled towards the nearest movable object, which happened to be the heavy brass tray on top of one of the Moroccan tables, and flung it at Dimitrios. The edge of it hit the side of his head as he was reaching for the revolver and he reeled; but the blow stopped him for barely a second. Latimer threw the wooden part of the table at him and dashed forward. Dimitrios staggered back as the table caught his shoulder. The next moment Latimer had the revolver and was standing back, still trying to get his breath, but with his finger on the trigger.

His face sheet-white, Dimitrios came towards him. Latimer raised the revolver.

"If you move again, I shall fire."

Dimitrios stood still. His brown eyes stared into Latimer's. His grey hair was tousled; his scarf had come out of his coat; he looked dangerous. Latimer was beginning to recover his breath, but his knees felt horribly weak, his ears were singing and the air he breathed reeked sickeningly of cordite fumes. It was for him to make the next move, and he felt frightened and helpless.

"If you move," he repeated, "I shall fire."

He saw the brown eyes flicker towards the notes on the floor and then back to him. "What are you going to do?" said Dimitrios suddenly. "If the police come we shall both have something to explain. If you shoot me you will get only that million. If you will release me I will give you another million as well. That would be good for you."

Latimer took no notice. He edged sideways towards the wall, until he could glance quickly at Mr. Peters.

Mr. Peters had crawled towards the divan on which his overcoat lay, and

was now leaning against it with his eyes half closed. He was breathing ster-
torously through the mouth. One bullet had torn a great gaping wound in the
side of his neck from which the blood was welling. The second had hit him
full in the chest and scorched the clothing. The wound was a round purple
mess about two inches in diameter. It was bleeding very little. Mr. Peters'
lips moved.

Keeping his eyes fixed on Dimitrios, Latimer moved round until he was
alongside Mr. Peters.

"How do you feel?" he said.

It was a stupid question, and he knew it the moment the words had left his
mouth. He tried desperately to collect his wits. A man had been shot and he
had the man who shot him. He . . .

"My pistol," muttered Mr. Peters; "get my pistol. Overcoat." He said something else that was inaudible.

Cautiously, Latimer worked his way round to the overcoat and fumbled
for the pistol. Dimitrios watched with a thin ghastly smile on his lips. Latimer
found the pistol and handed it to Mr. Peters. He grasped it with both hands
and snicked back the safety catch.

"Now," he muttered, "go and get police."

"Someone will have heard the shots," said Latimer soothingly. "The police
will be here soon."

"Won't find us," whispered Mr. Peters. "Get police."

Latimer hesitated. What Mr. Peters said was true. The Impasse was hemmed
in by blank walls. The shots might have been heard, but unless someone had
happened to be passing the entrance to the Impasse during the few seconds in
which they were fired, nobody would know where the sounds had come from.

"All right," he said. "Where is the telephone?"

"No telephone."

"But . . ." He hesitated again. It might take ten minutes to find a policeman.
Could he leave a badly wounded Mr. Peters to watch a man like Dimitrios?
But there was nothing else for it. Mr. Peters needed a doctor. The sooner
Dimitrios was under lock and key the better. He knew that Dimitrios under-
stood his predicament and the knowledge did not please him. He glanced at
Mr. Peters. He had the Lüger resting on one knee and pointed at Dimitrios.
The blood was still pouring from his neck. If a doctor did not attend to him
soon he would bleed to death.

"All right," he said. "I'll be as quick as I can."

He went towards the door.

"One moment, Monsieur." There was an urgency in the harsh voice that
made Latimer pause.

"Well?"

"If you go he will shoot me. Don't you see that? Why not accept my offer?"

Latimer opened the door. "If you try any tricks you will certainly be shot." He looked again at the wounded man, huddled over the Lüger. "I shall be back with the police. Don't shoot unless you have to."

Then, as he made to go, Dimitrios laughed. Involuntarily, Latimer turned. "I should save that laugh for the executioner," he snapped. "You will need it."

"I was thinking," said Dimitrios, "that in the end one is always defeated by stupidity. If it is not one's own it is the stupidity of others." His face changed. "Five million, Monsieur," he shouted angrily. "Is it not enough or do you want this carrion to kill me?"

Latimer stared at him for a moment. The man was almost convincing. Then he remembered that others had been convinced by Dimitrios. He waited no longer. He heard Dimitrios shout something after him as he shut the door.

He was half-way down the stairs when he heard the shots. There were four of them. Three cracked out in quick succession. Then, there was a pause before the last one. His heart in his mouth, he turned and ran back up to the room. It was only later that he found anything curious in the fact that, as he raced up the stairs, the fear uppermost in his mind was for Mr. Peters.

Dimitrios was not a pleasant sight. Only one of the bullets from Mr. Peters' Lüger had missed. Two had lodged in the body. The fourth, evidently fired at him after he had fallen to the floor, had hit him between the eyes and almost blown the top of his head off. His body was still twitching.

The Lüger slipped from Mr. Peters' fingers and he was leaning, with his head on the edge of the divan, opening and shutting his mouth like a stranded fish. As Latimer stood there he choked suddenly and blood trickled from his mouth.

Scarcely knowing what he was doing, Latimer blundered through the curtain. Dimitrios was dead; Mr. Peters was dying; and all he, Latimer, could think about was the effort required not to faint or vomit. He strove to pull himself together. He must do something. Mr. Peters must have water. Wounded men always needed water. There was a wash-basin and beside it were some glasses. He filled one and carried it back into the room.

Mr. Peters had not moved. His mouth and eyes were open. Latimer knelt down beside him and poured a little water into the mouth. It ran out again. He put down the glass and felt for the pulse. There was none.

Latimer got quickly to his feet and looked at his hands. There was blood on them. He went back to the wash-basin, rinsed them and dried them on a small, dirty towel which hung from a hook.

He should, he knew, call the police immediately. Two men had killed each other. That was a matter for the police. Yet . . . what was he going to say to them? How was he going to explain his own presence there in that shambles? Could he say that he had been passing the end of the Impasse and had heard the shots? But someone might have noticed him with Mr. Peters. There was the taxi-driver who had brought them. And when they found that Dimitrios had that day obtained a million francs from his bank . . . there would be endless questionings. Supposing they suspected him.

His brain seemed to clear suddenly. He must get out at once and he must leave no traces of his presence there. He thought quickly. The revolver in his pocket belonged to Dimitrios. It had his fingerprints on it. He took it out of his pocket, put on his gloves and wiped it all over carefully with his handkerchief. Then, setting his teeth, he went back into the room, knelt down beside Dimitrios and, taking his right hand, pressed the fingers round the butt and trigger. Removing the fingers and holding the revolver by the barrel, he then put it near the body on the floor.

He considered the *mille* notes strewn over the rug like so much wastepaper. To whom did they belong—Dimitrios or Mr. Peters? There was Sholem's money there and the money stolen in Athens in nineteen twenty-two. There was the fee for helping to assassinate Stambulisky and the money of which Madame Preveza had been cheated. There was the price of the charts Bulić had stolen and part of the profits from the white slave and drug traffics. To whom did it belong? Well, the police would decide. Best to leave it as it was. It would give them something to think about.

There was, however, the glass of water. It must be emptied, dried and replaced with the other glasses. He looked round. Was there anything else? No. Nothing at all? Yes, one thing. His fingerprints were on the tray and the table. He wiped them. Nothing more? Yes. Fingerprints on the door-knobs. He wiped them. Anything else? No. He carried the glass to the wash-basin. The glass dried and replaced, he turned to go. It was then that he noticed the champagne which Mr. Peters had bought for their celebration standing in a bowl of water. It was a Verzy, 1921—a half-bottle.

No one saw him leave the Impasse. He went to a café in the Rue de Rennes and ordered a cognac.

Now he began to tremble from head to foot. He had been a fool. He ought to have gone to the police. It was still not too late to go to them. Supposing the bodies remained undiscovered. They might lie there for weeks in that ghastly room with the blue walls and gold stars and rugs, while the blood congealed and hardened and collected dust and the flesh began to rot. It was horrible to think of. If only there were some way of telling the police. An anonymous letter would be too dangerous. The police would know immediately that a third person had been concerned in the affair and would not be satisfied with the simple explanation that the two men had killed each other. Then he had an idea. The main thing was to get the police to the house. Why they went was unimportant.

There was an evening paper in the rack. He took it to his table and read it through feverishly. There were two news items in it which suited his purpose. One was a report of the theft of some valuable furs from a warehouse in the Avenue de la Republique; the other was an account of the smashing of the shop window of a jeweller in the Avenue de Clichy and the escape of two men with a tray of rings.

He decided that the first would suit his purpose best, and, summoning the waiter, ordered another cognac together with writing materials. He drank the brandy at a gulp and put his gloves on. Then, taking a sheet of the letter paper, he examined it carefully. It was ordinary, cheap café notepaper. Having satisfied himself that there was no distinguishing mark of any kind on it, he wrote across the middle of it in capital letters: "FAITES DES ENQUETES SUR CAILLÉ—3, IMPASSE DES HUIT ANGES." Then he tore the report of the fur robbery out of the paper, folded it inside the note and put the two in an envelope, which he addressed to the Commissaire of Police of the Seventh Arrondissement. Leaving the café, he bought a stamp at a tobacco kiosk and posted the letter.

It was not until four o'clock that morning, when he had lain awake in bed for two hours, that the nerves of his stomach succumbed at last to the strain which had been put upon them and he was sick.

Two days later a paragraph appeared in three of the Paris morning papers saying that the body of a South American named Frederik Peters, together with that of a man, at present unidentified, but believed to be a South American also, had been found in an apartment off the Rue de Rennes. Both men, the paragraph continued, had been shot and it was thought that they had killed one another in a revolver fight following a quarrel over money, a considerable sum of which was found in the apartment. It was the only reference to the affair, the attention of the public being divided at the time between a new international crisis and a hatchet murder in the suburbs.

Latimer did not see the paragraph until several days later.

Soon after nine o'clock on the morning of the day on which the police received his note, he left his hotel for the Gare de l'Est and the Orient Express. A letter had arrived for him by the first post. It had a Bulgarian stamp and a Sofia postmark and was obviously from Marukakis. He put it in his pocket unread. It was not until later in the day, when the express was racing through the hills west of Belfort, that he remembered it. He opened it and began to read:

My Dear Friend,

Your letter delighted me. I was so pleased to get it. I was also a little surprised, for—forgive me, please—I did not seriously expect you to succeed in the difficult task which you had set yourself. The years bury so much of our wisdom that they are bound to bury most of our folly with it. Some time I hope to hear from you how a folly buried in Belgrade comes to be unearthed in Geneva.

I was interested in the reference to the Eurasian Credit Trust. Here is something that will interest you.

There has been recently, as you may know, a great deal of tension between this country and Yugoslavia. The Serbs, you know, have reason to feel tense. If Germany and vassal Hungary attacked her from the north, Italy attacked her through Albania from the south and by sea from the west, and Bulgaria attacked her from the east, she would be quickly finished. Her only chance would lie in the Russians outflanking the Germans and Hungarians with an attack launched through Rumania along the Bukovina railway. But has Bulgaria anything to fear from Yugoslavia? Is she a danger to Bulgaria? The idea is absurd. Yet, for the past three months or four, there has been here a stream of propaganda to the effect that Yugoslavia is planning to attack Bulgaria. "The menace across the frontier" is a typical phrase.

If such things were not so dangerous one would laugh. But one recognises the technique. Such propaganda always begins with words but soon it proceeds to deeds. When there are no facts to support lies, facts must be made.

Two weeks ago there took place the inevitable frontier incident. Some Bulgarian peasants were fired upon by Yugoslavs (alleged to be soldiers), and one of the peasants was killed. There is much popular indignation, an outcry against the devilish Serbs. The newspaper offices are very busy. A week later the Government announces fresh purchases of anti-aircraft guns to strengthen the defences of the western Provinces. The purchases are made from a Belgian firm with the help of a loan negotiated by the Eurasian Credit Trust.

Yesterday a curious news item comes into this office.

As a result of careful investigations by the Yugoslav Government, it is shown that the four men who fired on the peasants were not Yugoslav soldiers, nor even Yugoslav subjects. They were of various nationalities and two had previously been imprisoned in Poland for terrorist activities. They had been paid to create the incident by a man about whom none of them knows anything more than that he came from Paris.

But there is more. Within an hour of that news item reaching Paris, I had instructions from the head office there to suppress the item and send out a *démenti* to all subscribers taking our French news. That is amusing, is it not?

One would not have thought that such a rich organisation as the Eurasian Credit Trust would be so sensitive.

As for your Dimitrios: what can one say?

A writer of plays once said that there are some situations that one cannot use on the stage; situations in which the audience can feel neither approval nor disapproval, sympathy or antipathy; situations out of which there is no possible way that is not humiliating or distressing and from which there is no truth, however bitter, to be extracted. He was, you may say, one of those unhappy men who are confounded by the difference between the stupid vulgarities of real life and the ideal existence of the imagination. That may be. Yet, I have been wondering if, for once, I do not find myself in sympathy with him. Can one explain Dimitrios or must one turn away disgusted and defeated? I am tempted to find reason and justice in the fact that he died as violently and indecently as he lived. But that is too ingenuous a way out. It does not explain Dimitrios; it only apologises for him. Special sorts of conditions must exist for the creation of the special sort of criminal that he typified. I have tried to define those conditions—but unsuccessfully. All I do know is that while might is right, while chaos and anarchy masquerade as order and enlightenment, those conditions will obtain.

What is the remedy? But I can see you yawning and remember that if I bore you you will not write to me again and tell me whether you are enjoying your stay in Paris, whether you have found any more Bulićs or Prevezas and whether we shall see you soon in Sofia. My latest information is that war will not break out until the spring; so there will be time for some ski-ing. Late January is quite good here. The roads are terrible, but the runs, when one gets to them, are quite good. I shall look forward eagerly to learning from you when you will come.

With my most sincere regards,

N. Marukakis

Latimer folded the letter and put it in his pocket. A good fellow, Marukakis! He must write to him when he had the time. But just at the moment there were more important matters to be considered.

He needed, and badly, a motive, a neat method of committing a murder and an entertaining crew of suspects. Yes, the suspects must certainly be entertaining. His last book had been a trifle heavy. He must inject a little more humour into this one. As for the motive, money was always, of course, the soundest basis. A pity that Wills and life insurance were so outmoded. Supposing a man murdered an old lady so that his wife should have a private income. It might be worth thinking about. The scene? Well, there was always

plenty of fun to be got out of an English country village, wasn't there? The
time? Summer; with cricket matches on the village green, garden parties at
the vicarage, the clink of tea-cups and the sweet smell of grass on a July
evening. That was the sort of thing people liked to hear about. It was the sort
of thing that he himself would like to hear about.

He looked out of the window. The sun had gone and the hills were receding slowly into the night sky. They would be slowing down for Belfort soon.
Two more days to go! He ought to get some sort of a plot worked out in that
time.

The train ran into a tunnel.

JUDGMENT
ON
DELTCHEV

"Many things in your good people cause me disgust, and, verily, not their evil. I would that they had a madness by which they succumbed, like this pale criminal!"

NIETZSCHE: *Thus Spake Zarathustra*

One

Wᴴᴱᴿᴇ TREASON TO the state is defined simply as opposition to the government in power, the political leader convicted of it will not necessarily lose credit with the people. Indeed, if he is respected or loved by them, his death at the hands of a tyrannical government may serve to give his life a dignity it did not before possess. In that event his enemies may in the end be faced not by the memory of a fallible human being but by a myth, more formidable than the real man could ever have been, and much less vulnerable. His trial, therefore, is no formality, but a ceremony of preparation and precaution. He must be discredited and destroyed as a man so that he may safely be dealt with as a criminal. Sometimes he is induced to confess abjectly to the crimes of which he is accused; but unless he has himself been a member of the party that now seeks to destroy him, such confessions are not always believed by the people; and when, for example, he is the leader of an unliquidated opposition party, it is better to observe outwardly the old legal forms, to bring witnesses, produce evidence, and let him try to defend himself.

So it was with Nikolai Petkov in Bulgaria, with Julius Maniu and Ion Mihalache in Rumania, and with many other liberals in eastern Europe. Petkov they hanged. Maniu and Mihalache were condemned to solitary confinement for life. When Yordan Deltchev's trial took place, the pattern for such occasions had been already set.

The charges against him were of "treason and the preparation of a terrorist plot to assassinate the head of the state." The trial began before a People's Court on the 11th of June. He was described in the indictment as "president of the Agrarian Socialist Party and formerly a member of the Provisional Government of National Unity." In fact, he had been head of that Government and also its Foreign Minister. He was still the leader of the only effective opposition to the People's Party regime that remained.

I had been asked to attend the trial and write a series of articles about it by an American newspaper publisher whom I had met once or twice when he had been visiting London. The request had surprised me. I had never written anything of that kind before and had thought at first that my name had been mistaken for someone else's. There had been no mistake, however, and I had decided to accept.

At some time or other, I suppose, most writers who have never done newspaper work indulge in the belief that, should the occasion arise, they would make brilliant reporters. Some of them, of course, are right. My case is different. With a solemnity that in retrospect seems pathetic, I looked up an old *Times* article on Deltchev, bought some of the likely books, and lunched with an economist who had once read a paper before the Royal Institute of International Affairs. I felt that I ought to learn something about the country I was going to visit, its people, and its problems.

The odd part is that I did learn one thing. It was over that luncheon that I first heard about the Officer Corps Brotherhood. It was referred to as a kind of joke.

Originally, it seemed, this Brotherhood had been a welfare association formed to protect and to help financially the families of a number of army officers who had been shot after the Macedonian *Putsch* of 1925. The founders were brother officers of the victims and sympathetic to their cause; but they were not wealthy men and it was not long before some of them became convinced that the most honorable way of helping and protecting the bereaved families would be to kill those who had condemned their men to death.

By the early thirties the Brotherhood had become a secret society of reactionary extremists and been responsible for at least twenty-eight political murders. Moreover, it was concerned no longer with simple acts of vengeance, but rather with eliminating potential sources of injustice that would later call for vengeance. As in the Brotherhood's dogma any politician or highly placed official with even remotely liberal ideas was a potential source of injustice, the problem of the Brotherhood became a matter of interest to all parties.

Attempts made by successive prewar governments to bring actual murderers to justice and to suppress the organization had been only partly successful because never quite wholehearted. It was easy enough to disapprove of the Brotherhood, but courage was required to become actively concerned with an attack upon it. The Brotherhood had survived and although its earlier "officers only" membership qualification had been relaxed and psychotics from many other sections of the community had found it congenial, it had retained much of its traditional military background. The symbolic revolver and dagger of other Balkan terrorist organizations had become for the Officer Corps Brotherhood the symbolic rifle and bayonet, and during the occupation the Brotherhood had snobbishly preferred to collaborate with the German Army authorities rather than with the Gestapo.

This latter piece of discrimination, however, had not deterred the Provisional Government, set up after the liberation, from making the first serious effort to stamp out the Brotherhood once and for all. Emergency powers had been used to the full. Membership in the organization had been made a capital offense, and arrests, summary trials, and executions had continued over months. So effective, indeed, had been the Government's campaign that there was little doubt in most minds that the Brotherhood had been betrayed from within. Interest in this aspect of the affair, however, had soon faded. When, during the elections, there had been none of the usual Brotherhood murders, it had been assumed with general relief that the organization was at last dead and buried. Now, astonishingly, the corpse had been exhumed and was being declared alive. For part of the case against Deltchev contained the incredible allegation that he, who as head of the Provisional Government had set out to destroy the Brotherhood, was in fact a member of it and the organizer of a plot to assassinate the head of the People's Party Government.

I left London at the end of May and arrived in the capital the day before the trial began.

Two

~~~~~~~~~~~~~~~~~~

O VER MUCH OF south eastern Europe the heaviest summer rains have fallen by early June, and the hardening mud of the roads is being grated into dust. The tinted walls of the villages glow in the strong sun, and the shadows on them are black and sharply denied. Only the higher Balkan peaks still have snow upon them. The corn is becoming tall and rich, and in the river valleys east of the Yugoslav frontier the fields of roses and white poppies that you see from the train are alive with blossom. But in the cities the air is humid, and the insects that swirl in the sunshine over the refuse in the streets or crawl from the dark recesses of hotel beds are in their lush heyday. At that time the human animal has a strange feeling of lassitude; strange because, although the body is sluggish, the mind is uneasily alert, as if it fears that something is being prepared for its discomfort.

I was met at the Central Station by my employer's local representative. His name was Georghi Pashik.

I saw him standing on the platform as my train drew in: a short, dark, flabby man in rimless glasses and a bright seersucker suit with an array of fountain pens in the handkerchief pocket. Under his arm he carried a thin, black dispatch case with a silver medallion hanging from the zipper tag. He stood by a pillar gazing about him with the imperious anxiety of a wealthy traveler who sees no porter and knows that he cannot carry his own baggage. I think it was the fountain pens that identified him for me. He wore them like a badge.

I know a lot about Pashik now. I know, for instance, that the black dispatch case that he carried so importantly rarely contained anything but a stale meat sandwich and a revolver, that the seersucker suit was given to him when he was working in a Displaced Persons camp, that one of the fountain pens came from Passaic, New Jersey, and that those facts can be related directly to his death. I know now some of the ways in which his mind worked and of the strange fantasies that possessed it. Then he was merely a name in conversation—"our man there, Pashik, will fix you up with all the permits you need"—a figure waiting on a station platform. I was not expecting a man of destiny to meet me.

He shook my hand and smiled in a friendly way.

"I'm delighted to know you, Mr. Foster. Have you had breakfast?"

"Not yet. It's very kind of you to meet me."

He gestured a denial. "I have my car outside. We'll have to carry your luggage, Mr. Foster. There are no porters at this hour."

He spoke English well with an accent both foreign and American. He was not a prepossessing person. He had a plump, sallow face with several chins and a two days' growth of beard, and his eyes, as brown and limpid as a spaniel's, squinted slightly through the rimless glasses. He was businesslike and very courteous.

"Good journey, Mr. Foster?" he asked as we walked out to his car.

"Not bad."

"Any trouble at the frontier?"

"No more than usual, I imagine."

"I'm very glad of that."

In the station yard he put my suitcase in a battered Opel with no cushions on the back seats. He took my typewriter from me to put it with the suitcase and then paused, looking at it thoughtfully.

"You know, Mr. Foster," he said, "sometimes the authorities make a great deal of trouble for visitors who they think may not be favorable to the regime."

"Yes?"

"Oh yes." He put the typewriter in the car and then, with his hand still on the carrying handle of it, turned his head. For a moment he seemed about to say something very important. It was on the tip of his tongue. Then he changed his mind. He shrugged. "Things are difficult right now, Mr. Foster," he said. "I'm glad they made no trouble for you."

He had an office in a building just off the Boulevard Marshal Sokolovsky. He called himself the Pan-European Press Service and represented a number of American and a few British newspapers whose proprietors had not found it necessary after the war to re-establish their own offices in the capital. He was energetic and gave an impression of efficiency. I had to be registered as a foreigner with the police and as a newspaper correspondent with the Ministries of the Interior and Propaganda; I also had to have a special permit for the trial. It was early evening before we had finished.

Although there was a good deal of waiting about in the various offices we visited, as well as the ordinary opportunities for conversation, our relationship did not progress during the day. For the most part he remained courteous but reserved, avoiding all discussions of Deltchev or the trial on the grounds, plainly insufficient at times, that we might be overheard, and introducing me to officials with a measured politeness that took no responsibility at all for my subsequent behavior. He had very much the air of the man on the spot who, while giving the specialist from the head office all reasonable assistance, feels entitled to suspect that the results may not justify the trouble taken. This I could well understand; indeed, I would have shared the suspicion. What puzzled me as the day wore on was the growing realization that, understandable and appropriate though his attitude might be, it was only partly a disguise for professional jealousy and that he had some quite different anxiety about me to conceal. It manifested itself in curious ways: sudden bursts of cordiality followed by strained silences, moments when I looked up to find his brown myopic eyes contemplating me furtively, as if to assess my bank balance, and other moments, like that at the station, when he changed his mind about what he was going to say as he opened his mouth to say it. Evidently some bad news had arrived for me while I had been traveling, or he had a request to make that I would be likely to receive badly. The thought bothered me. Unfortunately, I already had a bad conscience about Pashik. I disliked him because of his smell.

I had become aware of it when we entered his car at the station. It was sour and musty and at first I was not sure whether it came from the car or its owner. I don't think that I have an unduly fastidious nose or that the stinks of urban humanity specially distress me. I have known other people afflicted with what is daintily called body odor without disliking them. Yet Pashik I did dislike. Perhaps it was that the personality expressed by his appearance and manner—the suit, the American glasses, the dispatch case, the touch of complaisance—did not in some peculiar way allow for a bad smell. I remember that when I found that he was the source and not his car, I took note of those with whom we came in contact in case what I was finding offensive was the body smell of a city rather than that of one particular inhabitant. But no; it was Pashik. And then, unreasonably, I had begun to dislike him and so was at a disadvantage for what followed.

The sun had not yet set, but the shadows of a church spire and the dome of a mosque stretched like a finger and thumb across the St. Mihail Square when we left the Propaganda Ministry for the last time that day and walked back to Pashik's car; but I had my permit for the trial.

He waved my thanks aside mock-modestly.

"We do what we can, Mr. Foster." He had one of his moments of cordiality. "If you do not mind coming with me and waiting while I clear up at my office, I will then take you to dinner. There is a special restaurant I use."

I should have liked to refuse; instead, I thanked him again.

There was a minute anteroom to his office, with a frosted glass door on which were painted the names of all the newspapers he represented. The list was long and imposing, and after it the office was an anticlimax. It contained a desk, a table, two chairs, and several filing cabinets. The window looked out on a tall fire-escape well. It admitted warm stagnant air and a gray twilight that left the corners of the room in darkness. Standing on one of the filing cabinets and framed as importantly as if it were a picture of his wife was a publicity photograph of Myrna Loy, with a reproduction of her signature on it.

He turned on the desk lamp and began to go through a pile of message flimsies. Most of them he crumpled and tossed aside; two or three he scribbled on and handed to a youth with a glazed peak cap who had been awaiting his return; others he clipped together in a folder. When he reached the last of the messages, he gave the youth some money and sent him off. Then he picked up the telephone and had a conversation, to me quite unintelligible, with a woman whose voice I could hear vibrating tinnily in the receiver. It ended with a brief crescendo of negatives. He stood up and began to tidy the desk. He was frowning and ill at ease.

I watched him from the darkness outside the ring of light shed by the desk lamp. His small hands no longer moved surely. He was making up his mind to a difficult task. He stopped tidying to look out at me. Then he sat down again, leaned back, and, taking out a packet of American cigarettes, began to open it.

"Mr. Foster," he said very carefully, "there is a matter about which I have not yet spoken to you."

Here it was.

"Yes?"

He kept his eyes on the cigarette packet. "The matter of censorship. You know there is a strict censorship here, of course?"

"I was told so."

"In the ordinary way the procedure is that I submit the matter to the censorship office and then file it as a cable or airmail it."

"I see."

"That is in the ordinary way." He laid peculiar emphasis on the words.

"You mean that you would like me to give my stuff to you for submission to the censorship and onward transmission. Is that it?"

He did not reply for a moment or two and began to rock slowly on the back legs of his chair. "Mr. Foster, these are not ordinary times here in this country," he said.

I waited. His glasses, reflecting the light of the desk lamp, winked steadily as he rocked. He went on: "As I understand it, your articles may contain satirical matter hostile and derogatory to this regime."

"They might do so, yes."

He shook his head solemnly. "I can tell you now, Mr Foster. That's out. Right out."

"Well, we'll see."

"Didn't they warn you at head office that things might be difficult here?"
I smiled amiably. "They said that you might be, Mr. Pashik."

He stopped rocking. "Oh now, Mr. Foster, please. You don't at all understand. The censorship is very powerful here. For writing matter antagonistic to the People's Party regime you would be liable under the February decrees to imprisonment and a heavy fine."

"Yes, but only liable."

"I agree. In your case there would naturally be no question of enforcing the decree, but your permit for the trial would certainly be canceled and you would have a very disagreeable interview with the police."

"I could make an article out of that, too."

His lips tightened. "Obviously your papers would be confiscated, Mr. Foster. If it amuses you to write articles so that they may be confiscated, that is your affair. I am concerned with practical newspaper work."

He had me there; I was not. But I felt that at the moment he was not either. I thought he was trying to show me how helpless I should be without him. I said as calmly as I could: "Very well, you're the paper's representative here and you tell me it's very difficult. I understand. Now, how do we get over the difficulty?"

I had to wait while he lit a cigarette and blew smoke at the end of it like a bad actor pretending to think. "You could try going down into Greece over Saturday night and Sunday and sending your work from there." He blew some more smoke. "Of course, the police would guess what you were attempting. An American on a Chicago paper tried it."

"Yes?"

Now he looked directly at me. "He just wasted a lot of time, Mr. Foster. Of course he had no written matter when they searched him at the frontier; it was memorized; but they made difficulties about his visa, took his passport away to get it fixed, and kept him at the frontier station for a week. He had a very uncomfortable time."

"I see. Well, now you've told me how it can't be done, what's the answer?"

He was rocking again. "There is no answer, Mr. Foster. Other ways have been tried. The crews of foreign air liners were used as couriers for a while, but no longer. It is too dangerous for them. I have tried to make all this clear to the head office, but what is real here does not seem so in New York and London."

"In fact, you think it's a great waste of time my being here at all."

"No, I do not say that."

"In effect you say it."

"You misunderstand me. I am in favor of these articles. This trial is *dramatisch*—er—" He broke off, feeling for the word.

"Theatrical?"

"Yes, theatrical. Thank you. The trial of a political leader on ideological grounds is most theatrical to Western ways of thinking. So I say that to have a distinguished playwright, such as you, Mr. Foster, write matter about the Deltchev trial is a very cute editorial idea. I am myself looking forward to reading the series. But—" he leaned forward impressively—"you cannot write it here and send or take it out of the country; that is, not unless you paraphrase the Propaganda Ministry's official matter and get every page stamped by the censorship. You must resign yourself to that."

"But—"

"See the trial, Mr. Foster, memorize"—he stabbed his forehead with a finger to show me where—"and then go home and write your articles. That is what you must do."

For a moment or two I did not answer.

I had been in a train for four days and had had very little sleep on the journey. I had arrived at seven o'clock that morning in a strange city under a hot sun and in a sticky, enervating atmosphere. I had left my luggage in a hotel that might, for all I could remember of the geography of the streets, be a hundred yards away or three miles from where I was now; and even if I found the hotel and remembered the room number, I would not know how to ask for the key. I had trailed round cafés and Government offices, listening to conversations that concerned me conducted in a language I did not begin to understand, at the heels of an aggrieved, self-important eastern European with fat hips and a bad smell. I had a blister on the sole of my right foot and a grimy face. I was also hungry and well on the way to wishing I had not come. Now I was being told that the fact that I had come at all was a pity, but that if I behaved myself and cared to waste my time, I might stay and see the fun. Or so it seemed to me then. I felt myself losing my temper and then managed to wait until the moment had passed before replying. I tried to keep my voice level.

"Mr. Pashik, you know as well as I do that these articles are meant for publication during the trial as a commentary on it. They'd be useless afterwards."

"Do you think so?" He looked knowing. "Deltchev will be condemned to death. Your articles will be part of the campaign against the sentence."

"That's not what I was told. I was asked to send the stuff in as I did it."

"And why?" He threw up his hands, smiling with teeth like salted almonds. "In case you, Mr. Foster, the distinguished playwright, should find time to enjoy yourself on the expense account, or get an idea for a new play about life behind that sinister Iron Curtain and forget your commission. Editors treat us all like children."

"Nevertheless, the articles are expected."

"No, Mr. Foster, they are not. I sent a cable to head office saying that they will not be available until you return."

"I think you should have consulted me before you did that."

"I am responsible, Mr. Foster."

There was a thin-lipped silence. Then I said: "Mr. Pashik, are you a member of the People's Party? I didn't think to ask you before."

He smiled again, but the American accent became more pronounced. "Ah, Mr. Foster, you are mad at me. I don't blame you. I will be frank with you."

"Good."

"If there is any trouble with the censorship over anything that goes out of this office, it will be closed up. That means that I will be closed up, finished. I am responsible."

"Then you'll still be responsible if the articles are published after the trial."

"Ah, no. If the Propaganda Ministry admits you to the country, it is their affair if you produce hostile matter when you leave. While you are here the responsibility rests with this office that you should not prejudge the trial by sending hostile matter." He shrugged. "It is no doubt for them an expedient. For myself, I am hostile to the regime; but I have been expelled for my opinions before, and Pan-European, representing twenty-seven foreign newspapers, has a responsibility to others besides your editor. So you see I must play ball with the regime, Mr. Foster."

I did not know quite what to say. My impulse was to take the trial permit from my pocket, put it on his desk, and say that I would leave in the morning. Certainly that is what he hoped I would do. It was only my awareness of disliking him for a poor reason that made me hesitate. He pushed the cigarettes toward me.

I shook my head. "When did you send that cable?"

"Four days ago, Mr. Foster."

"Why not before?"

"It was not certain that you were coming."

"It was settled three weeks ago that I was coming."

"I did not know that."

"Have you had a reply?"

"Yes, Mr. Foster."

"May I see it, please?"

"Certainly." He opened a drawer in the desk and brought out a cable and put it in front of me. I read:

Your 109 of 6 June understood advise Foster and
arrange air passage London soonest close trial.

"You could have shown me this before," I said.

"I did not realize that you did not trust me, Mr. Foster," he replied gently.

"The cable only says to advise you of something and secure an air passage for you. It does not explain what I have been telling you. You still have to believe that I am telling you the truth."

His smile said that this was the moment when I should feel silly and apologize. Perhaps it was the smile that prevented my doing so. Instead I said: "I take it that the other foreign correspondents will be under the same restriction?"

"If they are hostile to the regime they will have to be equally discreet."

"That story about the American who tried to go to Greece for the weekend—I suppose you made that up in case I thought of the idea myself and didn't tell you."

"It was a way of warning you that the method was known."

"You go at things in rather a roundabout way, don't you?"

He looked at me thoughtfully. "One gets in the habit of it, Mr Foster," he said, and then paused. "Roundabout ways are sometimes safer. However" —his expression changed and he stood up expansively, his smell billowing around him—"it is good to meet a person who cares for frankness. We can understand one another." He smiled cheerfully. "We shall get on well, Mr. Foster. We can help each other, and that is as it should be. I will show you."

He went over to a filing cabinet in the outer darkness, opened one of the drawers, and began to search through it.

"You know, Mr. Foster," he murmured as he picked through the files, "being expelled from a country is not dignified and not at all rewarding. For a few hours you are the brave man who dared to tell the truth. But the next day, when the handclasp of friends is forgotten, you are just another reporter without a job."

He came back to the desk with an untidy bundle of papers and a large envelope.

"When did it happen to you?" I asked.

"Italy, 1930. I was a married man then, too," he said. He hesitated for an instant, then stuffed the papers into the envelope and handed it to me with the rueful smile of a rich uncle for the rascally nephew whom he likes.

"The office file on Yordan Deltchev, Mr. Foster. It will help you."

"Thank you."

"Please." He put up a protesting hand. "I want to help you, Mr. Foster. And I want you to know that I want to. And that is frank. *Avanti*! Now we go to dinner, eh?"

That night I was too tired to sleep. For a while I tried to do so; then I gave up, switched on the light, and began to read the file Pashik had given to me.

At that point I still had the illusion that I could report the Deltchev trial.

Three

~~~~~~~~~~~~~~~~~~~~

THIS IS WHAT I learned from the file.

Until the spring of 1940, when his country had joined two of its Balkan neighbors in coming to terms with the Axis, Yordan Deltchev, although an important figure in the councils of the Agrarian Socialist Party, had had no popular following. Originally a lawyer by profession, he had been deputy for a provincial manufacturing area and then, having served the monarchy and later the Republic in various subordinate capacities, had become Minister of Posts and Telegraphs.

At that time he had been regarded by the knowledgeable as a very able man and as either honest or so far insufficiently tempted. That he was not then even considered as potentially a great popular leader is understandable. His special talent was for organization; and while as a speaker he was not without force, the cool logic, dryly delivered, that made him effective in debate seemed unlikely ever to capture the hearts of audiences of peasants. That it did ultimately do so was a phenomenon produced by a peculiar combination of circumstances. Deltchev himself had very little to do with it.

He had been one of the few deputies, and the only Minister, who had opposed the alliance with the Axis at all vigorously; and during the summer of 1940, at the request of the German authorities, he had been interned. Toward the end of the year he was released, but kept under police surveillance. Two years passed before the surveillance became sufficiently negligent for him to embark on the underground political activity with which his name was to become associated.

Before that time, opposition to the pro-German Government and its allies had been expressed chiefly by acts of sabotage against war-supply installations and by propaganda against the recruitment of divisions for the Russian front. This work had been done by groups led by militant People's Party men, but containing a good proportion of Agrarian Socialists. Yet, although it was sometimes spectacular and always dangerous, the amount of inconvenience it caused the enemy was small and its effect on popular morale disappointing.

To Deltchev's way of thinking, the policy of the underground opposition should be to leave the winning of the war to those who could fight effectively and to concentrate on planning for the future of the country during the period immediately following the inevitable German collapse. He saw that her fate at the hands of the victorious powers would depend very much on the speed with which she could herself establish a provisional government sufficiently uncompromised to negotiate without cringing and strong enough to prevent civil war.

The resultant Committee of National Unity was not created by Deltchev alone, but it was he who made it effective. Clandestine organizations are mostly recruited from among the dedicated, the romantic and the mentally ill-adjusted men and women of a community; and in them courage and devotion are more easily found than high-level planning ability and political skills. Because he was the clearest thinker the Committee had and the only member of it with any practical experience of government, Deltchev became in effect (though in fact he never held any specific appointment) its president, its secretary-general and, eventually, its spokesman. Hundreds of thousands of people who had never heard of Deltchev the Minister of Posts and Telegraphs now came to know of and exult in Yordan Deltchev the patriot. And when the time came for him to speak to them, the dry steady voice and the cool logic seemed, after the hysterical oratory of the war years, to derive from a special kind of sanity and goodness. They felt that he possessed the truth.

If the Provisional Government of National Unity set up by the Committee in the spring of 1944 had done no more than sue for peace so promptly, it would have justified its existence; for by this action it saved all but one of the northern frontier provinces from devastation and kept the minute army intact and available for police duties. Yet it did do more. It was able to secure recognition, qualified but sufficient, by the United Nations, and contrived, in those days of hasty negotiation and shifting authority, to confuse and postpone discussions of such matters as territorial claims and the dismantling of industrial installations. It ensured, at a minimum cost both to the national economy and to the national pride, that most of the vital decisions affecting the country's future were made not in the heat of the newly won battle, but in the milder atmosphere of delayed peace conferences. The credit for these benefits was given to Deltchev. He began to be nicknamed, affectionately, "Papa" Deltchev.

Perhaps but for that nickname there would have been no People's Party regime, and no Deltchev trial.

When the Provisional Government came into power, it was said by neglected members of his own party that the motives behind Deltchev's actions had all along been those of a shrewd, ambitious politician and that, while he could not be blamed for having had greatness thrust upon him, he should not now behave toward his old friends as if he had achieved it. They were soon to wish that they had been entirely right.

One of the main articles of the Committee's original program had been that of insisting on the need for free elections at the earliest possible moment. Its inclusion and the sanctimonious style of its wording were concessions to Anglo-American susceptibilities, which, it had been felt, could hurt nobody. Not that the men of the Committee were cynically indifferent to elections; it was simply that, faced with the task of planning for a great emergency of which nothing was then known and only the worst could be expected, they found such talk unrealistic. A cultivated sense of emergency is not easy to discard, and, later on, the early state of mind about elections tended to persist. When, therefore, the People's Party members of the Provisional Government began to press for redemption of the election promise, their action was interpreted, and correctly interpreted, as a demand for more power; that is, a larger share of the important posts. Only to Deltchev, apparently, did it mean anything different.

The People's Party had lately grown enormously in numbers and influence. The participation of the Agrarian Socialists in the formation and work of the Committee had achieved its object of enlisting wide popular support; but it had also had the secondary effect of making the Committee a powerful recruiting agency for the People's Party. This mishap had long been a subject of complaints and bitter exchanges within the Government, and on one occasion Petra Vukashin, the leader of the People's Party men, had been too frank. "If," he had said, "you are fool enough to introduce your wife to a handsome young man with a bad reputation, you must not complain when you find them in bed together."

When, to the manifest discomfort of Vukashin and the rest of the People's Party faction, Deltchev took the election proposal seriously and began to argue in favor of it, it was assumed at first by his pathetically gleeful colleagues that "Papa" Deltchev was merely calling the enemy's bluff. They knew, had known for some time, that the Provisional Government had the approval and support of the Western powers, who would not press for the promised elections while the country was in Soviet occupation. They had evidence that the Russians, not unimpressed by Deltchev's efficiency, were content to let things stay as they were for the present. Some of its members had even wondered if the word "provisional" might not be dropped from the title of a government with so rich an expectation of life. They could not know that their leader, Deltchev, had already numbered its days.

Many attempts were made later to offer more reasonable explanations of Deltchev's actions at that time than the one accepted by the simpler members of the public—namely, that he was a self-sacrificing patriot who had been directly inspired by God. Since, however, most of their other explanations relied on the assumption that he was monumentally corrupt, none of them was much more convincing.

The material facts were simple.

After the meeting at which the election promise was discussed Deltchev seemed preoccupied and unwilling to pursue the matter in private conversation. To one persistent man, however, he said: "If we have clean hands they cannot accuse us." The man took this to be a comment on the strength of the Government's position and the absurdity of the People's Party maneuver.

That was on a Thursday. For the next few days Deltchev was at home in bed with a severe chill. On the following Tuesday he was due to make a radio speech about a national campaign then in progress for conserving winter foodstuffs for livestock.

He came to the radio station straight from his bed, looking, according to the director of the station, "like a man who has been fighting with devils." In his speech he talked briefly about the conservation campaign and then, after a momentary hesitation, produced a handwritten script from his pocket and began to read a statement from it.

Five minutes later the people knew that, in the considered opinion of "Papa" Deltchev, the time had now come for the Government to redeem the Committee's solemn pledge to hold free elections at the earliest possible moment.

At the beginning of the statement he had declared that he was speaking only for himself and not for the Provisional Government of National Unity. This declaration was both seized upon as evidence of his cynical contempt for his audience and pointed to as marking his absolute integrity. For the former view it was said that no one but a fool would suppose that, whether he wanted to do so or not, Deltchev could in fact dissociate his private opinions on such a question from those of the Government he led; for the latter it was argued that if you accepted the fact of his honesty (and who could deny it?) you would see that his disclaimer was a simple statement of the truth, which he had been bound to make if he were not to deceive the public. As equally divergent constructions could be placed on every other sentence in the statement, neither side could score points. Deltchev himself had returned from the radio station to his bed and, having issued through his secretary the statement that the broadcast speech was "self-explanatory," remained there, silent and inaccessible. But by the time two days had passed, it was clear that the storm over the speech, which raged with mounting fury among the politicians, was no longer of interest to the people. In their eyes the Provisional Government was now committed quite irrevocably to holding elections in the near future and anyone who attacked Deltchev was attempting to deny the fact. Yet it was the People's Party that profited most from the situation.

Those of the unfortunate Agrarian Socialists who had the wit to see that, whatever they might now say in private about Deltchev, they could not hope to win without him as a figurehead were in the majority; but they were terribly hampered by a considerable and vindictive minority whose only concern now seemed to be to oppose and revile him in public. The People's Party, while taking full advantage of this mistake, took care not to make it themselves. By referring to Deltchev patronizingly but respectfully as a kind of elder statesman (he was in fact only sixty then) they managed to convey the impression that he was in a state of derelict senility, which could excuse his continued association with the Agrarian Socialists. Also, by securing the postponement of the elections until the early summer, they gave themselves time to prepare a *coup d'etat* that anticipated publication of the election results by a few hours. In the event, it was almost unnecessary. Thanks to Deltchev, they very nearly came into power by constitutional means.

His response to these events was at first curiously passive. True, he protested against the *coup d'état*, but rather formally, as if expressing an appropriate but not heartfelt sentiment; and in the Chamber his attacks upon the new Government had about them the studied moderation of a fencing master with a new pupil. For a long time he seemed unaware or unwilling to be aware of the Government's quick, wary moves to make themselves secure. Soon the anti-Deltchev faction within his own party began to find people ready at last to listen to their tale of a great fortune deposited abroad in Deltchev's name the day after his election statement. Even among the general public he seemed to be losing popularity. It was understandable that the Government's supporters should have come to think of Deltchev almost as one of themselves.

Then came the incident of "Deltchev's football match."

The occasion was the official opening of a sports stadium. It had been completed in 1940 and immediately requisitioned for use by the German Army as a transit camp. Later the Red Army had used it as a garrison headquarters. Its return was a gesture of Soviet goodwill, which the new Government had dutifully decided to celebrate with as much publicity as possible. It was probably the presence of Western diplomatic representatives at the ceremony that determined that Deltchev as leader of the "opposition" should be asked to speak.

He began, deceptively, with a tribute to the Red Army and expressions of his party's recognition of the generous motives that had prompted the early return of the stadium. He hoped that in the near future it would be the scene of a memorable football match with the local Red Army team.

Then, during the mild applause that greeted this suggestion, he moved nearer to the microphones. But this time he took no manuscript from his pocket. He knew exactly what he wanted to say.

"But meanwhile, my countrymen, there is another, more deadly battle for us to fight—the battle for freedom within the state."

He paused. There was a silence, in which the long banners could be heard flapping in the wind. He went on.

"Two days ago I was invited by the leader of the People's Party, Petra Vukashin, to take the office of Minister of Justice in the Government that now has power. My answer was promised for tonight. I take this opportunity of giving him the answer now. I answer that if he thinks that by so betraying my brothers in the Agrarian Socialist Party I should change in any way their determination to fight until this new tyranny is utterly destroyed—if he thinks that, then he is stupid. If our opposition to his party's criminal plans is such that he must try to buy us off with a share of the loot, then he is also frightened. My countrymen, there is no time to lose. These stupid, frightened men are dangerous, not for what they are now, but for what they mean to become—your masters. They are not . . ."

At this point the booming public-address system in the stadium was cut off. In the deathly pause that followed, Deltchev's voice, high and thin in the wind, could only be heard by those near him as he completed the sentence.

Then the cheering began. It came across the packed stadium as a rolling, sighing wave of sound that surged up and broke with a roar that shook the air like an explosion. It lasted nearly a minute and subsided only when another sound came to replace it: the steady, massive chanting of Deltchev's name. Suddenly on the far side of the stadium there was a wide swirling movement in the crowd as a fight developed, and from closer at hand there was angry shouting. Deltchev, who during the cheering had stood motionless in front of the dead microphones, now waved his hand and turned away. There was another tremendous cheer and more shouting. At that moment the officer in command of a Russian military band, which had been waiting to lead into the arena the squads who were giving the gymnastics display, decided not to wait for an order to do so. It was a sensible decision and probably averted serious trouble. As the band began to play and march in, the cheering became ragged and in places gave way to laughter and clapping. In less than a minute the incident of "Deltchev's football match" was over; over, that is, except for the breathless excitement of discussing it and of reporting it to those who had merely heard it on the radio. But nothing about it was forgotten and much that had not happened was remembered. "Papa" Deltchev had come back to them. He had spoken his mind and they had shown that they were with him in his fight against the "masters."

Four nights later an attempt was made to assassinate him.

His house was of the old kind with a walled courtyard. As he got out of his car to enter the house, a grenade was thrown. It hit the wall by the entrance and bounced back into the road before exploding, so that Deltchev, who had gained the doorway, was partly shielded from the blast. There were few people about at the time and the man who had thrown the grenade escaped.

The driver of the car was badly cut about the head and neck, but Deltchev, although he had been flung against the half-open door and much shaken, was not seriously hurt. In the ensuing confusion, however, his protests that the pain in his shoulder was caused only by a bruise were ignored and he was taken to a hospital with the driver. Within an hour rumors that he was dead or dying were circulating in the cafés, and a large crowd gathered outside the hospital. By this time Deltchev had returned to his home, where the police were collecting fragments of the grenade in the presence of an even larger crowd. There was a great deal of hostility toward the police.

It is said that when the Chief of Police reported to Vukashin later that night that the attempt on Deltchev was being described openly as the Government's reply to the stadium speech, the Minister exclaimed: "Did they think we would reply in the Chamber?" The story may be untrue, but, in the light of what followed, it is not incredible. Certainly from that moment on there was an ominous change in the Propaganda Ministry's public attitude toward Deltchev, and it is likely that the decision to try him was made at this time. The Ministry's official statement on the affair had a sort of angry jocularity about it that did nothing to change the general belief that the Government had known of the attempt in advance. It asserted that the grenade was of American manufacture, and went on to suggest that the obvious place to seek the criminal was in the ranks of Deltchev's own party, where there were many criminals with Anglo-American imperialist connections.

The editor of a newspaper that described this statement as "unsatisfactory, but significantly so," was immediately imprisoned. A series of savage attacks on the Agrarian Socialist Party now began. Their violent tone and the barely concealed threats that accompanied every allusion to Deltchev conveyed unmistakable warnings. The opposition had become intolerable and was going to be liquidated; but first Deltchev must be disposed of. He had a choice. He could escape abroad and be condemned or stay at home and be condemned. In any event he would be condemned.

Deltchev chose to stay. A month later he was arrested.

That was all. For a while I looked out of my hotel window across the flat roofs and Byzantine spires of the city, as still in the moonlight as the landscape of a dead world; and at last I became sleepy.

As I collected up the mass of news cuttings, notes, and manuscript that composed Pashik's file and began to put them back in the envelope, I noticed a paper that I had not seen before. It had been clipped to the back of a wad of sheets with cuttings pasted on them and therefore easily overlooked.

It was a page from a memo pad I had seen on Pashik's desk. On it was typed: "*Case of K. Fischer, Vienna '46—Aleko's hand?*"

For me, then, it was not the most interesting thing about the file. I went to sleep.

Four

~~~~~~~~~~~~~~~~~~~~~

PASHIK HAD PROMISED to drive me to the trial, and we met for breakfast. He nodded at the envelope I was carrying with the approving smile of a friendly schoolmaster.

"Ah, Mr. Foster, you have been reading."

"Yes. There's a lot of material there. Did you collect it?"

He fingered his chin self-consciously for a moment; he had shaved. "Why do you ask, Mr. Foster?"

"Because a lot of the unpublished stuff was obviously done by someone who knew Deltchev very well and liked him. You?"

"Ah, the memoir"; he looked embarrassed; "that was commissioned by one of my papers from Petlarov."

"Who's he?"

"He was Deltchev's secretary and friend—until the elections. Then they quarreled. He was paid for the memoir, but it was not used. It was not the moment."

"Where is Petlarov now? Is he here?"

"He may be."

"I should like to talk to him."

"He will know nothing about the trial, Mr. Foster."

"I'd still like to talk to him."

"He may not wish to see you."

"Then he will say so. You said you wanted to be helpful, Pashik. Here's your opportunity."

He wriggled unhappily. "Please, Mr. Foster. I see I must explain to you." He lowered his voice. "You do not understand. After the arrest of Deltchev, Petlarov was naturally arrested too. He is released now, but he is still suspect. It would be most indiscreet to have relations with him. I cannot take the risk."

189

"You don't have to. Just get a message to him from me. Ask him to tele-phone me at my hotel this evening."

He sighed. "Very well, Mr. Foster. But I think it will be useless."

I held up the envelope with the file in it. "We don't want to take this with us, do we? We could leave it at your office on the way and write a note to Petlarov at the same time. Your office boy can deliver it."

He pursed his lips together at this. "I see you still do not trust me, Mr. Foster," he said.

"What do you mean?"

He saw the danger of explaining just in time. "It is not important," he said with dignity.

He took the envelope from me. Then I remembered. "Oh, by the way," I said, "what does this refer to?" I showed him the paper with the *Aleko* note on it.

He looked at it blankly for a moment. "Oh, that, Mr. Foster," he said, and taking it from me put it in his pocket; "that is nothing. Something from another file."

When once you know how a person lies, it is difficult for him to deceive you again. With Pashik it was a special tone of voice he used for direct lies that gave him away—a cold, too matter-of-fact tone. He had used it before in telling me the untrue story of the American journalist who had tried to go to Greece for the week-end. I supposed the fact that he had lied about this piece of paper to be equally unimportant.

The large courtroom at the Ministry of Justice had been thought too small for a political trial of such moment. It was being staged, therefore, in the main lecture hall of the Army School of Aeronautics, a modern building on the outskirts of the city.

The walls, ordinarily decorated with engineering charts and war trophies, had been hung with flags—those of the Republic and of the Soviet Union, and, at greater intervals, those of the other sympathetic nations of eastern Europe. Just above and on either side of the judges' dais two draped Soviet flags bulged over (but, tactlessly, did not quite conceal) one of the trophies, the tail plane of a Russian aircraft, presented by a German flak unit during the war. Pinned to some of the flags were notices printed in four languages say-ing that smoking was prohibited. In the balcony a row of soundproof booths had been erected for the interpreters relaying translations of the proceedings to the earphones of the foreign diplomatic and press representatives below. In the balcony, too, on heavy stands or clamped to the balcony rail, were big floodlights pointing down into the court to illuminate it for the Propaganda Ministry's film cameras. Beside the judges' dais, on both sides of the prisoner's rostrum, at the corners of the hall, in the balcony, by the doors, and below every flag on the walls, guards were posted. They were all officers or N.C.O.'s and armed with machine pistols, which they did not sling, but held ready in their hands. It had been explained by the Propaganda Ministry that when the evidence against the criminal Deltchev was publicly known, attempts might be made by the people he had deceived to kill him before justice could be done.

The courtroom was crowded. My place and Pashik's were in the foreign-press section, below the edge of the balcony and to one side. In the center was the diplomatic section. On the ledge in front of each seat in these two sections were a pair of earphones and four plug sockets marked with letters distinguishing the Russian, French, English, and German interpretation channels. Also on the ledge was a duplicated copy of the indictment in French. There seemed to be no seats for members of the public without tickets, but several rows behind us were prominently labeled with notice cards bearing initials, which Pashik said were those of prominent trade-union organizations. The occupants of these seats were obviously in their best clothes and on their best behavior. They all wore badges, and in one row there was a group of peasants in national costume. They looked as if they were attending a prize-giving. The front rows, however, had a different look about them. These seats were reserved for the important party members and functionaries. Their occupants wore dark neat clothes and either sat with self-conscious, preoccupied frowns or conversed in *affairé* undertones with their neighbors. Aware of being in the public eye, they were concerned to show that they had business there and were not merely favored spectators. It was warm, and most of the women and many of the men had highly colored paper fans.

At about ten o'clock the floodlights in the balcony were turned on and the fluttering sound of film cameras began. A buzz of anticipation went round the courtroom; then, as the three black-robed judges came slowly in, all stood up. The judges went to their places on the dais but did not sit down until the national anthem had been played through a loudspeaker. It was all curiously reminiscent of a royal visit to the opera. Even the low murmur of conversation that began as we sat down again was familiar. All that was different was that instead of the lowering of lights and the rise of a curtain somebody stood up and called out the name of Yordan Deltchev, and all eyes turned toward a pair of glazed doors beside the dais. Then there was silence except for the sound of the cameras and the distant throbbing of the generator set that supplied the power for the floodlights.

After a moment or two the glazed doors were flung open and three men entered the court. Inside the door they paused for a moment blinking in the lights that poured down on them. Two of them were uniformed guards, tall, smart young fellows. Between them was an elderly man with a thin gray face, deep-set eyes, and white hair. He was short and had been stocky, but now his shoulders were rounded and he was inclined to stoop. He stood with his hands thrust deep into his jacket pockets, looking about him uncertainly. One of the guards touched his arm and he walked over to the rostrum and stepped onto it. A chair had been placed for him, but for a moment he stood there looking round at the flags upon the walls. He smiled faintly. He still had his hands in his pockets. Then, with a curt nod to each of the judges, he sat down and closed his eyes. This was Yordan Deltchev.

There were twenty-three counts listed in the published indictment against him. They charged (principally in count number eight, though the same charge was paraphrased in two other counts) that he had "prepared terrorist plots against the state and conspired with reactionary organizations, including the criminal Officer Corps Brotherhood, to secure, for financial and other personal advantages, the occupation of the motherland by troops of a foreign power." There were other charges concerned with terrorist activity, the smuggling of arms, and plots to assassinate members of the People's Party Government "in particular P. I. Vukashin." Sprinkled throughout were dark references to "various confederates," "notorious foreign agents," "hired saboteurs and murderers," "reactionary gangsters," and so on, while the name of the Officer Corps Brotherhood recurred with the persistence of a typewriter bell. It was soon evident that the indictment was a propaganda document intended for foreign consumption. It said, in effect, or hoped to say: "He is the kind of man against whom such charges may seriously be brought"; and: "He is accused of so much that of some he must be guilty."

The public prosecutor conducted his case in person. His name was Dr. Prochaska and he was one of the few members of the legal profession who had joined the People's Party before it had come to power. He was an authority on questions of land tenure, and most of his practice had been concerned with cases involving them. He had had little experience of court advocacy of any kind and none at all in criminal proceedings. A stout, pugnacious-looking man with quick, jerky movements and a habit of licking his lips every few seconds, he seemed more concerned to defend himself against accusations of weakness than to present his case effectively. He made scarcely any reference to the official indictment and dealt with only two of the charges in it. If he could prove, or seek to prove, those, then Deltchev would stand convicted on the whole indictment. That, at least, was the impression I had of it. From the commencement of his long opening address he adopted a tone of ranting denunciation that carried little conviction and confused even the more reasoned passages. In spite of the earphones on my head, and the voice of the interpreter quietly translating the speech, I was constantly distracted by the sight and half-heard sounds of its originator.

His case, however, was dangerously simple.

It was generally known that at the time of the German retreat in 1944 Deltchev, who had been secretly in touch with both the Russians and the Western powers, had gone to great lengths to secure Anglo-American rather than Soviet occupation of the country. Against the wishes of a majority of the Committee of National Unity, he had at one point gone as far as to propose to the Western powers that the national army should continue to resist the Russians in the north so as to give the Americans and British time to prepare an airborne invasion from Middle East bases.

It was now suggested by the prosecution that this proposal had come in fact from the Western powers themselves and that Deltchev's support of it had been bought with the promise that he would have control of the reallocation of the German oil concessions. In other words, he had tried to sell his countrymen's lives for money and power.

The other favored charge was the one that had so amused my economist friend. It was that Deltchev had planned to assassinate Vukashin, the head of the People's Party Government, and that he was, in fact, a member of the Officer Corps Brotherhood. If this could seem to be proved, he could quite legally and with full popular approval be sentenced to death. The case against Deltchev was designed to destroy both him and his Agrarian Socialist Party forever.

I left the court that day in a peculiar frame of mind. I felt as if I had been to the first night of what had seemed to me a very bad play only to find that everyone else had enjoyed it immensely. A Propaganda Ministry Bureau had been set up in a room adjoining the court. On the way out Pashik stopped to get the official bulletin on the day's proceedings. The room was crowded and I waited in the doorway. There were a number of tables, each signposted with the name of one of the official languages. As I stood there, I saw a bald young man whom I thought I knew coming away from the English table. I had noticed him earlier in the day and been unable to place him. Now as he pushed his way out we came face to face. He nodded.

"You're Foster, aren't you?"

"Yes. We've met before."

"Sibley, Consolidated Press."

"Oh yes." I remembered, too, that I had not liked him.

"What are you doing here?" he asked. "Getting local color for a new play?"

I explained. He raised his eyebrows. "Very nice too. Still, I expect you'll make a play out of it sometime, won't you?"

"I don't know."

"I should have thought that there were masses of material for you. It'd make quite a nice little paragraph, your being here. Do you mind if I use it?"

"Yes, I do." I smiled as I said it, but not very cordially.

He laughed. "All right, I'll spare you. But it'd be nice to send something even a *little* more interesting than these handouts." He waved the sheets in his hand. "I'm at our Paris office really. I've been lent for the trial. Why I can't think. An office boy could file this junk for all of us." He turned his head as Pashik came up. "Hullo, Georghi, we were just talking about you."

"Good evening, Mr. Sibley. We must be going, Mr. Foster. I have to get to the office."

"That's our Georghi. Always on the job." Sibley grinned. "Where are you staying, Foster?"

I told him.

"We must have a drink together," he said.

In the car Pashik gave me the bulletin. I glanced through it. Most of it was composed of extracts from Dr. Prochaska's address. They were even more idiotic to read than to listen to. I put the bulletin down. The streets leading back to the center of the city were narrow and crowded and Pashik was a driver who twitched at the wheel instead of steering with it. He squeezed his way none too skillfully between two carts.

"Mr. Foster," he said then, "there is a suggestion which I think I must make to you." He looked round at me soulfully. "You will not, I hope, be offended."

"Not at all. Look out."

He twitched away from a cyclist just in time. The cyclist shouted. Pashik sounded the horn unnecessarily and put on speed.

"It is a small thing," he said—the car swayed unpleasantly across some protruding tram line—"but I would not, if I were in your place, be too friendly here with Mr. Sibley."

"Oh? What's the matter with him?"

"It is nothing personal, you understand."

"But what?"

"He drinks too much and becomes indiscreet."

"I don't see that that has anything to do with me."

"His associates will be suspect."

I thought for a moment. "Mr. Pashik," I said then, "as a newspaperman don't you think that you're a bit too anxious about the censorship and the Propaganda Ministry and the police and all the rest of it?"

A woman missed death by an inch. He sounded the horn absently and shook his head. "I do not think so. It is difficult to explain."

"What's so difficult about it?"

"You are a stranger here, Mr. Foster. You look on our life from the outside. You are interested in the trial of a man whose name you scarcely know because his situation seems to you to contain the elements of a spiritual conflict. Naturally so. You are a writer of fiction and you make the world in your own image. But be careful. Do not walk upon the stage yourself. You may find that the actors are not what they have seemed."

"Is Sibley one of the actors?"

"I was speaking generally, Mr. Foster."

"Then I'm sorry, but I don't understand what we're talking about."

He sighed. "I was afraid not. But perhaps it does not matter."

I let that one go. A few moments later he pulled up outside my hotel. I got out of the car.

"Shall we meet for dinner, Mr. Foster?"

I hesitated. The air outside the car smelt good. I shook my head. "I think I'll get to bed early tonight," I said.

Five

~~~~~~~~~~~~~~~~~~

THE HOTEL BORIS had been built by a German company in 1914 and was one of those hotels in which footsteps echo and only the sound of a toilet flushing in the distance reminds you that you are not alone there. The foyer was a cavernous place with a tessellated floor and a hydraulic lift in a wrought-iron cage. The reception clerk was a slow-moving, mentally deficient youth with a charming smile. He spoke a little English.

"There is a message for you, sir," he said. He glanced at the scrap of paper that he had taken out of the key rack. "Mr. Stanoiev called to see you and will call again."

"Stanoiev? I don't know anyone of that name. Are you sure it was for me?"

He looked stupid. "I don't know, sir. He went away."

"I see."

The lift was deserted. I walked up the wide shallow stairs to the sixth floor.

My room was at the end of a long corridor with upholstered benches set against the wall at intervals along it. As I started down the corridor, I noticed that at the far end there was a man sitting on one of the benches. He was reading a newspaper.

It made an odd picture; one never expects corridor furniture to be used except as shelves for trays and chambermaids' dusters. As I approached he looked up casually, then went back to his newspaper. I glanced at him as I passed by.

He was a thin, dried-up man with pale, haggard eyes and gray hair cropped so that the bone of his skull was visible. He had a peculiarly blotchy complexion like that of someone just cured of a skin disease. The hands holding up the newspaper were long and yellow. There was a black soft hat beside him on the bench.

I went past him to my room. I put the key in the lock and turned it. Then someone spoke from just behind me.

"Herr Foster?"

196

It made me jump. I turned round. The man who had been on the bench was standing there with his hat under his arm.

I nodded.

"Petlarov," he said, and then added in German: "I can speak French or German, whichever you prefer."

"German will be all right. I'm glad to see you." I finished opening the door. "Will you come in?"

He bowed slightly. "Thank you." He walked in and then turned and faced me. "I must apologize," he said in a clipped, businesslike way, "for answering your note in this fashion. A native of this country would not find it strange, but as you are a foreigner I must make an explanation."

"Please sit down."

"Thank you." In the light of the room his clothes were shabby and he looked ill. His precise, formal manner, however, seemed to ignore both facts. He chose a hard chair as if he did not intend to stay long.

"First," he said, "I think you should know that I am under surveillance; that is to say, I have to report to the police every day. Second, I am officially listed as an 'untrustworthy person.' That means that if you were to be seen entering my house or talking to me in a public place, you would attract the attention of the police, and yourself become suspect. That is why I have used this unconventional means of seeing you. I discovered your room number by leaving a note for you in the name of Stanoiev and noticing which box it was put into. Then I came discreetly up here and waited for you to return. You need therefore have no fear that my name is in any way connected with yours or my presence here known about." He bowed curtly.

"I am most grateful to you for coming."

"Thank you. May I ask how you obtained my address?"

"From a man named Pashik."

"Ah, yes. I thought it must be him." He looked thoughtfully into space.

"Do you know him well, Herr Petlarov?"

"You mean what is my opinion of him?"

"Yes."

He considered for a moment. "Let us say that I do not subscribe to the common belief that he is merely a disagreeable person whose political views change with the person he talks to. But now that I am here, what do you want of me?"

I had held out my cigarettes. His hand had gone out to them as he was speaking, but now he hesitated. He looked up from the cigarettes, and his eyes met mine.

"I have some more," I said.

He smiled in a deprecatory way. "If you had perhaps a bar of chocolate or a biscuit, Herr Foster, it would, I think, be better for my stomach than tobacco."

"Of course." I went to my suitcase. "I have no chocolate, but here are some biscuits."

I had a box, bought in Paris for the train journey and then forgotten. I opened it. The biscuits were the kind with pink icing sugar on them.

"Not very good for a bad stomach," I remarked.

He took one with a polite smile. "Oh yes. Excellent." He nibbled at it with very white false teeth.

"Pashik gave me your piece on Deltchev to read," I said.

"Oh, yes? It was considered unsuitable for publication."

"By Pashik?"

"Yes, but I was not surprised or upset. I knew that it had been commissioned in the belief that because I had had a difference of opinion with Yordan I would therefore write about him in an unfavorable way. If Pashik had asked me, I would have told him what to expect. Fortunately he did not ask."

"Fortunately?"

"If he had known he would not have commissioned the article, and I needed the money."

"Oh, I see. I have a bottle of whisky here. Would it be safe to ask the floor waiter for some glasses?"

"I think not. Perhaps I may have another biscuit."

"Of course, please help yourself. You know, Herr Petlarov, I came here to write a series of articles about the trial of Deltchev. But Pashik seems afraid that I shall offend the censor if I do them here."

"He is probably right," he said calmly. "He is usually right about these things. Yes, I can see. If you offend he will be blamed."

I must have looked disbelieving. He took another biscuit. "I will tell you a little story about the regime. A member of the People's Party wrote a novel about the fight of a group of workmen with the capitalists who wished to close a factory. It was a naïve story in which the capitalists were all monsters of evil and the workmen's leader a People's Party man. The Propaganda Minister, whose name is Brankovitch, would not, however, allow its publication. He said that the hero was not positive."

"I don't understand."

"The author had not demonstrated that the hero member of the party was a *good* man."

"But surely that was inferred."

"Brankovitch would say that you were in intellectual error, Herr Foster. Inference is not positive. The public must be *instructed* that the man is good, as they must be instructed in all things."

"You must be exaggerating."

"In London or New York I would be exaggerating. Here, no. The sequel to this is that the writer was angry and made a little propaganda of his own. He has now been sent to forced labor. Pashik does not see that fate for himself. You see, Herr Foster, those who must be persuaded to obey are no longer important, for shortly we shall cease to exist. Our liquidation has begun." He smiled significantly.

"What do you mean?"

He took another biscuit and held it up. "This is the third biscuit I have taken," he said. "There are twenty-one left in the box. I can eat nine more."

"You can have the box."

He inclined his head. "Thank you. I had hoped that you would give it to me. I had based my calculations on your doing so. If I eat nine more I shall have eaten twelve. That will leave twelve for my wife. Luckily we have no children to share with us."

I was silent.

"I will explain. It is quite simple. Persons who are listed as untrustworthy are not allowed to work at anything but manual labor. I tried that, but I am not strong enough. So, as I cannot work, my wife and I may not have ration cards. We are, of course, very often hungry, and that can make a good argument for obedience."

I got up and went to the wardrobe for the whisky. Out of the corner of my eye I saw him reaching for another biscuit. He glanced over his shoulder at me.

"Please do not distress yourself, Herr Foster. A bad conscience can, I know, be as unpleasant in some ways as an empty stomach, and the person with the biscuits so often has a bad conscience. The trouble is that most of us with empty stomachs also have bad consciences. That combination will prove deadly."

"I have a metal cup," I said, "and also a tooth glass. If you like whisky—"

"I tasted it once," he said courteously. "I thought it better than schnapps and more interesting than our plum brandy. You need not fear, however, that I shall insist on taking it away with the biscuits."

I gave him the tooth glass. He took a small sip and looked at me. "I know that you will forgive my telling you that before I came to see you this evening I looked up your name in an English reference book I have."

"You'd like to know what a playwright is doing writing articles about a political trial?"

"Oh no, I see the connection. I was putting myself in your place for a moment. You have been in this city for two or three days perhaps. You do not know the country or the people. You are present at a trial that is like a game played for counters of which you do not know the value. Yet you have to interpret it for Western eyes."

"Something of the kind has already been said to me once today."

He nodded calmly. "As a guide you have Pashik, a man so preoccupied with a problem of his own—self-preservation possibly, but we cannot be sure—that he can lead you only to the counter of the Propaganda Ministry." He took another biscuit. "Have you seen the official bulletin of the trial today?"

"This?" I took it out of my pocket. "They gave out copies as we left the courtroom."

"They will do so every day. Tell me, Herr Foster, what will there be in your articles that a clever, malicious journalist sitting in London could not contrive for himself from a set of these reports?"

"I'm sure you have your own answer ready."

"Ah, I have offended you." He smiled. "But not seriously, I think, if you reflect. What I am suggesting to you, Herr Foster, is that you might find it useful to employ my services."

"Yes, that's what I thought you meant. How?"

"As a guide. I make this suggestion without embarrassment. You were kind enough to invite me to tell you some things about Yordan and of course I will do so." He touched the biscuit box. "I should have been well paid for that. But I think that I could be of further use to you." His haggard eyes looked up at me with a cold little smile in them. He licked a crumb off his lower lip.

"I'm sure you could," I said, and waited.

"For instance," he went on, "I wonder if you have considered that some of the evidence against Yordan Deltchev might not be as stupid as the prosecution makes it." He looked into the tooth glass.

An unpleasant suspicion crossed my mind. "Your difference of opinion with him," I said, "was over his radio speech approving the election, wasn't it?"

He was very quick. He said calmly: "If I were an enemy of his I would not need to beg a gift of biscuits, Herr Foster. I should be a witness at his trial. And if, as your caution may suggest, I am here as an emissary of the Propaganda Ministry to try to corrupt your judgment, then you cannot yet have identified the man whose task it will be to do so."

"I'm sorry. I don't know what you're talking about. What man?"

"Our friend Brankovitch has been forced to admit a number of hostile foreign journalists for the purpose of reporting this trial. Do you suppose that while they are here he will make no attempt to neutralize their hostility? Of course, he must try. I can even tell you the procedure he will adopt. Tomorrow perhaps, or the next day, after Vukashin's evidence has been heard, Brankovitch will call a foreign-press conference and answer questions. Then, perhaps the next day, someone will approach you privately with a great secret. This person will tell you that he has discovered a way of getting uncensored messages out of the country. He will let you persuade him to share the discovery. Of course, your messages will not be sent, but they will serve as a guide to your intentions, which can then be anticipated in the official propaganda. Brankovitch likes, for some reason, to use *agents provocateurs*." He looked at me sardonically. "I know his sense of humor. It was I who recommended him to Yordan for a place on the Committee."

I offered him a cigarette again. He hesitated. "If I might take two?" he said.

"One for your wife?"

"Yes."

"Please take the packet."

"Thank you."

It was not quite full. He counted the cigarettes in it carefully.

"How did you meet Deltchev?" I asked.

He looked up. "He was my partner," he said. He seemed surprised that I did not know.

I gave him a box of matches and he lit a cigarette.

"Thank you." He blew smoke. "When Yordan first practiced as a lawyer, I was his clerk. Later I became his partner. When he was appointed Minister of Posts and Telegraphs, I became his assistant and secretary. I was also his friend."

"What sort of man is he? Superficially, I mean."

"Quiet, deliberate, very patient. A sound lawyer. If you were a journalist interviewing him in his office, you would probably be irritated by a habit he has of looking past you when he is talking. He keeps his desk very tidy and empties the ashtray as soon as you have put your cigarette out. Yet polite. He would tend to put words into your mouth—criticisms of himself—and then answer them. A bad habit for a lawyer, that. A man with a family—wife, son, daughter—of whom he is very fond, but not a family man. A good man, but not at ease with himself."

"The sort of man who would betray a principle for a bribe?"

"Yordan has never valued money enough to be corrupt in that way. Power might have tempted him once. You speak, of course, of his actions over the election promise."

"Yes."

"If he was paid to make that radio speech, he gave up what he might value— power—to gain what he did not value—money." He shrugged. "I have had plenty of time for thinking, and much bitterness has gone. At one time I thought of killing Yordan for what he did then, but even in hate I never supposed that he had been bribed."

"What is your explanation?"

"I have none. Yordan was often accused of being merely a shrewd politician. In retrospect that seems as ridiculous as the accusation now that he is a murderer. By unnecessarily bringing about the November elections he committed political suicide and betrayed all the people who were loyal to him. You ask for an explanation." He threw up his hands. "It is as easy to say that he was insane as to deny that he was bribed. When I faced him in his room that night he did not look insane. He looked strangely at peace with himself. That made me more angry, and, you know, in anger many things seem clear. 'Why?' I shouted at him; 'why?' 'It is better so,' was all he replied. Then, when I had finished abusing him, I said: 'Papa Deltchev has gone and the Minister of Posts and Telegraphs has returned. Papa Deltchev was not strong enough to bear a people's love!'" Petlarov looked across at me and smiled slightly. "But now I cannot remember what I meant," he added.

After a moment I asked: "Will the election matter be raised at the trial?"

He shook his head. "Not by the prosecutor. For the regime, the less said about the election the better. But they might tolerate the defense's making play with it to suggest Yordan's fundamental sympathy with the regime."

"Who is defending?"

"His name is Stanoiev. It amused me to use it here. He is the party member appointed to defend. His arguments in mitigation will be given prominence. They will serve as the final condemnation." He frowned. "What I do not understand is this affair of the Officer Corps Brotherhood. Yordan's attitude toward Soviet occupation—yes, that is something to argue and misinterpret, to deal with speciously. But the Officer Corps Brotherhood is another matter. They make so much of it that they must have something. Yet the idea is absurd."

"Surely it's easy enough to manufacture evidence?"

"Yes, but that is not their way. Consider the case of Cardinal Mindszenty. He was accused of an offense against the currency regulations. We know that it was only technically an offense and not committed for his own gain, but he was guilty of it and that was the reason it was used. If he had been charged as a corrupter of youth it would have made better propaganda, and no doubt the evidence could have been manufactured. But no—the currency offense could be proved. The lie stands most securely on a pinpoint of truth." He took the last of his twelve biscuits and shut the box. "What do you want of me, Herr Foster?"

"You have already given me a great deal."

"I have a suggestion. Why do you not talk to Madame Deltchev?"

"Is it possible?"

"Yes, for you. She and her household are under protection—that is, they are not permitted to leave the house, which is guarded—but your permits will allow you to pass. I will give you a letter to her. She will see no other journalist, I assure you. You will make a coup."

"Yes, I see that. What kind of woman is she?"

"She was a schoolteacher in the town where we practiced years ago. She came of a Greek family. If she had married me instead of Yordan, perhaps I should have become a minister. But better that you should form your own opinion. If you wish, I will come here every evening at this time to give you what information and comment I can." He leaned forward and touched my knee with his forefinger. "Is it agreed?"

"Agreed. But what is my part of the agreement?"

He hesitated. "Money—a little, what you consider fair—and your ration card. Not the restaurant tickets—those you will need and I could not use—but the ration card for bread, meat, butter, milk, eggs, and green vegetables. As a foreigner, you have one on the highest scale, I think."

"Yes."

"You still have it? You have not already disposed of it?"

"No. It's yours. I'll get it now."

He sighed. "It is as well that my wife is not here," he said. "She would weep."

Later, when he had gone, I sat by the window and had a whisky and water in the tooth glass. I was beginning to feel perceptive and understanding.

That was the point at which I should have packed my bag and gone home.

Six

I**N THE AFTERNOON** of the second day of the trial the prosecutor completed his opening address to the court and began to call witnesses.

The first was Vukashin, the head of the Government. There was a stir as he went into the witness box.

He was one of those politicians who in their dealings with the public are like small-part actors who specialize in playing such things as shrewd lawyers, family doctors, and wise fathers; their mannerisms of speech and gesture have been cultivated to fit the stock characters their physical peculiarities suggest. He was square and solid, with a short neck, and he stood awkwardly in the witness box, his big hands clasping the ledge in front of him, the shoulders of his ill-fitting jacket hunched about his ears. He had blunt features, with a muscular jaw and full, determined lips. His forehead was low and permanently knitted in a frown of concentration. In the popular edition of his biography published by the Propaganda Ministry he was referred to as a "veteran front fighter in the class struggle," and from the illustrations you received the impression that he had spent most of his life marching up steep hills at the head of fist-brandishing processions of angry revolutionaries. The role he affected was that of "simple workman."

In fact he was not simple nor, strictly speaking, had he ever been a workman. His father had been a small but fairly prosperous tradesman, and Vukashin himself had been a bookkeeper in a timber warehouse during the early part of his political career. It had been a natural talent for accountancy and office organization rather than revolutionary ardor that had raised him first to the secretaryship of a trade union and later to leadership of the party. He had a reputation for the kind of wit that makes a political statement in terms of some excretory or sexual function. He was a powerful man physically and was said to have once made a brutal assault on a colleague who had opposed him. But it was also said that the victim had been alone in his opposition and unpopular and that the assault had been calculated quite coolly for its disturbing effect on the morale of other intransigent colleagues. He was a brusque, direct speaker and very effective with big audiences. "What are the *real* facts behind this problem?" he would shout; and although he never answered such questions, the sturdy conviction with which he pretended to do so, and his way of enumerating his sentences so emphatically that they sounded like hammer strokes of logic, usually concealed the deception.

The prosecutor's self-effacing deference to him was so abject that it was not even amusing. From a ranting bully who at least existed, Dr. Prochaska became suddenly no more than a disembodied, impersonal voice, a prompter who fed the witness with a short question and then waited until the speech in reply was over and another question was wanted from him.

"Minister Vukashin, in March of 1944 when the armistice negotiations began, what was the attitude of the prisoner, Deltchev?"

"Our policy was peace, immediate peace to save the country from devastation by reactionary-led forces seeking to continue their losing battle with our Soviet ally. Every hour of it meant another cottage, another farm destroyed, every day a fresh horror for our peasant workers in the frontier areas. Who could have said 'Go on'? Not a man with heart and bowels! Only a blood-maddened beast. But there was such a creature. His name was Deltchev!"

"Minister Vukashin, in what ways did the prisoner Deltchev work against the peace?"

"It would be easier, Public Prosecutor, to tell the court in what ways he did *not* work against the peace, for then I could answer shortly: 'in *no* way.' From the beginning of the negotiations he used his position on the Committee to hinder their conclusion. You may ask why this was tolerated, why he was not immediately removed from his post. The answer to that is simple. We believed at that time that he was in misguided but honest doubt about the terms of the negotiations that were under discussion. We were a responsible group acting not for a defeated country—we were never defeated—but for a resurgent nation. The terms offered us by Russia, however, contained, as was natural in the circumstances, military clauses that involved our surrendering certain rights of government. The interpretation put upon them depended upon one thing and one thing only—whether or not Russia could be trusted. We of the People's Party did trust Russia, and in the event we have been justified. All the rights surrendered by us then have now been restored. The prisoner took a contrary view—or said that he did, for we know better now—and it was this view that he urged upon us as a justification for delay and for continuing his negotiations with the Anglo-Americans."

"Did he contend that better terms would be obtained from them than from our Soviet ally?"

"No. The terms were no different in essence. They had been agreed to by the Foreign Ministers at the Moscow Conference of '43. According to the prisoner, what would be different was the way in which they would be enforced. Or so he said."

"Minister Vukashin, did the prisoner take part in the discussions with Soviet representatives?"

"Very little. He was too busy licking the backsides of the Anglo-Americans."

Laughter.

"Minister Vukashin, in presenting his arguments for negotiations with them, what advantages did the prisoner claim would follow?"

"He claimed so many advantages that you would have supposed us conquerors about to impose our will upon the defeated. But what were the facts at that time? First . . ."

The earphones softly droned out the translation, but above this sound his own voice persisted. It was loud and, in the harsh, penetrating quality of its lower notes, disquietingly aggressive. He claimed hostility as urgently as another might claim love, and to hate him was to submit to a seduction. In a way he was impressive.

The voice went on and the grotesque rubbish it talked was passively received in evidence. I watched the judges' faces as they listened.

The floodlights for the cameras were on all the time now. The day was warm, and soon, as the afternoon sun poured in through the high steel-framed windows, those in the lights began to sweat. Most of them wiped their heads frequently and fanned themselves; but the judges, sweltering in their black gowns and biretta-like caps, seemed unwilling to acknowledge their discomfort before the eyes of the cameras. They had been judges before the People's Party had come into power and it was known that all such appointments were under review by the Government. Later, perhaps, in a cool cinema at the Propaganda Ministry, the film would be examined by subtle, hostile men able to construe the wiping of hands or forehead as gestures of disrespect to the Minister and his evidence. No momentary relief from discomfort was worth that risk to the judges. Two of their older colleagues had already been dismissed for showing reluctance to preside at this trial. Now, behind the sweating impassivity of those who had not shown reluctance, there was the terrible anxiety of men who, having sacrificed their principles, fear that the sacrifice may after all go unrewarded.

Only the prisoner did not sweat. He sat with his hands in his jacket pockets and his eyes closed, the back of his white head resting against the wooden rail that separated the lawyers' tables from the body of the courtroom. His face was livid in the glare of the lights and he looked as if he might faint; but, incredibly, he did not sweat. But for the pricking of your own skin you might have fancied that the heat of the place was an illusion and that all the perspiration you could see was simply a visible manifestation of collective guilt.

The afternoon crept on and the shadows moved slowly across the courtroom until there were only narrow strips of sunlight on the walls. There were no more than ten minutes to go before the day's adjournment when the "incident" occurred.

Vukashin had almost completed his evidence and the prosecutor was asking him a series of questions about the meeting of the Committee at which it had been finally decided to accept the armistice terms.

"Minister Vukashin, what was the attitude of the prisoner when it was clear that the majority of the Committee favored acceptance?"

"As always, he attempted to obstruct the wish of the majority. He repeated all his former arguments, and when these were rejected again by the rest of the committee, he said that he had had further discussions with the Anglo-American representatives and that something might yet be done with them."

"He gave the impression that he was making these proposals to them?"

"He had always given that impression. But now in the heat of the moment he made a slip that revealed his true intention. He said that the Anglo-Americans were only waiting for the word and at the snap of his fingers they would come."

At that moment a strange voice in the court said something loudly and sharply, and, in the dead silence that followed, the interpreter automatically translated:

"That is a lie."

Deltchev had risen to his feet and was facing the witness box. His hands were still in his jacket pockets, but he was standing very straight.

Vukashin looked startled for a moment, then turned his head to the judges.

"The prisoner objects to the truth."

The center judge leaned forward. "The prisoner will be silent."

Deltchev took no notice. "I do not object to the truth," he said. "Nor do I object to the fantastic perversions of the truth that the court has been listening to today, for no person in his senses will accept them. I do, however, object to lies that attribute to me statements which I have never made."

The judge shouted angrily: "Be silent. You will have an opportunity of speaking later."

"Will the Minister Vukashin be available to me for cross-examination?"

"Your counsel may examine the witness if he wishes to do so."

"He does not propose to do so. He values his own skin too much."

There was a commotion at this, and the thin, dark man whom I took to be Stanoiev began to make some sort of appeal to the judges. As several other people, including Dr. Prochaska, were speaking at the same time, the interpreter became tongue-tied. One of the judges began to shout.

"The presiding judges call for silence," said the interpreter.

Vukashin had been standing in the witness box looking on with a grim smile. Now he raised a hand and, as the noise subsided, spoke: "I have given my evidence. Let him say what he wants."

Deltchev faced him again. There was complete silence now. The prisoner's voice was light but very clear and precise.

"Minister Vukashin," he said, "was it with the Committee's knowledge that I made the proposal to the Anglo-American representatives in 1944 that we should fight a delaying action in the north?"

Vukashin hesitated a fraction of a second. "Be careful how you answer," Deltchev put in quickly. "The facts can be checked. The minutes of the Committee still exist."

Vukashin made an impatient gesture. "I am aware of that."

"Then you see the need for caution. Will you answer the question, please?"

"The reply is not as simple as you try to suggest. The Committee was aware that a proposal was made, but it was not aware that you hid instructions from your Anglo-American friends to make it appear that the proposal came from the Committee."

"Your answer is that I *was* authorized by the Committee to make the proposal."

"Yes, but . . ."

"Let me continue, Minister. If the Committee authorized the proposal and if, as you say, the Anglo-American representatives wished it to be made, will you explain then why they did not immediately accept it?"

"Do not please ask me to explain the actions of the Anglo-Americans."

Laughter.

"It is not the actions of the Anglo-Americans I am asking you to explain, but your own account of them."

Vukashin turned angrily to the judges. "I am here to give evidence, not to answer political riddles. That is enough."

"You have been very patient. The court thanks you, Minister. The prisoner will be silent."

Vukashin left the witness box and sat down. As he did so, Deltchev turned with a pale smile to face the courtroom. "The Minister is afraid to answer," he said.

It was at that point that Dr. Prochaska made a foolish mistake. He had been standing there impotent and forgotten during this exchange. He was irritated. He was the prosecutor and yet matters had been taken out of his, the responsible, hands, and an important battle of words had taken place without him. More serious still, the Minister, whom he should have protected, had had the worst of the battle. Now he saw his chance of retrieving not only his own dignity but that of the Minister as well. Never once since the trial opened had Deltchev taken his hands from his pockets, and Dr. Prochaska had found the fact irritating. He suddenly thought he saw just how he might humiliate the prisoner.

"Afraid?" he exclaimed derisively. "The Minister is *afraid* to answer?" He gave a short laugh. "It is not the Minister who is afraid. It is you, Deltchev! No wonder you seek to accuse and discredit the witnesses against you. You are in fear of your life. No wonder you tremble. No wonder you keep your hands in your pockets. Do you think we do not notice? Ah, but the people have eyes, Deltchev. You cannot deceive them forever. You may disguise your fear in other ways, but your trembling hands you dare not let us see. Come, show us your hands, Deltchev. Or else be silent while justice is done."

In the breathless hush that descended, there was one single quickly suppressed giggle and then no sound but the fluttering of the cameras. The prosecutor had a hard, ugly little smile on his lips. At that moment he was not absurd. Vukashin looked down at his own hands, frowning. Deltchev stood quite still, his face expressionless. He was making up his mind.

Then he took his hands out of his pockets and held them out, palms downward, in front of him. They shook with a coarse tremor that must have been visible at the back of the court.

"The prisoner's hands are more truthful than his tongue," said the prosecutor.

Without a glance in his direction Deltchev put his hands back in his pockets and raised his head.

"I speak," he said loudly, "to the members of the diplomatic corps present here and to the representatives of the foreign press."

There was another commotion in the front of the court, and the prosecutor began to protest to the judges. The interpreter began to translate the protest and I took my earphones off. Others beside me were doing the same. Deltchev had spoken in German.

"You may have formed your own conclusions," he went on, "about the quality of the evidence that will be given by the prosecution in this court. In case you are in doubt, this demonstration will convince you. The evidence of my own hands has now been offered against me. I will explain what it is worth."

With an elaborately satirical bow in the direction of the diplomatic and foreign-press sections, the prosecutor abandoned his protest and stood, his arms akimbo and an unsuccessful attempt at a smile on his face, looking up at the ceiling.

"I make no defense of myself in offering this explanation," Deltchev was saying; "my defense is in the safe hands of the prosecution." He smiled faintly. "But perhaps you will be interested in this fact. I give it to you merely as a point of interest."

He paused and then went on very deliberately: "Gentlemen, I am a diabetic and have been so for several years now. That has meant, of course, a careful diet balanced with injections of insulin. The amount of insulin I need is not great—twenty units in the morning and twenty at night. I can, of course, call medical witnesses to prove this. When I was first arrested, the prison doctor was authorized to supply me with insulin. He even increased the injections slightly to compensate for the change in diet. Five weeks ago I was moved to another part of the prison and was not allowed to see the prison doctor. For just over four weeks I have been without insulin. The symptoms of diabetes have therefore returned—thirst, fatigue and other disagreeable manifestations, which I shall not trouble you with. The trembling of my hands is part of my general weakness and debility. If the prosecutor had asked me to show you my knees, you would have seen that they also tremble." He looked round at the prosecutor for a moment and then turned back to us. "I think that if he had known of this illness he would not have drawn your attention to it in this way. It is no part of his task to create sympathy for me. I merely ask you to note that he makes wrong deductions even from facts. The fantasies that he will create from the falsehoods his case rests upon I leave to your imagination."

Then he sat down.

The prosecutor said something quickly to the judges. The center judge said something in reply. I put the earphones on again and caught the translation.

"The presiding judges rule that the remarks of the prisoner shall not be entered in the record, as they were made in a foreign language not intelligible to the court. The case is adjourned until tomorrow."

The court rose.

When the judges had gone, Deltchev stepped down from the rostrum and with his two guards walked slowly toward the glazed doors. Nobody else in court moved. They watched him. At the door he paused and looked back. Then with a small, friendly nod he turned away again and went on through the doors.

I looked at Pashik. He was standing stiffly and awkwardly as if caught in the act of rising. He did not seem to notice his discomfort. He looked at me rather strangely. "A good man, Mr. Foster," he said softly; "in his way a great man."

But I did not pay much attention to him. Even now I can remember everything I thought during that next half-hour. I was very shocked by what I had seen and heard and full of hatred for the People's Party regime. I think that if I had met Dr. Prochaska in the corridor outside the courtroom I should have hit him. But soon I began to think more reasonably.

Nobody, I thought, could share the experience I had just had without also sharing my passionate indignation at what was being done in that sunny courtroom. If I could convey the scene with even a tenth of the impact it had in reality, I would arouse a storm of anger that might damage the regime appreciably. And then an idea began to form in my mind of how I might write about the Deltchev trial.

This, I thought suddenly, was more than just the crooked trial of a politician by his more powerful opponents. Here, epitomized, was the eternal conflict between the dignity of mankind and the brutish stupidity of the swamp. Deltchev, sick and alone, knowing that nothing could save him from a verdict and a sentence already decided upon, was yet prepared to go on fighting for the truth he believed in. Dimitrov at the Reichstag fire trial had fought for his life and won. Deltchev's life was already forfeit, but he was fighting none the less and might win a greater victory. And the fight was of his own choosing. Months back he could have escaped abroad and made the Government's task easy. He had not done so. Long-forgotten sentences began to run through my mind. *"Will you then flee from well-ordered cities and virtuous men? And is existence worth having on these terms? Or will you go to them without shame, and talk to them, Socrates? And what will you say to them? What you say here about virtue and justice and institutions and laws being the best things among men? Would that be decent of you? Surely not? . . . Will there be no one to remind you that in your old age you were not ashamed to violate the most sacred laws from a miserable desire of a little more life?" . . . This, dear Crito, is the voice I seem to hear murmuring in my ears, like the sound of a flute in the ears of a mystic. . . ."*

I was deeply moved. I was also beginning to enjoy myself.

And then I got back to my hotel, and Petlarov was waiting in the corridor. We went into my room and I told him what had happened.

He nodded coolly when I had finished. "Oh yes. Poor Yordan. He is certainly not strong. But how foolish of them not to tell Prochaska how the victim was being prepared! But we may expect foolishness. You see, they have always been able to rely before upon the folly of others. Now that they have to rely on themselves, their deficiencies are revealed. Of course an incident like that will make no difference to the outcome of the trial."

"No, but it will make a great difference to the comments on the trial in the Atlantic countries."

"The comments of the West did not save Petkov or Mindszenty. I think it is interesting, however, in quite a different way." He smiled thinly. "Why do you think Yordan made this demonstration? What did he hope to gain by it?"

"He saw an opportunity of hitting back and he took it. Surely, that's obvious. It was splendid."

"He saw an opportunity and took it, certainly. What exactly did he say finally—the last two sentences?"

I had scribbled down Deltchev's words as he had said them. I read the last two sentences again. " 'I merely ask you to note that he makes wrong deductions even from facts. The fantasies that he will make from the falsehoods his case rests upon I leave to your imagination.' "

Petlarov showed his white teeth. "What a clever lawyer Yordan is!" he said. "Do you not see what he has done, Herr Foster? Oh, certainly he has won the sympathy of the foreign diplomatists and press representatives, and that is very nice; but what else?"

"He made the prosecutor look a fool."

"He did more. Consider. He makes the speech in German. Why?"

"Obviously so that he would be allowed to speak. The interpreters didn't relay what he said, of course. As far as the public was concerned, he was unintelligible. Obviously it was the American and British representatives who mattered to him, and Vukashin and the judges and Prochaska didn't want to antagonize them unnecessarily by shutting him up. If they don't care much anyway about Western opinion, they could afford to let him talk."

"If it was the American and British who mattered, why did he not speak in English? Yordan speaks very good English."

"Oh."

"The educated persons of most small nations need a second language to their own. With us it is mostly German. Many of the party members in that courtroom speak German, and some of them are not unfriendly to Yordan. Those were the persons who interested him. What he wanted to do—and what he has done, perhaps—is to discredit the prosecution's evidence in advance."

"That's not difficult. It discredits itself."

"So far, yes. But perhaps Yordan was wiser than we yet know."

"I don't understand you."

"It is quite simple." He leaned forward with a chilling smile. "You see, Herr Foster," he said, "some of the evidence against him may not discredit itself. Some of it may be true."

Seven

〰〰〰〰〰〰〰〰

DELTCHEV'S HOUSE WAS on the edge of the city in an old residential quarter behind the Presidential Park. Petlarov had drawn a sketch map for me of the way there, and after an early dinner I walked to it from the hotel. There was a slight breeze and the air seemed cooler. The main streets and cafés were full of people, the women in their shapeless dresses and cheap wedge shoes, the men in their cloth caps, with their jackets over their arms, and their shirts undone at the neck; but beyond the park, where there were few shops and scarcely any cafés, the streets were almost deserted and the only sounds came from the radios in apartment houses.

I found the quarter without difficulty. It was off the Boulevard Dragutin; six quiet streets, paved for a short distance from the boulevard and then ending casually in a hillside wasteland of scrub and tamarisks. The streets were lined with plane trees and with square, solid old houses, each isolated within its own courtyard by a high wall with a heavy wooden door in it. The spaces between the walls of adjacent houses formed narrow lanes, some of which connected parallel streets but mostly were shut off by tall iron gates and choked with wild vines.

The numbers on the houses were on blue enamel plates over the wall doors, and when I came to the right street I saw that Deltchev's house must be the last in it. But the setting sun was in my eyes and I did not see the guards outside the house until I was nearly upon them."

They were standing in the shadow of the plane tree just by the door. The trunk of this tree was scarred and the lower branches were leafless; the grenade of American manufacture must have exploded just by it. The guards' faces turned toward me as I approached.

They were in the uniform of what I referred to in my own mind as the "military police," though perhaps "*gardes mobiles*" would have contained a more accurate comparison. They wore the same gray-green uniform as the court-

213

room guards; but these had rifles instead of machine pistols, and instead of
tunics they had blouses bunched in at the waist by greasy leather belts with
ammunition pouches. From a difference in their badges I guessed that they
were a corporal and a private. They were young, bronzed, and rather stupid-
looking. Our eyes met as I came up, and I nodded, but they did not reply in
any way or make any movement to intercept me. I stopped by the door, looked
up at the plate to confirm that I was at the right house, and then reached up to
pull a bell handle bracketed to the wall.

The next moment I received a violent blow on the shoulder. The shock of
it made me gasp. I lurched against the door and twisted round. The private
had his rifle raised to prod me again. The corporal had his rifle pointed at my
stomach, and his finger was on the trigger. I raised my hands.

The corporal shouted something and took a pace backwards. I moved away
from the door. I started to say in German that I did not understand what
he was saying, but he shouted again, and this time I caught the word for
"papers." With the heel of my hand I indicated my breast pocket and said:
"*Papieren.*" The private jabbed the muzzle of his rifle into my ribs. Then the
corporal, stepping forward, tore open my jacket, snatched out my wallet, and
stepped smartly away from me.

It all happened in a few seconds. I was absurdly shaken. I must have looked
it, for the private grinned at me then in quite a friendly way as if my discomfort were a tribute to his efficiency. The corporal was frowning over my press
permit. He looked at the photograph on it and he looked at me. Then he folded
the permit, put it back in the wallet, and, coming up to me, began to speak
very slowly and distinctly, waving the wallet under my nose to emphasize
what he was saying. It was clearly an admonishment. I nodded. Then he gave
me back the wallet, saluted negligently, and moved away. Behind me the
private stretched up and pulled the bell handle. A bell clanged inside the courtyard. Then he, too, went back to his post under the tree.

They watched me as I waited, the private still grinning, the corporal frowning coldly. My shoulder hurt abominably and I badly wanted to rub it; but a
curious shame and perhaps, too, a fear of pleasing them prevented my doing
so. I was disconcerted by these unfamiliar and, I could not help thinking, rather
childish emotions. I had behaved stupidly and had been roughly treated and
humiliated in consequence; but it was no use; my hatred of them welled up
like a sickness.

Then I heard footsteps crossing the courtyard inside: the clacking, slither-
ing footsteps of wooden-soled sandals without heel straps. There was a pause
and a rattling of bolts. Then the door opened a few inches and an old woman
looked out. She had a face like a walnut shell, with woolly gray hair and bright
little eyes very deep in their sockets.

She looked past me to the guards.

"I should like to see Madame Deltchev," I said in German.

She snapped out a reply I did not understand.

From behind me the corporal shouted something. I looked round in time to see him raise his rifle threateningly. She snapped again, then very slowly she opened the door. I heard the private laugh as I went inside.

The wall of the courtyard was about fourteen feet high and decorated all the way round with big frescoes of pastoral scenes: peasants dancing, a young man wooing a dairy-maid, a village wedding. They were crude and conventional like the decorations on Russian toys. The predominant colors were cobalt blue, terracotta, and ochre, but in some places the paint had flaked so badly that only a faint discoloration of the stones showed where it had been. The floor of the courtyard was paved with square flags, on which stood potted plants of various kinds, some of them in brilliant flower. Out of a square space in the flagstones grew a big cherry tree. Beyond it, in a corner, there was a neat woodpile, with vine poles leaning against the wall by it.

The old woman had stopped to bolt the door again, but now she straightened up and faced me grimly, her arms folded, her eyes bright and full of malice. She said something that must have been: "Well, now you're in, what do you want?" In German I replied that I did not understand. She did not understand that. I got out Petlarov's letter addressed to Madame Deltchev and gave it to her. She took it in her clawed, arthritic hands and looked without comprehension at the writing. I guessed that she could not read. She looked up at me suspiciously for a moment, then held up a hand for me to wait and clacked away round the side of the house.

I rubbed my shoulder and looked at the front of the house. It was about twenty feet from the wall, a blank symmetrical façade in gray stone with white painted metal shutters fastened over all the windows. Double steps curved up to the front door, which was flanked by potted azaleas and looked as if it were rarely opened. I heard the old woman's footsteps on a bare floor inside and a distant murmur of voices. Then for a bit there was silence. I was a small boy again, calling for a friend with rich parents.

The breeze stirred the leaves of the cherry tree and there were other footsteps inside the house. A moment or two later the front door opened and a girl came out. At the top of the steps she paused.

"Herr Foster?"

"Yes."

She came down the steps with the preoccupied frown of a busy person whose time is being wasted. She was in the early twenties, dark and very pale, with high Slavic cheekbones. It was an intelligent face, too, but had an expression of bland self-assurance too determined to be real.

"I am Katerina Deltchev," she said.

"I'm glad to meet you." She had only a remote facial resemblance to her father.

"What is it you wish, Herr Foster?"

"To see your mother. Perhaps Petlarov's letter did not explain that." I knew that it did.

"At the moment I am afraid that is quite impossible. She is very upset, you understand."

"Naturally. Is she specially upset today?"

"Please?"

"I am sure that these are all terrible days for her. I merely wondered if the proceedings today had specially affected her."

"I don't think so."

"Then perhaps you would ask her when I may see her, Fräulein."

"I can tell you anything you wish to know, Herr Foster." She smiled, but not very warmly. "Would you like a drink?"

"No, thank you. Are you quite sure that your mother wishes to be protected from someone who may be of help to her?"

"I don't understand."

"If you will take Petlarov's letter to her, I'm sure she will explain to you." She stopped smiling. "My mother does not see journalists."

"So I believe. That is why Petlarov gave me the letter to her."

She hesitated, then pressed her lips together. "Very well. Please wait."

She turned on her heel and went into the house again. She was wearing neat white shorts, a *maillot*, and sandals. I felt a little sorry for her. It is difficult, even for an attractive young woman, to make a dignified exit in shorts.

I waited a few more minutes. The light was going. Then the front door opened again and this time the old woman came out. She beckoned to me and I followed her.

Inside, there was a large hallway, with curtained doorways on either side and a slippery hardwood floor. There was a radiator against the wall between two of the doors. It was all very clean and smelt of polish. Motioning me to follow her, the old woman climbed up the stairs. On the landing there was a shuttered window, and by the half-light filtering through the slits in the metal I could see a passage running along the width of the house. The old woman turned to the right along it and, going to a door at the end, scratched on the panel. There was a voice from within. She opened the door.

Red light from the setting sun streamed into the passage through tall unshuttered windows in the room beyond, and as I came to the doorway I could see the bare khaki hills outside the city.

The windows gave onto a wooden terrace with an awning and vines growing over trellises at the sides. There was an iron table there with books on it and some cane chairs.

The room was large and filled with massive red plush drawing-room furniture of the kind made for the wealthy tradesmen of pre-Sarajevo Vienna. On the walls there were heavy gilt mirrors and girandoles, and colored prints in polished wood and ormolu frames. Overhead there was a large gilt electric chandelier. The upholstery was red cut velvet. In winter the room could be quite cheerless, but now with the windows opened on the terrace and with the gilt touched by the glow of the sunset it had a certain richness and warmth.

As I came into the room, a woman sitting just out of the sun by the far window put a book down and rose to her feet.

I had a slight shock.

She was someone who had once been a provincial schoolteacher. Petlarov had said: "Perhaps if she had married me instead of Yordan, I should have become a minister." There was the diabetic husband under sentence of death. There was my pilgrimage to this old house to see her and my interview with the attractive young woman whose mother did not see journalists. There was the quiet shuttered house, the smell of furniture polish. Out of all these things an image of the Madame Deltchev I would find had been composed in my mind's eye. She had been an old woman with white hair, in a wheel chair perhaps or even bedridden; a wiry matriarch with the evidence of her youthful beauty still discernible in her face, and the vitality, which had served the young lawyer and then driven the ambitious politician, still there in the brightness of her glance and the impatient directness of her speech. How this irascible crone had borne a daughter twenty years ago or what disease now immobilized her my untidy imagination had not troubled to inquire. What I was prepared for in Madame Deltchev was the female counterpart of the gray, shaking man I had seen in court that day and with whose mystery and fate I was preoccupied; and I had visualized no other.

What I saw was a slim, erect woman of about fifty in a striped silk blouse and well-cut skirt, and with sleek, black hair only slightly touched with gray. Her forehead was broad and high and she had gentle, very intelligent eyes. The bold regular features, which her daughter had inherited, were in her more masculine, but her complexion was perfect.

She smiled politely as she greeted me. "Herr Foster, I'm so sorry that you were kept waiting outside."

"It's very kind of you to see me."

"Please sit down." She sat down again herself. She had a small lace fan that she fluttered unobtrusively by the side of her face farthest from me. "My daughter had the best of intentions, but she did not understand Petlarov's motives."

The girl stood behind the chair. She did not look at me.

"With Petlarov," she said angrily, "there is only one motive. He does only what he is paid for."

Her mother said quietly: "Please get us some tea, Katerina."

Katerina laughed shortly. "English journalists drink only whisky, Mother. It is traditional." She went over to the samovar. "Isn't that right, Herr Foster?"

Madame Deltchev frowned and said something quickly in their own language. The girl made a sharp retort. Madame Deltchev smoothed her hair.

"I think that Herr Foster will excuse you, Katerina, if you wish to leave us to talk," she said calmly.

The girl stood still looking at her for a moment, her face dark with anger. Then with a bang she put down the tea glass she had been holding and walked out of the room.

Her mother rose and, going over to the samovar, began to pour the tea herself.

"All nerves in this house," she said, "are greatly strained, Herr Foster."

"Yes, I can imagine."

"For my daughter it is perhaps most difficult," she went on; "unfortunately she is in political disagreement with my husband. She sympathizes with that section of the Agrarian Socialists which blames Yordan for the present situation. So her love for her father is in conflict with her feelings toward the man who betrayed his party. It is difficult for her and I cannot help much." She handed me some tea. "You see, Herr Foster, it is not without reason that I avoid speaking to journalists. I do not guard my tongue. The regime would be glad to use the fact that Yordan's own children oppose him politically. But Petlarov says that you are friendly and to be trusted."

"I was wondering, madame, what there was about Petlarov's motives to be understood."

She took her tea back to her chair. "Petlarov is a good friend," she said. "Even after his disagreement with Yordan he remained a friend. When he was released from prison I was able to see him for a short while and I asked his advice about the press. We were already an object of interest, you see. He told me that I should see no one until he sent somebody who could be trusted."

"That is very flattering, but, frankly, I do not see the reason for his choice."

"Did you not read his letter?" She held it up.

"I'm afraid I couldn't."

"Oh yes, the language." She looked at the letter. "He says that you are going to write a series of articles about the trial and sentence which will be published in America and England. He says that your articles will be well written and acceptable and that although they will be politically naïve—" She broke off and looked at me apologetically. "He means, of course, that he does not regard you as primarily a political person."

"He's right."

She smiled. "So many of our circle would be offended." She returned to the letter. ". . . although they will be politically naïve, their simplification of obvious issues and the evident sincerity of their indignation will be admirably suited to the campaign against the outcome of the trial." She folded the letter. "Petlarov is interesting, is he not?"

"Very."

"So very wise, and yet not a whole man." She picked up her tea reflectively. "His nerves were never strong enough for power."

"Unlike your husband's."

She looked up, a little sharply, as if I had interrupted a train of thought. "Yes, let us talk about Yordan," she said; "and about the trial. That is why you are here."

"I don't wish to distress you, but I should like you to know about something that happened today."

She nodded. "Yordan made one of his demonstrations. I already know about it."

"It wasn't in the official bulletin."

"No. Every evening since we have been under house arrest an old friend of our family has come to see us. Every evening he is searched by the sentries and every evening the sentries find some money in his handkerchief. They let him pass."

"I see. The demonstration was very moving."

"Yes, I was told that. It is a great relief. After this they will not dare to withhold his insulin injections."

There was a curious lack of emotion in the way she said it. We might have been discussing a common acquaintance.

"Do you think that was all he hoped to gain from it?"

"What else is there, Herr Foster? Please do not think that you must spare my feelings. Yordan will be condemned."

"Petlarov had another explanation. He said that your husband seized the chance of discrediting the evidence of the prosecution."

"Yordan is a good lawyer."

"From the way your husband used his opportunity Petlarov deduced that there might be some evidence against him that can only be dealt with by discrediting it."

She looked slightly puzzled. "Evidence that can only be dealt with by discrediting it?" she repeated.

"Yes."

She shrugged. "There will no doubt be many things too absurd even for denial."

"There is no true evidence that can be brought to support any of the charges?"

She looked surprised. "Of course not."

"No facts at all that could be twisted into evidence of corrupt negotiations in 1944?"

"Most facts can be twisted, Herr Foster."

"But in this case not credibly?"

"No."

"That would be true also of the alleged association with the Officer Corps Brotherhood?"

"Doubly so. The idea is absurd. My husband was the man primarily responsible for the destruction of the Brotherhood."

"You think that false evidence will be brought?"

"They have no alternative," she said with a touch of impatience.

"Then it will be easy for your husband to disprove the evidence?"

"If he is allowed to do so, yes. But I do not follow the trend of your questions, Herr Foster. The charges are obviously absurd."

"That is what troubles me, Madame. If there is no vestige of a case to support them, they are too absurd. As Petlarov points out, if they had to fake evidence, there were less fantastic charges available."

"Petlarov is sometimes too clever. It is perfectly simple. Association with the Brotherhood is a capital offense and today also a disgrace."

"You do not expect to be surprised by any of the evidence?"

"Nothing that the People's Party can contrive would surprise me."

For a moment or two I sipped my tea. There was something difficult I wanted to say. She was sitting attentively waiting for me to go on. The sun was dying and in the faint after-light her face was astonishingly youthful. I might have been looking at the young schoolteacher whom the lawyer Deltchev had married, the young woman of Greek family whose lips may have had even then the same gentle, inflexible determination that I saw now.

"Madame Deltchev," I said, "when you were speaking of your daughter you referred to your husband as the man who betrayed his party."

"I was representing him as my daughter sees him."

"But you do not see him that way?"

"I understand him better than that, Herr Foster."

"That might not be a reply to the question, madame."

"Is the question important for your understanding of the trial?"

"I do not know your husband. It seems to me important that I should."

She sat back in her chair. She had just put her tea down on the table beside her, and her hands rested lightly on the chair arms. There they could reveal nothing.

"You saw my husband in court today. You could see the evidence of most of the qualities you wish to know about—his courage, his cleverness, his sense of timing, his determination. One thing the circumstances would not let you see—his absolute integrity, and I, who know his heart, will vouch for that."

The light was very dim now, and in the shadow of the chair her face was difficult to see. Then she leaned forward and I saw her smile.

"And in case you wish to ask me about his weaknesses, Herr Foster, I will tell you. He cannot accept people as they are, but only as his reason dictates they should be. Feeling he suspects, reason never, and the idea that in him the two may be connected he rejects completely. Therefore he is often mistaken about people and just as often about himself."

I was silent for a moment. Then I got up to go.

"May I come and see you again, Madame?"

"Of course, Herr Foster, please do." Then she paused. "I shall in any case be here," she added.

"Afterwards, if you are allowed to do so, will you leave the country?"

"When Yordan is dead, do you mean?"

"When there is no more to be done here."

"Then I shall go on living behind our wall," she said. "Did you not notice our wall?"

"It's very fine."

"You will see such walls round most of our old houses. In Bulgaria and in Greece, in Yugoslavia, in all the countries of Europe that have lived under Turkish rule it is the same. To put a wall round your house then was not only to put up a barrier against the casual violence of foreign soldiers, it was in a way to deny their existence. Then our people lived behind their walls in small worlds of illusion that did not include an Ottoman Empire. Sometimes, as if to make the illusion more complete, they painted the walls with scenes of national life; but only on the inside, for that was where life was lived. Now that we are again inside our walls, the habits of our parents and our childhood return quietly like long-lost pets. I surprise them in myself. This room, for instance. Since Yordan's arrest it has been the only room on this floor of the house that has had the shutters open in the daytime. My feelings tell me it is better so. But why? No reason except that from all the other windows on this floor one can see the street."

"Isn't it dangerous to deny the street?"

"For my children, yes. For me, no, for I shall not try to impose my private world upon the real. My son Philip is a student in Geneva. He will be a lawyer like his father. Already he promises to be brilliant, and Switzerland is a better place for study than here. I hope to make it possible for Katerina to join him there." She paused. "Yes, by all means come again, Herr Foster. When you wish." She pressed a bellpush. "Rana will unbolt the doors and show you out. I will tell her also to admit you if you come again."

"Thank you."

We shook hands and said good-night. As I went to the door I heard the old woman's sandals flapping along the passage outside.

"Herr Foster."

"Yes, Madame?"

"It might be misleading to pay too much attention to Petlarov's views."

"I will remember what you say. Good night."

"Good night."

The door opened and a shaft of electric light from the passage struck across the darkened room. I glanced back; I wanted to see her face again in the light; but she had turned away.

I went past the old woman into the passage and waited while she was given her instructions. Then she shut the door of the room and led the way downstairs.

The girl was standing in the hall. She was waiting for me. She had changed into a blouse and skirt.

"Herr Foster, may I speak to you a moment?"

"Of course." I stopped.

She said something to the old woman, who shrugged and went away.

"I will show you out myself," the girl said; "but I wanted to speak to you first. I wanted to apologize to you for my behavior."

"That's all right."

"It was unforgivable."

She looked so solemn that I smiled.

Her pale cheeks colored slightly. "I have something to ask of you, Herr Foster."

"Yes, Fräulein?"

She dropped her voice. "Tell me, please. Were you searched by the guards when you came in?"

"No. One of them pushed me in the back with his rifle and they looked at my press permit, but that's all."

"A foreign press permit. Ah, yes." Her eyes became intent. "Herr Foster, I have a favor to ask of you." She paused, watching to see how I took it.

"What is it you want me to do?"

"To deliver a letter for me."

"What letter?"

She took a letter from her blouse pocket.

"Can't you post it?"

"I am not permitted. Besides—" She hesitated.

"You just want me to post it for you?"

"To deliver it, Herr Foster."

"Why can't I post it?"

"There is internal censorship."

"Where is it to be delivered?"

"Inside the city, Herr Foster," she said eagerly. "Near the station."

"Who is it to?"

She hesitated again. "A young man," she said.

"Supposing I'm caught with it?"

"You will not be, Herr Foster. Rana said that when she opened the door the guards were friendly to you. Please, Herr Foster."

I thought for a moment of the guards and of their friendliness. The muscles in my shoulder had stiffened slightly.

"All right, Fräulein. A pleasure."

"Thank you, Herr Foster."

I took the letter and glanced at the envelope. The address was in block letters and quite clear. I put it in my pocket.

Her smile was replaced suddenly by a look of anxiety. "When will you deliver it?"

"Tomorrow sometime. When I can."

She would have liked to ask me to deliver it that night, but I was not going to do that. I made as if to go.

"Thank you," she said again. "I will show you out now if you wish."

She had a small hand-lamp. We went out and across the dark courtyard to the door in the wall. She undid the bolts.

"Good night, Herr Foster," she whispered, and then, standing behind the door so that she could not be seen from outside, she opened it.

The beam of a powerful flash shone in my face, blinding me. I stepped through the wall, and the door closed behind my back. I stood still.

"*Papieren*," said a remembered voice.

I got out my wallet and opened it with the press permit showing. The private was holding the flashlight. The corporal came into the beam of it. He glanced at the permit without touching it and then, smiling at me grimly, he nodded and with his thumb motioned me on my way. He said something and the private laughed. They were pleased that I had so quickly learned my lesson.

It was only as I walked away up the street and the beating of my heart began to return to normal that I realized that, for a moment or two, while the light had been shining on my face and while I had wondered if they might be going to search me after all, I had been very frightened. I fingered the pocket with the letter. It crackled faintly. I smiled to myself. I was childishly pleased. I did not know that I had just performed one of the most foolish actions of my life.

Eight

As USUAL NOW, I had breakfast with Pashik. "Last night, Mr. Foster," he said, "I telephoned your hotel."

"I was out."

"Yes. It does not matter." In his brown eyes was the faint hostility of the lover determined not to be possessive. "It was to tell you that Monsieur Brankovitch, the Minister of Propaganda, has called a foreign-press conference for this evening. We, of course, have been invited."

"Oh?" What Petlarov had said about the tactics of the Propaganda Ministry came into my mind.

"Monsieur Brankovitch will speak and also answer questions," said Pashik solemnly. "It will be very interesting. The food and drink will be excellent."

"And there will be a collection taken for the poor of the parish."

"I beg pardon."

"Nothing. A bad joke."

"The conference will be in the state rooms of the Ministry at six o'clock."

"Good ."

He dabbed his bread in his coffee. "Have you seen Petlarov again, Mr. Foster?"

"Yes. I thought you'd rather not know about it." For a moment I wondered if I should also tell him that I had been to see Madame Deltchev, and then decided not to.

"As long as there is no indiscretion, Mr. Foster."

"He comes privately to my hotel room. The reception clerk does not know him."

He sighed unhappily. "No doubt he will be discreet for his own sake. Is he still of interest to you?"

"Yes. He is an intelligent man, don't you think?"

"If he had used his intelligence, Mr. Foster, I should be more sympathetic towards him."

225

"You mean if he had played ball with the regime?"

"Of course. That is the realistic attitude."

We went off to the trial.

That day, the third, six witnesses were heard. All of them had been members of the Committee of National Unity, and all, except one, were members of the People's Party. The exception was a man named Lipka, and he was a member of the anti-Deltchev section of the Agrarian Socialists.

For the most part, the evidence consisted of repetitions of the assertions made by Vukashin the day before. A mass of documents, including the minutes of the Committee meetings for the critical period, was produced, and there was a great deal of pseudo-legal fuss about which documents could and which could not be admitted as exhibits. The minutes were naturally well to the fore. As minutes they were quite often worse than useless, but as ammunition for the prosecutor they were just the thing. I remember one typical item: "After some discussion the Committee agreed that Y. Deltchev should meet again with the Anglo-American representatives and urge them to delay the final decision on the proposals previously made." The prosecutor's witnesses declared that the "discussion" in question had been an effort by Deltchev and his henchmen to stampede the Committee into accepting a set of Anglo-American proposals it had not even seen and that the Committee's decision had made Deltchev "grind his teeth with rage." The judges had a word or two to say and even the defendant's counsel, Stanoiev, felt it safe to join in this sort of argument. At one point, indeed, there was a fair simulation of a legal battle between the two advocates—a battle between two clowns with rubber swords—and, in the approved fashion, high words were exchanged.

The only effective witness was Lipka. He was one of those angry, embittered men who bear the news of their defeat in their faces; prepared always for hostility, they succeed in provoking no more than weary impatience. A talentless but ambitious man, he had been an Agrarian Socialist deputy for many years without achieving office, and his membership on the Committee had seemed to him the long-awaited recognition of his worth and the beginning of his period of fulfillment. In fact, his value to the unconstitutional Committee had resided simply in his status as an elected deputy, and when posts in the Provisional Government were being allotted he had been passed over without a thought. From that moment he had nursed an almost pathological hatred of Deltchev. At one time that hatred had been something over which people smiled and shrugged. Now, at last, the People's Party had turned it to account. His mode of attack was stupid but damaging.

Most of those whose work is directly related to the moods and behavior of the public are inclined to refer to it on occasion in disparaging, even insulting terms. But, while a gibe at popular stupidity from a harassed bus conductor may be amusing, the same gibe from the mouth of a leading politician has, for many, an uglier sound. What Lipka did was to quote Deltchev's private comments on various matters and contrast them with public utterances made by him at the same time.

"Papa" Deltchev had made a speech officially regretting an incident in which some peasants, misunderstanding or ignoring a Red Army order to keep out of a certain area, had been shot down by Russian sentries. In private he had said: "It might not be a bad thing if a few more of the damn fools were shot." After a speech congratulating the farmers on their public-spirited efforts to send more food to the towns "Papa" Deltchev had said privately: "Thank God, they've had sense enough at last to find the black market." On his own proposals for dealing with the fuel shortage "Papa" Deltchev had remarked: "And if they're still cold we can always print a few more copies of the regulations for them to burn."

There were altogether about a dozen examples given of the prisoner's "contemptuous disregard of the welfare of the people whose interests he pretended to have at heart." No doubt there were, as Lipka claimed, many others that could have been quoted. The muttered asides of an overworked minister of state grappling with administrative chaos are unlikely to be distinguished for their sweetness or reason, and if he is an impatient man with crude notions of humor, they may be better forgotten. Certainly they cannot fairly be used as evidence of his true mind and intentions.

In his only interruption of the day Deltchev made this point himself. He said: "The doctor called out in the middle of a cold night may privately curse all mankind, but that curse does not prevent his doing his best for the patient."

This remark was immediately excluded from the record as irrelevant. It had its effect in court, but I was beginning to see that it was not in the court that Deltchev was being tried.

Petlarov's comments were not reassuring.

"After sitting for three days in that courtroom," he said, "you may realize that not one single piece of evidence that could be called evidence in a civilized court of law has been offered in support of the charges and that the only piece of sense uttered has been supplied by the prisoner in his own defense. And yet already much damage has been done. The grocer I now visit again—thanks to you, my friend—is an intelligent man and a supporter of Deltchev. He detests the People's Party and suspects what he reads in the controlled press. Yet the trial is important to him, and as he cannot attend in person, he must read the official reports in the newspapers. He reads with great suspicion, of course, and he discounts much of what he reads. But where is his standard of measurement? How can he discriminate? He reads that Minister Vukashin's evidence proves conclusively certain accusations against Deltchev. Can he ask by what rules of evidence Vukashin's statements are held to constitute a proof of anything except their own dishonesty? Of course not. He is a cautious man and hard to convince, but when I ask him today what he thinks, he is uneasy and does not like to meet my eye. 'Evidently,' he says to me, 'there was much evil that we did not know about. Even if these pigs must find it out, it is best that we know. We are in a mess all right.' And you know, Herr Foster, for the Vukashins and the Brandovitches, that is success. The disillusioned do not fight."

"I thought that it was the possible truth of some of the allegations that was worrying you."

"The foreign press is not so easily disturbed by official bulletins, as my grocer. What did Madame have to say about the Brotherhood?"

"She said quite confidently that the charges were absurd."

"Did you believe her?"

"I believe she sincerely thinks they are absurd."

"You were impressed, eh?"

"Yes. She said she thought you were being over-clever."

"It is possible. I hope so. But remember that the only parts of his indictment which make statements that can be proved or disproved are those referring to the Brotherhood. You may create a haze of misrepresentation to prove that a man had evil intentions and cast doubts on his denials; but if you claim that on a certain date he went to a certain place and saw a certain person and he can prove that he did not, you are lost. Because the court invites your contempt, do not suppose that Prochaska and Brankovitch are fools."

"What does Katerina Deltchev do?"

"She was an art student."

"Was?"

"Is, for all I know. But of course she cannot attend classes at present." He looked at my wrist watch. "It is time for you to go. You must not miss Brankovitch."

I went to the press conference in a gloomy frame of mind.

The Ministry of Propaganda occupied one of the wings of what had once been the royal palace. It had been built, during a period of national prosperity toward the end of the eighteenth century, to the design of an Italian architect who had seen Versailles. Only a quarter of the building planned had been completed, but the resultant structure was imposing and quite large enough to contain three ministries and the national bank. The Propaganda Minister's press conference took place in a large state room with a painted ceiling and two vast chandeliers. Chairs had been ranged in a semicircle round the marquetry desk at which the Minister was to stand. To one side there was a long table arranged as a buffet, with napkins covering the food on it.

Among the American and British correspondents Brankovitch was known as Creeping Jesus; he had a peculiar way of walking with his head and shoulders slightly in front of the rest of his body while his arms remained at a position of attention at his sides. By the French correspondents it was said that the posture was imposed upon him, as, in his imagination, Brankovitch carried two portfolios under his arms: that of his own Ministry on one side and that of the head of the Government on the other. He was a pale, dark man with a massive head and supercilious eyes. A graduate of Warsaw University, he had once been a mining engineer and his connection with politics had begun with pamphleteering. He had made a name for himself before the war as the arch-opponent of the foreign oil companies. He was a clever, ambitious man who never missed a chance of referring most emphatically to his loyalty to and admiration of Vukashin. There were many jokes made about these fulsome references to his leader; but it was said that, while he did not laugh at the jokes when they were reported to him, neither did he frown. It was believed that Vukashin disliked him personally but respected his judgment.

There were about sixty persons in the room; about half of us were foreigners. Brankovitch came in briskly, followed by two male secretaries bearing files and notebooks, and those who had been standing about, talking, took their seats. Brankovitch waited, looking round, until the movements had ceased. Then he began.

"Gentlemen of the press," he said in German, "I have invited you to meet me here with three objects in mind. First, I wish to help you as far as possible in your work by giving you certain information necessary to your understanding of the evidence soon to be given in the criminal trial you are reporting. Next, I wish to give you an opportunity of asking me questions on matters of fact, and also"—he smiled slightly—"on matters of opinion to which you may feel you already know the answers. Thirdly, I wished for the pleasure of renewing acquaintance with those of you I already know and of meeting those I don't know. But business before pleasure, as the English say. I will speak briefly and then there will be time for questions."

He glanced at his watch. He had a sort of brusque amiability that was not displeasing; he did not much care what we thought of him or mind if his amiability were not reciprocated. He was the busy man prepared to waste a little time on fools and so, logically, indifferent to foolishness.

"Let me tell you," he said, "about the Officer Corps Brotherhood; not about its origins—I feel sure you know about those—but about its later activities and its methods. Terrorist societies are not recent institutions. Most countries have suffered from them. Many countries, including the United States of America, still do suffer from them occasionally. It is the duty of all civilized governments, when these occasions arise, to seek out and destroy the criminals. It is the duty, I say; yet, of course, the duty is not always performed. Sometimes the government is itself terrorized. In other cases the government may sympathize with the terrorists' aims and secretly wish them well. I need hardly tell you that the Government of the People's Party is neither intimidated by nor in any degree sympathetic to the Officer Corps Brotherhood. We will not tolerate crime of any sort. The workman who kills his mate in a moment of rage and the fanatic who kills his ideological enemy in cold blood shall have the same justice."

"From a People's Court?" somebody in the row behind me murmured; but if Brankovitch heard, he took no notice. He went on:

"Under the reactionary governments of the prewar years the Brotherhood became a great and terrible burden to our people. It is not known for certain how many murders it was responsible for. Without doubt the number must be reckoned in hundreds. I can tell you with more precision that the number of violent attacks on the person committed by the Brotherhood in the ten years between 1930 and 1940 was about one thousand four hundred. This figure includes only those cases serious enough to need hospital treatment. The reason for the greater precision is, of course, that those persons lived to explain what had happened. The injuries included bullet wounds—approximately six hundred cases; stabbings—approximately two hundred cases; acid-throwing—approximately thirty cases; flogging—approximately two hundred cases; and severe bruising and beating with truncheons, rods, and other weapons made up the remainder."

He had been referring to notes in front of him. Now he pushed them aside.

"But statistics can give little idea of the emotional consequences of this state of affairs, of the hatreds and fears aroused and of the effect on the social life of the community. I will tell you, therefore, of one typical case among the known cases and leave the rest to your imaginations. It is the case of Kyril Shatev, who was prefect to this city in 1940. A man named Brodno, a criminal pervert and a member of the Brotherhood, had been arrested on suspicion of murder. There was plenty of evidence on this occasion and Shatev determined to bring this man to trial. Immediately he began to receive the usual threats from the Brotherhood. He ignored them. I will be quite honest with you; past experience told him that when the case came for trial the attentions of the Brotherhood would turn from him to the judge trying the case. The judge might yield, but that was not Shatev's business. However, he miscalculated. The probability is that the evidence against Brodno incriminated senior members of the Brotherhood and was for them too dangerous to be heard. The Sunday before the date of the trial was to be set, Shatev, with his wife, his two young children, and two female servants, was at his house about ten kilometers out of the city. They were about to sit down to the midday meal when a car drove up and three men got out. They said they wanted water for the car. A servant unthinkingly opened the outer door and the men pushed past her, knocking her senseless with a pistol butt. Then they went into the house. Shatev tried to defend his family and was immediately shot. Unfortunately for him, he did not die at once. The men had a bayonet, and the two children were killed with it. Shatev's wife was then forced to witness her husband's sexual mutilation, also with the bayonet. She was then killed herself. The other servant was not harmed. She was to serve as a witness, they said, that the sentence of the Brotherhood had been carried out. She was threatened, however, that if she attempted to identify the murderers she too would be killed. The murderers were never identified and Brodno was never tried."

He paused for a moment and looked round. "One typical case," he said, and sighed. "No doubt," he went on, "much could be said about a government that allowed itself to be intimidated by such means, but it is easy to miss the point. There were, in fact, many members of the Brotherhood in Government circles. This we have found out later, for, of course, membership was always secret. Who were these men? We know of two who were ministers and twenty-seven in posts of high authority in the civil service, the police, and the army. There were certainly others in these high places. The plain truth is that membership in the Brotherhood ran through every class of our society except that of the ordinary workman. This Brotherhood is a bourgeois disease. It is difficult to conceive, I grant you, that a man, presumably of more than average intelligence and ability, who has made his way to a position of authority and responsibility, could have any direct relationship with, for example, the murderous perverts who entered the Shatevs' house that Sunday or with others equally vile. But we found it so. When, during the life of the Provisional Government, we began the attack upon this evil, we had many terrible surprises. Yes, I say, *terrible*. To despise a man politically is one thing. To discover that he is a criminal lunatic is another. It is difficult to believe the most incontrovertible evidence in such cases. Yet we must."

He paused again and there was dead silence. We knew that now he was talking about Deltchev. He clasped his hands in front of him.

"Let me give you an example from history, gentlemen," he said; "not the history of our own country, but that of Italy and France. In 1830 there was in Italy a young exile named Louis Bonaparte, a nephew of the first Napoleon and once his adopted grandson. In Italy also at that time there was a secret terrorist society called the Carbonari—the Charcoal-Burners. Among the members were nobles, officers, landlords, Government officials, peasants, and priests. The members called each other 'cousin' and the only form of resignation ever accepted from a member was his death. This young Bonaparte became a member of the Carbonari and a year after was imprisoned by the Austrian police for his part in a murderous affair. He was not then a very important or responsible person. But twenty-eight years later, when that same man was Napoleon III, Emperor of France, the Carbonari had need of him and sent a reminder by an assassin named Orsini. The reminder was a gift of three bombs, and they exploded one evening in the January of 1858 as the Emperor was arriving at the Opéra in Paris. Eight innocent bystanders were killed and a hundred and fifty wounded, but Cousin Bonaparte was quite safe. What the Carbonari wanted from him was help to make a bourgeois revolution in Italy. He did not hesitate. The responsibilities of Napoleon III, Emperor of France, toward the people he ruled were as nothing beside those of Cousin Bonaparte toward the Carbonari terrorists. And so the Italian Risorgimento was paid for with the blood of the French soldiers that soaked the fields of Montebello and Turbigo and Solferino. It is not a pretty story—no prettier than that of Shatev and his family."

There was silence for a moment.

He added quietly: "Gentlemen, our people will fertilize no more fields for the 'cousins' or 'brethren' of this century. We intend to seek out all the murderers whether they sit on café chairs or on the thrones they have made for themselves above the heads of the people. The People's Party and its great leader Vukashin are pledged to that." He looked round at us again and then sat down. "I will answer questions," he said.

It was quite well done and for a space nobody moved; then an American in front of me got up.

"In December of last year, Minister," he said, "the People's Party Government announced that the Officer Corps Brotherhood had been completely—*eliminated*. I think that was the word used. Are we to understand now that that announcement was incorrect?"

Brankovitch nodded. "Unfortunately, yes. At the time, of course, we believed it to be true. Later developments have shown that we were mistaken."

"What later developments, Minister?"

"I would prefer not to anticipate the court proceedings."

A small dark man got up.

"Minister, was not Deltchev himself responsible for the very vigorous proceedings taken to eliminate the Brotherhood?"

"He was certainly responsible for the action against the Brotherhood that we now know to have been ineffective, but the decision that there *should* be action was taken by the Provisional Government as a whole. In other words, the People's Party participated in the decision but not in the carrying-out of it."

Others began to rise and now the questions came quickly.

"Minister, can your allusion to Napoleon III be taken to mean that the Government links the allegations about Deltchev's peace negotiations with the allegations about his membership in the Brotherhood?"

"You may draw that conclusion if you wish."

"The charge is that Deltchev was to be paid for his efforts. Aren't the two suggestions inconsistent?"

"Possibly. But remember that Napoleon III also had his reward—Nice, the Riviera, Savoy."

"Minister, do you consider that the evidence heard so far in court has gone any way toward proving any of the charges against Monsieur Deltchev?"

"The evidence must be considered as a whole."

"By whom was defending counsel appointed, Minister?"

"By the Government. In all cases when a prisoner fails to appoint counsel to defend him that is done."

"Did this prisoner fail to appoint counsel? Did he not, as an advocate, wish to defend himself?"

"On a criminal charge a prisoner is not by law permitted to conduct his own defense. The law was made for the benefit of poor persons certain of conviction who feared to burden their families with legal costs."

"Minister, could not the law, clearly not intended for persons in Monsieur Deltchev's position, be waived in this case?"

"Are laws waived in England for the benefit of persons in high position?"

"Then you agree, Minister, that it would be to Monsieur Deltchev's benefit if he could defend himself?"

"It would be to the benefit of you gentlemen, I have no doubt. I apologize for our reluctance to have the court turned into a circus entertainment."

"Will the Minister say if, as a result of the prosecutor's unhappy efforts yesterday to provide the court with entertainment, the prisoner will not be allowed proper medical attention in the prison?"

Brankovitch rose to his feet with a smile. "The prisoner is receiving ample medical attention," he said, "and as much insulin as he wishes. It was nothing more sinister than a stupid administrative blunder that prevented his having attention for a few days. Disciplinary action has been taken against those responsible. Naturally the prisoner took the utmost advantage of his plight to gain sympathy—"

"When driven to do so by the prosecutor?"

"Or when a favorable opportunity presented itself." Brankovitch smiled again. "We interpret motives from the standpoint of our own prejudices. But please note that the prisoner was not prevented from addressing you."

"What he said was not reported in the official press, Minister."

"Quite properly. The fact that a man is diabetic surely does not affect his responsibility to the community for criminal acts. Gentlemen, perhaps you would care to continue our discussion over the refreshments. I hope you will not think I am attempting to corrupt you if I say that there is champagne and caviar for you to sample. I am merely performing another of my functions as a Minister in introducing to you two products of our agricultural and fishing industries which we are anxious to export. The champagne is not French, of course, but it is a dry, sparkling wine of pleasing character and I think you will like it."

There were one or two murmurs of amused assent and a scraping of chairs. Waiters entered, obviously in response to a signal, and whisked away the napkins from the buffet.

"He is clever, the Minister," said Pashik seriously.

"Yes, he is. Shall we go?"

He looked shocked. "Do you not wish to ask questions, Mr. Foster?"

"What about? Napoleon III?"

"I think it would be impolite to go," said Pashik earnestly. "The Minister will surely wish to meet you. There is protocol to be observed."

"There are others going." Though most of those present had moved over to the buffet and stood in groups talking, I noticed several making unobtrusive exits.

"Those are local agency men, Mr. Foster. They have met the Minister before."

"All right. Shall we go over?" Brankovitch was talking to a group that included Sibley, the man who drank too much and was indiscreet.

"No, Mr. Foster. Let us quietly have some refreshments. Presently matters will arrange themselves."

We were joined after a moment or two by an American I had chatted with once or twice at the courthouse. A waiter brought us wine and caviar sandwiches. One of the secretaries delivered copies of a long blood-curdling piece on the Officer Corps Brotherhood.

"Did you know that Byron was a member of the Carbonari?" the American was saying. "I think we ought to rechristen our friend Brankovitch. When Ferdinand of Italy tried to liquidate the Carbonari he had his Minister of Police set up another secret society called 'the Braziers of the counterpoise,' *Calderai del Contrappeso*. The Minister recruited all the worst characters in the country for it and what they did to the Italian liberals makes Little Bopeep of that Shatev story. The Minister was a man called Prince Canosa. What about Creeping Canosa for our friend?"

Pashik had left us. I talked to the American and ate sandwiches. After a few minutes Pashik came back rather breathlessly with one of the secretaries, a stony-eyed young man with over-neat clothes.

"This is Monsieur Kovitch," he said; "he is of the Minister's bureau." The secretary bowed and we shook hands. "The Minister is most anxious to meet you, Herr Foster," he said stiffly.

"I shall be honored." I caught the American's eye and he put his tongue very obviously in his cheek.

The secretary stared hard at me. "Have you yet had time, Herr Foster," he said, "to visit any of the well-known beauty spots that abound in the vicinity of our city?"

"I'm afraid I haven't."

"At this time of year," the secretary continued steadily, "there are many varieties of the most remarkable rose blooms in the world to be seen and savored. Our country is very beautiful. However, it is to be hoped that you will wish to be present on Saturday at the official parade and celebration in honor of the twenty-seventh anniversary of the founding of the People's Party."

"I don't—"

"Herr Foster's special pass has already been applied for," Pashik put in smartly.

"Ah, then he will see some of the beauties of the country brought to the city," pursued the secretary steadily. "This year the parade will be a symbolic integration of peaceful husbandry and armed might—the plow and the sword in harmony together."

"Very interesting."

"Yes. It is of the utmost importance that all our visitors leave us with a correct impression. I will myself see that you have an advantageous place, Herr Foster. Here, now, is the Minister."

He stepped aside nimbly, like a *compère* effacing himself for the entry of the star. Brankovitch, with the other secretary in attendance, had stopped to say a word to a Scandinavian group. Now he turned in my direction. The secretary beside me said something in his own language with my name in it. Brankovitch held out his hand and turned on a watery smile.

"How do you do?" he said in English. His warm hand released mine almost as soon as it touched it. He nodded to Pashik as I answered him. "You have not been to our country before, Mr. Foster?"

"No, Minister. But I'm finding my first visit most interesting."

He nodded. "Much fiction has already been written about it, but mostly by strangers. Now that cultural activities are being widely encouraged, however, perhaps a native school of writers will emerge. There is the language difficulty, of course. A knowledge of our language is rare. Yet Ibsen, also writing in a narrowly spoken language, achieved world fame."

"Ibsen's heroes and heroines were not obliged to be positive, Minister."

"Ah, I see you have heard of our special problems. Yes, we are compelled to consider the standard of education of the public here. We must pay still for past injustices. The percentage of illiteracy is high and those who are literate are for the most part still uneducated in the Western sense of the word. But in other cultural fields—the visual arts and music, for example—greater freedom is already possible."

"Ideas do not have to be expressed in words to be dangerous, Minister."

"We do not hinder truth, Mr. Foster—only the facile repetition of lies. But we must have a long undisturbed conversation about such things, for I would be glad to hear your opinions. Tell me, how did you find Madame Deltchev last night? In good health?"

I sensed rather than heard Pashik's sharply in-drawn breath. Brankovitch's gaze rested on me with unwavering affability.

"She seemed very well."

He smiled again. "She is not being persecuted?"

"Not that I'm aware of."

"We have tried to spare her as much as possible. Naturally her position is difficult and we have to protect her against possible demonstrations. But I am glad to hear that she is well. You are the only journalist who has interviewed her, I think."

"I think so."

He nodded vaguely. "I am so glad to have had this opportunity of meeting you, Mr. Foster," he said. "We must have another talk. Most interesting."

He nodded again and turned away. The secretary slid past me after him. The interview was at an end.

I looked at Pashik. His face was quite expressionless. He stepped up to me.

"Do you wish to go now, Mr. Foster?"

"Yes, I think so."

"You did not tell me that you had seen Madame Deltchev," he said as we walked away.

"No. I thought you'd prefer not to know."

"We must hope no harm is done."

"What harm can be done?"

He shrugged. "Such things attract attention."

"Does that matter?"

"We must hope not. But I would have preferred that you had told me. I could at least have prevented the embarrassment."

"What embarrassment? The sentries on the house looked at my permit. They reported. What of it?"

"You do not understand."

"I'm afraid I don't. I think you're over-anxious, as I've said before."

"I think my opinion about that may be better informed, Mr. Foster."

"I'm sorry, Pashik. I certainly have no wish to compromise you, but I have a job to do."

"I have the responsibility, Mr. Foster."

"You must try to shoulder it."

Before he could answer, there were quick footsteps behind us. Pashik turned round as if he expected to be attacked. It was Sibley.

"Hullo there," he said breezily; "how are you, Foster? And you, Georghi my friend? What a dreadful party! When are we going to have that drink? Now? I feel the need."

"Please excuse me," said Pashik hastily, "I must go to my office. Mr. Foster, you have messages to send."

"I'll see you tomorrow."

He hesitated. We had reached the door. He gave up. "Very well. Good night, Mr. Foster. Good night, Mr. Sibley."

"Good night."

He went, leaving a slip-stream of malodorous disapproval.

Sibley chuckled. "Poor little man," he said.

Nine

We WENT TO a near-by café and ordered drinks. Then Sibley disappeared to make a telephone call. When he came back the drinks had arrived. He picked his up, peered into it as if it were a crystal ball, then downed it at a gulp.

"Well, what do you think?" he said grimly.

"About this evening's performance?"

"Performance! Exactly." He snapped his fingers at the waiter for another drink. "Incredible, isn't it?"

"In what way do you mean?"

"Oh, all of it. That old, old routine! Prejudice, friends? Not a bit of it! Anyway, judge for yourselves, friends. Here are the simple facts given as simply as we know how—the facts about the Brotherhood. What has that to do with Deltchev? Who said it had anything to do with him? You're drawing the conclusions, friends, not us. We're only giving you the nasty facts. And to show you that the facts are really nasty we'll pull an old atrocity story out of the bag. Castration and rape, friends! Yes, we thought that'd get you where it hurts. What has that to do with Deltchev? Well, we don't say definitely that it *has* anything to do with him but—well, you're drawing the conclusions and we can't stop you, can we? In fact, although we're not exactly saying so, the same ugly thought is beginning to cross our minds now. How clever of you to think of it first, friends! But it does seem fantastic, doesn't it? Though, wait! Isn't there a historical precedent that fits the situation like a glove? Of course it does. In fact, there is one point of coincidence we didn't mention. When Murat decided to destroy the Carbonari he gave the job to his police chief. The police chief destroyed a lot of people, and Murat thought the job was done until he found out that the police chief had always been a Carbonaro himself and that the cousins were stronger than ever. Strange, isn't it, friends? How clever of you to remember without our telling you! Any more questions? Yes? Well, let's not get into tiresome arguments. Let's have some caviar and a nice glass of aerated cat water. They make me tired." He swallowed another large plum brandy and sat back.

"Another drink?"

"For God's sake, yes." He leaned forward, his face slightly flushed, his lips still wet with brandy. "How does one deal with it, Foster?"

"Brankovitch's press conference?" I signaled to the waiter.

"All of it. The whole phony business. Perhaps it's all right for you. You've got plenty of time. A series of articles, weeks hence. But I'm supposed to be sending news. All I've got through so far are those damned official bulletins. I suppose Pashik sends those to your people?"

"Yes."

"Do you know what I'd like to do?" His dull, hot eyes brooded on mine.

"No, what?"

"I'd like to put it across them. I'd like to split the whole damn business wide open." He frowned suddenly as if with irritation at himself. "Take no notice. I had drinks before the party." He smiled slyly and lowered his voice. "Can you keep a secret, Foster?"

"Yes."

"The funny thing is I can do it."

"Do what?"

"What I said—break it open." He looked round cautiously and leaned farther forward. "I've found a way round this bloody censorship."

"Oh, yes?" My heart began to beat rather unpleasantly.

"I can't tell you the details because I swore not to, but there's a little man in the Propaganda Ministry who doesn't like the regime any more than we do and he'll play. Of course, if he was found out he'd be lucky if they hanged him quickly, but he's prepared to take the risk. There's only one snag." He paused. I waited. "He can't do it more than once and the deadline's tomorrow."

"That should give you time."

"It's a risk." He frowned at the table as the waiter put fresh drinks down. "A big risk. If I'm caught, I'm out. Of course, that wouldn't matter to you. It's not your living. But, by God, it's a risk I'd like to take."

"The little man in the Propaganda Ministry must think it worth while."

He laughed shortly. "You're right. It's funny, isn't it? One minute I'm breathing fire and murder, and the next I'm worrying about a little risk." He laughed again. His performance was deteriorating rapidly. I was not helping him and he would have to come to the point himself. I waited, fascinated.

"Would you take the risk?" he asked suddenly.

"I don't know. The question would have to arise."

"All right, supposing"—I thought I detected a note of genuine exasperation in his voice—"just supposing you had a chance to file a short message with mine. Would you take it?"

"Is that an offer?"

"Don't be silly. Why should I give you a beat?"

"I don't know. Why should you?"

"You'd have to make it worth my while."

"What's that mean?"

He did not answer. He was pretending to debate with himself. "Look, Foster," he said then, "let's be serious for a moment. If I'd thought you were going to fasten onto the thing like this, I tell you frankly I wouldn't have mentioned it." He paused. "But since I have, I tell you what I'll do. If you'll undertake to confine your message to pure comment on the trial as a whole, I'll get it through with mine."

"If you do send one, of course."

"Oh, I'm going to send it all right. Don't you worry. And now you can buy me another drink." He sat back with a tremendous air of having sold his birthright. "I make only one stipulation. I'll have to read your stuff before I pass it on. Honestly, I wouldn't trust my own brother in a thing like this. Right?"

"I understand." To give myself time to think I looked round for the waiter. I had had it all now: the confidence-promoting diatribe against the regime, the brandy-laden indiscretion, the indignant denial, the burst of generosity, the second thoughts, the grudging commitment. Petlarov would be amused. Pashik would purse his lips. I looked at my watch. I did not want to have to talk to Sibley any more. The waiter had disappeared. I put some money on the table.

"I have to go," I said.

It took me five minutes and another hastily swallowed drink to do so, but at last I stood up and put on my hat.

"About you-know-what," he said; "you'd better give me the stuff tomorrow morning. Two hundred words maximum."

"Oh, that." I smiled and shook my head. "I don't think I'll bother."

"Are you mad?"

"No. It's different for you. For me it's not worth the risk."

He looked at me coldly for a moment. Then very elaborately he shrugged. "As you will, *mon brave*," he said.

"Good night."

Still seated at the table, he gave me a heavily ironic bow. "Don't change your mind tomorrow, Foster *mio*," he answered, "it'll be too late."

"I won't change my mind." I nodded to him and walked out of the café. Outside I hesitated. Now that the disagreeable part of the encounter was over,

I was curious. Sibley the *agent provocateur* and employee of Brankovitch interested me as Sibley the breezy newspaperman never could. I had an impulse to go back into the café, sit down, and try to lure him into explaining himself. I did look back. He was sitting looking down at his drink, his elbows on the table, the thin, fair down on his sunburnt scalp glistening faintly in the evening sun. As I looked, he put his hands up to his head and there was something so hopeless about the gesture that it was quite moving. Then one hand dropped to the stem of his glass and twirled it between a finger and thumb. The other came down too. The money I had put on the table was still there, and now a finger of this other hand crept out rather stealthily toward it and gently sorted it over to see how much was there. Then he looked round for the waiter. I turned away. For the moment there was not much more I wanted to know about Sibley.

I went back to my hotel. I did not eat much dinner. I remembered that in one dim corner of the hotel foyer I had seen a framed map of the city on the wall. After dinner I went to it and got out Katerina Deltchev's letter. The address on the envelope was short: "*Valmo, Patriarch Dimo 9.*"

With some difficulty I located the street on the map and set out. The girl had said that the street was near the station. It was, but it was also on the other side of the main line, and to get there I had to make a wide detour through a crowded street market to a bridge and walk back along the far side of a freight yard. By the time I had found the church that I had noted as a reference point on the map, it was almost too dark to read the lettering of the street names.

It was not an inviting locality. On one side of the main road there were tall warehouses and a power station interspersed with ugly apartment blocks; on the other side were small shops and steep lanes of wooden houses, the roofs of which were patched here and there with sheets of rusty corrugated iron; the old slum. There was a tram terminus a short distance down the road and I considered riding straight back into the city without troubling further about the letter. Then I decided to give the search for the street five minutes. If, as I hoped, I had not found it by then, I would go back. I found it almost immediately.

The street of the Patriarch Dimo was one of the steeper and shabbier lanes. There was a dimly lit wine shop at the corner, and behind it a decrepit wooden building that seemed to be used as a stable for oxen. I walked up the hill slowly. The girl had said hesitantly that her letter was to "a young man." I had, I think, imagined Valmo to be a fellow art student of hers, a handsome lad with other girl friends who would have no scruples about taking advantage of Katerina's enforced absense. Now my ideas had to change.

Number 9 was a house much like the rest, but with the ground-floor shutters crossed with planks and nailed up. There were no lights in any of the upper rooms and the greasy-walled entrance passage at the side was littered with pebbles and marked with chalk lines as if children had been playing a game in it. The house looked empty. I walked along the passage to the door and struck a match.

At some time recently the building had been a lodginghouse, for there was a board with names painted on it. The match went out and I struck another. None of the painted names was Valmo. Then, as the second match was going out, I saw it. The top name had been scratched over with the point of a knife and under it the word "Valmo" was crudely written in pencil. I dropped the burnt-out match and stood in the darkness for a moment. I was becoming curious about this Valmo. By the light of another match I looked for a bell and, seeing none, tried the door. It was open.

I went in.

There was a small lobby with a flight of stairs in it. The place was quite still and seemed deserted. I looked round for a light. On the ceiling there was a hook and a smoke shield, but no lantern beneath it. I went up the stairs striking matches. There were two doors on the first landing, both open. I looked in. The rooms were empty. In one of them some floorboards were missing. I went on up. I did not stop on the next landing; obviously the house was abandoned. Only one thing delayed my turning back. The rooms I had seen had been deserted for many months. But Katerina had not been confined to her house that long. It was possible, therefore, that Valmo had only recently moved away and had left a notice of his new address.

As I went up the last flight of stairs. I noticed a peculiar smell. It was ammoniac and very sickly. It became stronger as I reached the landing under the roof. I struck another match. There was only one door here, and it was shut. There was no notice on it. I knocked and waited. The match burned out. I struck another and turned the handle of the door and pushed. The door opened. Then I had a shock; the room inside was furnished.

I raised the match above my head and moved forward into the doorway. As I did so, I became aware of a sound; there were flies buzzing in the room.

In the small light of the match I saw an unmade bed, a deal table, and a chair with some newspapers piled on it. There was also a packing-case.

The match burned down and I dropped it. Then, by the pale arc of light it made as it fell, I saw on the floor a dark mass like a crumpled curtain.

As I struck the next match I took a pace foreward into the room. The light from the match flared up.

The next instant my heart jolted violently. It was not a curtain on the floor. It was a man; and his face was black.

I stepped back quickly and with some sort of shout, I think. The movement blew the match out or I should have run. I fumbled desperately with the box and managed to get another match alight. I forced myself to look again.

His hair was close-cropped and white except where the blackness spread. The blackness was congealed blood, and it lay on and about him like spilled wax. His mouth was open and there was a gaping wound by his ear. There was no telling what he had looked like. He was lying on his right side, his knees drawn up to his chest and his elbows nearly touching them. He had a dark serge suit and leather sandals, but no socks. He had been small and thin. The flies buzzed round him. He had been dead for more than a few hours.

I began to retch and went out on the landing.

A minute passed and I was beginning to get my breath again when I thought I heard a sound from below.

The blood was thudding in my head so loudly and my breathing was so quick and shallow that it was difficult to be certain. Then I managed to hold my breath for just over a second and heard the sound again. Very slowly and quietly somebody was coming up the stairs.

I don't know who I thought it was; the murderer, I suppose; at that moment I would have panicked if a fly had settled on my hand. In the darkness I stumbled back into the room, shut the door, lighted a match, and looked feverishly for the bolt. There was a bolt, but the socket of it was missing. I looked round desperately for something to jam the door with. I tried to use the chair, but the door handle was too low. The match I was holding went out. I fumbled with the box again, opened it upside down, and the matches spilled on the floor. I was shaking with fear now. I went down on my knees and started to pick the matches up. At that moment I heard the footsteps on the landing just outside the door. I remained motionless. Under the door I saw a light flicker. The person outside had a flashlight.

Then the light went out and the door opened.

There was silence for a moment. Suddenly the flashlight went on and swept quickly round the room. It stopped on the body. Then it moved again quickly and stopped on me.

The end of a revolver barrel gleamed just in front of the flashlight. I did not move.

A voice said: "What are you doing here, Mr. Foster?"

It was Pashik.

Ten

≈≈≈≈≈≈≈≈≈≈

I GOT TO my feet.

"Why are you here, Mr. Foster?" he repeated.

"I don't know," I said. "Do you mind taking that light off my face?"

He turned the light down to my feet. I could see him now and the revolver in his hand was still pointing at me. He had his dispatch case under his arm and the medallion on it winked faintly.

"Well, Mr. Foster?"

"I might ask you the same question."

"I followed you, Mr. Foster."

"With a gun?"

"It was possible that we might not be alone."

"We're not." I looked at the dead man on the floor, but he did not move the light from my feet.

"I want to know why you are here, Mr. Foster, and who told you of this place. And I want to know right now." There was a very sharp edge to his voice.

"Katerina Deltchev asked me to deliver a letter for her. This was the address on it."

"Show me the letter."

"Pashik, do we have to stay in this room? Can't we go outside? Anyway, shouldn't we be calling the police? This man's been murdered."

"No, Mr. Foster, we should not be calling the police. Show me that letter."

I got it out. He came forward, took it from me, and turned the light on it.

"She told me that it was to a young man," I said.

Without replying he put the letter in his pocket and swept the light round the room.

"Have you touched anything here, Mr. Foster?"

"This chair. Why?"

"What did you touch it for?"

"When I heard you coming up the stairs I tried to jam it under the door handle."

"Wipe the chair where you touched it and also both sides of the door with your handkerchief. Then pick up all the matches you dropped, including the burnt-out ones, please."

I obeyed him. Just then the wish to get out of the room was stronger than my disposition to argue. He held the light down while I picked up the matches.

"Did anyone know you were coming here?"

"Only Katerina Deltchev."

"You told nobody?"

"No."

"Not Petlarov?"

"No."

"Mr. Sibley?"

"Nobody."

"Did anyone see you come in here?"

"I shouldn't think so. There weren't many people about."

"Your clothes are noticeably foreign. Did anyone turn to look at you?"

"You should know if you were following me."

"I was not close enough to see. Was there anybody in the passage below when you arrived?"

"No." I had collected all the matches. I straightened up. "I can't stay in this room any longer," I said, and went out on the landing.

"Wipe the door, Mr. Foster."

I did so. He ran the light round the room again and came out. "Shut the door with your handkerchief in your hand, please. Yes, that will do. Now, Mr. Foster, my car is at the end of the street by the wine shop. You have your matches. Go down as you came up, walk to my car, get in it, and wait for me."

"What are you going to do?"

"We must not be seen leaving together."

"Why not?"

"Get going, Mr. Foster."

He still had the revolver in his hand and he handled the thing as if he were used to it. Oddly, there was nothing incongruous about the look of Pashik with a gun.

He held the light for me as I went down the top flight of stairs. After that I struck matches again. It was a relief to get into the street. By the time I reached his car I had done a good deal of thinking.

I smoked the greater part of a cigarette before he joined me. Without a word he climbed into the driver's seat, took his gun and flashlight from the dispatch case and, putting them in the door pockets, stuffed a greasy rag over them. He started the car. "And now," he said, "we'll go see a friend of mine."

"What friend?"

"He will advise us what we must do. He is of a special kind of police."

"What special kind?"

"You will see, Mr. Foster. Perhaps the ordinary police should be told. I do not know."

He twitched the wheel suddenly, swerved across the road, and swung round uncertainly into a turning on the left.

I threw away the cigarette I had been smoking and lit another.

"Why did you follow me, Pashik?"

"I had a hunch that you might be about to do something foolish, Mr. Foster."

"But you did follow me?"

"You will agree that I was justified."

I looked at him. "I came through a street market that was difficult to get through on foot. How did you follow me in a car?"

I can't answer questions while I am driving, Mr. Foster."

"Then let's stop for a few minutes. I have lots of questions and they won't keep."

He drove on in silence.

"You've been to that house before, haven't you?" I said after a moment or two.

"Why should you think that, Mr. Foster?"

"You knew that that man's body was there before you came in. That is, unless you're quite used to finding corpses with shotgun wounds lying about. You paid no attention to this one."

He had been driving toward the center of the city. Now we lurched into a quiet boulevard with trees along it.

"Another thing," I said: "if you'd followed me and expected to find me there, you wouldn't have shown your gun. As you came up the stairs you heard me move about. If you'd known it was me you'd have called my name. You didn't follow me. You went there on your own account and for your own reasons. What were they?"

"You are making things very difficult, Mr. Foster," he said gloomily.

"Yes. Who was the dead man? Valmo? Who killed him? You?"

He did not answer. Behind the trees that lined the road there were houses with portes-cochères. He slowed down, then turned suddenly into a space between the trees and drove through into one of the courtyards. He stopped and immediately turned off the lights. We were in pitch-darkness.

"Mr. Foster," he said, "you are arrogant and very dumb. If I were truly a murderer you would be already dead. I have been very patient with you. Now we will see my friend."

He switched on the flashlight and I saw that he had his revolver again. He put it in his dispatch case and we both got out. I looked up. The bulk of quite a large house was visible against the sky.

"Where is this?" I asked.

"My friend has an apartment here. This way."

I could see very little. We went through a side door down some tiled steps to a small hydraulic lift with a rope control. The cage bounced as we got into it. Pashik hauled on the rope and we shot upwards with a faint hissing sound.

At the top floor the lift stopped automatically and we got out on a bare stone landing with a small doorway in it and a steel ladder up to a skylight. Pashik knocked on the door.

After a moment or two a woman in an apron opened the door. She had gray hair scragged back into a bun, and a bitter mouth. She obviously knew Pashik. He made some explanation to her. She nodded and looked at me curiously as we went in; then she led the way along a narrow passage and showed us into a drawing-room. She switched on the lights and left us, shutting the door behind us. If there had been a faint smell of disinfectant in the air, it would have seemed like an appointment with a dentist. The room we were in, indeed, had very much the look of a waiting-room. The chairs stood round the walls and there was a large table in the middle with one small ashtray on it. All that was wanting was a selection of magazines.

"What's your friend's name?" I asked.

Pashik sat on the edge of one of the chairs. "I will introduce you to him, Mr. Foster."

"What did you go to that house for?"

"You do not believe me when I answer your questions, Mr. Foster." His brown eyes looked at me mournfully. He took off his glasses and began polishing them.

"You never do answer them. Why didn't you tell me that Sibley was working for the Propaganda Ministry? You must have known."

"How do you know that, Mr. Foster?"

"Petlarov warned me to expect an approach from someone pretending to have a way round the censorship. It came from Sibley. If you knew, why didn't you warn me?"

"Would you have believed me if I had, Mr. Foster? No. You would have thought that I was trying to stop you sending news out."

"Yes, I'm afraid you're right. I'm sorry."

"It is unimportant, Mr. Foster. It is simply that you do not like me." He put his glasses on and stared at me. "I am used to being disliked," he added; "I no longer mind."

But I was spared the deathly embarrassment of replying to this. The gray woman appeared at the door, nodded to Pashik, and said something. He got up and turned to me.

"My friend wishes to see me privately for a moment, Mr. Foster," he said. "Perhaps you will wait."

He picked up his dispatch case and went out of the room.

I sat down.

Until that moment I had been feeling all right. Now, suddenly, the smell of the dead man was in my nostrils again. I felt sick and giddy. I put my head between my knees and tried to think of other things. I suppose that if Pashik had not arrived on the scene I should have hurried back to my hotel, had several large brandies and a sleeping-pill, and gone to bed. Instead I was sitting in a strange room in a strange house with a desperate feeling of having lost all contact with reality. At that moment I would have given anything to be back in London, quietly doing in my own way the work I understood. I had realized that the delayed reaction to the horror of finding a decomposing corpse in a dark room was only the surface of my discomfort. Beneath, there were fears of another kind. I had thought to write about the trial and condemnation of an innocent man. Now, in spite of the obvious injustice of the trial itself, I was having to accept the disagreeable possibility that really the man might not be innocent, that the rubbish Prochaska was talking might have a basis in fact, that the trembling hands of the diabetic Deltchev might have clasped in brotherhood those of the murderers of the Shatev family; and the foolish trouble was that if those things were true, I feared to know about them. Petlarov's grocer, I reflected bitterly, was not alone in his ill-informed uneasiness; Mr. Valiant-for-Truth, the great journalist, had also caught a whiff of the odor of corruption and was wishing his delicate nose elsewhere. It was curious how preoccupied I had become with smells; they seemed easier to deal with at that time than other ideas; the smell of the dead man, the smell of Pashik, the smell of furniture polish in Deltchev's house; those three things were related. And if I looked for reassurance to the other senses, I could recall the taste of the plum brandy I had had with Sibley, the feeling of the sentry's rifle on my shoulder, the image of Petlarov's white false teeth, and the sound of his voice saying: "Some of the evidence may not discredit itself. Some of it may be true."

I got up and began to wander round the room. I knew now that the train of thought I had been avoiding could be avoided no longer.

If you accepted the seemingly incredible proposition that Deltchev was, and for years had been, a member of the Officer Corps Brotherhood, it was possible to explain some things about him that had hitherto defied explanation. To begin with, you could explain the inexplicable election affair; Deltchev had done what he did, not because he had thought it right or necessary, or because he was a saint, or because he had been bought; he had done it in obedience to the orders of the Brotherhood. And having said that, you could also explain why he himself had been able to give no explanation for his action. You could explain, though with difficulty, how a prosaic, undistinguished Minister of Posts and Telegraphs had been able to become the leader of a secret nationalistic revolutionary movement and ultimately seize power. You could even explain the "football match" incident in that context; the fanatically nationalistic Brotherhood, having through fear of the growing People's Party misjudged the election timing, had commanded their puppet Deltchev to retrieve the position. Napoleon III had done more for the Carbonari. Besides, had not Petlarov himself admitted that power was a bribe that might be used with Deltchev? In a fantastic way it all fitted. It might be objected that, as a lawyer, Deltchev would not have qualified for membership in the early days of the Brotherhood; but the class distinction between professional men and army officers was not great. His membership was not impossible. It was certainly not improbable. Idealistic young men very often joined societies supposedly dedicated to the human struggles for freedom and justice; and very often, too, they later regretted having done so. When, I wondered, had Deltchev begun to regret the association? Then another objection occurred to me. Why, if the Brotherhood had supported Deltchev, had it also collaborated with the German occupation forces? But this I disposed of easily. What better cover could there have been for the subversive activities of the Brotherhood than half-hearted collaboration with the German Army? Not with the sharp and skeptical Gestapo, mark you, but with the army. It would be interesting to know about the men who had made the Brotherhood's policy. Perhaps the trial would reveal them.

But meanwhile Deltchev's daughter had sent a letter to a cheap lodging where there was a murdered man. I thought about that. Who was Valmo? Katerina's middle-aged lover? I doubted it. This rather too knowing young woman had offered me a drink because she had thought that the engaging way with an irritable reporter; she had said that the letter was to "a young man" because she had thought, perhaps less incorrectly, that that was the engaging way with a reluctant letter-smuggler. If I had had the presence of mind to do so, I might have looked more closely at the room for signs of a relationship with Katerina; her photograph perhaps, or a letter in her handwriting. A letter. And that brought me back to Pashik.

I had made a mistake about Pashik. I had thought of him as one of those hapless, over-anxious persons who cannot help entangling themselves in systems of small, unnecessary lies. It had not occurred to me that he might have anything of more than private importance to conceal. Now I had to reckon with the news not only that could he be concerned quite calmly with the body of a murdered man but also that his tiresome preoccupation with "discretion" had its origins in something very unlike the old-maidish timidity to which I had attributed it.

At that moment, with a jolt, I came out of the haze of cowlike rumination in which I had been lost and began to think clearly. If Pashik had known that the body was there before he came to the house, why was it necessary to consult his "friend in the special police" so urgently? Answer: because I had been there, because I had seen the body, because I had seen Pashik, because I had drawn certain conclusions, because I might be indiscreet.

I had been pacing up and down the room. I stopped, then went to the door. From another part of the apartment there came very faintly a murmur of voices. I glanced at my watch. Pashik had been gone five minutes. I was suddenly convinced that it would be wise to leave without waiting to be introduced to Pashik's friend—to leave now, quietly. I hesitated momentarily, then I made up my mind. I put my hand on the doorknob and turned it gently. Then I began to pull. But the door did not move. I had been locked in.

Eleven

FOR A MOMENT or two I stood there looking stupidly at the door as if I expected it to open itself. To find oneself locked in a room and know that the locking cannot be accidental or a practical joke is an extraordinary sensation. My feelings were confused and are not easily described; I was angry and frightened and depressed all at once. Then I broke out into a sweat. I tried the door again, then turned away from it. The room suddenly looked different, very large and empty, and I could see every detail in it. There was something familiar and yet not quite right about it.

When I had been walking about I had noticed an inch or two of string looped round one corner of the carpet. Now I saw it again; I was standing on the hardwood surround just by it. At that moment I was wondering if I should hammer on the door and demand to be let out, or sit there quietly and pretend not to have noticed that I had been locked in. Absently I reached down to pick up the string. I wanted something to fidget with. I got the string, but the corner of the carpet came up with it. The string was threaded through the edge of the carpet and tied to a label. The label had some figures written on it and a printed name, obviously that of the dealer who had sold it. It was an expensive carpet, a Sparta, yet the owner had not troubled to remove the price tag. It had simply been tucked away out of sight. I was puzzled. I let the carpet fall back into place and walked round the room again. At one end by the windows there was a buhl cabinet. I opened one of the drawers. There was a small brass screw in it and some dust. I tried the other drawers. All were empty except one, which contained a price tag from the same dealer who had supplied the carpet. I went round quickly looking at the wood of the chairs. They had been used a lot and yet there was a certain *un*used look about them. And then I knew what was familiar about the room: it was like a stage set when all the furniture has just been brought in and placed in position.

At that moment I heard voices and footsteps in the passage outside. I sat

251

down. They came to the door and there was a slight pause. I knew why. The person who was about to open the door was preparing to turn the knob and the key simultaneously so that the sound of the latch would conceal that of the unlocking. If I did not know that I had been locked in, they did not want to tell me of the fact. My heart beat faster.

The door opened and after a momentary pause Pashik came in. He was followed slowly by a small man in a loose tussah suit and a black tie. I stood up.

Pashik put his hand on my shoulder and enveloped me in a broad smile. "Herr Foster," he said in German, "let me introduce you to Herr Valmo."

I had no time to digest this surprise. The other man came forward with a polite smile and held his hand out tentatively.

"So pleased, Herr Foster," he said.

He was about fifty, short and very slight, with wispy and receding gray hair brushed back from a sunburnt forehead. It was a thin, pointed face with large, pale blue eyes and an expression that might have been cruel or amused or both. He looked like a retired ballet dancer who has taken successfully to management. In his hand was Katerina Deltchev's letter. It had been opened.

"Herr *Valmo*?" I said.

He smiled. "I am afraid a little explanation is due to you, *mein Herr*." He had a quiet, monotonous voice.

"It was not possible for *me* to explain, Herr Foster," said Pashik. "I could not break a confidence."

"Please sit down, Herr Foster, and you, my dear Pashik. A cigarette? Ah, you are already smoking. As our friend Pashik explained to you, I am, you might say, some sort of a policeman, a very"—he made a belittling gesture with his hand—"a very confidential sort of policeman." The woman appeared at the door with a tray and he glanced round. "Yes, come in, Mentcha. Put it down." He turned again, pulled round a chair, and sat facing me. "Coffee and a little brandy, Herr Foster. You have had a very upsetting experience, our friend tells me. Thank you, Mentcha. Shut the door. And now," he went on as she went out, "we must set your mind at rest. In the coffee, the brandy?"

"Thank you."

Pashik was sitting deferentially by as if at a conference between his superiors. The hand holding his cigarette was trembling slightly.

Valmo handed me a cup and went on talking as he filled the other two. "There is one thing," he said, "that I must ask of you, Herr Foster. That is that you respect the confidence of what I am about to tell you." He held a cup out to Pashik but he looked at me. "Pashik tells me that you are not friendly to the regime here. I understand. But I am not a politician. I am a civil servant. Our country is a center for many conspiracies against the law and it is my task to destroy them. Can I be certain that you will respect my confidence, Herr Foster?"

"Yes." I tasted the coffee.

"Very well." He put his cup behind him on the table and then leaned forward toward me with his elbows on his knees and his hands together. "In my role of policeman, Herr Foster, it was my duty to seek out the perpetrators of the bomb outrage against Herr Deltchev that took place shortly before his arrest. I made certain secret inquiries and investigations. It was believed that the criminals had had the Deltchev family under surveillance, and members of the family co-operated with me in identifying them. I have said that my function is not political. Herr Deltchev's trial does not relieve me of the responsibility of tracing these criminals. You understand?"

I nodded.

"For reasons with which I will not trouble you," he continued, "it became necessary for me to install an agent in the Patriarch Dimo. For convenience and identification, the agent employed my name. Very well. Three days ago my agent reported to me that he had news of the men we were after. That night he was killed." He paused impressively.

"Who found him dead?" I asked.

He stared at me for a moment. Then he turned round and picked up his coffee cup again. "I did, Herr Foster," he said blandly. "However, let me continue. The agent had collected certain documentary evidence against the conspirators, which he kept hidden in the room. I discovered that this had not been stolen. Therefore, I argued, they did not know of its existence. Therefore, if they were made aware of its existence they would return for it. Therefore I replaced the true documents with some false ones that I prepared and sat down to wait for results."

"You mean you put a secret watch on the house to catch the murderer when he returned?"

He smiled gently and shook his head. "I am afraid you do not know the street of the Patriarch Dimo, Herr Foster," he said. "That sort of secret could not be kept there. No. I set a different kind of trap. All I wanted was to get the false documents into the conspirators' hands. I had reason to believe that in fact that had happened. Tonight I asked Herr Pashik, who is a friend of mine and also sometimes a helper, to go to the house and make sure." He spread his hands out like a conjuror. "He finds you there."

"With a letter addressed to you."

"Exactly. Katerina Deltchev had recalled an important piece of evidence. She wrote to tell me of it."

"Through your agent."

"Naturally. This address is most confidential, Herr Foster. So you see how it has happened and the need for your discretion." He sat back with a smile, clicked his lighter, and held the letter in the flame of it. As it caught fire, he smiled at me again. "I'm sure you do," he added.

I thought quickly. It was just not quite good enough. The man who called himself Valmo and said that he was of the secret police had had a certain initial advantage; he did not look like the conventional secret policemen of fiction. If he had been vaguer and more mysterious about his story, it might even have been convincing. There would have been nothing unlikely about a secret policeman who was secretive. But this man had seen the holes in his story as he was telling it and instead of leaving them had tried to cover them up. For instance, having indicated an official connection between the Deltchev household and Patriarch Dimo Street he had decided that it did not satisfactorily cover Katerina's letter, so he had added another detail: that weak one about her recalling an important piece of evidence. It would have been better to let me see the hole and question it. He could then have replied with a knowing shake of the head that he was afraid he could not permit himself to give me that information. And that, in turn, would have prevented my asking the awkward question I did in fact ask.

"Herr Valmo," I said, "what I don't understand is why Fräulein Deltchev, who is under house arrest, has to get me to smuggle out a letter to the head of the secret police. Why didn't she just give it to one of the sentries?"

He crushed the ashes of the letter onto the tray. "She is a girl. No doubt she was afraid I would not get it."

"She seemed more concerned about the censorship than anything else. She made me promise to deliver it by hand."

"Confinement affects some people strangely."

"Shall you go to see her?"

"It may be necessary. I do not know." He was getting confused now. He pulled himself together a trifle impatiently. "Those, however, are not matters of immediate concern, Herr Foster. It is your position that we must make clear."

"Yes?"

"I have given you a great deal of confidential information. It must, please, remain confidential." His pale eyes stared at me coldly. "I may add, Herr Foster, that if you were not a distinguished journalist, it would have been considered advisable to put you in prison for a short while to make sure of your behavior. That, however, we need not discuss. You have already assured me that you will be discreet. I require now three further undertakings from you. First"—he held up a finger—"that you will not return to the house in the

Patriarch Dimo or tell anyone of it. Secondly, that you will not again visit the Deltchev house. Thirdly, that you will make no attempt to identify this house and that you forget its existence, and mine."

I did not reply immediately. I knew now the kind of conversation that must have taken place between Valmo and Pashik while I was safely locked up and waiting. My one desire was to get out of the place as quickly as possible. But I had the sense to realize that if I showed my anxiety and agreed to the terms too hastily, they would not feel quite safe. They were both watching me narrowly. I frowned, then looked up and nodded.

"All right," I said curtly. "I agree. And now, if you don't mind, I'd like another brandy."

Valmo stood up. "Yes, of course," he said perfunctorily. He poured a small one. He could not wait to get rid of me now. "Herr Pashik?"

"Thank you, no."

They stood looking at me impatiently while I sipped the brandy. It was the only moment of enjoyment I had had in the whole evening and it lasted about ten seconds. As I swallowed the first sip, I heard the front door of the apartment open and close and footsteps in the passage outside.

"It is my brother," said Valmo quickly.

Then the door opened and a young man came into the room. He saw me and stopped.

"Good evening, Jika," Valmo said. "We are talking a little business. I shall be with you in a minute."

He was about twenty-five, dark and very tired-looking. He had a raincoat on and his hair was blown about as if he had been in an open car. He looked at us suspiciously. For a moment he did not move; then he turned away slowly and went to the door.

"Don't be too long, Aleko," he said. "I have something for you."

I raised the brandy to my mouth again. I was not looking directly at Pashik, but I could see his face and it had gone the color of mud. He knew that I had seen the "Aleko" note in the Deltchev file and for some reason was terrified lest I had remembered it. Aleko himself was waiting for me to finish my drink. The use of his Christian name had not visibly upset him. But the situation was delicate. I had seen something I should not have seen, but Pashik did not know if I realized it. The main thing then was to get out of the apartment before he could make up his mind what to do. I drank the brandy at a gulp and held out my hand to Aleko.

"Thank you, Herr Valmo, and good-by."

He smiled agreeably. "I hope your stay is pleasant here, Herr Foster," he said.

I turned to Pashik. "Are you going to drive me back to my hotel, Pashik?"

"Yes, Mr. Foster, yes," he said heavily.

We went along the passage to the front door. Aleko came out to the lift with us. Aleko shook my hand again.

"I have liked you, Herr Foster," he said; "and with a journalist that is a new experience for me. I have faith in you. Good-by."

He might have been sending a promising young dancer on a first international tour.

Pashik was already in the lift. I got in after him. We went down in silence.

It was not until we were in his car and out on the road again that I broke the silence.

"Aleko Valmo," I said. "A curious name."

"In these parts it is quite common, Mr. Foster," he said calmly.

He had made up his mind that I had forgotten the other name.

I was not feeling very friendly toward Pashik, and for a moment or two I toyed with the idea of asking him suddenly: "What was the case of K. Fischer, Vienna '46, about, Pashik, and what had Aleko to do with it?"

Then I decided not to. We did not speak again until he drew up outside my hotel. As I went to get out, he put his hand on my arm, and his brown eyes sought mine.

"Mr. Foster," he said, "it has been a lousy experience for you this evening and no doubt you will wish to forget all about it. That is, if you are wise."

I did not answer. His voice took on its cautious roundabout tone.

"I wish only to tell you," he said, "that I understand your feelings and share them. But you have your own profession and need not trouble about what happens to dead-beats and bums far away from your home. Men are dying all over the world for the causes they believe in. You cannot fight their battles."

"Are you telling me that I should mind my own business?" I asked.

"Ah, please, Mr. Foster!" He spread his hands out. "You are mad at me."

I was exasperated. "I'm not mad at you, Pashik. I'm merely trying to get you to say straight out what you mean without all this double talk. I don't mind being advised to mind my own business. That's all right. I don't have to take the advice if I don't want to. I'm still capable of deciding what is my own business and what isn't. I'm not fighting any battles. I'm trying to find out what goes on here."

"That is what I mean, Mr. Foster. It does no good to try."

"You mean I won't be able to find out?"

He looked away from me and picked at the steering-wheel. "You force me to be frank, Mr. Foster."

"What's the matter with frankness? Why has it to be forced?"

"You say you fight no battles, Mr. Foster," he said quietly; "but I tell you, you are wandering like a fool between the opposing forces of those who are. That is a crazy thing to do. Once, years ago in Vienna, I saw street fighting between troops and revolutionaries. The fighting went on for many days. But there was one street that was swept equally by the fire of both sides, and neither could advance. Then one afternoon something very silly happened, as so often it happens in war. Into this empty, silent street there came a man. We heard his footsteps first. Then we saw him. He staggered from a side turning right into the middle of the street and stood there swaying. He belonged to neither side. He was drunk and did not know where he was or what he was doing. He began to sing and wave and call out for a woman. At first the soldiers laughed and shouted jokes at him. But after a while their officer noticed that the enemy was taking advantage of the distraction to run across the far end of the street in ones and twos so as to outflank the troops. He shouted a warning and they opened fire. The enemy replied with covering fire and the street was swept from end to end with machine-gun bullets. The drunk was killed immediately. You see, Mr. Foster?"

"Which side were you on?"

"I was a soldier then. I have been many things, Mr. Foster."

"Yes. Tell me. The reason that your friend Valmo doesn't want me to go to the Deltchev house again is that he doesn't want me to ask Katerina Deltchev to confirm his story, isn't it?"

"I don't know, Mr. Foster. As long as you keep faith with Mr. Valmo it does not matter. One thing I have to ask of you myself, however. I thought it discreet not to mention your connection with Petlarov; it would have complicated the affair. None of these things must on any account be mentioned to Petlarov. Or Mr. Sibley. That is most important."

"All right." I was tired of the whole business now. I wanted to get to bed. I opened the car door. Pashik put out his hand again.

"You will think over what I said, Mr. Foster," he said anxiously. "It is for your own good I ask."

I got out of the car. "I'll be very sober," I said. "That I promise you. Good night."

I was about to slam the door. He leaned across and held it open. His glasses flickered in the light from the hotel entrance as he looked up at me.

"I hope so," he said slowly. "But if you do not intend to take my advice, Mr. Foster, it might be less painful to be drunk. Good night."

Then he shut the door and drove off.

I did not sleep well that night.

Twelve

I T WAS ON the fourth day of the trial that the evidence connecting Deltchev with the Brotherhood was given.

When the court opened, a man named Kroum was called into the witness box. He was about fifty, with a bald head and glasses and an erect military appearance. He looked shrewd and brutal. He described himself as a brigadier of police in the detective department of the Ministry of the Interior. He was carefully washed and brushed and his manner was irritatingly complacent.

Prochaska began his examination in what was for him an unexpected way.

"Brigadier Kroum, how long have you been a member of the police?"

"Thirty years, sir."

"How long have you held your present appointment?"

"Twelve years, sir."

"Are you a member of any political party?"

"No, sir."

"Have you any political affiliations?''

"No, sir."

"None at all?"

"I do not interest myself in politics, sir. I have my work to do."

"An excellent citizen! Have you ever arrested a man or ordered his arrest for political reasons?"

"The only reason for any arrest, sir, is that a man breaks or is suspected of breaking the law. I do not make the law. It is my duty simply to enforce the law under the constitution. That is the duty of every police officer," he added.

Someone near me sniggered at this; but my impression was that Brigadier Kroum meant what he said.

Prochaska glanced at a paper. "In March," he said, "were you concerned with the arrest of eight persons on the charge of trading illicitly in prepared opium?"

"I was responsible for the arrests, sir."

"Did you also examine the prisoner?"

Kroum hesitated. "Unofficially, sir, and solely for the purpose of obtaining information about other members of the gang. The examining magistrate was responsible, of course, for the official interrogation."

"You were not usurping the magistrate's function, but merely doing your duty as a police officer. Is that correct?"

"Yes, sir. That is correct."

"But you gave the prisoners the impression that they were making official depositions?"

"It is sometimes necessary, sir."

He had a blubbery mouth with bad-tempered creases round it. Interrogation by Brigadier Kroum would not be an agreeable experience.

"Was one of those arrested a man named Rila?"

"Yes, sir."

"Did you interrogate him?"

"I did, sir."

"Tell the court about this interrogation."

"Yes, sir. This Rila is a criminal well known to the police. He is an old man who has served many prison sentences. I knew that his eldest granddaughter was pregnant for the first time. I told him that this time he would surely die in prison and never see his great-grandchild, but that if he assisted the police by telling all he knew, a permit might be obtained for the child to be brought for him to see." He looked doubtfully at the prosecutor. "It is customary to offer such inducements to prisoners. No regulations would be broken, sir."

"No, no. Continue please."

"At first he refused to talk. Said he knew nothing. The usual." Kroum was gaining courage. "But the following day, when I saw him again, he was in a better mood. He had thought over my offer and he was worried. After a while he asked if I would protect him from any consequences there might be of his talking. That, too, is usual with criminals informing," he added confidentially.

"Yes. Continue please."

"I asked him for the names of the other members of the gang. He said there were no other members and that we had them all and that there was no information he could give about that case. But he wanted to see his great-grandchild and there was other important information he could give in return for the concession. I said that if the information was valuable it might be possible."

"Continue."

"He then told me that there was in existence a conspiracy to assassinate Minister Vukashin and that the conspirators were members of the Officer Corps Brotherhood." He paused.

"And did you believe him—this criminal who wished to purchase a concession with information?"

"No, sir. At first I thought it was merely an impudent lie and sent him back to his cell. But on thinking it over I decided to question him again. Even though I thought that what he had said must be fantastic, the suggestion was so serious that I felt it necessary to make quite sure. I felt it my duty," he added virtuously.

"Yes, yes. So you questioned him again."

"Yes, sir, and again he began by asking for protection. Again I reassured him. Then he told me a strange story. He lodged in a house in the Maria Louisa quarter. One of his fellow lodgers was a man named Pazar." He paused. He was at his ease now, talking more as an experienced policeman and less as an applause-hungry functionary. "We know that house," he went on; "it is a place for crooks; and because we do know it we let it be; but anyone living there is automatically suspect. Pazar, however, was new there. Rila was curious about him. For Rila there was always the possibility that a stranger might be a police spy. So he took note of this man's movements and was watchful. All he discovered to begin with was that on certain evenings Pazar would be visited by three or four men unknown in the Maria Louisa quarter. They did not look poor, and Rila wondered what they were up to. It is probable, I think, that all along he had an idea of joining in what he thought might be a profitable racket, but this, of course, he denied when I suggested it. He gave another explanation. However—"

"Just a moment, brigadier. What was the explanation he gave?"

Kroum looked embarrassed, "He said, sir, that he was only interested in human nature."

There was some laughter. Prochaska frowned. "Go on," he said shortly.

"Yes, sir. Rila said that Pazar had been living there for about a month when one day he stopped Rila on the stairs and asked to speak to him privately. Rila agreed and they went to his room. After a lot of talk Pazar came out with what he wanted. Someone had told him that Rila dealt in illicit drugs and Pazar wanted some heroin for a friend. Rila's first thought was that Pazar was a police spy after all and he pretended to be shocked. But after a little more talk Rila became convinced that Pazar himself was a heroin addict and needed the stuff badly. Now Rila is quite frank about what followed. Pazar had little money and asked for credit. Rila refused. With heroin addicts one might as well give the stuff away as give credit. Instead he referred to Pazar's well-dressed visitors and said that if he, Rila, could afford smart clothes like that he would be very grateful to the person who had helped him. In other words, he asked for a share in the profitable business he thought was being done by Pazar's friends. Pazar refused angrily and went away. Rila shrugged and waited. Pazar would have to have his stuff, and if he had been driven to asking Rila for it, that meant that his old source of supply had for some reason been stopped. Two days later Pazar came again to Rila, who repeated his price. Pazar again refused, but this time he did not get angry; he pleaded with Rila. His friends, he said, had nothing to do with any trade. They were political. He went on pleading and Rila went on refusing until Pazar became desperate. He begged on his knees, and when Rila told him to go away he broke down and wept. Then it came out. Pazar and the friends who visited him were members of the Brotherhood."

Kroum paused. He had his audience now. There was dead silence. He went on:

"At first Rila did not believe him. When he did believe, he was worried. Our criminals have never liked the Brotherhood. They have been resentful of the extra vigilance it has caused, but also they have been afraid. It is curious," Kroum went on thoughtfully; "a man who kills for money they understand, but the Brotherhood killer troubles them. This old criminal Rila talked about the Brotherhood as a boy might talk about ghosts and demons."

"Yes, yes. Continue."

"Pazar worried him very much, for he knew the ways of heroin drug addicts, as I have said, and he knew that they were treacherous and spiteful. If he refused Pazar and Pazar told his mysterious friends of the Brotherhood that their secret was known to Rila, then Rila would be in danger. So to keep Pazar quiet he gave him some heroin. After a few days Pazar came back for more, and soon Rila was supplying him regularly. Pazar would come into his room and stay and talk and gradually he became more indiscreet."

That word! I glanced at Pashik next to me. His face was quite impassive, but his hands were tense.

Kroum had paused again. Now he went on very slowly:

"One day—Rila cannot remember which day—Pazar began to tell him of something he called the secret of power. He was very mysterious about this secret, but Rila let him talk and after a while Pazar took a round of machine-pistol ammunition from his pocket. 'This is the secret of power, my friend,' he said, 'for this beautiful little thing can make a revolution.' Rila was afraid to ask him what he meant, but Pazar told him eventually. The Brotherhood were planning to assassinate Minister Vukashin."

The prosecutor nodded and looked up at the judges. "The man Rila made a deposition to the effect of what the witness has told the court," he said. "The deposition is signed by him and properly witnessed." He picked up a bundle of papers. "I submit it to the court in evidence, together with three certified copies."

The copies were passed to the clerk of the court, who handed them up to the dais. The center judge glanced at the top paper, nodded gravely, and said something.

"The presiding judges accept the documents in evidence," said the interpreter's voice, "and call upon the prosecutor to continue."

Prochaska turned to the witness box again. "Brigadier Kroum, what action did you take as a result of what you had heard?"

Kroum had prepared this answer: "I considered it my duty, sir, to inform the Minister of the Interior at once so that those responsible for the protection of Minister Vukashin might be warned."

"And then?"

"Then, sir, I set about investigating the truth of the story."

"You doubted it?"

Kroum very nearly permitted himself a tolerant grin. "The police, sir, are obliged to think suspiciously of persons who wish to help them," he said, "especially if they may gain an advantage by doing so."

"Very well. You investigated. What did you discover?"

"That there was a man named Pazar at the house in Maria Louisa, that he did occasionally receive the kind of visitors described, and that he had a reputation for drug-taking. He was not known as a criminal. He was believed to have been at one time a schoolmaster. He had also made a living as a language tutor."

"And then what did you do?"

"There were three possible explanations, sir: that Rila had made up the rest of the story or that Pazar had invented it to impress Rila and get drugs from him; second, that Pazar was mentally unstable as a result of drug-taking and not only invented the story but also believed it to be true; thirdly, that it was in fact true. Although we believed this last possibility unlikely, we decided that no harm would be done by acting upon it. We therefore set a watch on the house with the idea of identifying Pazar's visitors and possibly confronting them in Pazar's room. On the evening of the third day Pazar did not return to the house at the customary time. That same evening a man arrived at the house and was identified by the woman who kept it as one of the regular visitors. He went straight to Pazar's room, which was on the second floor. He received, of course, no reply to his knock and waited for a time. Then he decided to go. When he was stopped by one of my men, he immediately drew a revolver and began to shoot, wounding two policemen. He then attempted to escape, but was shot down. He was identified as a man named Eftib, a university student with a reputation for fanatical views of the kind associated with the Officer Corps Brotherhood."

"He was killed?"

"Unfortunately he died before we could question him, sir."

"Continue."

"The fact that Pazar had not returned and that only Eftib had arrived for a meeting suggested to us that Pazar had been warned of our activity and had passed the warning to the other conspirators. This view was confirmed by the fact that Eftib had been visiting his parents in the country and had only that evening returned. He, therefore, had not received the warning. In any case, our interest in the house was now exposed. We therefore entered Pazar's room and made a search of his belongings."

"And you found?"

"The complete dossier of a conspiracy to assassinate Minister Vukashin on the occasion of the anniversary celebration, including a plan of the operation and detailed orders for the five men participating in it."

A stir ran round the court. Prochaska looked up at the judges. "I ask the court for discretion in this matter," he said. "I have the dossier here and will with permission proceed to offer it in evidence. I ask leave, however, to withhold that part of it concerned with the actual plan of the attempt. It is of great ingenuity and, for reasons that will appear in a moment, unsafe for publication at present. It is in any case not essential to the prosecution's case."

"The permission asked for is granted by the presiding judges."

A bulky file was handed to the clerk of the court. Prochaska continued: "The witness is, of course, not quite accurate in describing what he found as a dossier. He found the operation plan concealed under the floorboards of the room and in other hiding-places a number of documents. These things were later collected into dossier form."

The center judge nodded.

Prochaska turned to Kroum again. "I will ask you now to identify the various items. Item one." He nodded to the clerk, who handed Kroum a clipped wad of papers.

Kroum looked at it.

"Do you recognize those papers?" asked Prochaska.

"I do, sir. I identify them as those I found concealed beneath the tiles of the stove in Pazar's room."

"Have you ever seen papers like that before?"

"Yes, sir. These are pledge forms used as part of the initiation ceremony of the Officer Corps Brotherhood. I recognized them at once. They were secretly printed by a member of the Brotherhood now dead. His name was Markoff. He was arrested, tried, and hanged in January '45. But these were his work."

"Read the pledge to the court."

Kroum cleared his throat. He said: "The form is headed: *Brotherhood of the Officer Corps for the Holy Protection of all Kindred Families and of the Sacred Motherland which gave them Birth and Honor.* Then follows the pledge: *I, Brother X, having, from the dictates of my own heart and conscience and for no other reason, submitted myself to the judgment of my Brethren in honor, and having, through the mingling of my blood with theirs, received absolution before the Mother of God for all acts committed in their name, do hereby dedicate my soul and body to the service of the Brotherhood until and unto death. Recognizing that between Brothers thus specially united by ties of blood there may be no contention or preference or inequality, I swear unconditional and immediate obedience to all orders given to me by Brothers to whom authority has been delegated by the Brethren assembled, and should authority be so delegated to me I swear to accept it and use it faithfully in the knowledge that the responsibility is shared by all equally and that my loyalty to the Brotherhood is superior to all other loyalties and avowals, private or public. My reward for faithful service shall be the honor and love of my Brothers and their protection of me and of my family. But should I betray or in any other way fail the Brotherhood, my own death will be only part of the price to be paid for the offense, for by this oath now taken I bind my whole being, and in betrayal of it all that I hold dear is forfeit. All this I understand and accept. All this I believe just. All this I freely swear to on my blood, my honor, and my life and by this act become of you my Brothers.*" Kroum looked up. "That is all, sir."

"A license to commit treason and murder," commented Prochaska, "as the acknowledged crimes of this fraternity have long since proved." He nodded to the clerk, who handed up another document to Kroum.

Kroum looked at it.

"Do you recognize that document?"

"I do, sir. It was hidden in Pazar's room with the papers I have just read from."

"What is it?"

"A list of names under the word 'Active.'"

"Is the name of Pazar there?"

"It is."

"And Eftib?"

"Yes, sir."

"Is there any other name there familiar to the police?"

"Yes." He hesitated. "The name of Deltchev."

There was dead silence in the court now. Deltchev was sitting in his usual position with his eyes closed. He did not move.

"Is there any other peculiarity about the list?"

"Yes, sir. Certain names on it are underlined."

"Which names?"

"Those of Pazar, Eftib, Vlahov, Pechanatz, Radiuje, and Deltchev."

There was a faint murmur in the court. Deltchev opened his eyes and looked at Kroum thoughtfully.

"Did you say that the plan to assassinate Minister Vukashin required five persons to operate it?"

"Yes, sir."

"Then the sixth person might be the leader?"

"It seemed likely, sir."

"What action did you take?"

"I informed the Minister of the Interior, and warrants for the arrest of Pazar, Vlahov, Pechanatz, and Radiuje were issued."

"Did you execute the warrants?"

"Pechanatz and Radiuje were found to have already left the country. Vlahov was arrested while attempting to do so. It was at the airport and he was placed in the waiting-room to await an escort. The arresting officer had neglected to search him and while in the waiting-room he shot himself. Pazar has not yet been traced."

"What action has been taken about the other names on the list?"

"I ask permission not to answer that question, sir."

"I understand, brigadier." He turned to the judges. "I would point out to the court that at least one man connected with the conspiracy is still in the country and free and that he may attempt to find other confederates even now. It is for that reason that all information cannot yet be made public."

"The presiding judges acknowledge the point."

Prochaska bowed and nodded to the clerk. More papers were handed to Kroum.

"Do you recognize those documents?"

"Yes, sir. I identify them as from Pazar's room."

"Describe them."

"They are messages, mostly typewritten or inked in block letters on plain paper."

"Read from them."

"The first reads: *'Meeting for Thursday to take place Friday. Notified V. and P.'*"

"No signature?"

"None is signed, sir."

"Continue."

"The second reads: '*Await advice as arranged.*' The third: '*P. remains incomplete. Progress others.*' The next: '*V. unsuccessful. Will expedite.*' Next—"

Prochaska interrupted him. "One moment, brigadier. I do not think we need trouble you to read all the messages. I wished only to show their character. They continue like that?"

"Yes, sir. There are over thirty of them."

"Do you understand their meaning?"

"I think so."

"They have a direct bearing on the assassination plan?"

"Yes, sir."

"Then we will be discreet. I come to another point. Do these messages constitute a correspondence or are they only messages received?"

"Messages received, sir."

"What initials appear in the messages?"

"V., P., E., R., and D."

"Referring to?"

"Vlahov, Pechanatz, Eftib, Radiuje, and Deltchev, I believe."

"It seems likely. What is the general character of these messages? Are they, for example, instructions?"

"I would say they are reports."

"To the leader of the conspirators?"

"I think not, sir. It is difficult to say, but in my opinion Pazar, who received the reports, was responsible for coordinating the information. We learned that he received no messages at the house. My belief is that the others used a café or a shop as a post office and that he collected the messages from there, copied them, and redistributed them for information to those concerned. The nature of the plan would call for constant communications of that sort during the period of preparation. No doubt each conspirator had an accommodation address."

"Very well. The messages have been numbered for convenience. Please find message number twenty-seven."

"I have it here."

"Read it please."

"It reads: '*V. in difficulty. Advise D. urgent.*'"

"Is that written or typewritten?"

"Typewritten."

"Is there anything else on the paper?"

"Yes, sir, some pencil writing."

"Read it please."

"It reads: *'Strumitza, twelve.'* "

The courtroom stirred.

"Is that an address?"

"Yes, sir. It is the prisoner's address."

"What explanation have you for its being there?"

"It is in Pazar's handwriting. I suggest that as the message was urgent he did not deliver it to the usual accommodation address for the prisoner, but took it direct to his home. The pencil note was a memorandum of an address that Pazar would not normally use."

I looked at Deltchev. His eyes were closed again. He had not moved. It was impossible to believe. And yet—

Stanoiev did not cross-examine. Kroum left the witness box reluctantly, like an aging prima donna on a farewell tour, and one of his colleagues took his place. The questioning was resumed. What Kroum had said was now elaborately confirmed. I no longer paid much attention. I was trying to digest what I had already heard.

Thirteen

~~~~~~~~~~~~~~~~

IT WAS TRUE; of that I had little doubt. Prochaska had an air of confidence that was not of the kind he could assume. Perhaps clever cross-examination could have made much of Kroum's evidence look weak; Deltchev was not an uncommon name, and when you pointed out that the prisoner's identification with the D. of the messages rested solely on a penciled note of an address alleged to be in the handwriting of a man who could not be produced, you might have shaken a jury's belief in the whole story. But here there was no jury to be shaken and, after the massive certainties of Vukashin and the rest, the very flimsiness of the thing gave it probability. Someone named Deltchev who lived in Deltchev's house had been in close touch with persons desperate enough, as Eftib and Vlahov had been, to shoot when confronted by the police or to commit suicide when arrested. Madam Deltchev? Absurd. Katerina Deltchev? By the time the luncheon break came, I thought I was ready for Pashik.

"Well," I said, "what do you think?"

"It is very interesting."

"Yes. Where do you think Pazar is now?"

He shrugged elaborately. "It is a mystery."

"So they say. When do you think they'll find that man in Patriarch Dimo?"

The brown eyes looked at me steadily. He did not reply.

I stared back at him. "I would guess that it's Pazar's body in that room, wouldn't you?" I said.

"What makes you think that, Mr. Foster?"

"Just an association of ideas. Someone in Deltchev's house sent messages to a man named Pazar. That man is now missing. Someone in Deltchev's house sends a message by me to a man who lived in Patriarch Dimo. That man is now dead."

"That is bad logic, Mr. Foster."

268

"It might be good guessing. Do you believe that Deltchev was in a conspiracy to assassinate Vukashin?"

"It could be so."

"Yes, it could be, but do you think yourself that it was so?"

"Who else could there be, Mr. Foster?"

"Katerina Deltchev could be the D. of those messages."

He showed his brown teeth in a smile. "A nice young lady of twenty in a Brotherhood conspiracy? That is a very funny idea, but it is no more than funny. The Officer Corps Sisterhood! Ah, please, Mr. Foster!"

"Yes, it's silly. I'm trying to find a reasonable explanation, that's all."

"The reasonable explanation is the one already given. Mr. Foster, we are newspapermen, not attorneys for the defense. We need only observe and report. We are lucky."

He had a bland, noncommittal look on his face. At breakfast I had not mentioned the events of the night before. In the morning light they had assumed the proportions of a bad dream, and until I could talk to Petlarov I was content to leave them so. Besides, I was tired of Pashik's denials and warnings and had made up my mind to discover something about the case of "K. Fischer, Vienna '46" before I tackled him again. It looked now as if he thought I had taken his advice. I put aside a temptation to correct the impression.

"What was the Brotherhood plan they're being so secretive about?" I asked.

"I know no more than you, Mr. Foster."

"Doesn't Valmo know? Surely a man in his position would know such things?"

"I am not in his confidence to that extent."

"Did you know Pazar or Eftib?"

To my surprise, he nodded. "Eftib I knew. He was a young man with a great dislike of dogs. A dog he found tied up one day he beat to death with a piece of chain. The other students disliked and feared him. He was not sane, I think."

"How did you know him?"

"The dog he killed belonged to one of the professors at the university. There was a scandal. I reported it for a newspaper, but his family paid to avoid the publicity. By now," he added thoughtfully, "they may wish he had been safely put in prison."

The waiter came up with our food. This particular section of the restaurant was reserved for the pressmen attending the trial and across the room I could see Sibley talking earnestly and confidentially to one of the Americans. Then out of the corner of my eye I saw Pashik looking at me. He looked away almost as I saw him, but not quite fast enough. He had to cover up.

"Yes," he said, "Mr. Sibley is busy still. He may succeed with someone who has no reason to suspect him. It is very strange."

I smiled. "There's something I find even stranger, Pashik."

"Yes, Mr. Foster?" He was on his guard again.

"I find it strange that although you are quite ready to serve someone you say is of the Government secret police, you put obstacles in the way of Sibley, who is trying to serve the Propaganda Ministry."

He stared at me for a moment and I thought he was about to reply. Then he changed his mind, cleared his throat, and picked up his knife and fork. "Mr. Foster," he said heavily, "I think we should get on with our eating."

I could get nothing more out of him. After the luncheon break the conspiracy evidence was resumed. Now that he had something like real evidence to deal with, Prochaska spread himself. Every detail of Kroum's evidence was sworn to by three or four different persons, every document certified and proved. Had you not heard the earlier days of the trial, you might from Prochaska's attitude have supposed the judges to be pettifogging martinets hostile to his case. When you remembered the rubbish that had already been admitted as evidence by that pathetic trio, the present solemnity was funny. But not for long. Presently it became boring. Only one thing kept me there: the possibility of Deltchev's speaking in his own defense. But he seemed as bored as I was. As witness after witness was brought in to swear to the authenticity of the message with his address on it, I expected a protest from him. It would have been easy enough:

"These conscientious policemen swear to the presence of my address on this piece of paper. Nobody disputes that it is there. Why waste the time they might be devoting to more useful duties? Produce a really serious witness: the man who wrote it or who saw it written or, even better, the man who can tell us *why* and in what circumstances it was written down there. Those questions are important, gentlemen, for I, too, have been plotted against by assassins. They threw a bomb and badly wounded my chauffeur. That was outside my house, and to find my house you need the address, and to remember it you have to write it down. I have no wish to deprive Minister Vukashin of his martyr's laurels, but if I am to be convicted of plotting against his life, at least make sure that the evidence you use is not part of an old plot against *my* life. For a new plot new evidence should be manufactured. Economy in such matters is discourteous."

But Deltchev said nothing at all and the afternoon drowsed on. Curiously, it was only the diplomatic and press sections who seemed bored. For most of the spectators it was an exciting afternoon. As each witness appeared, there would be a buzz of interest, then dead silence while he gave his evidence, then breathless whispering as he stepped down. It was the factual nature of the evidence that did it. There must have been many in that courtroom who had been unwilling to believe in Deltchev's guilt and privately uneasy about the trial. Now they were enjoying the illusion that the legal forms were being properly observed and that they were free of the responsibility of condoning an injustice. I was glad when the afternoon was over.

Pashik had nothing to say as he drove me back to my hotel. He knew that I was going to see Petlarov and he was saving himself for a farewell admonishment on the subject of discretion; so I thought, at least; and I was tired of him; I was tired of his smell, of his admonishments, of his evasions and mystery-making, of his long-suffering brown eyes, of his dirty seersucker suit, and of his bad driving.

He stopped jerkily outside the hotel and turned to me. "Mr. Foster—" he began.

I interrupted irritably. "Look, do you have to go on calling me 'Mr. Foster' all the time? Can't you make it 'Foster' or 'you'? It would be easier for you and I shouldn't feel so stiff-necked."

He began again picking at the vulcanite covering of the steering-wheel. He already had most of it off and the metal beneath looked bare and squalid.

"I am sorry, Mr. Foster," he said, "I wished only to be polite."

"Yes, of course. It's not important."

But he was upset. "I am afraid you are not a good-tempered man, Mr. Foster," he said.

"No, I'm not. I apologize. You wanted to tell me to be discreet again, didn't you?"

He picked for a moment or two in silence. He was working on a big piece and it peeled away like a strip of sunburnt skin.

"I don't know what more I can say to you, Mr. Foster," he said. "I have tried to warn you, not because I like you or even because I have a responsibility to the New York office, but in the spirit of any man who sees another by accident going into a danger he does not realize. I can do no more. There are things more important than the safety of a stranger. You will not take the advice; then you must take your chance. I will not discuss the case with you further. The services I am paid for are yours, however. Tomorrow I will be getting your press ticket for the anniversary celebration. When the end date of the trial is known, your return passage by air will be available. If there is any other service you wish performed, you must tell me. Meanwhile, when we meet we can talk of other things." He turned and looked at me. "Good night, Mr. Foster."

"Good night."

I got out and went into the hotel. I was both impressed and depressed. As I walked up the stairs I decided that I would take his advice. I told myself that it was only my personal dislike of the man that had prevented my taking it before. That was really stupid. My task was to write articles about the trial, not to play policeman. I had stumbled on a political murder in a country where political murder was a commonplace. The fact that for me it was a novelty did not give me a license to inquire into it. I should remember that I was a foreigner, there on sufferance, that I had a very lucrative profession to return to, and that in my temporary role of newspaper reporter I had done very well to get an exclusive interview with Madame Deltchev. That was enough. I would now mind my own business. And it might be a good idea to apologize to Pashik. He had been very patient with me and I had behaved with the bumptiousness of an amateur. And, by the way, since when had Mr. Foster been entitled to object to being called Mr. Foster by someone who wished to be courteous? Mr. Foster was making a very tiresome fool of himself. He'd better stop.

Petlarov was sitting stiff and straight on his usual seat in the corridor. Without speaking he followed me into my room and sat down. I went to the wardrobe and got out the whisky. He took the tooth glass with his usual polite bow and then glanced up at me.

"You look tired, Herr Foster."

"I've had a tiring twenty-four hours."

He nodded politely. He did not even look a question.

"What about today's evidence? What do you think?" I asked. "It's more or less what you feared, isn't it?"

He considered for a moment, then he shook his head. "No. I don't think it is. You see, I expected something possible. I thought that Yordan might have committed some indiscretion capable of being shown badly. But not this. It is really very funny. I know Yordan and I know that he is incapable of this kind of association. And with men of the type of Eftib and Pazar it is grotesque."

"He associated with Vukashin and Brankovitch."

"He did not like them, but he recognized their importance. Both are considerable men, leaders. But conspiracy with this delinquent riffraff? It is impossible! Yordan is too much of a snob."

"What sort of indiscretion did you expect?"

He shrugged. "Many things are possible. For example, it would not have greatly surprised me to learn that some of the exiles were planning a *coup d'état* and had nominated Yordan their leader. If they appealed to him he would be flattered. He might temporize, but he would treat with them. In transactions of that kind many foolish things are written. Now with this, all is different. We have circumstantial evidence of the kind that is used to convict ordinary criminals—the piece of paper with the note on it, the scribbled address, the conspirators who escape and those who do not, the mysterious Pazar, who is missing but really dead—it is all of a different pattern." He shrugged again. "But that is only what I feel."

"What did you mean by saying that Pazar is really dead?"

"If he were alive they would certainly have found him before the trial. They could not risk his being found unexpectedly. He might be an inconvenient witness and it would look bad if he, too, were killed resisting arrest."

So then of course I told him. Whatever else was not my business, the problem of the evidence against Deltchev certainly was, and I had come to rely upon Petlarov's opinions. I told him about the letter I had carried, of the dead man in Patriarch Dimo 9, of Pashik's arrival, of the visit to Aleko, and of the Aleko note. He listened in silence and was silent for a time when I had finished. I noticed that he had gone very pale. Then he put down his drink and stood up.

"Herr Foster," he said slowly, "I too have something to tell you. Every two days I have to report to the police to get my papers stamped. It is part of the control to which, as an untrustworthy person, I am subject. Today when I reported, I was warned. I was told that I had recently made an undesirable association and that if I did not wish to be removed with my wife to a labor camp, the association must cease. That was all. Your name was not mentioned." He hesitated. "When I came here this evening, Herr Foster, I had almost made up my mind to ignore the warning. I thought that if it had been a serious matter I should not have been warned but arrested. I see now that I was wrong."

"What do you mean?"

But he did not reply. He was fumbling agitatedly in his pocket. He got out the ration card I had given him and held it out to me.

"I am sorry, Herr Foster," he said; "I cannot keep our bargain."

"That's all right. I understand." I didn't, but he was so obviously upset that I wanted to soothe him. "Keep the ration card anyway. I don't want it."

He shook his head. His face looked pinched and there was sweat on his forehead. I had a curious sense of shock. I had come to think of Petlarov as some kind of genie who inhabited the corridor outside my hotel room, ready to explain, to enlighten, to serve when I needed him. Because his own account of himself had been quite calm and impersonal, because he had not exuded the self-pity I should have been so quick to condemn, I had not found it necessary to think of him as a human being. Now suddenly he was very much a human being; he was frightened. The realization gave me a curious feeling of discomfort.

"Herr Foster," he said, "please take the card. I cannot use it any more, and if I am arrested I do not wish to have it found in my pocket."

I took it. He picked up his hat and went to the door.

"Just a moment," I said.

He stopped. The effort he made to control his agitation was almost painful to watch. He just wanted to be gone.

"Can't you give me any idea what this is all about?" I asked.

For a moment I thought he was going without answering. Then he swallowed and licked his lips. He looked at his hat as he spoke. "I will tell you one thing, Herr Foster. K. Fischer, Karl Fischer, you mentioned him." He hesitated before he went on with a rush. "He was a Left-wing politician, very popular in the working-class quarters of Vienna. A good man and a fearless speaker. He was in principle for the Soviets, but still in '46 he protested against the Soviet kidnappings of Austrians from the American sector. An honest man. He did what he thought right. He was murdered." He hesitated and swallowed again.

"Yes?"

"In September it was," he said. "He went out one evening to see his married daughter in Favoriten. Next day the railway police found his body behind a shed in the marshaling yard outside the Ostbahnhof." He paused and looked up at me. "You said that the man you saw at Patriarch Dimo had been killed by a bullet wound in the back of the head, by the ear."

"Yes."

He nodded. "That was how Karl Fischer died," he said. "That was the hand of Aleko."

Then he went.

Fourteen

〰〰〰〰〰〰〰

T HAT WAS ON Friday, the 14th of June. The assassination took place on the Saturday.

I have since been described in the People's Party press as "a well-known agent of the English secret service," "the leader of a foreign murder gang," "Anglo-American spy and pervert," and in other less reproducible ways. In one article the fact that I am a writer was acknowledged by a reference to "the notorious pornographer and English murder-propaganda lackey Foster."

That part of it has been less amusing than I would have thought. Some of the stuff was reproduced in London papers, and among my friends the "notices of Foster's Balkan tour" were quoted hilariously for a day or two. But when the news of the Deltchev verdict came and the mass executions of Agrarian Socialists began, the attacks on me became related to events that were anything but funny. I began to be asked questions that the Foreign Office had suggested I should not answer.

With the newspapers it was not difficult; I did as I had been asked and referred them to the Foreign Office. With friends and acquaintances it was less simple. It is, I find, extraordinarily embarrassing to be described in print as a member of the British secret service. The trouble is that you cannot afterwards convince people that you are not. They reason that if you are a member you will still presumably have to say that you are not. You are suspect. If you say nothing, of course, you admit all. Your denials become peevish. It is very tiresome. Probably the only really effective denial would be a solemn, knowing acknowledgment that there *might* be some truth in the rumor. But I can never bring myself to it. Foreign Office or no Foreign Office, I have to explain what really happened.

To begin with, I think I should make it clear that I am not one of those persons who enjoy danger. I take pains to avoid it. Moreover, my timidity is speculative and elaborate. For instance, in Paris at the time of the Stavisky riots I was living in a hotel room overlooking a street in which the police fought a revolver battle with rioters. My first impulse was to lean out of the window and watch. The firing was several hundred yards away and I knew perfectly well that at that distance a revolver is about as dangerous as a water pistol. What I remembered, however, was that the author of *Way of Revelation* had had a similar impulse of curiosity in Mexico City and died of it, absurdly, with a stray bullet through his head. Instead of leaning out of the window, therefore, I had knelt on the floor by it and tried to use my shaving-mirror as a periscope; but by the time I had arranged all this, the battle was over and I saw nothing but an indignant woman with an upset shopping-bag.

The war did nothing to make my attitude to danger bolder or more philosophic. I do not have heroic impulses. The news that a bomb had killed my wife in our London flat had many other effects on me, but it did not send me out in a murderous rage to exact retribution of the enemy, nor did it make me volunteer for some suicidal duty. For a long time my life felt less worth living than before, but I did not for that reason become careless of it. Accounts of great bravery sometimes move me deeply, but they arouse in me no desire to emulate them. The spirit of romantic derring-do runs somewhat thinly in my veins.

The truth about my part in the Deltchev affair is untidy. I did not even blunder into the danger; I strayed into it as if it were an interesting-looking tangle of streets in an old town. Certainly I had been warned that they were dangerous; but only to those who warned, I thought, not to me. When I found out that I was mistaken and tried to get out, I found also that I was lost. That was how it felt. The last moment at which I could have turned back was when Petlarov went out of my room that evening. If at that point I had shrugged my shoulders, had another drink, gone out to dinner, and spent the evening at a cinema, I should have been fairly safe. And I very nearly did do that. I had the drink—it was the last of the whisky—and I looked at a cinema I could see from my window. It was called LUX and was playing a dubbed version of a German film called *La Paloma* that I did not want to see. I considered opening a bottle of plum brandy I had bought, decided against it, and then caught sight of the typewriter I had brought with me but not yet used. I thought of the solemnity of my departure with it from London ten days or so before and felt absurd. Images came into my mind of those groups of toys you see mounted on highly colored boards in the shops at Christmas time; the Boys' Conductor Set (complete with ticket punch), the Boys' Detective Set (complete with three disguises), the Boys' Tank Commander Set (complete with binoculars). I spent a self-abasing minute or two thinking of a new one: the Boys' Foreign Correspondent Set, complete with typewriter, whisky bottle,

invisible ink, and a copy of John Gunther's *Inside Europe*. Then I did a foolish thing: I decided to pull myself together and be sensible.

What, I asked myself over dinner, were the facts? Quite simple. I was supposed to be reporting the trial of a man named Deltchev who was accused
of planning an assassination. Probably he was innocent. Yet some of the
evidence against him had a ring of truth about it. Moreover, his daughter had
been in touch with someone concerned in the assassination plan. I had found
that person dead, killed in the same way as an Austrian politician and most
likely by the same man, Aleko. Aleko had pretended to be of the secret
police but was probably an agent of another kind. Who had employed him?
Deltchev? Or the People's Party to implicate Deltchev? But why should
either employ Aleko when they had dangerous psychotics like Eftib and Pazar
ready to hand? It didn't make sense. And where did Deltchev come in? That
was the important thing. I was preparing to defend him before a very large
public. It might be just as well (might it not?) to make sure that I had the
facts right. *Might* be! A fine fool I should look if the noble Deltchev I had
postulated turned out to be in reality as murderous as his persecutors but rather
cleverer at concealing the fact. "Mr. Foster, what steps did you take to check
the validity of your impressions?" "Well, none really. I thought it better not
to be inquisitive. Too risky." Oh dear, oh dear! By the time the wine arrived I
no longer had any doubts. Nothing I already knew about the case seemed
either logical or in any other way satisfactory. Far too much was hidden. Well,
it must be revealed; and if the intimidated Petlarov did not want to help me, I
would find it out for myself. The first thing for me to do anyway was to see
Madame Deltchev at once—that evening—and hear what she had to say about
the day's evidence. Then I would give myself the pleasure of an interview
with little Miss Katerina, tell her the news about her friend Valmo, and ask
her the questions that Aleko did not want me to ask. After that I would
decide what to do next.

I finished my dinner and walked out to the Deltchev house. As I turned
into the street where it was, the mood of hearty resolution in which I had
started out suddenly weakened. The guards I had passed before might not be
on duty. A different set might have taken over. Then, as I approached, I saw
that the same guards were there. It made no difference; my anxiety deepened.
I realized that the real source of it had nothing to do with the guards but with
the undertaking I had given to Aleko and my too ready disposal of it. If, I had
reasoned, Aleko had really had any police powers he would not have asked
for an undertaking not to visit the Deltchev home again; he would simply
have issued an order to the guards not to admit me. Therefore, I had concluded, he had no police powers and I might call his bluff. But it was one

thing to have arrived at a theoretical conclusion and quite another to act upon it in this way. All sorts of unconsidered possibilities occurred to me as I walked toward the house. Supposing, for instance, he really did have police powers and had planned to test my good faith by including this prohibition to the undertaking. For a moment I hesitated and was about to turn back; then I realized that the corporal had seen and recognized me. Retreat was impossible now. I walked on up to him and took out my press permit. He nodded curtly, but examined the permit carefully again while the doltish private stood grinning at me. At last the corporal handed back the permit with a faint shrug (ominous?) and nodded to the private. The latter hitched his rifle sling more snugly on his shoulder and, crossing to the door in the wall, pulled the bell.

It was as before. I waited. They watched me. There was the clacking of old Rana's sandals on the paving of the courtyard. The door opened cautiously. But then she recognized me and held the door for me to go in. Inside she said something and signed to me to wait. She was not long. Soon I heard her sandals flapping down the stairs inside the house. She opened the front door and beckoned me in.

I went upstairs. The same slippery floor, the same smell of furniture polish, but this time no Katerina. She, I thought, would be standing with her man-of-the-world air behind her mother's chair. I hoped, uncharitably, that my arrival would alarm her.

But Madame Deltchev was alone. She was standing facing me by the window as I came in. The light was behind her, but there was tension in the way she stood. On the table by her were two empty tea glasses. The old friend had delivered his report for the day.

She turned quickly. "Good evening, Herr Foster. It is good of you to call again."

"You are very kind, madame. I am afraid I have more questions."

"Naturally. Please sit down."

"Thank you."

There was a *grande dame* artificiality about her manner that accentuated the feeling of strain she meant it to conceal. "Although," she went on, "I think it unlikely that I shall be able to give you the information you need. Tea?"

"No, thank you."

"Of course. You have dined, and the English do not drink tea after dinner." She smiled mechanically and, picking up one of the glasses, went over to the samovar. "With us it is a habit," she said; "Russian, of course. Most of our habits are Russian or Turkish or German or Greek. We have few of our own." Boiling water spluttered from the tap into the glass. "You see now why our patriots mean so much to us here. Their unquestioning belief that we are indeed a nation with our own cultural and political identities, and not merely a marginal tribe with some curious ethnological affinities, is a great comfort. The truth about many of our great traditional patriots is ugly or ludicrous; but it makes no difference. They are defended angrily. National feeling in small states is always angry; it must be so, for its roots are in fear and self-doubt, and for those things reason is no protection."

She spoke as glibly as a journalist quoting without acknowledgment from an article he has just written. I was not sure whether she was talking for concealment or whether I was being offered an elaborately wrapped hint. Was there perhaps an ugly truth to be known about patriot Deltchev?

"Your husband has meant a great deal to his people," I said carefully.

"Yes, yes, he has." She had carried her tea over to her chair. Now she sat down facing me. "They will not give him up easily, no matter what lies are told about him. A cigarette, Herr Foster?"

"Thank you; I'm sure you are right. Have you heard about today's court proceedings, madame?"

"Yes, I have heard about them."

I lit the cigarette she had given me. "Do you consider that the evidence was false in itself or that it was false only in relation to your husband?"

"Some of his witnesses may be truthful, but their testimonies compose a lie."

"May I put a hypothetical question? Supposing that the evidence were all true, that your husband had in fact been involved in this plot, would you have known about it, madame? Would he have confided in you?"

She did not answer immediately. Then: "He always confided in me. I should have known."

"It would be a dangerous secret to confide to anyone."

"If it had existed; yes, very dangerous."

"For comparison's sake, madame, can you tell me if your husband confided in you his intention to make that radio speech about the elections before he made it?"

She sat quite still for several moments, staring out through the window at the bare hills. I almost wondered if she had heard what I had said. She had heard, I knew, and understood too, but her air of preoccupation was very nearly convincing. Then, with a slight puzzled shake of the head as if to banish other thoughts and face the immediate reality, she turned her gentle, intelligent eyes toward me.

"I am very sorry, Herr Foster," she said with a faint, confused smile, "I am afraid I was not paying attention. I had other thoughts." She put her hand to her forehead as if she had a headache. "It was inexcusable."

It was not badly done; I have known actresses make a worse job of it; but if I wanted to parody a particular style of drawing-room comedy I would have that speech, and the performance that goes with it, well in mind. She must have seen it in dozens of bad plays. Probably she was expecting from me one of the two conventional reactions to it; the guilty ("Forgive me, you're tired") or the aggrieved ("I'm a busy man and my time is valuable"). However, I felt neither guilty nor aggrieved. I did feel intensely curious.

I repeated the question.

Her lips twitched with annoyance. "Herr Foster, what is the point of this question? Please be honest with me."

"Certainly. You deny that there is a word of real truth in the evidence put before the court today. I wish to know what value I may put upon that denial. Is it based on knowledge or an emotional conviction? You must see that that is important."

"What I see, Herr Foster," she said coldly, "is that this trial is beginning to have the effect intended by the Propaganda Ministry."

I felt myself flush with anger. By the light of the setting sun she did not see that, but I did not reply and after a moment she began to apologize. I must forgive her; she was tired and overwrought; she had not slept for many nights; she was distracted with worry. I listened carefully. What she was saying was all quite reasonable and genuine, but it was also a protective screen. Something had happened to her since our first meeting; some inner certainty had gone. Before, she had been facing with calm courage the prospect of her husband's conviction and death. Perhaps that courage had rested upon a belief in his innocence which no longer went unquestioned. Perhaps the unworthy doubts of which she now accused me were merely the projections of her own misgivings.

I tried a different way.

"In the theater," I said, "a little fact will sustain a lot of illusion. As Petlarov says, 'the lie rests most securely on a pinpoint of truth.' Brankovitch is not a fool. He knows that although he can impose any nonsense he likes upon the people of his own country, abroad it will not be so easy. With that trumped-up case he cannot hope to deceive the outside world. But what he can do is to confuse it by mixing with his lies a little truth. This plot against Vukashin. Why is it there? To prove that your husband is a member of the Brotherhood? Nonsense! Better evidence could be invented. Besides, even a stable government will regard an assassination plot as bad propaganda and try to conceal it if they can. No, this evidence is there because it is specially valuable. It is valuable because it is true. And those in court today recognized that it is true. It was not much—a few statements confirming a small set of facts—but it was true, and already in their minds this truth had grown and obscured the great mass of falsehood that surrounds it. You say, madame, that there may be truthful witnesses but that they compose a lie. But how much of a lie? Where does the truth end and the lie begin? You cannot defeat the prosecution's case with blank denials. It is not as simple as that. You have to give the whole truth, and that is what I want."

There was a long silence. She looked stonily out of the window, and when she spoke she did not turn her head.

"Herr Foster, there is not a court of law in the civilized world that would accept the case against my husband. I have been well advised of that."

"No civilized court of law is going to be asked to accept it," I retorted. "If the truth is not told, the final judgment will be delivered here. A few persons may doubt and speculate, but they must all come to the same conclusion."

"What conclusion?"

"That there must have been something in the accusations against Deltchev, that the conspiracy evidence was never seriously disputed, that if he wasn't the criminal they tried to make him out, he was something very nearly as bad—a fool. Forgive me, madame, but what you do not seem to realize is that any protest against your husband's trial is a political act. No foreign office and no responsible newspaper is going to make that protest unless it is absolutely certain that he is innocent. They must know the truth."

"It isn't true. The case against him is a lie. What else can I say?"

"To what extent did your husband confide in you?"

"What does it matter? If I tell you that he always confided in me you will say that this particular matter might have been too dangerous to confide. If I say that he did not confide it, it is no different."

"If he were in any way involved in this conspiracy would you have known?"

"Yes. He was not involved."

"Did you know that he was going to make that election broadcast before he made it?"

"Yes, I did."

"Did you know why he was going to make it?"

"Yes."

"Why was it?"

She shook her head hopelessly. I knew she was lying.

"Was it because at one time, long ago, your husband had been a member of the Officer Corps Brotherhood?"

For a moment she was quite still. Then, slowly, she raised her head and stared at me. "Is that a serious question, Herr Foster?" she asked coolly.

I knew suddenly that it was not a serious question, but part of a fantasy in a locked room. I began to mumble: "It was a faint possibility, madame." She still stared at me. "It could have been a youthful indiscretion, a mistake. . . ." I petered out.

She smiled in a twisted sort of way. "Yordan does not make that kind of indiscretion. He is always an intelligent man. Are there any other questions, Herr Foster?" she added.

If I had had any advantage it was suddenly quite gone. "Have you ever heard the name of Pazar before?"

"It is a Turkish name. I know no one who has it."

"Or Eftib?"

"No. Nor any of the other persons mentioned today."

"Aleko?"

"Was that name mentioned?"

"No. Do you know it?"

"It is a short name for Alexander. That is all I know."

"Valmo?"

"It is a fairly common surname, but it means nothing in particular to me. Should it do so?"

"I don't know." I stood up. "Thank you for receiving me, madame."

"It is nothing." She stood up too and switched on a reading-lamp.

"Before I go, I should like, if I may, to speak to your daughter," I said.

She stiffened. "Why?"

"I should like to ask her some questions."

"Perhaps I can answer them for you."

"Perhaps." I hesitated. "When I left here two nights ago, madame, your daughter asked me to take out a letter for her and deliver it to a man named Valmo." I paused.

She tried unsuccessfully to smile. "My daughter is an attractive young woman. She has her affairs of the heart."

"Yes, that was the impression of the letter she succeeded in giving to me. I agreed to take it."

"That was chivalrous of you."

"The address on the letter was Patriarch Dimo, nine. I found the place. It is a disused house in a slum."

"And did you find the young man?"

I shook my head. She relaxed perceptibly.

"If you will give me the letter, Herr Foster, I will see that it is returned to my daughter. It was good of you to take so much trouble." She held out her hand.

I said: "I did not find a young man, madame. I found a dead one. He had been shot."

Very slowly she sat down. "Had he shot himself?" she asked softly.

"No. The wound was in the back of the head."

She did not move. "A young man?"

"No. Gray-haired, about fifty I should think. Why do you ask?"

She straightened up a little. "I thought perhaps some poor young student—" She broke off and drew a deep breath. "There are so many tragedies. You must have gone to the wrong house, Herr Foster."

"No. It was the right house. But if the dead man was the person who had called himself Valmo, then your daughter knew Pazar. For that was the dead man's real name."

There was a silence. She did not look at me.

"Did the police tell you that?" she said at last.

"I did not go to the police. It would have been difficult to explain how I came to be visiting the Brotherhood assassin they are supposed to be searching for. Difficult and embarrassing for us all."

"We are in your debt, Herr Foster."

"Perhaps you would prefer your daughter to explain," I said.

She looked at her handkerchief. "My daughter is not here."

I was silent.

She looked at me. "I am speaking the truth, Herr Foster."

"I understand that everyone here was under house arrest."

"My daughter is not here. She has gone."

"Do you mean that the police took her away?"

"No. She escaped."

"How? What about the guards?"

"Katerina has lived in this house all her life, Herr Foster. There are other ways of leaving it than by the gates."

I hesitated. "A few minutes ago, madame, I asked you if you had heard of Pazar before. You said that you had not. Do you still say that?"

"Yes. It is the truth."

"But others in this house do know him?"

"I do not."

"Do you know where your daughter has gone?"

"No."

"When did she go?"

"This evening."

"Can you think of any reason why she should go?"

"Herr Foster, I am very tired."

I waited a moment or two, but she did not look up again. "I'm sorry," I said; "I think I might have been of help to you."

"I have told you all I can."

"You have told me all you think it advisable for me to know, madame."

"Good night, Herr Foster." She pressed the bellpush.

I said good night and picked up my hat, but as I got to the door she spoke again.

"Herr Foster."

I stopped.

"My daughter's letter. Will you give it to me, please?"

"It is burned."

"Are you sure?"

"Quite sure."

She hesitated. "Forgive me, but do you know what was in it?"

"I did not open it. In any case I cannot read your language."

She came a little way across the room toward me. "Herr Foster," she said, "I have not been helpful to you, but I would not like you to think that I am ungrateful for your kindness and patience. I do most sincerely thank you."

I bowed. I could not think of anything coherent to say that would not have deepened my embarrassment. The sound of Rana's sandals flapping along the passage outside came like the answer to a prayer.

"Good night, madame," I said, and got out of the room as quickly as I could. It did not occur to me until I was walking down the stairs that my twinges of guilt were unnecessary. Beside the monumental evasions to which I had been listening for the past half-hour my own reticences were trivial.

Fifteen

IT WAS VERY dark outside the house. The old woman had no lamp to guide us and I blundered rather than walked after her across the courtyard. The fact contributed somehow to the feelings of inadequacy, futility, and blank exasperation which were beginning to grow in me.

I stubbed my foot against the edge of a flagstone and said: "Damn!" violently. The old woman opened the door in the wall and the flashlight from outside shone in my face. I scowled at it and hauled out my wallet as the door closed behind me. The light left my face and I saw the corporal.

"*Passieren, vorwärts!*" he snapped, and waved me on peremptorily.

"Don't you want to see my permit, you fool?" I inquired in English.

"*Passieren, passieren!*" he repeated, and waved me on again.

"Grinning lout," I said with a smile to the private.

He nodded, grinning, and saluted.

I walked away. The corporal was not troubling to examine my permit any more. The corporal had decided that I was harmless. The corporal was absolutely right. Tomorrow, I decided, I would send a cable to the man who was paying me, tell him that he was wasting his money and my time, then take the first plane I could get out of the place. It was high time I stopped this foolishness and got back to work again. Not, I thought savagely, that the trip had been a complete loss. I had increased my knowledge of Napoleon III. I had also had two interesting experiences: that of finding a dead body in a strange house, and that of being locked in a room in another strange house. In the unlikely event of my ever wanting to write the kind of play in which incidents like that occurred, the knowledge would be useful. Meanwhile, to hell with it!

I turned into the Boulevard Dragutin.

It ran in a gentle curve round the high boundary wall of the Presidential Park. It was a wide road, lined with big plane trees and cobbled. Most of the buildings in it were apartment houses; there were no shops or cafés. The lights were on tall standards set among the trees on the building side of the road. I walked on the other side. Beneath the dense foliage of the trees it was very dark.

I walked slowly. The air was pleasant and after a while something happened to make me forget my immediate troubles. Before I had left London I had been trying to write the third act of a new play and had got into difficulties with it. Indeed, I had practically made up my mind to scrap the whole thing. The commission to report the Deltchev trial had come at an opportune moment; it had given me a reason for suspending work on the play that left the real reasons for doing so in abeyance. But now, quite suddenly, I found myself thinking about the play again and seeing quite clearly the point of the problem that I had missed before. The shape of a third act began to emerge. Of course! The wife's lover wasn't her own choice, but her husband's, and it was her realization of this fact that made it possible for her to leave him. Of course! It was the key to her whole attitude toward her lover. He was not *her* choice. Of course! How curious it was I had practically sign-posted the thing all the way through without realizing the fact. Why? My mind nosed round the discovery suspiciously like a terrier at a strange lamppost. There must be a mistake. But no, it was all right. I had been too close to it before and too anxious. Now all was well. I drew a deep breath. Forgotten were the Deltchevs and the enigma they represented. I had just finished a play. I felt light-hearted and alive. I quickened my pace.

Then I heard it. It was only a slight sound and it went almost immediately; a sort of ringing of my footsteps on the paving stones. But I was very much aware of everything at that moment; of the soft, warm breeze that was beginning to stir the air, of the smell of the trees, and of the slow movement of a distant point of light. At this moment of heightened sensibility the ringing of my footsteps was a matter for appreciation and curiosity. The pavement was solid enough. Where did the rest of the sound come from? I slowed down a little and heard it again, a kind of echo. From the wall? I stepped out again, but in a more emphatic way this time. Then I understood. It was not an echo I was hearing. Someone was walking behind me.

It is easy to separate sounds once you know they are there. As I walked on, I could hear the other set of footsteps quite plainly. I slowed down again. The sounds separated and then again they coincided. Even then it took me a moment or two to grasp what was happening. The person behind me was varying his pace with mine. He did not want to change the distance between us. I was being followed.

My heart suddenly beat faster. I looked round. I could just see him, a faint thickening of the shadows under the trees about thirty yards behind me. I walked on, fighting down a desire to run. Perhaps I was imagining it all, like a neurotic spinster with fantasies of being raped. But no; the footsteps kept pace with mine. Wild ideas of turning quickly and challenging the follower went through my mind, but I kept on walking for a bit. The calves of my legs began to ache. Then, suddenly, I turned and crossed the road to the lighted side. Out of the corner of my left eye I tried to see if he was crossing too. I could hear his footsteps. They had slowed down. He wasn't going to cross. He was going to stay among the shadows. For a moment or two a feeling of relief flooded over me. It was not until I was nearly to the pavement that I realized why he had not crossed. A hundred yards or so ahead there was a stretch of road with no buildings and no lights. I remembered walking along it earlier. He was going to cross there.

I reached the pavement and hesitated. Then I bent down and pretended to tie my shoelace. I wanted time to think. If I went back the way I had come, I could stay in the lights. I remembered also that I had seen two policemen yawning and spitting on a corner. But what was I to do then? Explain to them? But there was nothing to explain. The only thing was to wait about like a frightened child until someone else came along with whom I could walk in company through the dark. Ridiculous! What was there to be afraid of? Someone was following me. Very well. Let him follow. What did it matter? There was nothing to be afraid of in that. Nothing at all.

I stood up again and walked on stiffly toward the darkness.

It lay at the end of the lighted strip of pavement like the black mouth of a tunnel. The building I had to pass before I reached it was a huge baroque mansion that, judging from the lighted windows, had been converted into flats. I looked across the road. I could see him moving along under the trees now, a little behind me but at the same speed. The darkness came nearer and I began to see a short way into it. The footpaths ran on between a stone wall and the trees, but the surface of it changed from stone pavement to dust. At the end of the pavement I paused. The leaves above stirred faintly; there was a radio playing somewhere and the breathing sounds of distant traffic, but that was in the background; the darkness before me was quiet and still. The gritty dust crunched beneath my feet, and the branches seemed to close in as I walked on again. I had gone about thirty paces when I heard the sound of an approaching car. It passed, going in the opposite direction. Then, as the sound died away, I heard footsteps on the road; the man from the shadows was crossing it behind me. I went on faster, stumbling slightly over the swellings in the path made by tree roots. My heart was beating sickeningly now and I could feel the cold sweat stealing down my body. I fought against the desire to run.

It was absurd, I told myself. I had been in situations fifty times more danger-ous. Here there were no mines or alarm wires to tread on, no machine guns or mortars waiting to open fire. All I had to do was to walk along a path beneath some trees in a badly lighted city street, followed by someone who might or might not be ill-intentioned. He might be a detective, one of Brankovitch's men instructed to report on my movements. Petlarov had been warned off me by the police. They might now be checking to see if I had any other contacts. Indeed, the man could have been following me about for days without my having noticed the fact. Yes, that must be it. I almost chuckled with relief and slowed down, listening for the footsteps behind me. But there were none. Perhaps they were muffled by the dust. Perhaps—

I stopped dead. Something had moved in front of me.

I stood quite still for a moment, trying to control the thudding of the blood in my head so that I could hear. Something had moved—a shadow, some-thing. I took a step forward and my foot grated on a pebble. The next instant there was a blinding flash of light.

It came from a powerful hand-lamp a few yards in front of me and lasted for less than a second. And that, too, was the time I took to react. As the light went out I fell sideways, sprawling at the foot of a tree.

I only heard the first shot, a thudding crack that made my ears sing; but the next two I saw—yellow blots of flames that seemed to be exploding in my face as I rolled over and clawed for cover behind the tree. Then there was a silence.

I was gasping for breath as if I had been held under water, but my brain was working all right. He had missed me three times and then lost track of me. He would have to risk another flash from the lamp to locate me again, and it would be a risk; he could not be sure that I was unarmed. In any case, I was prepared now, and unless he was a first-rate shot or very lucky he had not much of a chance. For the moment I had forgotten the man behind me.

Five seconds went by. I was slowly straightening up and easing round away from the tree when the light flashed on again. It was not directly on me, and in the fraction of a second it took him to realize that, I had begun to move. I was halfway toward the next tree when he fired. The bullet whipped past my head. I reached the tree and swung round it as if to take cover again, but immediately scrambled on to the next one. The shot he fired at that moment was yards wide. But he had learned one thing; I was not going to fire back. The lamp shone out again, and this time it stayed on. He did not fire. He moved forward. He was going to make sure of it this time. Bent double, I scuttled on again. I saw my shadow twist among the long casts of the trees as the light swung round. Then, as I pulled up against the next tree, a different pistol fired.

The bullet tore through the bark an inch or two from my right eye, and a splinter of wood stung my cheek. I dived for the ground again. The other gun, I thought, had been a .38, but this had a heavier sound. I could see how it was. If I had not crossed the road, the man behind me would have shot me in the back. The second man had been there to make sure I did not get away. Probably he had crossed ahead of me while I was still in the lighted section.

I was out of the light for a moment now, but both pistols fired again and the bullet from one of them ricocheted off the road. They were getting worried. Nearly half a minute had gone by since the first shot, and I could hear shouting in the distance. The lighted stretch was only a hundred yards away now, but if I broke cover and made a dash for it, I would have to pass the heavy pistol with the other man's light behind me. It would not do.

At that moment the man with the light began to run forward, yelling hoarsely. The heavy pistol fired again as I rolled sideways and found myself on the edge of the road. I hesitated for only a split second. Then I scrambled to my feet and ran, swerving like a rabbit, for the trees on the other side of the road. They both fired, but by then I was a hopeless target for a pistol. I dived through the trees, came up against the boundary wall, and ran along it toward the lighted section.

I was safe now. I stopped to get my breath. There were people from the houses standing on the pavement opposite, talking and pointing toward the trees where the sound of the firing had come from. The two policemen I had passed farther back were approaching at a run. I was out of sight. My breath was beginning to come back, and with it my wits. I had not seen either of the attackers. I had no information about them to give. But even that would take a lot of explaining to the police, and they would certainly detain me while an interpreter was found and my story checked. If I could avoid the police altogether, I should do so. If, while they searched among the trees for the dead and wounded that were not there, I could make myself scarce, I would be saving them trouble. If, in fact, I now did what I should have done five minutes earlier—kept my head, walked back to a café, and there telephoned to the hotel for a car to fetch me—everyone would be much better off. I had begun to tremble violently. My ears were singing and felt deaf. I leaned against the Presidential wall fighting down a desire to vomit. Through the singing in my ears I could hear shouts from farther up the road. Then my head began to clear. Reaction or no reaction, if I was going to get away unobtrusively I would have to be quick about it. Keeping close to the wall, I started to walk.

It was an hour before the car arrived at the café, and by that time I had had several plum brandies. I was not drunk but I felt sleepy. It was silly of Aleko, I thought, to want to kill me. Very silly. I was perfectly harmless. However, I had now acquired another useless piece of information: I knew what it felt like to be shot at in civilian clothes; it was exactly the same as it felt when you wore a uniform. That was interesting. In the car I went to sleep and had to be wakened by the driver when we got to the hotel.

The reception clerk was asleep. I took my room key from the rack myself. The lift was not working. I walked upstairs slowly, yawning. I was really very tired. I was also beginning to feel stiff and bruised. If the water was hot (and late at night when nobody wanted it, it usually was hot) I would have a bath and attend to the knee I had cut on a stone. My suit was a mess too, but that could wait until the morning. A bath, then sleep; that was it. I felt curiously relaxed and happy. The odd thing was that this feeling had almost nothing to do with the plum brandy. It was because I had survived an ordeal.

I opened the door of my room. There was a small foyer with a cupboard and a hat rack between the door and the bedroom itself. I switched on the foyer light, remembered with a twinge of irritation that I had lost my hat and would have to buy one of the local Homburgs next day, and went into the bedroom.

My hand was on the bedroom light-switch when I saw what was there. I stood quite still.

A woman was lying face-downwards across the bed. By the foyer light I could see that she had a loose raincoat of some kind spread about her as if it had been thrown there to cover her up.

I pressed the light-switch, and the room was flooded with the bright hard light from the naked lamps in the gilt chandelier.

Her hair was dark and one of her tightly clenched hands concealed her face. I walked over to the bed, and a loose board cracked loudly. I looked down.

She stirred. Her hands moved and she rolled onto her side. The light poured down in her face and she raised a hand to shield her eyes.

It was Katerina Deltchev.

Sixteen

I SHOOK THE bed, not gently, and she sighed. Then, with a start and a gasp, she was awake. She sat up quickly and the thin raincoat she had thrown over her slipped to the floor.

"Good evening," I said.

For a moment she stared at me, then she scrambled off the bed and looked round defiantly.

"There's no one else here," I added.

She drew herself up as if she were about to deliver an oath of allegiance. "Herr Foster," she said formally, "I must apologize for this intrusion, but it was unavoidable. I will explain. I—" She broke off and looked down as she realized that she was in her stockinged feet.

"They're down there," I said. Her shoes had slipped off while she had been asleep and were lying beside the bed.

She opened her mouth to say something, then shut it again, went over to the bed, and put her shoes on thoughtfully. She was a young woman who was used to being in charge of a situation; now she was casting about for a way of taking charge of this one.

"I am sorry—" she began.

"Quite all right," I said. "You wanted to see me, so you came here. I was out. You waited. You fell asleep. I am afraid I can't offer you anything but a cigarette. Will you smoke?"

For a fraction of a second she weighed the possible moral advantage of a refusal; then she shrugged her shoulders. "Yes. Thank you."

She took a cigarette and I lit it for her. She sat down again on the bed and looked at me calmly.

"Herr Foster," she said, "it is not really quite as simple as that for you, is it?"

"No, not quite."

291

I went into the bathroom, dipped a towel in water, and wrung it out. Then I went back into the bedroom, sat down in the armchair, rolled the trouser leg up, and went to work with the towel on my cut knee. She watched uncertainly.

"Who told you I was staying here?" I asked.

"There were three hotels where you might have been staying. This was the second one I telephoned."

"How did you know the room number?"

"By asking for another room number when I telephoned. Of course I got the wrong number. The operator corrected me."

"Who let you in here?"

"The floor waiter. I said I was your lover and gave him some money. Does it matter?"

"Not a bit. It's just that at the moment I am in a suspicious mood. Now, then. How do you get out of the house without being seen? What do you do?"

"Our neighbors are friendly. Between our walls and theirs there is a tree. With two vine poles one can crawl from the top of our wall to the tree. From the tree one uses the branches to reach their wall. For a child it is easy. For a heavier person there is some danger, but it can be done."

"Then why did you ask me to deliver that letter for you, Fräulein. If it was so important you could have delivered it yourself."

"I did not wish to risk my life if there was another way."

"Are you risking your life now?"

"Yes, Herr Foster. I am also risking yours."

"That I guessed."

"But only if I am found here."

"Splendid."

"If I get back tonight without being seen, I shall be safe too. The guards inspect us only in the morning."

"Good."

"I would not have come, Herr Foster," she said severely, "if it had not been absolutely necessary to see you."

"You didn't have to leave the house to do that. I was there myself an hour ago."

She shrugged. "I did not know. I wished to see you because—"

I interrupted her. "Do you know a man named Aleko?"

"Aleko? It is common."

"Who was the Valmo you sent that letter to?"

"I don't know."

"I see."

"It is true. Valmo was only a name I was given to send letters to. The letter was for someone else."

"Who?"

"My brother, Philip."

I sighed. "The one who's studying law in Geneva?"

"He is not in Geneva."

"Your mother said he was."

"My mother was lying."

"I didn't think so."

"She did not intend you to think so. Will you please listen to me without interruption for a moment?"

"All right, I'm listening."

"My brother has been in hiding here since before Papa was arrested. My brother, Herr Foster, had five friends. Their names were Pazar, Eftib, Vlahov, Pechanatz, and Radiuje."

I dropped the towel. "Do you know what you're saying?"

"Perfectly. That is what I came to tell you. This evidence that they have brought against my father is quite true. Only it is not he who is guilty. It is my brother, Philip."

I sat back and stared at her. She was telling the truth. A lot of things were suddenly and appallingly clear.

"When did your mother find out?"

"She did not tell me."

"Does your father know?"

"He must have known from the beginning of the trial, or guessed. But what can he do? He cannot accuse his own son, and Brankovitch would certainly not let Philip give evidence."

"Nobody would believe it anyway. They'd laugh. Dutiful son takes blame for father's crimes? I'd laugh myself." I thought about it for a moment. It explained quite a lot of things, but not everything by any means. I looked up at her again. "What's the idea of telling this to me, Fräulein?"

"I want you to publish my brother's evidence."

"Does he want to give it?"

She set her lips firmly. "He must."

"Does your mother know of this idea?"

"I would not tell her. She would say that it would not help Papa, only condemn Philip."

"She'd be right."

"But abroad they must know the truth."

"Would your mother agree with that?"

"I do not know. She is too clever to be simple. She would discuss the idea and think of possibilities nobody else had dreamed of. Then she would say she was tired. You would not know her real thoughts."

"What was your brother up to? Is he crazy?"

She shook her head slowly. "When Papa betrayed the party," she said, "he and Philip quarreled. They were always in conflict, but this time my mother could do nothing." Tears came to her eyes. "We were all against him, even I was; and when the People's Party came to power, Philip joined a student political club that had for secretary this man Pazar. Pazar always needed money, but the students liked him. He talked very amusingly and they used to pay him for coaching. When they formed a club they would sometimes make him secretary and give him a commission on the subscriptions. Philip soon felt that the club was not serious, but he became very friendly with Pazar. Then, one day, Pazar told him that he was a member of the Brotherhood."

"There must have been pleasure in telling that to the son of the man who had done so much to destroy it," I remarked. It was all too easy to catch the flavor of those dangerous exchanges of confidences between the middle-aged drug addict and the fanatical youth.

She shrugged. "Perhaps. I know that when Philip joined the Brotherhood it was only to revenge himself on Papa. He did not mean then to do more than join."

"But once he had joined, he found that they expected more than a gesture. Was that it?"

She nodded. "There were six of them elected, and Philip was named the leader. Their task was to kill Vukashin at the anniversary-celebration parade. But—"

"Just a moment. Who was the man who gave them the job?"

"It was not one man, but a group of men. They called themselves the Survivors."

"When did Philip tell you all this?"

"Before he went to Switzerland. Mamma had become worried about him. He looked so ill and tired. She persuaded Papa to send him there to study. Naturally, he refused to go at first, but after a day or two he said no more. That was at Christmas. He had arranged to return in secret when Pazar sent for him." She paused before she added: "I knew then that he was not the real leader, but had been given the role of leader because of his name."

"Did you say that to him?"

"He already knew it, I think. But if I had said it he would have made some

other foolishness to prove to me that I was wrong. Besides, I thought that in
Geneva he might change his mind and forget about it."

"But he didn't."

"No. We had arranged a code for our letters, and when the attempt on Papa
was made, I heard from him that he was returning. I only saw him once. We
met secretly at a place near the station."

"Patriarch Dimo 9?"

"No, another. But he gave me two addresses which I might send letters to.
Valmo, Patriarch Dimo 9, was one of them. The other he told me I must use
only in case of an extreme emergency if I had to find him."

"What was in the letter you gave me?"

"I begged him to escape to Greece and publish the truth about the conspiracy against Vukashin from there."

"What made you decide to come to me?"

She frowned impatiently. "Today's evidence, Herr Foster. Surely you see.
The police know everything. Philip and Pazar are the only two left. They must
be in hiding somewhere, helpless. Philip can do nothing now even if he wished.
It must be done for him."

I thought hard for a moment or two, then I shook my head. "I don't think
that it's as simple as you believe, Fräulein."

"What do you mean?"

"Well, to begin with, Valmo was the name Pazar was hiding under. When
I tried to deliver your letter, I found him dead. He'd been shot through the
back of the head and had been there some days."

"What happened to my letter?"

"That was burnt by a man named Aleko who said that he was of the secret
police and that *his* name was Valmo. He also said that your letter was addressed to him and was something to do with the attempt on your father." I
described Aleko. "Does that mean anything to you?" I added.

She looked utterly bewildered. "No, Herr Foster."

"What does your brother look like?"

She gave me a description.

I nodded. "A young man who looks like that came into Aleko's apartment
while I was there. I only saw him for a moment. Aleko called him Jika."

She stood up quickly. "That is Philip. He likes his friends to call him that.
Herr Foster, where is this place?"

"I don't know for certain, but I should think that it may be the other
address your brother gave you. Have you got it?"

"Philip made me remember it. He said it was too dangerous to write down."

"What is it?"

"Pashik, Pan-Eurasian Press Service, Serdika Prospek 15," she said.

I went to the wardrobe, got out the bottle of plum brandy, and poured myself a big drink.

"Do you like this stuff?" I asked.

She shook her head.

"All right, Fräulein. You'd better go back now. I think I know how to reach your brother."

Seventeen

PASHIK LIVED IN a modern apartment house near his office. He had pointed out the place to me on the day I had arrived. I thought now that I could find it without much difficulty. There were no taxis. I walked.

The way there lay through the business quarter, and by that time the streets were mostly empty and still. Earlier that day they had been decorated in preparation for the anniversary parade, and the bright moonlight striking obliquely through the flags overhead cast a multiplicity of shadows that stirred and twisted in the warm breeze. It was like walking through the dark forest of a dream. But I had gone some distance before I became frightened.

It was a very unpleasant sensation. The brandy-engendered resolution with which I had set out seemed to drain suddenly away. I began to shiver uncontrollably and an icy, numbing kind of logic invaded the small corner of my conscious mind not whimpering with the effort required to keep on walking. What I was doing was incredibly foolish. Not three hours ago two men had tried to kill me in the street. I had been very lucky to escape. Now here I was in the streets again, giving them another chance. For obviously they must be waiting for me. Ruthless determination of the kind they possessed would be intensified by failure. They would not fail a second time.

Soon every shadow had become a man with a gun, every doorway the place of an ambush. I kept on simply because I was afraid to go back. I walked now simply because I was afraid to break into a run that might precipitate action. My legs ached with the strain. My shirt clung to my back. I had so completely lost my head that I went on fifty yards past my destination without seeing it. There was a frantic ten seconds on the corner of the Boulevard Sokolovsky while I got my bearings. Then I saw the apartment house from a familiar angle. I ran the fifty yards back.

It was a tall, narrow building with massive ferroconcrete balconies, from the sides of which rusty weather stains drooled down the walls. In the daylight these stains gave the place a tired, unhappy air—you wanted someone to wipe its face for it—but in the moonlight, they were hard shadows that made the balconies seem to project like freakish upper lips. The main entrance doors, ornate affairs of wrought iron and rolled glass, were still open, and the lobby beyond was dimly illuminated by a light from the concierge's room.

As I stood for a moment or two recovering my breath, I looked back along the street. There were two or three empty cars parked in it, but they had been there already. Nobody had followed me. I went in and pressed the concierge's bell. Nothing happened. After a minute or so, I went over to the lift. Beside it was a list of the tenants. Pashik was on the fourth floor. The lift did not work, of course. I found the stairs and walked up.

At the moment of deciding to see Pashik that night I had had a clear image of the sort of interview it would be. I had seen him already in bed and asleep when I arrived. In response to my insistent ringing he had at last appeared, a bleary, nightshirted figure (I had been sure he wore nightshirts), fetid and protesting. I had cut through his protests decisively. I had given him no time to build up his defenses. I had pelted him with the facts I had discovered and watched his features grow pinched as he realized how much I knew. Then, at last, wearily he had shrugged. "Very well. Since you already know so much, Mr. Foster, you had better hear the rest." And I had sat down to listen.

The reality was somewhat different.

The door to his apartment was at the end of a short passage near the main staircase landing. As I turned into the passage, I saw that the door was ajar and that there were lights in the apartment. I went along the passage and up to the door. Then, with my hand on the bell, I paused. Inside, someone was speaking on the telephone. Or listening rather; there was a series of grunts, then two or three words I did not understand. The voice, however, was not Pashik's. I hesitated, then rang the bell.

The voice ceased abruptly. There was a movement from within. Then silence. Suddenly the door swung open and clattered gently against a picture on the wall behind it. For a moment the small lobby beyond looked empty. Then I saw. Between the doors of the two rooms facing me was a narrow strip of wall. On the wall was a mirror, and, reflected in it, the face of the man who had pushed the door open with his foot. It was Sibley.

He moved slowly out from the wall just inside the entrance and looked at me. There was a heavy bottleglass ashtray in his hand. He put it down on the hall table and grinned.

"Well, Foster dear," he said archly. "This *is* a nice surprise! A small world,

I always say. Do *you* always say that? Of course you don't! Come to see our smelly friend?"

"Naturally. What are you doing here?"

He looked at me oddly. "I've come to see him too, and also naturally. Doesn't seem to be about, though, does he? I've looked high and low."

"Who were you expecting to have to beat over the head with that ashtray?"

"Somebody else who shouldn't be here. Like me. You're quite a logical visitor, of course. Been here before, I shouldn't wonder."

"No."

He grinned again. "I thought not. Come on in and make yourself at home. I was telephoning."

"Yes, I heard."

"Don't speak the language though, do you?"

"No."

"I thought not. This way."

He went through the left-hand door. I hesitated and then followed.

It was a sitting-room that had obviously been furnished by the owners of the building. There were built-in cupboards and bookcases and a built-in sofa. There were cube-like easy chairs, glass-topped circular tables, and an oatmeal-colored rug. You could have seen the same sort of things in any other furnished apartment building in any other European city. The extraordinary thing about this room was the decoration of the walls.

They were covered, every square foot of them, with pages cut from American magazines and stuck on with scotch tape. There were pictures of film stars (all women), there were near-nude "studies" of women who were not film stars and there were artlessly erotic color drawings of reclining seductresses in lace step-ins. All would have looked quite at home in the room of an adolescent youth. Yet that was the comprehensible part of the display; it was not remarkable that Pashik should have the emotional development of a sixteen-year-old boy. The startling thing was that for every Ann Sheridan, for every sandal-tying beach beauty, for every long-legged houri, there was a precisely arranged frame of advertisement pages. The nearest Betty Grable was surrounded by Buick, Frigidaire, Lux, and American Airlines, all in color. A sun-tanned blonde glistening with sea water had Coca-Cola, U.S. Steel, Dictaphone, and Lord Calvert whisky. A gauze-veiled brunette with a man's bedroom slipper in her hand and a speculative eye was framed by Bell Telephones, Metropolitan Life Insurance, General Electric, and Jello. The baffling thing was that the selection and grouping of advertisements seemed quite unrelated to the pictures. There was no wit, no hint of social criticism, in the arrangements. Many of the advertisements were not particularly distinguished as such. It was fantastic.

Sibley had gone back to the telephone. He had said something into it, listened again, and then, with a last word, hung up. He flicked his fingers at the wall as if he were launching a paper pellet.

"Lots of fun, isn't it?"

"Lots. How did you get in?"

"The concierge has a pass key and is corrupt. Would you like a drink? There must be some about." He opened one of the cupboards and peered inside.

"Do you know Pashik well?" I said.

"Would you believe me if I said yes?"

"No."

"Then let's say that I think I know a bit more about him than you do. Cigars but no drinks," he added, producing a box. "Cigar?"

"No, thanks."

"No, it's a drink you need. You're not looking your usual cheerful self, Foster dear. A bit pinched round the gills and upset. Let's try this one." He went to another cupboard.

"I take it you're not afraid of Pashik's suddenly turning up and finding you here searching his room. That wouldn't embarrass you?"

"Not a bit."

"Was that why you came? Because you knew he wouldn't be here?"

He looked up from the cupboard he was searching and shook his head. "No, Foster *mio*," he said softly, "that wasn't why. I just wanted a little chat with him. When there was no answer, I had another thought and fetched the concierge. Silly of me, wasn't it?—but I actually thought our Georghi might be dead."

"Why should you think that?"

"It was just a thought I had." He straightened up suddenly with a bottle in his hand. "There now! Our old friend plum brandy!" And then he looked directly at me. "You know about Pazar, of course?"

"What about him?"

"Tonight's police statement that they've found him shot in a derelict house."

"Oh yes, that." I tried to make it casual.

He reached down and brought out two glasses. "A house in some street with a funny name," he said slowly. "What was it?"

"Patriarch Dimo." My voice sounded unnatural to me.

"That's it. Who told you? Georghi?"

"Yes. He had the statement."

He brought the bottle and glasses over and put them on the table. "When did you see him?"

"Oh, earlier on."

He shook his head. "It won't do, Foster dear," he said. "No, don't get cross. I set a little trap and you fell into it, that's all. That statement was only issued half an hour ago. I was on the phone to the office when you came in. That's how I know." He thrust his head forward. "How did *you* know?"

I was feeling sick again. I sat down.

"*Did* Georghi tell you?"

I shook my head. "I found him by accident."

He whistled softly. "My, my! You *do* get around! What sort of an accident was it that took you to Patriarch Dimo? The same sort that got you into the Deltchev house?"

"Not quite."

"Doing a little private investigating perhaps?"

"That's the idea."

He shook his head regretfully. "Someone must be very cross with you."

Another wave of sickness came. I drew a deep breath. "Then that's probably why someone's just tried to kill me," I said.

He stared at me expressionlessly for a moment. "A joke, Foster dear?" he said gently. "A joke in bad taste?"

"No joke."

"Where was it?"

"In that road that runs round the park."

"When?"

"An hour or two ago."

"One man or two?"

"Two."

"One of them couldn't have been Georghi by any chance?"

"No."

He seemed to relax again. "Well, well! Poor Foster! No wonder you look peaky. And here I am chattering away instead of pouring the much-needed drink. There."

I swallowed the drink and sat back for a moment with my eyes closed. I hoped he would believe that I was feeling faint. I had to think and it was difficult. Sibley was Brankovitch's paid man and already I had given myself away appallingly. Pashik was involved with Aleko and Philip Deltchev in a Brotherhood plot to assassinate Vukashin. The wreckage of that plot was being used to convict the elder Deltchev. Now the dead Pazar, probably murdered by Aleko, had been officially discovered on the eve of the anniversary parade at which Vukashin was to have been assassinated. There was a contrived, bad-third-act feeling about the whole thing; as if . . .

"Feeling better?" said Sibley.

"Yes, thanks." I opened my eyes. He was looking down at me coldly. I had not deceived him. He smiled.

"What a busy week you've had! Have you any idea, I wonder, what you know that makes you worth killing?"

"None at all."

He sat down opposite me. "Maybe if you were to tell me what you do know, I could make a suggestion about that."

"Or perhaps find a way through the censorship with it? By the way, how is your little man at the Propaganda Ministry?"

He drank his drink down and looked at the empty glass as if waiting for someone to fill it. "Do I detect a note of bitchiness and distrust, Foster dear?"

"Yes, you probably do."

He looked at the bottle and poured himself another. "Drink will be the death of me," he said. "I was tiddly, of course, but it seemed such a good joke at the time. Although, Foster *amigo*, I won't deny that I should also have been interested to see what your angle on the affair was going to be."

"My angle was and is that your little man in the Propaganda Ministry was Brankovitch."

He giggled. "Who told you they played that trick? Georghi?"

"Not Georghi."

He giggled again. "Oh dear! Not Georghi, you mean, but someone else whose name you don't want to mention in case I'm a Ministry spy who might get him into trouble. Oh dear, oh dear! I do see. I played right into your hands, didn't I? No wonder you were so maddening. The thing was that they'd tried it on me days before. I could send anything I wanted if I knew how. That was the line. It would cost a bit, of course, but that was to make it sound right." He sighed. "I don't like being taken for a fool, do you? I was a bit vexed, so I decided to amuse myself. I thought at first of pretending I'd fallen for it and sending a really dreadful story I'd heard about Vukashin's sex life. Then I sobered up and thought again. In the end all I did was to lift their dialogue and try it on someone else. Georghi was my first customer and I frightened him out of his wits—or he pretended I did. And that was the crazy part of it; because it wasn't until I saw him looking at me with those big brown eyes of his and got a breath of that subtle perfume that I remembered where I'd seen him before. Do I convince you?"

"By no means."

He gazed upwards soulfully. "It's so sad. I can never make the truth sound convincing. Of course, I *look* so shifty. I should stick to lying, shouldn't I?"

"Where was it you saw Pashik before?"

"Ah, I have your interest. If only I can keep it until the knock-out drops that I slipped into your drink begin to work, all will be well."

Involuntarily I looked down at my glass.

He grinned. "You're really very tiresome, aren't you, Foster dear? If I didn't want badly to know what makes you worth killing, I wouldn't say another word."

"It's late. I'm very tired. And—"

"And it's always so upsetting to be shot at," he said quickly. "How inconsiderate of me not to remember that!"

"I wasn't apologizing."

"Of course you weren't. You were just hoping that I'd cut the cackle. I do understand. These affectations of mine are such a bore. All right. Let's talk about Georghi Pashik—why he exists and in whose image he is made. What has he told you about himself?"

"He was expelled from Italy for writing something Mussolini didn't agree with. He did his military service in Austria. He admires Myrna Loy. The last item I deduced for myself from a picture in his office."

"She must be his spiritual Mum, don't you think? All right, here it is. Technically, a stateless person. Born in the Trentino, of Macedonian Greek parents who were themselves of doubtful national status. He takes Hungarian nationality. Treaty of Trianon muddle. He does his military service in Austria. He goes eventually to Paris and works for Havas as a messenger. Intelligent, ambitious, a worker. He writes odd pieces. He gets on. Eventually they give him a job in the Rome office. He gets important. Then he's expelled, which is all very difficult because he's married an Italian girl and the *squadristi* make it hot for her family. He has a lot of trouble squaring things. After a bit his wife dies and he returns here to the home of his forefathers with very peculiar ideas about the way the world ought to be run."

"What sort of ideas?"

"I'm coming to that. Well, the war breaks out and in 1940 Georghi skips to Cairo. For a time he's on a newspaper there, then he decides that it's time to do a little war work and gets taken on as an interpreter by the British. Later on, when the United States Middle East contingent arrives, he is transferred to them. In 1945 he turns up in an American Civil Affairs unit in Germany."

"Still as an interpreter?"

"Still as an interpreter. Only by now he has a bastard sort of uniform and is working in a D.P. camp near Munich. He worked under an American major named Macready. I had business there, and that's where I first saw Georghi and got to know about him."

"What was your business?"

"Intelligence—the British lot." He caught a glance I gave him. "Oh dear me, no! Not any more. I was just the wartime variety, uniform and everything. I was liaising with an American who was on the same job as me—checking up on the bad boys who'd gone to earth in the D.P. camps and then digging them out—and it was this man who told me about Georghi. Another drink?"

"I think I will."

"That's good. There's another bottle in there if we run short or if Georghi comes home. All right, then. We go back to the time Georghi went over to the Americans in Cairo. Almost the first thing that happened was that he was sent up to a small hill town in the Lebanon with a lieutenant, a tech sergeant, and an enlisted man. The job was to operate a radio station monitoring an intelligence network operating in the Balkans. I believe there was some short-wave oddity that determined their position, but that's not important. The thing was that our Georghi was stuck out in the wilderness for nearly a year with three Americans who didn't like it either and talked about home. I don't know anything about the sergeant and the enlisted man, but the lieutenant was a radio engineer named Kromak and he came from Passaic, New Jersey. Do you know the Lebanon?"

I shook my head.

"In the evenings the sky is like wine and the shadows falling across the terraces have purple edges to them. Overhead, vines—grape and other things with big flowers and a wonderful smell. Everything is very still and warm and soft. It's the kind of atmosphere in which myths are born and the pictures in your mind's eye seem more real than the chair you're sitting on. I wax lyrical, you see. However, the point is that Lieutenant Kromak talked about Passaic, New Jersey, and read aloud his wife's letters while Georghi listened. He heard about Molly's graduation and Michael's camp counselor, about Sue's new baby and the seeding of the front lawn. He heard about the new refrigerator and the shortage of gasoline, about his friend Pete Staal, the dentist, and the Rotary Anns. He heard about the mouse in the cedar closet and the new screens that had been bought for the porch. And when the weekly letter was exhausted, the reminiscences would begin. 'Pete Staal, Pete Staal,' Kromak would say dreamily, 'a good dentist and a lovable son-of-a-bitch, but what a crazy guy! I remember the night Kitty and me, the Deckers, and the Staals went to Rossi's—that's an Italian restaurant at the far end of Franklin Street—and had ravioli. Ever had ravioli? At Rossi's they make the best ravioli in the world. Well, we didn't want to take two cars, so we rode down in mine. A Dodge I had then. Well, right after we'd eaten, Helen said she wanted to go over to the Nutley Field Club. That made Pete mad and he said that if she was going to Nutley he was going to fly down to Wilmington to see his mother. Of course, he knew what Helen really wanted—to see Marie and Dane Schaeffer—I told you about them, remember? Well . . .' And on he went while Georghi listened and drank it in. Do you know Passaic, New Jersey?"

"No."

"Chemical plants and some light industry and the homes of the people who have to work there. But to Georghi Pashik, looking through the eyes of Lieutenant Kromak, who wanted so much to be back with the wife and kids, it must have represented a paradise of domestic security and gracious living. You know how it is? Lots of quite intelligent Europeans have fantastic notions about the way most Americans live. Sitting on that terrace in a Lebanon hill town, poor, unhappy, exiled Georghi must have been a pushover for the American way of life. Just to put it in terms of food—reason might tell him that the ravioli he'd get in Rossi's on Franklin Street, Passaic, would not be as good as he'd eaten already in Rome and Florence, but Rossi's ravioli had become the desirable ones. They had the approval of those legendary figures the Staals, the Deckers, and the Schaeffers, and that was what mattered. He began to understand why the Americans didn't like the Lebanese they came in contact with. Lebanese standards of sanitation and behavior are not those of Passaic, New Jersey. Georghi heard local ways that he had accepted or failed even to notice condemned quite angrily. He was troubled and began to question himself. You see what was happening, of course? Along with his dream of Passaic, New Jersey, he was beginning to acquire an American conscience."

He paused for a moment to swallow another drink and fill my glass.

"How much are you embroidering this story?" I asked.

He shrugged. "Not much. But the man who told me was an American and he could reproduce that Kromak stuff so you'd think you were really listening to him. I just give you the bits I remember and fill in the rest. The effect's the same, though. Anyway, after nearly a year of the American Way and Purpose according to Lieutenant Kromak, Georghi was shifted back to Cairo. Americans again, only this time the high priest was a dairy chemist from Minnesota and the dream was in a slightly higher income bracket. Georghi read the Declaration of Independence, the Constitution of the United States and the Gettysburg Address. After that there was a filling-station proprietor from Oakland, California. He was followed by an insurance man from Hagerstown, Maryland. Then came 1944 and the surrender negotiations between Deltchev and the Anglo-American representatives. There was a British military mission operating with the partisans in Macedonia at that time. They controlled quite a large area and had a landing strip, so it wasn't too difficult to arrange the meetings. The Anglo-Americans flew in from Foggia. Deltchev traveled overland somehow. They met in a village schoolroom. Georghi was one of the interpreters. It was after the second meeting that Georghi's little cap went over the windmill."

"Wait a minute. Had he known Deltchev before?"

"Known of him, that's all. Well now, we get to the second meeting. They had their meeting all right, but storms delayed their return and they had to wait for twenty-four hours in the village. The atmosphere of the negotiations had been quite friendly and the wait produced a lot of general conversation about conditions inside the country, the problems, what was to be done about them, and so on. The man who told me this was on that trip. Anyway, one of the subjects discussed was the Officer Corps Brotherhood. Deltchev was very frank about the problem and the difficulties of dealing with it. Some of his revelations, in fact, were deeply shocking to the Anglo-American brass and they didn't hesitate to tell him so. Deltchev must have wished he hadn't mentioned the thing. But that night Georghi went to see him privately. It must have been a curious meeting. After extracting from Deltchev a lot of secrecy and immunity pledges, Georghi revealed that he was a member of the Officer Corps Brotherhood, had been one since he had returned to the land of his fathers from Italy in '37. I told you he'd had peculiar ideas then about the way things ought to be. He'd expressed them by joining the Brotherhood. But now, he told Deltchev, all that was changed. He'd seen the light of Western democracy—all the way from Passaic, New Jersey, to Hagerstown, Maryland, he might have added—and wanted to make reparation. The long and short of it was that the Provisional Government's big clean-up of the Brotherhood was made possible because Georghi turned stool pigeon."

"How do you know?"

"Because the man who told me was the officer Deltchev went to for a check-up on Georghi. The old man's first idea, of course, had been that Georghi was either an *agent provocateur* or crazy. So he was very careful. But after the next meeting he had another talk with Georghi and a plan was made." Sibley grinned. "You know, Georghi did a very brave thing really, when you come to think of it. He could have stayed safely with the Americans. Instead he asked them to lend him to Deltchev and came back here. The risk was really appalling, when you think. For all he knew, the Brotherhood might have already condemned him as a traitor. He'd not stayed to collaborate. He'd been in the service of a foreign army. And now he'd turned up again, safe and sound at a time when for a civilian the journey from Athens was all but impossible. However, he took the risk and got away with it. I suppose that outside this place the Brotherhood's intelligence system didn't operate, and in all the confusion nobody bothered to ask many questions. Georghi rejoined his cell and the game began. There were ten Brothers to a cell. Georghi would turn in the names of seven of them to Deltchev. Then the three survivors, Georghi among them, would attach themselves to another cell and in the next cell-purge the survivors of the first one would go with the rest. All except Georghi. He was the permanent survivor. But because of the secret way the Brotherhood was organized, nobody could know how many purges our man had survived. He always arrived with the credentials and code words of the cell just betrayed and he'd always see that those who came with him were at the top of his next list. So there was never anyone to say that where he went disaster followed. It was always the first time with him. But still risky. After a time the word got round that there was treachery, and the remainder of the Brotherhood disintegrated. As a safety measure, Georghi had himself arrested on suspicion and then released. He'd done all he could. Deltchev had him quietly shipped back to the Americans. That's when I met him."

"But why didn't you recognize him at once?"

"He had a mustache then and, as I told you, a uniform. As a matter of fact, he was so American it was difficult to believe that he'd never been out of Europe. His boss in Germany, Colonel Macready, was the last of the prophets as far as Georghi was concerned. He came from Texas. You know that seersucker suit Georghi wears? Macready gave it to Georghi as a going-away present. It came from a department store in Houston. It was also a kind of consolation prize. Georghi had tried every way he could to get a quota number for America, but it was no good. So he came back here and claimed his reward." He paused.

"What do you mean?"

"Well, just think. Four or five years ago he came back here without a penny to his name. Now he's got this place, which I can tell you is quite expensive by local standards, and an established press agency with a dollar income. How did he do it?"

"He's quite efficient."

"But no genius. Besides, the Pan-Eurasian was a going concern long before the war."

"You know the answer?"

"Yes. I did a bit of checking up. The Pan-Eurasian was originally a French company incorporated in Monaco. It took a bit of doing, but I managed to find out all about it through our Paris office. I got word today from them. Like a little surprise?"

"Yes."

"All right, then. All the shares in the Pan-Eurasian Press Service were purchased in 1946 from the French syndicate that owned them. Forty-nine per cent of them are in the name of Georghi Pashik. All of them were bought with a draft signed by the person who owns the other fifty-one per cent." He stopped and grinned again.

"Well, who is it?"

"Madame Deltchev."

My mind turned a somersault. "Are you sure?"

"Sure? Of course I'm sure."

"She'd be a nominee, of course."

He laughed. "Nominee? That woman? Don't be silly. She ran Papa Deltchev as if he were a family business. And if you've fallen for that holier-than-thou line of hers, you'd better think again. I'm a newspaper reporter, Foster, dear, and I've met some very tough ladies and gentlemen, but that one is up near the top of the list. When I was here two years ago, she was running the country. If there were any nominees around they were her husband and that secretary of his, Petlarov. She did the thinking. She wrote the speeches. She made the policy. Do you think that dried-up little lawyer could have got to power on his own? Not on your life! The only thing he ever did without consulting her was to make a damn-fool radio speech that virtually handed over the whole country to the People's Party. Papa Deltchev? Don't make me laugh! They're not trying a man in that courtroom. It's a legend they're after and I bet she's still fighting like a steer to preserve it. Why shouldn't she? It's her work. She's the only Deltchev they're sitting in judgment on."

I shook my head. "Oh no, she isn't."

He stared. "No?"

"No. You may be right about her husband, but she didn't control all the Deltchevs."

"What are you talking about?"

"Her son, Philip. He's a member of the Brotherhood. He was recruited by Pazar. And he's the Deltchev who was the leader of the conspiracy against Vukashin. You see, they're using the evidence against the son to convict the father and they know it."

Sibley stared at me, his face sagging.

"What's more," I went on dully, "the conspiracy is still in existence. And Philip Deltchev is still alive. I carried a letter from his sister, Katerina, to him. The address was a Patriarch Dimo 9 and instead of Philip I found Pazar shot through the back of the head. Then Pashik turned up. Where he is in this I don't know. But he turned up and took me to see a man named Aleko, who says he is of the secret police, but isn't. In fact he's a professional assassin who makes a habit of shooting people through the back of the head. He seemed to be in charge of the whole affair. Philip Deltchev was there under the name of Jika. The Patriarch Dimo thing was explained to me as part of a cunning police trap to catch the man who tried to kill Deltchev before he was arrested. I pretended to accept that and agreed not to make any further visits to the Deltchev house. Of course, they didn't want me to ask Katerina any questions. Pashik warned me privately too."

"But, all the same, you went?" Sibley's face was the color of dirty chalk.
"Yes."

"And you wonder why they tried to kill you?"

"Not any more. Of course, if the fact that Philip Deltchev was the Deltchev of the evidence were known it would make the trial look rather silly."

He jumped up.

"Rather silly!" His voice rose. "You poor bloody fool! Don't you know anything about this country? Don't you see what's happened? The People's Party has taken over the whole conspiracy. Aleko's *their* man, not the Brotherhood's, and he's going to do the shooting. Young Deltchev's only the scapegoat."

"Scapegoat for what?"

"For tomorrow's assassination, you nitwit! Don't you see? It's Judgment Day! The People's Party is going to liquidate its boss, Vukashin!"

Eighteen

SIBLEY HAD HIS office car and he drove me back to my hotel or nearly to it. He was so frightened that I thought at first that he was going to refuse to do even this. But in my own panic I had made up my mind to kill him if he tried to leave me to walk, and he must have known it. From the moment we left Pashik's apartment until we arrived we did not exchange a word. He stopped at the corner of the street by the hotel. I looked at him.

"I'm not driving up to the entrance," he said curtly; "you can get out here."

"All right."

The moment I was out of the car he slammed the door and drove off. I could see his point. If Aleko's men were waiting at the hotel for me, it would not be a good place to stop at. I turned the corner and paused. There was a police van outside the hotel entrance. I walked slowly toward it. The revolving doors were set back slightly, and as I approached I saw the sleeve of a uniform in the recess. I walked on more boldly. If the police were there, there would at least be no gunmen in ambush.

I reached the entrance and went in, stared at by the policeman. Inside the foyer there was a group of military police and the night clerk in his shirt sleeves. They seemed to be questioning him. Then, as I came through the revolving doors, they all looked at me. The night clerk pointed.

"Herr Foster," he said.

An officer stepped forward and two of his men moved round behind me.

"Your papers please?" He spoke in German.

I fumbled them out somehow. My hands were trembling. He glanced at them, pulled my jacket open to see if I had a gun, then nodded to the men behind me. "You are under arrest," he said to me as the escort closed in. "You will come with us."

I turned round and walked toward the revolving door again. I just managed to get through it before, very violently and painfully, I vomited.

310

I sat with the escort on benches in the van. The officer locked us in and got up beside the driver. I did not see where we went. It was not far. I managed to recover sufficiently to ask what I was charged with, and found that the escort spoke no German. The van turned onto cobbles and stopped. I heard the officer get out. Then there was silence. We stayed there for about ten minutes. When the van was stationary, the roof ventilators did not revolve and soon the air inside became warm and stagnant. I could smell the uniforms and greased-leather equipment of the escort and their sour, wine-laden breaths. At last there were footsteps on the cobbles, and the door of the van opened. The officer shone a flashlight.

"Get out."

The escort clambered down and I followed. We were in a quadrangle with a high entrance arch. On the three other sides the space was enclosed by a building with barred windows. A prison, I thought. The only light came from a narrow doorway near the van.

"Forward!"

Going toward the doorway I stumbled on the cobbles and one of the escort held me by the arm. I shook his hand away and went inside. There was a long stone passage with the smell of a barracks about it. Led by the officer, we marched along the passage and up some stone stairs. Then there was another passage and more stairs. The place was certainly not a prison. At the end of the second passage there was a wooden door with a guard on it. As we approached he unbolted the door. The officer went through ahead of us, and the ring of his footsteps was suddenly muted. The corridor we now entered was carpeted. We walked on between heavily ornamented walls reaching up to a vaulted ceiling. At intervals there were marble pedestals with busts standing on them and gilt wall brackets with electric candle lamps. There were no doors. Before we reached the end of the corridor, however, we turned off into a narrow passage like the alleyway of a liner. Then there were several doors. The officer peered at each in turn, then opened one of them and motioned me in.

It was evidently a committee room. There was a long table with a dozen or so chairs placed round it, a table with a telephone, and a bookcase. Over the rich marble fireplace there was a portrait of Vukashin in a gilt frame draped with the national flag. There were green linen blinds over the windows, and beside the fireplace a curtained door. The room smelt of stale cigarette smoke.

The door by which I had entered shut behind me and I heard the key turn in the lock. I turned round and found that I was alone. I looked at the time. It was two o'clock. I sat down at the table. My head was aching and there was a horrible taste in my mouth. There was a water carafe and glass on the table in front of me. I drank some of the water. It was strongly chlorinated and made me want to be sick again. I lit a cigarette. Minutes went by. Every now and then I would hear a movement or a cough from the passage outside. The escort was still there. When I had finished one cigarette, I lit another. If I were going to be put into a jail, my cigarettes would certainly be taken away. I might as well smoke while I could. However, this feeble effort at a philosophical approach to the situation was not successful. Whether or not I had cigarettes to smoke would probably not seem of much importance in the near future. If Sibley was right—and I knew that he was—my arrest could mean only one thing: that Aleko, having failed to kill me himself, had left me to be dealt with by his employers. It was not a pleasant thought. On the other hand, the party might have decided that to murder a foreign journalist would not be a wise move at a time when they would be busy denying their guilt of a more serious crime. But supposing their wisdom was of a different kind. Supposing they decided that the inconvenience of killing somebody who knew too much was as nothing compared with the inconvenience of being revealed as the accomplices of their leader's murder. Death seemed very near at that moment. I hoped it would come mercifully. Perhaps if the hand were that of Aleko—

I turned sharply, my heart pounding, my skin crawling. The curtain over the door on the far side of the room had moved.

I stood up. The fantastic thought went through my mind that if I were going to be shot from behind the curtain, I must stand up so as to present an easy target.

The curtain moved again. A draft from somewhere had caught it. There was the sound of a door closing in the adjoining room, footsteps; then the door behind the curtain opened and a hand brushed the folds aside.

Brankovitch came into the room.

He glanced at me casually before turning to shut the door behind him; then he came round the table toward me.

"Sit down, Mr. Foster." He nodded to a chair and sat down himself facing me. His face was haggard and he needed a shave, but he did not look as if he had been roused from his bed. Probably he had been attending a meeting. The hours before a *coup d'etat* that was to begin with an assassination would be busy ones for a propaganda minister. I must be one of the inevitable hitches.

He sighed. "A cigarette?" He brought out a case.

"I have one, thank you." This was idiotic. "I'm glad to find that you allow prisoners under arrest to smoke," I added.

He pursed his lips. "I think it will be better, Mr. Foster, if you avoid facetious comment. You are being treated with great consideration, as I think my presence here indicates. It would be polite of you to recognize the fact. You realize, I hope, that you are in a very serious position."

"It's difficult for me to realize anything, Minister. All I know is that I have been arrested and brought here. I should like to know what the charge against me is and I should like the British Consulate informed."

His dark, supercilious eyes stared at me coldly. "It would be convenient if you would abandon your pretense of innocence, Mr. Foster. It wastes time. If you prefer to be treated as a common criminal, that can be arranged. If you will recognize the fact of my sitting here talking to you as evidence of consideration toward a distinguished foreign writer, we may make progress."

I was silent.

He lit a cigarette. "Very well, then. Early tonight on the avenue that runs round the Presidential Park, shots were fired by two men at a third. Police pursued the men who had fired the shots. They escaped. So did the other man. But something was found by the police. A hat. It had your name in it, Mr. Foster. Was it your hat?"

I hesitated. "Yes, it was my hat."

"Why do you hesitate? Were you thinking of lying, Mr. Foster?"

His eyes were on mine and at that moment I understood the nature of the interview. Brankovitch knew what Aleko knew. He knew about the letter to Philip Deltchev and my finding of Pazar. He knew that Aleko had forbidden me the Deltchev house and that I had that night ignored the prohibition. He knew that Aleko had tried to kill me and failed. He might know that Katerina had talked to me. What he was trying to find out now was how much I knew, how dangerous I was. If I did not know the truth about the conspiracy against Vukashin, I was unimportant. If I did know or if I had an inkling of the truth, I must be eliminated.

I leaned forward and put my cigarette out in the ashtray by him. Then I smiled ruefully. "Surely you understand my position, Minister. The last thing I want to do is get involved in police proceedings. Two armed men attempted to hold me up. Luckily, I managed to get away from them. It happened on a very dark stretch of road. I didn't see either of their faces. What use would I have been to the police?"

"It was your duty to report the occurrence to them. By running away in that fashion you have raised a grave question in the minds of the police."

"What question?"

"It might be that you were one of the men who fired shots."

"Do you believe that, Minister?"

"What I believe is not important. This is a police affair. It is referred to me initially as a matter of policy because of your status here as a newspaper representative. But I cannot prevent their dealing with you as a criminal. I can merely advise them of my opinion."

"If I were a criminal, Minister, would I have been so careless as to leave behind a hat with my name in it?"

"The police argue from the stupidity of the criminal, not from his cleverness. But assuming, Mr. Foster, that your version of the affair is true, what do you think was the motive for this attack on you?"

Here it was. I looked puzzled. "Motive? Robbery, I imagine. What else could it be?"

He pretended to think this over. Then: "You have not, for instance, made any enemies here?"

I felt relieved. If this was the best he could do, I had nothing to worry about.

"Enemies? I don't think so."

"You have been involved, for instance, in no unusual circumstances that might give a clue to the police?"

I hesitated again.

"I should advise you to be frank, Mr. Foster. You see, armed robbery of that kind is a most unusual crime here. I do not imply that we have no violent criminals, but that it is unusual for them to be armed with revolvers. The reason is that to carry a revolver here is in itself an offense punishable by death. The law was made to deal with the Brotherhood criminals, but of course it applies to all. Robbers would try to kill you with knives. These men did not. If they were not robbers, then who were they? That is what the police ask."

I still hesitated. I was in a terrifying quandary. Obviously, the "unusual circumstances" he was inviting me to tell him about were my finding of Pazar and my meeting with Aleko. But to which would it be better to pretend— frankness or cunning? Which would conceal from him more effectively my actual knowledge? Frankness had its dangers. He would be able to cross-examine and perhaps catch me out. Or he might decide from my manner that I was less artless than I seemed and unlikely to have been genuinely taken in by Aleko's explanation of the affair. Perhaps an obstinate silence would be better. The silence itself would have a useful meaning. It would say to him: "This man does not know that I know what he is concealing. His pretense of ignorance shows, therefore, that he is truly ignorant of the important facts." But it might also add: "And that is just what he hoped I would think. Clearly he is bluffing."

"Yes, Mr. Foster?" He was watching every movement of my face.

Suddenly, hopelessly, I decided. I drew a deep breath. "Very well, Minister. I will be frank. I have a confession to make."

"A confession, Mr. Foster?"

"Yes." And then I had a desperate inspiration. I looked at him angrily. "That was what you were expecting, wasn't it?"

"Expecting?"

"Minister, with all due respect, I've had enough of this cat-and-mouse game. I've been silly. I stuck my nose into something that was none of my business and found out some things that I wasn't supposed to know. All right, I admit it. I didn't think Herr Valmo would bother you with it. I was hoping he wouldn't. But since he has, I'm sorry. One thing I can promise you is that no reference to it will be made in any of my articles. I can't say more than that."

He stared at me. The skin of his face was stretched tightly. It was for a moment a most extraordinary and horrible mask. The lips moved.

"Can't you, Mr. Foster?"

"What is there to say? I found a dead body that your secret-police people had baited a trap with. Naturally Herr Valmo was annoyed. But he didn't blame me. I acted in all innocence. I don't see what all the fuss is about."

"Did you make certain very solemn promises to Herr Valmo?"

I looked embarrassed. "Yes, I did."

"And yet you again went to the Deltchev house."

"Unfortunately, I did."

"Why did you go?"

"I felt I had to have Madame Deltchev's comments on the trial evidence. To be quite frank, I thought it more important to have those comments than to obey an instruction I couldn't really see the point of."

"Did you speak to Katerina Deltchev?"

I looked puzzled. "No, it was the old servant who let me in."

"Who do you think were the two men who tried to kill you tonight?"

"I've no idea. I told you. I didn't see their faces."

"I think you are pretending to be more stupid than you really are, Mr. Foster. How on reflection do you explain those men? If they weren't robbers, what were they?"

For an instant I thought that I had failed after all. It was the phrase "on reflection" that did it. If he was thinking ahead to a moment when, with Vukashin assassinated, I was beginning to put two and two together, I was really done for. If he thought that there was the remotest chance of my getting at the truth, he would decide against me. I made a last attempt.

I stared at him with sudden horrified comprehension. "You mean that they were Brotherhood men?"

For about ten long seconds he did not answer. Then, slowly, he nodded. "You see, Mr. Foster, this prohibition of Valmo's that you so irresponsibly ignored was not without reason. Naturally, Valmo did not tell you all the facts, but there was reason to believe that the Brotherhood was interested in reaching Madame Deltchev. You were mistaken tonight for one of Valmo's men. You are lucky to be still alive."

He had swallowed the suggestion whole. And he had given himself away. I sat back with a sigh which would have meant anything but which came actually from a feeling of relief that was almost painful. Fortunately, I still had my wits about me. There was one thing he had not mentioned. If he did not bring it up I would have to and I did not know how. I took another risk.

I frowned suddenly. "There's only one thing I don't understand," I said. "Your office issued a statement this evening saying that Pazar had been found shot. The details sounded as if he was the man *I* found. Why didn't Valmo tell me who he was? Why the secrecy?"

"Would you have respected the confidence, Mr. Foster?"

"Of course."

"As you did your undertaking to Herr Valmo?" He was quite sure of me now.

I tried to look embarrassed.

He smiled unpleasantly. "I will speak plainly, Mr. Foster. I think your behavior here has been, to say the least of it, unethical. If you were a professional newspaperman I should make a very strong complaint both to your employers and to the British Embassy. As it is, I shall recommend to the police that you are released in the morning. However, I shall withdraw from you all facilities for attending the Deltchev trial. I also advise you unofficially to leave the country immediately—let us say by tonight's train at the latest. In case you decide to ignore that advice, I propose to have your visa and *permis de séjour* canceled forthwith. Do I make myself clear?"

I protested as convincingly as I could, demanded that an official expulsion order be issued, became angry, and finally pleaded. He was obviously and satisfactorily bored with me. It has occurred to me since that he must have been nearly as relieved as I was that the problem I represented had been disposed of. He may even have disliked the idea of having to have me killed. It is possible. The last thing he said to me could be taken that way. To stop me talking he rapped on the door to summon the escort. When they came in he gave them an instruction and turned to go. Then he paused and looked back.

"Mr. Foster," he said, "I once saw a performance of a play of yours and I enjoyed it. Why not stay in the theater? I think, for you, it would be much safer."

I was taken out of the building by the way I had come in. It must have been a wing of the Propaganda Ministry. There was another ride in the van, another oppressive wait, then a cell in a police station. The cell had a bug-infested plank bed, but I was too exhausted and shaken to care much about bugs. As the patch of sky I could see got lighter, I fell into a headache-ridden doze. I even slept a little. At nine o'clock the cell door opened and I was taken to a sort of waiting-room near the entrance.

There, dirty and unshaven, in his seersucker suit with the three fountain pens in the pocket and his briefcase resting on his knees, sat Pashik.

He rose to his feet as he saw me, and nodded.

"Good morning, Mr. Foster."

"How did you get here?" I said.

His eyes flickered warningly in the direction of my escort. He spoke in German. "I have just been informed that you were arrested by mistake and were here. I understand that an apology has already been given and accepted."

"Yes. Am I free to go?"

"I am told so."

I shook hands with the escort and followed Pashik down the steps into his car. He drove off and turned a corner before he spoke. His tone was bleak and noncommittal.

"What happened, Mr. Foster?"

"I was interrogated by Brankovitch."

"Yes?"

"He wanted to find out how much I knew and how much I suspected."

He turned to look at me. The car wandered in the direction of an obelisk.

"If we're going to talk hadn't you better stop?" I added quickly.

He straightened up but did not stop. "And what did you know and suspect, Mr. Foster?"

"That the Brotherhood plot to assassinate Vukashin has been taken over by the anti-Vukashin movement in the People's Party. That Aleko has been brought in to organize the job efficiently. That Philip Deltchev was involved in the original plot and is still involved. That when Vukashin is assassinated at the anniversary parade today, Philip Deltchev will be executed for the crime. That story will be that when his father was arrested Philip took over the conspiracy and with the knowledge and approval of the Agrarian Socialist executive carried it through. That the Agrarian Socialist Party will be made illegal and liquidated. That Brankovitch will take over the Government."

He kept his eyes on the road. "And what did you tell him you knew?"

"Only what he must have been already told by Aleko—that I found the body of Pazar and believed Herr Valmo's explanations."

"And you convinced him?"

"Do you think I'd still be alive if I hadn't?"

"No, Mr. Foster, I don't. May I say that I have always had the greatest respect for your intelligence?"

"Thank you."

"You must have talked with Mr. Sibley, of course."

"Yes."

"I was sure he had recognized me and that someone had been indiscreet. How much does he know, do you think?"

"He's got the general idea. And he's very frightened."

"I see. We have much to tell each other, Mr. Foster."

"Yes. By the way, my permit for the trial has been withdrawn and I've got to be out of the country tonight."

He nodded. "That was to be expected. There is a train for Athens at five, which I strongly recommend."

"Athens? Why Athens?"

"Because that is where Philip Deltchev is."

I stared at him. He had a curious smirk on his face. He even began a wheezy kind of chuckle.

"What on earth are you talking about?" I demanded.

He swung exuberantly into the street that had the Hotel Boris in it. Already crowds were beginning to line the roads in preparation for the parade. He looked at his watch and nearly mowed down a family group in national costume.

"It is now twenty of nine," he said. "In an hour Philip Deltchev will be at the Hotel Splendid Palace in Athens. Apart from Madame Deltchev and myself, you are the only person who knows this. You can be the first news-paperman to interview him, the first to expose the People's Party's political murder conspiracy."

"But how did you know?"

"I think you could have guessed, Mr. Foster. I saw him across the frontier myself last night."

Nineteen

WHEN PASHIK WAS secretly rewarded for his services to the Provisional Government with shares in and management of the Pan-Eurasian Press Service he was not unduly grateful. He had risked his life to serve a political ideal; but it was an ideal that in his mind belonged exclusively to the United States of America; elsewhere it was not valid. He had performed his service somewhat in the spirit of the prosperous immigrant to that country who endows a public library or a childbirth clinic in his native land. The act is charitable, but it is also a reparation, a propitiatory rite that makes the separation final and complete. For Pashik there was little satisfaction in the knowledge that his contribution had been so frankly and practically recognized. His pleasure in the gift resided in the fact that the agency's clients were nearly all American and that he could feel, not preposterously, that as their representative he was in a sense an outpost of the American way of life. One day, perhaps, he would go on a visitor's visa to America; and, perhaps one day, before he was old, he would get an immigration quota number. Meanwhile he was in touch. For Pashik, who had learned not to expect too much of life, that was a singular blessing and he enjoyed it. After a while he could almost forget that the Brotherhood had existed.

The reminder that it had indeed existed and the news that in an attenuated way it still did exist came as a blow. The messenger was Pazar. He told of cautious overtures being made, of small, tentative meetings, of wary soundings, and of half-formed plans. It was as if the Brotherhood had been decimated by a plague and as if the survivors had now begun to raise their heads and look about them, uncertain whether or not the infection still persisted. Gradually, in an atmosphere of intense suspicion and extravagant fears, contacts were being re-established. The security precautions were formidable. All surviving members were invited to reapply for membership and submit to the most searching investigation. Refusal to reapply when asked was to be deemed

319

evidence of guilt. There had been no refusals so far, Pazar told Pashik grimly. The Brothers awaited him.

Pashik nodded and went to see his principal shareholder, Madame Deltchev. This was just about the election time and Madame Deltchev advised Pashik to reapply. Apart from the fact that it would be dangerous for him not to do so—Pashik did not think that this alone would have weighed heavily with Madame Deltchev—she felt that it would be advisable to be informed of the new Brotherhood's activities. She had always had in mind the possibility of the People's Party's manipulating the Brotherhood for its own ends. This resurgence might not be merely what it appeared.

So began again a double life for Pashik. He was reinitiated into the Brotherhood and sat in judgment on the applications of others. The purges had proved fatal for nearly all the senior members and soon he found himself being admitted into the higher councils of the organization. Some two months before the arrest of Yordan Deltchev he heard of the membership of Philip and of the plot against Vukashin.

For once Madame Deltchev was at a loss. She had already planned the football-match incident and was maneuvering as best she could to bring about an Agrarian-Socialist coup before the People's Party was quite secure. Her son's activities imperiled everything. Whether he succeeded or failed, it made no difference. As far as the people were concerned, Philip Deltchev was an extension of Papa Deltchev. The murder of Vukashin by Brother Philip would serve to unite the People's Party as never before and shatter the Agrarian Socialists irretrievably. She could not betray the boy, for to do so would bring the same evil consequences. It was useless, she knew, to attempt to persuade him, for he was too deeply committed. She could not even discuss it with him lest he should identify Pashik as her informant. Not that she would have minded sacrificing Pashik; it was simply that she saw no point in sacrificing him to no purpose. All she could do was to instruct Pashik to work within the Brotherhood to keep in touch with Philip and perhaps undermine his belief in the project. It was a feeble plan, but for the moment she could think of nothing better. Then events began in the most curious way to play into her hands.

In the days before the purges Pazar had been a comparatively unimportant member of the Brotherhood whose weaknesses had been clearly perceived and carefully reckoned with. He would certainly not have been allowed so much as to know about a plan as important as that he now administered. That he should tell someone of it was inevitable. That it should be the petty crook Rila whom he told was very nearly lucky. If Rila had not happened at that time to get into the hands of the police, things might have turned out very differently.

The casualties in the assassination group put the Brotherhood in a panic. The survivors had raised their heads only to find that the plague was still with them. It was another betrayal, another purge. Within a few hours the great majority of the readmitted Brothers were dispersed and in hiding. The rest— those who had no means of hiding—sat in their rooms rehearsing denials. Only Pashik was in a position to know that the plague had not returned and that there must be a more banal explanation of this disaster. He made his report to Madame Deltchev and waited.

A week later, things began to move. One night Philip Deltchev came to see him. He brought news. He and Pazar had escaped and were for the moment safe. Meanwhile the Brotherhood had reorganized. Pazar had been superseded as administrator—his nerves were bad—and a new man had taken over. His name was Aleko and he was a dynamo of a man with great determination and drive. But others were needed. Several Brothers had refused, cravenly. Would he, Pashik, come in with them? The plan would now go on to success, in which all would share.

Pashik accepted and reported to Madame Deltchev. She agreed with him that the whole affair felt peculiar. Their suspicions were aroused in the first place because of the failure of the police to arrest Pazar and Philip. Pashik knew that there was documentary evidence against them and that in such a dangerous case—a Brotherhood plot against Vukashin—the price of conceal- ment was beyond the fugitives' capacity to pay. And there was Philip's name. Why was the People's Party not publicizing the affair? By way of reply to this question Madame Deltchev produced her theory that the People's Party would ultimately take over the Brotherhood. Pashik listened respectfully. But he had an unworthy thought: that Madame Deltchev's preoccupation with the idea was dictated by her annoyance at having failed to take over the Brother- hood herself. She was, to Pashik's way of thinking, a remarkable woman, but inclined to underrate the cleverness of others.

A day or two later he was summoned to meet Aleko. The meeting took place in the apartment I had been in, and it was soon evident to Pashik that Aleko was not what he pretended to be. For one thing, he noticed—as I had noticed—that the furnishings had been assembled from second-hand stores and arranged hurriedly in an unlikely way. But there might have been rea- sonable explanations for that. What decided him was Aleko's way of talking. Pashik had met many members of the Brotherhood and he had learned to rec- ognize the habits of thought and speech that were the private currency of their relationships. For instance, the Brethren scarcely ever talked of killing any- body without at some point using the phrase "removing an obstacle." Aleko used the word "eliminate." It was a small difference, but it was one of many.

And there was a mannerism he had that was peculiar. When he spoke of firing a gun he would point with his forefinger at the back of his head and make a clicking noise with his tongue. For the Brethren a gun was a serious matter; you did not click facetiously with your tongue to convey its moment of power. The whole gesture reminded Pashik of something he knew he would remember later. By the end of that meeting he was sure that Aleko was not a bona-fide member of the Brotherhood. Yet he was dispensing money and making sound plans to assassinate Vukashin. In the early hours of the morning Pashik came to the conclusion that Madame Deltchev had been very nearly right. Someone had employed Aleko; someone who could hamstring police action and also pay well; someone in the People's Party. But not necessarily the People's Party as a whole. A faction within the party, then? It was probable. Somebody was going to get killed and somebody else was paying for the event. Pashik decided to learn more before deciding upon the identity of the principal.

The attempt to assassinate Deltchev was organized, Pashik thought, by Vukashin himself and without Brankovitch's knowledge or approval. The press releases that came from the Propaganda Ministry bore marks of haste, improvisation, and uncertainty of line which suggested that Brankovitch had been caught unprepared. Moreover, Aleko was disconcerted and talked vaguely about "bungling." The term could have referred to the failure of the attempt, but Pashik's impression was that it was more in the nature of a comment on a situation that permitted the attempt to take place at all. That was interesting because if the impression was correct, it meant that Brankovitch and Aleko had one thing at least in common—ignorance of Vukashin's intentions. And that in turn might mean that they had other things in common too.

The arrest of Deltchev created a new problem for Pashik. Hitherto he had had no difficulty in arranging for private meetings with Madame Deltchev. Now that she was under house arrest, it was impossible for him to see her personally. He knew that all visitors would be reported and he could not afford to have his name on the list. His whole position was, indeed, highly equivocal. He was certainly known to Aleko's employers as a member of the Brotherhood. The faintest breath of suspicion as to his motives would result in his being informed upon and promptly hanged. He had Philip Deltchev on his hands and an obligation to extricate the young man if he could. He did not know exactly what was afoot. He was without allies. All he could do for the present was to remain as inconspicuous as possible, cultivate Philip Deltchev, and check up on Aleko. But for a while he did not make much progress with either intention. Philip Deltchev did not like him. The best he had been able to do about Aleko was to remember what the gun-pointing gesture had reminded him of. The "K. Fischer" note that I had found was the result. It was Pazar who finally supplied the essential information.

When Aleko had taken over the conspiracy, Pazar had been in a pitiable state of exhaustion and terror. The arrest of Rila had cut off his drug supplies. He was without money or lodging and was hunted by the police. Philip, who then had (in the name Valmo) the room in the Patriarch Dimo, had taken him in, and for nearly a week the two had remained there, hungry, because they feared to go out to buy food, and in constant fear of discovery. The night Aleko arrived on the scene, Pazar had collapsed and was in a state almost of coma. It took him several days of ready access to the supplies of heroin that Aleko had miraculously procured to bring him back to anything like normality; and when he did come back, it was to find that he had been superseded.

Pazar was not unintelligent. Quite soon he perceived what Pashik already knew—that Aleko was not of the Brotherhood—but, unlike Pashik, he drew a wrong conclusion. His drug-twisted mind linked his discovery with his own fall from power and also with the memory of the traitor who had never been unmasked. All the paranoid projections of his mind focused suddenly upon a single object—Aleko. From that moment he began to plot against Aleko and to spy on him. Philip had moved into Aleko's apartment, and Pazar had the Patriarch Dimo room to himself. It was easy, therefore, for him to keep track of Aleko's movements outside the apartment. One night he followed Aleko to a house in the suburbs. It was a big house and there was a car outside of the kind that usually has a chauffeur. Aleko was there an hour. When he came out Pazar did not follow him, but stayed to watch the house and the car. Ten minutes after Aleko had gone, a man came out, got into the car, and drove off. As he passed by, Pazar recognized him. It was Brankovitch. Two days later, seething with malice and excitement, he told Pashik of his discovery.

It took Pashik ten seconds to make up his mind what he had to do. The first thing was to control Pazar and urge discretion. The second thing was to make him tell the story to Philip Deltchev in Pashik's presence so that while the boy would at last realize what was really happening, his desire for revenge could be usefully canalized. Obviously, Brankovitch's idea was to destroy his rival within the party and to put the guilt for the crime on the Deltchev family. In other words, he could manipulate the original conspiracy so as to convict the father and use the second conspiracy, his own, to dispose of Vukashin and have in his hands the perfect scapegoat, Philip. Pashik's idea was to remove the scapegoat when it was too late to change the assassination plan and let the whole affair recoil on Brankovitch. What was more, Pashik knew just how the idea could be put into practice. But everything depended on Philip.

It was a ticklish business. When Philip's first neurotic outbursts were spent he lapsed into a hopeless depression, which persisted for some days and which was noticed by Aleko. Fortunately, Pashik had managed to make his proposals understood, and Philip Deltchev had presence of mind enough to play the part he had been given. It was not too difficult. All he had to do was to continue to appear fanatically devoted to the task of killing Vukashin; and fanatics do not have to make much sense. The problem was Pazar. His hatred of Aleko soon wore so thin a disguise that an outburst of some sort was inevitable. All Pashik could do was to remind him constantly of the need for absolute secrecy, and hope that when the explosion came, Pazar the drug addict would be more in evidence than Pazar the conspirator. And so it turned out. The occasion was one of the biweekly meetings at which Aleko insisted on going over the entire plan of campaign afresh and rejustifying each part of it. The plan itself was simple enough, and clearly the object of the meetings was to keep the conspirators in hand; but that night Pazar chose to put a different interpretation on the meeting. Quite suddenly and fantastically he accused Aleko of having police hidden in an adjoining room to listen to the conversation. Without a word Aleko rose and showed the next room to be empty. Pazar replied that there were microphones hidden and began to tear up the carpet to prove it. Philip Deltchev sat as if he had not heard. Pashik sat sweating for what was to come. Aleko watched with a smile, but listened attentively to Pazar's babbling. There was just enough sense in it for him to guess what Pazar had discovered. When, in the end, Pazar collapsed, sobbing, Aleko gave him a big injection of heroin. When Pazar was quiet, Aleko looked at the others and shook his head. "We cannot rely upon him," he said. "He will compromise us all."

The other two nodded quickly. They were in heartfelt agreement.

Aleko smiled. "Leave everything to me," he said.

At the next meeting Pazar did not appear and Aleko announced briefly that he had committed suicide in his room, that the body would be left for the police to find, and that, as his services had never really been necessary, no Brother would be sought to replace him.

It was on the day after that meeting that I arrived.

I presented a serious problem to the harassed Pashik. To have someone in and about his office, poking and prying, hampering his movements, possibly endangering his neutral relations with the Propaganda Ministry—that was bad enough. To have someone directly concerned with him in contact with Petlarov was alarming, for who knew what that might not suggest to Brankovitch? He had already recognized and been recognized by Sibley, whom he remembered as one of the intelligence officers who could know his story.

Sibley knew me. Another potential danger. Especially as I was inquisitive.

My interview with Madame Deltchev threw him into a panic. The night he learned of it, he faced Aleko with his gun in his pocket instead of in his briefcase. But nothing unusual happened at that meeting. It was after it that Aleko took him aside, gave him a wad of papers, and asked him to put them in Pazar's room to "mislead" the police who found them. Pashik guessed that Brankovitch wished to take the opportunity afforded by Pazar's death of planting further incriminating evidence against Deltchev. When he got to Pazar's room, he found me there.

His dilemma was awful. I could be explained in several ways. I was telling him the truth or I was lying. But even if I was telling the truth I might still be an unwitting agent of Brankovitch's and this might be a trap to catch him out. On the other hand, I was doing work for one of the American clients and was therefore under the protection of the Pan-Eurasian Press Service. If this was a trap, then the only safe thing to do was to take me to Aleko for questioning. If it was not a trap, however, he might be taking the representative of an American client to his death.

"What made you decide to take me?" I asked.

Pashik blinked at me sheepishly. "I did not quite decide, Mr. Foster," he said; "I compromised. I left part of the decision to you."

"What do you mean?"

"While I hid the papers Aleko had given me in the room, you were walking to my car at the end of the street. I thought you might take the opportunity to escape. If you did not—" He shrugged.

"Do you know why I didn't run?"

"Because you were not alarmed?"

"No. Because I wanted to ask you questions."

He sighed. "You have been very lucky, Mr. Foster," he said. "It was difficult to persuade Aleko that you were harmless, and very embarrassing when he found that you were not. I certainly did not expect to find you alive this morning. And when you tell me of Katerina's foolishness I marvel."

"I suppose she got back all right."

"If she had not done so you would not be here. The check on the Deltchev house is carried out at eight every morning."

"Does Madame Deltchev know what's happened?"

"I have been able to send her brief messages."

"By that old friend of the family who drops in for tea?"

"You are too well informed, Mr. Foster."

I finished my fourth cup of coffee. "When you begin to make flattering remarks, I am suspicious," I said. "You really mean that I still don't know at all what's going on."

His brown eyes contemplated me through his rimless glasses. He was smelling strongly that morning. The seersucker suit was horribly dirty. He shrugged. "As for instance, Mr. Foster?"

"As for instance—why are you here at all at this moment? Why aren't you in Athens with Philip?"

We were in my hotel room. He opened his briefcase, took out a battered meat sandwich, and began eating it. He had his mouth full before he answered. "You forget, Mr. Foster, that there is to be an assassination here today."

"I hadn't forgotten it. What I was wondering was why you've been so cagey about it. What exactly is going to happen? What's the plan? When did Philip come into it? What happens now he isn't here?"

"They do not know he is not here. He did not leave until after the final meeting last night."

"But what's going to happen?"

"I will tell you. Pazar's original plan was simple and stupid. The celebration march takes place in the St. Mihail Square. The parade marches in along the boulevard and out along the prospect. The saluting base is the stone platform halfway down the great steps that lead up to the portico in front of the Ministry of the Interior. It was the main state entrance to the old palace. From the bronze statues at the bottom up to the platform there are forty steps. On these occasions the steps are flanked with troops, forty each side. They are a bodyguard and they are armed with machine pistols. It was Pazar's idea to kidnap four of these men and replace them with his men. They would shoot Vukashin as he stood on the platform and hope to escape in the confusion, because it would seem to be the real troops who had fired. This, I may tell you, was the plan that the prosecutor at the trial did not wish to explain."

"Why not?"

"Because the absurdity of it would make people laugh. Does it not make you laugh, Mr. Foster?"

"It might have worked."

He shook his head mournfully. "I can see, Mr. Foster, that you would not be a good conspirator. One has only to think for a moment of the kidnapping—"

"What were all these messages about?"

"The uniforms, naturally. They could not buy them. Instead they stole them from the soldiers' brothels. It was all very childish. When Aleko took over he made a new plan. Uniforms were wanted, but those of ordinary line troops, not those of the bodyguard. Three men only would be needed. It was a good plan. You know, when there is a parade great care is taken to guard against assassins. The occupants of rooms overlooking the square are carefully checked by the police, and the flat roofs of the buildings round it are guarded by troops from outside the city. The first part of the plan was to conceal a machine gun and ammunition on one of the flat roofs. Then just before the parade men in uniform would go up to the roof and tell the troops already there that the guards were being doubled as trouble was expected. As the real troops were from outside, these would not expect to recognize men who said they were from a city battalion. The false men would have bottles of brandy and things to eat in their haversacks. After a while they would offer to share it. The brandy would be heavily dosed with morphine. The soldiers would go to sleep; the gun would be produced and set up and trained on the platform. All would be in readiness for the appearance of Vukashin. And when the thing was done, escape would be possible. It would be difficult in the surprise and confusion to say exactly where the shots had come from. The troops on near-by roofs might think they were from a window below. But there would be doubt. And while there was doubt, there would be time for us to descend to the street and mingle with the crowd. Who is going to suspect three soldiers? Until the real ones wake up, hours later, nobody will know how it was done, and by then it will be too late."

"Philip Deltchev will have escaped?"

"Exactly, Mr. Foster. That was why the plan seemed so good at first to Philip and Pazar and so strange to me. Until I knew that Brankovitch was deeply involved and saw that it would be quite easy for him to arrange for the police to be warned that, say, thieves disguised as soldiers would be raiding such-and-such a building during the parade and that a patrol waiting at the exits could catch them red-handed."

"So as there will be no Philip, there will be no assassination. Is that it?"

"No, Mr. Foster, that is not it. There were to be three on the gun—Philip, myself, and one of Aleko's men."

"One of those who tried to kill me?"

"That is so. But there is another man and Aleko himself. What, I asked myself, would they be doing while Vukashin was being assassinated?"

"Leaving the country, I should think."

"Yes, I thought that. But three days ago there was a serious complication. Aleko told us that there would be a second gun on another roof and that he and the other man would man it. Philip would have the honor of firing first, but Aleko would be there in case of an emergency. What would that suggest to you, Mr. Foster?"

"That he was suspicious? That he didn't trust Philip?"

"Yes, I considered those possibilities. But then another thought occurred to me, a very interesting idea. Luckily I was able to check it. The following night the guns were hidden on the roofs we had selected—"

"Which are they?"

He smiled. "That I think I will not tell you, Mr. Foster. You will discover."

There was something very disturbing about that smile. I suddenly became uneasy.

"Go on," I said.

"The guns were wrapped in sacking and hung by wires inside the brick chimneys. Very early in the morning I returned by myself and examined them." He paused, smiling again.

"And—?"

"The gun on Philip's roof had no firing pin. It had been taken out."

I looked blank. "I'm sorry. I don't see—"

"Don't you, Mr. Foster?" His eyes gleaming through the spectacles were no longer sad. "Power is a great thing, you know. To be able to move and control great affairs—not the characters and situations on a stage, Mr. Foster, but the real—that is the greatest of all pleasures. You feel it in the stomach." He patted his own. "Here. I feel it now."

"Yes?" I wondered suddenly if he were mad.

"Consider." He stood up and strode over to the window. "A man in Aleko's profession is always in a difficult position. He must always be sure that his master has the power to protect him. He must always be sure that the master wishes to protect him. And he must consider the future. It is dangerous for him to serve one powerful person at the expense of another who may later do him harm. Aleko is clever. He would not have survived if he had not been. He is used to weighing advantages. And so I ask myself questions. Why are there two guns? Why is there no firing pin in a gun that Aleko expects to pour bullets into Vukashin. I answer, because it is Vukashin who is Aleko's best master and has been so perhaps from the first. What ultimate chance has Brankovitch in a struggle for power over Vukashin's dead body? None! He would go down in the end. His own intelligence would trip him. The sort of brutal cunning that lets him dig his own grave will always win. That is Vukashin's strength and Aleko knows it. Philip would have pressed the trigger of a gun aimed at Vukashin and nothing would have happened. Aleko would have pressed the trigger of the second gun, aimed at Brankovitch, and the gun would have fired. Philip and I and Aleko's man would have been arrested and hanged. The gun that would be used in evidence would be the one Aleko left on the other roof. The two murderous Deltchevs would hang together. The murderous Agrarian Socialists would be punished. Vukashin would be secure both from the opposition and from the plots and ambitions of Brankovitch. Aleko, who loves skiing, would be waiting, rich and happy, for the snow at St. Moritz. A pretty picture, Mr. Foster!"

"Yes." There seemed nothing else to say.

"But a picture that will not be seen."

"Because Philip is in Athens."

He held up a finger. "And because I am here."

"I don't understand."

"You will see now why I wish you to understand. The one obstacle is Aleko's man—one of those who tried to kill you—the one who was to have been with Philip and me. In one hour's time he will go to a rendezvous to meet us. If we do not arrive he will go to Aleko to warn him, and when Aleko knows that Philip is not there he will not fire. Brankovitch's life will be saved."

"I see."

"But if I stop this man, Aleko will fire. Brankovitch will die, and because there is no Philip to arrest, Vukashin will have to take Aleko. And when Philip has told his story to you and it is ringing round the world, Vukashin's day will begin to end. That is, if I stop this man."

I said nothing.

For a moment he continued to stare out of the window; then he turned to face me, his self-assurance gone, his face working grotesquely. "Do I stop him, Mr. Foster?" he demanded. "*You* tell me!"

I stared at him, and he read my thoughts.

He shook his head. "No, Mr. Foster, it is not in your hands. There is nobody here for you to tell this story to. That is if you yourself wish to live. Warn Brankovitch, and you will be rewarded by him with a bullet. Warn Vukashin and it will be the same. You know too much for either's safety."

"There's our Embassy. They could warn Brankovitch."

"Then you would be killing me instead. I do not think you will choose that alternative. You have no moral dilemma, Mr. Foster. It is my own I put to you."

I was silent.

He sat down and gazed suddenly into space for a moment. "Do you know America well?" he asked suddenly.

"Not very well."

"No," he said slowly, "neither do I."

He was silent again. I did not speak. I know, as if he were thinking aloud, that he was submitting his problem to the judgment of Passaic, New Jersey, Oakland, California, and Hagerstown, Maryland. It was perhaps as good a way of resolving it as any other.

When at last he stood up he was as calm and businesslike as the day we had met. He took an envelope out of his pocket and handed it to me.

"Your ticket for the press box at the anniversary parade, Mr Foster. I should have given it to you before. Even after what has happened, I do not see that there can be any objection to your using it. Your train, I would remind you, is at five. Have you money?"

"Yes, thanks."

He held out his hand. "I will try to get to the station to look after you, but there will be the cables and so on to attend to. You will forgive me if I cannot make it?"

I shook hands with him. "Yes, of course. Thank you very much for all your help."

He put up a protesting hand. "A pleasure, Mr. Foster."

He turned away briskly, picked up his briefcase, and walked to the door. Then he paused.

"You're welcome," he added, and went.

Twenty

~~~~~~~~~~~~~~~~~~~~~~

THE PARADE BEGAN at two o'clock.

It was only a quarter of a mile or so from the hotel to the square, but the crowds along the route of the parade and in the streets approaching the square were dense. It took me a long time to get through. The day was very warm and I felt tired and ill and frightened. I had not eaten any lunch. My legs were like paper and I kept thinking that I had lost something valuable. The sensation was curiously familiar. I had felt like that once before. And then I remembered: it had been when I was walking back to a hotel in Seville after seeing my first and only bullfight.

The press box was in a wooden stand built over the cathedral steps and at right angles to the front of the palace. The parade would pass below it, then bear left to march past the saluting base halfway up the palace steps. There a waist-high balustrade had been erected. It was draped with flags, and on the step below, flowers were banked to give an appearance of depth to the structure. Behind and above it were the crowded boxes of the lesser dignitaries. The whole square was a mass of flags and brilliantly colored flowers. The façades of the buildings that formed the square were mostly of a honey-colored stone, but the paving had been spread with white sand, and in the bright hot sunshine the effect was dazzling.

It was five minutes to the hour when I got there, and all but a few seats in the box were already filled. I could see the back of Sibley's head near the front. Nearly everyone had sunglasses, but I had forgotten mine, and the glare from the sand was painful. Somewhere a military band was playing, and every now and then a section of the crowd would raise a cheer. Heads would turn at the sound, but the cheer would die away. I looked at the rooftops. There was a canopy over the stand I was in and I could see only a small section of them. From there to the saluting base was a little over two hundred yards. At that range even a recruit could hit a man with one burst from an automatic gun. Perhaps even now an eye was peering through sights at the palace steps.

I wiped my face and neck with my handkerchief and looked at the official program. A duplicated translation had been slipped into it for the benefit of us foreigners. The parade would symbolize the plow and the sword in harmony together. First would come the floats carrying the tableaux of the various industries and crafts. Then the massed representatives of sport and culture. Finally the parade of military and air power. The whole parade would be led by a special tableau depicting the victory of the People's Party. This tableau would halt before the Ministry of the Interior to summon the party leaders to witness the parade, the visible demonstration of the triumph of their work for the motherland.

I had seen this float lurking in a side street just off the square. It was a huge affair mounted on a platform carried by an aircraft transportation truck. Art, Science, Industry, Agriculture, and Armed Might, each with its subsidiary tableau, were grouped round a white flag-decked plinth supporting a huge Winged Victory in wood and plaster. The subsidiary tableaux had the usual props: for Industry there was an anvil, for Science a retort on a bench, for Agriculture a plow, and so on. There were brackets and ledges jutting out from the sides of the plinth obviously for the use of the girls in voluminous white robes who would presently drape themselves round the feet of the Victory.

At eight minutes past two another band entered into the square and formed up round the statue in the center. Then the bodyguards marched in with machine pistols at the ready and to the accompaniment of excited cheers took up their positions on the steps below the saluting base. The stage was being set. At two eleven a squadron of cavalry clattered round from the far side and halted in line beneath the stand I was in. An order was shouted. The cavalry drew their sabers, and a single note on a bugle sounded. With a crash the bands began to play the national anthem. All those who had seats rose to their feet. Then with a roar of cheering, a waving of flags and hats, and another crash of music the Winged Victory float began to move into the square.

My heart was beating so quickly and the blood was thudding so violently in my head that the din of brass bands and cheering was like a continuous rushing sound. I sat down, but it was no better. I stood up again. A man's voice came through the loudspeakers. He was talking very quickly—giving a description of the tableaux, I suppose. The Victory, preceded by a small detachment of troops on foot, turned jerkily and passed our stand. The statue was wobbling as it moved along and the girls posing on the plinth wobbled with it; but I had no desire to laugh. I found myself staring at the tableau of

Industry on one corner of the platform. A man in a leather apron had a sledge hammer raised above the anvil as if to strike. His arms were already feeling the strain and I watched the head of the hammer gradually getting lower. Then the float began to turn again and he was out of sight. On the far side of the square, troops presented arms as the Victory came into view. It crawled on until it was nearly level with the center statue, then swung across to the foot of the steps exactly facing the saluting base and stopped. The girls on the plinth took up a new pose so that they all faced the palace.

Suddenly there was a tremendous roll of drums, and over the entire square the crowd fell silent. The drums ceased abruptly. Then the bands began to play the People's Party marching song. All heads were turned toward the palace portico and the aisle of steps that ran down between the upper boxes to the saluting base. Through the loudspeakers came the sound of a choir singing the song. The crowd joined in. The air seemed to quiver with the sound. Then, as the song reached its climax—the great shout of affirmation that came on the final note—Vukashin appeared at the top of the steps and the cheering began.

He was wearing a black suit and had a cloth cap in his hand. For a moment he stood there motionless. Then he raised a hand in salute and began to walk down the steps toward the saluting base, while the cheering swelled up. When he was about two steps down, a man in the uniform of a marshal stepped from the group behind him and began to follow. The Minister of the Interior came next. And then Brankovitch started down.

He, too, was dressed in black, but very neatly, and he wore a gray Homburg. He walked down slowly and deliberately as if he were unaware of what was going on in the square below. As he passed the upper boxes, the occupants of which were clapping, he nodded casually to someone he knew there.

Vukashin had reached the base. Now he walked forward to the balustrade and looked down. A fresh storm of cheering greeted him. The marshal and the Minister of the Interior moved to left and right of him. Brankovitch moved to the balustrade beside the Minister of the Interior and said something to him. The latter smiled and pointed to the Victory. By this time the whole length of the balustrade was occupied. There were two or three uniforms, but most wore dark suits with gray Homburgs. There was only one cloth cap— Vukashin's. On the other side of Brankovitch was a stout man who held himself as if he had a boil on his neck. They were about a foot apart. Brankovitch turned sideways to say something to him.

Vukashin raised his hand in acknowledgment to the Victory tableau, and with a jerk it set off again. At the same moment the bands struck up and the main procession began to move in.

It was headed by a detachment of men in white dungarees marching eight abreast. But I barely noticed them. My eyes were on Brankovitch. He was still talking to the man at his side.

As clapping and cheering broke out again, I began desperately to try to reassure myself. It just could not be! I had been listening to the babblings of a lunatic. Or—better, far better!—the verdict of Passaic and Oakland and Hagerstown had been that those things which were God's should be rendered unto God, that—Article something-or-other-of-the-Constitution-of-the United-States-of-America—nobody can do anything that affects the life, liberty, or person of anybody, without the aforesaid democratic procedure is properly and faithfully observed, and that the best thing Georghi Pashik could do would be to get his fat arse the hell out of it and send that suit to the cleaner's.

I was suddenly sure that it was going to be all right. At any moment now Pashik would appear beside me, businesslike, courteous, and all for playing ball with the regime. I almost laughed with relief. The time was two nineteen.

And then it happened.

The head of the parade had curved into the straight in front of the saluting base, and Brankovitch turned to look at them. For a second or two he stopped talking and was absolutely still. The next moment the toneless, tearing rattle of a burst of Spandau fire echoed round the square. And almost, it seemed, before the echo of the first had done one leg of its journey, a second burst came.

I had my eyes on Brankovitch. There must have been some sort of stool or bench behind each of them to rest against during the parade, for he lurched back as if he were falling and then stopped for a moment. I saw the second burst hit him in the neck. Then he turned slightly sideways as if he were going to talk to the Minister of the Interior again and crumpled out of sight behind the balustrade.

The man with the boil was the quickest-witted. He took cover behind the balustrade a second after Brankovitch fell. There might, after all, have been other bullets on the way. The Minister of the Interior just stood staring. Vukashin gave one quick look round, then went as if to help Brankovitch. I think that for about ten seconds only a very few of the spectators realized that there was anything amiss at the saluting base. Most of them had just shifted their attention to the parade. But someone screamed. At the same moment men began shouting above the noise of the bands, and the bodyguard closed in defensively round the saluting base with their guns pointed at the crowd. Then a wave of panic came.

All at once everyone seemed to be shouting or screaming. The bands stopped and the parade slowed uncertainly. The Winged Victory, now on the far side of the square, jerked to a standstill. I saw one of the girls fall off the plinth as a great mass of people trying to get out of the square surged forward round the thing. A man near me in the press box was shouting like a maniac. I was very near the exit. I stumbled to it and got down the steps. An official coming up shouted something and tried to stop me, but I pushed past him and made for the narrow street that ran between the cathedral and the adjoining building in the square. This street had been closed by the police and made to serve as a main entrance for box-ticket-holders and I thought that if I could get behind the cathedral before the crowds in the square were completely out of control and the surrounding streets impassable, I might reach the hotel in time to finish what I had to do.

Others in the boxes had had the same idea. The street was filling rapidly and most of the people were running. I began to run too. By the time I reached it, the police barrier at the end had been swept away and people were clambering over the remains of it to join the frantic stream pouring out of the square. It would have been difficult to walk then even if I had wished to, for to the shouting and screaming in the square behind us was now added the sound of shooting as the bodyguard fired over the heads of the panic-stricken crowd. Everybody ran. I must have run about a quarter of a mile before it seemed safe to walk. People had begun to sink down exhausted on the pavements. Many of them were crying. I walked on and found myself in a street of small shops. I had no idea whereabouts I was. The shopkeepers had put their shutters up for the day and I did not want to try asking directions of anyone who knew what had happened. It was not a good moment to reveal oneself as a foreigner.

I walked on aimlessly, looking for a familiar landmark. What I felt I had to do was to see Madame Deltchev and tell her about Pashik before I went. In the confusion I had had the absurd idea that I might get my bag and typewriter from the hotel, be driven to the Deltchev house in a hotel car, and go straight on to the station from there. I knew now that that was out of the question. Even if I managed to find my way to the hotel and hire a car, the chance of getting anyone that day who was willing to drive to Yordan Deltchev's house was small. And that made me realize something else. Unless I could get to the house before news of the assassination reached the sentries on the door, the chances were that I would not be allowed in. It was twenty to three now. Almost certainly the radio had shut down the moment the thing had happened. It would be at least an hour before any official statement was issued; but meanwhile the news and wild distortions of it would be spreading all over the city by word of mouth. I would have to be quick.

I hurried on. The sun was in my eyes. If I kept on walking west I must eventually come to the wall of the Presidential Park. Then, if I followed the wall round, I must come eventually to the quarter in which the house was.

I got there, but it took me well over half an hour and toward the end I began to think that I must be too late. The atmosphere of the city was extraordinary. Just by looking along a street you could see that something serious had happened. People stood about in small groups on the pavements outside their houses, talking very quietly. I had guessed right about the radio being off. Not a sound came from the open windows of the apartment houses. There were armored cars about, too, parked at road junctions or slowly cruising. Vukashin must have been ready to put a standard emergency control plan into operation the instant he got back into the Ministry. As I walked along in the hot sun, I began to see that I might have difficulty in leaving the city that night.

To my dismay, there were several groups of people standing about outside the Deltchev house, and as I drew nearer, I saw that there were extra guards on the door. I wondered if Vukashin yet knew that there was no Philip Deltchev to be arrested. The chances were that, with Vukashin unable to admit to any precise understanding of the situation, things at the palace were still confused. The people waiting here in the street must have heard fantastic rumors and gravitated to the Deltchev house simply because it was the nearest place with important political associations. I could even reflect brutally that, with Brankovitch dead, the worst thing that could happen to me here now was that I would be refused admittance. The same corporal was there. He was looking more sullen than usual and anxious. That probably meant that he knew nothing. I went up to him and he recognized me with a nod. I produced my papers. He glanced at them doubtfully and handed them back, but made no signal to let me through.

"I don't know, *mein Herr*," he said in German. "I must await orders."

"What orders?"

"Something has happened."

"What?"

He shook his head uneasily. "There are many rumors."

"You mean the riot?"

He looked at me keenly. "You know what it is?"

"There was a riot in the square during the parade. The troops had to fire."

"A riot? You are sure it is nothing more?"

"It was very serious, I heard. Many were killed."

"But a riot?" he insisted.

"But of course. I was told by an officer ten minutes ago."

"An officer told you?"

"Yes. I have said—"

He sighed impatiently. "These sheep!" he exclaimed, nodding toward the waiting people. "These silly sheep, with their gossip! They tell me the Agrarian Socialists have attempted a coup and that a revolution has broken out. Sheep!" He spat and then grinned. "A riot, you say. I know a way with rioters."

I grinned back. He nodded to one of the sentries. The bell pealed and after a bit came the familiar sound of Rana's sandals in the courtyard. I felt the eyes of the street upon me as I went in.

There was the same smell of furniture polish and the same slippery floors. There was the same room, and she rose from the same chair to greet me. There were the same gentle, intelligent eyes below the same broad forehead and there was the same polite smile. And yet for me nothing was the same; I saw her now in a different context.

The smile went out. "Herr Foster," she said quickly, "I am so glad you have come. What has happened? Something has. Rana says that there are people waiting outside in front of the house and additional guards. I don't understand it."

I did not answer for a moment. Then I said: "If you are asking me whether Aleko has succeeded, the answer is yes."

"Aleko?"

"I have a train to catch, madame. Perhaps it will save time if I tell you that Pashik and I have talked very frankly to each other and that at this moment, and because it has been difficult for Pashik to keep you fully informed, I know a great deal more about the affair than you do. I came to tell you what you don't already know."

She stared at me and then very calmly sat down. "I see. You are a messenger from Pashik."

"No. Pashik doesn't know I'm here."

"Where is he? With my son?"

"Your son is in Athens. Pashik is in the city somewhere."

"You tell me Vukashin is dead. You saw it happen?"

"I did not say Vukashin was dead, madame. I said that Aleko had succeeded. Brankovitch was assassinated just about an hour ago."

"Brankovitch?" Her hands came down on the wooden arms of the chair with a violence that would have been painful if she had been able to feel pain at that moment.

"Yes, Brankovitch."

"You saw it yourself?"

"Yes."

"Well? Go on."

I went on. It was difficult, for she kept interrupting with questions to not all of which I knew the answers. I said nothing of Katerina's visit. There was no reason to do so. She probably knew of it anyway. When I had finished, she sat back slowly and shut her eyes. Her face was very smooth and beautiful.

"I am leaving for Athens on the five-o'clock train. That's if they'll let me out, of course. I'll see Philip tomorrow. His signed statement and mine will be in New York, Paris, and London by Tuesday at the latest. That will give Vukashin two days to make a fool of himself. After that he hasn't got a chance."

Slowly she opened her eyes. "My dear Herr Foster," she said wearily, "do you suppose that you can defeat men like Vukashin with external propaganda? The conception is naïve."

"I rather thought it was yours."

"Mine?" She stood up angrily. "Pashik's, perhaps. Not mine. Don't you understand? They have defeated us."

"Then you were defeated anyway."

She shook her head. "No. You see, Herr Foster, we could have come to terms with Brankovitch. He would have needed the Agrarian Socialists. He would have thought he was using them."

"And your husband?"

She looked vague. "Agreement could have been reached about that. An acquittal and then temporary retirement."

In a very short space of time a lot of things went through my mind. Above them all, however, was the memory of my own voice asking if it were not dangerous to deny the street, and of the reply, the beautiful, saintly reply: *"For my children, yes. For me, no, for I shall not try to impose my private world upon the real."*

I was aware then of a profound dislike of her and did not trouble to keep it out of my voice.

"Do you really believe that?" I answered.

She turned away to the window. "Herr Foster," she said thoughtfully, "do you think you are safe here?"

It was very unexpected. My wretched stomach jerked unpleasantly. "Safe?" I said.

"Aleko must realize by now what has been done by Pashik. You say he has already tried to kill you once. He might guess you were here."

I saw then. I was being punished. I laughed. "If Aleko realizes what has been done, he will be far too busy getting out of the country to trouble about me. I can't hurt him. If he doesn't know what's happened, then he is most probably under arrest by now. In that case I don't think he would talk until he knew whether Vukashin was going to save him or not."

"You are very confident," she said coldly. "I think you are unwise to stay here."

"Then I shall go. I should like to say good-by to your daughter if I may."

"I will give her your message."

"Is there any message you would like me to give your son?"

"Yes, Herr Foster. You may tell him if you will that he did well and that it is not our fault, his and mine, that we are defeated. If it is possible Katerina and I will join him soon in Athens."

"I'll tell him. There's one thing I should like to know."

"Yes?"

"What induced your husband to make that election speech? What had gone wrong?"

"Nothing that would make a newspaper story, Herr Foster."

"It is for my own information that I ask."

She shrugged. "As you please. It is no longer important, I suppose, what sort of man my husband was."

When she had told me, I left.

I did not go back to the hotel. I reached the station with half an hour to spare. My passport got me on the train. The delay was at the frontier. It took me thirty-six hours to get to Athens, and by that time the Vukashin account of the Brankovitch assassination was out. The assassin was a man named Alexander Gatin and he, together with an accomplice named Pashik, had been shot and killed while resisting arrest.

Philip Deltchev was a pompous but amiable young man and very grateful for his mother's message. He said that it made him feel much better about everything. He was quite sure that she would contrive to join him. He did not mention his father.

Twenty-one

〜〜〜〜〜〜〜〜〜〜

I SAW THE end of the Deltchev trial in the projection room of a newsreel company in London.

In the hard blacks and whites of the Propaganda Ministry's cameramen the scene looked more real than the one I remembered. Perhaps the film gave it an authority the original had lacked. Or it may have been the sound-track that produced the effect; there was no interpreter to divide one's attention. With the six reels of film that Brankovitch's successor had selected for foreign consumption a translation of the proceedings had been sent; but for the moment I wanted just to look at it, and to look at Deltchev.

There was not a great deal of footage that included him. Only one of the three cameras had covered the dock, and the film had been received in an edited form that favored the judges and Dr. Prochaska; but during one evident denunciation of the prisoner there was a shot that showed him frowning anxiously and shifting his position in a way that made him look guilty. Most likely the shot had some other true explanation—boredom or some physical discomfort—but for me, as for the Propaganda Ministry, it had another significance. The Propaganda Ministry saw a scheming villain brought to book. I saw a prewar Minister of Posts and Telegraphs struggling to be a statesman. But then, I had listened to his wife.

It was the word "Papa" that defeated him.

The first time Deltchev saw the word printed in front of his name it pleased him; for, knowing his countrymen, he recognized the note of wry affection in it. It meant that they trusted him and that, although they might grumble, they would accept hardship at his hands and would not hate him too intensely. With amused pride he showed the newspaper to his wife and son. The small pang of anxiety he experienced he found unaccountable and ignored.

The nickname soon gained currency, and its use was no longer an occasion for comment; but he did not, for some reason, get used to it. On the contrary;

as time went by, he began to experience discomfort whenever he saw it or heard it used. It had begun to feel to him like an accusation.

"Yordan always invites criticism," his wife had said, "and always fears it."

Deltchev was aware of the jokes about his motives and had hitherto thought himself a better and not more prejudiced judge of them. Shrewd he might be; yet in 1940 he had opposed the Nazis, not for any personal advantage—unless internment and oblivion were advantages—but because he had thought it right to do so. Ambitious he might be; yet he had organized the Committee of National Unity, not for the risk of dying a martyr's death at the hands of the Gestapo, but because he thought it right to do so. But now, with his power increasing daily and that word "Papa" fastened to his name, he was no longer sure of himself. The whole climate of his thought and feeling seemed to be changing. If he were held in affection, trusted, he must be worthy. His conscience told him that he was not.

"Yordan is a self-torturer," his wife had said.

A terrible conflict now began within him; and the battleground chosen was the question of the election promise.

Reason and experience told him that the Provisional Government was the best that could be devised for the country in the present situation and that elections might well mean the accession of the People's Party to power. He believed that would be a disaster for the country. Reasoning, a lawyer's reasoning, told him, too, that the promise had been one of *free* elections and that the essential condition of freedom was not at present obtainable.

Yet the other voice, the cruel, accusing, contemptuous, punishing voice that haunted him, offered arguments of a different kind. "Why are you so anxious?" it inquired. "Why do you hesitate? Is it because you know in your heart that you have become corrupt and that these reasons you invent for keeping the power in your hands are mere devices to conceal the fact? Is it? You dictators are all the same! You whine that what you do is for the people's good and that they love and trust you. But when there is a chance that you may have to put that love and trust to the test, you find reasons—oh, excellent reasons!—why you should not do so. And the reasons are always to the same tune. It is for the people's good, you cry. That, my friend, is the spiral of corruption you are ascending. Government by consent of the governed! You know the phrase? Who are you to determine what government they shall consent to? Your power and their trust in you give you a responsibility above your party interests. You see now the distinction between a statesman and a politician. The statesman has courage. Did you speak? Ah no! Not the courage of his convictions. (How you twist and turn, my friend, to avoid the truth!) The statesman has the courage to be impartial—even at the risk of his own destruction."

He told no one until after it was over, and then he told his wife.

"My hands are clean," he said. It was as though by violating all his own beliefs and interests, as well as those of other honest men, he had performed an act of absolution for some unnamable sin.

"Last reel," said the cutter who was supervising the running. "Judges' summing up and sentence."

I looked at the screen again. I looked at the tired shell of a man who had been Yordan Deltchev and at the presiding judge delivering the sentence of death by hanging, which had since been carried out.

There was silence in the courtroom after the sentence. Probably the spectators were expecting him to say something. But there was nothing. He nodded his head slightly and turned to go. The guards stepped forward. Then he climbed down from the dock and walked slowly away between them.

I recalled another departure he had made from the courtroom and the parallel I had attempted to draw from the trial of Socrates. My memory of it was better now. There were words more apt than the others I had chosen.

"But, sirs, it may be that the difficulty is not to flee from death, but from guilt. Guilt is swifter than death."

"That's the lot," said the cutter. "Would you like to see the assassination of Brankovitch? I've got it here."

"No, thanks," I said. "I've seen it."

PASSAGE
OF
ARMS

passage . . .

9. A mutual act or transaction; something that goes on between two persons mutually; a negotiation; an interchange or exchange of vows, endearments, or the like; an interchange or exchange of blows; encounter; altercation; a fencing, as in argument; as, a passage *at or of arms.*

Webster's New International Dictionary

One

ALL THAT MR. Wright, the rubber-estate manager, ever knew of the business was that an army patrol had ambushed a band of terrorists within a mile of his bungalow, that five months later his Indian clerk, Girija Krishnan, had reported the theft of three tarpaulins from the curing sheds, and that three years after that someone had removed the wheels from an old scooter belonging to one of his children. As it never occurred to him to look for a possible connection between the three incidents, he remained unaware even of that knowledge. In Malaya, at that time, there were more important facts to ponder and attempt to correlate. Stolen tarpaulins and missing scooter wheels were trivial mysteries; and, although the ambush itself was not forgotten, it was remembered more for its proximity than its novelty.

Mr. and Mrs. Wright had been at breakfast when they heard the sound of firing. It began with a flurry of submachine-gun bursts and continued intermittently for about two minutes.

The truck which took the tappers out to the work areas had not yet left the compound; and, although there was a lot of shouting and excitement, there was no panic and little confusion. Almost before the firing had ceased, the barbed-wire barricades were in position and the inner defense posts manned. During the long silence that followed, Mrs. Wright, a woman of character, calmed the servants and ordered fresh toast and tea so that she and her husband could finish breakfast.

At eight-thirty the patrol appeared: fifteen Malay infantrymen under a British subaltern, and two R.A.F. radio operators. They had been in the jungle for several weeks and their success that morning would probably earn them a rest period. They were smiling and talking as they toiled up the steep track to the compound.

Shortly after they arrived, Girija was summoned to the bungalow. As he went up the veranda steps he could see the officer, a downy, blue-eyed

PASSAGE OF ARMS

Englishman with paratroop wings, on his jungle-green bush shirt. Mrs. Wright was pouring him a cup of tea.

"All Chinese, and on their way to mine the main road, by the look of things," he was saying. "We got the lot."

"Nice work," said Mr. Wright.

"Could have been better, sir." The young officer grinned. "They were all killed outright. You can't ask them questions about their chums when they're dead."

Mr. Wright chuckled and then, seeing his clerk waiting outside, beckoned him in.

"Girija, this is Lieutenant Haynes. He's just wiped out a gang of terrorists. I said we'd let him have some men to help bury them. Will you see to it?"

"Certainly, sir." Girija turned with a slight bow to the officer.

Lieutenant Haynes nodded genially. "I left two men there on guard," he said. "They'll give your chaps a hand if you send extra spades. The ground's quite soft, I think. Shouldn't take long. If you'll speak to my sergeant, he'll detail a guide for you."

"Thank you, sir. I will make all necessary arrangements."

The officer's grin faded slightly. "Seen many dead terrorists around these parts?" he asked.

"No, sir. Have not had that pleasure."

"Well, mind you spread the good news."

"I understand, sir. Two men from each kampong?"

"That's the idea. And tell them they'll be seeing plenty more before we're done."

Girija smiled politely and withdrew to organize the burial party.

He was well aware of the reason for it. The Malay villages in the area had long been suspected by the authorities of aiding the Communist guerrillas with food and shelter. It was not that the villagers approved of the invaders, but simply that the savage reprisals that could follow any refusal of aid were more intimidating to contemplate than the possibility of having fines or other collective punishments imposed by the British. They were not warlike people; their villages were often isolated; the British forces were scattered. In the past, glib official assurances that the police and army were at last gaining the upper hand and able to protect the outlying areas from the terrorists had been given too often, and too often proved baseless. Now, the villagers believed only what they saw themselves, or what had been seen by their own people. Dead terrorists had to be shown to be dead. The burial party was in the nature of a morale-building or public-relations device.

Girija found the head tapper and explained what was wanted: two men from each of the four neighboring villages, and picks and shovels. Then he went to the Malay sergeant and secured a guide. Within twenty minutes the party was ready to move. The head tapper was obviously hoping to go with it, but Girija sent him off with the truck and the remaining men to the work areas. He had decided to take charge of the burial party himself.

The action had taken place in a deep gully carved out of the red laterite hillside by the monsoon rains, and flanked on both sides by bamboo thickets, tree ferns, and dense tangles of croton undergrowth. It was a natural route for men to use on that otherwise trackless hillside, and a perfect site for an ambush.

There were ten bodies there: four within a few feet of one another, and the rest scattered along the gully for a distance of some twenty-five yards. It was easy to see what had happened. Concealed in the undergrowth along both lips of the gully, the patrol had been able to open fire at point-blank range without fear of hitting each other or the smallest chance of missing the enemy below them. One or two of the dead men were lying in attitudes which suggested desperate split-second attempts to claw their way to cover behind the roots of a fallen tree. One had been hit in the back as he turned to run. One, the farthest away, had tried to return the patrol's fire; there were empty shells scattered on the ground by him; but he was as dead as the rest. Nobody in the patrol had been hit.

The two Malay soldiers left on guard were squatting on their heels by a Sterno fuel stove, heating cans of tea and smoking. They took no notice of the burial party. Beside them, on a ground sheet, were stacked the arms and equipment collected from the dead: machine pistols, boxes of ammunition and road mines, and canvas belts with pouches containing hand grenades.

The soldier who had guided the party from the compound joined his friends at the stove. Girija knew that they would not help with the digging unless he told them what Lieutenant Haynes had said; but he made no attempt to do so. During his brief inspection of the gully he had made two small discoveries. They had aroused his curiosity and made him wish to know more about the dead terrorists. He put the burial party to work and sat down on the ground nearby.

The first thing he had noted was the fact that, although the bodies had been searched and stripped of all arms and equipment, there had been no cooking utensils of any kind found on them. This meant almost certainly that they were within a day's marching distance of their camp; which meant, in turn, that they had probably been living off one or more of the four villages near the estate. They would be known, if only by sight, to at least two members of the burial party.

His second discovery had to do with the arms and equipment. He was sure that the machine pistols were new; not new in type necessarily, but newly acquired. His father had been a subahdar in the British army, and Girija had spent his childhood in barracks and cantonments. He knew the look of a new gun and how soon it acquired the patina of use from normal cleaning and handling. At least three of the machine pistols on the ground sheet had been so recently unpacked, and so little used and cleaned, that traces of brown preservative grease were still visible on them. The ammunition boxes, the mines, and the grenades were also new. The grenades were of an old type with cast-iron fragmentation cases; but the gray paint on them was fresh and the pins were clean and bright.

The gully was only partly shaded by the overhanging trees, and by eleven o'clock the sun was shining directly into it. The tappers were craftsmen, used to the careful work of milking rubber trees without damaging them. Digging graves on a hillside, and in ground which, despite Lieutenant Haynes' assurance, had proved to be rock hard, was not a job which they could be expected to tackle with enthusiasm. The excitement of the occasion and the sight of ten bloody corpses were novelties that had soon paled. By the time the third grave had been dug, most of the men had lost their customary good humor. Criticism began to be voiced of the soldiers squatting in the shade and drinking tea while others cleaned up the mess they had made. There was even an exchange of remarks, meant to be overheard, to the effect that the tuan's clerk might, without serious loss of face, enhance his already considerable popularity by taking a shovel and doing a bit of digging himself.

Girija was able to ignore this unworthy suggestion with equanimity. The tappers' complaints interested him for reasons other than their substance. He was almost certain now that he knew the area in which the band had made their headquarters. Only two of the burial party had remained cheerful. Malays were not good at concealing their emotions, and although these two were trying hard to conform to the mood of the others, their satisfaction with the turn of events and the task in which they were engaged kept showing through their scowls. Girija watched them dump one of the bodies into its grave with unmistakable gusto, and then glance round guiltily when they caught themselves grinning at one another.

The two men came from a village named Awang on a river three miles away to the west. Once there had been tin mining in the district, but falling yields and rising operating costs had made the mines uneconomic. The small labor force of Awang had been gradually absorbed by the rubber estates.

Girija had been to the village once or twice to pay sick benefits to the families of men in hospital, but he did not know it well. It was at the end of a secondary road which had degenerated in recent years to no more than a cycle track. Beyond the old tin workings the jungle-covered hills stretched all the way to the borders of Thailand. In that lush wilderness, small groups of disciplined men with minds and bodies adapted to the environment could remain healthy and mobile almost indefinitely. At that period it was impossible either to police the area effectively or to halt the stream of Chinese militants filtering down the peninsular from the north. Villages like Awang became staging points for the terrorist bands cautiously working their way southward toward the politically more sensitive areas of Selangor, Negri Sembilan, Malacca, and Johore. The men now being buried had probably made their camp within a mile or so of it, going in at night to receive food, gather information, browbeat the headman, and talk earnestly to potential recruits.

Girija walked over to the two tappers and stood watching them as they filled in the grave. They had fallen silent as he approached. After a moment or two he moved in closer.

"A good day's work," he remarked.

They looked at him warily.

He smiled. "The past buries itself."

That raised a sheepish grin.

"And honest men are free again," he added.

They went on working. The body was covered now.

"The tuan was pleased," Girija said thoughtfully; "pleased that these pigs were all foreigners. To him that proved the loyalty and courage of our men here."

They looked at him again. One of them mumbled: "The tuan is a father to us."

"It is unfortunate," Girija went on, "that the lieutenant tuan does not agree with him."

They stared at him in dismay.

Girija shrugged. "He said that this gang was new to the district. He said that a week was no test of loyalty."

He had them now. Dismay gave way to indignation.

The man who had spoken before spoke again. "The tuan was right," he said firmly. "The lieutenant tuan does not speak the truth."

Girija shrugged again. "It is not important."

"The lieutenant tuan is wrong," the man insisted. "It was many weeks."

Girija made sympathetic sounds.

"Many weeks," repeated the other man emphatically.

Girija spread out his hands. "It is not my business. Perhaps you should tell this to the lieutenant tuan." He saw the sudden panic in their eyes and went on smoothly: "Myself, I do not think it necessary, or wise. The pigs are dead. They are best forgotten."

"Yes, yes. It is best. We will forget."

Girija smiled benignly and moved away. He knew that they were watching him and wondering fearfully if he would betray them to the lieutenant. He had no intention of doing so; but there was no point in telling them that. They would not quite believe him; and in any case they had served their purpose. He had found out what he wanted to know.

ii

Girija was born of Bengali parents at Cawnpore in the United Provinces of India. He had five sisters but no brothers. When he was six his father, the subahdar, went to London with a detachment of his regiment to march in the Coronation procession of King George the Sixth. During his stay the subahdar was taken on a conducted tour of the city, which included visits to the Tower of London, Westminster Abbey, the Houses of Parliament, the British Museum, the Law Courts, Battersea power station, and, for some obscure reason, a factory in Acton where bus bodies were made. He returned to India laden with souvenirs and fired with ambition for his only son. The Law Courts had particularly impressed him. Girija would become a lawyer or, failing that, a policeman.

Girija became neither. The subahdar was killed at the battle of Alamein, and Girija spent the next three years in a military orphanage at Benares. When the war ended, however, his mother wrote to a brother, who had a cotton-goods business in Singapore, explaining that she had only her widow's pension and asking if she might join him with the children. The prospect of securing this windfall of cheap labor appealed to the brother, and he replied sending passage money. In December 1946 the family sailed as deck passengers from Calcutta. With them went the subahdar's medals and the precious souvenirs of his visit to London: the Coronation mug, the picture postcards, the newspaper cuttings, the photographs, the ash tray from the warrant officers' mess at Chelsea Barracks, and the bus-body manufacturer's catalogue.

In his last year at the orphanage Girija had been taught bookkeeping, office organization, and the jargon of commercial letter writing. The uncle in Singapore found him useful—so useful, indeed, that after three months he got rid of the bookkeeper to whom he had been paying forty dollars (Straits) a week and replaced him with Girija, to whom he paid twenty. Girija was sixteen then. He stayed two years in Singapore. During them he learned Malay and a smattering of Cantonese and made friends with a Parsee who worked in the offices of a Chinese financial syndicate.

At that time, shortage of capital, ill health brought about by internment, and sheer hopelessness engendered by the early successes of the terrorists were persuading many British rubber planters in Malaya to sell out. The Chinese syndicate was buying. It was through his Parsee friend that Girija heard that the new manager of a recently acquired estate in the north was asking the Singapore office for a clerk.

His uncle was angered by Girija's decision to leave him, and talked darkly of getting a court order requiring Girija to repay the cost of his passage from Calcutta. To his astonishment, the bluff failed. Girija, whom he had come to regard as a pliant and somewhat timid young man, not only laughed loudly and made a disrespectful noise with his lips, but also threatened to take his mother and sisters north with him unless their wages were immediately doubled. There was a shrill Bengali family quarrel during which Girija uttered a further and more compelling threat. He had made a secret analysis of his uncle's accounts which he was prepared to send to the Inspector of Taxes. The uncle wept and spoke of ingratitude, but capitulated. Girija's mother embraced her son proudly and said that he was his father's true heir.

When the time came for Girija to leave, however, he asked her for only one thing that had belonged to his father: the bus-body manufacturer's catalogue. His sisters were relieved. They had been afraid that, as a man, he would feel himself entitled to the subahdar's medals.

The catalogue was a quarto-size book with a brown cover on which the name of the manufacturer was embossed in green. Inside there were forty-eight pages of thick, shiny paper displaying the specifications of twenty different types of buses together with color illustrations of the exterior and interior of each. There were double-deckers and single-deckers, buses designed to enable the driver to collect the fares, and buses designed to carry conductors. There were twelve-seaters, twenty-four-seaters, and sixty-seaters. There were buses for long distances and buses for local service in cities, for cold climates and for hot. The cover was dog-eared from much handling, and some of the pages were loose. There was an inkstain on the title page. It was Girija's most treasured possession.

As a small boy he had sat for hours turning the pages, studying the illustrations and rereading the text. He had, in the end, come to know it by heart. At the orphanage, when he had been separated both from his mother and from the catalogue, he had found comfort in reciting it to himself, beginning with the Foreword by the Chairman (*"In presenting to our customers all over the world this, the Eighteenth Edition, of our Catalogue and Price List, we are proudly conscious that . . ."*) and finishing with the specifications of a forty-seat medium-range staging coach (available on A.E.C. or Commer chassis) *"as supplied to the Argentine Government. Price £8,586, f.o.b. London."*

One day in the streets of Benares he had seen a new bus that he thought he recognized as a modification of one of those listed in the catalogue. It had been just starting away and he had run for almost half a mile before he had caught up with it at a stopping place. Breathlessly he had searched for the body manufacturer's name plate. The bus had been moving off again before he had found it; but it had been the right plate. A wave of excitement had swept over him. From that moment he had known exactly what he wanted to do in the world. He would operate a bus service.

His first letter to the body manufacturer had been written from Singapore on his uncle's business stationery. He had been aware for some time that the original catalogue from London, precious though it was and always would be, was now very much out of date. Nevertheless, the decision to send for the latest edition had not been easily taken. For some reason that he had been unable to account for, it had seemed almost like an act of treachery.

However, the arrival of the new catalogue had given him other things to worry about. The catalogue itself had been magnificent. Unfortunately, it had been accompanied by a courteous letter from the sales manager, informing him that the company's Far Eastern representative, Mr. W. W. Belden, would shortly be visiting Singapore and would take that opportunity of meeting Mr. Krishnan and discussing his fleet requirements with him personally. For weeks Girija had gone in fear of W. W. Belden's arrival at his uncle's office and the humiliating scenes that would ensue when the truth was known. But Mr. Belden had never come, and eventually Girija had drawn the correct conclusion. Mr. Belden had investigated the financial status of this new prospective customer and decided not to waste his time.

His prudence had been understandable. The cheapest twenty-four-seater now cost over three thousand pounds—almost double the price of the cheapest bus in the 1937 catalogue. But one thing in the new edition had caught Girija's eye: a quotation from a trade journal devoted to the interests and activities of road-transport operators. Girija had found that this journal could be obtained in Singapore and had bought a subscription. From the articles it published he began to learn about the economics of public transportation. By the time he went to work for Mr. Wright, he had acquired a reasonably realistic view of his chances of achieving his life's ambition. Unless he could find a working capital of at least twenty thousand dollars (Straits), his chances of starting even the most modest country bus service were nonexistent.

iii

Girija had a one-room atap house in the estate compound, and an arrange-ment with one of the servants at the Wrights' bungalow to keep it clean. There were Indian families of his own caste living in a village six miles away, and on Sundays he would cycle over there for tiffin. One of the families had an attractive daughter named Sumitra, whom he thought he would one day marry. However, during the week the curfew kept him at home, and there he always cooked his own food. Sometimes he would go back to the office after he had eaten his evening meal and do some more work before going to bed; at others he would listen to Radio Malaya and read and dream.

On the evening of the day of the ambush he stayed late in the office, trying to make up for the time he had lost by going with the burial party. The following morning he would have to drive in with Mr. Wright to the bank at Bukit Amphu to cash the weekly wages check, and he had not yet completed the time sheets.

The work required care and concentration, and he was glad of it, for it postponed the moment when he would have to entertain once more the dangerous thoughts which had come to him in the morning.

The things he had observed at the scene of the ambush, and learned from the two tappers, had made it possible for him to reconstruct the recent history of the dead men with reasonable certainty.

They had only recently arrived from the north and were relatively inexperienced. Of that he was sure. Their use of the easy route offered by the gully showed that. True, they had had a lot to carry, but that did not excuse carelessness. In an area where British patrols were being supplied by the R.A.F., a fact which they could scarcely help knowing, they had not even troubled to send scouts on ahead to feel the way, but had blundered straight into the ambush in a body.

The Lieutenant's opinion was that they had been on their way to mine the main road. Girija did not agree with that. The quantity of ammunition they had been carrying was out of all proportion to the needs of such an operation. And how was the absence of cooking utensils and food supplies to be explained if they were going so far from their base? To Girija there seemed only one possible explanation. What the Lieutenant's patrol had ambushed was a supply column on its way to deliver mines and ammunition to another gang operating farther south.

It had been at this point in his argument with himself that Girija's heart had begun to beat faster, and that an unpleasant sensation had come to his stomach. If his reasoning were correct, it could mean only one thing. The base camp near Awang was a guerrilla arms dump.

He finished his work, locked up the office, and walked slowly back across the courtyard to his house. It was a warm, humid night. He took off his shirt and khaki drill shorts, washed himself carefully all over and then put on a dhoti. There was some lentil soup in an iron saucepan. He lit the oil burner under it and sat down to wait.

What had disconcerted him had been not so much the nature of his thoughts as the way in which they had presented themselves. He did not regard himself as being fundamentally honest or dishonest, idealistic or corrupt, lawabiding or delinquent. He did not think of himself as definable in such terms. His dilemmas had always been capable of resolution into simple questions of choice. Choice A would be wise (advantageous). Choice B would be stupid (disadvantageous). The discovery that his mind could explore enthusiastically the possibility of his committing a major crime, with only a belated and distasteful glance at the path of rectitude, had been disturbing.

And a major crime it undoubtedly would be.

He had heard about these dumps and caches. It was known that the arms were brought in by professional smugglers operating from beyond the Thai border and employing different routes from those used by the guerrillas. A number of consignments had been intercepted, but it was generally believed that a far greater number always got through. Terrorists captured far to the south in the Kuala Lumpur area had been found to be in possession of substantial quantities of weapons, ammunition and explosives of the same pattern as those intercepted in the north. It was said that there were not enough troops in the whole of Malaya to patrol the border with Thailand effectively.

Just before the burial party had finished its work that morning the Malay sergeant and four more soldiers had arrived with packing crates strung on bamboo poles. When the ammunition and grenades had been loaded into the crates, they were taken off to the compound. While the machine pistols were being gathered up, Girija had asked the Sergeant a question.

The Sergeant had looked down at the machine pistol in his hands and shrugged. "How should I know what they cost?"

"But don't you know how much your own cost, Sergeant? Supposing a man lost one."

"He would be court-martialed."

"But surely he would have stoppages of pay, too?"

"Oh, yes. Two hundred dollars perhaps."

"So much?"

"They do not grow on trees."

The Sergeant had gone. Girija had turned and looked at the row of graves. Each man had had a machine pistol, and ammunition was costly stuff. It was more than likely that what the ten men had been carrying between them was worth anything up to three thousand dollars. It would be interesting to know how much more there was where that had come from.

The soup began to bubble. He poured it into a bowl and, when it had cooled a little, began to eat.

The penalty for being found in the illegal possession of arms was death.

Whether or not knowledge of the whereabouts of smuggled arms would constitute possession, and whether concealment of such knowledge carried the same penalty he did not know. One thing was clear: the illegal *selling* of smuggled arms would certainly be a hanging matter—at least while the emergency regulations remained in force. The best thing he could do was to go to Mr. Wright immediately and make a clean breast of the matter.

But a clean breast of *what* matter? He did not really *know* anything about an arms dump. He only believed one to be there. And where was "there"? Assuming that his deductions were correct, the dump was concealed in an area of jungle covering at least three square miles. It might prove quite impossible to find. Mr. Wright would not thank him for starting a wild-goose chase, and neither would the police. When the time came for him to apply for a local bus-service franchise, they might remember the trouble he had caused and hold it against him. No. The best thing he could do was nothing.

He finished his soup and felt better. He was an innocent man again, quietly digesting his evening meal. What did he want with smuggled arms? Could he ever have sold them? Of course not. Who would buy? And supposing others knew of the dump, if dump there were. Ten men had been killed; but supposing that other members of the guerrilla band had stayed behind. It might be highly dangerous to start searching in the area for their camp. Besides, there was always a chance that one or two of the men living at Awang already knew where it was. Not a very big chance, perhaps; the guerrillas would not have trusted their unwilling hosts to that extent; but someone might have found out by chance. Naturally, no man or woman from the village would dare to go to the police with the information—or not immediately, anyway. A decent interval would have to elapse before the dump could be discovered "accidentally." More likely it would just be forgotten. And that perhaps was what he should do: forget about it. After all, he could always remember again later, if he wanted to.

There was a metal trunk in one corner of the room. In it he kept his catalogues and trade papers and the schedule of a projected daily bus service linking ten of the principal rubber estates in the district with Bukit Amphu sixteen miles away. He took the schedule out, read it through very carefully, and then began to make one or two long-contemplated modifications

iv

A month went by before Girija made any move to locate the arms dump.

There had been no reports of any special patrol activity in the district, and guerrilla attacks in the province had been concentrated on areas nearer the

coast. He had watched the men from Awang carefully without detecting anything unusual in their demeanor. But such reassurances came mingled with
doubt. If no dump had been discovered, it could well be for the simple reason
that none existed.

It was, in fact, the growing conviction that he must have been mistaken
that gave him the courage he needed to go on. If there were nothing to find,
he argued, there could be nothing incriminating in the search.

The first part of his plan called for a satisfactory cover for repeated visits
to the Awang area. He might avoid going through the village itself, but he
would have to use a mile or more of the road leading to it. Encounters with
men who knew him, and who might gossip or ask questions, would be inevitable. The difficulty had seemed insurmountable at first; but finally he had
had an idea.

The latex produced by the estate went thirty miles by road down to the
port of Kuala Pangkalan and from there was shipped to Singapore. Since the
emergency, the trucks from the coast had had to be provided with armored-
car escorts and, consequently, did not make the journey so often. Mr. Wright
had been talking for some time, and writing to Singapore, about the need for
additional storage sheds. The Singapore office had been reluctant to authorize the expenditure. Girija's idea was to make the new sheds an excuse for
his trips to Awang.

Near the abandoned mine workings there were a number of derelict corrugated-iron buildings which had been used as offices, stores, and repair shops.
Girija wrote to the head office of the mining company in Kota Bharu and
asked permission to inspect the property with a possible view to making an
offer for the material of the buildings.

He did not tell Mr. Wright. If Mr. Wright found out, no great harm would
be done. Indeed, Mr. Wright would probably give him a pat on the back for
his zeal and initiative in attempting to solve the problem of the new storage
sheds. But Mr. Wright would also tell him something he already knew: that
the mining company's rust-eaten buildings were not worth the cost of dismantling them, and that it would be a waste of time for him to go and inspect
them.

The mining company replied with understandable enthusiasm that
Mr. Krishnan had their full permission to inspect the buildings any time
he liked. That was all he needed. No one person he might encounter there
would know exactly how many visits of inspection he had made, or how many
might be necessary. It would be assumed that he was acting on Mr. Wright's
instructions. If he were ever challenged, he could produce the letter.

The following Sunday he cycled out to Awang. Just short of the village he turned off the road onto the overgrown track which led to the mining company's property. He met nobody on the way.

Ground sluicing had cleared some twenty acres of land in the bend of the river. No topsoil had been left for the jungle to reclaim, and the brown scars of the workings were still visible beneath a thin film of scrub and weed. Girija walked along the riverbank until he came to the shell of a building that had housed a big rotary pump, and went through the motions of inspecting it and taking notes. This was for the benefit of anyone who might have seen him and be watching from across the river. After a few minutes he moved away, circling out of sight of the riverbank until he reached the cover of some trees.

He had thought long and carefully about the problems of searching the area. The only large-scale map which covered it, and to which he might ordinarily have had access, was an ordnance survey sheet marked with the estate boundary lines. Unfortunately, a strict security regulation governed the distribution and custody of such maps at that time, and it had to be kept by Mr. Wright in his personal safe. Girija was forced to rely on his none too vivid recollection of it.

The picture in his mind was one of three parallel ridges, rather like steps, with contour lines very close together. That meant, he knew, that the sides of the ridges were steep and that there were deep ravines between them. It was not much to go on; but it was something. He did not believe that even inexperienced men would choose the floor of a ravine for a base camp, any more than they would choose to perch on the summit of a ridge. To that extent the likely areas of search were limited. And there was another factor to be considered. Even if they had had only small quantities of arms and ammunition to store, they would have tried to find a place for them which gave some protection from the weather. He thought it unlikely that there were caves there; but on the steeper hillsides there would be sizable hollows made during the monsoons, when the heavier trees fell and tore their roots out of the ground. Such hollows could easily be made into shelters. All in all, it seemed sensible to start the search by working along the upper slopes.

He attempted to do so; and that first Sunday expedition was very nearly the last. It took him an hour to climb three hundred yards up the side of the first ridge, and almost as long to get down again. He tore his clothes, scratched his arms and legs, and ended by becoming completely exhausted. He also became frightened. If some patrolling policeman were to ask him to account for the tears and scratches, he would be hard put to it to invent a convincing explanation.

He succeeded in getting back to his house unobserved, but the experience had thoroughly unnerved him and he decided to abandon the whole project.

For several days he did succeed in putting it out of his mind. Then, as the scratches on his arms and legs began to heal, he began to think again. None of the ambushed men had had scratches on arms or legs. That meant that they must have found an easy route to and from their hiding place. The beauty of this deduction restored his confidence.

The next time he made no attempt to penetrate the jungle. Instead he worked his way around the fringes of it, looking for easy ways in. He found several and noted them for future reference.

The following Sunday he began a systematic probe. He had learned well from his initial mistake. When the going became too hard, he made no attempt to force a path through, but went back and tried a different or more circuitous way. He knew by now that he could never hope to cover anything like the whole area, but he had become philosophical about the search; it was a kind of game now, and although he did not expect to win, he had not yet reached the point of conceding his defeat.

Eight weeks after he began, he received his first piece of encouragement. He had been following a dry stream bed up a fold in a hillside. On both sides there were cane thickets of a kind he had learned to avoid. It was useless to try to push your way through. You had to go around them, and they often covered wide areas. Then, as the stream bed bore away sharply to the left, he paused. There were a few pieces of dead cane lying on the ground. At first he thought that they had been broken away by some animal grubbing for food among the roots. Then he saw that they had been cut.

He stood still for a moment, staring. There was no mistaking the marks on the cane. They had been made by a metal cutting edge. He examined the border of the thicket carefully. For a distance of about two feet the cane was thinner and greener, and near the ground he could see short stumps of older cane in among the new growth. At some time in the not too distant past someone had cleared a path there.

It was getting late, and he was a mile and a half or more from the tin workings and the shed where he had left his bicycle. He decided to leave further investigation until the following Sunday. During the week, on the pretext of checking an inventory, he went to the tool store, borrowed one of the long chopping knives, called parangs, that the estate workers used for clearing underbrush, and hid it in his room. On Sunday morning he wrapped the parang in newspaper, tied it to the crossbar of his bicycle, and set off early for Awang.

He found his way back to the cane thicket without difficulty and started hacking a path through it with the parang. The new growth had not yet had time to harden, and the going was fairly easy. He had no fear of running into surviving members of the band. If this were indeed the way to their camp, it had not been used for several months.

The path was uphill. After he had gone fifteen yards, the cane thinned out and he found himself on a shallow ledge from which he could see down into the stream bed. On the ground there were some dead tree branches arranged to form a sort of chair. It looked as if the ledge had been used as a vantage point from which a sentry could cover the approach along the stream bed. A well-worn track led off to the right. He followed it, his heart pounding.

The camp was in a clearing shielded both from the sun and from air observation by the branches of a large flame-of-the-forest. The jungle apes had been there before him. Pieces of clothing had been torn apart and scattered over the clearing amid cooking pots, an earthenware chatty, and empty rice bags. The only thing that seemed to have escaped the apes' attentions was a metal box. It was full of leaflets, printed in Malay and Chinese, calling upon the people of Malaya to rise against the imperialist exploiters and establish a people's democracy.

There was another path leading down from the clearing, and Girija followed it. It ended at the hole which had been dug for use as a latrine. He walked back slowly to the clearing. In the long search for the camp site his doubts had been forgotten. Now he remembered them and faced the bitterness of defeat. Lieutenant Haynes had been right. He, Girija, had been wrong. Sunday after Sunday he had exchanged the pleasures of tiffin with his future mother-in-law, and the soft glances of Sumitra, for senseless walks in the jungle and the pursuit of an illusion. There was no arms dump; there never had been.

He had started to retrace his footsteps when his foot struck something that tinkled. He looked down. Lying on the ground was a brass cartridge case. As he bent down to pick it up, he saw another one. A minute later he had found three more. He stared at them, puzzled. They were of .303 caliber. He went over the ground again and found what he was looking for: the clip which had held the five rounds.

There was no doubt about it. A .303 rifle had been fired there. But no rifle of any kind had been found at the scene of the ambush. And none of the weapons had been of .303 caliber. Where, then, was the rifle?

He searched the camp site thoroughly first. He found a small fixed-frequency radio in a teak box, but no rifle. He began to search the hillside above the camp, taking any route that looked as if it might conceivably have been used before. After about an hour he came upon a clump of bamboo from which a number of thick stalks had been cut. Then, about twelve yards away, he saw what he had been looking for.

Braced between the steep hillside and the trunk of a tree was a triangular roof of bamboo. Cane screens had been plaited to enclose the sides of the structure and form a shelter.

Girija scrambled toward it, slipping and sliding about on the spongy carpet of dead leaves and slashing wildly with the parang at the undergrowth in his path. When he reached the shelter, he stood for an instant, breathless and trying to prepare himself for the crushing disappointment of finding it empty. Then he pulled one of the screens aside.

There was a sudden, swift rustle and his heart leaped as some small brown animal rushed out past him. He pulled the screen back farther and looked inside.

The hillside beneath the roof had been dug out to make the space roughly rectangular. It was about six feet high and ten feet long and filled from floor to roof with wood and metal packing cases.

He sat down on the ground to get his breath back and stared at the cases. A number of them, he could see, were long and narrow and had rope handles. One of these was near the screen and looked as if it had been opened. He crawled over to it and prized the lid off with the parang.

Inside, carefully packed on slotted wood bearers, were six .303 rifles. Five of them were heavily greased and wrapped in thick oiled paper with the name of a Belgian manufacturer printed on it. One had been unwrapped. Girija took it out and opened the breach. It had been fired, presumably down at the camp site, and put back without being cleaned. The barrel was corroded.

Girija clucked disapprovingly. That was no way to treat valuable property. He returned the rifle to its case and began to examine the rest of his find. He soon discovered that there was more there than he had at first supposed. There were ten cases of rifles and at least thirty other boxes and cases of various sizes, in addition to ammunition containers.

He began to move some of these so as to get a look at the stenciled markings on the bigger cases, and then stopped. He would have to start back soon and there was no hope of taking an inventory that day. Besides, he had no need of an inventory.

He knew that all he had really found was hope. Of course, it would have been agreeable to dream of what was there in terms of wealth; but wealth that could only be realized, if at all, in some unmeasurable fullness of time was meaningless. It would be the hope that mattered in the days to come; and if he could draw from it the strength to go on quietly reading his transport trade journals, and turning the pages of his catalogues, and revising notional timetables, and faithfully continuing to serve Mr. Wright—if, in short, he could be patient and discreet—he might perhaps one day fulfill himself.

v

He waited, patiently and discreetly, for three years.

In the beginning it had been comparatively easy. There had been practical matters to attend to.

First, he thoroughly cleaned and greased the rifle that had been fired; then he gave some thought to the long-term problems of storage and preservation. The monsoon rains would arrive shortly, and the bamboo roof was not waterproof.

He decided to reconstruct the shelter. One Sunday he moved all the boxes out of it and laid a framework of bamboo on the ground to ensure a proper circulation of air. Over this he put a heavy tarpaulin taken from the estate compound, and then rearranged the boxes on top of it. Another tarpaulin went over the boxes and was lashed down firmly with wire rope. A third tarpaulin he incorporated in the roof. He also repaired the screens.

Thereafter, he only went to the place once a month to make sure that all was in order. He would have gone more often if he could have trusted himself, but, rather to his surprise, he had found patience easier to cultivate than discretion.

In spite of his initial resolution, it had proved hard not to take an inventory of what was in the shelter and keep it in his tin trunk. He knew that such a document was premature and pointless. He knew that if, through some mischance, Mr. Wright happened to see it and ask questions, his lies would be unconvincing. Yet the temptation had persisted. There had also been an insane desire to confide in Sumitra, to bask in her admiration and flattery, and bind her future more securely to his. He knew that she would certainly tell her mother, who would tell the father, who worked in the bank at Bukit Amphu and was a notorious chatterbox; but that temptation, too, had continued to haunt him.

During the second year he had other troubles. His mother died; and two of the cases resting on the lower tarpaulin were attacked by termites. Fortunately, he noticed the fact in good time and was able to minimize the damage. The ammunition boxes were metal, and, having given them a thick coat of bitumen paint, he moved them to the bottom of the stack. The damaged boxes he repaired with strips of teak, and sprayed all the wood containers with a powerful solution of benzine hexachloride.

The second year went by; and the third. General Templer's policy of winning the co-operation and goodwill of the people of Malaya and enlisting them in the fight against the terrorists began to succeed; and, as success snowballed into victory, curfews were lifted and road blocks removed. Areas free of terrorists were declared "white," and restrictions on unescorted civil transport movements canceled.

The day that the province in which he worked was declared "white," Girija wrote to England for a new bus-body catalogue. The following Sunday he went to the shelter and spent two of the happiest hours of his life, taking an inventory.

Two
~~~~~~

WHEN THE RUBBER estates in the Pangkalan district had latex for shipment, they generally notified the Anglo-Malay Transport Company at the port
of Kuala Pangkalan. The company would then send their trucks to collect the
latex, store it temporarily in their godowns, and finally, when instructions came
through from Singapore, ship it out in one of their big motor junks.

The founder, manager, and sole proprietor of this useful enterprise was a
Chinese, Mr. Tan Siow Mong.

Mr. Tan had been educated at a mission school in Macao, and spoke Hokkien
and Portuguese as well as Cantonese, Malay, and English. His father had owned
a fishing junk, and had divided his working year between snapper fishing and
carrying cargoes of rattan up the coast to Hong Kong. When he died, in the
early thirties, Mr. Tan and his two brothers had taken over the junk and turned
to the more lucrative business of opium smuggling. They had been caught, in
the end, by a British gunboat, and their junk had been impounded. By that time
they had had a substantial sum of money saved and could accept the forfeiture
of the junk with equanimity. However, a family council had considered it
advisable for the Tans to leave the China Coast for a while and seek their
fortunes elsewhere. One brother had gone to Singapore, another to Manila. Tan
Siow Mong, the eldest, had taken his mother to Kuala Pangkalan. There, with
his share of the family capital, he had started to deal in copra and lend money
to Malays at forty per cent. During the Japanese occupation he had accepted a
disused godown in discharge of a debt. After the war he had tried to sell it.
Unable to find a buyer, he had eventually decided to make it pay for itself. The
Anglo-Malay Transport Company had grown from that decision.

Mr. Tan was in the late forties now, with graying hair and rimless glasses.
He wore well-cut tussore suits, and was never seen without a dark tie even
in the hottest weather. He had an air of well-bred dignity that was much
admired in the Chinese business community of Kuala Pangkalan.

His office was so placed that he could, without moving from his desk, see
the trucks in the unloading bay of number one godown and the wooden quay
at which the junks discharged and took on cargo. By turning his head he could

also see, through a glass panel let into the wall beside the door, his four Chinese assistants. Mr. Tan did not believe in elaborate organization. Working sixty-five hours a week, the four assistants were well able to take care of most of the routine paper work of the business. The accounts he preferred to look after himself.

Two of the trucks were unloading bales of latex which had come down that afternoon from one of the Chiang Thye Phu Syndicate estates, and he could see the Indian clerk from the estate office checking off the weights with the godown foreman.

Mr. Tan did not like that. Mr. Wright, the estate manager, had always, and rightly, trusted the company before. Why had he suddenly felt it necessary to send his clerk to check the weighing?

The clerk and the godown foreman had evidently agreed the figures now, for, as Mr. Tan watched, the clerk smiled and turned away. Mr. Tan had made a note to ask the foreman what reason, if any, had been given for this uncomplimentary change of procedure, when he saw that the clerk was walking across the yard towards his office.

Mr. Tan looked down at the papers on his desk. It would be undignified to be seen peering out. A moment or two later, one of his assistants came in to say that Mr. Krishnan desired the pleasure of a few moments' conversation with him.

Mr. Tan disapproved of Indians. He had often found them to be disagreeably acute in business matters. He also disapproved of estate clerks, who, if they were not given occasional presents, could delay the payment of accounts and cause other inconveniences.

This one he remembered only from having seen him with Mr. Wright, the estate manager. He was lean and very dark, with bright, intelligent eyes and a predatory mouth that smiled too much. It would be interesting to discover how accurately he would estimate his nuisance value.

He greeted Girija with grave courtesy and asked him to sit down.

"It is not often," he went on in English, "that we have the pleasure of seeing you, Mr. Krishnan."

Girija smiled. "Thank you. Mr. Wright sends all compliments and best favors."

Mr. Tan congratulated himself on choosing English for the conversation. His own, he knew, was excellent. The clerk's was little better than the illiterate commercial patois that the British called "Babu." It placed him at a disadvantage, small but possibly useful.

"And are Mr. and Mrs. Wright well?"

"Both very well. We hope ditto for Mrs. Tan, self, and family."

364 PASSAGE OF ARMS

"Thank you, yes."

Tea was brought in from the outer office and served in minute cups. Tentative moves might now be made toward a discussion of the real object of the visit.

"This must be a busy time for you at the estate," observed Mr. Tan.

What this banality was in effect asking was why Mr. Wright had thought it necessary to waste his clerk's time by sending him in to Kuala Pangkalan to supervise a normal warehousing operation.

Girija smiled and answered in Malay. "With the rubber market so firm, we are always busy now."

Mr. Tan nodded. He was wondering if by some faint flicker of expression he had revealed his amusement at the clerk's English. The Malay was fluent. Courteously, he answered in the same language.

"Let us hope the bad times are ended for good."

"Good business for one is good business for all," said Girija.

"Very true." Now, Mr. Tan decided, they were coming to the point. Reference to mutual advantage was the accepted preliminary to a squeeze.

"This tea is excellent, sir," said Girija.

Mr. Tan instantly sent for more. This again postponed pointed discussion, and further inanities were exchanged. Grudgingly, Mr. Tan had to admit to himself that the young man was handling the interview well. He found himself becoming interested.

When they were alone again, he said: "Mr. Wright is a very good manager. It must be a pleasure to work for such a man."

Girija nodded. "Indeed it is. He is, as you say, a fine manager. But he is also a man of good heart."

"I can well believe that."

"In fact," Girija went on, "when I asked him if he would allow me to come down to Kuala Pangkalan on personal business, he did not even question me before giving his permission."

"One has always known that he values your services highly." Mr. Tan was making the pace again now. The use of the phrase "values your services" would, he was sure, bring the matter to a head.

"And yet," said Girija, "I was glad he did not ask me questions." He paused.

Mr. Tan was silent. He was certain that the moment had arrived.

Girija flashed a smile. "For if he had, I would have been forced to hurt his feelings or to lie. I would not wish to do either of those things."

"Both are offenses against good taste," agreed Mr. Tan sententiously.

"Mr. Wright has been my father," said Girija. "How could I tell him that, being in need of the wisest advice on a matter of great importance, I was turning not to him but to Mr. Tan Siow Mong?"

Mr. Tan said nothing. He had nothing relevant to say. He was hurriedly revising his estimate of the situation. If the clerk were choosing this way of leading up to a request for money, he must have some absurdly large sum in mind.

Girija leaned forward earnestly. "Nowhere in Kuala Pangkalan is there a wiser head in important matters of business," he said. "It is well known."

Mr. Tan noted the qualifying phrase, "in important matters of business." He said: "You pay me an undeserved compliment."

"My friend," continued Girija, "could think of no one else whose advice on this matter would be so valuable."

"Your friend?" Mr. Tan was becoming confused again and in consequence also a little annoyed; but his tone remained polite.

"You do not know him, sir," said Girija, "and he knows you only from your high reputation. When I said that I would ask your advice on this important matter that is troubling him, he begged me not to mention him by name. The matter is highly confidential."

"Most business matters are." Mr. Tan spoke dryly. He guessed that "confidential" in this context probably meant "criminal."

Girija's smile became tentative. For the first time Mr. Tan saw him ill at ease, and decided to offer a word of reassurance. It would be irritating if the man took fright and left without revealing the object of his visit.

"If your friend respects my wisdom," he remarked, "he must also acknowledge my discretion."

Girija's smile went back into place and his eyes met Mr. Tan's. "Of course. But he is a nervous man. You will see why when I explain." He paused to choose his words before going on. "It appears that some years ago, during the emergency, when the terrorists were bringing in arms from the north, my friend found some of these arms—rifles machine guns, ammunition." He looked up to see how Mr. Tan was taking this.

Mr. Tan smiled, but very faintly. "And so he turned them over to the police?"

"That, of course, is what he should have done." Girija shrugged. "But, as I said, my friend is a nervous man. He did not wish to call attention to himself. At the time, it seemed best to do nothing. Now he is in a difficulty."

"Yes?"

"My friend is in need of money. He thought of these arms. If he told the police about them now, there would be questions and trouble. But if a buyer for the arms could be found, perhaps his debts could be paid, and no one would be the worse. The emergency is over. No harm could come of it, only good for my friend."

Mr. Tan sat very still. "You wish me to advise your friend?"

Girija nodded. "That is what he hopes you may do, sir. Yes."

"He should still take the matter to the police. It would be very wrong to try to sell them. He need not say that he found them long ago, but he should certainly go to the police."

Girija spread out his hands. "But, sir, my friend has debts."

"It is better to go to a money lender than to risk going to prison."

Girija smiled triumphantly. "That was exactly my own advice to him, sir. To risk going to prison for a few hundred dollars is the act of a fool. I told him so."

Mr. Tan hesitated. The agreement baffled him. He knew instinctively that somewhere, somehow, he had mismanaged the conversation. He knew that he was left with only one question to ask, and that when he had asked it he would have lost a battle of wits. But he also knew that his curiosity would have to be satisfied. Mentally he shrugged off the humiliation.

"And what was his reply?" he asked.

Girija's hand went to the row of ball-point pens in his shirt pocket and drew from behind it a folded sheet of paper. He opened it out and handed it across the desk.

"This paper, sir," he said. "My friend gave me this paper."

Mr. Tan took the paper, spread it out on the desk in front of him, and looked down. It was a typed list with the word INVENTORY at the head of it. He read on:

Description	Type	Quantity	Today's Free Market Value ($ Straits)
Rifles	.303 Military S.A. Belge	54	16,000
.303 Ammo	For above	5,000 rds	6,000
Machine pistols	Schmeisser	25	18,000
.300 Ammo	With magazines for above	8,000 rds	7,000
Bazookas	U.S. Govt. pattern	4	6,000
Ammo for same	" " "	35 rds	1,000
Grenades	Mills unfused	} 100	2,000
Fuses	For same		
Land mines	Teller	40	4,000
		Total	60,000
		Equals £ (Sterling)	7,500
		Equals $ (U.S.)	21,000

Note   All items in brand new mint condition in original mnfrs. packings, containers, etc.
Prices   All prices f.o.b. vicinity Kuala Pangkalan
Terms and Conditions   Items sold separate subject 20% increase.

Mr. Tan looked up.

"You see, sir," said Girija softly, "I was wrong. It is not just a matter of a few hundred dollars, but of many thousands."

Mr. Tan pretended to read the list through a second time in order to give himself time to think. He had little doubt that the "friend" for whom the clerk claimed to be acting was nonexistent. The Indian must have been desperate for money to take the risk of approaching a comparative stranger in this way, or very sure of himself as a judge of character. Mr. Tan had an uneasy feeling that the latter explanation might be the more likely. The fellow looked confident enough, and not at all desperate. Of course, he could be lying, and the whole story could be a mere trick to get money; but Mr. Tan did not really think so. In any case, it would be simple to find out. He looked up again and met the clerk's yes.

"My friend," said Girija, "would be willing to pay a commission of fifty per cent to anyone who found a buyer, and who would take delivery of the goods."

Mr. Tan shook his head. "But this would be a serious criminal matter. Does your friend not understand that?"

"That was my first thought, too," said Girija approvingly, "but he did not agree. This is not stolen property, he says. It has no owner. If it should leave the country, the police would have no interest in it. The emergency is over."

"But the laws remain."

"That is true." Girija nodded thoughtfully. "You think, then, sir, that I should tell my friend that you advise him to go to the police?"

"I think you should tell him to put the whole matter out of his mind." Mr. Tan paused and then added: "Perhaps later the law will not be so strict."

"Yes, that is so."

"Such merchandise as this is always saleable." Mr. Tan looked down again at the list. "Have you seen any of these items?"

"My friend is naturally careful."

"But do you believe him? You say he wishes to find a buyer. A list is not proof that there is something to sell. Could he produce samples?"

"He would be more than ready to do that, sir."

Mr. Tan refolded the inventory. "I know little about these matters," he said, "but I have heard that buyers in this market are not easy to reach. Contacts must be found. Time must be spent. There can be no urgency."

"My friend is very patient."

"Then, do as I suggest. Tell him to forget for a while." He looked up at Girija. "You agree?"

"Of course, sir."

Mr. Tan held up the list. "And I may keep this paper?"

It was a test question.

Girija smiled. "My friend will be happy for it to remain in such wise hands, sir."

He rose. The interview was over. When the usual courtesies had been exchanged, he left.

Mr. Tan watched him walk away across the yard, then sent for the Chiang Thye Phu Syndicate estate's files.

The first thing was to find out whether the clerk's discretion and sense of self-preservation were as lively as they had appeared to be. If he had been foolhardy enough to type out his list on Mr. Wright's estate-office typewriter, and then leave it with someone who could, if it seemed advantageous, go to the authorities and gain credit by reporting the incident, Mr. Tan wanted no more to do with him and would burn the paper at once. If, as he suspected, the young man had been careful to leave himself in a position to deny effectively all knowledge of the conversation they had just had, and of the list, then something might be made of the situation.

He looked through Mr. Wright's office consignment notes and compared the typing on them with that of the list. It was obvious that the list had not been typed on the same machine. So far so good. He read through the list once more and then locked it in his private office safe.

Later that day, when he had had further time to think, he wrote to his brother in Singapore.

ii

Tan Yam Heng was the disreputable member of the family. Such, at least, was the view of his brothers in Kuala Pangkalan and Manila.

He was one of the founders of the Singapore Democratic Action Party and organizer of a waterfront trade union which, though small in membership, had sufficient nuisance value to levy tribute on two of the bigger stevedoring companies. As the fruits of these negotiations were always handed over to him personally, privately, and in cash, he did not consider it necessary to report their receipt either to the union auditors or to the income-tax authorities. He had no time to waste on the pettifogging rituals of accountancy and other hindrances to social progress. He saw himself as a man of power, a manipulator of puppets, choosing to work behind the scenes until the strategic moment came for him to step forward and lead his party on to victory.

If that had been all there was to say of him, his brothers would have been

content. His political pretensions they could ignore, and, devious men themselves, they did not seriously object to his methods of augmenting his income.
What they did object to, strongly, was what he did with it.

Most Chinese like to gamble, and with some this liking becomes an addiction as compulsive as those of drugs or alcohol. Yam Heng was a gambler of
this kind. Moreover, he was a stupid gambler. Games of chance are at least
subject to the law of averages, race horses do sometimes run true to form,
and skill can often qualify bad luck at poker; but Yam Heng's conceit and
fantasies of omnipotence had in the end demanded more esoteric gratifica-
tions. He had taken to gambling on the "pickle" market.

This unofficial market in raw rubber is conducted by freebooters operating
outside the respectable Singapore brokerage houses, and they are speculating
on small price fluctuations over short periods. On the pickle market a consignment of rubber in transit may theoretically change hands several times
in the course of a day. Large sums of money are made and lost on feverish,
bull-and-bear transactions. The successful speculators are Chinese with great
experience, cool heads, and reliable intelligence organizations. Much use is
made of the time difference between the London and Singapore markets, and
a few minutes' lead on a piece of cabled information can make thousands of
dollars for its possessor. It is the efficient who generally win; the gamblers
who generally lose.

The pickle market was no place for Yam Heng. The acquaintance who had
introduced him to it was one of a syndicate of small men, and they had been
perfectly willing to let an outsider buy in; the stronger the syndicate, the
better; but his arrogant impatience with their wariness and caution had soon
antagonized them. Eventually he had taken his money out of the syndicate
and started to operate on his own.

If he had immediately and heavily lost, the blow to his self-esteem might
have caused him to think twice about continuing. Unfortunately, he had won.
After that, it had been too late for second thoughts.

His early appeals for loans had been received by his brothers with frater-
nal tolerance, and responded to in the belief that the money lent would be
repaid. They had known, of course, that he was overfond of gambling, but
had believed his profligacy in that respect to be confined to horse racing or
fan-tan. The discovery of the true nature of the "investments" they were so
innocently subsidizing had been a disagreeable shock; so had the realization
that Yam Heng had been deceitfully making his applications simultaneously,
and in identical terms, to both of them.

There had been worse to come. In the face of their joint refusals to lend
him another cent, Yam Heng had blandly informed them that the various union

funds in his charge were some thousands of dollars short, and that unless the shortages were made good before the annual audit, the consequences for the Tan name might be serious. There had been hasty consultation between Kuala Pangkalan and Manila. The brothers had paid up in the end, but only after both of them had been to Singapore and personally checked the union books. The days when Yam Heng could be trusted had gone. Thereafter, he had the status somewhat of a poor relation—a responsibility to be discharged as inexpensively as possible.

It was with this responsibility in mind that Mr. Tan had written his letter. Some weeks earlier he had received one of Yam Heng's periodic requests for money and noted a veiled belligerence in the wording. It had reminded him that the annual audit of the union books was due shortly, and that Yam Heng would soon be making his annual attempt to extort money by hinting at another raid on the union funds. Mr. Tan's nerves were strong, and for the previous three years he had successfully refused to be intimidated; but he knew gamblers, and there was always the chance that one day Yam Heng might become desperate.

At that moment, in fact, Yam Heng was merely depressed. He had had two small wins in the past two weeks and a bigger loss which had canceled out the winnings. His brother's letter annoyed him.

It contained a polite inquiry after his health, a detailed account of their mother's most recent illness, and a proposal that he visit Kuala Pangkalan at a convenient moment in the near future. It mentioned that the junk *Happy Dawn* would be unloading in Singapore the following week, and that the master would be instructed to offer him a free passage. It gave no hint of a possible reason for the visit.

Yam Heng knew his brother too well to suppose that the visit had been proposed for any social or family reason. Their mother was senile. Her current state of health could only have been mentioned to make the invitation seem logical to some stranger reading the letter. Yam Heng disliked having his curiosity aroused unless he had the means on hand to satisfy it. The offer of the junk passage irritated him also. It was his brother's way of saying that if he wanted to travel in comfort by train or plane, he could pay his own fare. He considered sending a dignified reply regretting that pressure of work compelled him to decline the invitation; but, finally, curiosity and the faint hope of another loan decided him to accept. He had just enough money for the train fare.

His brother met him at the station, greeted him warmly, and drove him to the ornate brick-and-stucco house in Willoughby Road. The first evening was spent in celebrating the family reunion. Old Mrs. Tan emerged from her room, an elaborate dinner was consumed, the young children made their Uncle Yam tell them about Singapore, and the eldest son showed his Voigtlander camera and some of the colorslide photographs of birds which he had made with it. Yam Heng found it all very agreeable. His brother remained friendly and courteous. There were no references, oblique or otherwise, to their long estrangement, or to the reasons for it. He permitted himself a few restrained smiles, some delicate compliments to his sister-in-law, and a joke or two with the younger children.

It was not until the following day that his brother revealed the reason for the invitation. In the morning they toured the godowns, visited the truck-maintenance shed, and watched one of the junks unloading fifty-gallon drums of fuel oil. Then they went to the office and tea was served.

"And how," Siow Mong inquired at last, "is the pickle market?"

Yam Heng gave him an impassive stare.

"I ask," Siow Mong continued after a pause, "not in a spirit of criticism, but because I want information."

For one wild moment Yam Heng wondered if his brother were contemplating a foray of his own. Then he shrugged. "Some make money, some lose."

His brother nodded sagely as if he had had a suspicion confirmed. "I did hear," he went on, "that there is another thriving market now in Singapore."

"There are markets there in most things."

"Yes. But I heard—I cannot remember from what source—that the market in arms is particularly active at present."

"Oh, yes." Yam Heng spoke indifferently. "The Indonesian rebels are trying to buy. They have several purchasing agents there."

"Several?"

"There is one from Sumatra, one from Java, another from Celebes. They are united only in their opposition to the central government."

"They compete?"

Yam Heng shrugged. "They must. There is not so much to buy. It is not easy."

"How do they pay? Rupiahs?"

"Nobody would take rupiahs. Pounds or dollars, I suppose."

"Dollars U.S.?"

"Straits or Hong Kong dollars, I would think. Why?"

"Cash?"

"I suppose so."

His brother nodded approvingly. "I would think this a very satisfactory business."

"No doubt it is."

"These agents you speak of—you know them?"

"I know who they are, yes."

"Have you not thought of taking an interest in the business yourself?"

Yam Heng smiled sourly. "The peddler cannot do business with an empty tray."

"And if the tray were to be filled?"

Yam Heng hesitated. His brother was not in the habit of making idle remarks. "That would require capital," he said cautiously.

"Not necessarily."

Siow Mong went over to his private safe, got out the piece of paper Girija had left with him, and handed it to Yam Heng.

"That was brought to me by a man who wants a buyer for those goods," he said.

Yam Heng read the list through carefully. His expression did not change. When he had finished, he glanced up at his brother. "It says that delivery must be taken in the *vicinity* of Kuala Pangkalan. What does that mean?"

Siow Mong told him about Girija's visit and summarized the conversation they had had.

Yam Heng listened without interrupting, and then read through the list again. He spoke as he read.

"Is this Indian to be trusted?"

"I think so. If he gets what he wants."

"I know very little about this market. Are these prices realistic?"

"I was able to make only one inquiry. There is a dealer in machinery here who used to import sporting rifles. Naturally, I had to be careful how I asked, but from what I was able to learn I would think these prices are three times what they should be. But in a sellers' market, who knows?"

"I could find out in Singapore." Yam Heng paused. "What is your proposal?"

Siow Mong sat down behind his desk and leaned forward across it. "You are a gambler, brother," he said pleasantly, "and you know what I think of that. Especially as, in the game you play, you cannot win. I am inviting you to try a different one."

"Selling arms is no game."

"It can be very profitable." Siow Mong's smile faded. "Let us have no misunderstandings. I have a good business here. I do not like risks. I do not have to take them. If you can find a way to handle this transaction without personal risk to me, I will help you, for a small handling charge of ten per cent. But I must know exactly what you intend to do, first. If I agree with your plan, I will put you in touch with the Indian. Is that understood?"

Yam Heng had been listening absently and did not reply to his brother's question. "There are two problems here," he said slowly. "The first is to get the goods out of the country. That is a matter of careful organization. The second problem is more difficult. They must be made respectable."

Siow Mong waited. Yam Heng might be a fool in many respects, but he could sometimes be shrewd.

"You see," Yam Heng continued after a moment or two, "if *I* were to sell these goods in Singapore, I might never receive payment. They would deal, yes; but these are not normal business dealings. There is no trust. 'Payment on delivery,' they would say. But when I had delivered, they could give me a five-thousand-dollar tip and tell me to go to the police for the rest. What could I answer in such a case? You say that these are not stolen goods, and no doubt you are right. But I would be as helpless as if they were, if I had to deal illegally."

"What is the alternative? How do you make such property respectable?"

"There must be an intermediary, someone who will sign papers, admit ownership if necessary, and take perhaps five per cent for his trouble."

"A Frenchman or an American, perhaps?"

"What sort of person? An Englishman?"

"It would be better if he were not a subject of the Federation or of Singapore. I am thinking of the emergency regulations."

"There are Americans doing such business."

"Could you approach one of them?"

Yam Heng pursed his lips. "This would be too small for those men, I think. Besides, they would want too much for themselves. We do not need an experienced man."

Siow Mong thought for a moment. Then he asked: "Have you met Khoo Ah Au?"

"Who is he?"

"I was forgetting that you have been out of touch with family affairs. He married our niece in Manila last year. They live in Hong Kong now. Perhaps he would know of a suitable American. I shall be going there next month. I might discuss the requirements with him. Possibly . . ." He broke off. "But this is all talk. You say that to ship the goods is only a matter of organization. How would you do it?"

Yam Heng told him.

His brother listened and was impressed. "It might be done," he admitted grudgingly at last.

They discussed some details, and later that day Siow Mong telephoned Girija. He referred to their recent conversation and then said that although he, Mr. Tan, could do nothing in the matter, he had heard of a Mr. Lee who might be able to give useful advice. A meeting was arranged.

iii

Girija never guessed that "Mr. Lee" was Mr. Tan's brother. Mr. Tan was refined. Mr. Lee had coarse, heavy features, a sullen expression, and a hectoring, impatient way of speaking that bordered on rudeness. Girija did not like him.

They met at a rest house not far from the estate. Mr. Lee had taken a room there for the night, and they identified one another without difficulty.

The first meeting was brief. Mr. Lee produced Girija's list and asked him if he were prepared to prove the existence of the items listed by producing a sample of any one of them that Mr Lee himself selected.

Girija nodded. "I have already said that my friend could give a sample if required. I ask only that the item chosen should be small and light."

"How small? How light?"

"Small and light enough to be carried in the pocket. You would not ask me to cycle along the road with a rifle on my back."

"Is a machine-pistol loading clip small enough?"

"Yes. And I will bring a few rounds of ammunition with it."

"When?"

"Monday."

"Today is Thursday. Why not tomorrow?"

"It cannot be arranged before Monday."

"Very well. But I have no time to waste."

On Sunday Girija went out to Awang and made his way up to the dump. It was several months since he had last repaired the shelter, and the screens were in a bad state. The termites were back again, too. He hoped that Mr. Lee was in as much of a hurry as he professed to be.

On Monday he met Mr. Lee again and showed him some ammunition and a clip.

Mr. Lee wiped the grease off the clip and examined the German markings carefully. Finally he put the clip in his pocket.

"That would seem to be in order," he said. "Naturally, I will have to check these marks. In the meantime I must have some information. Where would delivery take place?"

"In this area."

"What do you consider would be needed to transport the goods?"

"One thirty-hundredweight truck."

"Are the goods near a road?"

"Not at present. They can be brought to a loading point fifty yards from a road, but that operation will require three days' advance notice."

"That may be difficult."

"It must be allowed for." Girija spoke with assurance. He had had three years to solve this problem in logistics, and knew that there was only one answer to it.

"You say fifty yards from a road. Would you and your friend be there to help with the loading? It would have to be done at night."

"I or my friend would be there. Two men could do the loading in less than an hour. The heaviest boxes are those with the rifles. There are nine of them, and they weigh about forty pounds each. But they have rope handles."

Mr. Lee looked at him with interest. "You speak as if you have had experience before."

"I am a businessman, Mr. Lee." Girija paused. "Perhaps, now that you have examined the samples, we should discuss financial arrangements and terms."

Mr. Lee took the list from his pocket. "These prices you mention are foolish. You knew that, of course."

Girija smiled. "I knew that you would say they were foolish, Mr. Lee. And, of course, I understand. These are always difficult goods to sell. The right buyer may not be found immediately. The demand fluctuates. Handling and storage charges are high. You must work on a very small margin of profit. That is why I am prepared to pay fifty per cent of these estimated prices to the selling agent."

"*You* are prepared, Mr. Krishnan? What about your friend?"

Girija was not disconcerted. "I am authorized to speak for him at present," he said. "I say 'at present' because my friend is considering the possibility of going to Singapore and investigating the market personally."

"Could your friend move the goods?"

"He is a patient man. He could wait."

Mr. Lee did not reply immediately. He was tired of Girija's toothy smile and the knowing lilt in his voice. "Your prices are foolish," he repeated coldly.

Girija smiled again. "Then I will reduce them, Mr. Lee. I will accept thirty thousand dollars Malay net."

"That is an insignificant reduction."

"It is the only one I can make."

"I will pay twenty thousand."

They compromised in the end on twenty-five thousand, to be paid one month after the goods were handed over. A protocol for the transaction was also agreed. Under this, each of the high contracting parties was protected against murder or trickery on the part of the other. The meeting ended in an atmosphere of goodwill and mutual respect.

The following day Tan Yam Heng took the train back to Singapore.

The following week Tan Siow Mong flew up to Hong Kong. He was there for only two days; but he was able to spend an entertaining and constructive evening with his niece and her husband, Khoo Ah Au.

Three

TWELVE HOURS OUT of Kobe, the *Silver Isle* ran into bad weather and more than half her ninety passengers took to their cabins.

She was owned by the Isle Line, which operated a freight run between San Francisco and Calcutta, calling at Yokohama, Kobe, Hong Kong, Manila, Saigon, Singapore, and, occasionally, Rangoon. With the growing popularity of round-the-world trips, the company's passenger traffic had increased rapidly, and they had refitted two of their newer ships so as to enlarge and improve the cabin accommodation. The *Silver Isle* was one of these. Unfortunately, the improvements, which included an extra deck, had also added considerably to her top hamper, and in any but the calmest sea she rolled heavily.

For Greg Nilsen, however, the bad weather came as a blessing. Both he and Dorothy, his wife, were good sailors and could go down to the dining room with their appetites unimpaired. True, Dorothy did complain that the incessant rolling made her tired; but he could only view that as a minor inconvenience. As far as he was concerned, any weather conditions that kept Arlene Drecker confined to her cabin were fine.

Greg was an engineer and the owner of a precision die-casting business in Wilmington, Delaware. He and Dorothy had been planning their round-the-world trip for over two years—ever since their younger boy had gone to college.

They could have done it earlier if they had been prepared to fly most of the way, but Dorothy had said no. She had wanted to do it properly—by sea, and in small, slow boats.

"After all," she had said, "we're only going to be able to do it once in our lives. All the tourists go to Tokyo and Hong Kong and Paris and Rome, places like that. I think we ought to see some of the little out-of-the-way places as well; the ones most people just read about, or see pictures of in photographic books; wonderful places like Tahiti, where the cruise ships don't go."

Greg had agreed with her. However, a few evenings spent with maps, sailing lists, and an eighteen-inch globe had modified their views. They had found, for example, that if they wanted to go to Japan and Hong Kong, a one-day visit to Tahiti would add two weeks to their travel schedule. In the end it was plain that, even if they compromised on the size and speed of the boats, confined themselves to the regular ports of call, and cut out South America completely, the trip would still take at least two months. If they did not want to spend all the time traveling, it would take three.

Greg had some very capable men working for him, but, at the management level, Nilsen Die-Casting and Tools was very much a one-man business. A three-month vacation could not be embarked upon just when he felt like it; and although he had for some time been planning a reorganization that would enable him to delegate more responsibility, it involved changes that could only be made gradually. He had allowed two years—one in which to make the changes, and one in which to see that they worked—but, even so, it had still not been easy to get away. There had been some moments in the month before they had sailed when difficulties over a new government contract had made it look as if the trip would have to be called off. However, the difficulties had been ironed out in time and they had left Wilmington early in October. Because of the amount of baggage they were taking, they had gone by train to San Francisco. They had sailed on the seventh.

Neither of them had traveled much by ship before. During the war Greg had gone to Europe on a troopship. Together they had been to England and France and back on the *United States* and the *America*. That was all. They had received much advice from more experienced friends. One of them, Greg remembered later, had had a solemn warning to deliver.

"It's the first two or three days you want to be careful of," this man had said, "and especially the first day just after you sail. You're going to be with those people for weeks. But you'll be feeling strange and want to be friendly. You'll go into the bar and have a drink to celebrate the start of the trip. Watch it. Don't start getting friendly with anyone. Wait. You start talking to someone, and before you know it, bingo, you're stuck with the ship's bore. It can ruin a trip."

Arlene Drecker was not the ship's bore, but, as far as Greg was concerned, she became an even more maddening affliction.

After the ship had sailed, he and Dorothy had stayed on deck until they had cleared the Golden Gate. They had promised the boys to make a complete photographic record of the trip, and Greg had been up on the boat deck with the 16 mm. Bell and Howell for the best part of an hour. It had been a sunny day, but with a cool breeze. They had been glad, when there was no more to see aloft, to get down into the warmth of the bar for a pre-lunch drink.

Arlene had been sitting by herself at a small table about six feet away from them. She had been writing radio telegrams and sipping a Martini. Then the pen she had borrowed from the writing room had run out of ink, and she had looked round in exasperation. Greg had politely offered her his. She had accepted. Later, when she returned his pen, she had asked them to have a drink.

"No, no. You join us," Dorothy had said.

Arlene had smiled. "You know, a gal traveling alone has one big problem— how to persuade people to sometimes let her buy a drink."

Nevertheless, she had joined them and had another Martini. They had gone down to lunch together. Later that day the chief steward had approached Greg with the permanent seating plan for the dining room and asked if he and Mrs. Nilsen minded having Miss Drecker sit at their table. There were no single tables, he had explained, and Miss Drecker did not want to be with a crowd. Greg had had little choice but to agree.

That night, when they went down to dinner, there had been a bottle of champagne on the table—to thank them, Arlene had explained, for letting her sit with them, and to drink a toast to the voyage.

Later, in their cabin, Greg had grumbled about this. He did not care for champagne, which always gave him indigestion; but Dorothy had not been sympathetic. It showed, she had said, that Arlene did not intend to impose on them. The champagne had been a very nice way of telling them that. The fact that it gave him indigestion was beside the point. Dorothy had taken a liking to Arlene.

She was a tall, angular blonde with large white teeth, a beige complexion, and very thin legs. Dorothy deduced from things said that she was probably in her late forties, but she certainly looked younger. She dressed smartly and in a vaguely masculine style that suited her, although she was inclined sometimes to overload herself with chunky gold bracelets and wear earrings which accentuated the narrowness of her head. She talked freely, and not unamusingly, about herself in a carefully mellifluous voice which creaked slightly on each change of register. Her father had been a Los Angeles real-estate man. During the war she had been in the American Red Cross and had stayed on with that organization in France and Germany until '47. Then her father had died and she had gone back to California. She had a house in Palm Springs now, which she rented when she went away on her trips. She had never had any great desire to get married, although she liked married people and was crazy about kids. But things had to work out right, or it was no good. She had a sister who had been married four times, and what a mess and misery all that had been. Her attitude toward men was one of sardonic camaraderie tinged with disdain.

By the fourth day out, Greg's dislike of her had become intense. The bottle of champagne had been a minor irritant; but when at dinner on the second night a bottle of claret had appeared, he had objected.

"It was very thoughtful of you, Miss Drecker," he had said, "but Dorothy and I don't drink wine as a regular thing. So if you don't mind . . ."

"But the steward's already opened it. Oh, come on, Mr. Nilsen. Live dangerously."

Dorothy had giggled. The steward had smiled and poured the wine.

"Now, look, Dorothy," Greg had said when they were alone, "Arlene Drecker can drink all the wine she wants and so can you, for that matter. But I'm not having her tell me what I'm going to drink."

"She didn't mean it that way."

"I don't care what way she meant it. The way it worked out was that I had to drink something I didn't want or seem boorish. Dammit, she's not our hostess on this ship. I wish she'd stop behaving as if she were."

"She's only trying to be friendly."

"Listen. If you want wine or we want wine, *I'll* order it."

The following night Arlene had ordered burgundy; but Greg had taken the precaution of ordering in advance a bottle of *rosé* and the two wines arrived together.

"Too bad," Greg had said blandly. "What about joining us and having rosé, Arlene?"

"Rosé with roast beef?" Arlene had raised her eyebrows. "Thanks, I prefer burgundy."

But the next night, when the steward had produced the partly consumed bottle of burgundy, Arlene had not pressed them to share it with her. Greg had succeeded in making his point. It had not been until later in the evening that he had discovered that she had paid his bar bill for the day. Dorothy had not been able to help laughing.

Two days before they had reached Yokohama, a notice had gone up announcing that, during the ship's stay in port, conducted sightseeing tours ashore had been arranged. Those passengers wishing to take advantage of the special rates offered should inform the purser's office within the next twenty-four hours.

Greg had put his and Dorothy's names down. At lunch Dorothy had mentioned the fact.

Arlene had stared at her incredulously. "Sightseeing tours! Honey, you must be out of your mind."

"What's wrong with sightseeing tours?" Greg had asked. "After all, that's what we're making the trip for—to see sights."

"Oh, Greg!" Arlene had laughed tolerantly. "Have you ever been on a Japanese sightseeing tour?"

"Have you?"

"Yes, and I can tell you it's the end. They just cram you into a bus, give you a box lunch, and then drive you from one clip joint to another. They don't want to show you what you want to see. They just want you to buy things—cameras, fans, bits of fake jewelry."

"That's not what it says on the notice board."

"Naturally. Look, if you want to go rubber-necking, let me take you. I've been before. All you do is hire a car and have the man drive you around. You're on your own. You can stop when you want and go on when you want."

Dorothy had turned to him uncertainly. "What do you think, Greg?"

"Well, we've put our names down now."

Arlene had sighed. "Well, take them off again. Why not? If you want to be tourists, you may as well do it properly. This is not the best time of the year to come to Japan, but, since you are here, at least make yourselves comfortable."

Unhappily, she had been right. Those who had gone on the sightseeing tour had returned exhausted, ill-tempered, and late for dinner. Dorothy had had a fascinating day and bought a pair of carved soapstone hairpins which the barman said were worth at least three times what she had paid for them.

The following day, and then later at Kobe, the performance had been repeated. It could have been his fancy, but Greg suspected that both Dorothy and Arlene had a tacit agreement to ignore his leadership and run things their own way. When the table steward had reported that Miss Drecker was staying in her cabin, seasick, it had required an effort of will to utter the appropriate words of regret.

The bad weather lasted for two days and Greg thoroughly enjoyed them both. When on the third day Arlene made a wan appearance at lunch, he was almost as solicitous as Dorothy.

Then came the misunderstanding over the ship's shuffleboard tournament. The doctor had wanted Greg and Dorothy on his team, and Greg, without consulting Dorothy, had accepted. When the first round was announced over the ship's loudspeakers, Dorothy was missing. Greg found her eventually in Arlene's cabin playing Scrabble. By the time he had explained what had happened and they had reached the deck, the teams had been rearranged and they were out of the tournament.

Greg was annoyed. He did not mind about the shuffleboard, which he thought an old man's game, but he did mind having to apologize to the doctor.

Dorothy was very reasonable about it. "I'm sorry, dear, but you didn't tell me, did you?"

"I thought you were around on deck."

"Well, you were reading and Arlene suggested Scrabble. I know how you hate that, so I didn't bother you."

"Did you have to play down in the cabin?"

"She's got a very comfortable cabin. You haven't seen it. It's twice the size of ours. Look, dear, I'm sure the doctor didn't mind a bit. He understood."

"Yes, I know. But all the same . . ."

All the same, he was annoyed. That evening, when Arlene and Dorothy began to talk about the shopping they were going to do in Hong Kong, his annoyance returned.

"The big stores are in Victoria," Arlene was saying. "That's on Hong Kong island itself. But for us gals the best places are over in Kowloon. That's on the mainland. There's one called Star of Siam in the Peninsular Hotel that's a must."

"Shops in a hotel?" asked Dorothy.

"That's right. There are two whole floors of them."

"Sounds like a tourist trap to me," said Greg.

Arlene smiled at him. "What would you say to a suit in the best English tropical worsted, made to order, for twenty-five dollars?"

"Oh, sure, I know all about that. They just copy a suit you have and it falls to pieces the first time you wear it."

Arlene smiled again, very gently. "Is that what happens? I've never heard that, not from anyone who's really been there and bought one."

"Why don't you try, dear?" said Dorothy. "I mean, twenty-five dollars for a suit is cheap. And you do need some more summer outfits."

"Brooks Brothers is good enough for me." He knew it was a dull, foolish remark even as he said it.

"Well, it's not important." Dorothy spoke a trifle grimly.

Arlene's silence was monumentally tactful.

It was a Sunday night and there was no dancing after dinner. When Arlene had gone to her cabin, Dorothy suggested a walk around the deck before they went to bed.

After a while she said: "Darling, I'm worried. I'm having a good time, a wonderful time. You don't seem to be."

"Because I don't happen to want to buy a suit in Hong Kong?"

"Now you're being tiresome."

"All right. That woman gets on my nerves."

"Arlene? But she's really a very nice person."

"Well, I don't like her and I wish she'd get out of our hair."

"She's not in *my* hair. I think she's being very sweet and helpful. Can you imagine what it would have been like in Tokyo if we hadn't been lucky enough to have her to show us around? It couldn't have been very exciting for her. She'd seen it all before. She went to a lot of trouble for us."

"Well, I wish she'd go to a lot of trouble for somebody else. Anyway, if she's seen it all before, why does she come on the trip?"

"Greg, dear, you're usually more understanding and tolerant. She's a very lonely woman."

"And for some very good reasons."

"That's an unkind thing to say. It doesn't sound like you."

"Well, it is me. I told you, I don't like the woman. The chief steward told me she didn't want to sit with a crowd. Why not, if she's so lonely? Why did she have to pick on us?"

Dorothy did not reply immediately, and they walked once around the deck in silence.

"Look, darling," she said finally, "we didn't come on this trip just for a vacation, but because we wanted to travel and because we wanted to see something of the world outside America. If we were multimillionaires, maybe we could have done it in our own private yacht. As it is, we have to go with other people. We're not in a position to choose our traveling companions, any more than they're in a position to choose us. So, we've all got to make the best of one another. Isn't that common sense?"

Greg chuckled. "It's a poem, and beautifully delivered."

"Greg, I'm serious."

"I know you are, dear." He drew her arm through his. "That's why you're so cute."

He had recovered his good humor. Dorothy's homilies usually had that effect on him. Before they were married, she had taught at a kindergarten school, and in moments of stress traces of the old Montessori manner were still discernible.

"You're maddening," she said.

"I know it." He stopped and kissed her cheek. "All right, darling, we'll be nice, well-behaved American tourists spreading sweetness and light and hard currency wherever we go."

"If you'll just spread a little of that sweetness in Arlene's direction, that's all I ask."

"You said make the best of one another. Okay, I'll make the best of her, whatever that is."

"Thank you, dear."

He sighed. "Anyway, I'll try."

And, for some days, try he did.

The *Silver Isle* was to be in Hong Kong for forty-eight hours, discharging and taking on cargo, and she docked on the Kowloon side of the harbor by the wharfs on the Canton Road.

This was convenient for the passengers. They could go ashore any time they wanted, and were within easy walking distance of both the ferry to Victoria and the Peninsular Hotel.

Left to themselves, Greg and Dorothy would probably have taken the ferry straightaway and gone across to see Hong Kong itself; but Arlene led them first to the hotel.

"There'll be plenty of time for sightseeing later," she told them. "Let's get organized first. I suppose you've heard that these Chinese can make anything from a pair of earrings to a man's tuxedo overnight. Well, it just is not true. If you want anything properly made, you have to give them at least thirty-six hours. So let's do our shopping first, and then we don't have to worry."

They window-shopped for a while in the hotel, and then the girls left Greg with a tailor named Mr. Yu and went back to the Star of Siam to order Thai silk skirts. They had arranged to meet in the hotel lobby. When Greg had chosen his suit materials and had his measurements taken, he made his way down there.

He knew that he had at least half an hour to wait. It was too early for a drink. There was a row of travel agents' booths in the lobby, most of them offering sightseeing tours. It might be a good idea, he thought, to see about renting a car and driver.

The moment that thought came into his head another one followed it: "Maybe I'd better check with Arlene first." It was enough. He said "God dammit" between his teeth, and went over to the nearest booth.

A Chinese in a black business suit came forward.

"Good morning, sir. What can I do for you?"

"I want to rent a limousine with a driver to take us around. Do you have cars?"

"We do not have our own cars, but we can arrange that for you, sir. An American car, if you wish. When and for how long would you want it?"

"Well, we only have two days. We'd like to see as much as we can. We could start right after lunch from here."

"Then I would suggest, sir, that this afternoon you go across on the car ferry to Hong Kong and drive up to the Peak. There is a magnificent view from there. After that I would suggest a drive to Deep Water Bay and Repulse Bay, with tea at the hotel there. Tomorrow you could tour Kowloon and the New Territories."

"Would that take us as far as the Red Chinese border?"

"Certainly, sir. And you could lunch at Shatin. But I will get you a good driver who will know all these things and make helpful suggestions."

"How much would it cost?"

By the time Arlene and Dorothy arrived it was all settled.

Arlene clearly resented having the arrangements taken out of her hands in this fashion, but had difficulty in finding anything in them to criticize. She did the best she could, however.

"We didn't have to have a car this afternoon," she said. "We could have gone across to the island by the Star ferry and taken a cab on the other side."

"In all this humidity?" said Dorothy. "It's worse than August in New York."

"Humidity?" Arlene smiled knowingly. "You wait until we get to Singapore."

Greg congratulated himself on this small rift in the female alliance; but his satisfaction was short-lived. They went to a Chinese restaurant for lunch and Arlene insisted on their all using chopsticks. It was considered discourteous, she said, to use a fork. Dorothy thought it great fun; but Greg, who liked Chinese food and was hungry, became impatient and dropped some egg on his tie.

After lunch they went back to the Peninsular Hotel to pick up the car and driver.

The car proved to be a three-year-old Chevrolet Bel-Air, and Arlene looked at it disdainfully. The driver was a young Chinese wearing gray flannel trousers, a dark blue blazer, and a chauffeur's cap. He took off the cap and stood respectfully at attention as he held the rear door open for the ladies.

"Want me to go in front with you?" Greg asked him.

"If you do not object, sir, I think you will be more comfortable."

"Okay."

When they were in the car the driver turned to him.

"I see you have a camera, sir. There are certain places on the road up to the Peak where particularly good shots can be obtained. Would you like me to stop at those places?"

"That'd be fine. By the way, what's your name?"

"My Chinese name is Khoo Ah Au, sir." The driver smiled. "American clients find it easier to call me Jimmy."

iii

Khoo Ah Au liked American tourists. He found them, on the whole, generous, easygoing, and completely predictable. They were rarely ill-tempered, as the British often were, or eccentric in their demands, as were the French. They did not harass him with questions he had not been asked before, and listened politely, if sometimes inattentively, to the information he had to impart. They used their light meters conscientiously before taking photographs and bought their souvenirs dutifully at the shops which paid him commission. Above all, he found their personal relationships very easy to read. It was probably a matter of race, he thought. His own people were always very careful not to give themselves away, to expose crude feelings about one another. Americans seemed not to care how much was understood by strangers. It was almost as if they enjoyed being transparent.

This American and these two women, for example. You had only to listen for a few minutes to what they said and how they said it, and everything was clear. The woman called Arlene was attracted to the wife, and the husband was jealous. Possibly he had no cause; possibly the two women had done no more than exchange confidences or touch each other's hands; but he was jealous. And the hungry woman was jealous of him. Only the wife, personable but middle-aged, seemed unconcerned. She did not appear flattered by the situation, or even aware of it. Perhaps she was more subtle than she sounded. When he had listened a little more, he would be able to decide.

They were on the car ferry when he heard something that interested him keenly. "If we'd gone across by the passenger ferry," the Arlene woman was saying, "you'd have been able to get a beautiful shot of the boat in dock."

"Well, maybe I'll do that tomorrow," the American said. "Anyway, there'll be plenty of chances of seeing her in dock."

It was the word "boat" that had interested him. He had assumed that the trio were staying at the Peninsular Hotel because he had been engaged from there. The possibility of their being transit passengers off a boat had not occurred to him.

"You've come by boat, sir?" he inquired diffidently.

"Yes, the *Silver Isle*. Know her?"

"Oh, yes, sir. And are you staying here?"

"No, we're going on in her. Manila, Saigon, Singapore, Rangoon, Calcutta. My wife and I are on a world trip."

"Ah, that is very nice."

They were coming in to the landing ramp now, and his passengers had plenty to engage their attention. It gave him time to think.

Almost two months had elapsed since his wife's uncle had visited them; and, so far, all his attempts to find an American who would meet Mr. Tan's specifications had failed. Moreover, his last attempt had been a frightening failure. The American, a department-store executive from Cleveland, had accused him of trying to work a confidence trick and threatened to go to the police. After that, he had made up his mind to do nothing further in the matter. Unfortunately, Mr. Tan was a highly respected member of his wife's family, and she had begun nagging him about it—not in an angry way, but reproachfully, intimating that his failure to do what her uncle wanted would cause her to lose face. There was also the money to be considered. With the five hundred dollars (Hong Kong) that Mr. Tan had offered for the service, he could go to Cheong Ming and Co. and buy a hi-fi set. But was it worth the risk?

He began to study the American beside him.

He was tall and thin with loose-fitting clothes and short, graying hair. He spoke quietly and with a slight smile in one corner of his mouth. His eyes were watchful and shrewd; but there might be innocence there, too. Not an easy man to deceive; but one who might sometimes deceive himself.

Ah Au drove up toward the Peak. Near the lower cable-car station he stopped so that they could admire the view of the port from the road. The American took his camera and got out of the car.

The Arlene woman said: "There's a much better view from the top."

She and the wife stayed in the car.

Ah Au went over to the American and began pointing out various landmarks in the panorama below them.

"Yes, it's a great place," the American said. "By the way, Jimmy, *is* the view better from up top?"

"There is a fine view there, too, sir, which I will show you in a minute, but this is better for photography. From the Peak there is more haze."

"I see." He was winding the camera.

"Are you using Kodachrome, sir?"

"Yes. Why?"

"From here, sir, at f. eight with a haze filter you will get a very good picture."

"Thanks. You take many pictures?"

"No, sir, but I have such information for my clients."

The camera whirred. As they were walking back to the car, the American said: "Is this your car or do you just drive for someone else?"

"It is my car, sir. I like to give personal service to clients."

"I expect you make more money working for yourself, too."

Ah Au smiled. "There is also that, sir."

The American smiled back.

Ah Au drove on up to the Peak. Some progress had been made, he thought. They had established a personal relationship.

The tour continued. His passengers had tea at the Repulse Bay Hotel. Then he drove them on to the fishing village of Aberdeen and showed them the floating Chinese restaurants. At the Arlene woman's suggestion, it was decided that he should drive them out there to dine the following night. It was on the way back to the ferry that Jimmy had the glimpse of his client's mind for which he had been hoping.

He was driving along Connaught Road, by the long quay where the junks tied up for unloading, when the American turned to him.

"Jimmy, what are all those barges lined up along there? I mean the green painted ones with the yellow stars on them."

"They are junks from Canton, sir."

"But that's in Red China."

"Yes, sir. Canton is only ninety miles away."

"Stop the car. I've got to have some shots of this."

Ah Au parked the car and, leaving the women sitting in it, walked back along the quay with the American. The man seemed curiously excited and was almost tripping over himself in his eagerness to get a closer look at the junks.

"What are they doing here?" he asked.

"They come and go all the time, sir."

"Doing what?"

"Carrying cargo." Ah Au was puzzled. He could not understand why the man was so interested.

"What sort of cargo?"

"Any sort of cargo, sir. That is rattan cane they are unloading. It is made into chairs and baskets here."

"But I don't see any police about. Do you mean they're allowed just to come and go as they please?"

"They are ordinary people. They make no trouble, sir."

"Well, I'll be . . ."

He began to take pictures. When they got back to the car, Ah Au listened thoughtfully as the American told his wife and her friend what he had found out.

The women were interested, and the Arlene one said that it showed what the British had come to when they didn't worry about Communists going in and out of one of their Colonies; but they were not interested the way the man was. As they drove on toward the ferry, Ah Au saw him looking about him intently, as if he were discovering a new meaning in everything he saw.

By the time they reached the mainland Ah Au had decided to take matters a stage further. As he drove them back along the Canton Road to the ship, he asked a question.

"Tomorrow morning, sir, for your tour of the New Territories, do you wish me to go to the Peninsular Hotel, or shall I take the car to the ship?"

"Can you do that?"

"Oh, yes, sir. If I have your name to give at the dock gate."

"My name's Nilsen. Would ten o'clock be okay?"

"Perfectly, sir." He frowned as if making an effort of memory. "Mr. Nilsen, there was another Mr. Nilsen here last year. He was in the textile business. He had a big plant at a place called Dayton, I think. Perhaps you know him."

Mr. Nilsen smiled tolerantly. "No, Jimmy, I don't. I'm an engineer and I have a small die-casting plant at a place called Wilmington. Nilsen's a pretty common name in the United States."

"I beg your pardon. I did not know that. Someday, perhaps, I will be able to go to America."

He congratulated himself. The chances of his being caught out in the lie about a textile man named Nilsen from Dayton had been small. The information gained had been reassuring. Mr. Nilsen was neither a government official, who might consider it his duty to notify the authorities, nor a newspaperman, who might become indiscreet in other ways. He was a respectable businessman of just the type that Mr. Tan had described, and traveling by just the specified route. The problem now was to find a way of putting Mr. Tan's proposition in an attractive light without being either compromised or misunderstood.

When he returned home, Ah Au said nothing to his wife about Mr. Nilsen. He had already decided to make this further attempt to oblige Mr. Tan; but only if a favorable opportunity presented itself. The pressure of her expectations could distort his judgment.

During the night he lay awake for an hour, going over every moment of the afternoon and re-examining his image of Mr. Nilsen. When he was sure that nothing had escaped his attention, he went back to sleep.

The Arlene woman was late, and they did not leave the dock until nearly ten-thirty. Mr. Nilsen controlled his impatience too obviously. It was an inauspicious beginning. Ah Au wanted Mr. Nilsen in as relaxed a mood as possible, and took an early opportunity of suggesting that, as they had plenty of time in hand, they might like to stop at the Castle Peak Hotel for coffee. It was about four miles out on the Tai Po Road, and they would be passing it anyway.

Mrs. Nilsen thought this a good idea, and the tension seemed to slacken. By the time they left Castle Peak and were heading for the frontier, the atmosphere had improved still further. Soon, as they began to pass farms and paddy fields, Ah Au was hearing the familiar exclamations—*Look at that wooden plow! This is really old China! What about those hats with curtains! My God, the smell!*—which told him that his passengers were enjoying themselves.

He drove absently, answering the questions put to him promptly and fully, but not elaborating on his answers. He was waiting for a British army truck to come along. Presently they overtook one, and he slowed to stay behind it. It was, happily, full of troops.

He glanced at Mr. Nilsen and smiled. "We are getting near Red China," he said. "This is the beginning of the military zone."

Mr. Nilsen was leaning forward, staring at the truck. "Are those British troops?"

"Yes, sir, a Scottish regiment. There is a camp farther along this road."

"How many do they have to guard this frontier?"

"One or two battalions, I think."

"One or two battalions!" He turned around. "Did you hear that, Dorothy? Only one or two battalions to guard this frontier. My God, the Reds could walk in here any time they wanted. Isn't that right, Jimmy?"

Ah Au smiled. "Oh, yes, sir. But I think they could do that even if there were two divisions to guard the frontier."

Mr. Nilsen nodded grimly. "You could be right at that. How near to the frontier can we get?"

"About a mile, sir. It is dangerous, you see."

"How dangerous?"

"Sometimes they shoot from the other side at persons moving too close to the frontier line."

"Nice people."

The army truck turned off the road into the camp entrance, and Ah Au put on speed again. He could feel the mounting excitement of the man beside him and wanted to satisfy it.

About a mile and a half from the frontier the road turned sharply to the right and ran parallel to it. However, there was a narrow cart track heading straight on, and Ah Au drove down it until they reached a small farmhouse. The track continued, but a few yards past the house there was a large signboard prohibiting movement beyond that point. Ah Au stopped the car, took a pair of binoculars from the glove compartment, and they all got out.

For about a mile ahead the landscape was flat. Then there was a line of low hills, the sides of which were dotted with groups of burial urns, and a ridge. Along the ridge and near the top of it ran a thin black line.

"That is the frontier, sir." Ah Au handed Mr. Nilsen the binoculars.

"That black line?"

"Yes, it is a barbed-wire fence. There are machine-gun towers, too, but you cannot see them well from here."

Mr. Nilsen scanned the line of the fence from side to side, then handed the binoculars to his wife and got out his camera.

"F. eleven with the haze filter," Ah Au murmured.

Mr. Nilsen nodded and went to work. He did a panning shot first, beginning close on his wife as she looked through the binoculars, then going on to the signboard, then moving into an extreme long shot of the frontier. Then he switched the turret onto the telephoto lens. He used two magazines of film before he was finished.

The Arlene woman became bored and went back to the car. Small children from the farmhouse came out to peer at her through the car windows and hold out their hands for money. Ah Au had to chase them away.

Mr. Nilsen returned to the car reluctantly, and insisted on taking some shots of the farmhouse and the giggling children before he could be persuaded to leave. Even as they bumped along the track back to the road, he kept looking over his shoulder toward the frontier. Ah Au was pleased with the impression it had made.

When they passed the Kowloon-Canton Railway where it curved toward the frontier station, there were more questions.

"Is there a lot of railroad traffic between Kowloon and Canton?"

"Oh, yes, sir. People go to see friends and family in Canton."

"I don't get it. You mean they just go?"

"They must get a permit from the Chinese government office in Hong Kong, but it is quite easy."

"Hear that, Dorothy? So that's the bamboo curtain!"

"You wish to go to Canton, sir?"

"Me? No, thanks!" He laughed. "I have United States government contracts to think about."

They stopped at Tai Po market so that the two women could look at the small shops there and buy coolie hats. Ah Au bargained for the hats and, when they had been paid for, took them back to the car.

He was about to return and render further assistance when Mr. Nilsen joined him.

"They've gone into a silk shop," he said "They're not going to buy, but they'll be there an age. You smoke?"

"Not when driving, sir. But now, thank you."

They sat in the car and smoked. A ring of children collected to stare at them, but Mr. Nilsen took no notice.

"Have you ever been to Canton?" he asked.

"No, sir. I have been to Macao, where my wife has some relatives, but my family is in Manila."

"Is that so? Don't you like the Philippines?"

"My family went there from here, sir. But I was born here and I am British. There are more opportunities here, I think."

"I don't get it. I should have thought this was the last place where you could look forward to any sort of security for your family. This section, for instance. You call it the New Territories. But it's leased, isn't it, from the government of China?"

"Yes, sir, in eighteen ninety-eight. It was leased for ninety-nine years."

"So in nineteen ninety-seven you'll have to give it back to the Reds, if they're still in business."

"That is so."

"Or if they don't walk in and take it back before?"

"There is always that possibility, sir, but I do not think the risk is great. Hong Kong is no danger to them and it is a useful outlet to the West. That is why, too, the Portuguese are allowed to stay in Macao."

Ah Au spoke almost without thinking. He had planned to wait until after lunch at Shatin before attempting to broach the subject of Mr Tan's proposition. Now, he was being offered an opening of a kind he could not possibly have contrived. His heart began to beat faster. Then, he made up his mind.

"All that could change overnight," Mr. Nilsen was saying. "Some shift in the Cold War or another Korea over the Formosa situation, and I wouldn't give you a nickel for the Peninsular Hotel."

Ah Au smiled. "You are probably right, sir. But, meanwhile, there are advantages to both sides, and not only for the big bankers and trading companies here."

"That so?"

"In fact, I can tell you a story that may amuse you, sir."

"What's that?"

"Well, sir, it is a little confidential, but you are not a policeman or a newspaperman, so I can tell you." He paused.

"Sure, go ahead."

"You see, sir, we Chinese are all pirates at heart." He shrugged. "Chinese piracy is as old as history. When the Reds began sending arms and ammunition down by sea in junks to the terrorists in Malaya, there were naturally some men, both here and in Macao, who thought it a pity that such valuable cargoes should arrive at their destinations. It was a great temptation. So as often as they could, they . . ." He spread his hands deprecatingly.

"They hijacked them?" Mr. Nilsen smiled.

"Yes, though that was not the best part of the joke, sir. You know that arms and ammunition are very valuable in this part of the world."

"They are in most places."

"Particularly in the Far East, sir. But the trouble is that there are government regulations and embargoes that make it difficult to sell equipment. It was not easy to seize these cargoes, and although the Reds could not make international complaints without admitting openly that they were supplying the terrorists, these pirates, these hijackers you would call them, they ran great risks. There had to be profit." He paused again. He could see that he had Mr. Nilsen's whole attention.

"Well, how did they get rid of the stuff?"

"It was very simple, sir. They took the Communist arms down to Indonesia and sold them to the *anti*-Communist rebels."

Mr. Nilsen stared and then began to laugh.

Ah Au sighed inwardly with relief. He saw the holes in his own story so clearly that he had been afraid Mr. Nilsen would see them, too.

He did see one an instant later. When he had stopped laughing, he said: "What I don't see is why the Reds sent the stuff down by sea at all. What about the British navy? Couldn't they intercept the shipments to Malaya?"

"They intercepted many, sir, but, you know, there are a lot of junks in the China Seas. Last year there were over twenty-five thousand of them using Hong Kong alone. You cannot intercept and search every junk at sea between here and Singapore."

"I suppose not."

"Though you are right, sir. The illegal arms traffic was stopped in the end. A friend of mine in Manila was very sad about that."

"Yes?"

"Some time ago he took a shipment of arms and ammunition out of a Red junk off Hainan. It was modern equipment—rifles, machine guns, bazookas— worth sixty thousand dollars. And it is still in Manila."

"Why? Aren't there any more anti-Communists in Indonesia?"

"Plenty, sir, but it is not as simple as it was before. This is no longer a small business. The buying agents for the rebels are in Singapore, and they must be careful. They will not buy illegal arms any more. My friend has tried to sell. Now he says he must try to make the arms legal."

"How does he propose to do that?"

But Ah Au had seen the two women approaching and was already getting out of the car to open the door for them. Mr. Nilsen's forecast that they would buy nothing had proved incorrect. His wife had a Shantung dress length and the Arlene woman had some jade earrings. They got into the car, showing their purchases and chattering about the other things that the shop had for sale.

Ah Au drove on toward Shatin.

The interruption of his conversation with Mr. Nilsen had not dismayed him. On the contrary, he was glad of it. He was quite sure that Mr. Nilsen was sufficiently intrigued to want an answer to his last question, and it was much better that he should be the one to return to the subject.

Ah Au did not have to wait long. When the three Americans had had lunch at the Shatin Hotel, the women went for a walk in the gardens overlooking the valley. Mr. Nilsen had gone to the toilet, but when he came out, he did not join the women in the garden. Instead, he came out to Ah Au, who was sitting in the car.

Ah Au got out to open the door, but Mr. Nilsen waved him back.

"I've seen enough sights for the moment," he said with a smile. "I want to hear more about your friend in Manila."

"Yes, sir?"

"What did you mean about making that shipment of arms legal?"

"You understand, sir, this is very confidential."

"Sure, I understand."

"For arms to be legal, sir, they have to have a legal owner and a legal place of origin. What my friend needs is a nominee."

"How do you mean?"

"What my friend would like to do is ship the arms to be held in bond at Singapore, and then sell them."

"Why can't he do that?"

"Sir, the authorities at Singapore would not accept the consignment in bond without a proper certified bill of lading from a reputable shipper at the port of origin. Unfortunately, residents of Manila cannot trade in arms without a government permit. That is difficult and expensive to obtain. So, he must have a foreign nominee."

"Why? I don't get it."

"After the war in Manila, sir, a lot of surplus American war material was sold to dealers who exported it. The regulations about permits do not apply to non-resident foreigners exporting arms."

"I see."

"Also, sir, the nominee would have to go to Singapore to sign clearance papers. My friend has tried to find the right person, but although he is willing to pay as much as five per cent for the service, he has been unsuccessful. He will not deal with crooks."

"Hijackers aren't usually so particular."

"A crook would cheat him, sir. Once the papers are signed, what is to prevent the nominee from claiming the goods are his and keeping all the money? Sixty thousand Straits dollars is a lot. Twenty-one thousand dollars American."

"And five per cent of that is a thousand and fifty." Mr. Nilsen grinned amiably. "Jimmy, you couldn't be telling me all this for a reason, could you?"

Ah Au's heart missed a beat. Was Mr. Nilsen going to be like the man from Cleveland after all?

"A reason, sir? But you asked me."

"I know it. But you sort of raised the question in the first place, didn't you? Come on, now, Jimmy. Didn't you have some idea that I might be suckered into acting as your friend's nominee?"

Ah Au looked amazed. "You, sir? I had not thought of it."

"All right. Never mind." He started to turn away.

Ah Au spoke quickly. "But would you consider such a proposition, sir?"

Mr. Nilsen looked at him coldly. "What's the angle, Jimmy?"

"Angle, sir?"

"What's your friend in Manila trying to smuggle? Opium?"

"Sir, that is not a good thing to say. You asked me questions. I answered the truth."

"All right. Let me ask you some more questions. What's your friend's name?"

"Sir, if you believe that he is smuggling opium, you will go to the police. How can I tell you?"

"All right, I promise not to go to the police. What's his name?"

Ah Au hesitated, then bowed slightly. "As you promise, I must accept your promise. Please note that, sir. His name is Mr. Tan Tack Chee."

"Right, then why does Mr. Tan Tack Chee have you touting for him? Why doesn't he find a nominee himself?"

"Because he has no contacts, sir, with passengers off boats. He cannot go up to strangers and make his request. And it has to be someone who is going to Singapore. How would he know?"

"Why doesn't he get hold of an officer on one of the ships and ask him to do it?"

"A ship's officer dealing in arms would be an object of suspicion to the authorities in Singapore, sir."

"So would I."

"No, sir. Many of the dealers in war material are American businessmen. You are an engineer with a business in America. You would be perfectly acceptable."

"Don't you mean innocent-looking? Don't you mean I'd be a good cover?

You say no opium. Okay, but there are other kinds of contraband. How do I know what'd be in that shipment."

Ah Au smiled. "Mr. Nilsen, sir, no person who wished to make an illegal shipment of any kind would describe it on a bill of lading and a ship's manifest as arms and ammunition. That is asking for it to be examined by port authorities."

"Is that how it would be described?"

"Of course, sir." Ah Au spread out his hands. "That is my friend's need, to be able to have the shipment legally bonded in Singapore. I explained this."

Mr. Nilsen thought for a moment, then nodded. "Yes, you did. This Mr. Tan, now. You say he's a friend of yours. How did you get to know him?"

Ah Au drew himself up a trifle stiffly. "He is my wife's father, sir," he said.

Mr. Nilsen began to laugh, then checked himself. "Sorry, Jimmy, I was just amused at the idea of a man calling his father-in-law his friend."

"You are not friendly with Mrs. Nilsen's father, sir?"

"Oh, sure, but . . . no, skip it. I'd better go and see where those women have got to."

He had started to go. Ah Au followed him.

"Then you will consider the proposition, sir?"

Mr. Nilsen grinned affably. "Oh, sure, I'll consider it."

"When will you decide, sir?"

"I'll let you know tonight. Now back the car up, Jimmy, will you? I have to stop off at the Peninsular Hotel for a fitting at the tailor's."

iv

Greg was feeling good that evening. The idea of his having been asked, in all seriousness, to act as front man for a Chinese pirate had appealed to his sense of humor.

At least, that is how he chose to explain the sudden lightness of heart that had come to him as he was changing for dinner. He regarded himself, not without reason, as a mature and level-headed man. If anyone had suggested that somewhere in the back streets of his mind another Greg Nilsen—a roistering, romantic, ten-year-old swashbuckler—had escaped from custody and was out enjoying a game of cops and robbers, he would have been angrily incredulous. It had not yet occurred to him to ask himself why, if the whole thing were simply a good joke, he had not told Dorothy about it.

Jimmy Khoo brought the car to the boat at seven o'clock and drove them across to Aberdeen.

The trouble with Arlene started in the sampan which took them out from the quayside to the floating restaurant. Halfway out across the harbor, she suddenly jumped up out of her seat.

"I've been bitten," she said to Dorothy.

"Oh, no!"

"I've been bitten."

"Where?"

The light sampan rocked dangerously.

"Better sit down," Greg cautioned them. "You're rocking the boat."

Dorothy sat down, but Arlene ignored him. "I've been bitten," she repeated maddeningly and, pulling up one side of her skirt, began examining the back of her leg.

The sampan lurched over in the other direction. The Chinese girl, standing on the stern counter with the oar, was thrown off balance. The old woman who owned the sampan screamed. Greg felt the wicker chair he was sitting on start to slide. He grabbed at the side of the boat.

"For God's sake, sit down!" he shouted.

Arlene sat down, the Chinese girl giggled, and a minute later they were at the restaurant steps. Greg paid off the sampan and joined Dorothy and Arlene on the veranda. They appeared to be having some sort of argument.

He heard Dorothy saying: "I'm sure Greg didn't mean to . . ." And then Arlene turned to face him. Her nose and mouth were pinched and white with anger.

"I'm not used to being yelled at like that," she said.

"Arlene, I only asked you to sit down. That sort of boat upsets pretty easily."

"There was no need to yell at me like that."

"I yelled because I didn't want to have to swim the rest of the way."

"Oh, really, Greg!" This was Dorothy. "I do think you ought to apologize to Arlene. I know you meant well, but it wasn't very polite."

"All right, I'm sorry. Now, for goodness' sake, let's go eat."

It was not a gracious apology and nobody attempted to pretend it was. The situation was not improved when they found that the desirable tables on the upper deck were all reserved, and that they would have to sit down below surrounded by very noisy mah-jong players. Arlene had said that it was unnecessary to make table reservations. Greg pointedly refrained from reminding her of the fact. The critical moment came, however, when they went with the waiter to the big traps moored alongside the vessel to choose the fish they would eat.

There was a man with a long-handled landing net standing by the traps. As the customers pointed to the fish they wanted, he would scoop them dextrously out of the water and fling them on to a long tiled slab which led to the kitchen.

One of the fish he pulled out was some kind of grouper. It was a heavy fish and it landed on the slab with a force that stunned it. For a moment or two it lay there almost still, its eyes staring vacuously, its big slack mouth gaping in an expression of the deepest gloom.

Arlene glanced at Dorothy. "Isn't that someone we know?" she asked slyly.

She did not look at Greg; but Dorothy did, and then burst out laughing.

"Oh, really, Arlene," she said, "he's not looking as miserable as all that."

Then she squeezed Greg's arm in affectionate apology; and, of course, he had to laugh, too.

But there was murder in his heart, and at that moment a resolution was born. Somewhere, somehow, their plans, his and Dorothy's, would have to be changed. He was not going to go all the way to Calcutta in the *Silver Isle* with Arlene Drecker.

When they arrived back at the ship, the two women went on board while Greg stayed to settle the account with Jimmy. He added a generous tip.

"Thank you very much indeed, sir." Jimmy took off his cap and bowed, but made no move to leave. He was looking at Greg expectantly.

Greg smiled. "Oh, yes. You want to know about that proposition."

"I hope you can accept, sir."

"Well, I don't know, Jimmy."

"Sir, all that is necessary is that you sign some papers in Manila and Singapore."

"People have been hanged before now just for signing papers, Jimmy."

"In this case, sir . . ."

"No. I tell you what I will do. When we get to Manila I'll see your Mr. Tan, if you'll have him contact me on the ship. And *then* I'll decide. Okay?"

Jimmy beamed. "Certainly, sir. That will be entirely satisfactory. Thank you very much indeed, sir."

"There's nothing to thank me for. And mind you explain the exact position to him. I don't want any misunderstandings."

"There will be none. And may I say what a pleasure it has been to serve you, sir?"

"The pleasure's mutual. Be seeing you again someday, maybe."

"I sincerely hope so, sir."

When Greg got back on board, he found that some mail had been sent up to the cabin from the purser's office. Among it was a progress report from his vice-president in charge of production. Everything at the plant was running smoothly. He didn't have to worry about a thing; just enjoy the trip.

v

The following morning Khoo Ah Au dispatched two cables: one to his wife's father in Manila, the other to his wife's uncle in Kuala Pangkalan.

The cable to Mr. Tan Tack Chee read:

CONTACT POSSIBLE PROSPECT MR. G. NILSEN PASSENGER S. S. SILVER ISLE ARRIVING MANILA 14TH RESPECTFUL AFFECTION WIFE AND SELF. KHOO.

The cable to Mr. Tan Siow Mong read:

HAVE ADVISED MANILA SUITABLE PROSPECT ARRIVING S. S. SILVER ISLE 14TH RESPECTFUL AFFECTION WIFE AND SELF. KHOO.

That night Mrs. Khoo had the unusual and elevating experience of receiving an overseas telephone call from her father in Manila. The only disappointing thing about it was that more time was devoted to the business talk with her husband than to the discussion of her possible pregnancy.

Four

TWO DAYS LATER the *Silver Isle* docked in Manila, and hordes of scarlet-shirted Filipino stevedores swarmed on board. They seemed to penetrate into every corner of the ship. Some even found their way into the writing room, where they lounged with their feet up on the tables until indignant stewards shooed them away.

The passengers had been warned that Manila was one of the worst ports in the Far East for pilfering. Greg was depositing a package containing Dorothy's jewelry in the purser's safe, when a steward came up with the message that Mr. Tan Tack Chee would like to see him. The gentleman was in the bar.

Dorothy was waiting for him by the notice board. They—or, rather, they and Arlene—had decided not to go ashore immediately, but wait until after lunch. When the purser's clerk had made out the receipt, Greg went over to her.

"Darling, I meant to tell you before. There's a man here who wants to see me on business. It'll only take a few minutes. I'll see you up on the sports deck."

Dorothy pulled a face. "Business? I thought we'd left that behind."

"It's nothing important."

"I didn't know you did any business here."

"It's just a man I promised to see." There was nothing untrue about the statement; nevertheless, he did not feel quite easy about it. "I'll tell you the story later," he added. "Look, darling, do you mind holding on to the camera for me?"

He went up to the bar. It was crowded with dock police, customs officials, and the usual collection of "business" visitors thirsty for free drinks. The steward who had brought him the message pointed to a table in the corner of the bar. Greg made his way over.

Seated at the table with an open briefcase in front of him was a middle-aged Chinese. He wore a well-pressed light gray suit and thick tortoise-shell glasses. He was writing busily in a loose-leaf notebook. As Greg approached, he glanced up.

"Mr. Tan?"

"Mr. Nilsen?" As he spoke he rose and they shook hands.

Mr. Tan's voice and manner were subdued, and his hand was like a soft bag of chicken bones. It would have been difficult to conceive of anyone less piratical. Greg, whose imagination had had three days to prepare for the encounter, was disconcerted.

"My son-in-law in Hong Kong cabled me that you would be passing through Manila," Mr. Tan said easily. "He hoped that I might perhaps be of some service to you and Mrs. Nilsen."

"Well, that's very kind of you, Mr. Tan. But I rather understood that there was a matter of business you wanted . . ."

"Do you or Mrs. Nilsen know Manila?" Mr. Tan's interruption was so gentle in tone that Greg scarcely noticed the firmness of it.

"No, we don't."

"Then, may I make a suggestion? I have my car on the wharf. It would be a favor if you would allow me to place it at your disposal."

"Mr. Tan, I don't think . . ."

Mr. Tan held up a slender hand. "And an additional favor if you would allow me to be your host at lunch. You understand, I do not have the professional skills of my son-in-law, but my driver knows Manila well and can show you what there is to see."

"As a matter of fact, Mr. Tan, we've sort of committed ourselves to taking another passenger along with us. A lady."

"She is included in the invitation," Mr. Tan said promptly.

"I think . . ."

"I understand perfectly, Mr. Nilsen. Please feel free to consult with your wife before you accept."

Greg hesitated. "Mr. Tan, I think I had better explain that I have not mentioned to my wife the business we might have to discuss."

"Naturally, Mr. Nilsen, one does not trouble ladies with business." He smiled. "I am in the so-called import-export market. That is a very loose term covering everything from powdered milk to earth-moving equipment."

Greg nodded uncertainly. "I guess so. If you'll excuse me, I'll go and find my wife."

Half an hour later the four of them left the ship and walked along the quay to the car park. As they approached, a pink Cadillac swung out of the parking line and pulled up alongside them. A Filipino driver sprang out to open the doors and they all got in.

Mr. Tan took them to his house for lunch. It was in the Spanish style and built on a hillside overlooking the bay. Mrs. Tan, obviously a second wife, proved to be young, very attractive, and a graduate of the University of Southern California. She wore toreador pants, and barbecued steaks for them on the patio. Arlene was enchanted. Mr. Tan talked about Philippine politics, skin diving, and the amusing misfortunes of an American motion-picture company who were trying to shoot on location up in the hills. He did not once mention business.

After lunch the car dropped him back at his office, which was in a modern, American-style building, and then the Filipino driver took them on a tour of the city. When they returned to the office Mr. Tan's secretary informed them that he had had to go out, but that he hoped Mr. and Mrs. Nilsen and Miss Drecker would dine with him that evening. The car would call for them at seven. Mr. Tan would wear a white tuxedo.

Dorothy glanced at Arlene with a smile of triumph. "We're certainly getting the full treatment," she said. "He must want those die-castings pretty badly, eh, darling?"

Even Arlene was looking at him with approval.

Greg mumbled something noncommittal He was feeling thoroughly confused. His neglecting to tell Dorothy about the conversation with Jimmy Khoo in Hong Kong had been natural enough, he assured himself. The commercial technicalities about nominees, manifests, and shipping in bond would only have bored her; and, besides, they had agreed from the start that business talk was to be taboo on the trip. The last thing he had been prepared for was having to account for Mr. Tan in the role of a generous host. When he had first reported the invitation to lunch, Arlene had been there, and it had been impossible to go into long explanations. "He's in the import-export business," had been all that he had said; but Dorothy had jumped to the conclusion that the man wanted to buy die-castings.

He had not realized it until later, or he could have said something to her in time. As it was, the first he had heard about it had been during the afternoon's sightseeing. He had been listening to the driver talking about the village he came from, when a fragment of conversation from the back seat had caught his attention.

"You see," Dorothy had been saying, "Greg's plant only does this special precision work. Most of his contracts are with the government, or people like airplane manufacturers, or those other people who develop the missiles. He's never had much time for export business before."

"Well, you ought to encourage it."

"Why?"

"Won't it make part of your trip tax-deductible?"

Dorothy had laughed. "I'd never thought of that."

"I'll bet Greg has."

Greg had pretended not to hear. An explanation at that moment would merely have made his wife look foolish and gratified Arlene's appetite for discord.

Now he was almost sorry that he had not taken the risk. He had maneuvered himself into one false position where Dorothy was concerned; and it looked very much as if Mr. Tan had maneuvered him into another. It was going to be embarrassing now to say "no" to Mr. Tan, or even to question him closely, when the questions could only imply doubt of his good faith. The fact that Mr. Tan's hospitality had a clear purpose was beside the point. Wisely or unwisely, the hospitality had been accepted; and so, an obligation, of courtesy at least, had been incurred.

Dinner was at a country club just outside the city, and had been specially ordered by Mr. Tan. The rum drinks were innocent-tasting but very potent. Toward the end of the evening Arlene became emotional and, in trying to express her gratitude for the wonderful day she had had, was moved to tears of joy. Her mascara ran and she was forced to retire to the powder room Mrs. Tan and Dorothy decided to join her there. Greg and Mr. Tan were alone.

There was a pause.

"This has been a very enjoyable day," Greg said.

Mr. Tan smiled. "For me, too, Mr. Nilsen. Although—" he smiled again— "it would have been more enjoyable if you had not been so troubled by your suspicions."

"Suspicions?"

"My son-in-law in Hong Kong is a very praiseworthy young man. He is not a man of great substance as yet, but he is honest and hard-working. Otherwise, I would not have allowed my daughter to marry him. But he has a weakness."

"Oh, yes?"

"A taste for melodrama. Did he mention piracy, Mr. Nilsen?"

"He did, yes."

"I was afraid so. He lives in the richly flavored past of lions and dragons. It is an engaging weakness, but embarrassing in business."

"I guess it would be."

"You know, Mr. Nilsen, this small parcel of arms was acquired by accident, but, as far as I am concerned, perfectly legally. I will confess to you that its existence is inconvenient, and I would like to disembarrass myself. A technicality makes this difficult. You, as you know, are in a position to overcome the technicality. That is the length and breadth of the problem."

Greg pushed his drink away. "Mr. Tan, are you on the level?"

"Sir?"

"I want to get this straight. These are arms from Red China originally intended for Red terrorists in Malaya. Is that correct?"

"Perfectly correct. As I said, they fell into my hands by accident."

"What sort of accident?"

"The man who seized them off Hainan left them with me as a pledge for a loan. Later, I am afraid, he went bankrupt."

"And now you want to sell them to the *anti*-Red people in Indonesia. Is that correct?"

"Entirely correct, Mr. Nilsen."

Greg considered for a moment and then nodded. "Okay, it's a deal."

Mr. Tan stroked his chin thoughtfully before he said: "Very well. I will bring the papers to you to sign in the morning." He hesitated and then went on. "I will be frank with you, Mr. Nilsen. I am not entirely happy with this arrangement."

Greg stared at him. "You mean you've changed your mind?"

"Indeed no. On the contrary, I am quite satisfied with the arrangement as far as it goes. My regret is that it does not go further."

"How do you mean?"

"My brother in Singapore is capable of handling the shipping and delivery arrangements, but when it comes to dealing with the buyers, I am not sure that he is the best man. An American can always drive a harder bargain in that business. How long will you be in Singapore, Mr. Nilsen?"

"Two days."

"Not very long. I had hoped you might consider conducting the negotiations personally. For an additional consideration, of course."

Greg shook his head. "I don't think I'm qualified to do that, Mr. Tan. And, as you say, I won't be there long enough."

"I quite understand. Ah, here are the ladies."

The ship was sailing at midday. At ten-thirty Mr. Tan arrived with the papers for signature.

The first was a consignor's note requesting the Anglo-Malay Transport Company of Kuala Pangkalan to ship the goods listed from the Tak Wah Godown and Storage Corporation, Manila, to the Chen Warehouse Company, Singapore, to be held in bond there pending further instructions. The second was an export license giving Greg's name and address in the United States and a list of the goods to be exported. This required his countersignature and passport number to become effective.

When Greg had signed, Mr. Tan gave him copies of the documents. "As soon as you arrive in Singapore, Mr. Nilsen," he said, "my brother, Tan Yam Heng, will contact you. I have written his name down here. He will have copies of the bill of lading, and go with you to make the proper customs declaration. He will then ask you to sign a paper transferring the ownership of the goods in bond to a company or person to be designated later. When you have signed that paper, he will hand you a check for one thousand and fifty dollars U.S."

"Not going to have any trouble with the customs people, am I?"

"No. The goods are being held in bond. It is merely a formality." Mr. Tan stood up. "It has been a pleasure to meet and do business with you, Mr. Nilsen."

Dorothy was ashore with Arlene, doing some last-minute shopping and arranging for flowers to be sent with their note of thanks to Mrs. Tan. She did not get back until half an hour before the ship sailed. By that time Mr. Tan had left.

"What a pity," she said when Greg told her. "I think he's nice. I hope you decided to let him have his castings after all."

Greg hesitated and then side-stepped the question. "As a matter of fact, he wanted to see me about something else, something he wants me to do for him in Singapore."

"Are you going to do it?"

"I think so."

Dorothy nodded approvingly. "After all, they did put themselves out for us, didn't they?"

ii

That afternoon a cable went from Manila to Kuala Pangkalan:

DOCUMENTS SIGNED AIRMAILED YOU TODAY. TACK CHEE

That evening Girija was in the estate office when the telephone rang. As he lifted it off the cradle he heard the operator telling Kuala Pangkalan to go ahead.

"Mr. Krishnan?" said a voice a moment later.

"Yes."

"I am speaking for Mr. Lee."

"Yes?" He did not recognize the voice, which was that of Mr. Tan Siow Mong's eldest son.

"Mr. Lee wishes for delivery three days from now of the goods previously discussed."

"Very well."

"Mr. Lee will be at the rest house on Thursday evening at eight o'clock, if you will meet him there."

"Very well."

The caller hung up.

Girija sat down again at his desk. His heart was pounding, but whether from excitement at the prospect of having a long-cherished dream realized, or from fear of the things he would now have to do, he did not know. He sat there for a while until he felt himself calmer. Then he looked at his watch.

It was half past six. He had three nights in which to move the arms and ammunition to the pick-up point near the road. If everything went according to plan, that was only just sufficient time. His instinct was to lock the office and set out at once for Awang; but he restrained himself. The first thing to remember was that his behavior must not appear in any way unusual.

At seven o'clock he left the office and went to his house. There were the remains of some food which he had prepared at midday, and he forced himself to eat it. At eight o'clock he took his bicycle and left the compound.

His first care was to see that he was not followed. The possibility of Mr. Lee's attempting to discover where the arms were hidden, so that he could remove them without payment, had to be considered. All appeared to be well, however, and he reached the tin workings without encountering anyone he knew on the way.

He had been up to the camp site at night only once before. That had been months ago, when he had been planning the operation; but he still remembered the panic that had seized him when he left the open ground by the tin workings and entered the terrifying blackness of the jungle. The track to the lower end of the dried stream bed was the worst part. It was too near the village for him to risk using a flashlight, except intermittently, and, well as he knew it in daylight, at night there was always the danger of his getting lost. Above all, there was his fear of leopards. It was at night that they raided villages on the edge of the jungle, carried off chickens and goats, and killed men. He knew the fear to be largely irrational—there had been no reports of leopards in the area for some time—but still it haunted every step he took. He plunged on desperately along the track, living for the moment when he would reach the stream bed and be able to keep the flashlight on all the time.

His plan for moving the boxes of arms and ammunition fell into three parts.

On the first night he would move them from the shelter to the cane thicket at the edge of the stream bed. On the second night he would move them to the foot of the stream bed where it met the track. On the third night he would move them to the pick-up dump that he had contrived in one of the derelict mining-company buildings.

It had taken a long time to prepare the dump. The building he had selected for it was a windowless Nissen hut that had formerly been used as a store for drums of diesel oil. The corrugated-iron sections were so badly rusted that it was possible to put a fist through them in most places; and there were several big holes near the ground where the rusting process was more advanced and the metal had simply disintegrated. From Girija's point of view, it had three things to recommend it. There was still enough metal there to prevent a casual passer-by seeing inside; it contained some empty oil drums which had been punctured for some reason, and so had not been stolen for use as waterbutts by the villagers; and it had a door with a hasp on it to take a padlock.

Once the arms and ammunition were out of the shelter, the risk of their being discovered increased as they were moved nearer the road. While they were in the cane thicket, the risk was small. The second stage at the foot of the stream bed was a greater risk, but, for twenty-four hours, an acceptable one. For the third stage, however, there had to be an effective hiding place. Girija had never read *The Purloined Letter*, but the technique he employed was similar in principle to that used in Poe's story: concealment by familiarity.

The first thing he had done was to buy a padlock, grease the interior mechanism carefully, and leave it in the underbrush for the exterior to rust. Then, one day he had gone to the oil store and padlocked the door. A gleaming new padlock would have excited too much interest in a passer-by. The rusty one, if noticed at all, would only arouse mild curiosity. When he had returned a week later, the padlock had still been there; but there had been signs that someone had crawled through one of the holes near the ground to find out what was behind the locked door. As there had still been nothing inside but the useless oil drums, nothing had been touched. Girija's next move had been to move the oil drums about inside, so as to cover the bigger holes in the corrugated iron, and draw a series of squares and circles on the dirt floor with a stick, to make it seem as if children had been playing there. The following week he had found that one of the drums had been pushed aside. He had replaced it. He had considered defecating on the floor as an additional discouragement to the curious, but had finally decided that it would require too many visits to make that form of deterrent completely effective. In the event, additional measures had not been needed. That had been the last time he drums had been touched. The former oil store with the padlocked door had become accepted as a place where children sometimes played, containing nothing worth stealing and nothing of interest. It would look no different during the twenty-four hours it held the arms and ammunition.

By the time he reached the camp site, it was after nine thirty; but he rested a few minutes before starting work. He had calculated that it would take him less than two hours to move all the boxes to the cane thicket, and was determined to reserve his strength as much as possible. The hardest part of the job would come on the third night, and he must be prepared for that.

The problem of handling the boxes, he had solved almost by accident. At intervals Mr. Wright received catalogues from a mail-order house in Singapore, and in one of them Girija had seen a device that had interested him. It was a gadget for those with heavy suitcases who could not afford porters, and consisted of a strap attached to a bracket with two small trolley wheels mounted on it. The strap was fastened lengthwise around the suitcase, with the wheels at one corner. There was a handle on the strap. The owner of the suitcase simply grasped this handle and walked along, trailing the case behind him, with half the weight of it carried on the trolley wheels. The price was six dollars.

Girija had sent for one and experimented. The thing worked on firm ground; but up at the camp site, and with a heavy box of rifles, the small wheels sank into the spongy surface of the hillside and were useless. Larger wheels with broader tires were needed. He had found them eventually on the estate. Before the Wright children had been sent away to school in England, one of them had had a scooter. It had been left in Mr. Wright's garage, and Girija had had no difficulty in removing the wheels. Mounted on an axle made out of a spare jack handle, they worked quite well.

The transfer to the cane thicket was completed by midnight, and Girija began the journey back. In spite of his resolve to conserve his energies, he was very tired, and realized that he could no longer rely upon his wits to see him through. Now it would be a question of stamina.

There was a compensation. As his weariness increased, his fears seemed to diminish. By the time he had completed the next night's work, he had forgotten about leopards, and feared the dark track from the stream bed to the tin workings only because it threatened his powers of endurance.

The nine boxes containing the rifles were the most awkward to handle, and only one could be moved at a time. It required twenty stumbling journeys each way to shift all the boxes and ammunition containers, and the final move from the stream bed to the oil store took five and a half hours. When he had secured the padlock he sank down onto the ground in a state of collapse. It was another hour before he could summon the strength to get on his bicycle and ride back to the estate; and only his fear of being seen returning to the estate compound at daybreak, and before he had had time to wash and put on clean clothes, drove him to make that final effort.

He was in the office that morning on time, as usual, but he knew that unless he could get some rest during the day, he would be unable or unfit to keep his appointment with Mr. Lee in the evening. If he pleaded sickness, Mrs. Wright, a keen amateur physician, would dose him with pills and order him to bed; and she would see that he stayed there, too. In the end, on the pretext of looking into some minor pay dispute among the tappers, he left the compound, walked to a part of the estate which he knew was not being worked, and went to sleep under the trees. He awoke at sundown and hurried back to the office. His body ached almost intolerably, but he was no longer stupid with fatigue. When Mr. Wright looked in at the office on his way to the bungalow, Girija was able to report, with his usual air of efficiency, that the pay dispute had been satisfactorily settled.

Girija's business arrangements with Mr. Lee were somewhat complex.

When they met at the rest house, Mr. Lee would give him a draft on the Hong Kong and Shanghai Bank for twenty-five thousand Straits dollars, postdated thirty days and guaranteed by Mr. Tan. He would also give him a receipt for the arms and ammunition. Girija would, in return, give Mr. Lee a promissory note for twenty-five thousand dollars, acknowledging the sum as a loan repayable within thirty days. Then, Girija would return alone to the estate compound, put the check in an envelope marked "To be opened in the event of my death," and leave it in a safe place of his own choosing.

An hour later he would meet Mr. Lee at a rendezvous on the Awang Road. Mr. Lee would have a truck. Guided by Girija, they would then drive to the dump, where Mr. Lee would be allowed to inspect what he was buying.

This would be a critical moment for both of them; but both would feel reasonably secure. If there were no arms and Girija had brought Mr. Lee there merely in order to kill him and keep the check, Mr. Tan would know and be in a position to inform on Girija. If, on the other hand, Mr. Lee contemplated killing Girija and making off with the arms, there would be the telltale check to accuse Mr. Lee. The promissory note and the receipt were safeguards of a more genteel nature. The promissory note was Mr. Lee's insurance against Girija's making off with the check and failing to deliver the goods. The receipt for the arms was Girija's insurance against Mr. Lee's declining to return the promissory note when the arms had been delivered. These two documents would be formally exchanged at the conclusion of the transaction.

Girija reviewed the procedure once more as he cycled out to the rest house. He knew that Mr. Lee could trust him; he was quite certain that he could not trust Mr. Lee. His tired mind began to imagine new ways in which he could be betrayed. Supposing Mr. Lee had henchmen hiding in the truck. What was there to prevent their pouncing on him, retrieving the receipt for the arms, and then seizing the whole consignment? Mr. Lee could still use the promissory note, and Girija would be in no position to complain to the police of what had happened. Or supposing Mr. Lee had a confederate in the estate compound who would watch where he put the check, and then steal it while he was away delivering the arms. There were countless opportunities for treachery remaining in the situation. Only one possibility did he refuse to consider: that the check guaranteed by Mr. Tan might not in the end be honored.

Mr. Lee was already at the rest house when he arrived. His attitude was wary but businesslike. He merely grunted a greeting and handed Girija the promissory note to sign. He then produced the check and the receipt. When the documents had changed hands, he nodded.

"That is satisfactory. Now, where do we meet?"

"At the twenty-one-mile post near Awang."

"Where is that?"

Girija told him how to get there, and then stood up to go. His whole body was aching, and a spasm of pain shot up his spine as he moved.

Mr. Lee was eying him thoughtfully. "Are you sick?" he asked.

"No, I am tired."

"Will your friend be there?"

"No, but I will help you load the boxes."

"Then I will meet you in one hour's time."

The whole transaction had taken no more than five minutes. Girija cycled back to the estate compound and went to his house. When he had written the inscription on the envelope, he put the check inside and locked it in his tin trunk. If he did not return, Mr. Wright would probably take charge of the trunk and ultimately hand it over to the authorities. It was not an ideal arrangement, but it was the best Girija could think of. As long as Mr. Lee did not know how he had disposed of the check, that was all that mattered.

He had ten minutes to wait before setting out for the rendezvous. He considered opening up the tin trunk again and passing the time with his bus catalogues, but made no move to do so. Through his weariness, he knew that the time for dreams was over. The next time he looked at the catalogues, if there were to be a next time, he would be seeing them through different eyes. There was half a tin of butterscotch on the table by his charpoy. He sat and ate that until it was time to go.

The truck was already at the rendezvous when he arrived. About a hundred yards short of it, he dismounted, switched off his bicycle lamp, and walked along the edge of the road. As he approached, he saw that the canvases above the tailboard of the truck were drawn and tied. He did not like this, and made up his mind to see that the truck was empty before they moved off.

Mr. Lee looked out of the driver's cab window as Girija came up.

"You are late," he said.

"I am two minutes early," Girija replied evenly. "Would you open the back of the truck, please?"

"Why?"

"I wish to put my bicycle inside."

"Why can't you leave it among the trees there? No one will steal it. We have to come back this way."

"I prefer to have it with me."

Mr. Lee got down impatiently and went to the rear of the truck. Girija joined him. In silence they unfastened the tailboard. Girija knew the truck. It belonged to a copra dealer in Kuala Pangkalan. The Anglo-Malay Transport Company hired it sometimes when their own trucks were busy. Mr. Lee must have learned of it from Mr. Tan.

The back of the truck was empty. Girija put his bicycle inside and they set off. Mr. Lee was a fast and bad driver. Luckily, they met little traffic on the way. After ten minutes they reached the road leading to the tin workings.

"You turn off here," said Girija; "and I must ask you to put your lights out."

"On this cart track? We shall run into a tree."

"If you drive slowly, you will be all right. If you keep your lights on, we may be seen from the kampong and someone will come to see what is happening."

Mr. Lee grumbled, but submitted. The truck ground along the road as far as the derelict pump shed.

"We stop here," said Girija.

They got down from the cab and Mr. Lee looked around. "What is this place?"

Girija told him. "We go this way," he added.

"One moment. Are the cases open?"

"Of course not."

Mr. Lee took a case opener and a hammer from the cab of the truck. In his hands they looked like weapons. Girija's scalp crawled as he led the way to the oil store. However, Mr. Lee's main concern at that moment seemed to be to avoid tripping on the uneven ground beneath the scrub. He muttered a complaint about the darkness.

Girija took no notice. Not until they were inside the oil store with the door firmly shut did he switch on his flashlight.

Mr. Lee looked at the stacked boxes. "Is this all of it?"

"Everything on the list is there."

Mr. Lee produced the list from his pocket. "Which are the rifles?"

"Those long boxes there."

Mr. Lee began opening them. He opened every one. When Girija suggested that this was a waste of time, Mr. Lee straightened up.

"Cases full of stones have been sold before now," he said. "I am buying only what I see. If you want to save time, you can refasten the cases after I have examined them."

When he had finished with the rifles, he went on in the same methodical way with the rest—the machine pistols, the bazookas, the grenades, the land mines. Only when he approached the ammunition did Girija protest again.

"If you open those, Mr. Lee, you will not be able to reseal them. You will reduce their market value."

Mr. Lee looked at the ammunition boxes. They were airtight metal containers with soft inner lids which had to be cut or torn open with a tool. He nodded reluctantly.

"Okay. I will accept them unseen. Now we can start loading."

He grabbed the rope handle of one of the rifle boxes and looked up at Girija.

Girija smiled, but made no move to take the other handle. Once the boxes were in the truck, there was nothing to prevent Mr. Lee's hitting him on the head with the case opener and taking the receipt from him while he was unconscious. He had a feeling that Mr. Lee was aware of the fact.

"Do you not think, Mr. Lee," he said, "that we should complete our business first?"

"There is plenty of time for that."

Girija held up the flashlight. "By the time we have finished the loading, this battery will be very weak. Let us complete our business now, Mr. Lee, while there is light."

Mr. Lee stared at him resentfully, then shrugged. "As long as you help with the loading, I do not care."

"I will certainly help you." Girija produced Mr. Lee's receipt from his pocket and held it up.

Mr. Lee shrugged again and got out the promissory note. The two pieces of paper changed hands. The moment he had his note, Girija lit a match and burned it. Mr. Lee did the same with his receipt. The transaction was complete.

It took an hour to load the truck, and Mr. Lee became abusive over Girija's refusal to use the flashlight to guide them across the scrub. When the job was finished, Girija went back alone to the oil store to replace the padlock on the door. As he did so, he heard the truck start up and drive off. Mr. Lee had not had the elementary courtesy to wait and say good-by.

Girija went back to the track, picked up his bicycle, and started for home. When he had gone about a mile, he remembered that he had left the trolley with the scooter wheels in the oil store. For a moment or two he wondered if he should go back and get rid of it; then the absurdity of the notion struck him. What could a pair of wheels and a strap tell anybody? He had nothing to hide any more; nothing, that is, except a check for twenty-five thousand dollars.

When he reached his house he examined the tin trunk to see that the lock had not been tampered with. He did not open it. He did not even wait to undress before he lay down on the charpoy and went to sleep.

iii

It was one in the morning when Tan Yam Heng drove the truck up to the gate of the Anglo-Malay Transport Company's compound. The Sikh night watchman came out of his hut and opened the gate. Yam Heng told him to remain at the gate and then drove through to the unloading bay of number-two godown.

The unloading platform was level with the tailboard of the truck. It did not take him long to drag the boxes out and stack them inside the two large machinery crates he had brought in some hours earlier. He had only been able to guess at the various dimensions of the boxes, and they had to be wedged and braced inside the crates; but he had anticipated this, and had provided himself with the wood and tools he would need to do the job. By two thirty both crates were ready to ship. He left them on the platform and drove himself in the truck back to his brother's house. Tan Siow Mong had waited up for him.

"Was everything in order?" he asked.

"Yes."

"Were the goods according to specification?"

"I opened and counted everything except the ammunition. Those boxes are sealed."

"And he has the check."

"Of course."

"You do not seem pleased. Has anything gone wrong?"

"That Indian clerk is insufferable. He treated me as if I were a crook."

His brother nodded calmly. "I warned you he was no fool," he said.

The following morning Tan Siow Mong had a brief interview with Kwong Kee, master of the Anglo-Malay Transport Company's motor junk *Glowing Dawn*, just back from her weekly run to Manila.

Kwong Kee was a square, pot-bellied man with a cheerful disposition and a veneral appetite that bordered on satyriasis. He was not greatly interested in the commercial reasons Mr. Tan gave him for switching the *Glowing Dawn* temporarily to the Singapore run. Nor was he interested in the cargo she carried. And if Mr. Tan's young brother were fool enough to want to go home by sea instead of comfortably by train, that was no business of his either. He was quite content to do as he was told. It was some time since he had sampled the Singapore brothels.

The *Glowing Dawn* sailed that afternoon with a cargo of latex and two machinery crates. When she was well out to sea, Yam Heng went down into the hold and stenciled the consignee's name and address on the crates: "G. NILSEN, C/O CHEN WAREHOUSE CO. SINGAPORE. IN BOND."

iv

The night before the *Silver Isle* reached Saigon, there was a ship's gala dance. The notice had said: "Fancy Dress Optional."

On the advice of his cabin steward, who had lived through many of these occasions, Greg went as a Spanish hidalgo. It was easy. All he had to do was wear the black pants belonging to his tuxedo, an evening dress shirt with a black string tie, and two cummerbunds instead of one to raise the waist line. The steward provided the extra cummerbund and also a flat-topped black hat with a wide brim. He always carried them in his baggage. They had earned him many an extra tip. As he explained to Greg, the advantage of the costume was that a gentleman did not have to wear a jacket with it, and in the steamy heat of the South China Sea that was a real blessing. Dorothy painted on the long sideburns he needed with her eyebrow pencil.

She herself had been undecided what to wear. She had discussed the problem with Arlene; but Arlene had been curiously unhelpful, and had even refused to say what she was going to wear herself; she wanted it to be a surprise. Finally, with the aid of the stewardess, Dorothy had settled for a German doll costume. The stewardess happened to have the dirndl skirt and the blouse with embroidered smocking. Dorothy made herself a coif with two white napkins from the dining room, and put big dabs of rouge on her cheeks.

Both she and Greg were ready early, but lurked in their cabin with the door on the hook until, by watching their fellow passengers passing along the alleyway outside and listening to their conversation, they had assured themselves that they were not going to be the only ones who had opted for fancy dress. Then they went up to the bar.

Most of the passengers had decided on some form of fancy costume for the evening, and, although many had contented themselves with funny hats, false noses, and other easily discarded fripperies, a few had allowed their enthusiasm to run away with them. In the bar, the pirates, Al Jolsons, hoboes, and Indian maharajahs were already drenched with sweat and in difficulty with their burnt-cork make-ups. Over their Martinis, Greg and Dorothy congratulated themselves on having hit it off just right; they had taken trouble, but not too much trouble; and they were comfortable.

Arlene did not appear until just before the ship's speakers announced dinner. Then she made a slow, regal entrance through the double doors leading to the lounge. She was wearing a *cheong sam*, the silk formal dress with the high collar and split skirt that Chinese women wear, and long jade earrings. Just inside the door, she stopped and smiled as if expecting a round of applause.

The *cheong sam* can be an attractive and becoming garment; but it makes certain demands on the wearer. She must be small-boned and very slender, with invisible hips and near-to-invisible buttocks, a flat stomach, and minute breasts. Her arms and neck must appear fragile, and her face must be round with high cheekbones. She must, in other words, be Chinese. On Arlene's shapely but large and well-padded body, and surmounted by her equine head, it looked grotesque.

Greg said: "My God!"

"She bought it in Hong Kong," muttered Dorothy. "It's the most lovely material."

"It still looks ridiculous."

"I didn't see it on her at the fitting."

"She must be out of her mind."

Arlene's entrance created a minor sensation, and there were one or two uncertain whoops of gallantry as she swayed over to the Nilsens' table. If she were kidding, everyone was prepared to laugh. If she were serious, they were ready to be polite. Meanwhile, they were embarrassed.

Arlene sat down beside Dorothy and the splits in her skirt gaped to reveal, on Greg's side, a large area of thigh and one pink suspender. She smiled archly.

"Well, what do you think of Chinee laundly girl?"

"It's a lovely dress," said Dorothy eagerly.

"It certainly is," said Greg. "Martini?"

"No." Her smile was challenging now. "Tonight I am drinking champagne."

They went down to dinner twenty minutes late, and had to run a gauntlet of eyes as they crossed to their table. Arlene's half-bottle of champagne seemed to have gone to her head, and she began calling Greg "Don Gregorio" and Dorothy "Gretchen." She was thoroughly pleased with herself, looking about her with the calm assurance of a woman who knows that she is the most attractive in the room.

When the dancing began, she became skittish, breaking away from her part-
ners to execute little hip-waggling solos in the middle of the deck. Greg and
Dorothy, dancing sedately on the outskirts, glanced at one another.

Dorothy was worried. "I don't understand it," she muttered; "she usually
has such good taste in clothes."

"Yes."

"Well, you must admit she *has*."

"If you ask me," said Greg, "she had a few belts in her cabin before she
came up."

"Now, darling, that's a nasty thing to say."

"Well, look at her."

Arlene, with her arms stretched out wide, her head turned over her right
shoulder, and her chin tilted imperiously, was now dancing a flamenco. Her
partner, one of the ship's officers, was rotating around her somewhat helplessly. He had an uneasy grin on his face.

"She's just a little excited," said Dorothy defensively. "Anyway, she's
having a good time."

"In my opinion, she's making a horse's ass of herself."

"Really, Greg!"

Arlene did not return to their table. When a "Leap Year" dance was
announced, she made a beeline for the Captain. After that dance she returned
with him to his table; whether by invitation or not it was impossible to
determine.

The following morning, when they were going up the river to Saigon, she
did not appear at her usual time; but Greg and Dorothy were too busy shooting with their movie camera and watching the sampans and the riverbanks go
by to give her much thought. They found her, immaculate but a trifle pen-
sive, sitting in the bar after the ship had docked.

"What happened to you last night?" she asked Dorothy as they joined her.

"We went down around eleven thirty."

"Four o'clock, me," Arlene said grimly. "The barman opened up a can of
wienies. He's got an electric grill back there. That was after I'd switched to
Scotch."

"Who else was there?" Dorothy asked.

"Nobody. Just the barman and me. He comes from L.A. and he's a Dodger
fan," she added sourly.

But after lunch she felt fine again and they all went ashore. At Arlene's
suggestion, they crushed into a small Renault taxi for a tour of the city.

It was insufferably humid, and the driver, a handsome young Vietnamese,
smelled peculiarly of rotting fish. Arlene explained that the smell came from

a sauce used in all Vietnamese cooking and was no reflection on the driver's personal cleanliness.

The driver grinned. "Is made from fish," he said suddenly in English. "You like me show where make it?"

Up to that moment he had spoken nothing but French, and Arlene had been the interpreter. Nobody had troubled to ask him if he understood English, Greg remembered. Arlene, proud of the French she had acquired in her Red Cross days, had just gone ahead and spoken for them. As a result, they had unwittingly hurt the man's feelings. That was precisely the sort of stupid incident, Greg thought, that made Americans unpopular abroad.

However, the driver did not seem offended. "I show you on way back ship," he went on. "Make bad smell, but many vitamins."

"That so?"

They were traveling along a broad, tree-lined street that reminded Arlene and Dorothy of Paris, when the driver turned to Greg.

"Now I show you where Quiet American made bomb explosion," he said.

"How's that?"

"That café there." The driver pointed. "That was where Quiet American made bomb explosion. Many killed."

They were crossing a square now. Greg looked from the café to the driver.

"But *The Quiet American* was a novel," he said.

"Yes, sir. That is café back there. I was near at time of explosion. Was very bad."

"But it was fiction," Dorothy said. "It didn't actually happen."

"Apparently there was a bomb explosion there," Arlene explained. "I had this when I was here before. Somebody told me Graham Greene was in the city at the time."

"Graham Greene, yes." The driver nodded emphatically. "Presently I will show you bridge where Fowler found dead body of correspondent, and place where there was restaurant where they talk. Real restaurant now gone, pulled down."

"You mean people here believe that story?"

"Is true, sir. I show you the place."

"But it was just a novel."

"Look," said Arlene impatiently, "if you go to Marseille, they take you out to the Chateau d'If and show you the hole in the wall that the Count of Monte Cristo made when he scratched his way through to the Abbé Faria. They show you the dungeon occupied by the Man in the Iron Mask. It doesn't mean anything. It's just to make the tourists feel they're getting their money's worth."

"But that was an anti-American novel. If they believe all that stuff, my God! We're giving these people millions in aid."

"That's right," said Dorothy.

Arlene smiled. "I can see you two have got a few surprises coming to you on this trip."

They returned to the ship hot, tired, and out of temper. On their way down to shower and change, Greg and Dorothy had to squeeze their way past a pile of baggage in the alleyway. Their steward told them that three new passengers had come on board. When they went up on deck, they saw Arlene sitting talking animatedly to a florid, thick-set man in a khaki bush shirt. They were drinking Pernod.

At cocktail time Greg and Dorothy were sitting in their usual corner when Arlene appeared with the same man. He had changed into a white sharkskin suit. Evidently he was one of the new passengers. They came over.

"Ces sont mes amis Greg et Dorothy Nilsen," said Arlene. "Je veux vous présenter Monsieur Seguin."

"How do you do?" said Monsieur Seguin.

They shook hands. Greg said: "Will you join us?"

"Thank you." With a courteous bow to Dorothy, Monsieur Seguin sat down.

He had small blue eyes, a merry smile, and large pudgy hands with little mats of gleaming blond hair on the backs of them.

"Monsieur Seguin est ingénieur civil," Arlene explained. "Il va nous accompagner jusqu'à Calcutta. Monsieur Nilsen est ingénieur aussi."

"Indeed?" Monsieur Seguin looked interested. "In what branch of our profession, sir?" His English was excellent.

"How do you say die-casting in French?" Arlene asked.

Greg shrugged helplessly.

"Oh, but I understand," said Monsieur Seguin affably. "Mr. Nilsen makes the small pieces of all those things that the world thinks of when it hears an American use the phrase 'standard of living.'"

Arlene laughed heartily. Greg and Dorothy smiled. More Pernods were arriving.

"Isn't it lucky?" Arlene said. "I had a word with the chief steward and he's fixed it for Monsieur Seguin to sit at our table."

The *Silver Isle* was an American ship and most of her passengers were Americans. Not unnaturally, the cooking was American, and served in the American style.

Monsieur Seguin did not like it. He did not like the shrimp cocktail and tried to remove all the sauce from it. He asked for his steak *bleu* and, when it came rare, regretted that it had been overcooked. He did not want his salad on the side, but as a separate course, and requested that the slices of avocado pear be removed. He ignored the baked Idaho potato, and refused the ice cream.

He took one mouthful of the Wisconsin Brie, made a face, and ate no more. However, he remained, apparently, good-humored. His only comment seemed mild enough for a Frenchman who had not enjoyed his dinner.

"I needed to lose some weight," he said with a smile. "This ship will be very good for me. Here it will be easy to maintain a regime."

"I don't know what they think they're doing," Arlene burst out angrily. "You could get better food at a drugstore."

Dorothy chuckled. "The other day you were saying you thought the food was great."

"Great is a relative term, dear. Even an American chef must be able to cook eatable food *one* day in thirty." She was sharing a bottle of wine with Monsieur Seguin, and now she drained her glass.

Monsieur Seguin refilled it. "Mademoiselle, I think you are being very unfair to America," he said. "She has made some very important contributions to world civilization. Let us see—" he pretended to search his memory—"she has given us chewing gum, and Coca-Cola, and gangster films, and she has given us atomic bombs." He smiled slyly at Greg. "As well as a lot of advice."

Greg raised his eyebrows. "Aren't you forgetting popcorn?"

"Ah, yes. Pardon. And I was forgetting democracy also. McCarthy style, of course."

Arlene laughed. "That's telling 'em!"

Dorothy's face froze.

Greg smiled placidly at Monsieur Seguin. "I expect you have a lot of jokes about American tourists, too. And foreign aid."

Monsieur Seguin shrugged. "It is sad," he said. "You Americans give away billions of dollars to defend yourselves against Communism, but you ask everyone to believe that you give it because you are good and kind. Why?"

"Because big daddy-o wants to be loved," said Arlene promptly.

"America," said Monsieur Seguin, "is rich, and behaves like the rich always behave. When they begin to fear death, they become philanthropists."

"Well, most Americans aren't rich," said Greg, "and they certainly don't feel particularly philanthropic when they're paying their taxes."

"That's just childish," snapped Arlene. "Monsieur Seguin was talking about us as a nation."

Dorothy's face went pink. "I don't think Greg's the one who's being childish," she said.

"What I meant to say," Monsieur Seguin went on evenly, "was simply that American foreign policy has always, from the first, been made by men who saw the world through the eyes of money, of riches."

"If you don't mind my saying so, Monsieur Seguin," said Greg, "that is one of the stupidest remarks I've ever heard."

Monsieur Seguin smiled. "You know, Mr. Nilsen, there was an American who owned fifteen thousand acres of some of the best land in America. He owned land in New York and Pennsylvania and Virginia and Maryland and the city of Washington. When he died he was one of the richest men in your country."

"Who was that, Rockefeller?"

"His name was George Washington," said Monsieur Seguin quietly; "but, of course, you knew that."

Arlene laughed so much that she had the whole dining room looking at their table.

Dorothy sat with a face like stone.

After dinner she and Greg went straight to their cabin.

"I think Arlene behaved disgustingly," Dorothy said; "and as for that ghastly little Frenchman . . . Was it right what he said—about Washington, I mean?"

Greg shrugged. "Probably. He's the sort of man who collects facts of that kind. Of course, they weren't relevant to the point he was trying to make, but that wouldn't interest him. He's a debater."

"It's Arlene I don't understand. Encouraging him to go on talking all that anti-American nonsense. And on an American ship, too. I mean, it's such bad taste. And how dared she ask the steward to put him at our table, without even consulting us?"

"I tell you one thing, dear," said Greg, "and you'd better be ready for it. The next time that guy starts any anti-American stuff, I'm going to take a poke at him."

"You mean we have to go on eating with him?" Dorothy demanded.

Greg stared at her, a wild hope surging through him. "Darling, the ship's full. You know that. They can't rearrange the seating now."

"You mean we're stuck with them all the way to Calcutta?"

"Unless we complain to the purser and make a personal issue of it, I'm afraid we are."

"Oh, Greg!" She sat down miserably on her bed. "Our lovely trip!"

He sat down beside her and put his arm around her waist. "You said it yourself, darling. We're not in a position to choose our traveling companions."

Dorothy stuck out her chin. "Maybe not. But we *are* in a position to choose the way we travel."

"Darling, we're booked through on this ship to Calcutta."

"Maybe we are, but we can change our minds. We could stop over at Singapore, take a side trip or two, and then go on by air to Calcutta. You said you were going to do something for Mr. Tan in Singapore. All right! It's business. If you explained that, I know we could get a refund on the passage."

Greg had never loved her more. "That's right. Pan-Am and B.O.A.C. go via Bangkok. Maybe we could stop over there instead of Rangoon before we go on to Calcutta."

"Bangkok! That would be wonderful!"

"As a matter of fact, it wouldn't cost us any extra, even allowing for side trips. I didn't tell you, but this business that Mr. Tan asked me to do will net me a thousand dollars."

"Hong Kong?"

"No, real American dollars. And I could make a thousand more if we spent a day or two extra in Singapore."

"How?"

"Signing papers. Anyway, I'll tell you about that later. The main thing is that we enjoy ourselves. We don't have to worry about the extra expense. If we decide we want to get off at Singapore, then that's all there is to it."

Dorothy was silent for a moment. Then she said: "I know you never liked Arlene. I suppose she's not really a very likable person. I think that's why I felt sorry for her."

Later that evening Greg had a talk with the purser and then sent a radiogram to Mr. Tan Tack Chee in Manila.

Five

AT THE UPPER social levels of the British community in Singapore, Colonel Soames was known as "The Policeman."

There was nothing derogatory about the name. It had been applied originally to distinguish him from another Colonel Soames, who had been a retired Ghurka officer and a prominent member of the Turf Club. The fact that its use had continued after "Ghurka" Soames' death, however, had been only partly the result of habit. Although Colonel Soames' status as a senior police official was well known, the nature of his duties was not. He never discussed them, and any attempt to draw him out on the subject was met by him with a frosty silence. It was generally assumed that he was not, strictly speaking, a policeman at all, but something to do with Intelligence. To go on calling him "The Policeman" was a mildly sardonic way of underlining that assumption.

It was, in a sense, correct. Singapore was a naval, military, and air base of crucial importance to the British Commonwealth; but it was also a free port and a trading post, largely dependent for its economic existence on international commerce. In the latter capacity it was obliged to receive many strange guests. Colonel Soames' job was to detect the undesirables among them, and to see that their interests and those of Singapore as a whole did not seriously conflict. He worked in collaboration with the immigration department, the service intelligence organizations, the port and airport authorities, and the customs. He never ordered arrests. If any major criminal activity came to his attention, he either turned the facts over to an appropriate colleague for action, or, if, in his judgment, inaction would be more productive, he merely watched and waited. Occasionally he might suggest a deportation or the refusal of an entry permit; but most of his results were obtained simply by contriving to let the objects of his attentions know that they were observed and understood. Officially, he was in charge of a branch of the internal security forces. His own definition of his function was "discouraging the bad boys."

His second-in-command was a plain-clothes inspector named Chow Soo Kee. Every morning at ten they met to discuss the reports of the previous day. It was at one of these meetings that the name "Nilsen" first came to Colonel Soames' attention.

They had reviewed the current activities of a Belgian who was attempting to set up a central distribution agency for "blue" films from Bangkok, an Austrian who was buying girls for a new brothel in Brunei, and an Australian couple who seemed to be doing too well at the badger game. They had discussed the steps to be taken in the case of the consul of a Central American republic who, comfortably shielded by his diplomatic immunity, was making money in the opium market. It had been decided to advise a man posing as a theatrical booking agent that his record had been forwarded by Scotland Yard. Inspector Chow was getting up to leave, when he remembered something.

"By the way, Colonel," he said, "we have another arms dealer."

"Not that Italian again?"

"No, sir, a new one. Customs told me about him. There was a parcel of arms consigned in bond to a G. Nilsen from Manila."

"How big?"

Inspector Chow told him. "Probably Korean war surplus," he added. "They could be samples."

"Rather a lot for samples, don't you think? Sounds more like a small man trying to get his toe in."

"Well, that's the funny thing, sir. He isn't the usual type. Full name is Gregory Hull Nilsen. American citizen. Engineer. Comes from Wilmington, Delaware, where he has his own light-engineering business. Traveling with his wife. They arrived on the *Silver Isle* two days ago. Staying at the Raffles Hotel. They have an air-conditioned suite. Highly respectable sort of people, apparently."

"Well, that's a comfort."

"Yes, sir." Inspector Chow paused. "Except for two things. He made a false statement to the immigration people. Said he and his wife were here just as tourists. Made no mention of the arms business."

"How long did he ask for?"

"Two weeks. Immigration visa'd them for thirty days. The other thing was that he was brought to the hotel by Tan Yam Heng."

"You mean that union thug who's always losing his shirt on the pickle market?"

"Yes, sir. Apparently on friendly terms with him. That's what I didn't like. Tan's a member of the Democratic Action Party."

"Who else has this man seen?"

"Nobody, as far as I can gather. Yesterday he and his wife hired a car and drove round the island—to see the sights, they said. The driver says that's all they did do."

"Could be establishing their cover. I wonder why he lied, though. Stupid thing to do, if he's just a dealer. Who'd be in the market now for what he's got to sell?"

Inspector Chow thought for a moment. He knew that what he had to say would not please Colonel Soames, and he wanted to phrase it as delicately as possible.

Indonesia, the young republic which claimed sovereignty over the three thousand islands of the former Dutch East Indies, was an uneasy neighbor. The Central Government in Java was weak, unstable, and hag-ridden by Communism. In the big outer islands, especially Sumatra and Celebes, there were powerful revolutionary movements demanding secession and independence. The political thinking of these movements was religious in tone and strongly anti-Communist; and they had made fighting alliances. For three years or more, parts of Sumatra and Celebes had been virtually in a state of civil war, with insurgent forces in control of large areas and Central Government troops having in some places to defend even the big towns. With the long coastline of Sumatra only thirty miles away across the Straits of Malacca, Singapore was, whether it liked it or not, the natural supply base for the Sumatran insurgents. Their "liaison officers" and purchasing agents were the bane of Colonel Soames' existence.

"As you pointed out, sir," Inspector Chow said finally, "it is a small consignment. I don't think the Darul Islam people would be interested at present. You know they had a shipment of eighty machine guns and fifty three-inch mortars three weeks ago."

"Not through here, I hope."

"No, sir. Direct from Macao."

"That Dutchman handle it?"

"Yes. But he shipped the ammunition separately—over three tons, apparently—and an Indonesian Government destroyer intercepted it. They'll be wanting to replace that ammunition first. I don't think they'll bother about a few more rifles. I would say that at the moment the most interested buyer would be Captain Lukey."

He was careful to say the last two words very casually. Captain Lukey was the liaison officer and representative in Singapore of a small insurgent force that had recently begun to operate in Northern Sumatra. Colonel Soames's dislike of him was personal and intense.

Herbert Henry Lukey had been a regular soldier in a British county regiment, and commissioned as a lieutenant quartermaster during World War II. He had served, without distinction, until 1950, when the final period for which he had signed on had expired. His regiment had been stationed in Egypt at the time, and much of his last six months of service had been spent answering questions at Courts of Inquiry appointed to investigate the virtual disappearance of a number of emergency gasoline storage dumps of which he had been in charge. His answers had revealed qualities of imagination and ingenuity not hitherto apparent in his military career; and a secret, though unauthorized, investigation of his bank balance had shown him to be in the possession of funds far exceeding his total army pay for the previous five years. However, the smoke screen of confusion which he had succeeded in creating had, in the end, led to the inquiries being abandoned for lack of evidence. The gasoline losses had been written off, in the way he had originally advocated, as "due to evaporation." He could, and frequently did, claim that his army record was as clean as a whistle.

His subsequent record, as a civilian in North Borneo, Malaya, and Singapore, was not. He had worked in minor executive posts for several big trading concerns, most of which had, like the army, suffered some evaporation of assets before dispensing with his services. Eventually one of them had thought forthrightly and unconfusedly enough about its losses to go to the police. There had been talk, too, of forged references. He had left Singapore hurriedly, and after a while the charges against him had been dropped. Occasional inquiries over the next three years from police authorities in Colombo, Cape Town, Mombassa, and Bombay had made it possible to chart his subsequent progress. The report of his return to Singapore had been referred immediately to Colonel Soames.

"The Policeman" was not an intolerant man. He disapproved of the crooked and the *louche*, but he did not generally dislike them. Admittedly, his attitude was not as objective as he thought it was, and had a paternalistic, schoolmasterish quality about it; but that was largely a result of his training. He had come late to police work, and was inclined to treat most of the adult transgressors who came his way as if they were delinquent members of a regiment of which he was in command, and to which both he and they owed a common loyalty.

However, with Captain Lukey it was different; and the difference resided in the word "captain."

The day after Lukey had returned, Colonel Soames had summoned him to his office for an interview.

"According to your statement to the immigration authorities," Colonel Soames had begun, "you are here as a liaison officer and purchasing agent for the armed forces of the Independent Party of the Faithful of North Sumatra. Is that correct?"

"Perfectly correct."

"You say you are a liaison officer. What is the liaison between, may I ask?"

"The army of the Party of the Faithful and other forces in Sumatra hostile to those Commies in Djakarta, sir."

"I see. And in your role as purchasing agent, what are you intending to purchase?"

"Supplies, Colonel."

"Arms?"

"Supplies of various kinds, Colonel."

"Do you have funds for these purchases?"

"Naturally, Colonel."

"And where do these funds come from?"

"They are subscribed by loyal Sumatrans and certain friendly parties."

"Have you a banking account?"

"Yes, Colonel. Hong Kong and Shanghai, Orchard Road. All perfectly respectable."

"Are you empowered to sign checks?"

"With a counter-signature, yes."

"Whose counter-signature?"

"A member of the Executive Committee of the Party of the Faithful."

"Is the Committee aware of your previous record?"

"My British army record, Colonel? Certainly."

"I was thinking more of your record here, and in Borneo."

"I wasn't aware that I had one, sir."

"Weren't you?"

"I don't think I understand you, Colonel. Are you suggesting I have a criminal record in Singapore?"

That had been just what Colonel Soames had been suggesting, but he knew better than to say so. There had been no convictions recorded against the man in that area.

"All I am suggesting is that while you are in Singapore you are careful to respect the law. Do you understand, Mr. Lukey?"

"*Captain* Lukey if you don't mind, Colonel."

Colonel Soames had smiled unpleasantly. "And that brings me to another point. I don't think that there is much sense in my pointing out that the use of a military title to which one is not entitled is bad form and caddish. Perhaps I should simply remind you that it is an offense in law."

Captain Lukey had smiled back, equally unpleasantly. "And perhaps I should simply tell you, Colonel, that the British army isn't the only army in the world. Here, take a look at this."

He had handed over a paper. It had been a commission from the Commander in Chief of the army of the Independent Party of the Faithful of North Sumatra, appointing his loyal servant Herbert Henry Lukey a staff captain.

It had touched Colonel Soames in a very sensitive place. He had lost his temper.

"This is meaningless. You cannot accept such a commission."

"Why not, Colonel?"

"In the first place, you are a British subject. In the second place, you are, unhappily, an officer of the armed forces of Her Majesty the Queen."

"Not any more, Colonel."

"You may not be a serving officer, but you are on the reserve. You could be recalled to active duty if necessary."

Captain Lukey had grinned. "Do you take me for a fool, Colonel? I came off the reserve two years ago. I'm over age."

"Well, that's something to be thankful for, but don't expect me to recognize this rubbish." Colonel Soames had tossed the paper contemptuously back across the desk.

Captain Lukey had picked it up, folded it carefully, and put it back in his pocket before speaking. Then he had said: "Is that your considered opinion, Colonel?"

"It is."

"Then you won't have any objection, I take it, if I report it back to my commanding officer in Sumatra as the official British view."

Colonel Soames had hesitated. The Independent Party of the Faithful was probably little more than a gang of dissident Sumatran officers greedy for the spoils of local political power. But in Sumatra anything might happen. Within a few months those same officers could be members of a lawfully constituted government. A senior Singapore police official who had gratuitously insulted its leaders would find himself most unpopular with the British Foreign Office, to say nothing of Government House. The fact that H. H. Lukey was, in his opinion, a cad would not excuse the indiscretion.

He had swallowed his annoyance. "No, it's not an official British view. It merely represents my personal opinion of you."

Captain Lukey had not been deceived by the evasion. He had grinned infuriatingly. "Good show, Colonel. I'll tell my masters I'm getting full cooperation and all proper respect."

"You can also tell them that if there's any hanky-panky here you'll be out on your ear, and pretty damn quick."

It had been a feeble threat and Captain Lukey had known it. He had still been grinning when he left.

Colonel Soames had not forgotten the humiliation. He looked up sharply at Inspector Chow. "Why Lukey?"

"He doesn't seem to have much money to spend, sir. I should think he could just about manage this deal, though. Another thing: he's been trying to buy three-oh-three ammunition. They must have rifles of that caliber already. It would make sense to buy more. Most of the stuff going about at present is three-oh-oh."

"I see." The Colonel was thoughtful for a moment, then he nodded. "Put a man on to Tan Yam Heng. See if he tries to contact Lukey. Keep me posted."

"Very good, sir."

"What did you say that American's name was? Nilsen?"

"Yes, sir. Do you want me to . . . ?"

"No. I think I may look into that myself."

ii

Greg and Dorothy were enjoying Singapore. They had made two tours of the island and also crossed the causeway into Johore; and although they had had to admit to themselves that there was not really all that much to see, they were so glad to be on their own again that it did not seem to matter. In any case, they were having fun arranging side trips. There was a Garuda Indonesian Airways flight that could take them down to Bali, and they had made provisional reservations for early the following week. The only snag was that they would have to have an Indonesian tourist visa, and that took several days to get. Until it came through they would not know for certain what their plans were. So they had applied for the visa and decided that, if it did not come through in time, they would console themselves with a trip up to Penang. The man in Thos. Cook's had shown them some pictures of the island that made it look almost as enchanting as Bali.

The only area of dissension between them was that surrounding the Tan arms deal.

When Greg had, finally, explained it to her in detail, Dorothy had stared at him almost incredulously.

"But, darling, it sounds to me completely crooked."

"What's crooked about it? It's just a question of helping Mr. Tan to avoid a technicality in the Philippine law. Nothing more."

"Well, that's something, isn't it? It's their law."

"It wasn't made to cover this sort of eventuality."

"What sort is that?"

"Well, I think the idea of selling Communist arms to the anti-Communists is a pretty good idea."

"Maybe. But how do you know they *are* Communist arms? Who told you they were? How do you know he's telling the truth?"

It had been a long, inconclusive, and uncomfortable discussion. One passage of it had stayed in his mind to trouble him later.

"Supposing someone back home had come to you with a proposition like this," she had said.

"How could they?"

"But supposing they did. You know what? I think you'd call the police or the FBI."

"Well, this isn't America, and the circumstances and the people are all entirely different."

She had nodded calmly. "That's just my point."

"I don't get it."

"Maybe we don't know *how* different they are."

Their first encounter with Mr. Tan Yam Heng in Singapore had not improved the situation. They had found his appearance unprepossessing and his manner furtive. Indeed, when he had contacted them on the boat, Greg had at first mistaken him for some sort of tout. Then he had tried to hustle them through the immigration and customs before they had had a chance to say good-by to anyone on the ship. Greg had had to be very firm.

Later, at the hotel, Tan had produced an airmail letter from Manila confirming that Greg would act as sole selling agent for Mr. Tan Tack Chee, and revising their financial arrangements accordingly. That had been all right; but, although the letter had been addressed to Greg personally, Tan Yam Heng had already opened it and read the contents.

When he had gone, Dorothy had raised her eyebrows. "Not much like his brother, is he?"

"No."

"Do you think opening other people's letters is an old Chinese custom?"

"Well, I don't suppose it matters. By the way, Mr. Tan sends you and Arlene his best wishes."

The meeting at the Customs House the following morning had been no more propitious. After Greg had signed the appropriate papers, they had gone outside.

"The next thing, Mr. Nilsen," Tan Yam Heng had said briskly, "is for me to arrange meetings with buyers."

Greg had smiled and shaken his head. "No, Mr. Tan. The next thing is for you to give me a check for one thousand and fifty dollars."

"But that is not until you sign the papers transferring ownership of the goods. That is the arrangement."

"That *was* the arrangement. You read your brother's letter. The arrangement is changed. The first five per cent is to be paid over on signature of the customs documents. The *second* five per cent will be paid when ownership is transferred to the actual buyer."

It had been at that moment that Greg had understood why Mr. Tan in Manila had been so anxious for him to act as his agent. Under the earlier arrangement, there would have been nothing to stop Mr. Tan in Singapore from completing the blank transfer of ownership in his own favor. Under the new arrangement, ownership would only be transferred to the buyer. The explanation was simple: Mr. Tan in Manila did not trust Mr. Tan in Singapore, and probably for very good reasons.

Tan Yam Heng had scowled almost threateningly. "Between associates in business enterprise," he had said, "there must be trust and personal dignity in all negotiations."

"I couldn't agree more. And I think the best way of keeping that trust and personal dignity, Mr. Tan, is for everyone to do just what they've agreed to do right along the line. No more, no less."

Mr. Tan Yam Heng had had the check, drawn on the Manila office of an American bank, ready in his pocket, and had handed it over in the end, but with a bad grace. He had left, saying that he would telephone when he had arranged the meetings.

Since then, two days had elapsed and Greg had heard nothing. He had not told Dorothy about the argument over the check; nor had he thought it necessary to discuss with her his other misgivings. He was on the point of cabling to Mr. Tan in Manila to remind him of the time limit they had agreed on, when Tan Yam Heng called.

"Mr. Nilsen," he said, "I have an interested buyer."

"Oh."

"He would like to meet with you and discuss the proposition."

"Who is he?"

"A British army captain, now acting for a group in Indonesia."

"What sort of group?"

"I think it is religious."

"What do you mean, religious?"

"Does it matter? We wish to sell, he wishes to buy."

"It matters a great deal. Anyway, what's the man's name? How do I meet him?"

"His name is Captain Lukey, and, if convenient, I will bring him to your hotel this afternoon at five."

"Okay."

"And the price is agreed?"

"We ask seventy-five thousand, accept anything over sixty."

"Yes. This is very confidential."

"I'll see you at five."

He told Dorothy.

"What's a religious group want with rifles and machine guns?" she asked.

"How should I know? I don't think Tan knew what he was talking about. Anyway, there's a British officer acting for them, so they must be fairly respectable."

"I suppose you'll have to see him alone."

"You can stay in the bedroom and listen through the door, if you want."

Tan Yam Heng arrived ten minutes early, looking more furtive than ever.

"I wished," he explained, "to find the best route from the courtyard entrance to your suite. As soon as he arrives I will bring him straight here without telephoning from the reception desk first, if you agree."

"It's all right with me."

"The fewer people who see us together, the better."

"Why all the cloak-and-dagger stuff?"

"In such negotiations it is important to be secret. If some spy of the Indonesian Government got to know of this, it would be dangerous."

Greg avoided looking at Dorothy. "I see."

"Captain Lukey may wish to search the suite before discussions begin."

"Well, he can't. My wife's going to be in the bedroom."

"These are serious matters. I am sure Mrs. Nilsen understands."

"Look, there's not going to be any searching, and if the gallant captain doesn't like it, he can lump it. How well do you know him?"

"I have talked to him."

"Did he say he wanted to search the place?"

"No, but . . ."

"Then supposing we let him speak for himself. He'll be here in a minute. Now, why don't you just go down and wait for him, Mr. Tan?"

Tan Yam Heng went, sullenly. Twenty minutes later he returned with Captain Lukey.

The Captain was a tall man in the late forties with a slight paunch, a florid complexion, graying brown hair, and a large handlebar mustache stained on one side by nicotine. He wore the Singapore business uniform—white duck slacks, white long-sleeved shirt with breast pockets, and a regimental tie. He had a reverberating voice and a hearty manner. He came into the room with hand outstretched.

"How do you do, Mr. Nilsen? Sorry I'm late. Got held up in a spot of traffic."

"Glad to know you, Captain," said Greg. "Won't you sit down?"

Captain Lukey seemed not to have heard the invitation. He smiled broadly, put his hands on his hips, and looked around the room. "Well, now," he said, "the last time I was in this suite, General Blacklock had it. That was before he became C. in C. of course. I was his A.D.C. for a time. Rum bird, old Blackie."

"Can I get you a drink?" Greg asked.

"Very handsome of you. I'll have a stengah, if you don't mind."

"That's Scotch and soda, isn't it?"

"Little Scotch, lot of soda. Got to keep the old waterworks going in this climate."

"Oh, yes, I see." Greg was having trouble placing Captain Lukey's accent. Behind the stage British there was another intonation that he could not identify. Colonel Soames could have told him that it came from Liverpool.

"You know," said Captain Lukey, "lots of people say business before pleasure." He sat down heavily. "Never been able to understand it myself. But then people say all sorts of things they've never thought about. They've got rule-of-thumb minds. The shortest distance between two points is a straight line. Agreed?"

"Agreed."

"Is the hypotenuse of a right-angled triangle a straight line?"

"It is."

"And the sum of the lengths of the other two sides is greater?"

"Yes."

Captain Lukey gave him a cunning leer. "Yet the *square* of the hypotenuse is *equal* to the sum of the squares of the other two sides. How do you account for that?"

"Euclid accounted for it quite satisfactorily." Greg put some more soda in the Captain's drink. He was wondering if the man were as sober as he had at first appeared to be.

"Euclid!" The Captain laughed shortly, as if Greg had mentioned some long-discredited mutual acquaintance, and glanced over his shoulder at Tan Yam Heng. "You never bothered your head about that sort of thing, eh, Tan?"

"I do not understand." Tan Yam Heng had stationed himself in front of the door like a character in a trench-coat melodrama.

The Captain eyed him sourly. "I'll bet you don't. Shortest distances, maybe. Straight lines? Don't make me laugh."

"Are you meaning to insult me, Captain?"

"Me? Perish the thought."

Greg finished mixing the drinks and crossed over to them.

"Shall we talk business?" he said. There was a touch of impatience in his voice that he could not quite conceal.

Captain Lukey chuckled. "That's what I like," he said. "American hustle. Okay, brother, where do we go from here? You name it."

He was speaking now with what he evidently imagined to be an American accent.

Greg smiled. "All right. I understand you're in the market for small arms and ammunition. Did Mr. Tan show you a list of the stuff I have in bond here?"

"Yup," said Captain Lukey sportively.

"He's told you the price?"

"Yup."

"And I gather you're interested."

"Nope."

Greg stared at him coldly. "Then, why are you here?"

"Because I just *might* become interested." He had abandoned his American accent.

"In what circumstances?"

"Well, if the stuff were really new and not re-conditioned, for instance."

"You can inspect it."

"And if you cut your asking price by fifty per cent, so that I could make a reasonable offer at something like the current market price."

"There is no current market price."

"Mr. Nilsen, I'm just a simple soldier, but even I know better than that. I can buy rifles at twenty dollars apiece."

"Then you should."

"I'm not all that interested in rifles. Now, if you were to put a fair price on the machine pistols, we might talk. As it is . . ." He broke off, swallowed the rest of his drink, and got to his feet. "Tell you what. You think it over and we'll be in touch tomorrow. What do you say?"

"I might come down a little, but the price'll still be in the same range."

Captain Lukey nodded, almost appreciatively. "Well," he said, "there's no taste in nothing."

Greg found the statement obscure, but he, too, nodded. The Captain wrung his hand and went, exuding good will.

The moment the door had shut, Tan Yam Heng went to it, listened, and then flung it open suddenly.

The corridor outside was empty.

Tan shut the door again and turned to Greg. "Of course, he is bluffing," he said.

"How far? You did check the going prices thoroughly, I suppose?"

"Oh, yes. If he does not come back to us, it will only be because he does not have the money to pay."

"What happens in that case?"

Tan looked shifty. "There is another buyer, but he is away in Macao at present."

"When's he coming back?"

"Next week, perhaps."

"Well, he won't find me here. All right, Mr. Tan, we'll check in the morning."

When he had gone Dorothy came out of the bedroom.

"What a curious man," she said. "Do you think he really is a British officer?"

"Why not? I've met some pretty curious American officers in my time. Why shouldn't the British army have some dogs, too?"

The telephone rang. Greg answered it.

"Mr. Nilsen?" It was Captain Lukey.

"Yes."

"I'm speaking from downstairs. I wonder if I could slip up and see you again for a tick."

"Very well."

"Be up in a brace of shakes."

Greg looked at Dorothy. "Lukey again."

"I'll go back into the bedroom."

"No, you stay here."

Captain Lukey returned looking bland and businesslike. When he saw Dorothy, however, he became stickily gallant.

"Well, this is a delightful surprise. I'd no idea."

Dorothy said: "How do you do, Captain?"

The Captain did not miss the lack of warmth in her tone. "Terribly sorry to butt in like this, Mrs. Nilsen. Frightfully bad form, but I did want another word with your good husband. Ghastly shop talk, I'm afraid."

Dorothy sat down. "That's quite all right, Captain."

"I'm afraid Tan's not here," said Greg.

"I know. Saw him go." The Captain smiled boyishly. "As a matter of fact, I waited downstairs until he did."

"Oh?"

"Mind if I sit down?"

"Do."

"You see, it was a bit awkward."

"What was?"

The Captain smoothed his mustache. "Well, it's a funny sort of game, this. I didn't know quite what to expect here. No offense meant, of course. As soon as I met you, I knew that you were a good type." He hesitated.

"But . . . ?" said Greg encouragingly.

"Well, as I say, it's awkward." Captain Lukey gave the impression of a simple man wrestling with an unfamiliar problem in ethics. "I'm no saint myself, and if you tell me to run along and mind my own confounded business, I'll understand, but I do think white men ought to stick together a bit. Nothing against Asians, mind you, but, well, sometimes . . ." He broke off, his pale, anxious eyes searching Greg's face for understanding.

"Captain, if you'll just tell me what you're talking about."

The Captain turned apologetically to Dorothy. "So sorry about all this, Mrs. Nilsen."

Dorothy smiled sweetly. "Oh, I'm just as interested as my husband."

The Captain did not seem reassured. He went on with knitted brow. "Well, it's awkward, you see," he said again, and then appeared to make up his mind. "Look, Nilsen, man to man, how long have you known this fellow Tan?"

"Three days. Why?"

"I see. Thought it might be like that."

"Like what?"

"Nilsen, I'm not asking you how you came to meet him or who put him in touch with you or who recommended him as a contact man." He paused and then added somewhat unexpectedly: "Ask no questions and you'll be told no lies, I always say."

Greg shrugged. "I may not answer your questions, Captain, but I'm certainly not going to lie to you."

"Very decent of you to put it that way." Captain Lukey seemed genuinely pleased.

"Is it?"

"Frankness begets frankness, Nilsen. So I'll be frank with you. How much do you know about Tan?"

"Very little."

"Do you know what he does for a living?"

"Import, export—at least, that's what I gathered."

"Did he tell you that?"

"Not in so many words, no."

"What would you say if I told you that he ran a labor protection racket down at the docks?"

"How do you know?"

"Made inquiries about him. You see, I know most of the people in this business. Part of my job. I didn't know you and I didn't know him. Could have been a trap."

"A what?"

The Captain looked surprised. "Well, of course. Naturally the Indonesian Government knows what's going on. You know as well as I do that they've only got a few old destroyers and gunboats to patrol a huge area. They can't stop more than a fraction of the stuff getting through. So, naturally, they go for our weak spot."

"What's that?"

"Money. If they can get me tied up in a phony deal, they will."

"I'm afraid I don't get it. Are you suggesting I'm operating a phony deal?"

"Good God, no! Please don't misunderstand. This is nothing personal."

"Then, what's the problem? You inspect the stuff first. You don't pay until you take delivery, do you?"

"No. But I take delivery in bond. As soon as I start to move it, things happen. First some cheap lawyer comes along and claims that the goods have been obtained by trickery and gets a court order holding them. By the time that's straightened out, there's some other stooge claiming that all the ammunition is phony, and that instead of having cordite inside them the cartridges are loaded with morphine. So then the narcotics people have a go. And so on."

"But the stuff gets there in the end."

"If you're lucky."

"But you said yourself that the Indonesian Government can't maintain an effective patrol."

"If they know exactly when the stuff is going, the size of the consignment, and the approximate delivery area, they've got at least a fifty-fifty chance of intercepting it. It stands to reason."

"You said money was the weak spot."

"You don't know these people, Nilsen."

"What people?"

"The people I work for. Oh, they're good types in lots of ways, but when they pay out money, that's something special."

"Who are they? Tan said something about their being a religious group."

"They're devout Moslems, if that's what you mean. Most of the anti-Communists are. That doesn't mean they're not tough, though. Life and death don't mean much to them. They'd kill a man or be killed themselves without turning a hair. But they're funny when it comes to money. If things go badly, they give up."

"And you think Tan's working for the Indonesian Government?"

"I don't know. In my opinion, he's the type who'd work for anyone who paid enough. Anyway, I don't want to risk it."

"Then you don't want to deal?"

"I didn't say that. I said I don't want to deal with Tan."

"But Tan already knows about all this. If what you say is true, he can cause just as much trouble, whoever deals."

"Not if you're the principal. Are these goods bonded in your name?"

"They are."

"Then we don't need Tan at all."

Greg was silent. He was inclined to believe what the Captain had said, or some of it, anyway; and his own instincts were against having business dealings of any kind with Mr. Tan. Unfortunately, they were almost equally against having dealings with Captain Lukey. And there was the overriding complication of the fact that he was not in reality a principal at all, but an agent. To some extent he was deceiving Captain Lukey. He temporized.

"I'll have to think about that, Captain."

"Sure. Don't get me wrong—" the Captain was Americanizing again—"I'm not trying to pressure you, old boy."

The sudden lapse into British made Greg smile. "Oh, I didn't think you were, Captain," he said hastily.

His smile and his tone of voice combined to create an effect he had not intended.

"No need to apologize," said Captain Lukey cheerfully. He suddenly snapped his fingers. "I tell you what. Have you and Madame made any plans for the evening?"

Greg looked quickly at Dorothy. "Well, we . . ."

But it was too late. The Captain swept on enthusiastically. "I tell you what. Why don't we stop talking shop now and all go out to dinner, the four of us?"

"Four?" For one wild moment Greg thought that the Captain was proposing to include Tan in the invitation.

"I know my good lady will be dying to meet you. She's mad about America. Do you like Indian food? I mean the real stuff, not those ghastly Madras curries the planters ruin their livers on. There's a little restaurant we found where it's absolutely the real thing. You know India, of course?"

"Well, no But I'm sure you don't want to . . ."

"Then that's settled, then." The Captain smiled broadly at them both. "Sorry to butt in again like this. Supposing I pick you up at seven. No jackets. Just a tie. We might have a spot of the cup that cheers first."

He gave them a mock salute and left.

Greg looked at Dorothy. "Sorry, darling," he said, "I didn't think fast enough."

But Dorothy did not seem unduly put out. "Well, at least we'll go somewhere we wouldn't have been to on our own," she said. "I wonder what Mrs. Lukey's like."

Promptly at seven Captain Lukey called up from the lobby and they went downstairs. He was alone.

"Left my good lady outside in the taxi," he explained.

It was dark, and Mrs. Lukey was sitting in the shadows at the back of the taxi; but even in the brief glimpse Greg had of her as they were introduced, he saw that she was strikingly beautiful. Her husband got in beside the driver and told him to go to the Cathay Hotel. On the way there he talked almost continuously, identifying buildings which they could not see, and having rapid conversations in Malay with the driver which they did not understand. Dorothy, sitting next to Mrs. Lukey, exchanged one or two brief courtesies with her. From her English, which was fluent but overprecise, Greg deduced that Mrs. Lukey was not British. It was not until they were in the elevator which took them up to the Cathay Hotel bar that he saw her clearly.

She had dark hair, cut short, and a long face with a delicate, high-cheeked bone structure that reminded him of a bust of Queen Nefertiti which he had seen illustrated in *Life*. Her skin was pale without being pallid. She wore no powder and very little lipstick. Her figure was slender, with a small waist that the flared silk skirt she was wearing made seem even smaller. Only her legs were disappointing. Greg thought them too straight and shapeless. Nevertheless, she was an exquisite creature, and it was difficult to understand how she had been captivated by Captain Lukey. Beside her, he looked oafish and gross. She smiled readily, revealing excellent teeth. However, the smile did not reach her eyes, and at those moments she became less beautiful. It was possible, Greg thought, that she had a dull mind.

Her husband was an overpowering host. He drank deeply and talked incessantly, mostly about people whom he had known in South Africa and Egypt. Many of the stories he told seemed pointless to Greg until he realized that, in deference to Dorothy, and possibly also to his own wife, the Captain was censoring his tongue. He was the kind of man who has a stock of anecdotes packed away in his mind like the contents of a kit bag. He cannot rummage about and select what he wants; everything must be pulled out as it comes to hand, dirty clothes as well as clean. It was noticeable, too, as the evening progressed, that the social pretensions of those who peopled his memories became more and more modest. Brother army officers, generals, senior civil servants, important businessmen, and embassy attachés gradually gave way to sergeant majors, canteen managers, stewards, bartenders, and seedy men encountered in pubs. Captain Lukey's accent also deteriorated, or at least changed, earthier tones and racier speech rhythms replacing the plummy affectations of the afternoon. Greg and Dorothy found him easier to understand and, as some of his stories were quite funny, even began to warm to him. Captain Lukey the officer and gentleman might verge on the odious, but Lukey the soldier of fortune was not unengaging.

The Indian restaurant was in a street off Orchard Road. It was small and squalid. The waiters were Indians wearing dhotis and striped shirts with the tails hanging out. They spread sheets of white wrapping paper on the table instead of a cloth. A single fan stirred the warm, curry-laden air. There were a great many flies. Greg made up his mind that the first thing he and Dorothy would do when they got back to the hotel would be to take full doses of the Entero-Vioforme which they had bought in Saigon.

Mrs. Lukey ordered dinner in a language which she told Dorothy was Urdu. The food took a long time to prepare, and Captain Lukey had drunk four more stengahs and paid two trips to the toilet before it arrived. There were four dishes, two of them curries, and a bowl of boiled Patna rice. To Greg's surprise, it was all delicious. He often ate curried dishes—the University Club in Wilmington always had curried shrimps or curried turkey on the lunch menu—but he had never tasted curries like these. They were hot but not harsh, and there were undertones of flavor that he could not begin to identify.

"In the West you use curry powder already made," Mrs. Lukey explained. "Here the spices are ground fresh and mixed according to the needs of the dish. In this case, for instance, there is less turmeric and more cumin. That is what you taste."

A plate of Indian condiments was put on the table. Among the seeds and sauces and shredded coconut there were sliced bananas.

"If a curry is too hot," said Mrs. Lukey, "you add sliced banana and it becomes milder."

"You mean it seems milder?"

"No. It *is* milder. I do not understand why. Some say it is the juice of the banana. Try."

Dorothy tried and was impressed.

Mrs. Lukey smiled. "Some curries are so hot," she said, "that even I could not eat them without banana, even though I have lived many years in India."

The Captain, returning from yet another visit to the toilet, overheard her.

"If you think this is a good curry," he said, "you wait until you taste Betty's. She's a wonderful cook."

This was the first time they had heard Mrs. Lukey's first name. The

Captain's endearments, which had ranged from "darling" through "the memsahib" to "old girl," had not hitherto included it.

Suddenly the Captain slapped the table. "I tell you what. One night you must come over to our place and have a binge. The old girl will cook, and if we can still move afterwards we'll have a rubber of bridge. You play bridge?"

Greg admitted that they did.

"Then, it's a date. As a matter of fact, why don't we go back now and have a drink? It's only a furnished place we've taken while we look around, but it's not all that bad, and at least we'll be able to drink some decent whisky."

Greg had opened his mouth to hedge, but Dorothy spoke first. "I think that would be a lovely idea," she said.

The Lukeys' apartment was a few minutes' walk from the restaurant. It was over an electrical-appliance showroom and was approached by a long steep stairway at the side. The living room had pale green walls and contained a polished teak table and some bamboo-framed lounge chairs. In one corner there was a card table with some papers and a desk pad on it. Light came from a frosted-glass ceiling fitting. The effect was bleak.

"Make yourselves at home," said the Captain. Going to a wardrobe in the small hallway, he got out bottles and glasses.

Dorothy and Mrs. Lukey retired to the bedroom. Greg sat down in one of the lounge chairs.

"You know," Captain Lukey continued as he made the drinks, "the trouble with my job is that you never know where you're going to be next. Can't put down any roots."

"I suppose not." Greg had not thought of the Captain's occupation as one about which it was possible to generalize in such terms. Acting as purchasing agent for Sumatran insurgent forces scarcely seemed the basis of a career. Whether the insurgents won or lost, their need for a foreign representative with Captain Lukey's special qualifications seemed bound eventually to disappear; and, while there might be other insurgent forces in other parts of the world who could use his services when available, the business of contacting them would be hazardous as well as difficult. The Captain did not strike him as being a particularly robust type of adventurer. "How did you come to get into the job?" he asked.

"Oh, I don't know. Friends, influence." The Captain grinned. "Never could stand the ordinary desk job. 'Sing ho for the open road,' that's me." He reached for the soda siphon. "Say when."

"That's enough, thanks." Greg went over and took the drink.

"Yes, always on the go." The Captain shook his head ruefully. "Take next week, now. I'll probably have to go off to Macao for a few days."

"On business?"

"You can bet your sweet life I wouldn't go for pleasure."

Greg was beginning to understand the Captain. When dissembling he had the too artless look of a boy telling a lie.

"I shouldn't have thought there'd be much for you there at the moment," he said casually. "My information is that the buyers are all moving in here."

The Captain looked at him quickly. "The Dutchman's still there."

"I'm only telling you what I heard."

The Captain stared at him gloomily for a moment and then, with a visible effort, relaxed. "No shop in the mess," he said. "Cost you drinks all round in the old days. All the same, I'd like to know where we stand pretty soon. About Tan, for instance, you said you'd think it over. How long do you want?"

"Twenty-four hours."

"Cards on the table, Nilsen. Got another buyer on ice?"

"Could be." Greg was enjoying this.

"Is he dealing with Tan?"

"Look, I said I want twenty-four hours to think it over. Until tomorrow evening. I'd like to deal with you, Captain, and as long as there's no misunderstanding about price range, I'm sure we can work something out. If you want to save time, you can arrange with Tan to inspect the stuff at the warehouse in the morning."

"I told you, I don't want to deal with Tan."

"He's merely holding the customs documents at present. You wouldn't be committing yourself to anything."

"All right. As long as we understand one another."

The women came out of the bedroom and the Captain returned to his reminiscences. Soon Greg and Dorothy left.

As they were walking to the taxi rank by the Cathay Hotel, Greg told her about his brief business discussion.

"You know," he added, "I'm a bit sorry for that man."

Dorothy laughed.

"Oh, I know he's a phony," Greg said. "All that gobbledygook he talks, all those stories, all that false bonhomie."

"And all those trips to the men's room."

"It's not his fault if he has a weak bladder."

"He shouldn't drink so much."

"I think he's a pretty depressed character. I think he has to have a few drinks to stay in one piece. You know, he wants those arms badly and tried to pretend that he didn't. It was pathetic, bush-league stuff. It made me feel like a con man."

"Famous last words."

"All right. We'll see."

They walked on in silence for a moment or two. "I liked her," said Dorothy.

"Yes, what about that! How in the world did he do it? She looks like something out of *Vogue*. Do you think she really likes him?"

"Oh, yes."

"Attraction of opposites, I suppose. What nationality is she? 'Betty' sounds British enough, but she's got a funny sort of accent."

Dorothy glanced at him wonderingly. "You mean you didn't get it?"

"Get what?"

"She's Eurasian."

"She's what?"

"Well, Anglo-Indian, she called it. Her mother came from Bombay. She didn't say much, but I think it must have been very important to her to marry an Englishman."

"Even that one?"

"I told you, she's very fond of him."

He drew her arm through his. "I'm glad we came on this trip together," he said.

Dorothy smiled.

When they got back to the hotel, there was a message for Greg. Mr. Lane Harvey of the American Syndicated Wire Service had telephoned, and would call again in the morning.

Before he went to sleep that night, Greg booked a person-to-person call to Mr. Tan Tack Chee in Manila.

iii

While they were at breakfast the following morning, the Singapore overseas operator called to say that Mr. Tan was not then in Manila but was expected back that afternoon. Greg placed a call for 4:00 p.m. Manila time.

Just as he put the telephone down, it rang again.

"Mr. Nilsen? This is Lane Harvey, American Syndicated Wire Service."

"Yes?"

"You're from Wilmington, Delaware, I believe."

"That's right."

"And you have a die-casting business there?"

"Yes. What's all this about? The plant hasn't burned down, has it?"

Mr. Harvey chuckled. "No, nothing like that. It's just that I'd like to send back a story on you, if you could spare me half an hour sometime today."

"Well, yes, of course. But, Mr. Harvey, it's not a very big plant, you know, and I'm not an important man. Mrs. Nilsen and I are just tourists stopping over for a few days. I don't want to waste your time."

"Mr. Nilsen, you wouldn't be wasting my time. That's the very reason I want to talk to you. More Americans are traveling now than ever before. New York's doing a survey on the problems they run into, what they don't like, what they do like, and so on. We don't get many stopping over here in Singapore, so if you could spare the time I'd be grateful."

"Okay, if you think it's worth it. When do you suggest?"

"Well, let's see. Are you doing anything for lunch?"

"I don't think so."

"Then why don't you and Mrs. Nilsen come along to the American Club?"

"Well, that's very kind of you, but . . ."

"Mr. Nilsen, I've got to try and justify my expense account sometimes." Greg laughed. "All right, Mr. Harvey."

"Twelve thirty, then? I'll send the office car for you."

"We can take a cab."

"No trouble. The car'll pick you up at twelve thirty."

Greg gave Dorothy the gist of the conversation.

"Isn't it a bit unusual?" she said. "Why doesn't he just come over here?"

"I don't know. Perhaps that's the way they like to do things in Singapore."

Lane Harvey was a balding man of about forty with an unhealthy complexion and sleepy eyes. He spoke slowly and carefully, as if he were under some emotional pressure that he was striving to ignore, or as if he were listening all the time to the voice of a doctor telling him to relax or suffer the consequences.

"For a wire-service man," he said, "this place is Siberia. Politically, Southeast Asia is one of the most important areas in the world. In Vietnam, Laos, Cambodia, Thailand, Sumatra, Java, the Islands, everywhere around, there's history being made. But all around. Not in Singapore. We're in the eye of the storm here."

"So all you have to do is interview American tourists," said Dorothy. "It's a shame."

Lane Harvey smiled. "I'll tell you a secret, Mrs. Nilsen. It's more comfortable here than those other places, and I like being comfortable. But an American correspondent who doesn't wail for the dangers and discomforts of the battlefront is guilty of unprofessional conduct." He signaled to the waiter for another round of drinks. "Now tell me about your trip."

Greg began to do so. Lane Harvey listened attentively, nodding understandingly now and then, but asking no questions. After a few minutes Greg, beginning to hear the sound of his own voice droning on, broke off.

"Look, Mr. Harvey, this must be very boring for you."

"No, no."

"Isn't there something else we can talk about?"

"You've given me just what I wanted." He looked across the ranch-style patio. "By the way, I hope you don't mind. I asked someone else to join us for lunch. He's very British, pukka sahib and all that, but he knows a lot about Singapore. You might find him interesting."

A lean, gray-haired man with a long, narrow head and a receding chin was advancing across the patio toward them. He was one of the few men there wearing a jacket. He came up to the table.

"Hallo, Harvey. Hope I'm not late."

"Not a bit. Sit down and have a drink. Mr. and Mrs. Nilsen, this is Colonel Soames."

Over lunch, Lane Harvey insisted on telling the Colonel all about their trip, the details of which he recalled with remarkable accuracy. Greg became embarrassed.

"Now, wait a minute," he said. "Thousands of Americans must do this trip every year. There's nothing special about it."

"Yes, but we ought to do more about them in Singapore," said the Colonel. "All we get as a rule are the transient passengers off the boats. They buy a few batik sarongs and that's the end of it. Now, you, for instance—what made you decide to stay in Singapore? It would be interesting to know."

Greg glanced at Dorothy and grinned. "We were escaping," he said.

The Colonel looked startled. "Indeed?"

"From the ship's bore."

"Oh, now, that isn't fair," Dorothy protested. "Arlene may have been difficult, but she wasn't a bore." She turned to the Colonel "You see, we were going on to Calcutta, but—well, we thought it might be better to get off here and take a side trip. Anyway, there was some business Greg wanted to attend to here, so it fitted in quite well."

The waiter came over and said something to Lane Harvey. He got up apologetically. "Call from New York," he said. "I'll only be a few minutes, but don't you wait for me, please." He left them.

The Colonel nodded genially. "Nothing like combining business with pleasure," he remarked.

"Harvey was saying that you knew a lot about Singapore," Greg said. "Are you in the tourist business here?"

The Colonel began eating his steak. "I suppose you might call it that," he replied.

"Then I expect you know quite a lot of the local people."

The Colonel shrugged. "Big place, Singapore," he said. "Over a million now. Mostly Chinese, of course."

"I suppose you don't happen to know of a Chinese named Tan Yam Heng?"

Dorothy said: "Oh, darling, I don't think you ought to bother the Colonel with all that."

"No bother, Mrs. Nilsen," the Colonel said cheerfully. "As a matter of fact, I do happen to know the chap. Trade-union organizer. That the one you mean?"

"Well, I heard it put a little more crudely," Greg said.

"Labor thug?"

"Something like that."

"Who told you?"

"A Captain Lukey. Perhaps you know him, too?"

"Met him, yes. Having trouble with Tan?"

"It's a long story. I won't bother you with it. Captain Lukey doesn't want to deal with Tan. I wondered why. You confirm what Lukey said. That answers the question. I'm much obliged to you."

The Colonel gave him a toothy grin. "Could be another answer though, couldn't there?"

"How do you mean?"

"You're selling something?"

"Yes."

"Lukey wants to buy?"

"Yes."

"And Tan Yam Heng's the contact man?"

"Yes"

"Could be that Tan's trying to get a commission out of Lukey as well as you, couldn't it?" The Colonel smeared English mustard on a large piece of steak and popped it into his mouth.

Greg stared. "But . . ." he began, then stopped. The possibility had simply not occurred to him.

The Colonel chewed for a moment or two and then swallowed. "Squeeze," he said. "Old Chinese custom."

"But why didn't Lukey tell me that?"

"Might think you already knew. Might think you didn't want to know. Might think a lot of things. What's your impression of Lukey?"

"I only met him yesterday. We had dinner. Do you happen to know anything about these people he represents?"

The Colonel shrugged. "They're called the Army of the Independent Party of the Faithful," he said. "All I know about them is that their Committee seems to have some sense of self-preservation."

"Oh?"

"They don't allow Lukey to sign checks on his own. One of them has to countersign. Met that chichi wife of his?"

"Chichi, Colonel?" Dorothy said. "What does that mean?"

"Indian slang for Eurasian, Mrs. Nilsen." He grinned. "'Anglo-Indians,' as they like to call themselves nowadays."

The diversion had given Greg time to think. "Colonel," he said, "you told us that your business was with tourists. You didn't mean that quite literally, did you?"

"I said you could call it that."

"What are you really? Police of some kind?"

"I work for the government, yes."

"And this little party was prearranged, I take it." Greg's smile was wide but hostile.

The Colonel nodded. "We try to do these things in a friendly fashion."

"What things? Is there something wrong, Colonel?"

"Wrong? He appeared to consider the adjective. "That rather depends upon your point of view doesn't it? Of course, there are some cranks who think that gun running and the arms traffic are evil things in themselves, ethically indefensible. I think that's a lot of nonsense myself. In your country and mine the people can change their governments, if they want to, by voting. But there are a lot of places where it takes a revolution to do that. Look at Cuba. If somebody hadn't supplied that fellow Castro with arms, Batista would still be a dictator. Some people might say that those gun runners deserved a vote of thanks. Take Sumatra. The people there are afraid that Java's going to go Communist. They want to secede from Indonesia before that happens. Maybe they're right. Sumatra could be a self-supporting country. There are quite a few people here who think that she might one day join the Federation of Malaya. But, whatever they do, they'll have to win their independence first. They won't do that with words. Mind you, these are only my personal views."

"Do they conflict with your official views, Colonel?"

The Colonel shook his head. "No, Mr. Nilsen, they don't. And for a very simple reason. I have no official views. I am not entitled to any. My job is to obey orders. The British government recognizes the Indonesian government, and is in normal, friendly, diplomatic relations with it. That means that we don't like to add to its difficulties by helping its enemies. At the moment, that means you."

"Well, that's certainly laying it on the line, Colonel."

"I'll go farther." The Colonel took a cigar case from his pocket and offered it to Greg.

Greg shook his head. "No, thanks."

The Colonel took a cigar for himself and glanced inquiringly at Dorothy. "Do you mind, Mrs. Nilsen?"

"Not in the least." Dorothy's tone was icy.

"You were going farther, Colonel," said Greg.

"Yes. I should tell you that I was considering having you deported."

"I beg your pardon."

"Making false statements to the immigration authorities is a serious offense."

"False statements? What the hell are you talking about?"

"Steady, darling," Dorothy said quietly.

Greg took no notice. He was glaring across the table at tbe Colonel.

The Colonel stared back coldly. "Nature of visit—tourism. Isn't that what you told the immigration inspector?"

"Of course. It happened to be the truth."

"No. Only part of the truth. You are also here dealing in arms."

"Oh, for God's sake! Look, I also had a letter from the man I left in charge of my plant back in America. I even replied to it. So I'm in the die-casting business here, too."

"There's no point in losing your temper, Mr. Nilsen, and it's bad for the digestion. I said I had considered deporting you. Of course, now that I have met you and Mrs. Nilsen, I have no doubt of your good faith."

"Is that intended as a compliment, Colonel?"

"No, reassurance."

"The American consul will be glad to hear that."

The Colonel smiled. "You can't threaten me with your consul. I know him very well, and he doesn't have much patience with empty indignation."

"How does he feel about petty officiousness?"

"If I'd wanted to be officious, Mr. Nilsen, we would not be sitting at this table, but in my office. I don't expect you to like what I'm saying, but I think you might try to understand the political reasons for it. Singapore is a free port and a center of international trade. I admit that, legally, there is nothing to stop you or anyone else using its warehouse facilities as you are using them. But we don't like it, and you can't expect us to welcome your presence here." He smiled at Dorothy. "I'm speaking officially, of course, Mrs. Nilsen."

"But you don't disapprove of selling arms to anti-Communists?" demanded Greg.

"Personally, not in the least."

Greg laughed shortly. "You change hats rather easily, don't you, Colonel?" he said, and had the satisfaction of seeing the Colonel redden.

"I'm sorry you think that," he said stiffly. He looked at his watch. "I think it's time I was getting back to my office."

The look at the watch was evidently some sort of signal, for almost immediately Lane Harvey returned to the table.

"Sorry to have to leave you like that," he said when the Colonel had gone. "You know how it is."

"Yes," said Greg acidly. "The Colonel explained."

Lane Harvey was unembarrassed. He even grinned. "Funny old guy, isn't he?" he said. "I thought you'd like him."

iv

Late that afternoon Inspector Chow interviewed the driver of the American Syndicated Wire Service car. Then he reported to Colonel Soames.

"They went straight back from the American Club to the Raffles Hotel. The man was expecting a telephone call from Manila. The driver had no difficulty in hearing their conversation."

"Well?"

"The man was very angry, sir."

"I imagine he was."

"With Mr. Harvey, mainly. He used strong language and talked of reporting the incident to Mr. Harvey's superiors in New York, with a view to having him dismissed."

"He'll think better of that."

"Yes, sir. He spoke of humiliation and feeling ridiculous. He also apologized to the woman and talked of forgetting the whole deal. That was a reference to the arms, I take it."

"Pulling out, eh? Good show. I was pretty sure he was an amateur."

"Later, sir, he changed his mind."

"Oh?"

"The woman said that he had a business obligation to Captain Lukey."

Colonel Soames stared. "Mrs. Nilsen said that? Are you sure?"

"That is what the driver reports, sir."

"But she was on my side right from the start. I could see it."

"According to the driver, sir, Mrs. Nilsen made some highly unfavorable remarks about you. She appeared to think that you had insulted Mrs. Lukey."

"I?" Colonel Soames was genuinely bewildered. "I only asked her if she'd met the woman."

"Yes, sir." Inspector Chow's face was quite expressionless. "It appeared that you used the word 'chichi.'"

"What about it? She asked what it meant. I told her."

"She appeared to think that it was equivalent to using the word 'jigaboo' in America."

"What the hell does that mean?"

"I don't know, sir, but I assume that it must be something to do with the race question." Inspector Chow hesitated. "The woman used one very unladylike phrase."

"Well?"

Colonel Soames could not be quite certain, but he thought he detected a hint of relish in Inspector Chow's tone as he answered.

"She said you were a bigoted old bastard, sir."

Six

THE CALL TO Manila came through on time.

Greg was still out of temper, and cut through Mr. Tan's preliminary courtesies almost brusquely.

"Mr. Tan, I'll come to the point. The prospective buyer doesn't want to deal through your brother."

"Oh. Does he give a reason?"

"He says he doesn't trust him, but I have an idea that that's not the real reason."

"I see. And what do you think the real reason is, Mr. Nilsen?"

"Are you paying your brother a commission?"

"Of course."

"Well, I think he's trying to make the buyer pay him a commission for the introduction as well."

There was a pause. "What do you propose, Mr. Nilsen?"

"That I negotiate on my own with the buyer, and that you tell your brother to behave himself."

"Leaving everything in your hands, Mr. Nilsen?"

"You're covered. Your brother has the customs documents. He can hold on to those as security."

There was another pause before Mr. Tan said: "Very well. I will cable to my brother."

"Today?"

"At once. It is a pleasure to do business with you, Mr. Nilsen."

At five o'clock there was a call from Captain Lukey.

"Did you inspect the stuff?" Greg asked him.

"Yes. It seemed pretty fair. What about Tan?"

"He's taken care of."

"Good show."

450

"Do you want to talk business?"

"Be over in a jiffy."

Despite his admitted eagerness to buy, the Captain proved to be a stubborn bargainer. It took an hour and three stengahs to force his price up to fifty thousand dollars. His method of haggling was to isolate two items, the machine pistols and the bazookas, admit their worth, and then insist on putting a nominal valuation on the remaining items. He wore a tortured expression throughout, gnawed steadily at his mustache as if it were hurting him, and covered sheets of hotel stationery with pointless calculations. In the end Greg became impatient.

"Captain, we're not getting anywhere. Sixty-five thousand is rock bottom. If you don't want the stuff, just say so."

"But if we disregard the rifles . . ."

"Well, let's not disregard them. They're there, and that's the price."

Eventually, at sixty-two thousand five hundred, there was a meeting of the minds. When they had shaken hands on the deal, the Captain grinned.

"I'd have paid sixty-five if you'd stuck out."

"Well, I'd have gone down to sixty if you'd stuck out," Greg replied, "so we're both happy. Now, about terms. Cash on delivery, of course. Okay?"

"Okay."

"Good. If you'll get a certified check made out and meet me at the Customs House tomorrow morning, we'll square it all away."

The Captain stared at him indignantly. "I'm afraid I can't do that, old boy."

"Why not?"

"Well, I'm only the liaison officer, the agent. I have to follow the drill."

"What drill?"

"Well, I told you. Those people are funny about money. They like to do the paying out themselves."

"As long as it's clearly understood that the stuff stays where it is until I have sixty-two thousand five hundred dollars in my hand, I don't care who does the paying."

"You needn't worry about that, old boy. They want that stuff and the sooner the better. This is how we handle it. I give you a draft on the Hong Kong and Shanghai Bank, made out but unsigned. It requires two signatures, mine and a member of the Central Committee's. When you present that check to him, he knows that I've inspected the stuff and agreed to the price. He signs. Then you and I go down to the Customs House, you sign the transfer, I countersign the check, and Bob's your uncle."

"Will the check be certified?"

"We can go to the Bank and cash it first, if you like."

"Well, it sounds unnecessarily complicated to me, but if that's the way they want it, okay. Where do I see this Committee man?"

"In Labuanga."

"Where's that?"

"Oh, it's only half an hour or so by air. Anyway, my good lady will arrange all that side of it." He spoke rather too airily.

Greg was suddenly suspicious. "Where is it?"

"Just across the other side of the straits, opposite Penang."

"In Sumatra?"

"Well, naturally."

Greg took a deep breath. "Now, wait a minute. Why didn't you say something about this before? I'm not going gallivanting off into the wilds of Sumatra in order to get a check signed."

"Labuanga isn't in the wilds, old boy," the Captain said patiently. "It's a coast town with its own airport and a hotel. Pretty little place, as a matter of fact."

"I don't care how pretty it is."

"But that's the drill. There's nothing to it, really. It's always worked out fine. Don't misunderstand, old boy. I'm not asking you to pay your own expenses."

"I tell you, it's out of the question. Quite apart from anything else, I don't have an Indonesian visa."

"Well, that's easily fixed."

"Is it? I understood it took a week."

The Captain threw up his hands in exasperation. "Old boy, this isn't my idea. You want cash on delivery, Singapore. All right. Cash it is. I'm not arguing about that. But you've got to look at things from their point of view. They've been let down before now, and they like to know who they're dealing with. You only have to go the first time. After that it's plain sailing."

"Don't they trust you?"

"Of course they trust me. I tell them what to buy and what they ought to pay. They just finalize the first deal."

"Well, I don't like it. If you can't produce the money here without this drill, as you call it, the deal's off."

The Captain drew himself up. "I'm sorry, old boy, but I can't accept that. I thought we shook hands on it."

"We didn't shake hands on a trip to Sumatra."

"Old boy," the Captain said wearily, "there's a plane every day. You can be there and back in twenty-four hours. It's perfectly simple. Betty goes along with you, calls up when you get there, arranges the meeting, and takes you to it. You don't have to bother about a thing. Take Dorothy along with you for the ride, if you like."

"I don't get this. Why does your wife have to go? Why don't you go yourself?"

"I would, but the Indonesians won't give me a visa any more."

"Why not?"

"Naturally, they know what I'm up to."

"But they let your wife in?"

"She's got her passport in her maiden name. As a matter of fact, she looks forward to these little trips. Makes a change for her. Look, old boy," he went on persuasively, "you admit the deal's a good one for you. All I'm asking you to do is finalize it."

"You could have said something about this before."

"It never occurred to me that you'd object, old boy. Most of you chaps are popping in and out all the time."

"Well, I'm not."

"A half-hour plane trip, that's all. Surely, old boy . . ."

"All right, all right," Greg snapped irritably, "I'll think about it."

"I'll have to know tomorrow. They're waiting to hear about this stuff." He was looking troubled again.

"I understand."

The Captain smiled bitterly, shook his head, sighed, finished his stengah, and went.

Dorothy came out of the bedroom.

"You heard?" Greg asked.

"Yes. Do you think he meant that if I went with you he'd pay my expenses too?"

Greg chuckled. "I wonder. That colonel was certainly right about his needing a counter-signature on checks. What a way to do business!"

"What will you do?"

"I'm darned if I know. The trouble is that, as Mr. Tan's appointed agent, I'm virtually the legal owner, as far as Singapore customs are concerned. If I don't sell it to Lukey, what happens? After all, I do have an obligation to Tan. I can't just do nothing at this stage. As for that crooked brother of his, I'd be crazy if I expected him to find another buyer while I'm around to stop him picking up two commissions. It's got to be Lukey."

Dorothy shrugged. "Well, we'll never get another chance to see Sumatra."

"Are you serious?"

"Why not? Why shouldn't we both go? You know, while you two were arguing about money, the Cook's man called up. He said our Indonesian visa has come through. All we have to do is take our passport around in the morning."

ii

Mrs. Lukey, or, as her British passport somewhat incongruously proclaimed her, Miss Elizabeth O'Toole, met them at Singapore Airport with the tickets. The plane, a Garuda Indonesian Airways Convair with an Australian pilot, was reassuring. The discovery that the flying time to Labuanga was not thirty minutes, as the Captain had claimed, but a full two hours seemed a matter for amusement rather than annoyance. They were getting off the beaten track— and not merely as tourists, but in order to sell arms to a band of freedom-loving anti-Communists. Moreover, they were traveling at someone else's expense. The spirit of high adventure tingled in their veins.

Mrs. Lukey had explained the whole thing to them while they had been waiting in the departure lounge. The Captain's contact man in Labuanga was a Sumatran oil-company employee who had legitimate reasons for cabling regularly to Singapore. This man also had access to a clandestine radio, through which he kept in touch with insurgent headquarters in the hills. On these check-signing occasions he notified headquarters and arranged the rendezvous three days in advance. This gave the Committee member time to make the journey to the coast without running the risk of traveling by day.

"What sort of people are they?" Greg had asked her. "The Committee members, I mean."

"I've only seen two of them. One is a lawyer from Medan, the other is an army officer. I think those two are sent because they both speak English. A European comes with them, but only as a guard, I think. All the Committee members are Moslems."

"What sort of European?"

"He is Polish. Hamid, who is our contact, said that he had been in the French Foreign Legion in Indochina and was training them to use the arms."

The plane reached its cruising altitude and headed north along the coast of Sumatra. The Malacca Strait moved slowly beneath them, green among the shoals of the offshore islands, brown where the river mouths discharged the silt carried down from the hills, slate blue where the colder currents flowed down from the Bay of Bengal. Then, as the Strait widened, they altered course and began to fly over land. Soon, from their seats on the port side, all they could see below was something that looked like a vast sand dune covered with green moss.

"Jungle," said Mrs. Lukey.

The Indonesian stewardess began to serve bottled lemonade and stale cheese sandwiches. Twenty minutes before they were due at Labuanga they ran into a local storm and had to fasten their seat belts. The plane bucketed about wildly for a time, and they came in to land under a huge black cloud and in a deluge of rain. A sheet of spray went up as the plane touched down; but by the time it had taxied in to the arrival apron, the rain had stopped and the sun was out again. Their first impression of Labuanga airport was the smell of steaming mud.

It was the most favorable impression they received.

Mrs. Lukey had warned them about the immigration and customs officials. "They are appointed from Djakarta," she had said, "and they are not friendly to anyone here. Europeans especially they do not like. The last time I was here, they made two Europeans undress to be searched; but the papers in Singapore were very angry about it, and I do not think we shall be troubled in that way if we are careful. It is better not to smile or look impatient."

Greg and Dorothy did their best to remain impassive, but it was difficult. One immigration official took their passports away for examination and did not return. A second official then demanded the production of the passports. When Mrs. Lukey had explained to him what had happened, they were told to wait. It took an hour to recover the passports. Next the currency-control official ordered Greg to turn out his pockets and, for some unexplained reason, decided to confiscate his Diners' Club Credit Card. Finally, the customs inspector insisted on taking the lens numbers of his camera and impounding the exposed film in it.

Mrs. Lukey seemed to be as shaken as Greg and Dorothy by the experience. "I am sorry," she said. "They have never been so bad before."

"What the hell were they trying to prove?" demanded Greg. "Why take a credit card? I don't particularly mind. I can replace that. But what's the idea?"

"Darling, at least they didn't make us undress."

Greg, whose cotton and Dacron shirt was clinging wetly to his body, muttered that he wished they had. The loss of the film had particularly annoyed him.

The airport was three miles from the town, and the airline bus had already gone. There were no taxis. They found that they had to wait for another bus. There was a painful silence.

Mrs. Lukey made an unfortunate attempt to dispel the gloom. "Well, anyway," she said, "I don't suppose the same men will be on duty tomorrow when we leave."

"You mean we have to go through all that again?" asked Dorothy.

"If we are careful about our exit visas, it will be all right."

Greg swung around "What exit visas?"

"We have to get those tomorrow morning at the police office. As long as we give the man who makes them out a good tip, there will be no trouble." She gave them an anxious smile.

There was another silence.

As the mud dried, other, more human smells were beginning to emerge from the vicinity of the airport. The heat was stupefying. Dorothy could feel the sweat trickling down her legs. She made a determined effort to be objective.

"Well," she said lightly, "it's their country."

Mrs. Lukey turned to her eagerly. "Yes, they are really gay, laughing, happy people, but they are not always understood. It is the same in India. Because a European coming to Bombay cannot buy alcoholic drinks without a permit, he thinks that the Indians are not friendly people. That is not true. One must live in a country to know it. One should not judge a country from the airport. Nor from its customs officials."

She had spoken quietly and vehemently, and, in doing so, had suddenly become more Asian than European. It was a disconcerting transformation.

Dorothy started to make some sort of reply. Fortunately, a bus drew into the yard at that moment and she did not have to complete it.

Almost as soon as the bus left the airport they passed through a village. The houses were of the small teak-framed atap kind with which they were becoming familiar, but on most of them the atap was faded and torn or patched. Only one house looked new and cared for. There was a signboard across the veranda. On it, painted in Malay and English, were the words: LABUANGA DISTRICT COMMUNIST PARTY.

Dorothy and Mrs. Lukey were on the other side of the bus. Greg did not draw their attention to it.

iii

Labuanga was a port, and the terminal point of a system of pipelines connecting the oil fields in the area. The town sprawled over a broad alluvial tongue of land jutting out into the sea beside a river delta. It had been built by the Dutch, and the tree-lined streets and public gardens of the civic center had been laid out like those of a provincial town in Holland. The effect was bizarre. The trees were not lindens or sycamores, but casuarinas. Flower beds which should have contained orderly rows of tulips, narcissi, and hyacinths were lush with crotons, wild orchids, and scarlet lilies. Hibiscus rioted over the iron railings surrounding a plinth which had supported a statue of Queen Wilhelmina. The portico of the Stadhuis looked raffish under the burden of a monstrous bougainvillaea. The center of Labuanga was like a respectable Dutch matron seduced by the jungle and gone native.

Radiating out from it were the wide roads and bungalow compounds of the former European quarter. There were still a number of Europeans living there, mostly oil-company employees; but many of the buildings had been taken over by the security forces and other agencies of the Central Government. It was now called the "Inner Zone."

The change had a military as well as a social significance. The District of Labuanga covered an area of several hundred square miles and included oil fields, pipelines, copra plantations, over fifty villages, and substantial tracts of virgin jungle in addition to the city and port. An effective system of defenses against the insurgents operating from the hills would have absorbed at least three divisions of reliable and well-equipped troops. Major General Iskaq, the military governor of Labuanga, had at his disposal a garrison consisting of two demoralized infantry battalions, with three small field guns, ten decrepit armored cars, and sixty policemen. So far, the insurgents had confined themselves to night raids on outlying oil-storage installations, the dynamiting of bridges, and harassing reconnaissances in force. But the General knew that the day must come when the Party of the Faithful would feel itself strong enough to mount an all-out assault on the city, capture it, defend it against counterattack, and proclaim an autonomous regional government. When that day (or night) did come, the Inner Zone would become a fortress within which the garrison could hold out until help came from Medan. The problem had been to guard against surprise. At every road junction on the perimeter of the zone, concrete defense positions had been built. Now, at the first sign of any insurgent activity at all in the vicinity of the city, an alarm button was pressed, the defense positions were manned, and the rest of the garrison withdrew behind them. Only a small mobile column was left outside the zone to deal with the raiding party which had been the cause of the trouble.

The Inner Zone plan was one of those dreamlike pieces of military thinking which even their authors know to be unsound, but which are solemnly acted upon, nevertheless, because any plan is preferable to none. The General was well aware of the illusory nature of this one. The zone contained the police headquarters, the Stadhuis, and a number of office buildings and houses. From a tactical point of view, it was a mere geographical location, no easier to defend than any other part of the city. The power station, the water-pumping station, the port installations, and the telephone exchange were all outside it, together with the bulk of the population. But there were similar disadvantages to every other area that had been considered. The truth was that, with only two infantry battalions, ten armored cars, and three field guns, there was no right way of defending a place the size of Labuanga against superior forces.

General Iskaq was a cunning and ambitious man with a deep contempt for Djakarta politicians and a sensitive regard for his own interests. He knew that many of his officers were in sympathy with the insurgents and that he had only to hint at such a sympathy himself to initiate secret negotiations with the committee. He had a reputation as a patriot, and the price they would pay for his defection would be high. He had never heard the axiom "if you can't lick 'em, join 'em" expressed in just those terms, but it exactly described his own ideas about power. Only one thing secured his allegiance to the Central Government.

His father had been a Javanese coolie. All through his childhood the General had seen his father kicked, shouted at, and bullied by white men, or *mandurs* working for white men. There had been nothing strange about this. His friends' fathers had been treated in the same way. That white men should drive Javanese coolies to work, coolies who would otherwise have idled in the shade, had been in the natural order of things, just as it had been natural to stop work when a white man drove by in his car or carriage, and turn toward him, and bow. Then, one day, a white man who had drunk too much gin had accused the General's father of smiling at him. When the General's father had denied it, the white man had started to beat him about the head and shoulders with a thick cane. The General's father had been strong, but the cane had been stronger, and, as his face had become covered with blood, he had fallen to his knees crying like a child.

From that moment, and for many years after, the General had found nothing natural in a relationship with white men but hatred. It was not until the Japanese army had surrendered and the white men had tried to reclaim Java as a colony that he had been able to assuage much of his hatred by killing. What was left of it had in time been transformed into the irrational but unshakable belief that white men and Asians could have no interests in common, and that what was good for one must be bad for the other. The Party of the Faithful was financed by white men, its forces were trained by white men, and, if it came to power, it would be friendly with white men. For the General, the idea of coming to terms with such an organization was totally unacceptable.

His repeated requests to the area commander for reinforcements had been refused—and for a good reason. The area commander had no reinforcements to send. The General had been in a mood of bitter desperation when his new intelligence officer, Captain Gani, had come to him with an interesting proposal.

According to the Captain's estimates, the insurgents had roughly three thousand men in the hills and many unarmed sympathizers in the city, ready to help them when the time came. The General had only two thousand men at present. Yet, did he but know it, he could have a powerful ally with over fifteen hundred men to throw in on his side. That ally was the local Communist party. If the General were prepared to arm the Party men, he would have a disciplined auxiliary force at his side and superior fire power.

The General had stared at him angrily. "Are you mad?"

"Far from it, sir. What I am proposing is the creation of a loyal militia to meet an emergency."

The General had laughed harshly. "You know the area commander. He is one of Dr. Hatta's men. Are you fool enough to imagine that he would give me permission to arm the Labuanga Communists? He would have me arrested for suggesting it."

"You are responsible for the defenses here, sir, not the area commander. You are entitled to take emergency measures without consulting him. Besides, until it is equipped, the militia should remain a secret force."

"Only the area commander can authorize the issue of arms and ammunition. What is your militia to be equipped with? Stones?"

Captain Gani had had an answer for that, too.

Two months later the General had promoted him to major and made him his personal aide.

iv

The Harmonie Hotel was in the Inner Zone and consisted of a number of porticoed colonial bungalows built inside a rectangular, wire-fenced compound. The reception clerk, a handsome young Indonesian in European dress, was courteous but firm. The only accommodation he could offer them was a bungalow with three beds in it. All other bungalows in the hotel were occupied by permanent residents. This was by Government order.

Greg and Dorothy stared at one another in dismay, but Mrs. Lukey nodded as if she had anticipated the difficulty. "There is a sitting room," she said. "I can sleep in there."

The clerk took them along to the bungalow. The sitting room was an unscreened veranda with a tiled floor. The bedroom beyond contained three cubicles completely enclosed by perforated zinc screens and looking rather like old-fashioned meat safes. As the clerk turned on the ceiling fan, a thing like a soft-shelled crab with black fur on it flopped onto the floor at their feet and began scuttling toward the wardrobe.

Dorothy let out a yelp of fear. Giggling, the boy who had brought their bags in picked the creature up by one of its hairy legs and tossed it out through the sitting room.

"My God!" said Greg. "What was that?"

"They are quite harmless," Mrs. Lukey said. "It is better to leave them. They eat the insects."

But the thing had unnerved Dorothy. While Mrs. Lukey was away telephoning the contact man, she insisted on Greg searching every inch of the bungalow. He found some lizards and a mildewed slipper, but no more of the black creatures.

He did make the discovery that the bungalow contained no bathroom.

When Mrs. Lukey returned, she showed them the row of bathhouses, separated, for hygiene reasons, from the living quarters. One of those gloomy cement caverns had the number of their bungalow on it. Inside, there was a toilet, a large urn full of water, and a metal scoop.

"It is a Siamese bath," Mrs. Lukey explained. "You throw the cold water over you. It is very refreshing."

The rendezvous was for seven o'clock at a house outside the Inner Zone.

It was then a little after four. They had had no lunch. They bathed awkwardly and, when they had changed, walked over to the hotel restaurant. There was a noisy group of Dutchmen drinking in the veranda bar, and they did not stay there long. With some difficulty they found a waiter and persuaded him to produce some food. It was a warmed-over rice dish and not very appetizing, but they were hungry enough to persevere with it. While they were eating, darkness fell, and the square on the far side of the gardens, which had been deserted before, suddenly came to life. Market stalls were set up among the trees, people congregated, and food sellers appeared. A boy, squatting on his haunches by the roadside, began to play a bamboo xylophone.

It was a gentle, plaintive sound and curiously moving. Dorothy looked at Greg and he smiled at her understandingly. They were in a strange, far-off land, with no tourists within hundreds of miles of them. For a moment the discomforts of the day were forgotten. It was a brief moment.

Mrs. Lukey had said that it would take half an hour to walk to the rendezvous, and that they would probably be back at the hotel by eight o'clock. When they had had their coffee, they returned to the bungalow.

As soon as they switched the lights on, a large insect flew in and blundered about the sitting room, hitting the walls and light fittings with the force of a ricocheting pebble. Greg killed it eventually by knocking it down with a towel and treading on it. It was like a huge grasshopper made of brown plastic. Its hard shell crunched sickeningly beneath his foot. Two more came in immediately after.

Mrs. Lukey said that they were harmless and that it was best to ignore them; but Dorothy had seen the one Greg had killed and was afraid of the things getting into her hair. The prospect of remaining there by herself while Greg and Mrs. Lukey went off to their business appointment was becoming more unattractive every minute. She announced her intention of shutting herself inside one of the screened bed cubicles while they were gone.

Greg looked at Mrs. Lukey. "Is there any reason why all of us can't go? If we took a cab, Dorothy could sit and wait outside while we did our business."

"Of course, if she will not be bored."

"I'd sooner be bored than fighting these things," Dorothy said.

They had some difficulty in getting a taxi, but the reception clerk sent boys out and eventually one was captured. Shortly after seven they set off.

The taxi was a diminutive Fiat, and Greg and Dorothy, crouching in the back, found it difficult to see where they were going. After they left the Inner Zone there were fewer lights in the streets, and soon they lost all sense of direction. They had glimpses of the port, of the flashing beacon at the end of a mole mirrored in the water, and of a cluster of oil-storage tanks. Then they turned onto a road with a bad surface and broken fences on either side, bumped along it for two or three hundred yards, and stopped.

The house was about twenty yards from the road, and surrounded by an untidy litter of banana trees. It was built on teak piles and there were steps leading up to the veranda. Light showed through the plaited window blinds.

Greg pressed Dorothy's hand. "You'll be all right here?"

"Of course."

As Greg clambered out to join Mrs. Lukey, she said something to the taxi driver. He switched off his lights. As they walked toward the house, Greg asked her if she had used this rendezvous before.

"Once," she said.

The car's arrival had been heard, and, as they approached, a door opened and a man came out on the veranda. He had a flashlight in his hand. He shone it in their faces for a moment before motioning them up the steps.

He was very small and thin, with slightly bowed shoulders. He wore a black *petji*, a sarong, and bifocal glasses. He inclined his head courteously to Mrs. Lukey, and then looked at Greg.

"Mr. Nilsen?"

"Yes."

He held out his hand and said in good English: "I am Mr. Hamid. That is not my real name and this is not my house, of course, but you will understand that I have to be careful."

"Sure."

"Please come in."

The walls were of corrugated iron. Nightfall had not brought any noticeable drop in temperature, and the single room interior was like an oven. In
one corner there was a bed with a mosquito net looped back over it, but most
of the space appeared to be used as an office. There was a desk, a steel filing
cabinet, and a table piled high with small cartons apparently in the process of
being labeled. Against one wall were stacked some larger cartons with the
words FRAGILE—MADE IN JAPAN stenciled on their sides.

There were two men in the room: one Indonesian, one European. The
Indonesian was a slender, graceful man and tall for his race. The skin of his
face was stretched tightly over a prominent bone structure, and the veins on
his forehead stood out too plainly. There was a look of hunger and tension
about his face that seemed to contradict the ease and grace of his body. His
hair was long and unkempt. The European was thick-set and muscular, with
cropped gray hair, lined gray cheeks, and a thin half-smile which exposed a
set of stainless-steel false teeth. Both men were dressed in sweat-stained khaki
shirts and slacks, and wore pistol belts. The Indonesian was sitting by the
desk. The European lounged on the bed.

As Greg and Mrs. Lukey came in, the Indonesian got to his feet.

"This is Major Sutan," said Hamid.

The Major did not offer to shake hands. "The woman can wait outside," he
said.

Mrs. Lukey looked at Hamid, who nodded and ushered her out again. The
Major moved across and shut the door after them before turning to face Greg
again.

"Your passport, please," he said.

Greg took the passport from his hip pocket and handed it over.

The Major examined the photograph in it and handed it back. "This is
Captain Voychinski," he said.

Greg nodded. "How do you do, Captain?"

The man on the bed stared at him without speaking.

"Captain Voychinski is Polish," said the Major. "He is one of our technical staff advisers. Sit down, please, Mr. Nilsen."

He himself sat down behind the desk. Greg got the Singapore check out
and laid it on the desk. Major Sutan glanced at it.

"We have not done business together before," he said. "You will not object
if I ask you some questions?"

Greg smiled amiably. "As long as you don't object if I ask you a few, no."

Major Sutan considered him for a moment before he said: "Perhaps you
had better ask your questions first."

"All right. To begin with, why do I have to come all this way to get a check signed? Captain Lukey says you like to know whom you're dealing with. I don't get it. Don't you trust him?"

Major Sutan shrugged. "We trust ourselves."

Captain Voychinski got up off the bed and came over. "That's right, mister," he said. His English was only just intelligible. "That fool in Singapore know nothing."

"He knows how to drive a bargain."

"Does he know agent provocateur when he see?" Captain Voychinski demanded. He spat the French words out as if they were fish bones.

"Are you suggesting that's what I am?"

"How we know? You sell arms. How do we know you not take our money and tell the Central Government?"

"I went through all this with Captain Lukey," Greg said patiently. "It's not my business to deliver the arms here. I sell them in Singapore. When and how they reach you is your business."

Major Sutan leaned forward. "We have lost too many shipments lately, Mr. Nilsen."

"Sorry about that, but I don't know what it's got to do with me."

"I am explaining our caution, Mr. Nilsen."

"Well, I'm not proposing to tell the Indonesian Government about the deal, and I don't know anyone who is. That's if there is to be any deal to tell about."

"If, Mr. Nilsen?"

"That's right—if. You like to know whom you're dealing with. So do I."

Captain Voychinski laughed unpleasantly.

Greg turned and stared at him. "You're a long way from home, Captain," he said.

"Home?"

"Isn't Poland your home?"

"What is meant by that?" Captain Voychinski's hand had gone to his pistol.

Major Sutan intervened. "Captain Voychinski is an ardent fighter against Communism," he said. "He fought in Russia and Italy and Vietnam."

"Italy?" Greg raised his eyebrows.

"Captain Voychinski was an officer in a Polish division of the Wehrmacht."

"I see."

"Any more questions, Mr. Nilsen?"

Greg shook his head. Captain Voychinski smiled grimly and took his hand from his pistol.

"Very well." Major Sutan picked up the check and looked down at it. "Where did the arms come from, please?"

"Manila. Why?"

"You are not a regular dealer, Mr. Nilsen, and the composition of the shipment is unusual. Naturally, we are curious."

"I got the stuff from a man who'd taken it as collateral for a loan. He was left with it on his hands and wanted to get rid of it. I understand that it came originally from Red China."

"How?"

"I was told that it was intercepted at sea on its way to Malaya."

"At sea?"

"That's right. Does it matter? Captain Lukey has inspected the stuff."

"Arms from China to Malaya do not go by sea."

"Well, these did."

"What is the name of the person who told you?"

"Tan Tack Chee."

Major Sutan looked down at the check again and then took a pen from his shirt pocket. "I do not know this Tan, Mr. Nilsen, but I would suggest you do not deal with him again."

"Why not?"

"If you are not lying to me, then he lied to you. I do not think you can be lying."

"Thanks."

"On that point you would have no reason to lie." He signed the check and pushed it across the desk. "That is all, Mr. Nilsen. Will you be returning to Singapore tomorrow?"

"Yes." Greg picked up the check and slipped it inside his passport.

"Then the transaction could be completed the following day?"

"It could."

Major Sutan got to his feet and held out his hand. "Next time," he said, "I think that our dealings will be more friendly. It will not be necessary for you to come here again, I think."

"Thanks." Greg shook hands with Major Sutan, nodded to Captain Voychinski, and went to the door.

Mrs. Lukey and Hamid were waiting on the veranda.

"Is everything in order?" Hamid asked.

"Yes, the check's signed." Greg glanced at Mrs. Lukey. "Shall we go? Good night, Mr. Hamid."

They had reached the bottom of the veranda steps when he heard Dorothy cry out.

He started to run toward the road.

There were lights there now, and he saw the soldiers almost immediately.

Two of them were dragging the driver out of the taxi. Three more were coming toward him across the clearing. From behind, near the house, there was a sudden confused shouting and then the ear-shattering din of a submachine-gun burst.

At that moment one of the soldiers saw him, yelled to tho others, and started to bring his carbine up to his shoulder.

Mrs. Lukey was screaming at him to stop.

Greg stopped; and then, as the other two soldiers ran toward him, he took a step backward and put up his hands.

Seven

GENERAL ISKAQ ATE a second honey cake and poured himself a third cup of coffee. It was cool enough to drink, but he left it to get still cooler. He was in no hurry. He knew that he was going to enjoy the day which lay before him. A little delay in approaching it could only serve to increase the ultimate satisfaction. Meanwhile, there were more modest pleasures at hand. He picked up his binoculars.

From the window of his apartment on the top floor of the Stadhuis he could see the port, the river delta, and the sea beyond. The sky was cloudless, and at that early hour there was little heat haze. The previous day's rains were pouring down from the hills, and the silt-laden water was swirling out in fantastic patterns across the choppy waters of the bay. When the river was in flood like that, the currents interacted with the tides to produce a mill-race effect at the harbor mouth. Plans had been made to eliminate this navigational hazard by extending the mole; but the Government had refused to pay for the work. Now a tanker in ballast, trying to get alongside the oil company's wharf, was having to be warped in cautiously a foot at a time. The morning sun was glittering on her wheelhouse windows, and the General could see the white-topped caps of her European officers out on the wings of the bridge. Other white blobs on the wharf marked the presence of the oil company's Dutch undermanager and the English representative of the tanker's owners. They, too, would be impatient at the delay.

The General watched through his binoculars and was content. Admittedly, the situation had richer possibilities. For some minutes he had toyed with the vision of one or, better still, both of the warps parting under the strain, and of the tanker drifting helplessly across the basin to crunch into the side of a dredger moored there; but that, he knew, had been idle daydreaming. One should not expect too much of life. It was enough that the Europeans were inconvenienced and irritated. Enough for the present, anyway. One of them, the Englishman, was British vice-consul in Labuanga, and there were further tribulations in store for him.

The tanker was nearing the wharf now, and the brown water eddying around her sides was losing its power over her. The General continued to watch, but his thoughts began to stray. There was an important question to be decided. Whom should he tell first—the American vice-consul or his British colleague?

It was not easy. The Englishman, Mr. Wilson, was the local agent of the North Borneo and Federation Shipping Company, and his post as British vice-consul was merely honorary. In fact, it was said that the only reason for appointing a British vice-consul in Labuanga had been to enable Mr. Wilson to import his supplies of whisky and tobacco duty free. When told that a female British citizen had been arrested the night before and was in jail on charges of conspiracy against the Government, illegal trading in arms, illegal entry, consorting with criminals, and espionage, the inexperienced Mr. Wilson might well become confused and behave incorrectly. That would be most enjoyable. On the other hand, he might consult with the British consul in Medan or, worse, ask Mr. Hallett, the American vice-consul, for advice. They were very friendly. In that case, Mr. Hallett would have less of a shock when he discovered that there were two American citizens also in jail on similar charges.

The General wanted Mr. Hallett to have a big shock. Mr. Hallett's post was not honorary. He was a career member of the Foreign Service of the United States, and acted not only as his country's vice-consul, but as a local information officer as well, organizing subversive things like American book centers and documentary film shows, and corrupting promising young Indonesians by arranging for them to take courses in American technical institutions. He was also closely associated with the World Health Organization office in Labuanga, and had been known to accompany malaria-control and B.C.G. field units into the interior. On several occasions he had even penetrated into insurgent-held areas with such units, returning not only unscathed but impertinently unwilling to talk about what he had seen. There were a number of American tehnicians working in the oil fields; and when they came into Labuanga, they could be as riotous as Dutchmen. Mr. Hallett had a disagreeable way of making the arrest of one of these drunken gangsters appear as either a calculated affront to the President of the United States or the result of some ridiculous mistake on the part of the security forces under the General's command. The prospect of confronting Mr. Hallett with two American arms smugglers, disguised as tourists and caught redhanded in the company of notorious traitors, was infinitely alluring.

From the other end of the apartment he could hear his wife upbraiding one of the servants for not answering the doorbell promptly. A moment or two later he heard the voice of Major Gani. He decided to hear his aide's report before making up his mind how he would handle the situation.

The General did not really like Major Gani, who had spent a year as a student at a Japanese university and did not always trouble to conceal his belief that he was cleverer and more cultivated than his commanding officer. He had, too, an annoying habit of quietly snapping his fingers while the General was speaking. The General, a religious man himself, had also realized by now that Gani was a Communist. However, it was impossible to get rid of him at this juncture. The man had made himself indispensable; and so had the Communist Party.

The idea of seizing the insurgent arms shipments to the Labuanga area had been a good one; he was at once arming his secret militia and denying arms to the enemy; but without the Communist intelligence network to discover the times and places of the shipments it would have been impossible. The insurgents had lost four substantial shipments before they had changed their delivery arrangements; and now, thanks to Gani and the Party, the new arrangements would soon be as unpredictable to the Committee as the old.

It had been Gani, who had noted, in the immigration service's reports, the frequency and brevity of the visits to Labuanga of the British woman Elizabeth O'Toole. A more detailed study had then shown that O'Toole had always arrived from Singapore, and in the company of a male European of one sort or another. She had always left with him the following day. Out of five visits, one had been made with a Belgian, one with an Italian, one with a German, and one each with two different Australians. Since nobody in his senses, Asian or European, would regularly choose Labuanga as a place of assignation for any amorous purpose, Gani had made a further investigation and noted a relationship between the dates of three of O'Toole's visits and the dates of three interceptions of arms shipments. The Party had alerted the comrades in Singapore and inquiries had been made about her there. Two days ago a report of her true identity had been received, together with the information that she was about to make another visit to Labuanga. Arrangements had been made with the immigration service to delay the woman and her companion at the airport when they arrived, so that the necessary steps could be taken to place them under surveillance.

Major Gani came in briskly. As usual, his salute was more like an acknowledgment of applause than a mark of respect; but the General did not care today. He was hungry for information.

"Well, Major?"

Major Gani took off his cap and sat down before he answered. "The traitor

Hamid Osman," he said, "died of his wounds an hour ago, sir. It is a pity because I had hoped for much information from the man. The house they were meeting in belongs to a small importer. He is believed to be in Medan at the moment. We shall find out. Hamid Osman's house was most interesting."

"Ah."

"He is unmarried and lived with his brother, who is a radio technician. We found a radio transmitter there. It was still warm from use."

"You arrested the brother?"

"He had escaped. The two houses are only three hundred yards apart. He must have heard the firing."

The General frowned. "The radio was still warm, you say. Would he have had time to report to the traitors in the hills?"

"Perhaps."

"It would have been better if we could have had complete secrecy."

Major Gani shrugged. "There cannot be complete secrecy, sir. The American and British consuls here will have to be informed. And I believe there is a Polish consul in Medan." There was a hint of malice in the way he said the last sentence. The General would have to be careful. If it became generally known that there were four non-Dutch whites under lock and key in Labuanga jail on charges other than disorderly conduct, the area commander in Medan would remove them from the General's jurisdiction within hours. The area commander had a weakness for personal publicity and would certainly not permit a subordinate to take charge of a situation of such lively interest to the press.

"I will deal with the American and British consuls myself," the General replied casually. "They will want to be discreet. The Polish consul does not matter." He brushed the subject aside with a wave of his coffee spoon. "Now, about the prisoners. What information do we have from them?"

"It is a little soon, sir, to expect real information. I interrogated the taxi driver who took them from the hotel. He heard only that the house had been used as a meeting place once before. Nothing of value. I released him." He saw the General stiffen and added curtly: "He is a good Party member."

"But the O'Toole woman—what does she say?"

"Nothing, sir." Major Gani began snapping his fingers.

"And the Americans?"

"Also nothing. The man Voychinski advised them to say nothing until instructed by their consuls. It is not important. They are not important."

The General threw his coffee spoon down with a clatter. "Not important?" he demanded. "Four European gangsters engaged in smuggling arms to the traitors, not important?"

Major Gani sighed patiently. "Very important, sir, for propaganda purposes. But for our purposes we have someone much more useful—Major Sutan."

The General controlled himself. In his daydreaming about the white prisoners he had almost forgotten that a member of the insurgent Committee had been taken, too.

"What does Sutan say?" he asked.

"He refuses to speak."

"Where are the prisoners?"

"In the police jail, sir."

"Sutan as well?"

"Yes, sir." And then Major Gani made a mistake. "He is a strong man," he went on blandly, "and will not talk easily. I have put two good men onto the preliminary interrogating work, but we do not want to injure him too much, in view of the public court-martial that must follow, and it may be twenty-four hours or more before he can be persuaded. I thought it safer not to interrogate him at your own headquarters. He has many friends in the army."

"Yes." The General pushed his cold coffee away and got to his feet. "I was one of them."

"Ah, then you understand, sir."

Major Gani was an able and astute officer with a glib command of the Marx-ist dialectic and a keen eye for the weaknesses of other men; but he was also a deeply conceited man and in some respects grossly insensitive. To him, General Iskaq was merely a brutish and reactionary strong-arm guerrilla leader whom circumstances had thrust into a temporary position of authority—a thick-skulled clod to be deferred to and pandered to now so that he could be exploited later. The possibility of the General's disliking the idea of torturing a former comrade had not occurred to him.

The General looked him in the eyes. "Yes, I do understand. I shall take charge of these interrogations personally."

"In the case of the foreigners, sir?"

"In the cases of all these prisoners. Then we will see who will talk, and who will not."

ii

At the time of the arrest Greg had been too bewildered to be really fright-ened; it had been as if they were in some nightmare traffic accident involving a truckload of uniformed maniacs instead of another car. Later, when Dorothy and Mrs. Lukey were being yelled at, prodded with guns, and searched in front of a roomful of policemen, he had been too angry. The butt of a carbine slammed into the pit of his stomach had ended that phase. Out of the consequent pain and nausea had come at last a cold realization of their predicament—and, with it, fear. On the way to the jail Mrs. Lukey had wept hysterically. It had been Dorothy, calm and collected, who had found the words of reassurance. Handcuffed to Voychinski and Major Sutan, he had sat there in numbed silence.

At the jail, a single-story brick building in a walled compound on the outskirts of the town, Dorothy and Mrs. Lukey had been hustled off to the women's quarters. Major Sutan had been held in the control section. Greg and Captain Voychinski had been put into a cell containing one iron-framed bed, an urn of water, and a bucket. The whole place had a strong ammoniac smell thinly mingled with that of disinfectant.

Voychinski had taken their arrest philosophically, and, now that Greg's good faith had been so strikingly proved, his attitude became almost friendly. Unfortunately, he was one of those men who, in the face of danger, affect a sardonic facetiousness as nerve-racking after a while as any display of fear.

"How did they get onto us?" Greg asked him as soon as they were alone.

"When I know, I send you letter."

"What do you think they'll do?"

"To me? Pop-pop-pop." He grinned, showing his steel teeth. "Or perhaps . . ." He made the motion of castrating himself. "With you? Big trial after six months. After two years, perhaps, they let you go. With the women? If they let you go, they keep the women. If they let the women go, they keep you. Don't worry."

"Well, they'll have to inform our consuls, anyway."

"Oh, yes. Next week, perhaps."

"What about Major Sutan?"

"He no have consul here. Like me."

As there was nothing to sit on except the bed, neither of them had any sleep. Voychinski seemed unconcerned. He began to talk about his experiences with the German army in Russia and Italy. His facetiousness never flagged, but there was an unpleasant undercurrent of reality to all he said. Greg, who had served with the Fifth Army in Italy and understood what he was hearing about, listened with a mounting disgust that he found difficult to conceal. He had seen an Italian village after a unit of the sort Voychinski seemed to have enjoyed serving with had left it. He tried not to listen, and to pin his thoughts onto the moment when Dorothy and he would be regaling their friends with the hilarious account of how they were arrested in Labuanga and had to spend a night in the local hoosegow; but it was not a very convincing fantasy and was too easily overlaid by another in which Dorothy and he did not figure personally. In this, their friends were discussing with gloomy perplexity what the newspapers were referring to as "the Nilsen arms-racket inquiry" and wondering how come Greg Nilsen had made such a horse's ass of himself.

Soon after dawn a guard brought them a pot of rice and fish, which they had to eat with their fingers. Greg ate very little. His bowels were beginning to cause him uneasiness and he had been obliged more than once to make use of the bucket. Voychinski had some jokes to make about that, too. Greg's dislike of him was now complete.

The barred window of the cell gave onto an inner court, and as the sun rose, they were able to see through the zinc mosquito screen that it was an exercise yard. About twenty male prisoners, barefooted and wearing sarongs tucked between their legs like loincloths, wandered about aimlessly or squatted in groups under the supervision of guards with carbines. Inside the cell, the heat and smell were becoming unbearable. When, shortly before noon, a guard unlocked the door and beckoned to him, Greg's fondest hope was that he was to be allowed out into the yard with the other prisoners.

Instead, he was taken by two guards to a room off a corrridor leading to the main entrance. Except for a long table and six chairs, it was bare. The windows were barred. One guard entered with him, motioned him to a chair, and stood by the door with his carbine at the ready. After a brief interval the door opened and an army officer entered. Greg recognized him as the officer who had attempted to interrogate him the previous night, a handsome man with angry eyes and an air of carefully controlled impatience. Behind him was a man of Greg's own race, in a very clean white shirt and gabardine slacks. He was about thirty-five, stocky, and balding, with a round, chubby face and square shoulders. He stood in the doorway with a lopsided smile on his face and looked curiously at the guard.

As Greg got to his feet, the officer inclined his head. "I am Major Gani," he said.

Greg nodded. "Major."

"And this, as you requested, is the American vice-consul in Labuanga."

Greg gave an audible sigh of relief and smiled. "Am I glad to see you, Consul."

The man in the doorway nodded, but without looking at him. "I wish I could say the same, Mr. Nilsen. My name's Ross Hallett."

Greg started to move toward him, but the guard raised his carbine threateningly. Hallett took no notice. He looked from the guard to Major Gani.

"Good-by, Major," he said.

Major Gani's lips tightened and he began to snap his fingers. "The formalities have now been complied with," he said. "You have seen the prisoner. He is unharmed. It is now your duty to inform him that it is in order for him to be interrogated and to answer all questions."

Hallett shook his head. "Oh, no, Major. That isn't my duty."

"This is Labuanga, not Washington, Mr. Hallett. The prisoner is under our law, and so are you."

"Sure we are," Hallett replied easily, "and you have every right to ask Mr. Nilsen any questions you like. But that doesn't mean he has to answer them. You see, I've had no opportunity yet of talking privately to him. I don't think that I can advise him to co-operate with you at this stage."

He turned away as if to go, then paused as the Major said something sharply in his own language. Hallett answered him in the same language.

"What did he say?" Greg asked.

Hallett ignored him. Greg stood there, uncomprehending and irritated, while they argued. Finally the Major gave a reluctant nod and motioned the guard out of the room.

"You may have ten minutes," he said in English. "There will be a guard on the door."

He followed the guard outside.

Hallett's smile faded as the door closed.

"Sit down, please," he said.

"Now look, Mr. Hallett," Greg began, "all I'm worried about at the moment is my wife. You see . . ."

"I know, Mr. Nilsen. But we don't have that much time, so supposing you let me run things. I've seen your wife, and she seems to be okay. The British vice-consul is seeing Mrs. Lukey, and she's okay, too."

"You mean Miss O'Toole, don't you?"

Hallett sighed. "Mr. Nilsen, I don't have time for games. Whatever her passport says, these people know she's Mrs. Lukey."

"How did they find out?"

"I don't know. Anyway, that's unimportant. If you'll just answer my questions, we may get somewhere." He took a notebook from his pocket. "Now, then. Mrs. Nilsen gave me some basic facts, and, according to her, you have a joint American passport. Where is it now?"

"They took it away."

"The police or the military?"

"That officer who was just in here was in charge."

"What else did they take from you?"

"Everything—money, wallet, watch, the lot."

"They claim they have documentary evidence linking you with Major Sutan. What would that be?"

"I had a check for sixty-two thousand five hundred Malay dollars in my passport. It was drawn on the Hong Kong and Shanghai Bank and signed by Sutan."

Hallett's lopsided smile returned for a moment, but it was anything but friendly. "Do you know what sort of a spot you're in, Mr. Nilsen?"

"I have a pretty good idea."

"I wonder if you have. All right, give me the background. I want the whole history of this transaction."

Greg gave it to him.

When he had finished, Hallett was staring at him in sour wonderment.

Greg shrugged.

Hallett drew a deep breath. "Mr. Nilsen," he said, "I wish you could tell me something. Why is it that when an apparently normal, intelligent, law-abiding citizen like you gets hold of a passport and a steamship ticket, he suddenly turns into a juvenile—"

"Okay, Mr. Hallett," Greg broke in irritably. "You can't say anything I haven't already said myself."

"I wouldn't be too sure of that. Our country spends millions of dollars trying to help these people become a nation of free men, trying to give them confidence in democratic processes, trying to persuade them that some version of our way of doing things offers them a better chance of happiness than the Communist Party, and then people like you . . ." He broke off. "I'll give you the rest of the lecture another time. Right now we've got to try to get you and Mrs. Nilsen out of this mess."

"Well, Mrs. Nilsen, anyway."

"As they see it, she's guilty by association." Hallett leaned forward. "Now, tell me again. Your arrangement with Lukey was just as you've stated it? You had nothing to do with the delivery of this war material and know nothing about the arrangements that were to be made for that delivery? Is that right? Don't fool with me, Mr. Nilsen. I have to know. Is that the true picture?"

"It is."

Hallett sighed. "That's too bad."

"What do you mean?"

"The military governor's terms for your release are that you inform them when and how the stuff is being delivered, so that they can intercept and confiscate it."

"But that's crazy. How can I tell them? Lukey doesn't even own the stuff until that check is cashed in Singapore."

"They won't believe that."

"But they'll have to."

"There's no 'have to' about it."

"Major Sutan'll tell them I don't know anything. Voychinski, too."

"A traitor and a hoodlum? Why should they believe what they say?"

Greg was silent for a moment. Then he nodded. "I see. It looks as if my wife and I are going to be here quite a while."

Hallett made no comment. "How much money did you have with you?" he asked.

Greg told him.

"All right, I'll try to get that released. While you're held without trial you can pay for a more comfortable cell and have food sent in from outside, if you want."

"Will I be able to see my wife?"

"I'll ask, but I doubt it."

"I don't know how Mrs. Lukey's fixed for money. If we can get these privileges for her, too, I'd be glad to pay."

"I'll speak to the British consul about that. Now, then. You're going to be interrogated by the governor personally. His name is General Iskaq, and what he'd really like to do is beat the daylights out of you. He won't, because he knows I'd raise hell in Medan and Djakarta if he did, but bear it in mind and don't push him. Do you know what xenophobia is?"

"Yes."

"Well, the General has it badly. So watch yourself. Tell him the truth. He won't believe you, but go on telling it anyway. That check is your best talking point."

"How do you mean?"

"It substantiates your story that the transaction was incomplete, and that there were, therefore, no delivery arrangements. Tell him about the second signature needed. Say that, if he doesn't believe you, he should send the check to the Indonesian consulate in Singapore and ask them to try and cash it as it is. Ask him if he thinks you fool enough to trust Lukey with the goods before you had been paid."

"He knows Lukey?"

"Of course. Lukey's a crook. The oil company filed embezzlement charges against him two years ago, but couldn't make them stick. The Government deported him."

"I see."

"Another thing: don't get into any sort of political discussion. You had the stuff to sell. You were approached in Singapore. You thought you were dealing with an agent of the Central Government."

"You said I was to tell the truth."

"The Communist Party here will make all the propaganda use they can out of this. They'll try to say you're an American agent and that we're secretly backing the insurgents while pretending friendship with the Central Government. The less help they have from you, the better."

"How do I account for the meeting with Major Sutan?"

They could hear footsteps approaching along the corridor outside. Hallett began to speak quickly.

"You thought he was a Government official trying to get a secret commission on the deal. Play the innocent. You shouldn't find that too difficult." He waved Greg into silence with a gesture. "Do you smoke, Mr. Nilsen?" he went on loudly.

"A cigar occasionally. Why?"

"I'll send you in some cigarettes anyway. They are currency here. There's a pack to go on with. Liquor is not allowed, I'm afraid."

"Do you have something for an upset stomach?"

"I'll get you some pills from my doctor."

The door opened as he was speaking and Hallett got to his feet. Greg rose with him.

The man who came into the room had a stunted, barrel-chested body the ugliness of which was only partially concealed by an immaculately laundered uniform. He had a heavy, pock-marked face with thick, rubbery lips and ears. His eyes were watchful and his movements deliberate, like those of some powerful yet cumbersome animal. He wore a scrubbed webbing pistol belt, and carried a short leather-covered cane of the type Greg had seen carried by British officers during the war.

Just inside the door he stopped and looked distastefully from Hallett to Greg.

"This is Mr. Nilsen," Hallett said, and added to Greg: "The military governor of Labuanga, General Iskaq."

The General went over to the table and sat at the head of it. He was followed by Major Gani, who motioned to Greg to stand facing the General.

Hallett said: "General, I have advised Mr. Nilsen to make a frank and full statement."

The General seemed to take no notice.

"You will find that he acted in good faith and that no possible charge against him can be substantiated," Hallett continued.

Major Gani smiled ironically and began to translate what had been said into Malay. Only then did Greg realize that the General could not understand English.

When the translation was finished, the General looked at Hallett and said something in a harsh, guttural voice.

Hallett inclined his head politely and turned to Greg. "I am requested to leave now, Mr. Nilsen," he said. "You will, of course, answer the General's questions as best you can. I have no doubt that you and Mrs. Nilsen will be released very soon. In any case, I shall be watching your interests and will see you as often as I can. If it becomes necessary, I will get counsel for you."

"Thanks."

With a slight bow to the General, Hallett went. As the guard shut the door behind him, Major Gani sat down by the General.

Greg turned to face him.

Major Gani nodded. "We will begin," he said briskly. "First, let us hear what you and Mr. Hallett have arranged that you shall say. After that we will hear the truth."

iii

The General listened absently to the white man's voice speaking the language that always sounded to him like the chattering of apes, and watched the sweat pouring off him as he talked. In his mind's eye, however, all he could see was the room he had left ten minutes earlier, and his old friend Mohamad Sutan lying on the stone floor in a pool of bloody water, moaning and choking, with blood running from his mouth and nostrils and his stomach heaving. He had told the proudly smiling men who had done it to stop for the present and let the prisoner rest; but he could not leave matters there. Soon he would have to tell them to go on again. Unless, of course, one of the whites should talk first.

As Major Gani started to tell him what the white man was saying, the General picked up the cane he had placed beside him on the table and began to tap the palm of his other hand.

iv

"It's really my fault," Dorothy was telling Mrs. Lukey. "We'd been planning this trip and looking forward to it for so long that the reality was bound to be an anticlimax. I was prepared for that, but Greg wasn't, and I let him get angry and bored. I should have had more sense. When a man's worked so hard and successfully for so many years, and been such a wonderful husband and father, you tend to forget some things about him. Or maybe tell yourself that they're no longer there."

"What sort of things?"

Dorothy sighed inwardly with relief. After the American and British consuls had been there, Mrs. Lukey had been calmer for a while; but gradually the effect of their visits had worn off and she had begun to weep again. She was going to be tortured, she was going to be raped, she was going to be shot. She had done nothing. She did not want to die.

As almost everything she had said expressed Dorothy's own presentiments and fears, it had not been easy to reassure her with any sort of conviction. Despair can be infectious, and Dorothy had begun to cast about feverishly for some means of diverting her companion's thoughts from their immediate situation. She had found it, unexpectedly, in the subject of her relationship with Greg. Mrs. Lukey was almost avidly curious about it. Dorothy guessed that she was trying indirectly to find the key to a more secure relationship with her own husband. It was the difficulties of marriage that interested her most. Her eyes were dry now, and, although she still held the damp white ball which had been Dorothy's last piece of Kleenex, her nose had at last stopped running.

"What sort of things?" she repeated.

"Oh, I don't know," Dorothy said. "Nothing very bad, really. You know those dolls with round weights at their feet? The ones that always stand up straight again, however much you push them over? As long as he has work that's important to him, a man like Greg hardly ever does anything really silly. It's only when the weight is suddenly taken away that things go wrong. It was like that when he came home from the army. He'd been away four years working with mine-detection equipment and explosives. It was dangerous work, but it had fascinated him. All that time he'd hardly thought of anything else. When he came home safely to me and the boys, I was so happy. I thought that all our troubles were over." She paused. "The first thing that happened was that he fell in love with another woman—or, rather, a nineteen-year-old girl."

Mrs. Lukey looked at her quickly; but Dorothy's expression remained placid.

"I suppose that if it hadn't been for the children," she said, "we'd have broken up. But we didn't. Greg got his business going, and gradually everything was all right again."

"What about the other woman?"

Dorothy shrugged. "The last time we talked about it was five years ago. Greg became very upset."

"Because he was still in love with her?"

"No. Because he couldn't remember her second name."

Mrs. Lukey stared at her uncertainly for a moment. Dorothy was looking preternaturally solemn. Then Mrs. Lukey began to laugh. After a moment Dorothy began to laugh with her. They did not hear the footsteps of the guard approaching, and were still laughing when the cell door opened. Mrs. Lukey's laughter became a strangled cry as they turned.

Standing in the doorway were the old woman who acted as wardress and one of the armed guards from the control section.

The wardress said something in Malay, and Mrs. Lukey began to back away.

As Dorothy started to go to her, the guard came into the cell and, reaching out, grabbed Mrs. Lukey by the arm. She screamed and tried to pull away. With a shout he flung her across the cell to the wardress and then, using his carbine with both hands, thrust them out into the corridor. The cell door slammed behind him.

As the sound of Mrs. Lukey's screams receded, Dorothy sat down on the bed and searched her bag frantically to see if by any chance there was one more piece of Kleenex that she had overlooked. There was none. She sobbed once and tried holding her breath. Then she ceased trying. Kleenex or no Kleenex, it was better perhaps to cry.

v

When Greg was taken back to his cell, Voychinski was stretched out asleep on the bed.

He awoke at the sound of the cell door closing, but made no attempt to move. Greg took no notice of him. Heat, lack of sleep, stomach cramps, and the insistent questioning had exhausted him to the point of indifference to discomfort. When he had used the bucket, he sat down on the floor and rested his back against the wall.

Voychinski sat up lazily and yawned. Greg took Hallett's cigarettes and matches from his shirt pocket and tossed them onto the bed.

"Compliments of the American consul," he said.

Voychinski picked up the cigarettes and smirked. "You leave soon, hah?"

"Just as soon as I tell them when and how that stuff you were going to buy is being delivered."

"They think you know?"

"That's right. They think I know."

Voychinski swung his feet off the bed and looked down at him. "Who question you?"

"General Iskaq and that major."

"So!" The pale eyes searched for hidden clues. "What you say?"

"What could I say? I told them all I know. I told them fifty times."

"About the delivery?"

"I don't know anything about the delivery. You know that as well as I do."

"But you tell them something, a good story perhaps?"

"I told them what I know and that's all."

"Nothing about delivery?"

"That's right."

"You lie."

Greg shut his eyes wearily. "Anything you say."

Voychinski got up off the bed and stared down belligerently. "Gani would not permit you to say nothing."

"Gani wasn't conducting the interrogation."

"You are lucky."

"It's not Gani I'm worried about."

"That peasant Iskaq?" Voychinski spat derisively. "Listen, my friend. Iskaq is a soldier, a good soldier, but stupid politically. Oh, yes, he would wish to break your face, but he is not serious. Gani is the dangerous one. He want those guns to arm more of his Party men."

"What party men?"

"You do not know he is a Red?"

"How would I?"

"Mrs. Lukey know it."

"What difference does it make?"

"My friend, if Iskaq had political sense, he would have come over to the Committee. Now he secretly help to arm the Reds and think he is fighting us when he only make firing squad for himself. It is stupid." He sat down again and stared at Greg suspiciously. "You did not tell Gani anything?"

"About the delivery? Don't be silly. I don't know anything. Is there anyone who does? Does Major Sutan? Do you?"

Voychinski's eyes narrowed unpleasantly. "Did Gani tell you to ask that?"

"Oh, for God's sake!"

Voychinski shrugged. "When a man is afraid and has nothing to lose, he will do many things. And Gani mean to find out from one of us."

Greg glowered at him. "What do you mean, 'nothing to lose'?"

"Your arms are still in Singapore."

"Exactly! So there's nothing for Major Gani to find out. That's what I keep trying to tell you."

Voychinski sighed impatiently. "My friend, do you think that you are the only man in the world who sell us arms?"

It took Greg several seconds to get the point. Then he remembered something Captain Lukey had said. "You only have to go the first time. After that it's plain sailing." With only one deal to consummate himself, he had not taken much notice of it then. He looked up at Voychinski.

"You mean there's another shipment from someone else already on the way?"

Voychinski showed his teeth, but did not reply. From along the corridor there was the sound of a door opening and a rattle of keys. A moment later the cell door was opened and a guard outside motioned to Voychinski.

He got up slowly, stretched himself, and walked out. He did not even glance at Greg. The door shut behind him.

vi

Ross and Fran Hallett were playing bridge with Dr. Subramaniam, the Indian director of the tuberculosis clinic, and his wife that evening when the lights went out. It was a little before eight o'clock.

They were not unduly concerned. Power failures were common enough. Dr. Subramaniam lit some oil lamps, and they went on with the rubber. Twenty minutes later the lights were still out, and Dr. Subramaniam, wondering if the failure could after all be due to a fuse in his own house, went out to the road to see if there were lights elsewhere. He saw immediately that the failure was general; but as he walked back he heard the sound of distant machine-gun fire. It seemed to come from the other side of the town, by the port.

He called Ross Hallett. The sounds of firing were becoming more insistent, and intermingled with them now there were faint thudding noises.

"What is it, do you think?" asked the doctor. "Another raid on the storage tanks?"

"Possibly. Difficult to tell from here."

"What else could it be?"

"I wouldn't like to say. Anyway, I think I have to get back."

"Why? There's nothing you can do. We've got a spare bed you and Fran can have for the night."

Hallett shook his head. "I'll be grateful if you'd let Fran stay, but I have to get back."

"They'll have shut the Inner Zone."

"I'll get through on my pass."

Fran Hallett recognized what she called the "State Department" look on her husband's face when he returned to the house, and made no attempt either to dissuade him from going or to insist on going along herself. She did not even tell him to take care. She merely reminded him that there were fresh eggs in the water cooler and kissed him good night.

He drove very slowly. Once, when a column of army troop carriers began to pass him, he pulled off the road and stopped. During these emergencies the Labuanga garrison became trigger-happy, and moving vehicles, including their own, were frequently shot at. As he approached the Inner Zone check point, he became even more cautious. A hundred yards short of it, he stopped the car and, leaving the headlights on, got out and walked toward the guardhouse. With the lights behind him, the sentries could see clearly that he was unarmed and alone.

The N.C.O. in charge of the check point had never seen a diplomatic pass before, and could not read. An officer had to be summoned to approve the pass before Hallett was allowed through. The sounds of firing were louder there, and it was possible to determine the direction from which they were coming. The officer was excited and on edge, but Hallett decided to take a small risk.

"What do they want?" he asked. "To burn one more oil tank?"

There was a local joke implicit in the form of the question. From time to time Government spokesmen had accused the oil company of secretly subsidizing the Party of the Faithful. Insurgent propaganda leaflets had indignantly denied the charge and listed the attacks made on oil-company property. The list had been unconvincing, and a Government newspaper had run a sarcastic article about it. Why was it, the writer had asked, that the insurgents were never able to blow up more than one oil-storage tank at a time? Why didn't they use a little more explosive while they were about it and blow up two or three? And why did they bother with oil-storage tanks at all when they could, at much less risk to themselves, cut the pipelines? The writer had gone on to offer helpful suggestions of how this might be done, and to suggest that the insurgents apply to America for technical assistance. Even the strongly pro-Faithful had smiled a little at this.

The officer looked at Hallett uncertainly.

Hallett said: "Maybe they brought two sticks of dynamite this time."

The officer grinned. "Tuan, it will take more than two sticks to blow up the power station."

Hallett chuckled, but said nothing more. He had confirmed an earlier suspicion.

He went back to his car and drove through into the Inner Zone.

Eight

KEITH WILSON, HER Britannic Majesty's honorary vice-consul in Labuanga, had been born in Shanghai. When he was eight, his parents had sent him "home" to school in England. When he was eighteen, he had returned to the Far East. Most of his working life had been spent in Borneo and Malaya. He looked and, in a sense, was a typical middle-class, pipesmoking Englishman. His wife had died in a Singapore internment camp during the war, and he had never remarried. The ruling passion of his life was cricket, and his only complaint against Labuanga was that there were not enough cricketers there to form two teams. He had a powerful radio receiver and spent much of his spare time listening to broadcast cricket commentaries on the Australian and B.B.C. short-wave services. He held that the political stability of India and Pakistan owed as much to the legacy of cricket as to the existence of the British-trained Indian Civil Service. When not on the subject of cricket, he had an agreeable sense of humor. He also had the insight necessary to translate obscure Malay and Chinese jokes into meaningful English. The Halletts, who had read their Somerset Maugham, referred to him, not unaffectionately, as "The Taipan."

He answered Hallett's telephone call promptly. "I tried to get you at the Subramaniams," he said. "They told me you were on your way back. Are you at home now?"

"Yes." Hallett could hear the breathing of the switchboard operator listening to their conversation, and knew that Wilson could hear it, too. "What about a drink?" he asked.

"Fine. Why don't you come over here and enjoy the view?"

"Be with you in a couple of minutes."

Wilson's apartment was on the top floor of the oil company's building and overlooked the western half of the city. That was the area in which the power station was situated. Earlier, when the firing had started, he had been able to see through his binoculars a sparkle of tracer bullets in that direction. By the time Hallett telephoned, however, the firing had almost ceased. He had switched the radio over to battery operation, and was listening to the voices on the garrison communication frequency when Hallett arrived.

"What do you make of it, Keith?" Hallett asked.

"As far as I can gather, the Faithful sent a strong force in to take over the power station, and the army got in first. The Faithful took up encircling positions. Now they're all just sitting there. I don't understand it. If they wanted to dynamite the place, why didn't they use a small party and their usual hit-and-run tactics?"

"Why indeed?"

Wilson was lighting another candle. Something in Hallett's voice made him look up. "Any ideas?"

"A hunch. You know the night defense plan. The moment there's an attack alarm, the main body concentrates in the Inner Zone. No dispersal of forces. All that's left outside is the mobile column. Where's that now?"

"Holding the power station."

"Which is on the opposite side of town from the jail."

"What about it?"

"That power-station attack could be a diversion. The Faithful could be going for the jail to spring Major Sutan."

Wilson thought for a moment. "It's a possibility," he said finally. "Do you think Sutan's worth it to them?"

"He's an important member of the Committee. Besides, if they do nothing, don't they lose face?"

Wilson thought again. "If they did get inside that jail," he said, "what they'd do there wouldn't be very nice."

"That's what I was thinking. Once they started killing . . ."

"Yes. You know, I tried to call our consul in Medan earlier. I wanted him to go to the area commander and get Mrs. Lukey moved out of here. They wouldn't put me through. Said the line was down."

"I know. They gave me the same treatment. I'd made up my mind to fly over there in the morning if necessary. As it is . . ."

"What do we do? Call General Iskaq and request him to move troops out to the jail just in case?"

Hallett frowned. "I don't know. Let's think. Supposing he did take the idea seriously enough to send part of the garrison out there. Is that necessarily better for our people? Supposing the troops were given orders to shoot all prisoners in the case of an attack. It's happened before. Supposing someone like Major Gani decided to use them as hostages. Look at it another way. The more fighting there was, the more killing there would be after the fighting was over. After all, the jail doesn't matter to us, only those three persons inside it."

"I gather you're against requesting reinforcements," said Wilson dryly.

"I'm against hypothetical reinforcements in that hypothetical situation."

Wilson switched the radio off. "Well, it may be hypothetical, but I must confess you have me worried. Mrs. Lukey's a highly strung woman. Anglo-Indian, you know. Even with your Mrs. Nilsen to help, she's in a pretty bad state. I didn't like leaving her there today."

"Do you think she knows anything they want to know?"

Wilson hesitated before he said: "I'm afraid she might."

Ross Hallett nodded. Mrs. Lukey was a British subject and, common humanity aside, no concern of his. He thought about the Nilsens, who *were* his concern. To Fran he had referred to them as "rogue tourists." They had been irresponsible and stupid—more irresponsible and more stupid than the booziest oil driller spoiling for a fight. So far, he had been able to view their predicament with a certain amount of detachment. Now it was beginning to frighten him. Men like General Iskaq and Major Gani were not easily deterred from violence by the fear of diplomatic consequences. The Nilsens could be murdered that very night, and he would be powerless except to protest and listen to polite expressions of regret.

"I'm going out to the jail," he said. "Do you want to come with me?"

"What are we going to do?"

"Ask to see the prisoners."

"At this time of night? They won't let us."

"No, but we'll be there. It can't do any harm, and if there is going to be trouble, it just might do some good."

"Then we ought to put on a show. Flags on our cars, neckties, lots of protocol."

"Whatever you say, Sir Anthony."

They had to make a wide detour to avoid going through the Inner Zone, and approached the section in which the jail was situated from the Chinese quarter to the south of it. It was probably that which saved them. If they had been coming from the Inner Zone, they would almost certainly have been fired upon before they had had time to identify themselves.

As Hallett's car was the more imposing, it had been agreed that he should lead the way. Skirting the Chinese quarter there was a deep drainage canal that was bridged in only two places. He was driving very slowly over the ruts and potholes of the approach road to one of the bridges when something he saw in the headlights made him pull up quickly. He heard Wilson stopping behind him.

They were about fifty yards from the narrow earth ramp which led up to the bridge. At the foot of the ramp was an overturned cart completely blocking the way. Hallett got out of his car. Wilson joined him.

"What do you think, Keith?"

"We could probably move it out of the way between us."

"Think we ought to try?"

"I don't know. Does it look like an accident to you?"

"Pretty funny sort of accident."

On one side of the road there were a few small houses, but they were in complete darkness. The only sounds were those of crickets and of the car engines idling.

"What about leaving the cars here with the lights on and going a bit closer to have a look?"

"Okay."

They walked forward into the beam of the headlights, heard the quick rustle of sandaled feet, and saw the long shadows of the men behind them flickering across the road ahead. As they swung around and stopped with their hands in the air, the men closed in.

ii

It had been mid-afternoon when Voychinski had been taken away, and Greg had immediately used the opportunity to get some sleep.

It had been dark when he had wakened. Voychinski had not returned. After a while, a guard had come in with food and water. With it had been a package from Hallett containing a carton of cigarettes, two paper-backed novels, a tube of Entero-Vioforme, and a note saying that he hoped to secure further amenities the following day. The package had been opened and most of the cigarettes stolen. Greg had given one of the remaining packs to the guard and received in return a cup of weak tea. His watch had been taken from him with the rest of his personal belongings, and he had had no means of telling the time. It had been about two hours later, it seemed, when the lights had gone out. He had thought that this must be part of the jail routine. Then, through the grille in the cell door, he had seen oil lamps being brought to light the corridor.

The cells had been left in darkness. As he could no longer read, he had gone to sleep again.

To Dorothy the power failure had brought a curious kind of relief.

Some time after nightfall Mrs. Lukey had been brought back to the cell sobbing incoherently. It appeared that after being questioned for over two hours by Major Gani she had been taken to another room and confronted by Captain

Voychinski. Already he had been so badly beaten by his guards that he was scarcely able to stand; then in front of her, they had knocked him down and kicked him until he became unconscious. After that, she had been taken out and warned, meaningfully, that her own interrogation would shortly be resumed. Meanwhile, she should try to remember useful facts.

Dorothy had done her best to calm her, but without success. It had been all she could do to remain calm herself. If they could beat Captain Voychinski, they could beat Greg. The American consul had said that Greg would not be physically harmed; but how could he be sure? These horrible little madmen might do anything.

"But what do they want to know?" she had asked. "Mr. Hallett said he was going to tell Greg to make a full statement."

"There is another shipment already on the way." Mrs. Lukey had hesitated. "They want to know about that."

"Did you know about it?"

"Yes, I knew."

"Did you tell them what they wanted?"

"I told them what was in the shipment. That is all I know. But they want the route so that they can intercept it. They said that if I did not know the route myself, I must tell them who did know."

"What did you say?"

Mrs. Lukey raised her panic-stricken eyes to Dorothy's. "I told them Captain Voychinski knew."

"And *does* he?" Dorothy was beginning to feel sick.

"He might." The eyes pleaded for understanding and forgiveness. "I could not help it. I had to say something or they would have beaten me."

And then the lights had gone out, and Dorothy had no longer had to watch Mrs. Lukey's eyes and wonder if, the next time she were questioned, she would become desperate enough to implicate Greg as well as Captain Voychinski.

There were two beds in that cell. After a while Dorothy said: "It looks as if we're not going to have any more light. I think we ought to try to get some sleep."

"They will be coming for me again."

"If you don't listen for them, maybe they won't."

"I could not sleep."

"Try."

A few minutes later Mrs. Lukey began, in a quiet, ladylike way, to snore.

Dorothy dozed fitfully. Hours seemed to go by. She was half awake, half asleep, when she heard a sound like a huge air-filled paper bag bursting somewhere near at hand. A moment later the sound came again. This time the bed shook a little. Mrs. Lukey woke up and started to whimper.

iii

Only convicted prisoners serving sentences of less than ninety days, and suspects on remand or awaiting trial, were held in Labuanga jail. It was built around two small quadrangles which were used as exercise yards—one for the male prisoners, one for the female. Separating the two quadrangles was the so-called "control section." This contained the guards' quarters, some interrogation rooms, a kitchen, and the head jailer's office. A high outer wall enclosed the whole compound. The main gates, two imposing slabs of iron-braced teak, were opposite the control-section entrance.

What Dorothy had heard were the explosions of two P.I.A.T. mortar bombs, stolen some months earlier from a British army ordnance depot in Kuala Lumpur and purchased from the thieves by Captain Lukey. They were fired, with some accuracy, from a projector which looked like a truncated Lewis gun, and the first one hit the junction of the gates just by the drop bar. Two of the brackets which supported it snapped, and a piece of the flying metal wounded one of the duty guards. The second bomb completed the work. The drop bar fell to the ground, and one of the gates swung open. The unwounded guard was too dazed by the blast of the explosions to do more than stare as the attackers poured in. Then, as he turned and started to run, he tripped and fell to his knees. An instant later a parang sliced down into the muscles of his neck, and he slid forward to die.

Tho grilles at the entrance to the control section were less imposing than the outer gates, but more efficient. A Very pistol was fired to give the P.I.A.T. crew light to aim by, but the bomb only bent and jammed the long sliding bolts. A second bomb aimed at the hinges was equally unsuccessful. By this time, too, the defenders had come to their senses. A flare was lobbed from the roof of the building onto the road, and a burst of rifle fire from behind the grille forced the P.I.A.T. crew to take cover behind the outer wall, where they could do no more damage. The flare from the roof was now followed by grenades. Caught in the narrow space between the outer wall and the jail itself, the assault party began to suffer casualties.

However, they were well trained and ably led. The surprise attack having failed, they set about blasting their way in. With the aid of smoke grenades and covering fire from across the road outside, more men were rushed through the broken outer gates. They had orders to work around the sides of the building, deal with the defenders on the roof, and then dynamite their way through from the rear.

Inside the control section, Major Gani, whose interrogation of Voychinski had been interrupted at an interesting point, was on the telephone to General Iskaq at his headquarters in the Inner Zone.

"No, sir," he was saying, "I cannot tell you how strong the attacking force is. It is impossible to estimate. But they are well armed, with machine guns and an anti-tank weapon of some kind. Our guards are armed with only rifles and grenades. It is imperative that you send armored cars and troops."

"Anti-tank weapons?"

"They burst open the main gate with two shots."

The General hesitated. Only four of his ten obsolete armored cars were at that moment capable of taking the road. The rest had mechanical trouble of one sort or another. Three, which were awaiting spare parts from Italy, had been out of commission for months. The thought of exposing even one of the effective cars to the fire of anti-tank weapons made his heart sink.

He put a touch of impatience into his voice. "Unless they destroy the outer wall first, they cannot use such long-range weapons against the building. The jail is of brick. Every window is barred. You have the main gate covered. Why do you need more troops?"

"These guards are not troops," Major Gani replied. He knew that he had made a mistake in mentioning the anti-tank weapons, and tried to regain the initiative. "I must remind you, sir," he went on quickly, "that we are holding important prisoners here. This is an attempt to free them."

"Of course. But they will not be freed."

"Then send troops, sir."

"They will not be freed," the General repeated sharply. "Better if they should all be killed."

"You authorize me to kill those five prisoners, sir, including the American and British subjects?"

"It would be the insurgents who would be held responsible. But that will not be necessary. We will keep them. Has the white man talked yet?"

"No, sir. He . . ."

Somewhere overhead a grenade burst, and slabs of plaster fell down from the ceiling of the head jailer's office from which Major Gani was speaking. As the plaster dust billowed up, he heard the General asking if they had been cut off.

He managed to croak into the mouthpiece: "Send troops," before the dust forced him to start coughing; then he hung up. If the General were left wondering what had happened, so much the better. The troops would be dispatched with more urgency.

He had misread the General's thought processes. The General was a hard man to stampede. So far, only half of the available Party men had been armed with weapons from the intercepted shipments, and they had very little ammunition. Subsequent interceptions would no doubt improve that position, but, until they did, the "militia" was not effective. As far as the General was concerned, the Inner Zone plan was still in force. That meant that the garrison did not dissipate its small strength by chasing off in all directions to fight wherever the rebels chose to attack. The thrust at the power station was obviously a diversion for the attempt on the jail; but that knowledge changed nothing. The power station was difficult to defend. The jail was virtually a stronghold. Gani was an Intelligence officer, unused to battle and therefore overanxious. His reckless demand for armored cars showed that. He must learn that there was more to soldiering than he had realized. The experience might make him more respectful.

The General's only misgiving at that moment concerned his authorization to kill the white prisoners. It would be annoying if Gani lost his head and killed them prematurely. For a moment or two he considered telephoning the jail and countermanding the authorization; but he concluded finally that any hint of indecision on his part could be misinterpreted just then. If there were a serious change in the situation at the jail, Gani would obviously report it. Meanwhile, it was best to leave things as they were.

At that moment, in fact, the situation at the jail was changing more rapidly than even Major Gani knew. There had been fighting on the roof, and the jail guards up there had been cornered by the water tank. It was only a matter of time before the enemy winkled them out and gained access to the stairs leading below. With a steadiness and decision which would have surprised the General, Major Gani prepared to evacuate the control section and fall back behind the grilles and steel doors of the men's cell block. What he did not know was that, under cover of the roof fighting, a party had made its way to the rear of the building and was at that moment setting demolition charges in one of the drains.

Orders had been given to remove Sutan and Voychinski from the interrogation rooms and transfer them immediately to cells in the men's block, when the man who had tapped the charges lighted the fuse.

iv

Greg's cell was less than a hundred feet from the explosion. The blast wave slammed him against the wall, smashed the light fitting, and snatched the zinc screen out of the window embrasure as if it had been paper.

Since the attack had begun, he had been sitting there as wretched and perplexed as a child listening to a quarrel between adults. Outside in the corridor, there had been some confused shouting at first, and then the guards, apparently in response to an order, had all left. The other prisoners in that section had begun to carry on excited conversations in Malay through the door grilles. The exercise yard had been quiet. The sounds had been coming from the other side of the jail. He had started then to worry about Dorothy. If, as it seemed, there were some sort of jail riot going on, she could be in danger.

Now, as he got to his feet and went to the unscreened window, he could see a cloud of dust and smoke drifting across the moonlit yard. At the same moment there was the crash of a grille opening along the corridor behind him and the sound of running, struggling, shouting men. Then the air was shattered by a long burst of submachine-gun fire and the shouts changed to screams.

v

The Committee member in charge of the raiding force was a former army officer, Colonel Oda, whom Hallett had met on one of his trips into insurgent territory.

The Colonel had a protruding lower lip which curled inauspiciously at the smallest hint of opposition to his wishes; but he was not wholly unreasonable, and had been persuaded in the end that the proposal of his second-in-command to kill the American and British vice-consuls and commandeer their cars was both politically unsound and tactically unnecessary. On the subject of those in the jail, however, he had been adamant. He and he alone would decide what was to be done with them, prisoners and guards, white or brown. After further discussion he had agreed, reluctantly, to allow the foreign diplomatic representatives to accompany the attacking force. They would go as neutral observers of the justice meted out by the Committee of the Faithful.

The reason for even that concession had soon become apparent. Neutral or no, the observers had been ordered, before the assault began, to park their beflagged cars bumper to bumper fifty yards from the jail entrance, in order to provide cover for the Colonel's battle headquarters among the trees beside the road. During the early stages of the fighting, Hallett and Wilson had been obliged to crouch behind the cars while carbine bullets from the roof of the jail had ripped through the door panels into the upholstery.

Half an hour after the first P.I.A.T. mortar bomb had been fired, the demolition charge blew out the rear wall of the control section. Two minutes after that, the sound of firing ceased. There was some shouting. Then the second-in-command appeared at the main gate and called out that the place was taken. The Colonel walked across the road. He took no notice of Hallett and Wilson. They exchanged questioning glances, then left the cars and followed him.

As they went through the main gate, the damaged grilles beyond were being levered open by the men inside. Lanterns had been brought. By their yellow light it was possible to see a group of guards huddled by an office door with their hands clasped behind their heads. The bodies of the guards who had been killed in the forecourt were lying face downward at the foot of the steps. Their blood had drained into a broad puddle. The Colond did not trouble to walk around it.

The blast of the demolition charge had brought down a great deal of plaster. The dust of it hanging in the air made Hallett and Wilson cough. It did not seem to affect the Colonel. He was talking to his second-in-command. When he saw the captured guards, however, he stopped and glanced over his shoulder at Hallett.

"Do you know where your American and British prisoners are in this place?" he asked.

"I know where they were, Colonel." Hallett began coughing again.

The Colonel looked at one of the soldiers covering the guards. "Keys," he said.

The soldier looked at the six terrified guards. Three of them had long key chains at their belts. The soldier grinned and took out a knife. Then he stepped forward and swung the knife upward. The guard screamed as the double blade of the knife slashed through the belt and across his stomach simultaneously. As he doubled up in agony, the soldier snatched the belt away and handed the keys to the Colonel. The other two guards with keys hastily unfastened their belts and let them drop to the floor. The soldier with the knife laughed.

The Colonel pulled his lip in and nodded to Hallett. "You may release your prisoners," he said, "but do not try to take them away from here."

"Very well, Colonel."

But the Colonel was already walking on. "Voychinski can wait," he was saying to the second-in-command. "The one who matters is our Sutan."

The guard with the stomach wound had sunk to the floor and was looking down stupidly at the blood pouring over his hands. Wilson picked up one of the belts and took the key chain off it. His face was white as he looked at Hallett.

"If you want to see that Nilsen's all right," he said quietly, "I'll look after the two women."

Hallett nodded. "Okay."

He took the remaining set of keys and went on down the corridor. The demolition charge had wrecked the building here, and he had to pick his way over piles of rubble to get to the passage leading to the men's cell block. The soldiers there had seen him with their officers and made no move to stop him. In any case, they were too busy stripping the bodies of the dead guards to care much about a white man. He stumbled on, using the flashlight from his car to light the way and shutting his ears to the cries of two men who were not yet dead. From beyond the open grille ahead of him came the sound of prisoners calling to one another and pounding on the doors of their cells. One man was screaming hysterically that the place was on fire and that they would all be burned alive. As Hallett went along, trying to make out the cell numbers, he shouted in Malay that everything was all right and that all prisoners would soon be released. Under cover of the excited cries that followed this announcement he called out quietly: "Mr. Nilsen."

"Here."

He had already passed the cell. He went back, fumbling with the flashlight and keys, and called again. "Where are you? Keep talking."

"Right here. Is that Hallett? What's going on? Is my wife all right? What's happened?" He was trying, not quite successfully, to keep a tremor out of his voice.

Hallett began trying the keys. "Take it easy, Mr. Nilsen. I've got to find the right key. The jail's been taken over temporarily by the insurgents. The British consul's gone along to get your wife and Mrs. Lukey."

"Is she all right?"

"There was no fighting on that side. They may be scared, but I'm pretty sure they're not hurt. Wait a minute. This looks as if it might be the right one."

A moment later he had the cell door open and saw the prisoner's face livid and desperate in the beam of the flashlight.

Hallett made himself smile. "Dr. Livingstone, I presume," he said and then: "Steady, Mr. Nilsen. Sit down a moment."

"I just want to get out of here." But he did as he was told. "It sounded as if they'd blown the whole place up," he added weakly.

"Only a bit of it. Now, listen. We're in a curious sort of spot. Sutan's friends came to get him. Okay, they've got him. They won't hold this place for long, though. As soon as it starts to get light, they'll be high-tailing it back to the hills. Where that leaves you and Mrs. Nilsen, I don't know, unless you ask them to take you along. Even if they'd agree, I wouldn't advise that."

"You mean we've got to stay here in jail?"

"I hope not. I don't know. I'm just warning you. At the moment it's all up to the commander of the raiding party, and he's a tough proposition. I'm taking you to him now. He doesn't speak much English, so he won't question you direct, but don't say anything unless I tell you to. Above all, don't get mad or try to protest. Just keep quiet. Is that clear?"

"I don't have a protest left in me."

"Good. How's your stomach?"

"Queasy."

"Well, keep close to me and don't look around too much, or it may give you trouble."

He led the way out of the cell and back toward the control section. He went quickly, holding the flashlight ahead of him and ignoring the prisoner's complaints that he could not see where he was going. Hallett judged that the man had reached a point of mental exhaustion at which he could very easily become unnerved. Anger was sometimes a useful restorative.

"Come on," he said impatiently, "we don't have much time."

"Time for what?"

Hallett did not have to reply. They had reached the main corridor of the control section and Colonel Oda's second-in-command was approaching. He was a square, muscular man with a wispy mustache and bright, stupid eyes. He had not forgotten that the Colonel had earlier accepted Hallett's arguments in preference to his own. He looked at the prisoner contemptuously.

"Is this your American?"

"This is Mr. Nilsen, yes."

"You will both come to see the Colonel immediately."

"Very well."

The second-in-command turned on his heel, and they followed him along the corridor. Hallett felt the prisoner's hand on his arm.

"What did he say?"

Hallett frowned warningly and told him loudly in Malay to hold his tongue. The second-in-command spoke no English and Hallett did not want to irritate him unnecessarily.

The room into which they were taken was the one in which Hallett had last seen Major Gani; and Major Gani was the first person he saw there now. He was standing against one of the barred windows, with a soldier on either side of him and blood running from his head and left shoulder. Sitting at the table beside Colonel Oda was a man whom Hallett guessed to be Major Sutan. His head was drooping and his face a deathly yellow in the lamplight. It was obviously all he could do to remain upright. The Colonel was talking to him quietly.

Across the table from them was Wilson with the two women. Mrs. Lukey was crying. As soon as he saw his wife, Nilsen went over and put his arms around her. She began to cry, too. The Colonel looked up in exasperation.

"Ah!" He rapped on the table as if for silence. "I have told Mr. Wilson. Now I tell you, Mr. Hallett. Major Sutan has confirmed the friendly status of these European prisoners. You may take them with you and go. That is all."

Hallett's eyes met Wilson's. The latter shrugged resignedly.

The Colonel frowned. "That is all," he repeated sharply.

"Thank you." Hallett bowed slightly. "May I ask where you suggest they should go to?"

"That is their affair. They are free to go."

"Just a moment, Colonel." Hallet went forward to the table. "You asked Mr. Wilson and me to come here as neutral observers to witness the administration of justice by the Committee of the Faithful. You say now that Major Sutan has confirmed the friendly status of these persons. Yet you are prepared to send them away from here, without protection, to be rearrested by the Central Government, put back into prison like common criminals, perhaps shot as your collaborators. Is that the justice of the Committee of the Faithful?"

"They are free to go. I do not understand what you want."

"He understands, all right," Wilson said in English. "I've just finished explaining it to him."

Hallett kept his eyes on the Colonel. "It has been instructive to see how the Committee of the Faithful keeps faith with its friends," he said. He put a sarcastic inflection on the word "Faithful."

The second-in-command stepped forward. "You do not have to hear these insults, Colonel. Give the order and I will see that they cause no further trouble."

The Colonel ignored him. "What can we do?" he demanded angrily. "What do you expect?"

"A safe-conduct for these persons to the airport, and permission to embark on the first Malayan Airways plane to Pelnang or Singapore."

"You are a fool or mad."

"I don't believe so."

"This is a raiding force, not an army of occupation. Only General Iskaq could give such a safe-conduct."

"I know that."

The Colonel laughed shortly. "Then you must know also that you are wasting my time. We have released these persons. They are in your care. We can do no more."

"You can obtain a safe-conduct for them from General Iskaq."

"Impossible."

"Is it? Why not ask Major Gani?" Without waiting for a reply, Hallett looked across the room at the man by the window. "Major, do you think that General Iskaq values your services highly enough to grant a safe-conduct for Mr. and Mrs. Nilsen and Mrs. Lukey in exchange for your release unharmed?"

He saw Gani's eyes flicker. Then there was a crash as Colonel Oda stood up quickly and his chair shot back against the wall.

Wilson started to move toward Hallett. The second-in-command snapped back the cocking handle of his machine pistol.

Hallett looked from the machine pistol to the Colonel's lower lip and shrugged. "Violence is the fool's answer for every difficulty," he remarked. "I did not think it was yours, Colonel."

"Get out, before we think too much."

Hallett inclined his head. "Very well. It is a pity. I had hoped that Mr. Wilson and I could have been of help to you."

The Colonel's lip curled proudly. "We did not need your help to take this prison. We will not need your help to take all Labuanga when we wish."

"Maybe not. But you will find that taking Labuanga is easier than keeping it. One day—soon, perhaps—you will proclaim an autonomous government here and declare your independence of Djakarta and Medan. It is then you will need the help of friends."

"These are our friends." The Colonel tapped his pistol holster.

"They will not win your government recognition. Think, Colonel. The Central Government will denounce you as brigands and bandits and destroy you as they destroyed your comrades in Celebes. To whom will you appeal for justice? To the United Nations? The Central Government is there before you. To the Soviet Union? You are anti-Communist. The only ears that will hear you are in the United States and Britain. Our countries, Mr. Wilson's and mine, admire good fighting men, but they also value moderation. No doubt Major Sutan has been viley ill-treated by this man Gani. But how will you explain that, merely in order to have your revenge by torturing and killing Gani, you endangered the lives of two Americans and a British subject? Supposing General Iskaq puts them back here tomorrow, has them killed, and then tells the world that they were savagely murdered by you when the jail was attacked. How could you deny it?"

"You would know that was not true," the Colonel said indignantly.

"Would I? It seems to me that there is a very small difference between that and what you are planning. And how foolish that plan is. Simply by using Gani as a hostage, you could not only cause General Iskaq to lose face, but also show yourselves as humane and honorable men, infinitely more worthy of governing Labuanga than these lackeys from Djakarta. These things are not forgotten. When the day comes on which you need the friendship of the United States and the nations of the British Commonwealth, which memory will you prefer—that of killing Major Gani or that of having saved American and British lives?"

The Colonel stared at him for a moment and then sat down again. He looked at Sutan inquiringly.

Sutan's haggard eyes looked up at Hallett. "Captain Voychinski has died from the beatings this man gave him," he said slowly in English. "Perhaps the gentleman does not know that. Voychinski was a white man. Perhaps if the gentleman saw Voychinski's body, he would not feel so merciful."

"It's not mercy he's asking for," Wilson put in, "but some protection for these people who came here to do business with you."

"They came at their own risk."

"Oh, no. They came because you wanted them to. They were told there was no risk. Personally, I feel they were unwise, but I also feel that you people have a responsibility. Besides, have you thought about what would happen to your future arms deliveries if you turn these three persons over to the authorities? You wouldn't be able to buy a bow and arrow after that."

The Colonel hammered on the table with his fist. "We are *not* turning them over to the authorities," he shouted.

"In effect you are." Hallett had taken over again. "That is, unless they have a safe-conduct out of the country."

The Colonel turned to Sutan again.

Sutan shrugged wearily. "Gani learned nothing that matters. Do what is best."

The Colonel looked with disgust from the white men to Major Gani. His eyes hardened.

"We had good plans for you, Gani," he said. "Perhaps, if your General does not love you enough, we shall still carry them out. Or perhaps, if you stay in Labuanga, there will be another day."

"Perhaps," said Major Gani.

The Colonel motioned to the telephone. "Then, see if your fine General will speak to you."

vi

General Iskaq had not been unduly worried by the absence of news from the jail. An explosion had been heard in that direction; but the sounds of firing had later ceased. He had assumed that the situation at the jail was now similar to that at the power station. When he heard Gani's voice on the telephone, he was prepared to be calm and matter-of-fact. By making no reference at all to Gani's hysterical behavior earlier, he would emphasize its absurdity far more effectively than by drawing attention to it.

When he heard what Gani had to say, a spasm like an electric shock seemed to jolt him from his heels to the top of his head. His ears began to sing.

Through the singing he became aware of Gani's repeating urgently: "General! General! Can you hear me?"

He controlled himself carefully before he answered: "You say you are a hostage?"

"Yes, General. You see, sir, the position is this. . . ."

"Answer my questions!" He had heard the brisk self-assurance flowing back into Major Gani's voice, and, in a sudden rage, shouted the order.

"Certainly, General. But you see . . ."

"That steps were taken about the white prisoners?"

"Unfortunately, Captain Voychinski died. The others are alive. It is about those persons . . ."

"And Sutan?"

"Major Sutan is beside me, sir, and Colonel Oda."

"Why have they not killed you?"

"If you will permit me to explain, sir."

He explained.

The General listened with mounting bitterness. Fantasies began to crowd into his mind. He would countermand his standing orders about night operations and the Inner Zone, take his armored cars and field guns out, and blast the jail into a heap of rubble. He would kill everyone in it, including Major Gani. The anti-tank weapons of the raiding force would be crushed beneath the wheels of the armored cars. There would be a holocaust. Or, simpler, he would refuse the safe-conduct, tell them to kill Gani, and then hang the three whites publicly in front of the Stadhuis. Or, wiser, more cunning, he would put a cordon around the jail area, cover it with the field guns, and starve them all into submission. He knew that none of those things was really going to happen, that he could never be sure that the power station and jail attacks were not tricks to lure him out of the Inner Zone so that the garrison could be chopped to pieces by the main body of the insurgents. He also knew that, however much he might want to discard Major Gani, the time had not yet come when he could safely do so. Without Gani, the arming of the militia could not be completed, and he, the military governor, would be left again to plead impotently for reinforcements which would never arrive. He knew, too, that he could never justify, even to himself, the proposition that the life of one Indonesian officer was worth sacrificing for the pleasure of punishing three whites.

He heard himself saying: "Very well. I understand. But what guarantees do we have that they will keep the agreement?"

"One moment, sir."

"I had better speak to Oda myself."

"One moment, please, sir."

There was a pause and silence. Gani had had the impertinence to put his hand over the mouthpiece. Then another detested voice addressed him.

"General, this is Ross Hallett. I am at the jail in order to protect the lives of two American citizens. Colonel Oda, who commands the troops now in control of the jail compound, has requested my assistance and that of the British vice-consul in the matter of this proposed exchange of prisoners."

"What kind of assistance?"

"As referees, General. It will be five hours before a Malayan Airways freight plane leaves that could take Mr. and Mrs. Nilsen and Mrs. Lukey out of Indonesian territory. During that period Colonel Oda's troops will leave the jail compound. They will take Major Gani with them. So that there will be no misunderstandings or unfortunate incidents, Mr. Wilson will accompany Major Gani and remain with him. I shall remain at the airport with Mr. and Mrs. Nilsen, Mrs. Lukey, and three of Colonel Oda's officers until the plane leaves. I shall then telephone Mr. Wilson, and the exchange will be completed. Major Gani will report to you. Colonel Oda's officers will report back to him."

"You expect me to trust you?"

"Colonel Oda is prepared to trust us, General. However, should either side attempt to take advantage of the situation, Mr. Wilson and I will personally offer ourselves as hostages until the agreement is carried out."

The General thought for a moment. The possibilities of trickery inherent in such a situation were many. Mr. Hallett had obviously envisaged some of them. For instance, he had stipulated a Malayan Airways plane. That precluded the use of an Indonesian plane to take the prisoners into the air and set them down at Labuanga again after Gani's release. But, what was to prevent Oda, on learning that his white accomplices were free, from killing Gani and laughing at Mr. Wilson's protests? The lives of three expendable junior officers? The General laughed. He knew the answer to that. No insurgent leader who hoped to survive would dare to abandon so treacherously even the most useless of his men.

"How can I believe that you will not favor the traitors in arranging this exchange?" he said at last.

"Do you really believe, General, that Mr. Wilson and I are dishonest?"

The General examined his inner thoughts and found, somewhat to his surprise, that his truthful answer to that question would be "no." He decided to ignore it.

"Very well," he said coldly.

"Then perhaps I may discuss the detailed arrangements for the exchange with a member of your staff?"

"I will discuss the arrangements personally."

When the conversation was finished, the General made a few notes and sent for his senior colonel.

Only one thing puzzled him. Gani had tortured Sutan. Sutan and Oda were friends. How was it that such men, whom he himself knew and had once respected, could forgo the satisfaction of tearing Gani to pieces with their own hands in order to permit three whites to escape without a scratch on their ugly skins? It seemed incredible. And yet, from another point of view, it showed how easy Asians became weak and corrupt through association with white men. It showed how right he had been himself to resist the temptation to come to terms with the Party of the Faithful. The thought was comforting.

vii

It was four o'clock in the morning when Hallett set out in his bullet-scarred car to drive Greg, Dorothy, and Mrs. Lukey from the jail to the airport. Following him, in Major Gani's personal jeep, were the three insurgent officers who would replace them as hostages when the plane took off three and a half hours later.

Hallett had managed to retrieve the two passports and an envelope with the prisoners' valuables in it from the wreckage of the head jailer's office; but, at his lukewarm suggestion that some way might later be found of picking up their other belongings from the Harmonie Hotel, Greg had shaken his head.

"We've caused enough trouble," he had said. "As far as Dorothy and I are concerned, they can keep everything, camera included. We just want out."

Mrs. Lukey had not been so accommodating. Hallett had explained briefly to Greg and Dorothy the substance of the negotiations for their release; but Mrs. Lukey had understood them at the time and, as a result, had acquired an exaggerated idea of the strength of their position.

"I do not see why someone should not be sent from the hotel to the airport," she had said. "I have a very nice overnight case. It was very expensive. I do not want to lose it. These people are all thieves."

Hallett had started to remind her that the Inner Zone was still closed, when Dorothy had firmly taken Mrs. Lukey aside. Neither man had heard what she had said, but thereafter Mrs. Lukey had been subdued, and there had been no more talk of her overnight case.

The General had evidently decided that the opportunity of impressing three insurgent officers with the strength of the Labuanga garrison had been too good to miss, and the airport building was bristling with troops when they arrived. As Hallett presented himself to the officer in charge, an armored car moved in menacingly, if pointlessly, to cover the approaches to the bus yard.

They were taken to a large storeroom in the customs section to await the arrival of the plane. Hallett asked for food and tea, and, rather to his surprise, some was presently brought. Access, under escort, to a nearby washroom was also granted, providing that not more than two persons went at a time. Dorothy and Mrs. Lukey were away taking advantage of this concession when Greg raised a question that was beginning to trouble him.

"Does everybody know about all this?" he asked. "I mean, will it get in the newspapers back home?"

Hallett's smile was not entirely free from malice. "If it gets in the newspapers here," he said, "you can bet your life it'll be picked up back home. So far, it's all been kept secret. I don't imagine the General'll want to give it any publicity now. The press do what they're told here, anyway. Where you'll have to be careful is in Singapore."

"How do you mean?"

"Well, you'll be put on this plane under armed guard. You can't stop the crew talking when they get back. You might be questioned when you arrive. If I were you, I'd have a nice dull story ready in advance for the pilot."

"Like what?"

"Technically, your visa's not in order. You were only cleared for Bali. You've been held here under guard. You could be pretty mad about it. Why didn't Garuda Indonesian Airlines check your visa carefully before flying you out from Singapore? Goddam Asian inefficiency. That sort of stuff. I'm not telling you to say that, mind. That's just advice."

"Thanks. I wish there were something I could do for you."

"Don't worry about that, Mr. Nilsen. There's no real harm been done."

"Major Gani's going back to work, isn't he? That's harm. You can't have enjoyed making that deal."

"No?" Hallett laughed. "I was never so relieved in my life. When the General agreed to swap you three for that sadistic bastard, I thought he must be kidding."

Greg stared. "Why?"

"You don't know General Iskaq. I'd have said he'd have ditched his own wife for the chance of keeping his hands on you three. He hates the whites. Always has."

"So you said. But you knew he couldn't ditch Gani."

"Couldn't? I was almost sure he would. You don't know how lucky you are."

"But in view of what he and Gani are doing, surely he *had* to have him back."

Hallett frowned. "What are you talking about?"

"Well, aren't they hijacking all these insurgent arms shipments to arm the Communists? Isn't Gani the Party go-between?"

Hallett said nothing for a moment, then looked across at the three officers.

They were curled up on top of some packing cases, asleep. He looked again at Greg.

"Who told you that?"

"Voychinski. Didn't you know? He spoke as if it were common knowledge."

"Well, it isn't. Can you remember exactly what he said?"

Greg could. He would remember every moment he had spent in that jail for the rest of his life.

"Is it important?" he ended.

"If it's true—and that could easily be checked—it's important enough to relieve Iskaq of his job and start a clean-up. Assuming the area commander in Medan were to find out, of course."

"Will he?"

"That's not for me to say. All I'll have to do is send an information report through. You'll be quoted as the source, naturally."

"Do I have to be?"

"I'll have to send through a report about your arrest and the reasons for it." His smile was no longer unfriendly. "This could just about square the account," he added.

"That's something, I suppose."

"It is. By the way, was that check of Sutan's with your other things? I didn't look to see."

"I don't know." Greg got his passport out and opened it. The check was still there. He looked up at Hallett. "Did Major Sutan mention it to you at all?"

"No."

"That's funny. He must have known they'd found it, but he said nothing to me before we left. I know he was in pretty bad shape, but you'd think he'd have been anxious about that."

"Perhaps he took it for granted that an experienced arms peddler like you would have asked for another check if he needed it." There was a gleam of amusement in his eyes.

Greg was silent for a moment; then he folded the check carefully and put it in another pocket. "Did you see Voychinski's body?" he asked.

Hallett seemed to find nothing inconsequential in the question. He nodded. "Major Sutan evidently felt that a mutilated corpse ought to prove something about the Central Government. All it proves really, of course, is that in civil wars there are always men around like Major Gani."

"I think that Voychinski was that kind of man himself." Greg remembered something. "By the way, did you or Wilson tell Dorothy *how* he died?"

"I didn't, and I don't imagine Wilson would. Maybe Mrs. Lukey told her. Why?"

"Well, she didn't appear to worry too much about those guards who were killed. But Voychinski dying—that really seemed to upset her."

viii

The freight plane from Koetaradja and Medan landed at seven-thirty and took off again for Singapore at eight. The captain was a New Zealander. Greg had no difficulty in boring him with complaints about Indonesian red tape and a garbled tale of mislaid overnight bags. He listened absently, lent Greg an electric shaver, and returned to his seat in the nose. They did not see him again.

Most of the interior space was taken up by pieces of machinery going to Singapore and beyond for repair, and mail bags. The plane was unpressurized, cold, and noisy. They sat on the mail bags, dozing fitfully, until the Malay radio operator came aft to warn them that in five minutes they would be landing in Singapore. The plane taxied in to the freight sheds and the operator led them across to the passenger arrival section so that they could go through immigration and customs. He left them there, politely declining the tip Greg offered him.

It was the first time the three of them had been alone together and able to talk freely since the evening of their arrest. Mrs. Lukey, hollow-eyed and plaintive when she had been awakened on the plane, now became flustered and embarrassed. As soon as they were through the customs, she hurried off to telephone her husband.

Greg sighed. "Oh, my God! Do we have to wait for her? All I want in the world at the moment is the Raffles Hotel, a bath, and a drink."

"Me, too, darling," said Dorothy, "but I think we have to wait a moment."

"I suppose so. Don't you think one of us ought to tell her that we're not holding her responsible for anything?"

"I don't think so." Dorothy's tone was surprisingly firm.

"Just as you say. Only she looked perfectly miserable to me."

"I don't think we're feeling exactly gay, are we, darling?"

He kissed her, but she drew away.

"Don't. We both smell of that place still."

"I know."

They stood there unhappily until Mrs. Lukey returned.

"I had to telephone," she explained breathlessly. "I knew he would be terribly worried when we did not get back yesterday. He sent a cable off, but there was no reply. He is coming over immediately with the car."

Dorothy nodded. "That's good, but I don't think we'll wait, Betty."

"Oh, but you must."

"No. We'll get a cab to the Raffles."

"That's right," said Greg. "Maybe we'll talk later, or tomorrow morning when we're rested up a bit."

"But he said he wanted to see you."

"Sure, but not right now, eh? We'll be in touch."

She seemed both relieved and distressed to see them go.

In the taxi they were silent until, as they were nearing the hotel, Dorothy said: "Did you get that check back?"

"Yes, it was still in the passport." He paused. "We don't even have a toothbrush," he went on. "I suppose we'd better stop at a drugstore and buy a few things."

By the time they had bathed, it was twelve-thirty. Greg rang down to the bar for double dry Martinis, but neither he nor Dorothy wanted any lunch. While they were drinking the Martinis, he telephoned Cook's.

"This is Mr. Nilsen. . . . Yes, we're back from Indonesia. . . . Yes . . . Well, we decided to cut it short. Now, look. I'd like you to check up for me on boats sailing during the next couple of days for Calcutta. . . . No, that doesn't matter. British, Norwegian, German, anything you like, as long as it's comfortable. We'd want a large stateroom with bath, air-conditioned if possible. . . . I see. Okay, but not too slow, and it's got to be comfortable, with good food. At the same time, I'd like to know about flights to Calcutta. . . . Via Bangkok. We might want to stop over there for a couple of days. . . . Yes, that's right. . . . No, not today. We'll come around and see you in the morning. . . . Thanks."

He hung up and his eyes met Dorothy's.

"Could we afford the Bangkok trip?" she asked.

"I don't know. Let's see what it would cost, anyway."

He smiled at her, but she was looking down at her drink now.

"Greg, what are you going to do about Captain Lukey?"

He got up with a sigh. "I don't know. While we were in the plane I tried to think about it. We went to get a check signed and—" he hesitated—"got off the beaten track. Well, we did both. Logically, all I have to do now is go to the customs office with Tan and Lukey, sign some papers, and collect sixty-two thousand five hundred dollars. But . . ." He broke off.

"But you don't know if you want to be logical."

"That's right. What do you think?"

She went over and kissed his cheek. "Maybe we should get some sleep," she said.

Nine

GREG WOKE AT six-thirty in the evening. His body ached all over and he had a metallic taste in his mouth. Dorothy was still asleep. He went into the sitting room, shut the bedroom door softly behind him, and rang for some ice. When it came, he got out the remains of the bottle of whisky purchased for his first meeting with Captain Lukey, and made himself a drink. As he drank it, he realized that he would be feeling very hungry, but for one thing: he could still smell the jail.

He thought carefully about that. Before they had gone to bed, both he and Dorothy had thoroughly washed every inch of themselves, their hair included; and they had given every stitch of clothing they had been wearing to the room boy with orders to burn or otherwise dispose of it. There could be only one reason for the phenomenon. "Thank *you*, Dr. Freud," he muttered sourly.

He reached for the telephone and asked the operator to see if Mr. Lane Harvey of the American Syndicated Wire Service could be found at his office or at the American Club.

Harvey was at the club, and sounded as if he had been there for some time.

"And how was fabulous Bali?" he asked.

"Great."

"And those nubile young ladies with the fecund breasts and the sidelong looks? How were they? Or maybe I'd better ask Mrs. N. about them."

"Maybe you had. Look, I want to have a word with Colonel Soames. Do you mind telling me how I can get in touch with him?"

There was a momentary pause before Harvey answered. "The Policeman? Sure. Just call up police admin. They'll put you through to his office."

"I meant this evening."

"Oh. Well, I don't have my book with me right now, but I'll be going back to my office sometime. Supposing I call you later."

"Thanks. I'm at the Raffles."

"I'll call you."

His tone was careless and he hung up almost before the last word was out. Greg suspected that the promise had already been forgotten. He put some more ice in his drink and then looked up the word "Police" in the telephone directory. There was a long list of entries, none of which was "Police admin." He was edging his way through the listings under "Government" when the telephone rang.

"This is Soames," said a well-remembered voice.

"Colonel Soames, I was just trying to contact you."

"So I gathered. That's why I'm phoning. What can I do for you?"

"I need advice. I'd like to see you as soon as I can."

"Won't the morning do?"

"I was hoping . . ." Greg broke off. "Look, I've been in Labuanga. I got back today. It's sort of urgent."

There was a pause. "Very well, Mr. Nilsen. I'll meet you in the Raffles lounge in fifteen minutes. Will that be all right?"

"Fine. Thanks."

He went back into the bedroom. Dorothy was fast asleep. Very quietly he collected the clothes he needed and returned to the sitting room. When he was dressed, he left a note for Dorothy telling her where he was, and went down to the lounge.

ii

Colonel Soames arrived with the sandwiches Greg had ordered. He was wearing a white dinner jacket.

"Hope this won't take long," he said briskly. "I'm due at a dinner party at eight-thirty."

"It's a longish story," said Greg, "but I'll cut it as short as I can. What are you drinking?"

"Is that coffee you've got there?"

"Yes."

"I'll have some of that. Now, what's the trouble?"

The Colonel was a good listener. He did not stir as Greg told him the story of his dealings with the Tan brothers, Captain Lukey, and the Party of the Faithful. Twice only, he interjected brief questions to obtain a clarification of detail. Once he signaled to the waiter to bring some more coffee. When Greg had finished, he sat back.

"That all?"

"Yes."

"What did you say that fellow's name was? Gani?"

"Yes, Major Gani."

"Very interesting. Might come in handy to our people sometime. Much obliged to you." He paused. "You said you wanted advice, though."

"Help would be a better word."

"For a rank amateur, you don't seem to have done so badly without help. You've been lucky, of course, but didn't someone say luck was a form of genius?"

Greg leaned forward. "Colonel, you said at lunch the other day that you'd considered having me deported."

The Colonel chuckled amiably. "If I'd known what I know now, I probably would have. Can't have amateurs fooling about in the arms racket. Disgraceful state of affairs!"

"Supposing you had deported me," Greg went on, "and supposing I'd just been on the point of concluding a piece of business that netted me sixty-two thousand five hundred Straits dollars. Would I have been allowed to complete it?"

The Colonel's smile faded and he eyed Greg curiously. "That would have depended. I was only gingering you up a bit. You wouldn't have been deported unless the Indonesians had made a formal and specific complaint against you. In that case, naturally, we'd have tried to stop you completing."

"Once I was out, could I have come back?"

"Of course not."

Greg nodded. "That's what I wanted to know. Right, Colonel. As a favor to me, I'd like you to have a deportation order made out against me."

"I beg your pardon."

"Naturally, I'd like it done without any fuss or publicity. I figure there wouldn't be any, unless I tried to contest the order, and, obviously, I wouldn't do that. I'm sure that if I were to have a word with the American consul first there'd be no trouble there."

The Colonel was staring at him angrily. "If this is your idea of humor, Nilsen, I think it's in very poor taste."

"I'm quite serious."

"Then you must be up to some game I don't know about. I think you'd better tell me what that is."

"Certainly. I want to call this whole deal off."

The Colonel scowled. "I see. Had a better offer for the stuff. My dear chap, if you think you're going to use me to get you off the hook, you're very much mistaken."

"I haven't another offer. I don't want another offer. I just want out from the whole filthy business."

"But not neglecting to take your commission, I imagine."

"No deal, no commission, nothing."

The Colonel shook his head wearily. "All right, what are you up to? Come on, let's hear it."

"I've told you. I want out." Greg paused, then shrugged. "You may as well know the whole idiotic truth. When I went into this thing, it was a sort of a joke. I was told those arms had been hijacked from the Communists. I thought it would be highly amusing to help put them into the hands of anti-Communists. Don't ask me how I managed to sucker myself into thinking that I was doing something pretty smart. That's another cute little story. The thing is, I fell for all that double talk of Tan's in Manila like a kid. No, that's unfair. My own sons would have had more sense." He paused again. "Well, then I got what I deserved. I had a chance of seeing a bit of both sides of this fascinating little war. Oh, yes, I found a Communist bastard, all right, and he was right where you might have expected him to be. But I found a Fascist bastard there as well."

The Colonel laughed shortly. "And wasn't *he* where you might have expected *him* to be?"

"I guess he was." Greg's lips thinned. "But you have to remember this, Colonel. I'd been dealing in make-believe. Now, for a real hundred-per-cent Rover Boy like me, just a lick of reality can be terribly uncomfortable and disturbing. To say nothing of the fact that Rover Boy managed to put his wife as well as himself into a very dangerous situation, where they not only became a source of acute embarrassment to their country's representative, but had to be rescued by him as well. So you see, Colonel the joke's now over. My wife's a very tolerant woman. She hasn't said 'I told you so,' and she won't. But I have a bad conscience, and she knows it. I think she'd like me to do something about that. So, that's what I'm trying to do."

The Colonel sneered. "I see. You'd like to wash your hands of the whole thing and make believe none of it ever happened."

"Yes, that's about the size of it, I guess. More make believe, as you say. Well, maybe that won't work, but there are some things I can do."

"Like having yourself deported? What would that accomplish?"

"One thing. It would put Tan back right where he started. Originally, he couldn't move those arms from Manila because of some legal snag, or so he said. I'm his sole authorized agent. If I'm expelled from here, I can't sign them out of bond or transfer ownership. That means he can't move the arms from Singapore because of a legal snag. So he's back where he was before I came along, and those arms are back behind the eight ball. He can't take legal action against me because the circumstances are beyond my control. He can have his check for a thousand dollars back. Finish."

The Colonel looked perplexed. "I see your point, but, my dear fellow, you're not seriously asking me to have you deported, are you?"

"I am."

"I'm not Himmler, you know. I'd have to justify such a request, and I don't see how I could."

"Why not? You said yourself that a complaint from the Indonesian Government could do the trick. I bet there's one on the way right now."

"If what you say about General Iskaq is true, I should think that extremely unlikely. He'd have to send his complaint through Medan, and that'd mean he'd have to answer a lot of awkward questions first." He shook his head. "No, I'm afraid it won't do. If that's your idea of washing your hands, you can forget about it."

"Well, thanks for listening, anyway."

The Colonel glanced at his watch. "I'll have to be off." He hesitated. "Of course, it's none of my business really, but I can't help thinking that you're being a bit hard on yourself, Nilsen."

"Yes?"

"And on one or two other people as well."

"Including Tan?" Greg asked sarcastically.

"I wasn't thinking of him. You see," the Colonel went on thoughtfully, "I'm something of a prig myself, too, on occasions, so I can understand how you feel. But one thing I have noticed. When all the hand-washing, clean-slate stuff begins, it usually has the effect of landing someone else in the soup. Funny thing, moral indignation."

Greg said nothing.

"This idea of yours, for instance." The Colonel broke off to murmur something in Malay to a passing waiter. "It wasn't such a bad idea really, selling Communist supplies to anti-Communist forces, hoisting them with their own petards or whatever the phrase is. Not bad at all."

"Maybe. If they really had been Communist supplies."

"They were that, all right."

"You don't mean to say you believe that story of Tan's about collateral for a debt?"

"No, but I had one of my chaps take a closer look at the stuff. The types of weapons, the manufacturers, the ammunition batch numbers, the quantities— it all corresponds to a very familiar pattern."

"What pattern?"

"Terrorist arms cache. That's exactly the kind of parcel the Chinese were shoving across the Thai border into Malaya four or five years ago. Couldn't mistake it."

"Where did Tan get it, then?"

"How should I know? Probably stole it. Does it matter?"

"No, except that, if he did, that makes me a receiver of stolen goods as well."

The Colonel sighed. "As well as what, my dear fellow? Of what other crimes against God or man are you accusing yourself?"

"Arrogance, ignorance, stupidity, and trying to make a fast buck out of men trying to kill one another. Will that do for the moment?"

The waiter put down two stengahs in front of them.

"As I doubt if I shall reach my hostess in time to be offered a drink before dinner, this is just a precaution," the Colonel explained. "After all the breast-beating you've been doing, you could probably use one, too."

Greg was silent.

The Colonel drank half the contents of his glass, and then dabbed his lips with a black silk handkerchief. "Nowadays," he said, "we don't hear the phrase 'merchants of death' very much. It's all very sad. The idea that the act of selling arms somehow tricked people into making wars they didn't want never really stood up to very close inspection, did it? But it was good to have a fine, top-hatted bogeyman to put all the blame on. The trouble is we've learned a thing or two since nineteen thirty-nine. Now we can't even blame the politicians—not with much conviction, anyway. The real bogeyman crawled out of the mud with our ancestors millions of years ago. Well, we all have a piece of him, and when we start to put the pieces together, it's like one of those nuclear-fission things—when the mass reaches a critical point, a chain reaction starts, and poof!"

Greg raised his eyebrows. "I always thought there was a standard justification of any sort of illicit peddling, whether it was in drugs, smut, or arms. 'If I don't, somebody else will.' Isn't yours a bit new?"

"I wasn't talking about illicit peddling," the Colonel replied huffily, "and I wasn't attempting to justify anything. I was merely trying to correct your rather muddled view of your obligations at this moment. Selling arms or selling the wherewithal to make them—what's the difference? What does your government do with the die-castings you make for them—feed the hungry or put them into ballistic missiles?"

"The United States Government isn't selling arms for profit."

"I must remember that when the nuclear war starts. It'll be a great comfort."

Greg's temper was beginning to fray at the edges. "As I said before, Colonel, you change hats rather easily. Which one are you wearing at the moment?"

"Major Sutan's, probably."

Greg looked at him, startled.

The Colonel picked up his drink and examined it dubiously. "Of course," he said slowly, "you've had a trying time, a surprise or two, and not very much sleep. Apt to warp a man's judgment, those things. Same as a hangover. Alcoholic remorse and all that." He looked up with a small smile.

"What are you getting at, Colonel?"

"Well, now. Let's suppose I'm Sutan. Rightly or wrongly, I'm buying arms with which to fight for something—freedom, power, social justice, or one of the other delusions. You offer to sell me arms and I accept your offer. We're both men of good faith, eh? I give you a check. Then something unforeseen happens. As a result, I and my friends have a choice. We can wash our hands of you and your wife and leave you both to rot, or we can, at some cost to ourselves, see that you go free. It's not an easy choice, but we decide in your favor and you go free. To show your appreciation, you promptly call off the deal we've made, and try and arrange things so that nobody else can call it on again. How does that sound to you?"

Greg sighed. "As it was intended to sound, of course. However, the facts are a bit different."

"I'm sure they are. But you began by asking for advice. Then you asked me to help you. I couldn't do that, so perhaps you'll accept some advice after all. It's not your conscience that's troubling you, Mr. Nilsen, but a slight injury to your self-esteem. Officially, I'm not particularly interested now either in you or in what happens to those arms. Unofficially, though, I would suggest that you do something about recovering your sense of humor."

"So that I can laughingly go ahead with the deal as planned?"

"Oh, I've no doubt you'll find a way of penalizing yourself in the process, like sending that thousand-dollar check back to Tan." He got to his feet. "I really must be going now. I think I'll let you pay for my drink."

"Good-by, Colonel."

The Colonel hesitated, then sat down again. "I don't like to leave you in this despondent mood," he said. "If it's laughter you need, it's just possible that I may be able to help you."

"I'll stop you if I've heard it."

The Colonel ignored the remark. "What was your arrangement with Tan in Manila about payment?" he asked. "What were you to do with the money from Lukey?"

"Pay it into the Merchants' Security Bank here for the credit of his account."

"Was anything particular said about what you were to do if you received the money in cash?"

"No. Why? I seem to be missing the point of this story, Colonel. You know, I doubt very much if we laugh at the same things."

"How about poetic justice? That can sometimes be quite entertaining, can't it?"

"Oh, sure."

"Well, your Mr. Tan in Manila wasn't what you might call frank with you, was he? Don't you think you're entitled to a little joke at his expense?"

"What sort of joke?"

"You could give Tan Yam Heng here the money to bank for his brother."

"And give him a chance to take his double commission after all? Is that the idea?"

The Colonel pursed his lips. "Something like that. Of course, you'd make the fellow give you a receipt in duplicate for the full amount. Keep one copy for yourself, send the other to Manila."

Greg smiled doubtfully. "Well, it's not exactly the biggest belly laugh of the year." He shrugged. "In fact, it's sort of petty, isn't it?"

"I can assure you that Mr. Tan won't think so."

"You mean he'll lose face, or whatever they call it?"

"Undoubtedly."

"Well, I'll think about it. There's no chance of Tan Yam Heng being restrained by any feelings of family loyalty, I suppose?"

The Colonel grinned. "Don't worry. I know a little about that chap. No chance at all."

When he had gone, Greg remained there for a few minutes, finishing his drink and thinking about what the Colonel had said.

He had, he reflected, been called, directly or by implication, a prig, a simpleton, a hypocrite, a pompous ass, a self-satisfied ingrate, and a man who could mistake his self-esteem for his conscience. Together with the adjectives he himself had applied, it all made quite a picture. Dorothy would have been highly indignant. The odd thing was that he did not feel at all indignant himself. For the first time in several days, in fact, he felt like laughing—not at anything in particular, certainly not at the Colonel's feeble vision of poetic justice, but because he had suddenly seen his own face.

He signed a chit for the sandwiches and drinks, and went back up to the suite. Dorothy had not stirred. He undressed, brushed his teeth, and got back into bed beside her.

iii

The following morning he met Captain Lukey and Tan Yam Heng at the Orchard Road branch of the Hong Kong and Shanghai Bank.

The Captain was boisterously cheerful, and countersigned the check with a flourish. The "spot of bother in Labuanga," as he had called it over the telephone, had now, it seemed, been forgotten.

Greg watched Tan as the money was being paid out. His face did not move, but his eyes followed every bundle of notes as it was pushed across the counter, and the fingers of his right hand twitched in sympathy with the Captain's as he checked the bundles. It was more than likely, Greg decided, that the Colonel had been right. Once Tan Yam Heng had his hands on the money, brotherly love would not deter him from taking a triple or even quadruple commission if he had a mind to.

From the bank they went to the Customs House. There Greg signed the necessary papers transferring the ownership of the arms and ammunition to Captain Lukey, and received the bulky canvas bag containing the money.

Captain Lukey beamed. "Signed, sealed, and delivered," he said fatuously. "What about a drink to celebrate?"

They went to the lounge bar of a nearby hotel. When the drinks had been ordered, Captain Lukey left them to go to the toilet. Greg looked at Tan.

"I think this is where you give me another check for a thousand and fifty dollars," he said.

"Ah, no." Tan pointed to the bag on the table in front of Greg. "That must be paid into the Merchants' Security Bank first."

"Where is the bank?"

"In Coleman Road. We will take a taxi there."

Greg frowned. "I've got a lot to do today. Look, you're acting for your brother. Why don't I give you the money, and you pay it in? Then we can square everything away right now."

He had been prepared for some visible indication that the suggestion met with Tan's approval, but had not expected the reaction to be so manifest. It was remarkable. Not a muscle of the man's face moved; but suddenly it was glistening with sweat.

His lips moved slowly. "If that is what you wish, Mr. Nilsen, yes, I will go to the bank."

"Fine. Just a moment." Greg got up and, going over to one of the writing tables, wrote out on hotel stationery two copies of a receipt for sixty-two thousand five hundred Straits dollars cash received from Gregory H. Nilsen as payment in full for the goods listed on bill of lading number so-and-so, and the date. Then he addressed an envelope to Tan Tack Chee in Manila, marked it "airmail," and went back to the table.

Captain Lukey had stopped to talk to someone on his way back from the toilet, and they were able to complete the transaction before he returned. Tan filled in the bill-of-lading number on the receipts, signed both copies, and handed Greg a check for a thousand and fifty dollars. Greg put the check and one copy of the receipt into his pocket. Across the other copy he wrote "Compliments of Gregory H. Nilsen," then put it in the envelope and sealed it.

Tan was sitting tensely, watching. Greg pushed the canvas bag over to him and smiled. "I guess you don't want to count that again."

"No." Tan took the bag and rested it on his knees.

Greg held up the envelope. "You don't happen to have an airmail stamp for Manila, do you?"

"I will get one from the barman."

"Don't trouble. I'll get one later."

"No trouble, Mr. Nilsen."

Tan put the bag under his arm and went to the bar. Captain Lukey came back to the table and began talking about the "dear old chum" he had just run into. "White man through and through, which is more than you can say for some of the murky types who work for Afro-Asian nowadays."

Tan came back with a stamp and put it on the table at Greg's elbow. He did not sit down.

"If you will be good enough to excuse me now," he said with strained civility, "I think I will go to the bank."

"Won't you have a drink first?"

"No, I will go to the bank." He was still sweating, and obviously yearning to be gone.

"Okay. I'll be seeing you."

"Good-by, Mr. Nilsen, Captain."

He hurried away.

Captain Lukey chuckled. "You must have a trusting nature, old boy. If it was mine, I wouldn't let him hold that money even while I tied a shoelace."

Greg smiled. He was putting the stamp on the envelope. "I don't think I need worry," he said.

As they were leaving, Greg went over to the hotel mailbox. He was about to drop the envelope in it when Captain Lukey stopped him.

"By the way, old boy. Couldn't help noticing, but if you want that to go airmail to Manila you'll have to put some more stamps on. That's the surface rate. It may take a week or more to get there."

Greg shrugged and put the envelope into the box. "It's not particularly urgent," he said.

iv

On his way back to the hotel, Greg called in at the Chase National, who were his own bankers' agents, paid in Mr. Tan's two American-dollar checks, and asked for special clearance on them.

At the hotel he wrote out a check for two thousand one hundred dollars payable to the Wilmington Chapter of the American Red Cross. Dorothy, who knew a woman on the Volunteer Service Co-ordination Committee, wrote a covering letter. They mailed it on their way to see the man at Thomas Cook's.

Ten

T AN TACK CHEE and Tan Siow Mong were bland men with level heads and strong nerves; but the arrival of Yam Heng's receipt in Manila threw them into a state of flustered consternation that Greg would have found gratifying, if puzzling.

Tack Chee took one long, appalled look at the receipt and then put through an overseas call to the Raffles Hotel in Singapore. He was told that Mr. and Mrs. Nilsen had sailed two days previously on the *S. S. Camboge* for Colombo and Bombay. Next he tried to call Yam Heng at the union office where he worked. A clerk there told him that Yam Heng had not been to his office for several days. He was presumed to be indisposed. Yam Heng had no telephone at his home, and Tack Chee knew that it would be useless to cable. Despairingly, he put through a call to the Merchants' Security Bank. The manager was helpful and efficient. No payment of any kind had been made into his account for the past month. Tack Chee hung up, turned his air-conditioner on FULL, and told his secretary to place a person-to-person call to his brother in Kuala Pangkalan.

Siow Mong had not been unduly concerned at the delay in collecting the twenty-five thousand dollars due to him in respect of Girija's check. He had received a satisfactory progress report from Singapore, saying that the sale was about to be completed. As there was still a clear week to go before the Indian could present the check for payment, he did not expect to have to draw upon his own resources in order to honor it. Only one thing was troubling him a little. So far, the clerk had shown himself to be shrewd, careful, and discreet. But would he go on being shrewd, careful, and discreet with twenty-five thousand dollars in the bank? Money could affect people strangely, and for a young man in his position this would be a fortune. What did he propose to do with it? Something foolish, like buying an expensive sports car and driving about ostentatiously advertising his sudden wealth? And, if so, how

516

was he proposing to explain where he had got it? Tan Siow Mong had decided to have a talk with him before the thirty days were up, to caution him if that seemed necessary, and to make sure that any explanations the young man contemplated using did not compromise either the Anglo-Malay Transport Company or its proprietor.

The telephone call from Manila came through late on Thursday afternoon.

As soon as he heard his brother's voice, Siow Mong knew that something was wrong; but Tack Chee was an ingenious breaker of bad news, and it was two minutes before Siow Mong fully realized what had happened. Then he lost his temper, and for a further minute there was a loud and demeaning exchange of generalities in which words relating to the excretory organs and functions of the body were freely used. Finally, however, Siow Mong began to recover his self-possession and to think again.

"It is the American who is responsible," he declared. "If the money is gone, he must pay."

"Impossible," Tack Chee replied. "Yam Heng signed the receipt as my authorized agent. We can only hope that he has not yet lost it all. You must go to Singapore immediately."

"Both of us must go."

"My expenses in this business have already been heavy enough. Twenty-one hundred dollars American plus entertainment, and now overseas telephone calls."

"Those are trifles, brother." Siow Mong was becoming angry again. "When I stand to lose twenty-five thousand dollars Malay, plus five hundred dollars Hong Kong, plus shipping and other handling charges, I am surprised that you commit the indelicacy of speaking about them."

"There is nothing indelicate about two thousand dollars American. The whole transaction was your idea."

"You had no criticisms of it. If you had properly instructed this Nilsen . . ." He broke off. "There is no sense in our bickering. It is a waste of time. Obviously, we shall get nothing unless Yam Heng can be persuaded to cooperate. You know what that means. This time it may be necessary to bring in the police and threaten charges of embezzlement. You are the legal principal in this, and the receipt will be required evidence. You must be there."

"The police? He would know we were bluffing."

"I am not bluffing," Siow Mong said. "This time he has gone too far. Charges of misappropriation of funds brought against him by that union would have been damaging to our names. We should have lost face. Charges brought against him by us would give rise to no such indignity, except for Yam Heng."

"They might cause pain to our mother."

"She has endured worse," Siow Mong said unfeelingly. "If I leave immediately for Kota Bharu, I can get a plane to Singapore tonight. I will meet you at the Cathay Hotel tomorrow morning."

Yam Heng had had a bitterly frustrating week on the pickle market, and was querulous when the brothers eventually confronted him. He had, he explained indignantly, merely borrowed the money for a few days. Was not part of it due to him anyway, for all his work on their behalf? Why was he hounded in this way? Yes, he had incurred certain losses; but these would at any moment be more than offset by substantial gains. In three days' time he would be able to get them a hundred thousand dollars if they needed money so badly.

Mention of the police, however, changed the character of the debate. There was abuse, and much harsh, contemptuous laughter and snapping of fingers. It was only when he realized that his brothers were not simply ready to press charges against him, but beginning to feel vindictive enough to relish the prospect of doing so, that Yam Heng agreed sulkily to an accounting.

Of the sixty-two thousand five hundred dollars there remained seventeen thousand, three hundred; and threats of violence as well as police prosecution were necessary to persuade Yam Heng to part with that. His brothers left him, glutinous with self-pity, and returned to the Cathay Hotel.

Minor expenses disregarded, they were fourteen thousand dollars (Straits) out of pocket on the deal. They were also tired. They had little difficulty in agreeing how they should divide the salvaged remains. Tack Chee took the equivalent of eight hundred American dollars to set off against his outlay of twenty-one hundred. Siow Mong, as the heavier loser, took the balance of fifteen thousand dollars (Straits).

He arrived back in Kuala Pangkalan late on Friday night. When he went to his office the following morning, he found a message. Mr. Krishnan had telephoned and would like to see Mr. Tan. In the hope that Mr. Tan would find it convenient, he would call in on Saturday afternoon at four p.m.

ii

Mr. Tan, sitting gloomily at his desk, watched the Indian cross the yard from number-one godown and thought that he detected a certain impudent jauntiness in the fellow's walk.

In spite of its obvious absurdity, he could not quite rid himself of the fear that the Indian had somehow learned of the Singapore disaster and had come there merely to gloat over and humiliate him. If that should indeed be the case, he told himself darkly, the fellow would regret his temerity.

As matters now stood, he, Siow Mong, was prepared to be generous. The Indian would be solemnly warned of the dangers of so much sudden wealth, and of the impossibility of his being able to account satisfactorily to the police for its acquisition. It would then be relatively simple to persuade him to return the check. In exchange, he would be given a deed of annuity guaranteeing him a yearly income of two thousand five hundred dollars for ten years. Mr. Tan was reasonably sure that he could buy such an annuity for around fifteen thousand dollars.

Should the fellow be in any way disagreeable, however, Mr. Tan had an alternative scheme ready. He would stop payment of the check and invite the young blackguard to sue him in open court. There, if his challenge were accepted, he would tell the judge that the Indian had undertaken to buy for him, through a relative, a certain valuable tract of tin-bearing land, and that the postdated check had been written, at the Indian's request, to impress the relative and to use as a deposit if the purchase went through. When he had discovered that the Indian's land-owning relative was nonexistent, he had stopped the check. Perfectly simple. If the Indian chose to tell the truth, he would either be disbelieved and lose his case, or believed and prosecuted for selling arms. Mr. Tan did not think that he would be fool enough to risk either of those alternatives.

When he was announced, Mr. Tan assumed the mask of courtesy and ordered tea.

Girija flashed a smile as they shook hands. "I am sure that if Mr. Wright had been aware that I was to have the pleasure of seeing you, Mr. Tan, he would have wished me to convey his personal regards." He had a box file under his arm. He placed it on the floor beside him as he sat down.

"Mr. and Mrs. Wright are well and happy, I hope."

"Oh, yes, thank you. I trust that your own fine family are equally blessed."

The tea came and was consumed to further light conversation. Then Girija picked up the box file and rested it on his knees. Mr. Tan accepted this as an intimation that business might begin.

"I was hoping to have the pleasure of seeing you again in the near future, Mr. Krishnan," he said. "In fact, when I returned from Singapore yesterday, it was already in my mind to telephone you."

"Perhaps there was the same thought in both our minds, Mr. Tan."

Mr. Tan stiffened involuntarily.

"I refer," Girija continued, "to the thought, sad for me, that, under present arrangements, our very satisfactory association will shortly end."

Mr. Tan relaxed. He had noted the words "under present arrangements" and decided to wait for the Indian to explain them.

"I am assuming," Girija added politely, "that the association also proved satisfactory from your point of view."

"Oh, yes. Very satisfactory," Mr. Tan replied manfully.

"And Mr. Lee's?"

"Sufficiently so, I believe."

"I am glad of that," said Girija, "because it gives me the courage to submit a further problem to you, in the hope of receiving further good advice."

Mr. Tan was silent.

Girija flashed another smile. "I am so sorry to have to tell you that the friend I spoke of to you before has since died."

Mr. Tan permitted himself a faint twitch of the lips. "You have my sympathy."

"Thank you. However, as you know, my friend had money. That now passes to me. Unfortunately, he left no will. My difficulty at the moment is to find a substitute for that will."

Mr. Tan hid his satisfaction perfectly. "I can appreciate the difficulty," he said. "In fact, if you will allow me to say so, I had anticipated it. I even had a possible solution to suggest to you if you were interested."

"I am indeed most interested."

Mr. Tan proceeded, somewhat elliptically, to explain his annuity proposal. As he began to enlarge upon its virtues, however, he was disconcerted to see, for the first time, a smile of pure amusement spread over the Indian's face. He felt himself getting angry, and stopped in the middle of a sentence.

The smile vanished instantly and Girija leaned forward. "Mr. Tan, I beg your pardon. Perhaps I should have explained first. For the project that I have in mind, twenty-five thousand dollars will be the minimum capital required if we are to operate at a profit."

Mr. Tan never discovered whether the Indian had used the words "we" and "profit" at that moment intentionally; just as he was never quite clear how it had come about that, twenty minutes later, the contents of the box file had been scattered over his desk and he had been listening bemused to a dissertation on the economics of public transport operation in rural areas. It had been quite difficult to break in and regain the initiative; and even then he did not keep it long.

"Why don't you begin with one bus? Why must you have two?"

"People must learn quickly that the buses are reliable or they will keep to their bicycles. The service must become indispensable, Mr. Tan. With only one bus it cannot be guaranteed."

"But if you were to buy one new one, you would have the reliability you want."

"We cannot afford an experienced mechanic full time, to begin with. Therefore we cannot carry out maintenance at night, as the big operators do. What I propose is that we buy two of these reconditioned buses. I know this firm at Acton in London. They have long experience of the work. The chassis are old, but very good. The engines are new. The bodies have been adapted for Far East work. Look, here is a picture."

Mr. Tan waved the picture aside. "Yes, yes. It is all very interesting. But why have you brought this project to me?"

Girija returned to his seat on the other side of the desk before he replied, slowly and methodically: "Firstly, Mr. Tan, because a bus service such as I have described would be a logical extension of the Anglo-Malay Transport Company's business. Secondly, because of the trade journals I subscribe to, Mr. Wright knows of my interest in such matters. He knows of my respect for you. He would not think it too strange that a new bus company which you owned should employ me as manager. Thirdly, because if a new company called Kuala Pangkalan Transport Limited were formed, with a nominal capital of fifty thousand dollars, and if, in consideration of my signing a service agreement as managing director of that company, I were allotted fifty per cent of the ordinary shares free, I could return your check to you without presenting it for payment. Fourthly, because a company with your reputation behind it would have no difficulty in securing a franchise to operate the service. Fifthly, because I think you know that I can be trusted and would serve our interests well."

Mr. Tan thought carefully. What the Indian had said about the need for a bus service was undoubtedly true. As a business venture, it was probably sound. The capital of a new company would not have to be fully paid up. Fifteen thousand would buy the two reconditioned buses. On the other hand, if the project were a success, a fifty-per-cent interest in it was eventually going to be worth a lot more than twenty-five thousand dollars. He would certainly be wise to keep the ordinary shares in his own hands. A counter-offer of non-voting preference shares might be the answer. Ingeniously worked out, it could, he was sure, be made to seem advantageous. Meanwhile, he would employ delaying tactics, wear the Indian down by keeping him waiting, and then, if necessary, dictate the terms. He fingered the papers from the box file as if they were of small importance, and then pushed them aside.

"Very well," he said. "I will look through these estimates and proposals, and perhaps make some other inquiries. Later, possibly, we could meet again and continue the discussion."

Girija nodded. "Of course, Mr. Tan. On the terms I have mentioned, the whole matter can be very easily settled—" he paused and flashed his most annoying smile—"any day before your check falls due for payment next week."

iii

The day after Greg and Dorothy arrived back in Wilmington, Kuala Pangkalan Transport Limited took delivery of its first vehicle at Singapore.

W. W. Belden, the maker's Far Eastern representative, was on hand to promote an atmosphere of goodwill. The new owners' managing director, G. Krishnan, was there to sign the necessary documents on behalf of his company.

A ten-ton crane picked the bus off the deck of the ship and placed it on the dockside.

Privately, Mr. Belden thought that the thing looked like a cattle truck; but, as most of its passengers would presumably be coolies, that probably did not matter. The important thing was that the Indian seemed to be pleased. With all this German competition in the low-price field, you had to be on your toes. When the second reconditioned unit had been delivered, he would start plugging their own new economy job. Meanwhile, he had a luncheon date at the Yacht Club. As soon as he could gracefully do so, he left.

The two drivers Girija had brought with him had both spent some years on army vehicles, and knew the type of chassis well. When everything had been checked, the new battery installed, the temporary registration plates fitted, and the tank filled, the engine was started. It had a leisurely, powerful sound that was very satisfying.

One driver got up into the cab, the other sat behind him on one of the passenger benches.

The driver at the wheel grinned down at Girija. "Can we drive the tuan to his hotel?"

Girija smiled and shook his head. "I'll be waiting for you in Kuala Pangkalan," he said.

He did not ride in buses; he operated them.

But he stood there, listening and watching, as the big gears grated, the big tires began to turn, and the bus rumbled away toward the dock gates and the journey north. He wished that his father, the subahdar, could have been there.